# RAKE

## AND THE

# RECLUSE

### REDUX

*Jenn LeBlanc*

ISBN 13 : 978-0-9837954-8-3

The Rake and the Recluse - Redux (a time travel romance)
(Trade edition)

Published in the United States of America
•••••
This novel is a work of fiction.
The characters, incidents, places and dialogue are figments of the author's imagination
and are not to be construed as real.
Any resemblance to actual events or persons, living or dead, is entirely coincidental.

Title scripts used with permission:

*Jellyka Delicious Cake*

IVORY

# EDICATION

*This story was written for my Momma,*
*who may have been concerned but always believed in me.*


*This edition is dedicated to my friend Melinda,*
*who recently embarked on the greatest journey of her lifetime.*

# ACKNOWLEDGEMENTS

Over the past year I've received an incredible amount of support. This book would not be what it is today without the help of every single one of you.

A special thank you to Mr. LeBlanc, for continuing to support me.
Perhaps support is not the right word. Believe.
In the beginning it was support, but then he started to believe, and there is a difference.

Derek, my hero, there wouldn't be this book without you and there are no words
for what your friendship means to me.

Kati "McSquee" for her undying devotion to my story, my heroes, both my writing and my images and for her neverending promotion. You are more than an author's best friend and the first person I think of when ogling men on the internets.

Jamie Lynn joined forces with Kati to create Romancing Rakes For The Love Of Romance, and she brings it on home, the girl knows how to find men, and is one of the most excitable people I've ever met.

Rita Jett of Not Another Romance Blog for her amazing support and ridiculousness, there are no words for the tsunami that is you.

Though the pervy trinity is in retirement, the three of you have changed my life,
and I am blessed.

Heather of Book Savvy Babe, when you made TRATR your favorite read of August last year,
I thought I would die. You are an asset to the romance reviews community.

Elise Rome, an amazing friend and the best editor a girl could ask for

Melinda, Cora, Brandy, Auberry and Elena, thank you for all your help in studio and out.
Sarah Clark and Monika Graf, for the beautiful styling of hair and makeup.
You took my vision and made it your own, and with it created a masterpiece.

So many people helped to make the original edition of this book a success, there is no possible way for me to thank everyone here. But I invite you to visit my website and check out the links for all the places I've been, these bloggers have made this year the most exciting one yet.

Thank You

# CAST

His Grace, Gideon Alrick Trumbull, 10th Duke of Roxleigh : Derek Hutchins
Francine Adelais Larrabee : Cora Kemp
Lord Peregrine Afton Trumbull, Viscount Roxleigh : Derek Hutchins
Lilly Steele : Mary Cates

# TRUMBULL

Marcus Avris 6th D
Avris Marshall 7th D
Dorsey Aloysius 8th D
m. Allesandre D

**Aubrey Leigh**
m. Vincent Calder
Duke of St. Cyr, Viscount Briton.

**Darius Alrick 9th D**
m. Melisande D

**Helena Adeline**
m. Aloysius Marshall Diplot
Marquess of Cheshire

**Bridger Allen**
Earl of Beaumore
m. Tallop Cibblin

**Georgia Grace**
m. Jerrod Danforth D

**Lord Thorne Magnus**
The most Honorable the Marquess of Canford

**Gideon Alrick 10th**
Duke of Roxleigh, Earl of Kelso, Earl of Sussex,
Viscount Devon and Viscount Pembroke

**Peregrine Affton**
Viscount Roxleigh

**Lord Jerrod**
Baronet Galveston

**Lady Isadore Leigh**

**Lady Maeth**

**Lady Seoirse**

**Greyson Locke**
His Grace the Duke of Warrick

**Lord Didier Timothy**
The Most Honourable the Earl of Vaughn

**Lord Quintin Joseph**

**Lady Poppy**

# FREEDOM
## PART ONE

# PROLOGUE

*April, 1880*

**M**adeleine ran as if the devil himself were on her. She glanced back when she heard the hounds then tripped, scraping her hands as her head whipped forward. Her temple struck a tree root. She groaned, feeling the trail of blood marching slowly down her forehead, the coinciding beats in her skull growing with the advance. She crawled forward, slowly at first, dirt caking the scrapes on her palms before she gathered up her skirts and scrambled to her feet.

*He will never catch me. I will never go back, I will never be his. I will die first.*

She tried to catch her breath as she stumbled wildly. Tears spilled down her cheeks as she fought the barrage of low-hung branches and high-reaching roots. She leaned against a tree trunk to steady herself, her hand shaking as she yanked at her corset, trying to loosen it.

She heard the dogs to her right and concentrated on her bearing. This was her only chance. The Earl of Hepplewort became more daring and devious with every sunset and she didn't believe her fiancé intended to wait for the marriage before making her his own. She shifted direction to compensate for the chase and glimpsed the bright sunlight of a break in the tangled woods. She knew it wasn't far to the manor, but had no idea how she was to survive the run across open meadow with his hounds on her. Surely Lord Hepplewort would call them off before the duke discovered his trespass. Surely she would make it to safety.

She heard the group of hounds approach in the rustling of the underbrush with the snarling and snapping of jaws and her heartbeat rushed to her throat, forcing a scream that tore through her like a jagged knife. The rumble of a carriage gave her hope and she drove herself toward it through the trees as one of the hounds tore at her skirts. The horn blew, recalling the dogs as she launched herself from the protective covering of the forest—directly into the path of a pair of horses.

"Mon Dieu!" The words ripped through her as the large black

horses startled and reared, their frightened neighs filling the clearing with warning. She fell back as their front legs came within a hairsbreadth of her nose, then the first hoof came down, dispatching the hound by her feet with a horrid shriek. She flung her arms about her head and prayed for a swift end.

•••

*April, today*

The alarm went off at 5 a.m. and Francine hit the snooze. It went off again at 5:10 and 5:15. At 5:20 she rolled out of bed, bleary-eyed but moving. *I should just go back to bed*, she thought. *The office would miss me for exactly five minutes before some other up-and-comer like Isaac stepped up to steal my position.* She sneered. *Let him have it.*

She dressed in soft black yoga pants and a washed-out green tank and turned for the door of her bedroom as she slipped into her shoes. Grabbing her iPod, she hurried down the hall toward the fire escape. She ran nine flights down to the second floor landing, then back up and down four more times before returning to her apartment.

Still moving quickly, she stripped her clothes off and threw them, missing the basket by the bathroom door. Instead, they landed on the ceramic tiles with a sweaty thwack. She yanked the shower on and brushed her teeth as she considered the candles and bath oils she kept on a shelf by the tub, wondering when she would have the time, or inclination, to use them. She never seemed to make it past the browse, dream, purchase phase.

Thirty minutes later Francine looked at the clock and grunted, then gazed in the mirror and took a deep breath. Her short golden hair brushed her shoulders in gentle waves. Her wide mouth was held in a tight line of concentration.

She relaxed and smiled, checking her suit for stray hairs as she flattened the lapels and smoothed the skirt around her wide hips. She glanced up at her face, catching the shadow of insecurity in her own gaze. She poked her tongue out. "Blah!" she exclaimed, staring at the mirror. As if it wasn't bad enough that she was terrified of her presentation today, she had to be obsessing about looks, too.

*Today is the first day of my future. Today is the first day of my future*, she chanted. It was the culmination of years of hard work, so why was she questioning it? Her academic accomplishments had pushed her into an internship with an international firm, and that had led to a much sought-after—albeit temporary—position. She intended to make it permanent today. She was doing what everyone expected of her, on a track bound for certain glory: a high paying position, a big house in Cherry Hills, followed by—she mentally ticked off her fingers—husband, dog, children, fish, and happiness.

Going back to her dresser, she picked up the old family portrait that had been taken just a month before the accident. Her thumb rubbed over the glass. Her mom had been so pretty, so sure of herself. So happy taking care of her family and her home.

"I hope I make you proud today, Momma," she said quietly. When her parents were killed—and she was left a ward—the court had liquidated their assets to make her moveable life more manageable. Her only tangible legacy from her parents—beyond her blonde locks—was the trust fund that followed her from foster home to foster home, her father's thesis study journals—which weren't making much sense—and a miniature of a girl that looked like her, save for the hair and costume. Francine put the picture down and picked up the miniature. "Madeleine Adelais," she said, running her thumb over the engraving on the silver frame.

She sighed heavily and her shoulders fell. *How can I not know, at this point, that what I have been working for is what I want?* Mother-number-four had always told her that she needed to work hard in school and get a business degree so she could make enough money to have the happiness she wanted. But she'd done those things, and still she felt… nothing.

She was still constantly struggling for something: a little more composure, a little more concentration, a little more time. There was so much missing from her past that the pieces of who she was floundered about, impossibly fractured and incapable of coexisting.

She glanced at the clock and her heart skipped. "Crap!" She scowled as she grabbed her cell phone, ebook reader, and the last journal in her father's set and headed for the door. She passed a bookshelf full of the same classics that were on her reader and looked back to the mirror in the hallway one last time, bright from the reflection of all the white, barren walls, then grunted as she grabbed her briefcase and left.

She nodded at G.W. as he held the front door to the old building.

He always stood tall and *always* had a smile. She loved that he seemed to be here only because he liked it.

"Good morning, Miss Larrabee," he said.

"Good morning, G.W.," she replied with a smile, juggling her accessories.

"You look lovely today."

"Why thank you, G.W."

"Of course, miss. I've a taxi waiting," he said, then turned to open the car door.

"You've saved me once again." She ducked into the back seat.

He winked. "Good luck today."

She appreciated the way G.W. always thought ahead, paid attention to what she enjoyed and needed, and always knew when she was running late. He was the perfect replacement for a boyfriend: all the care and attention and none of the drama. *Maybe I could add him to the list,* she thought. *Husband, children, dog, fish—and G.W.* She smiled.

Francine gave directions to the driver, then was tossed across the backseat, dropping her reader, the journal, and the miniature on the seat as they sped away from the curb, the door not yet fully closed. *Shit.* She should have left that home.

She picked up the portrait carefully, inspecting the girl who gazed out from the frame. She looked so confident. There was something innately familiar about her, like she could see into her soul. "What is it you have to tell me, Madeleine?" she whispered.

The taxi darted through traffic and Francine swayed, throwing her arm out to steady herself. She shook off the reverie and called her assistant. "Julia, I forgot the meeting with my father's thesis advisor about this notebook. Could you call him to reschedule? I need to speak with him. The assumptions appear to be based in fact, but—well, you saw how preposterous they are." She paused, listening.

The journals detailed a time-shift within an unnamed lineage. It developed a theory that certain people within the family were born at the wrong time, and the universe was endeavoring to return them to the age when they should have lived. Or, more precisely, to whom they should have lived with. She'd grown up thinking her father was a brilliant anthropologist, but the journals made him sound like a loon.

Francine had shared them with her assistant at the firm since she was the closest Francine had to a friend. She laughed at her assistant's snarky response. "Thank you, really, like what we need to do here is make fun of the dead." She ran a thumb over the miniature again. "No doubt my father is living in the shoes of some ancestor in the middle ages. It was his favorite era for research, after all." She smiled. "Yes, yes, I'm on my way, I just—well you know. Please call the professor and—"

The taxi lurched to the left around a corner, then was brought to a screeching halt before it could crash into an overturned delivery van. Francine jolted forward against the safety glass, her phone dropping to the floor as she was thrown back on the seat like a rag doll.

As she shook off the confusion she could feel hands on her body, but she couldn't see. She strained to open her eyes, but they wouldn't cooperate. There were sounds of fabric tearing and people screaming. She tried to touch her face, but someone grabbed her hand and yelled for someone else to hold her down. She struggled and her head flew back, hitting the ground hard. Then everything went dark.

When she came around she was gasping desperately for air. She heard rushing footsteps and a rather loud stomping. Women screamed, men commanded and—horses? *We weren't close to the 16th Street Mall, were we?* She clutched her hands instinctively, but both the miniature and her phone were gone. Francine tried again to focus her eyes, but they deceived her. Instead of the city, she saw a picturesque countryside, a pair of horses rearing, and a man with bright green eyes and thick, dark hair spilling into his face as he leaned over her.

"No!" he yelled.

She heard fabric tearing and felt an intense pressure around her ribs, then suddenly air rushed to her lungs and she was arching into him with a powerful breath. "What the hell is this?" she asked, her voice rasping with pain. She frowned and reached up to her throat; the sound had barely come out.

He shook his head. "Gentry! Smyth!" The man's baritone rumbled deeply as he shouted. Her eyes went wide when he lifted her against his hard chest, and she latched onto his lapels as her vision spun against the thundering in her temple. She tried to stay lucid but lost the battle as she felt, more than heard, the man's voice commanding those around him.

# ONE

**H**is Grace Gideon Alrick Trumbull, the tenth Duke of Roxleigh, held a countenance both foreboding and powerful. His ability to terrify people with his demeanor only helped his business dealings, creating a sense of either security or terror—depending on which side of the table one was seated—and tonight he clearly seated himself on the wrong side of his own table.

He had nearly killed a girl. If he'd been paying more attention he was sure he'd have taken note of her sooner, but his mind was on the railroad plans. Now he paced nervously in the sitting room outside the guest bedchamber, raking his hands through his hair with a growl so deep in his chest it was nearly inaudible.

When his household manager Mrs. Weston emerged, he turned on her. She stood before him, her face stricken and pale, wringing her stout fingers together. She was a short but sturdy woman with graying, mahogany brown hair gathered in a knot above the nape of her neck. She had a muddled accent that belied her history; based in cockney, then thickening in Glasgow and finishing in the service of a blue blood. She'd attended the Trumbull household for most of her life after she met and lost her husband, helping to raise the children. In all the years Roxleigh had presented Mrs. Weston with the challenges of his adventurous youth she'd not generally been taken to fits of unease when faced with an injury, and that fact alone served to worry him further.

"Your Grace," she started, trembling. "Pardon, Your Grace," she said again.

Roxleigh slowly curled his outstretched hands into claws while she continued wringing hers. She peered around him, as if looking for someone to save her. He clenched his jaw.

"What is it, woman?" he bellowed.

"Beg pardon, Your Grace. I am not sure what to say."

"Well," he began, "let us start with something simple." He straightened, clasping his hands behind his back and squaring his shoulders.

Mrs. Weston squeaked.

"Is she alive?" he asked calmly.

"Well yes, Your Grace, she—she is that."

"Good." he responded, then waited. "How about this," he said a moment later, rather sardonically, "Is she speaking?"

Mrs. Weston shifted her eyes. "Oh well, that she is, Your Grace. Yes…quite." Her eyes grew as round as saucers. "She goes on and on about where she is, and where she should be and what year it is—and she thinks we have absconded with her! She wants us to *call* her office, and notify—"

Roxleigh cut the woman off with a drastic exhale, deflating his chest as though the world needed the air worse than he.

"Fine then, Mrs. Weston, she is alive and she is speaking." He paused. "Did you say 'what year it is?'"

Mrs. Weston nodded slowly and he paced again, then stopped, waving the statement off. "Indeed, and beyond that what exactly seems to be the difficulty?" He opened his arms. "I know she lost no limbs and seemed to be—"

He was interrupted by the loud crash of something hitting the wall directly behind Mrs. Weston, who jumped forward into his outstretched arms. They both glanced over her shoulder at the spot on the wall, then he caught her gaze with a silent, pointed question.

Mrs. Weston realized herself and pushed away from him, casting her eyes downward. "That is just it, Your Grace. You see, she is a bit upset. I mean—she is not quite herself. Well, we do not know who she is, so it is difficult to say that, exactly. But she does seem to be a bit—" She hesitated. "Cross."

"I see."

Mrs. Weston shook her head. "That is to say, she does not act quite as a lady should, of course, assuming that she is a lady. She is not very ladylike, certainly. There is something about her, the way she speaks, Your Grace. She is just not quite right. We have tried, Your Grace, truly, we have tried, but we cannot pacify—"

He placed his hands on her quivering shoulders in a last attempt to calm her.

"Oh, Your Grace, I cannot—I simply have never seen anything

so—"

"Well then." Roxleigh halted her meandering. "I will just have to see what *I* can make of it." He straightened and moved her aside. He opened the door to the bedchamber and nudged the silver tray on the floor with the toe of his boot, scowling as he looked back at his wall and spied the splintered panel where it had hit.

He scanned the room. The barefoot girl was pacing in front of the windows at the far wall of the bedchamber, explaining in a raspy voice— to no one in particular—that she didn't appreciate the assumptions being made. She had naught on but a thin, sleeveless chemise and ankle-length drawers, and her long brown hair was tangled with leaves and fodder.

Dr. Walcott stood to Roxleigh's right, in front of the hearth, his white comb-over floating in disarray. Two housemaids, Meggie and Carole, cowered behind the doctor like mice tracked by a tomcat. Meggie had hold of her apron, which she twisted relentlessly in her hands. Dr. Walcott saw Roxleigh and shook his head, his hair flying in tufts around his ears.

The girl turned on him. "You!" she said, her voice catching on the force of the word as she marched determinedly for Roxleigh. "Are *you* in charge?"

"Am I— Pardon?" His eyes narrowed. "This is my estate, my land, my manor, the seat of the Roxleigh dukedom. Everything you see from these windows is within my purview, if that is what you ask." He slid his gaze over her.

She stunned him. She was not a small girl, but rather tall, though not as tall as he. His eyes traveled her womanly curves, remembering the soft feel of her weight in his arms. He could see the gash on her forehead, but she otherwise appeared healthy—angry, but healthy. He shook off his improper gaze and looked at Dr. Walcott questioningly before walking toward the settee.

"Perhaps you should put this on," he said as he reached for a robe.

The girl walked directly to him, fisting her hands on her hips as she inspected him. He felt her gaze measuring, as if to determine his very soul, and he flinched. From the corner of his vision he saw the doctor drop his hands, which had been suspended in midair as if to ward off some sort of attack.

The strange woman caught up to him, her temper evident. "The fact that I have no clothes on is an issue for both of us, but I'm not doing anything until you tell me what the hell is going on! Where am I?" The words came out on a croak, and she poked him in the chest before continuing. "I don't know what kind of damn joke this is, but I've had enough!"

The doctor and two housemaids gasped at the boldness of her speech, and Roxleigh felt the tension of their reactions weigh heavily. He released the robe and slowly straightened again as the woman went on, apparently heedless of his growing ire.

"I don't understand the problem. I want to know where I am." She started ticking off fingers as she spoke. "I want to know how I got here, and these people," she ground out between her teeth, "won't explain anything to me. They just insist I cover myself, calm down, and get back in bed. Screw your bed!" she yelled toward Dr. Walcott, who winced in return before her gaze swung back to Roxleigh. "I had a presentation today. I've been working on this for months— No! Gah! My whole life!" Her voice broke on the last word and she rubbed her throat gently as she looked down. "I sound like I smoked a pack of reds." She straightened her spine and looked him square in the eyes. "This crap isn't funny. Explain how I ended up here in this drafty room, in someone else's underwear, and how you are going to get me home!" Her voice cut out again and she held her throat as she swayed, drifting closer to him, her other hand flattening against his chest to steady herself.

Roxleigh looked from the woman to the doctor, then back. He watched as she steadied herself, then clasped his large hands together behind his back as he considered her with narrowed eyes. She spoke French, but English as well, although he couldn't place the dialect. He took a deep breath to gather his frayed nerves. He didn't much care for surprises, and was having a difficult time reconciling the soft, injured figure he'd carried from the track with the angry young lady who stood before him now. He fancied himself quite a patient man, but this behavior was more than enough to cause his control to slip.

"First of all, miss, you must remove your prodding hand from my waistcoat and gather your wits. I am more than interested in assisting you, as *soon* as *you* are able to compose yourself."

Francine glanced at her hand and suddenly felt the heat of him sinking into her skin. She yanked the appendage back. *Compose?* Her gaze snapped to his. "Compose this, jackass!" she yelled, ignoring the searing pain that knifed through her throat and head as she flipped him off.

His jaw twitched.

Taking one more step forward, she drew herself up and let her hands fall to her sides. She realized, rather abruptly, that the difference between them was not slight and she wished she had her heels on so as to even it a bit. He must have been more than six feet, and it wasn't just his height that was overwhelming. He was broad through the shoulders, which was greatly emphasized by his stark white shirt, brocade vest, and well-tailored suit. *Was I at a wedding?*

She looked back up. His jaw was wide and sharp, his full lips drawn against a set of straight, gleaming teeth, and his dark hair curled at the ends. She met his eyes. They were curious but stern--deep pools of emerald green with a few hints of topaz near the edges. Her mind swirled.

She leaned toward him, inexplicably drawn as a fly to a web, and she closed her eyes, inhaling deeply. His scent was soap and spice, slightly dusty, with a hint of salty exertion and something else she couldn't quite place. She gazed into his face, and his tense expression had the most overwhelmingly comforting effect on her.

She took a deep breath and felt her eyelids start to flutter. He seized her by both arms above the elbows and pulled her toward his chest. He held a wide stance and lifted her, her thighs drifting between his as she worked to keep her toes on the ground.

"You will show some semblance of respect when you address me within the boundaries of my estate. Is that understood?" The words rolled from the depth of his cavernous chest as his eyes smoldered, and though it was posed as a question, there was no debating the rhetorical nature with which it was delivered.

Francine glanced to the servants, wondering if they would help or hinder her, but they were frozen in place. She tried to break free of his hold as she looked back to his ferocious countenance. She felt the corded muscles of his thighs surrounding her own, his proximity overwhelming as she tried to figure out what to do with her arms. She alternated pushing her hands against his hard, unforgiving chest, then curling them toward hers. Finally, his heaving breaths accentuating his strength, she began to hyperventilate.

"Calm yourself," he said fiercely.

She turned her head away from his brutal visage only to catch sight of herself in a tall polished mirror—then forgot him altogether. Her jaw dropped and she quit her struggle as she gazed at a woman standing in her place, half-naked and covered with bruises, her hair tangled with twigs and soil. But what troubled her most was the color and length. The deep brown hair fell like water cascading over rapids, well past her waist, the curling tips gently brushing her backside. "Madeleine," she said, sotto voce. The eyes in the mirror grew wide as she lost control of her breathing entirely and stared at the reflection of who she wasn't. She tried to scream, but the sound caught and heat flooded her throat as she fell limply against him.

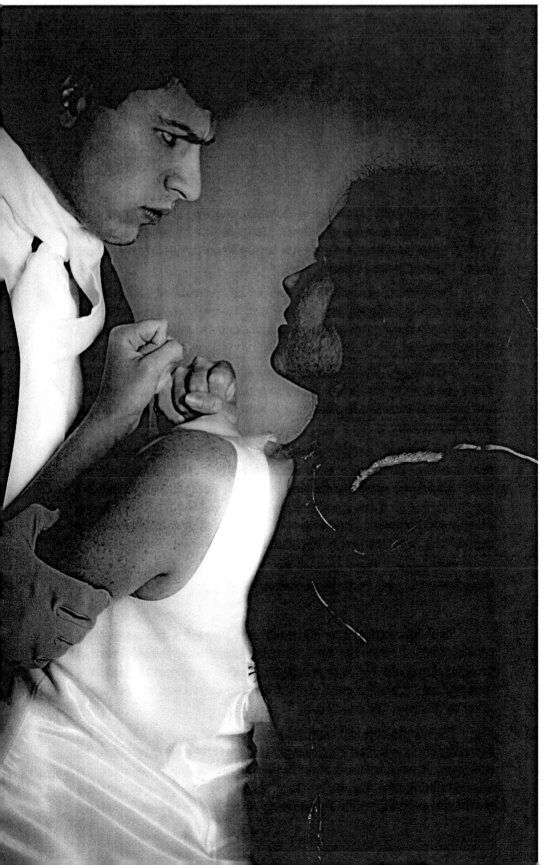

# TWO

"Bloody hell!" Roxleigh exclaimed, grasping at the wilted girl's shoulders as she slid down his front like a sack of bones. He bent one knee between her legs to brace her before she hit the floor. "Doctor, if you please."

Dr. Walcott smoothed his hair as he approached and grabbed her legs. When he finally had hold of her, Roxleigh marched with him toward the bed and released her as quickly as he was able, dropping her to the mattress.

"Thank you, Dr. Walcott, for your attention." He wiped his hands down the front of his jacket, partly to straighten his rumpled clothing and partly to erase the tingling that spread like wildfire from where he had touched her.

He turned swiftly, smoothing his disarrayed locks and straightening his waistcoat as he headed for the door. "I shall be in my study should you need me, doctor," he said as he closed the remaining gap to the exit in three great strides. He avoided the terrified faces of Meggie and Carole as he paused and looked back over his shoulder. "I expect to be kept apprised of the situation with the—uh, my...guest."

"Of course, Your Grace," Dr. Walcott replied. As the doctor leaned over the girl, Roxleigh turned and fled.

Roxleigh strode into his study and poured a fair amount of whiskey from the decanter, then turned to lean against the sideboard as he drank. He could still feel her softness pressed up against the length of him, and he rubbed his palm down his patterned waistcoat once again to try to dissipate the sensations.

He was furious at losing his composure in front of his staff. He felt so tightly drawn that if anyone came close right now they'd likely be in danger. Though it wasn't anger he felt for the strange woman—no, it was something else. The feel of her and the way she spoke to him was thoroughly perplexing. How dare she speak to him in so familiar a tone;

she was no one to him, but he was a peer. She had no right to address him without permission, much less rail at him the way she had.

He downed the last bit of whiskey and turned back to the sideboard, setting the glass down with a determined thud. He didn't understand why she affected him in such a manner. Whatever the doctor determined her malady to be, she would soon be sent away, regardless of whether he felt responsible for her injuries—

She could not stay here. He would see to it that she received the best possible care somewhere else. Somewhere far from Eildon Hill Park. Such a violently discomforting feeling had never besieged him, but he was certain once she left he would be set to rights. The Season was beginning soon and he had a wife to find. He could not be distracted with this girl.

"Your Grace, I have news," Dr. Walcott said from the entry.

"Come." Roxleigh motioned toward his desk.

The doctor scurried in as Roxleigh turned and leaned against the forward edge. He felt drained and was in no mood for further surprises. "Has she awakened so soon? I expected I would not hear from you for some time."

"Yes, Your Grace, she awakened momentarily."

"So she has gathered her wits?"

The doctor gave him a wary glance. "No, Your Grace. That is, she came about, but I gave her laudanum to calm her because she was contrary. I cannot attest to whether or not she has regained her wits, but I am of the opinion that she has not…and she will not," he said resolutely.

Roxleigh read the man's face, measuring the tension and judging the veracity of his pronouncement. In matters of the Crown he had the innate ability to precisely cut the chaff and remove the core of any situation, giving him not only a clear advantage but also the ability to complete transactions with lightning speed. He arrived, weighed, measured, decided, and departed, and in general those in his wake were left in awe. "What say you, then?" he asked, watching.

Dr. Walcott returned his gaze carefully. "She should be taken immediately to Bethlem Hospital for further evaluation, most likely for committal."

Roxleigh stiffened. His breath stilled with disbelief. She'd been irreverent, of course, but she otherwise seemed fit—except for the injuries of the collision. He could not relegate her to the devil's own crypt, no matter how contrary her nature. "No," he said harshly. The idea was untenable; he would not subject a person, a woman, to such a fate.

The doctor backed up a pace. "I beg pardon, Your Grace? I do not understand. The woman is quite obvio—"

"No," Roxleigh repeated, his voice strong and unwavering as he straightened to his full height. "I appreciate your help in this matter, and if you have completed your attentions, your services this evening are no longer required."

"Yes. Yes, Your Grace." The doctor appeared stunned. "I should mention that she seems to have damaged her voice. She should not be speaking. Since you choose to tend to her, I will prepare a list of instructions. But if you should need—"

Roxleigh dismissed him with a gesture. "I will send for you, of course."

Dr. Walcott whirled and left the study.

Roxleigh walked back to the sideboard, leaning over the whiskey decanter, his mind racing. *What have I done? If she is that far gone, there is no way for me to help her. I know nothing of this girl; I have no relation to her. Why must I feel obligated to protect her?*

But he knew why. After what seemed hours instead of minutes, he straightened once more and rang for Mrs. Weston.

"Your Grace?" she asked warily as she entered the study.

"Mrs. Weston," he said without turning from the sideboard. "It seems our guest will remain with us for a time. She has the physical mien of a lady, and shall be treated as such. She should be made as comfortable as possible and given every freedom in the manor, save one. She must never be left alone. She is your charge. Make the necessary arrangements."

"Gid… I… Your Grace?" Mrs. Weston sputtered. "Are you quite sure 'tis safe?"

He turned on her, seeing her unnerved expression. But it was not her right to question him; while he'd known Mrs. Weston for the entirety of his life, he was at this point her master and expected certain formalities. He cast her a firm sideways glance to remind her of her place. "I will not send her to Bedlam," he said quietly.

She drew a sharp breath, understanding blossoming across her features. Righting herself quickly, she replied, "Of course, Your Grace, I will see to everything. She will be well cared for here." Mrs. Weston gave a hasty curtsey and retreated from the room.

Bracing himself, he let out a deep, guttural moan, closing his eyes tightly against their sting. He turned, straightening his waistcoat once again and smoothing his unruly hair. There was no more time he could give to the matter. Yet though he had much work to accomplish, now he was entirely too agitated. He needed to ride.

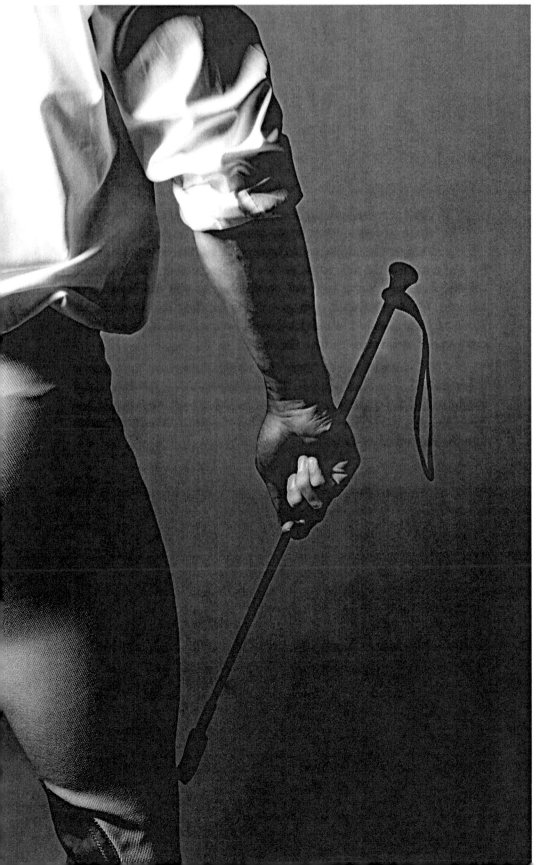

# THREE

Francine stirred as a ray of sunlight warmed her face through the window. *What day is it? No alarm—must be Sunday.* Keeping her eyes closed, she smiled and giggled at the ridiculous dream her unconscious had unleashed on her the night before. She stretched, curving her back like a cat, and reached up to rub the sleep from her eyes, wincing as her fingers grazed the bandage on her forehead. Hesitantly, she looked through her lashes. Seeing the rich brown velvet comforter that covered the bed, she froze.

"No," she whispered. There was a swift movement from across the room and she sat up suddenly. The pain lanced through her forehead and branched out in delicate webs throughout her body. She clasped her head, pressing the heels of her hands to her temples as she fell sideways into the mound of pillows.

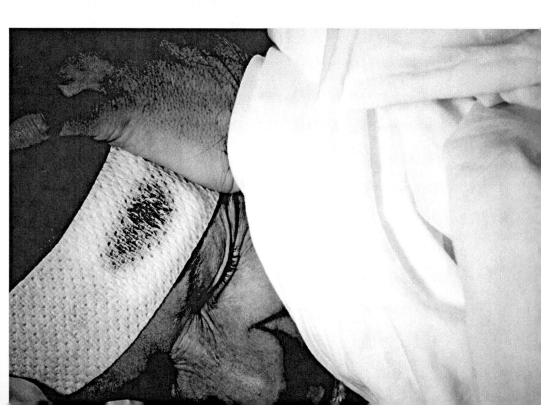

She heard someone approach, but kept her eyes shut tight against the light.

"Miss," the gentle voice said. "Miss? Is there something I can do?"

Francine groaned into the pillows as she waved one of her hands above her head.

"Is it the light, miss?" the voice asked.

"Mmmuuuh," was all that she could say, nodding her achy head as she tried to swallow. The maid quickly released the tent from the bedposts and drew the curtains closed around Francine, who relaxed immediately, letting out a desperate sigh as she sank into the mattress.

*This is not happening.*


Mrs. Weston was preparing a breakfast tray for her new charge when the small chime rang, calling her to the main guest suite. "Ah, Your Grace, I hope this girl is worthy of your kindness," she said under her breath. She hurried through the kitchen, seeing that dinner was being prepared in a timely manner, and walked out to the entry, pausing only to inspect the new day's work.

The great entrance of Eildon Manor opened to the morning and Mrs. Weston liked to see it cleaned early so Roxleigh could enjoy the sunrise. Enormous, solid cherry doors graced the front, surrounded by leaded glass windows. The room itself was a rotunda, everything about it meant to set off the large, round table centered in the entry, which would easily seat thirty guests. It had been designed, constructed, and inlaid with more than fifty types of wood that were brought as tributes from around the world to Roxleigh's great-great grandsire, Marcus Avris Trumbull, the sixth duke, who had designed and built the manor. Above the table, floating below the large, stained-glass dome, hung a crystal chandelier of the same scale.

Across from the entry loomed the grand staircase, which mirrored the shapes of the table and the chandelier. It protruded into the perfect circle of the room at its first step and rose, gently narrowing to the first floor, where the dark wall panels concealed a private parlor. The only evidence of the parlor was the row of high placed windows that signified a great, airy room which overlooked the whole of the valley at the back of the manor.

The sweeping design of the grand staircase masked the private stairways that led to passages woven throughout the walls. They ensured the servants could carry out their duties as masters required: quickly, quietly, and efficiently.

Nearly every bedchamber—almost thirty of them—consisted of an intricate suite of rooms branching off from winding hallways in awkward patterns. It was an annoyance for guests who came to Eildon, as they often became lost and had to ring the servants' bells to summon a rescue. The sixth duke, Marcus, had designed the layout in order to skulk around the manor to watch his guests, and all the goings-on, without being noticed. It also allowed him to keep both a mistress and a wife under the same roof.

Mrs. Weston turned from her inspection and shuffled for the first floor guest suite, gathering her skirts. As she turned toward the wall to enter the passage behind the grand staircae, she noted Roxleigh's curious glare from the door of his study. She nodded. He didn't move, and she could feel him watching as she ascended the stairs and disappeared into the wall.

Francine could see the maid next to the door through a breach in the curtains. She was wringing her hands as an older woman entered, the one from yesterday.

"Mrs. Weston, ma'am, she only just woke. She hasn't said anything yet, just groans and such. The light seemed to bother her, so I fell the tent."

Mrs. Weston nodded and carefully made her way across the room. "Miss," she said as she pulled the curtain back on one side of the giant bed. "I am Mrs. Weston. I shall be attending you. If there is anything you need, please never hesitate to ask."

Francine buried her head in the pillows and closed her eyes. *This isn't possible. This is a dream.*

"You have had a terrible fright, I imagine, miss. His Grace would like to notify your family that you are safe."

Francine opened one eye and looked at the woman. *Where the hell am I?* She shook her head and closed her eyes again. Even if she understood the circumstances she was currently faced with, there was no one to notify. Wherever in the world she was, she was completely alone.

She studied her surroundings. The solid wood furniture was thickly cushioned with deep cinnamon hues. She'd been surrounded with what seemed like a houseful of British and Scottish servants, a tired doctor who wouldn't listen to her pleas, and an incredibly powerful and domineering man that she could only assume was this 'His Grace' person they all kept referring to.

Her pulse quickened as she remembered him. He was straight and tall, broad and dark, the very definition of masculinity. For some reason she remembered the smell of his skin, spicy from soap and tangy from sweat. She remembered the endless depths of his eyes, swimming with anger at her outburst, but hinting of some other, deeper emotion. Most of all she remembered his grasp on her arms as he caught her and drew her up to him—flush against him from her chest to her knees—before her mind had faded. She grunted and tried again to sit up, this time a bit more slowly.

Mrs. Weston reached for the pillows at the head of the bed to help. "Here, miss, let me. 'Tis what I'm here for. His Grace has seen fit to put me at your will. There's a pull just on your right, and another by the door."

Francine opened her mouth to speak, then thought better of it. It hadn't done her any justice the last time, and at odds as she was with her current predicament, keeping her mouth shut might be the best course of action. She snapped it closed, then tried to clear her throat and instead felt it tighten. She frowned and touched her forehead then brought her hands together in her lap. She implored the woman with her eyes, hoping beyond reason that she would understand and could oblige her even a little.

"Hmm, yes... You are not remembering anything?"

Francine shook her head.

"Well, His Grace was out in the curricle yesterday. From what I gather, you came from the wood, startled the horses, and fell under hoof." Mrs. Weston gently pushed Francine's hair back from her face and examined the bandage, then the scrapes and bruises on her cheek. "One of them got you good, miss," she said. "But 'tis a miracle you weren't trampled to death."

Francine looked away. *I wasn't in a forest. I was in a taxi. I was in a taxi, and I was headed to work and then—then, what then?* She closed her eyes, trying to remember, but the memory wouldn't come. "Where am I?" she croaked, the words barely recognizable.

Mrs. Weston grimaced at the sound. "You are in the manor at Eildon Hill Park, home of His Grace, the Duke of Roxleigh."

Francine closed her eyes then looked at her again, confused. Mrs. Weston cleared her throat. "County Lanarkshire." She paused. "United Kingdom," she said finally.

Francine felt the shock cross her features and Mrs. Weston patted her hand reassuringly. "Now then, we can worry about the rest of it later."

Francine's confusion bloomed, and, as though she felt the uneasy shift, Mrs. Weston moved to change the subject. "Meggie, let's help our miss get freshened up, shall we?" She gave a strained smile.

"Yes, ma'am," the maid replied, curtseying then leaving the room. Mrs. Weston looked at Francine, appeared to expertly take stock of her needs with a considering glance, and set about the room to serve.

Meggie returned with a footman, who pushed a heavy copper slipper tub, bright with polish and trimmed with a thick round edge to lean on, followed by a parade of more servants with buckets and steaming kettles. Mrs. Weston urged Francine to stand, lending her sturdy frame. Francine watched them pour the water, letting her thoughts dissolve along with the whorls of steam that rose and twisted.

When the tub was full and the door closed on the other servants, Meggie turned, reaching for the hem of the delicate ivory chemise that Francine wore. Francine squeaked and retreated, and a surprised Meggie silently beseeched Mrs. Weston for how to proceed.

Mrs. Weston waved her away. "Leave us, Meggie. I'll see to the miss." Meggie curtseyed and took up the rest of the kettles.

"You must feel desperately in need of a bath. I know if my head were full of twigs it would be the first thing I'd ask for. Modesty aside, miss, I see you're not familiar with being tended to, but here it's necessary. You must allow me to serve you, lest His Grace be angered."

Francine saw the lightly veiled worry on the housekeeper's face and flinched at the thought of Mrs. Weston going to tattle her behavior to that man. She nodded as a tremor started in her knees and traveled throughout her body. She allowed herself to be stripped of her drawers, then waited patiently, her eyes clenched, for Mrs. Weston to remove the chemise. She was astonished when Mrs. Weston merely nudged her toward the tub, and she went, fighting her body's urge to run.

She eased one toe into the water, only to feel the powerful wash of heat move swiftly up her leg, drawing her into the warmth. She settled into the tub and closed her eyes as Mrs. Weston set about carefully removing brambles before washing her hair.

Mrs. Weston handed her a lump of lavender soap then went to the wardrobe. "We have very little here for a lady to wear, I'm afraid. I've some older nightgowns and robes that have been forgotten by previous guests, but there are no day clothes. As it stands, you'll have to stay here discreetly, for propriety's sake. And His Grace would never allow a gentle lady to wander his manor in an untoward fashion. He certainly wouldn't want to be your ruination."

Francine watched her, thinking of how like a mother she was, or rather, how like a mother she would like, and it soothed her. She remembered the warm feeling of her own mother's hands moving over her shoulders and massaging her hair while she bathed as a child. She remembered the safe feeling of her mother's arms when she pulled her into an embrace, and the soft touch of her kisses that covered her face when she was frightened. Her eyes stung and her body trembled in a great sob that seemed to begin inside and extend out, creating a ripple of water in the tub that threatened to slosh over the edge.

"Please, dear one, do not cry," came Mrs. Weston's voice, then a pause. "I beg your pardon. I tend to be a bit forward even when I shouldn't. But I find there's no reason to skirt the issue." She wrapped a towel around Francine's shoulders and urged her to stand.

Francine had no idea how she came to be in County Lanarkshire in the United Kingdom. All she wanted was to go back to her small apartment on Lafayette Street in Denver, crawl into her pillow-top bed, and sleep until she woke up, exactly where she'd lay down.

She shuddered again and stepped out of the tub. Mrs. Weston loosed the neck of the chemise and let it fall to the floor at her feet then dried her off, wrapping the large, soft towel around her and steering her toward the dressing table. She sat her down in front of the mirror and Francine raised her hand to touch her face. It was beaten and bruised, but it looked like the face she remembered. She just could not reconcile the color and amount of hair that fringed it. Hers was short and blonde. She was most definitely no longer blonde. She stared into the eyes in the mirror and the girl in the miniature danced across her memory.

*Madeleine.*

Her studious silence was broken by Mrs. Weston's cheerful voice. "Don't you worry, miss, the doctor thought the bruises and marks would all heal well. In due time you'll have your pretty face back to rights. As well as your voice. He said you should not be speaking."

Francine looked at Mrs. Weston in the mirror's reflection as the older woman combed out the tangles from her long hair. "Francine," she said on a breath.

Mrs. Weston started, almost dropping the brush, her eyes growing wide as she looked in the mirror. "Beg pardon, miss, did you say something?" she asked as she leaned over.

"Francine," she said again, barely more than a whisper.

"Francine," Mrs. Weston said definitively. "Well, that is a beautiful name. French, yes?"

Francine shrugged, falling silent again.

"Well, beautiful in any regard, miss," she said with a big, gentle smile, one that Francine could not help but to return. "Might you have another name? One His Grace could use for contacting your family?"

Francine stiffened. What kind of difficulty would that bring? If she were here, if she was Madeleine, her last name was the same. That would bring Madeleine's family, her family, her ancestors. Or this was a dream and all of it irrelevant. But if it wasn't—she shook her head, hoping to put off—what? She didn't know. She wanted to go home, but logic told her that finding her ancestors would not make that happen. She had heard the doctor talking about Bedlam before that bitter drink he'd forced down her throat had put her back to sleep. She knew of Bedlam, everyone knew of Bedlam. She rather preferred to stay where she was for now, the devil you know and all.

She felt exhausted in every respect, physically, mentally, emotionally wrecked. She returned to the bed and slept most of that day, still hoping to wake up where she thought she belonged.


Roxleigh worked quietly in his study, waiting. He didn't know for what, exactly. He hadn't seen hide nor hair of his mysterious charge since the fracas in her suite two days ago. He couldn't concentrate, his mind addled with thoughts of the woman in his guest room.

Before her arrival he'd projected a quiet and powerful façade: always attentive, always watching, always in charge. He was born with the sole purpose of becoming the tenth Duke of Roxleigh, Earl of Kelso and Sussex, Viscount Devon and Pembroke. To that end he'd been trained from birth how to behave properly, to control people and situations, to intimidate for the Crown's gain and to manipulate outcomes to his satisfaction. He was not ruled by emotions, but by propriety, principle, and grace.

That was not how he felt now.

A knock on the door echoed through his study and he flinched, not entirely sure he was prepared for what was to come. He took a deep breath. "Enter."

Mrs. Weston entered the room, drawing her small frame as tall as she could before him, then visibly melting as her gaze met his. He realized he must be a sight, practically guarding his desk from an intruder, his arms stretched wide across his desk, his knuckles white with tension. He pulled his hands to his lap and massaged the tension away as she approached.

"Your Grace," she said in a tone of voice a bit too concerned for his spirit.

"Out with it, Mrs. Weston. I would prefer to be left to my work."

"Yes, Your Grace. I came about Miss Francine—"

"Who?" He sat forward to hear her better. For the love of all that was holy, he needed to calm his nerves so she would speak up.

"The lady, Your Grace. Her name is Francine."

"She told you that? I thought she was not able to speak." He played with her name in his mind, then concentrated on Mrs. Weston, who eyed him cautiously.

"Well, she shouldn't, Your Grace, and she only told me her Christian name. Nothing more."

"I see."

"I did ask, Your Grace, but she seemed confused so I assume perhaps she cannot currently remember much."

He nodded. "And Miss…Francine, she is well? I mean, she was well enough to let you know her name, so it would seem that she does have her wits then?"

"Your Grace, I am no doctor. I can't say more than I know. She seems reasonable, but I have thought that of others." The moment the words were out, she paled and Roxleigh stood, abruptly knocking his chair over as he dropped his guard, taken aback at her callous reference to a past better left alone, particularly now.

"Your Grace, I— I did not mean to... I beg your pardon, Your Grace. What I meant to say was—and I don't mean to be forward, and I don't mean any disrespect and you know that. I only meant to tell you in a way that I am sure will leave no doubt. I'm obliged to you. I'll follow your wishes—without heed for your reasoning—and you know this of me. But I cannot, and will not, tell you what I'm unable to, Your Grace. I do not know the state of the lady's mental faculties. Now, I've said my piece."

"I understand," he said as he righted the chair and took a seat. "Why have you come?"

"Your Grace, the lady needs clothes beyond a nightdress and a robe. The gown she had was ruined. She needs day gowns, as well as the—er, other necessaries. It's right improper for a young lady to be covered by others' leavings. If she had her own gowns and such she might feel better, and she needn't be hidden like an unwanted chore. It's only right, if she surely is a guest." He could see the challenge in her stare.

He considered Mrs. Weston as he shifted the papers on his desk with one finger. There was the gown he'd torn asunder on the track. Even though she was—at the time—unable to breathe, he did owe the woman at least that, if not more, and he and Mrs. Weston both knew it.

At last, he inclined his head. "So be it. You will see to her needs."

"Of course, Your Grace. She will be delighted." Mrs. Weston gave him a relieved smile, but something about that statement rankled and he narrowed his eyes on her. "Did she bid you come here to ask this of me?"

"No, Your Grace, she would not think of it. She's more than content to wander in a borrowed nightdress and drawers. In fact, she has difficulty accepting all offers of help. In fact, she's been quite timid," she said with concern.

He nodded and dismissed her with a gesture, but called her back before she reached the door. Mrs. Weston waited. His shoulders were tense; his troubles swam in his mind. His fingertips were once again white from being pressed into the surface of his mahogany desk, and he felt the muscles of his arms twitching as though he were wrestling with an unseen foe.

When he finally spoke, he rose and looked directly at Mrs. Weston. "I appreciate your effort. Please send Ferry to my quarters and have Davis ready Samson."

Not wanting to push his difficult mood, she curtseyed. "Yes, Your Grace," she said with a smile.

When Ferry entered Roxleigh's bedchamber from the door behind the large fireplace, Roxleigh had already managed to change into a pair of doeskin-lined riding trousers. A fresh white shirt hung open at his neck and sleeves. "My boots," he said as Ferry went to the wardrobe.

Roxleigh looked around his bedchamber as he waited. The paneling was dark imported cherry, deeply tinted with hues of burgundy. The center of the room was overtaken by a large fireplace that stood out from the wall, providing a passage in the depths beyond.

As a child Roxleigh had run the passages, hiding from his father who could never catch up to him. He remembered one time in particular, not long before he lost his mother. He'd run from his angry father who thought to ambush him at the front staircase, but Roxleigh ducked through a panel next to the great entrance and ran through the winding passages and up the stairs to the first floor behind the master suite, only to be caught up in a flurry of skirts by his mother coming from the other direction.

She'd kneeled, clutching him to her chest, wrapping him in her softness, kissing his tear-streaked face, quietly repeating his name to soothe him. He could almost smell her skin again, sweet and fresh, like the gardens. She swept him away, his face hidden against her neck, into a room filled with soft, translucent panels hanging throughout like a willowy maze. The breeze from a window he couldn't see moved the delicate fabrics, causing them to graze the floor.

She carried him deep into the room to a sitting area near a large white bathtub. It was covered with hand-painted tiles, tiny flowers in hues of purple, pink, and yellow dancing across the surface.

Roxleigh shook his head, forcing the memory away. He must have embellished it greatly, because no such room existed at Eildon Manor. There was no piped water in the manor; the estate had not been wealthy enough to make such improvements until recently, but the feeling of that one imaginary room was what he wished for the entire manor to be: safe, peaceful, and joyful. He frowned; *he* didn't fit into that picture very well.

Ferry set Roxleigh's well-worn top boots next to the bench in front of the fireplace and he pulled them on, still lost in his thoughts. He'd recently decided to rid the manor of its previous masters' deviousness by rebuilding parts of the interior. He didn't approve of the clandestine way the manor was used for improper pursuits.

He knew the past had kept many in the peerage away and he hoped he could turn it into a more inviting home, one that many guests would visit. He knew no proper lady would willingly wed him and make a home in such a wickedly deceptive place. To that end, he had invited one of the brightest new London architects, Amberly Shaw, to the manor to assist him.

He stood. His personal demeanor tended to be more off-putting than anything else, including the layouts of the guest suites that tended to bamboozle visitors. It was merely his status that drew them.

Ferry returned to the wardrobe to retrieve a neck cloth, cuff links, jacket, and riding gloves.

"Don't trouble," Roxleigh said. He left Ferry there, his finishing items hanging limply from his valet's hands. His eyes wide.

"Bollocks!" Ferry exclaimed after the door clicked shut.

Roxleigh paused momentarily, then moved on.


Roxleigh rushed out the side entrance of the manor, heading directly for the stables. "Davis! My steed!" he yelled.

"Here, Your Grace, warming in the paddock," Davis replied.

Roxleigh stabled nearly forty horses, some of them mares sent to him from as far away as the Netherlands to be foaled with Samson. He preferred Friesians, beautiful, large, strong, jet-black horses known for their carriage and manner. They had an inherently smooth gait and incomparable demeanor, and the fact that their presence was often viewed as both regal and foreboding was also an asset. He took a great deal of pride in his breeding program and in turn it brought success and notoriety to the Friesian line.

Roxleigh approached Samson, stroking his muzzle. At nearly seventeen hands, the horse was one of the largest riding Friesians in all of Europe. The steed bristled and whinnied. Samson was Roxleigh's champion and a proud and competitive horse. He didn't like to come in second— he didn't like to *run* in second. He knew when he was lagging and was more of a competitor than even his master. He was no match for the quarters and would never win a race, but yet he was a specimen unto himself.

Samson twitched and stamped his front hoof, eager to set out. "Yes, of course," Roxleigh muttered, placing one hand at Samson's crest. "We'll be off soon," he said, double-checking the saddle and rein. "How are Delilah and Kalliope?" he asked Davis.

"They are well, Your Grace," he said. "Only scrapes and bruises. There's no further evidence of damage to Delilah's cannon bone as feared. Both mares have recovered well."

"Good."

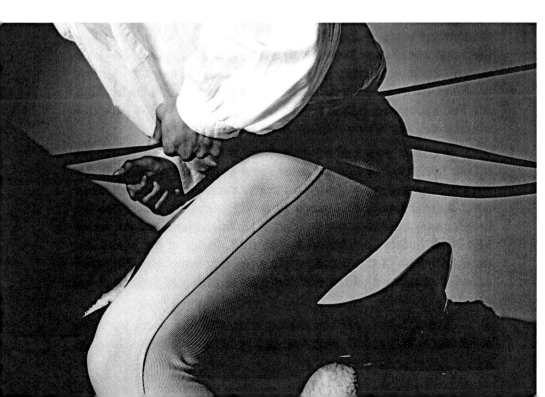

Though Samson and Delilah had yet to drop a foal, Roxleigh had found stunning success with Kalliope, who had been a broodmare when he purchased her not three years before. He was obsessed with replicating the depth he found in the tones of her sleek blackness, and the yearlings she had with Samson were of the best conformation and promised excellent action for many purposes.

His horses were his pride and were treated as extended members of his family. When he'd taken Kalliope and Delilah out to train with the curricle, he never expected the ruckus from the wood, or that the horses would have startled so badly as to nearly kill a woman and do away with a hound.

That foxhound still troubled him. He thought that if he discovered its owner he might have answers to some of his questions about—

"Francine," he whispered. She was like no one he had ever met. She cared not for his title or status. Waving them off like a fly at her tea.

"Pardon, Your Grace?" Davis said.

Roxleigh grunted. "We're off!" he said quickly, leading Samson through the paddock gate. He pulled himself up onto the saddle, the large horse bristling and whinnying with the excitement of the coming run. Roxleigh smiled at the way his muscles pulled in his thighs from the sheer girth of the horse. He needed to feel the tangible pull of muscles, the eventual soreness the work would bring him, and the exhaustive sleep that would greet him this night. Samson nickered and Roxleigh took up the reins, leaning into his knees. The horse needed no more prodding. He took for the open meadows at the base of the Eildon Hills at a heart-pounding gallop, toward the forest and river at a pace that would startle any other horse and rider.

Samson's grace and surefootedness at breakneck paces was the closest Roxleigh had ever come to some semblance of peace in his life. His head was never clearer, his nerves never calmer, and his mind never more unbound than when he rode Samson. He listened to the horse's steady breathing, the exertion of his exhalations, and the steady beat of his hooves, punctuated by the swift silence of the jumps and the exclamation of the landing—like a staccato symphony. His mind unfurled its stressed tethers with the smooth action of Samson at full speed.

Roxleighshire was the closest town and the ducal seat. His residence, at Eildon Hill Park, was one of the largest estates in all of the United Kingdom, including forest and field. The light this far north was surreal, crisp and clear, perfectly toned—not detracting from the natural colors of the world or inhibited by extensive amounts of coal smoke like the larger cities. The first of the three Eildon Hills was home to his manor, the second was the site of the ruins of an old Roman fort known as Trimontium, and the third provided a view of the expanse of his lands. The Ettrick forest at the base of the hills met the meadow in a dramatic, heavenly rise, sheltering the meeting of the Teviot Water with the River Tweed not far from the manor as they meandered through the wood and clearings.

Roxleigh was passionate about his land, his manor, and the people it provided for. The estate, and the privacy it garnered, kept him close to home. He didn't like to be disturbed, he wasn't keen to socialize, and he only traveled to London when his duties to the realm required it of him. He had currently been in residence for nearly seven months, leaving only to visit the towns, shires, and villages within his purview.

Roxleigh leaned into the steed as Francine's face hovered in his memory. He kept his eyes on the path ahead, attempting to clear his thoughts to everything but the sound of the ride.

After what Francine believed to be three days of sleep, but felt more like a century, Mrs. Weston allowed her to leave the guest suite. She followed the housekeeper along the upper balcony, marveling at the expanse of the entryway and the sheer beauty of its adornments. She was taken to the family parlor at the back of the manor, which looked out over an expanse of meadow and field beyond a maze of hedgerows. She could also see the two neighboring hills and the edge of the forest.

It really was a beautiful room with an incredible view, but there was only so much resting and looking Francine could handle. She curled up on a settee once Mrs. Weston left, picking at the trim on the back. She wanted to explore, but she knew she wasn't allowed anywhere else in the manor, save her suite, since she wasn't properly attired. She'd thought about sneaking around anyway, but there was always someone nearby, even when she thought she was alone.

She was terribly unnerved about being trapped in this unknown place, but had no idea what she could do about it. She had tried to get information from the doctor, but he had refused to answer her questions, instead demanding she rest, or cover herself, or calm down.

Mrs. Weston was comforting, and Francine knew she refused too much of her assistance, but she couldn't help it. She liked to take care of herself.

She stood and paced the length of the parlor, running her fingers over thick brocade cushions and soft damask upholstery. Everything was so precisely made, definitely not of the ready-to-assemble vein of her bookshelves and furniture. It seemed to be the stuff of a different era, which had occurred to her before, but the country she was in was so much older than hers to begin with that she had no way to measure. If her father's hypothesis was correct, she was not only in a different place, but also a different time. *A different time. A. Different. Time.* Her breath caught and her hand went to her chest where her heart skipped.

She considered everything her father had written in his journals about the unnamed family. She was told she was in the United Kingdom, and judging from the accents and behaviors of the people around her she believed it, but most likely it was a more recent era than the Jane Austen books she loved. Definitely more recent than Shakespeare. By the corsets alone she would think it Victorian.

Even so, Francine tried to convince herself that this episode was some sort of waking dream, or unconscious dream, or delusion, or—something. She must have pulled the scenario straight from the journals, and her appearance from the portrait. She wondered if this was really what her assistant had lovingly termed her family curse. She knew it was ridiculous, but if this was a dream, she hoped—for now—that it would last as long as her mind could will it to, and she wasn't entirely sure why. Seemed odd for a vacation. She wanted—no—needed to learn more of the duke.

Her attention was pulled toward the tall windows and doors lining the balcony by a giant black horse careening across the lush valley at the base of the rolling hills. It seemed impossible that a horse that large could propel forward at such a pace. The animal was nearly as beautiful as the rider it carried, at least what she could remember of him, and her breath caught on that twinge of remembrance as it sparked.

Most of her memories from that first day were faint, like looking through leaded glass, but his eyes were perfectly clear in her head, green and bright like polished emeralds shot through with molten topaz.

She placed both hands against the cool glass of the window and considered the horse and rider. The horse was black on black, gleaming brightly in the sun with his long waved tail and mane floating in the wind. The spray of silky hair above his hooves created a fluid look, like a hummingbird in flight. His step was sure and smooth, and the man, His Grace, floated along just above the saddle, with only his arms working to steady him.

Francine looked ahead of them and saw the forest looming dangerously. Her heart quickened as she scanned the tree line, then quelled when she picked out the small path that cut the dense copse. She raised a hand to her mouth as she waited, hoping he would break off and turn back. She imagined it would take a great deal of trust between an animal and its rider to be able to accomplish such a reckless pace through the thick forest. Even with a well-worn path there were treacherous limbs and roots that would change with the earth, requiring an immeasurably keen alertness.

Francine wondered what it would be like to put her complete trust in another being. She couldn't begin to fathom what that kind of freedom would feel like. She was suddenly saddened, realizing that in all her life she had never felt such a liberty; she had never run as fast as her legs could carry her or even driven a car to its limit. She felt a pang of self-pity, recognizing that in the absence of parents, she had kept herself overly safe. She suddenly, *desperately*, realized she wanted to be on that horse, riding hell-bent for leather, without a care as to destination or outcome. She wanted freedom from her ordered life, from the rooms she was restricted to, from the skin of her being.

Francine threw the window open and closed her eyes, feeling the cool breeze washing over her. She leaned past the edge as the wind flew up the side of the manor into the open window. She smelled the earthiness of the clearing and the damp of the woods beyond. She stood smiling, her arms held out, grasping at the air and the possibilities until a woman's terrifying scream jolted her from the reverie and she jumped back, losing her balance at the sill.

# FOUR

Mrs. Weston wandered the manor, surveying the work of the under servants. The past days had run into countless tense and nerve-racking hours of seeing to her new charge. She never knew quite what to expect from their guest, so she stayed up most nights keeping watch—and slept hardly at all during the days as well, tending her customary duties. She knew she was wearing thin.

Francine wasn't speaking and seemed fearful, but she had trusted Mrs. Weston enough to share her name and would soon begin to trust her with more, the housekeeper hoped. It wouldn't be long before everything would settle down or Francine's family would come looking for her.

The thought arrested Mrs. Weston and she suddenly frowned. She didn't want everything back to normal. She realized normal hadn't been all that wonderful; it had been mundane. The manor was run smoothly and efficiently; Roxleigh had seen to that. And he was a generous master and duke. The tenants had no complaints and when they did they were seen to. She itched for something to happen beyond the silver needing polished. Again.

Roxleigh had a novel way of running his lands, and his management had turned Eildon into a more profitable estate than it had ever been. She knew that Roxleigh's father, Darius—the previous duke—had very nearly driven the estate into the ground. He was resentful of his life and his station. He blamed the world for his misfortunes and didn't see the most blessed part of his life, his son, right before him.

It was a tragedy to see him work himself to an early grave, but there had been no helping him after—

*No.* She stopped that train of thought. Things were different. She could feel it in her marrow. There was something happening and it was all coming along with the girl upstairs.

Mrs. Weston finished her rounds and headed straight to the private parlor where she witnessed something she thought never to see again—and she screamed.

Francine stumbled from the window. She cried out, but the sound was trapped in her vocal chords, and she put one hand to her mouth, the other to her throat. Shaking from her toes to her shoulders with fright, she nearly fell to the floor as Mrs. Weston rushed over. She looked into the woman's round, gentle face and saw the infusion of fear. She dared not utter a word.

"Apologies, Miss Francine, you gave me a start. What were you doing?" Mrs. Weston asked nervously. Francine shook her head. She glanced at the window, trying to figure out what was so fearful as to cause Mrs. Weston to scream like that.

"Miss Francine," Mrs. Weston said with a disapproving look on her face. "I know you do not speak, but I also know you can. And if you do not tell me what you were doing at that window, I will have to inform His Grace about exactly what I saw. I cannot take a chance on this. Go back to your silence afterward if you must, but trust me now or there'll be hell to pay when he returns."

Francine looked into the woman's eyes, noting the well-masked concern. She certainly didn't want a bad word to get to *him*. She glanced toward the window. She was keenly aware that her existence here at the manor was conditional and if she disrupted him she might be sent away. It was that unknown that she couldn't bear, even though she had become accustomed to it. She'd faced that before, when the police came to take her away after her parents died, and now as a grown woman she dreaded it even more.

"I..." She cleared her throat gingerly. She could handle no more than a whisper, and even that strained and tightened the muscles of her throat to a thick, scraping ache.

"Go on now, out with it," Mrs. Weston prodded. Francine clutched her hands together.

"I don't want to be sent away," she cried, and with that she wept. Mrs. Weston put one of her soft arms around Francine's shoulders, pulling her down to the settee and cradling her against her ample chest.

"There, there, miss, don't fret. I will see that you stay. Why, only now I was looking to tell you that His Grace gave me leave to have some gowns made for you. Is that not a wonderful thing? If he was intending to send you away, would he be seeing to your comfort?" Mrs. Weston asked.

Francine shook her head. "No, I don't suppose so," she said.

"All right then, tell me, what has got to you? Why were you going out the window like that?" Mrs. Weston asked.

Francine stared at her. Out the window? She wasn't out the window; she was at the window. Wasn't she? She never went out the window. Realization dawned and she sat up straight, looking at Mrs. Weston in horror. "Oh, no. No! I wasn't going anywhere!"

She groaned and clasped her throat. She struggled to speak, both of her hands massaging, trying to coax the words out as she sought to explain. "I was only feeling the breeze, I—I just, felt the breeze, I felt—" She shook her head. "I saw him on the horse and—" She clenched her eyes against the pain and tried to continue. "They were running toward the forest and it looked so—" Her breath caught in her throat; her voice was done.

"All right, miss, calm yourself. There, there, calm yourself." Mrs. Weston moved Francine to a chair by the fireplace and rang for a maid.

"Meggie, put the kettle on and have tea sent up," she said when the girl entered.

When Meggie returned, Mrs. Weston poured some hot water into the teapot and the rest into a dish on the tray, soaking a soft cloth. She wrung it out and brought it over to Francine, wrapping it around her throat.

"There'll be no more words from you for a time, I'd say." Mrs. Weston considered Francine with a stern face as she stood directly in front of her. "I just have one question. I expect the truth from you, and if I don't get it, I will know it. Do you understand me, miss?" Francine nodded. "Did you intend to fall from the window, miss? Did you intend to die today?" she whispered.

Francine shook her head until her hair tangled around her fingers as they held the cloth at her neck. Mrs. Weston shook her head, too. "Oh, there now, miss, you're making yourself a fright. I believe you, just— I had to know. You see? I'm in charge of you, and I need to know if something is not as it should be. Do you understand?"

Francine nodded. "Please," she croaked, barely audible, her eyes stinging with tears.

Mrs. Weston pushed her long unruly hair out of her face. She loosed the knot, since it was halfway to being undone anyway, and smoothed the mane down her back.

"Settle there, miss. We'll talk again when you're ready. Don't try yourself further. I'm sorry if I caused you any pain. I will send for the doctor to come look at you, to see to your…" Mrs. Weston patted her own throat and Francine nodded, relaxing.

She looked up at Mrs. Weston, wondering why everyone seemed to have a deep spark of terror shielded in their eyes, as though she were completely naked, or bleeding profusely, or wielding a knife. No one seemed to have a peaceful moment around her; they were strained and overwrought, but she believed them when they said she wouldn't be sent away as long as she behaved, just like in the foster homes. She would stay here; Mrs. Weston would see to it.


Mrs. Weston poured a cup of steaming tea with honey to help relax Francine's strained throat and nerves. She glanced at Francine as she stirred the tea and set it on the table next to her. She believed Francine. She believed that the girl hadn't intended to throw herself from the window. The problem, however, was that she hadn't believed the Duchess of Roxleigh had intended to, either.

# FIVE

Roxleigh vaulted Samson into a clearing bordered by forest and river, then leaned back in the saddle, slowing him to a trot. This particular stretch of the Teviot Water was slow and peaceful, with very little slope to hurry it along. It widened, creating a welcoming pool, before it turned back into the forest where it began the descent to the River Tweed. He had visited this place all his life, swimming in the clear waters to find his own peace.

He dismounted, falling to the grass of the meadow, his thoughts still racing as Samson meandered close by, grazing and drinking from the pool. Although he couldn't stand the thought of the girl in his home, neither could he tolerate having her hauled off to Bedlam.

Roxleigh didn't have time for this preoccupation. He needed to be done with the entire situation.

He stood and checked Samson's hooves, then walked to the water's edge, his steed following faithfully. He was damp with sweat, his clothes stained from the leaves of trees—he was most thoroughly disheveled from the ride. He should never have left in such a hurry. At the least he should have finished dressing, retrieved his gloves and jacket, but he needed to be away. To ride the way he did through the forest was madness, and he knew it. He felt a mess: unfinished, improper, uncomfortable and, in general, confused.

He didn't *need* any more distractions right now. The architect was on his way to begin measuring and plotting the reconstruction of some of the unused and impossible areas of the manor. The work needed to be closely overseen if he was to host an extended house party at the end of the summer, something he was looking forward to with rampant trepidation.

He rolled his open cuffs to his elbows, examining the cuts on his forearms and hands from the whip-like tree branches that had assaulted him in the forest. He put his hands to his face and with a great roar crouched at the edge of the pond on his boulder. The rock was large and flat-topped, tilting into the water's edge. He threw water at his face, letting the rivulets course down his shoulders and chest.

He closed his eyes, allowing the serenity of the meadow to wash over him like the sound of the lapping pool. He rolled back on the rock and rested his head on his hands as his mind drifted to Francine and the day she came to Eildon Hill.

In his head he heard the crash of the tray against the wall and entered the room. She was completely alone and dressed only in a chemise so thin he could see through it. Her long, chestnut hair draped around her shoulders like a velvet cape as she stood quietly at the window, gazing out at his land.

The sun rose over the forest and golden light filtered through the silk, outlining her soft figure against the glass. The length of her hair gently brushed the curve of her backside as she shifted, forcing the muscles in his stomach to tense.

He imagined dragging his fingers across her waist, letting her curls fall back to her body, sending shivers across her flesh. He stalked across the room, his eyes taking in the curve of her ankle, the dimples behind her knees, the crease that met the sumptuous curve of her buttocks.

He longed to drag his fingers nimbly across that sensitive fold and, in a breath, he was kneeling before her as she turned toward him. His hands smoothed up her thighs, gathering the chemise on his forearms and leaving a trail of gooseflesh in his wake. Embracing her hips, his thumbs rested on the pulse points, which hastened with his touch at the seam between hip and belly.

His breath stirred the delicate fabric of her chemise as it rested on his arms, and he felt the muscles of her abdomen tense. He nudged it aside with his nose and placed his mouth on her skin, dragging his lips from one indented hip to the other, breathing heavy sighs of warmth into the triangle of curls at his chin. She wavered slightly and he moved one hand to her backside to steady her as he drew the other hand down her leg, gently lifting it over his shoulder.

She placed a hand on his head, tangling her fingers in his hair as he turned and kissed the inside of her raised thigh, stroking it with his fingers from one bend to the next. His cheek brushed against her and her hand fell to his nape, urging him on.

Taking her hips, he pressed her back against the window's edge, caressing her heated skin. The chill at her back from the window and the heat of his hands on her skin must have called forth the whimper that escaped her lips, and she dropped her head back against the fogged glass, streaking the dew.

He brushed his cheek across her thigh as her hair fell away from her shoulders. From this angle he could see the slow curve of her belly rising gently to the soft, round push of her breasts, the rosy pink buds straining against the translucent chemise.

The curve of her neck swept up to the defined triangle of her jaw, and he could see a swallow move her pulse, quickening in the twin veins that framed her throat as he stroked her. Her lips parted to sigh and he came undone. Standing, he felt a rush of cold flood his boots and he looked down. The room filled with icy water and she vanished with a jolt, his booted feet soaked by the water's edge when he stood.

"Ah, for fuck's sake!" He pulled at his boots, tossing them at the sun-heated stone, then watched the patterns of water dissipate in the heat.

He'd sent his mistress away in early December, not wanting to begin another year with someone who was easy to bed and slow to leave. He was determined to find a wife by the end of this year and there was no way he could do so with such trivial physical distractions. Here, at the onset of spring with this mysterious woman underfoot, he could see that the diversion of a mistress might have done him a favor in dealing with her. Had his need not been so deep, his want might be controlled.

"Come," Roxleigh grunted as he pulled his boots back on with great difficulty. Mounting the horse once more, he gave him his head to careen through the forest. He watched the trees and path closely, gently nudging the stallion with his knees to avoid any brambles that might trip him up. He did it mostly out of habit, knowing Samson would find the safest, fastest way home with no help from him.

He closed his eyes, gripping the reins in his calloused hands, feeling the sheathed muscles that moved beneath him, the rise and fall of the horse's gait, the smell of the trees, the dust and sweat rolling from his face with the wind they created. He breathed deeply and opened his eyes as they soared into the park at the base of Eildon Hill and continued at a great speed toward the manor. Roxleigh felt an electricity in the air and quickly sat back, pulling on the reins and bringing the massive beast to a halt.

He perused the outwardly graceful manor atop the hill. It was majestic, built of large light-grey stones quarried not far away. The strength of the stone and the flying buttresses at the sides and back gave them the ability to open the facing walls to the interior with spectacular windows. The architecture also provided for a sheltered pathway around the exterior that was used to create the sunrooms, including the breakfast room, and several greenhouses.

Roxleigh had never seen a manor in England that rivaled it. If it weren't for the passion he felt for this place, the land, and his people, he would have left and never looked back. He held several estates where he could reside, all of them closer to London, and thus more convenient. But along with the nightmarish visions of his youth came the wonderful ones, and every single memory involved Eildon because his family had never been attached to London society like the majority of the peerage.

While the exterior appeared powerful and protective, the interior was chaotic and beautiful. The complexity of it astounded him. He could never leave this place—at least not for long. He closed his eyes, taking a deep breath, and a scent caught him. He shifted his gaze, searching the gardens. He glanced toward the parlor balcony and saw the figure peering out.

The wind rushed up to her from the valley in greeting, sweeping her hair over her shoulders as she threw her head back. She leaned against the balustrade, putting her arms out to steady herself. She probably didn't think anyone would see her, but he did. She pressed herself toward him, her nightdress pulling tight against her chest, accentuating the gentle curves of her body beneath.

He groaned, and as if the wind carried the sound of his sigh to her ears, she became aware of him. She looked down as her mouth dropped open. Obviously flustered, she turned and tripped on the long borrowed nightgown, falling back into the depths of the parlor in a flurry of white fabric.

Roxleigh caught the scent of her again, lavender and rain. He let out another deep groan as she disappeared and he shifted his seat, trying to regain the comfort of his saddle. Watching the empty balcony, he leaned forward to drive Samson in an easy gait around the side of the manor to the stable, still without taking his mind from her supple figure. As he passed the paddock he called to Davis.

"Yes, Your Grace," Davis said, running from the stable.

Roxleigh slid from the horse, stroking his withers and neck before handing over the reins.

"Did he work hard for you, Your Grace?" Davis asked with a broad grin.

Roxleigh looked up at the horse. "As he does."

"Aye, he does, Your Grace. That he does." Davis walked Samson to the paddock to cool his muscles and rub him down before putting him up for the night.

Roxleigh turned and strode to the manor, rubbing his palms gingerly, feeling the newly sore calluses. He eased his cramped muscles as he walked and thought about the woman who had managed to turn his life upside down without so much as a full conversation. He decided it was time to change that. She would join him for supper.

Determinedly he walked in the front entrance before the butler could even see to the door. "Your Grace?"

"Stapleton, call Mrs. Weston."

"Yes, Your Grace." Stapleton bowed and disappeared.

Roxleigh looked down at his attire—his white shirt no longer crisp but hanging open at the neck and sleeves, his riding pants rumpled and untucked from his soggy, drooping boots. He still held the riding crop and grumbled. He should have left it in the stables. He swatted at the dust on his trousers with the crop and decided it was time for new boots. Disgruntled, he moaned at the thought of breaking a pair. He started to unroll his sleeves but was interrupted by the sound of footsteps coming from behind the grand staircase, and he looked up to find the housekeeper walking toward him.

"Mrs. Weston, I wish to have our guest to supper. Please advise me as soon as she is able."

"Yes, Your Grace," she said in a confused manner as she came to a stop, eyeing him.

"What?"

"Well, Your Grace, you're a sight," she began, then cleared her throat as if aware of her familiarity. "As you know, Miss Francine is not yet in any position to be at supper with a gentleman." She paused. Her left eyebrow rose nearly to her hairline. "Or anyone, for that matter," she finished with a stout nod.

He growled. "Of course," he said, unrolling his other sleeve.

"Shall I ring for Ferry?" she queried, the eyebrow still cocked in a curious gaze.

It bothered him the way Mrs. Weston sometimes took liberties, but occasionally overlooked it since she'd happened to be there when he was brought into the world and had cared for him thenceforth. "Has Dr. Walcott checked on our guest?" he asked, choosing to ignore the impertinence.

"No, Your Grace. He is expected within the hour."

When he finished unrolling his sleeves he clasped his hands behind his back and stood wide, tensing his muscles. The position drew his figure straighter and sturdier, making full use of his height and his broad shoulders. He latched onto Mrs. Weston's gaze and held it. "What has the girl said?"

Mrs. Weston became flustered. He knew she hated it when he used this tactic with her, mostly because it worked so well. There was nowhere for her to run and hide, and no way for her to lie or omit anything. "Well," she said, "she agreed to the visit from the doctor and she appreciates the gowns, though as I told you she is a bit unhappy about your generosity."

"What?" He released his hands and stepped forward.

Mrs. Weston held up a hand. "Sorry, Your Grace, I meant to say that she's overwhelmed by it, she doesn't want to be a bother. She doesn't seem to feel that she's worthy of the expense," she corrected.

He stopped cold. "I see. I—misunderstood." He paused. "You will send Dr. Walcott to me as soon as he is finished and you will let me know as soon as she is able to attend supper."

"Yes, of course, Your Grace," she said as he waved her off. She scurried for the servant's passage, her hand on her chest. "Oh Lord, you do work me, Your Grace," he heard her whisper as soon as she was out of sight. Odd how well sound carried in that particular room.

There was a soft knock at the door and Meggie entered with Francine's supper tray, setting it before the fire.

Mrs. Weston entered just as she was sitting down to eat. "I sent for the dressmaker in town when I sent for the doctor. She'll be up by week out, and Dr. Walcott should be here any time now."

Francine nodded resignedly and smiled. She was already receiving too much from the duke. His hospitality was more than any reasonable person would expect. She thought about the terrace, when he had seen her, and her face heated in a blush as she looked at her supper tray. The look on his face when he'd looked up at her still had her flustered.

The food here was unrecognizable—strange cuts of unknown meats, fancy colored gel-like substances filled with vegetables, and grey colored sauces that seemed to drown everything—as though it was merely the texture of the food that mattered and not the flavor.

Cynically, she thought it the best diet she'd ever been on, and she placed her hand over her mouth and laughed a bit. *If this is my dream, why can't I have a big New York strip with a buttered baked potato and glazed asparagus with lemon pepper?*

She clenched her eyes tight and envisioned it, willing the steak dinner to her plate. She sighed when she opened her eyes to the same colorless glop and then saw Mrs. Weston watching her quizzically. Francine realized she was only adding fuel to the fire of her own oddity. She shook her head and smiled at Mrs. Weston, then picked up the fork and tried to eat.

After supper, Mrs. Weston asked Meggie to fetch the slipper tub and prepare a bath. It had been a long day. Mrs. Weston was ready to be done with it, and she hoped that Miss Francine would feel the same. A nice warm bath would ease her muscles and ready their guest for bed—she was sure of it.

As Dr. Walcott examined Francine, Mrs. Weston turned the bed down and placed a warm brick at the foot. It wasn't quite summer yet, but her grandmother had always said that warm feet made a sleepy head, and what she needed right now was for Miss Francine to sleep so she could retire to her own bed. She'd arranged for Meggie and Carole to watch over her in shifts, sleeping in the adjoining servants' room and keeping an eye on her from the passageways whenever she wandered.

The doctor nodded when he finished, and Mrs. Weston let out a hearty sigh as he left.

Dr. Walcott knocked at Roxleigh's study before leaving the manor.

"Enter."

The doctor opened the door and Roxleigh stood, motioning him to the desk.

"You have already attended my guest."

"Yes, Your Grace. Her physical wounds seem to be healing nicely, but she isn't speaking, and that concerns me, considering her reaction—"

Roxleigh cut him off with a gesture. "I have heard, listened to, and understand your concern, Dr. Walcott—but we will not, again, discuss sending her to Bedlam. Is that understood?"

Dr. Walcott cringed, then nodded. "I have removed her bandages. I will return again at a later time to check on her—wounds," he said stiffly.

"As you see necessary, Doctor."

"Your Grace." And with that Dr. Walcott left.

# SIX

Francine was in a daze as the next days drifted slowly by. She awoke with the sun from the windows, breakfasted in her room, then sat in the private parlor watching the breeze stirring the trees, where she was currently. The most exciting moments were when Roxleigh left on his afternoon ride, though it never seemed as vigorous and fervent as the first time she saw him. She didn't dare venture outside on the balcony again.

He was infuriating. So pious in his demand for propriety. The fact that his wishes were constantly conveyed to her through Mrs. Weston was equally annoying.

*I should run through the house screaming like a banshee simply to get a rise out of him. Force him to confront me personally.* She let her mind's eye take him in—the soft dark brown of his hair; the beautiful deep green of his smoldering eyes; the straight, broad shoulders that cut off the sun behind him; the narrow waist tucked into the fine weave of his trousers. She gasped, catching her train of thought as it barreled down the wrong track. That was not exactly the kind of rise she should be considering.

She slapped her hands over her eyes and shook her head. Maybe if he never opened his mouth—no, actually his mouth was irrelevant, less than irrelevant. She shook her head. But those wide solid lips that more often curved down than up, the arc of his mouth—

She grunted and lay down, turning her face into the soft cushion of the settee. Who was she kidding? He couldn't possibly be more attractive. Her eyes glazed over and there he was again, standing before her. She desperately needed something else to occupy her addled brain.

Mrs. Weston felt terrible keeping Francine hidden away with nothing to keep her. She poked her head in the private parlor to see how the poor girl was doing and saw her lying on the settee, hitting the back with her fist. "Humph," Mrs. Weston mumbled. She closed the door quietly and descended to Roxleigh's study.

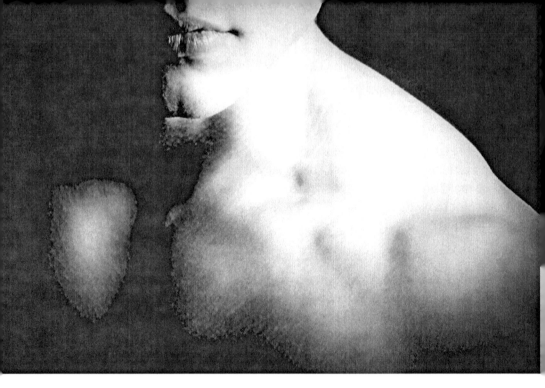

"Enter," he said gruffly.

He was in a mood; she could tell from that single word. She straightened her drab woolen skirts and opened the door.

"Your Grace," Mrs. Weston said.

He looked up at her warily, one eyebrow cocked.

She approached his desk, suddenly a bit nervous. These days he always seemed to be in a mood, but there wasn't much to do about that. *Maybe this wasn't such a good idea,* she thought. She panicked like a rat in a trap, the problem being he had her by the tail.

Roxleigh watched. "Out with it," he said finally.

"Your Grace, it's Miss Francine, she's— She's a might bored. She can't go anywhere, and the days are a trifle long."

He leaned back in his chair, holding her gaze.

"I thought, Your Grace, mayhap I can take her to the library, through the passages, so she can select a few books? I think if she'd a book to read it might be—"

"No," he cut in without hesitation.

Mrs. Weston's eyelids fluttered at his asperity. "But—but, Your Grace, she has naught to do, can you just imagine? All sh—"

"What I meant was, you may escort her to the library, but you will take her down the main stair. I do not wish her in the passages. I prefer she never see them. You have one hour."

Her feet stuttered. She wasn't sure whether to run straightaway, or thank him profusely first. She finally decided she ought to express her gratitude, lest he regret the decision. "Thank you, Your Grace. I'll see to it immediately."

"Mrs. Weston," he said, catching her before she could leave.

"Yes, Your Grace?" She turned back nervously.

"I will not find a nightgown-clad girl in any of the common areas of Eildon Manor. She is not to think that she can traipse around here simply because I allowed this one excursion. She should collect enough books to keep herself occupied. For a while."

"Yes, of course, Your Grace," she said as she scurried for the door.


Francine was still daydreaming when Mrs. Weston entered the private parlor. "Oh, Miss Francine, come. We've not much time, come, come!" Francine stood and Mrs. Weston shuffled her out of the room.

Francine panicked and turned away, but Mrs. Weston simply grasped her wrist and pulled her down the stairs, looking around as if to ensure they were alone. "His Grace said I can take you to the library. Come, we've only got one hour, miss."

Francine heard the words and stopped fighting Mrs. Weston, instead running down ahead of her. When she reached the bottom she looked at the circle of doors she was met with, wondering which was the library. Mrs. Weston caught up to her and took her hand.

"This way," she said.

At the first door Francine halted, pulling Mrs. Weston back. Her gaze drifted toward it as she rested a hand on the seam of the double door. Mrs. Weston went pale.

"Oh, miss, no. That's his study. His Grace is in there. Come away, please!" she whispered violently.

Francine looked at the door, hearing the panic in Mrs. Weston's voice. She couldn't help herself, though, she felt— What did she feel? She felt something, a connection, the feeling of him holding her as she collapsed, the shock of his hard muscles against her, the tremble of his voice against her body. She quietly exhaled, placing both hands against the door, listening.

Mrs. Weston grabbed her forearm and pulled her away and into the library, shutting the doors solidly. She peered through the crack between the double doors before she turned on Francine.

"Look here, miss! I took a great risk to even ask this favor for you, and you need to heed my warnings! Please don't tempt him. He's in an awful state, one you cannot imagine."

Francine turned to Mrs. Weston and placed her fist against her chest, sweeping it in a circle around her heart before looking back to the room. If she couldn't speak, she would sign, and they would learn.

Tall bookshelves lined the walls from floor to ceiling on two levels. Francine marveled at the collection, though she supposed if she lived in the middle of nowhere she might have such a wonderful library as well. She scanned the bookshelves, trying to determine the organization. She came upon a set of shelves with Byron, Chaucer, Dickens, Shakespeare, and Thackeray.

She had become used to searching titles on the Denver Public Library website, checking them out and downloading them to her ebook reader. She pulled a well-worn book off one shelf and smoothed her hand over the leather cover. She had forgotten what the weight of a book felt like, the smell of the fiber, the turn of the page. She smiled broadly and replaced it.

She pulled several familiar titles from the shelf and handed them off to Mrs. Weston, then reached for more. *The Taming of the Shrew, Vanity Fair, The Book of the Duchess, English Bards and Scotch Reviewers, The Marriage of Heaven and Hell, Pride and Prejudice, Emma, The Charge of the Light Brigade, Moby Dick, Candide.*

She opened the covers of first editions with personal inscriptions written by the authors. She added to her giant stack and roamed farther into the library. Then she saw it, up high on a shelf: *Madame Bovary*. She smiled, climbing the bookshelves to reach it.

"Miss Francine! You cannot do that! There's a ladder!"

Francine clutched the book and fell back to the floor with a quiet thud, then turned apologetically to Mrs. Weston who tugged on her sleeve, begging her to follow. "Come, miss, this must be enough for now. We need get back upstairs." Francine nodded and followed. They ascended the stairs quickly, Francine staring at the books in her arms, smiling. As they reached the top of the staircase Mrs. Weston pushed Francine into the private parlor.

Francine grinned from ear to ear as she sank into the settee and spilled books all around her. She looked back to the door, expecting to see Mrs. Weston right behind her, but instead she heard him. He was close. She tiptoed to the doorway as quickly as she could, peering through the crack behind the door to see him inspecting the books in Mrs. Weston's arms.

"I assume the outing was successful?" the duke asked.

"Yes, Your Grace. She seemed quite satisfied."

He looked at her armload and picked a couple of books off the top. "*Pride and Prejudice, Wuthering Heights.*" He grunted, then picked up the third book. "*The Divine Comedy?*"

Francine took the opportunity to appraise him. He wore dark grey trousers that strapped around his shoes, creating a sharp line to his leg; a crisp white shirt; a rumpled neck cloth; and a black waistcoat. The muscles of his thighs strained the fabric of his trousers, and as he leaned forward—reading the titles of the books—a lock of hair fell across his forehead, begging her to smooth it back.

He glanced toward the doorway and she jerked back and held her breath, feeling his gaze sweep the opening before refocusing on Mrs. Weston. He placed the books back on the stack and turned on his heel.

"Thank you again, Your Grace," Mrs. Weston called after him.

The duke simply waved a hand behind his head at her thanks and ducked swiftly through a doorway. As he walked away Francine marveled at the cocky way he didn't turn back. The only word that came to mind was *dashing*. No—*stunning*. Mrs. Weston, on the other hand, appeared frazzled.

Francine walked back to the settee and started organizing the books on the table, trying to calm her speeding heart rate.

"Miss, I have to see that supper is started. Will you be all right?" Mrs. Weston asked as she made her way over and put the books down.

Francine nodded and sat back, examining her treasure. She giggled and felt her throat catch slightly, then lifted a hand to massage it. She carefully rearranged the order with the addition of the new books, deciding to start with *Vanity Fair* since she had meant to reread that book ever since the movie came out.

She set *Madame Bovary* aside; she would read that one later. She suddenly realized she had been quite lucky to have had that particular novel in her stack instead of Mrs. Weston. If the duke had seen *Madame Bovary* she would have died of embarrassment. She sighed and looked out over the gardens before settling back to start reading.

She was disappearing into *Vanity Fair* when she heard it: the steady, powerful hoof-beats of the beautiful black horse and the infuriating—and striking—rider he carried. She stood and walked to the French doors, placing her hands lightly on the handles.

She wouldn't go outside—there was no way she would test the duke's patience again—but she did open the door a smidge to let the air in. He soon disappeared into the trees and she threw the door wide to feel the spring breeze before going back to her book. She needed someone else's conflict to occupy her mind for a while.

Roxleigh rode for the clearing. He wasn't getting any work done with her around. Today was the first time he'd ever used the passages for a nefarious purpose. He'd watched her in his library. She knew the titles, clapping her hands and pulling the books off the shelves to add to her stack.

He watched her read the pages, inspecting the personal inscriptions that were written to his father, grandsire, mother, grandmother, and others, delicately running her fingers over the pages as if each one was a precious treasure. He'd wondered what it felt like to be those pages, handled so delicately and with such care, then realized with his recent behavior that she might actually be wondering which circle of hell she found herself to be dwelling in here, at his manor.

He exhaled sharply as he entered the clearing. He truly needed to find some measure of calm. He was scaring the wits out of Mrs. Weston; he could see it in her eyes. He was ashamed by his behavior as of late, but he didn't know how to *be* around this woman. He climbed up on his rock and sat down, high and away from the water's edge.

All he could think about was the day she'd arrived. He'd cut her dress and corset loose and managed to revive her somewhat. Then he'd carried her from the edge of the clearing up to the manor and to the guest suite. He'd stayed with her, removing the remaining tatters of her bright satin dress while Mrs. Weston sent for the doctor and gathered supplies.

He'd watched her closely, trying to bring her around with gentle hands. He'd loosed her hair and tried to smooth the brambles from it. He'd massaged her back in slow gaining circles to calm her speeding heartbeat. Finally when her eyelashes fluttered, he'd soothed her with hushed words, caressing her face and her hair. When the doctor arrived and she began to come around in earnest, he'd reluctantly stepped out.

He didn't go far, pacing the hallway outside the room nervously until Mrs. Weston came out bearing news. He'd felt an extreme flood of concern for her, unlike he had for anyone before that day, but when he came back into the room and she was railing about being kidnapped and mistreated and *him*, he'd lost his wits.

Roxleigh shook his head, laying on the rock with his knees bent, his boots flat, well above the gently breaking water of the pond. He listened to Samson's quiet huffing and snickering as he grazed nearby, the sun warm and welcoming. He was tempted to slumber, but knew he needed to return to the manor. It was getting late, and he was exhausted from his sleepless nights, thick with dreams.

# SEVEN

r. Walcott had departed the duke's manor only to be caught by a messenger with a dispatch from Kelso. A town smaller than Roxleighshire by half, Kelso was a little more than an hour south by carriage.

He examined the girl as soon as he arrived. She looked like she had been flung about the woods like a rag doll. The visible damage was so extensive he had no idea where to begin, or where the injuries might end.

He finally decided the proper course was to clean the wounds as best as he was able, putting salve on and wrapping them up to protect them from air. If they were allowed to dry they would crack when she moved, causing her such a fright of pain she wouldn't survive. Sighing, he realized she might not make it regardless.

The girl's face was practically unrecognizable, but everyone here knew who she was and her parents were waiting just outside. Her mother was in such a state that Dr. Walcott gave her some laudanum to ease her so he could deal with Lilly. He motioned for the two girls at the door and quietly sent them for fresh linens, shears, and kettles of hot water. He rolled up his sleeves and settled in for a long night.

Roxleigh returned to the manor and vaulted up the stairs, energized from his ride. He paused on the landing to examine the chandelier, its lowest point at a height just above his head. He liked to watch as the sun set, sending shafts of light toward the crystals, painting the entry in rainbows of shattered light. The back of the manor faced west, the high windows above the private parlor allowing the setting sun to reach the chandelier.

At this time of year the light show went much unnoticed, as it happened just when everyone was preparing for supper. During the summer months the show would greet the guests arriving for suppers and balls, and in the winter months it warmed the occupants who were shut in from the cold.

Roxleigh turned and walked into his suite. A slipper tub steamed in front of the fire. His evening wear was laid out carefully, his robe on the settee next to the bath.

Ferry entered the room as Roxleigh started to remove his shirt, jerking it from his riding breeches and stretching as he pulled it over his head.

"I will take supper here, Ferry," Roxleigh said quietly. "Have a tray sent up."

"Yes, Your Grace. Do you require further assistance?"

Roxleigh stilled. He knew he was acting peculiar as of late and Ferry was not one to comment, but Roxleigh could see concern in his eyes and heard it in the way he spoke.

He shook his head and finished undressing. "No, Ferry, that will be all."

The valet bowed and disappeared.

Roxleigh's suite of rooms was much like the main guest suite, mirrored on the opposite side of the great entrance, but his suite was nearly twice the size of the other. He dropped his clothes where he stood and walked to the tub, scrubbing his fingers through his hair. He sank in, the steaming water washing over his aching muscles as he groaned and leaned back, resting his head on the edge. For the first time in several days, he started to relax as his mind drifted.

The only thing in attendance in his mind was her.

Gideon took himself in hand—and not at all gently. His tension mounted every time he thought on the girl in his manor. *Francine.* He had done his best to avoid her, and the fact that she was unable to wander from her rooms and the private parlor certainly helped in that endeavor.

Nonetheless, he found himself searching her out in the depths of the first floor balconies whenever he left his study, or walked the stairs, or went to the dining room. She had touched a nerve in him he never knew existed, and he was having a most difficult time in quelling his rampant need.

There was more. Certainly his cock twitched whenever he thought of her, but there was a knot in his chest where she was concerned as well. His position in the peerage, and her status as an unknown, drove him like nothing had in all his years as the Duke of Roxleigh.

He shifted in the bath. Water hit his chest like a waking slap and he released himself. What was he doing?

*Bloody hell and damn.* He finished the bath and toweled himself off, then wrapped it around his waist. Standing by the fire, he felt the heat singe the hair on his shins, the crackle dissipating his reverie and backing him up against the chaise. He fell into it, the towel falling open as he stretched out long, his ankles hanging from the end. He threw one arm over his eyes.

"Supper, Your Grace," Ferry said as he entered with a tray. Roxleigh couldn't even be troubled to grunt a response. Instead he left Ferry to his duty, listening to his footsteps slide across the floor, then become muffled by the rug. The delicate clink of china followed as he arranged the tray in front of the fire before leaving the way he came.

Roxleigh glanced at the tray and saw a missive set by the terrine of soup. He closed his eyes and returned to his thoughts.

Better not to think of her by name. Instead she would be *this girl.* This unwanted bit of distraction. That was what she was, that was how he had to think of her. No more, no less. She would be gone from his life soon enough, with all of her spit and fire with her.

He thought of the shock of her pulled up against him, neck to knee. Her indecision as her hands drifted between them, unsure whether to touch his chest or curl her fingers in retreat. He remembered the fight in her eyes, stolen by shock when she turned and glimpsed herself in the looking glass. He would have it destroyed. She had been moments from deciding to set him down good and proper, he was sure of it, and nothing in his life had stoked his passion as the anticipation of that set-down.

He felt his grin against his arm. This girl, this girl. God help him with this girl. How was he to survive in his own household? Part of him wanted to catch her somewhere she should not be, only for the chance to reprimand her, to see if he could get her to fight him again.

He growled. Picking fights with a girl? What was he, still in short pants? But she wasn't a girl; she was a woman, and he a man. One leg slipped off the chaise and he anchored himself, planting his foot on the floor next to him.

The fire warmed and dried his skin from the bath, and he felt it soak in through his inner thighs and up though his groin. He really should move. He really should eat his supper. He really should read the letter. At the very least he should cover himself like a proper gentleman instead of laying here in his glory for all his furnishings to see.

He grunted.

His jaw clenched.

He took himself in hand. This time, a bit gentler. His thumb notched the base of his manhood and he palmed himself in one long stroke. He smoothed his hand down, then back up again, and he spread his legs wider, pushing into the floor as his thighs tensed.

Her hair was the color of toasted butter and cinnamon, her eyes the varied colors of the sky, and her demeanor was just as changing. He'd felt her watching him ride across the valley to the wood, each of his nerves striking the hairs on the back of his neck as it took all of his concentration to stay his course and not turn toward her. The launch into the thick forest was a release as much as it was a disappointment to no longer feel her awareness prickling his skin.

When he returned to the manor to find her on the balcony, her breasts straining the fabric of her nightgown, the garment pulled tight as she leaned into the wind above him, he nearly lost himself on his mount.

He pulled at the favorite memory, his stomach dampening with the early proof of his desire as he shifted and strengthened his grip.

His other hand found the towel half beneath him and tangled in it, pulling and grabbing the soft fabric until the muscles of his arm strained.

"Francine."

He gasped at the rough gritty edge to his own voice and pushed his head against the cushions, his back bowing out from the seat.

*Sweet Francine.* Her eyes were like windows to the world, lips as softly tinted as the blush on a rose. Her sweet, terrified face interchanged with that fierce vixen who prodded his chest, demanding to know who he was and how he was going to help set her to rights.

This was not normal. This should not be happening to him. This was something he should easily be able to avoid. His life was beyond controlled, ordered, set, decided, simple.

He felt the knot in his abdomen tighten, a frisson of electricity coursed down his spine, and every muscle stiffened, then release washed over him as his hand stroked feverishly, working to his end.

He collapsed into the spasms, his jaw and fingers flexing as he pulled the towel from beneath him and threw it across his belly.

As he settled before the fire to sup he picked up the note from Dr. Walcott that had been brought with his tray. Roxleigh never liked receiving news that someone in one of the shires was injured, and this one in particular was terrifying. There was no reasonable explanation for the girl's injuries and no one could account for her whereabouts, leaving them no idea as to what had happened to her. He made a mental note to send a man to Kelso.

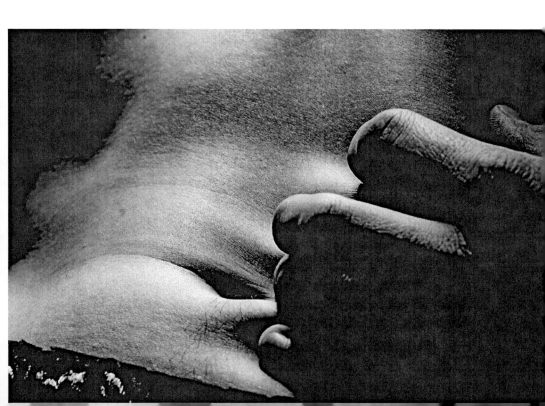

Francine's body was recovering well, even though her voice was not, and she yearned to be active. She couldn't very well run the halls or staircases as she did at home; she imagined that kind of behavior would be frowned upon. She wanted to explore the beautiful gardens visible from the family's private parlor, but there was no way she could go outside, either.

She stood in front of the fireplace in her bedchamber. Everything took such a great deal of time here. Sending for the doctor, requesting a dressmaker, visiting a neighbor. She missed e-mail and smart phones.

She started pacing in front of the windows and looked down at the nightdress and robe which were becoming entirely too familiar. It was a beautiful gown, but was so long she had to pull up the skirt in front to keep from tripping on the hem. The matching robe had a full skirt that gathered up to the bodice with a pink ribbon, and it reminded her of something from old Hollywood movies.

Francine paused at one of the windows and looked outside. It was twilight and the western sky was still streaked in yellow and violet. She knew the sky at the back of the house would have most of the remaining light, while the stars above would be glistening brightly like diamonds in velvet. She knew it would be beautiful, and she knew then she had to see it.

Everyone would surely be inside. She took a deep breath and turned, then bolted for the door, not stopping to give her mind a second chance. She ran through the entrance to the private parlor and straight to the wall of French doors that overlooked the balcony and gardens to the west. She stopped in front of one of the doors and held her breath as she reached out to try the latch. It opened easily with a quiet but sturdy click and she smiled. She slipped out, then gathered her skirts up in front of her and ran across the balcony.

Meggie woke suddenly. She thought she heard a door. Sitting up rigidly in the small bed, she placed her hand on the wall that joined the servant's quarters with the guest bedchamber, then swung her legs out of the bed and went straight in without hesitating to knock; it was empty. She wrung her hands in her skirts. Her eyes stung, her lips started to quiver, and her breath caught in her throat. She had only one job to do: to be there. Wherever Francine was, Meggie was to be there, and now she wasn't. She had fallen asleep and Francine was gone.

Meggie summoned courage from somewhere deep inside and ran to the bell pull to call for Mrs. Weston.

"She's gone, ma'am, I'm so sorry! I only just closed my eyes, but she's gone and I do not know where!" Meggie cried when she came to the bedchamber.

"Oh, Meggie, we must find her before His Grace finds out. Go gather the others, go!"

Meggie stared at her.

"Go!" Mrs. Weston yelled, pushing her toward the door.


Francine was a flurry of white. She'd seen stairs at both ends of the long balcony so she knew it didn't matter which way she went. She placed one hand on the stone balustrade and followed it to the end and down the sweeping staircase that curved its way out from the house, mirroring the other. The stairs surrounded a large terrace like protective arms and she descended the lower steps from the terrace into the gardens.

She suddenly realized how much her body and mind had been starved of movement. She'd made her escape and she was going to enjoy her moment of solitude in the moonlight, consequences be damned. She ducked behind a hedgerow leading to a tunnel blanketed in vine roses. The moonlight made the pale blossoms glow like lanterns, and the surreal landscape propelled her further down the lane.


Dr. Walcott watched the evening light wane through the western window, then turned back to his patient. He dabbed at Lilly's wounds with fresh linens, methodically pulling debris from the deeper cuts. Then he flushed the wounds with enough water to remove small fragments before putting salve and fresh linen over each one to protect them and keep them from drying out.

He worked half the night on her face, neck, and shoulders. He decided to simply cut her hair, to save the pain of brushing out the horrible tangles. She must have had clothes on at one point because there were no abrasions around her torso, but once he started cleaning her legs he noted that the gashes on her thighs were a great deal worse. He leaned back in the chair, rubbing his temples with the heels of his hands as he glanced over at her mother. She sat on the opposite side of the bed, her head resting on the pallet next to Lilly, more likely from his laudanum than her exhaustion. He bent back over the girl, picking up right where he left off.

Mrs. Weston watched Roxleigh from a passageway. The others started to move but she held them back with her finger at her mouth. A few minutes later, Roxleigh left the library and ascended the steps going to the door of the private parlor. He opened the door slowly—presumably to make sure his guest was not in there.

She rushed out of the passage as soon as he was safely in the parlor, ushering the other servants with her. "All right then, let's see to this. Meggie, you go wait in her room and ring if she returns. Davis, you go check the grounds, but don't go out back because the master will see you if you're out in the gardens. Ferry, you keep a look out for His Grace. I'm going to the lower north wing. Carole, you take the south." She paused after hearing a noise in the parlor and then quietly directed the other servants down various hallways, up and below stairs. At last she shooed everyone into action, watching them scatter like mice from the light.

Roxleigh ambled across the parlor to the French doors. The moon was out with the stars, waiting for the sun to take the last streaks of gold below the horizon in the west. The chill of early spring was starting to wane in the evenings, and this night was unseasonably warm, making it a rare one that was more midsummer than spring.

He opened the door and stepped onto the balcony, taking a deep breath. A scent captured his attention and he stilled, scanning the gardens. He caught a flash of movement out of the corner of his eye and left the book he'd brought from the library on the wide balustrade. He hurried down the stairs toward the hedgerow. Nobody would dare enter his maze at this hour; it wasn't safe. Only he knew the layout. He heard a quiet laugh carried to him by the breeze, and his eyes widened. It had to be her.

Francine laughed as she ran without consideration, her skirts gathered up almost to her waist, allowing her strong legs their freedom. The breeze through her hair lifted her spirits, the realization that she'd escaped the manor and was doing something reckless more than exhilarating. She felt like she'd shed all of her previous life's trappings and was free, finally free. She let out an excited cry that sounded more like a chirp through her wounded vocal chords and bolted around another corner, nearly losing her footing on the soft grass. She was ridiculously giddy and didn't care if she never came out of the gardens or returned to her stuffy old life. She felt drunk and wildly out of control as she ran through tunnels and around corners with no regard for where she was headed.

*What would those prim and proper people think of me running willy-nilly through the garden in a nightgown and no shoes?* She stopped abruptly. If I get caught, he'll send me away. Taking a deep breath, she forced the thought from her head before continuing on.

She was gasping hard and felt a stitch in her side, but she kept going: right, left, left, right, until she turned a corner and ran straight into what felt like a fabric-covered brick wall. She bounced off and was thrown back against the hedge wall. In a daze, she let go of the hem of her skirts and tried to catch her breath. Large hands seized her waist.

"No!" she cried as her breath hitched and she twisted in the grip. She tried to get a leg up to kick her attacker but he was too close, looming over her and backing her up against the hedge. She couldn't see his features, shadowed by the moonlight at his back, and she started to panic. Then he spoke.

"Quiet," he said. "I came to help."

She stilled instantly and looked up, straining to see his face as her ears pricked at the voice she knew she'd heard before. "No," she said gravelly. *Why him? Of all people to find me, why him?* "I'm fine," she whispered. "I just needed to get out." She tried to clear her throat. "I've been trapped for so long. I just thought—"

His head tilted toward her as if to hear her better. "You just thought— What?" he asked impatiently, cutting her off. "You just thought you would streak madly through a labyrinth you've never seen, in the dead of night, laughing like a madwoman the entire way? Is that what you thought?"

"No, I— You don't understand." She tried to wriggle free of his steely grip. "You need to let go of me!" she said as her voice broke, angered by his rigid hold. She tried to clear her throat but it tightened.

He released her and backed away, taking her hand. "This way." He moved before she was ready and she tripped as she tried to grab her skirts with her other hand. She could hardly keep up with his pace, but his strength pulling her through the turns helped her to regain some of the reckless freedom she'd felt earlier, save the guiding hand on her wrist. She covered her mouth with the edge of her skirts to stifle a heady giggle as he pulled her into a small clearing and let go of her abruptly, then strode a few feet away.

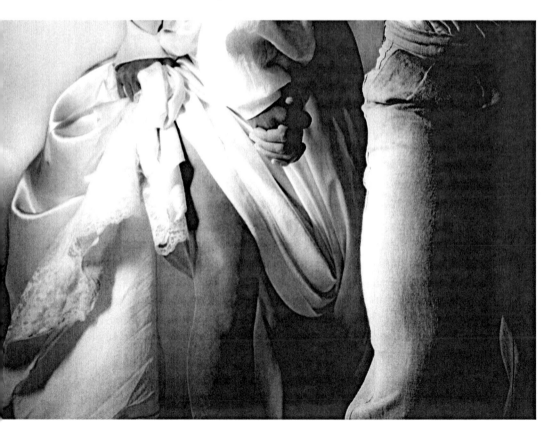

The clearing was circular and had several openings leading back into the hedgerow. In the center was a large white marble fountain with several terraces spilling water down into a raised pool at the base. She wanted to put her tired feet in, but she looked at the stiff back of the duke and thought better of it. She started to make a mocking face at him, but froze at the sight of tension stiffening his shoulders. He shoved his hair back from his face. She clasped her hands in front of her waist as he turned to face her, standing straight and tall.

"I apologize that we have not been, and now will not be, properly introduced. I am Gideon Alrick Trumbull, tenth Duke of Roxleigh. You have been a guest at my estate since an unfortunate accident. You ran from my wood, into my meadow, startling my horses and causing the death of an unknown foxhound." He paused, one eyebrow arched. She shook her head after a moment and he continued. "Mrs. Weston has been keeping me apprised of your continued recovery. It appears to me that you are, in fact, well recovered, since you are able to run haphazardly through my hedgerows with no regard for your safety. Now, why don't you tell me something of yourself?"

He challenged her with his gaze, with his stance—his legs spread slightly, his hands clasped at his back, his spine straight and his shoulders rigid. She exhaled slowly, gawking at the vision before her. But she advanced toward him, carefully attempting to speak.

"Well, um. Hmmm." She tried to clear her throat once more but failed. She patted it gently with her fingers then tried again. Finally she whispered. "My name is Francine Larrabee, and I have no idea how I came to be in *your* wood, on *your* estate, or under *your* horses," she said sardonically as she returned his gaze head on.

She caught the heady scent of him, an intoxicating blend of clean male skin matched with a spicy soap and the tang of sweat, and her skin pricked in reaction. His very presence was dizzying. She floated between his half-raised arms, electricity sizzling across her flesh. She blushed as he continued to stare at her, a half-terrified look on his face. There was something else in those eyes—anger, yes; trepidation, absolutely. But beneath those: fear, longing…and pain. She desperately wanted to allay his anxious demeanor.

"I was lonely," she whispered. "I very much appreciate everything you've done for me, and if there is any way I can repay your kindness—"

She looked down, breaking the connection, suddenly embarrassed by the expression on his face. She realized too late that she shouldn't have said something like that to this obviously virile man who also happened to be a complete stranger. "I just meant that someday, somehow, I would like to repay your kindnesses toward me, even if it is just a token."

When she lifted her chin she took in more of him. She liked the way his hair curled slightly at his nape and wanted to run her fingers through the thick waves. She wanted to smell it, rest her cheek against it, float her fingers across his skin. Before she knew it, she was moving forward again.

Francine realized how much pleasure she took in watching him. His movements made her skin over-sensitive, with a keen awareness that gathered in her belly. She could see he was concentrating greatly, his breath steady and determined, his muscles undulating the fabric of his shirt. She also noticed the outline of the large muscles of his legs against the fabric of his pants. She looked back up to his sharp white shirt, which fell open at the neck, and watched as his ribcage moved.

Roxleigh realized his posturing had done nothing to faze her as she quietly swept forward like a spirit. She drew up to him, whispering closely so he could hear her over the rushing water of the fountain. He felt a ripple of tension extend from his core, lifting his arms and tingling in his fingertips. He tensed as he looked into her eyes and stood perfectly still, hands flung out, entirely unsure of her nearness.

He nodded once, very aware of her proximity, and backed up a pace, then leaned against the edge of the fountain, drawing a broad smile from her. He cocked his eyebrow.

"May I?" she whispered, quietly motioning to the fountain. Her eyes were sparkling, the color of the sea washing up on a sandy beach, and he nodded, captivated by the intensity of her gaze. She took three steps and sat on the edge of the fountain, then swept her feet over the side and into the water, sighing heavily as she pulled her skirts up to her knees.

He watched her small feet, her delicate ankles and surprisingly muscular legs, as they lowered into the water. His gaze moved up as her legs descended, catching sight of the exquisite bones of her knee, the crease which circled the back of her leg and was covered with sensitive flesh. His mouth went dry and his stomach clenched as he imagined his finger running along that line. He jerked and turned, pushing away from the fountain as she looked up.

"You don't have electricity. How is this possible?" she whispered.

He looked back at her, puzzled, then glanced at the fountain. "A siphon, from the cistern built by the Normans," he explained before walking away. *Good Lord. How am I to survive this?* He strolled around the fountain, in desperate need of distance, watching her from the corner of his eye. It hadn't been even an hour since he had considered her while taking his pleasure. Her skin was creamy and freckled, with a subtle hint of pink flushing the surface from the chill of the water. Her arms and legs were long and lissome, but not as soft as most women of age. Her limbs had the shadows of definition that hinted at exertion. *She has strength, he thought excitedly. Could she possibly be a rider, or is she merely fond of walks? I did find her running through the maze—not exactly an acceptable form of exercise for a lady.*

He was mesmerized by her movements as she wiggled her feet back and forth rapidly under the water, then straightened her legs in front of her, letting the water run off her skin in rivulets, dripping to the surface of the pool and drawing quiet coos and sighs from her. He smiled at this small token of pleasure he had brought her, then scowled, wondering why he should care.

He turned away again, his breath becoming more rapid. He felt her gaze on him and looked back over his shoulder. She smiled as she watched the chilled water running off her feet. His breath caught in his throat as he felt his loins tighten with need. Or was it want? *How inconvenient.* He turned toward her and spoke, attempting to strengthen his voice with the appropriate firmness. "Miss, you should not uncover yourself in such a familiar manner. It is hardly proper behavior for a lady," he said stiffly.

Francine frowned and pulled her feet up to the bench. She tugged the nightdress down over her toes and leaned her chin on her knees, wrapping her arms around her legs and inspecting him.

*That was a mistake.* The way her lower lip jutted out in a frown made him want to nip at it. His lips pulled back from his teeth almost instinctively, as if to do so, before he turned his back once more. His chest tightened and he bent over, leaning his hands against his knees. *Bloody hell! Breathe, damn you.* He groaned. He'd never been affected like this. He glanced back at her.

She tilted her head, watching him, her brow furrowed. He could see her taking him in and her inspection only drove his passion higher.

After what seemed an eternity, he straightened and continued around the fountain, brushing past her quickly. He faced away from her, straight as an arrow, his arms crossed over his chest. He took a deep breath and turned toward her, bending one knee and resting his boot at the edge of the fountain, tapping his thigh with his clenched fist.

Francine reached toward him with one dainty hand, then drew back sharply when he raised his arm to block her. "Just—give me a moment," he said slowly, pleadingly, as his breathing began to slow. He was fighting to keep from being overwhelmed by his baser instincts, but just the smell of her at this point was enough to send him over the edge. Even so, he couldn't force himself to move away again.

How could the sight of one small, feminine ankle be enough to send all his blood rushing to his groin? He felt a deep pressure begging for release and he hoped he could steady his body enough for the passion to recede. It wasn't as if he hadn't seen at least that much of a woman's body before, and more. He was well practiced in the art of pleasure, but even more practiced in the art of discipline, and as such his body shouldn't react to this girl without his permission.

He saw her blush and turn her head from the corner of his eye, and even that small movement caused her scent to waft toward him. Lavender and rain. By all outward appearances, she was well bred and well learned. She should have had the proper studies in comportment and manner, but she seemed to have misplaced them. He looked down to see her toes at the hem of her robe, and he exhaled.

She waited so patiently for him. After a time he lowered his arm, attempted to relax his muscles,,and raised his head. He lowered himself to the edge of the fountain and leaned forward, his elbows on his thighs, his hands clenched.

"You don't seem to have morals," he stated bluntly.

Her jaw dropped and her spine straightened. He shook his head, to ward off her coming protest, then turned toward her. "When I—*we* found you, your manner of dress was that which would befit a lady. You were—are clean," he said, with a gesture to her countenance. "Your hair was made properly; your corset was such that you could *not* have dressed yourself. I should know because I had to remove it to allow you to breathe."

*This is not a proper conversation for an unmarried gentleman to have with an innocent girl.* His speech was entirely too personal, but he couldn't help it; he had an unwarranted desire to discover more about her.

She blushed and started to turn her head away, but he clenched his jaw and bid her hold his gaze. She bit at her lower lip, ducking behind her knees. He could see just her clear blue eyes peeking out at him and tried to steer the conversation to a more acceptable subject. "I thought I heard you speak French," he offered, hoping she would give more in explanation.

He waited—patiently, he thought—to no response.

He shook his head and closed his eyes. *It must have been the madness.* But wasn't the doctor's assessment based on the fact that she *wasn't* speaking? Or was it the way she spoke that had him more concerned? She was certainly an infuriating paradox.

He stood, circling the fountain again. He didn't know much about mental frailty. He only knew that those whose minds were in disrepair were taken from their families, never to return. Maybe he should trust Dr. Walcott; maybe she should be sent to Bedlam. He watched her, sitting peacefully on the other side of the fountain. No, it wasn't in him to relegate her to that.

He was restless and wished there was some way he could ease the tension. *There is one way*—he could throw her down on the grass here in the clearing and have her. He lifted his head, and she smiled at him. Mistake.

The twilight ended, but the moon and stars were bright enough that he could see her from the far side of the clearing as he paced, the moonlight reflecting into her face from the clear fountain water. She didn't budge, just watched as he moved toward her again. Perhaps he would slake this desire.

*No—the woman is damaged.* He shook his head as he admonished himself.

"I'm sorry," she whispered forcefully as he approached. She held her throat, hands shaking. When he saw the fear and anger wash across her face he halted in his advance. "Don't look at me like that. Don't look at me as though I have a broken wing. I don't know what has come over me, I don't know what to say to you. I am afraid every moment that I am doing something wrong which will cause me to be sent away from here and I don't—" Her breath caught. "I don't have anywhere to go. In all my life, I cannot remember ever feeling as safe as I do right now, in this strange place, and I don't understand why. Because regardless of your actions"—she turned on him and pointed—"your demeanor has been less than welcoming." Her voice cracked as she whispered. She took a deep breath and rubbed her throat with her hands.

He sat down and leaned toward her, trying to hear.

"I didn't mean to disturb you tonight. I have just been cooped up on the second floor of your—your palace, and I needed to get out," she pleaded. "I saw you earlier on that black horse, and you looked so free. I just wanted to feel the same. That's why I came out tonight. That's all."

He stared at her for a long moment as she pulled her knees up again. "I understand that feeling," he said, with a half grunt. "I hate being holed up in the manor—it is a manor, not a *palace*, mind you, but the, uh, *compliment* is well taken."

She made no reply.

"You have been held on the first floor, not the second," he said a moment later, as an aside. "I never considered that you would see me riding Samson. It scares the hell out of my staff, tears up my hands." He paused, rubbing his palms together, shocked at his own familiar tone.

She reached out and grasped one of his hands before he knew what she was doing. They were much larger than hers. Turning his hand palm up in hers, she gently stroked the rough calluses with her thumb.

He sucked in a breath as he froze, watching. "But—but I cannot help it." He exhaled strongly, then in a whisper, continued. "It's that feeling of freedom and peace, and I—I have no right to keep you from yours." *He* was breathless now. He was breathless now, his mind reeling from her touch and his disclosure. He reached out with his other hand, gently touching the abrasion on her forehead, then traced his fingertips down the frame of her jaw.

She smiled and he retracted his hands abruptly, folding his arms across his chest. She hid her face, resting her forehead on her knees.

"It's my understanding that Mrs. Weston has made arrangements to have some garments made for you, and that should ease the trouble. It shouldn't take long, but until then I must insist for your safety and out of common decency that you keep yourself covered as much as possible, and that you remain in the private areas of the manor. I have business associates that visit, not to mention all the servants and others within my purview. If they saw you, your reputation would be ruined, which would be a shame, because you will obviously make a fine wife someday—after we figure out where you belong or, I suppose, once we get you to where you belong or—" He realized he had rambled so far from the point that he finally drifted off into silence with a sigh. Why did he feel so terribly uncertain? He rubbed his fingers across his eyes and sighed again.

"Thank you," she whispered.

"For?" he replied, not looking at her.

"For everything. I don't expect anything from you, and I very much appreciate what you have done." She reached out to touch his arm. "I *will* repay you somehow."

"No, you won't." He looked directly into her eyes as he spoke, ensuring she understood his intention. "What I give, I give freely and expect nothing in return. The fact is, we don't know to whom you belong and it wouldn't be proper to just ignore your needs."

"To whom I belong?" Her head cocked to the side and her eyes widened, then she nearly yelled but for the broken voice. "To whom I belong! I belong to no one!" she tried to scream, but no sound came from her throat.

He panicked and tried to explain. "I meant your father or husband…of course. I already assumed you weren't a servant, not dressed like—" He stiffened when she reached out, grabbing his arm frantically as the color left her face.

In one swift move he stood and threw one of her arms over his shoulder, scooping her up to his chest. Already panicked by her pallid skin, the shock of her hand on his bare neck was enough to startle Roxleigh into a dead run. He skidded through the maze, slipping around corners as he held on to her, his boots slick on the lawn. The feel of her fingertips in his hair sent a shiver from his extremities straight to his middle, causing him to shift his grasp, pulling her higher up his chest and tighter to him as he lurched slightly going up the stairs.

He went all the way to the first floor without pause and burst into the private parlor with a yell. "Weston! Ferry! Meggie! Where the hell are you?" he yelled as he ran to the door, then stood at the crest of the grand staircase looking out over the entry. "Weston!" he bellowed, as loud as his lungs would allow.

She came up next to him. "Your Grace, you found her!"

"Yes, and it would have been quite nice to know she needed finding," he answered with a scowl.

Mrs. Weston followed him to the guest suite, running to keep up with his long stride. Roxleigh laid Francine carefully on the bed and she looked up at him with gentle eyes as she reached out, grasping one of his arms before he could move away. She held her right hand straight and flat, the tips of the fingers to her lips, and then moved it forward, but he only stared at her in confusion and worry. Then she mouthed the words *thank you*, and made the motion again.

He nodded to her, taking slight comfort in the fact that her pain seemed to have eased, and turned to Mrs. Weston. "We will discuss this on the morrow. Tonight she needs rest, and *you* will *watch her*," he said, emphasizing his potential displeasure should his wishes be disregarded again.

"Yes, Your Grace, of course. I'll not leave her side," Mrs. Weston replied, her voice quivering, and she went to warm a kettle on the fire.


Roxleigh left Francine propped up on a few pillows, waiting for Mrs. Weston to come back to the bed. When she did, he left and Francine reached for Mrs. Weston's arm. With her right hand she made a fist and motioned in a circle over her heart, mouthing the words *I'm sorry*. Mrs. Weston's expression flushed with confusion as Francine repeated the gesture, then understanding broke across her face.

"No, dear! No! *I* am sorry. I should have been close by your side the entire time. I never should've left you, and I won't make the mistake again," she said.

Francine knew that Mrs. Weston had no idea what had happened tonight in the garden. All she knew was that Francine had disappeared and been returned in the arms of an angry duke. There was no way for her to know of the time shared in the maze, the amount of care he took with her. Mrs. Weston did not know that it had actually been the best night of her entire life, the first night she'd ever felt truly free.

She considered Roxleigh's actions. No man had ever cared for her. She never had time to deal with them, and frankly they all seemed uninterested and a bit scary. But this one was different. He was concerned, not merely for her health but for her well being. He touched her without moving, her body aware of him regardless of proximity. She could feel him everywhere, and just the thought of him sent blood rushing to the surface of her skin.

She realized his anger was coming from concern and his agitation from some deeply seated emotion that she believed resonated from his gut—because right now, her gut was telling her the same thing.

# SEVEN

r. Walcott could see dawn breaking through the small gap in the heavy drapes and he heaved a sigh then stood, rubbing his back with stiff fingers. He turned to the girl that had helped him throughout the night and patted her on the shoulder. "Go rest. Send someone else to watch over her. I will give them instructions before I go. There is nothing more that can be done now, but perhaps to pray," he said quietly.

The girl nodded and took an armload of bloody rags with her as she disappeared. A few minutes later, another servant entered with Lilly's father behind her.

"Mr. Steele," the doctor said, shaking his head. "I cannot even fathom what it must take for you to look on your daughter like this. I must tell you that in all likelihood she'll not survive. I'll stay and see her through as far as I am able, but you should prepare her mother. I've never seen injuries as extensive as these, and I don't know how she's to survive… Or if she would even want to," he whispered.

Francine watched as Mrs. Weston pulled the drapes open on the windows, letting in the fresh morning sun, before stoking the fire in the grate and heating a kettle. The room warmed quickly and Mrs. Weston walked to the giant bed.

Francine groaned and rubbed her hands over her face, then cocked an eyebrow as she looked around. She was still here, wherever *here* was. She'd tossed and turned all night, in and out of dreams, her mind replaying the events in the maze. She believed half the images must have been imagined, because she certainly wasn't aware of the duke being attracted to her before. She decided the excitement had colored her memories, making them more vivid than they actually had been and, in truth, the parts that she knew to be accurate were rather unbecoming and a bit insulting.

Had he actually said that she had no morals? *Yes, he did,* she thought. *He really said that.* Obviously he wasn't taken with her as much as embarrassed for her sake—or maybe simply for propriety's sake. Good grief, he was ridiculous. She had never met a man who was so concerned with what others thought.

Francine sat up, looking for Mrs. Weston again. She spied her behind a footman who was pushing in the slipper tub, and she smiled.

"The dressmaker should arrive today, so we should get you all cleaned up."

Francine watched as Mrs. Weston moved around the room and a parade of housemaids came in through the passage behind the fireplace carrying kettles. Francine sighed as the steam rose, blotting out the countryside as it peeked through the windows. Mrs. Weston added some oils to the bath and then went to help Francine to the tub.

They were starting to get used to each other, and Mrs. Weston turned away politely as Francine disrobed and stepped into the warm bath, then returned and fussed over her hair, straightening tangles and getting it washed.

Francine reached up and patted the hand that gently pushed her forward in the tub.

"Oh dear, sweet. Don't you worry, miss, we're going to take good care of you, no matter," she said.

Francine smiled, leaning her chin on her knees and letting Mrs. Weston take care of her as her mind drifted back to the garden. She closed her eyes, saw him leaning on the wall in front of her, his breathing labored, his movements determined. And his body—aroused? *Is that what I saw?* she thought as she flushed. *Yes, it was.* She could feel the blood tingling close to the surface of her skin, raising goose bumps and tightening her nipples. She leaned back in the tub at Mrs. Weston's urging, shaking her head under the water to clear her thoughts and rinse the soap from her hair.

"Oh, miss! You've caught a chill," Mrs. Weston said. Francine blushed harder, sending Mrs. Weston in a flurry, yanking the curtains closed and stoking the fire. Francine sat up, giggling, and Mrs. Weston walked over to her. "Are you feeling well?" she asked.

Francine nodded as she glanced up at Mrs. Weston and signed *thank you.*

"You did that last night, miss. You used your hands to tell me something. What was that?" Mrs. Weston asked.

Francine was surprised she remembered any sign language since she hadn't used it in years. But she used it naturally, as though she had never stopped. One of the girls in the foster home where she was taken after her parents died had been profoundly deaf, and she had learned from her. Francine shrugged, unable to tell Mrs. Weston about it, and signed *thank you* again, this time using both hands for emphasis.

"Well, miss, how do you say you're welcome?" Mrs. Weston asked.

Francine repeated the sign for *thank you.*

"'Tis the same?" Mrs. Weston asked. Francine nodded and Mrs. Weston smiled. The housekeeper handed her the bar of lilac soap and turned to ring for her breakfast tray. Francine rubbed her hands around the bar, squeezing to make it spin. She closed her eyes tightly and chanted to herself, *iPod iPod iPod iPod.* She opened her eyes and looked down. *Soap.* She sighed and watched Mrs. Weston as she walked back to the tub.

"Gideon?" Francine whispered, wondering when she would see him again.

Mrs. Weston's eyes widened. "You must not use his Christian name, miss," she said stoutly. Francine nodded. "My, but I believe you're taken with His Grace," she continued quietly. "Understandable, yet to use his given name would be improper. You cannot do that, and besides, you're not to speak."

Francine nodded again and sank into the tub, thinking about the duke, while a broad smile spread across Mrs. Weston's face.


"Ferry!" Roxleigh sat on the edge of his bed, not bothering to reach for the pull because he felt like yelling.

"Should I have Samson readied?" Ferry asked when he entered.

"No. I'll be going to London. Pack my things."

"Yes, Your Grace," Ferry said, turning to the wardrobe. "What of the architect?" he asked.

"I'll leave everything he requires on the grand table," Roxleigh said.

"Yes, Your Grace."

Roxleigh had business to attend to in London that had been waiting for too long, and a few days away from the manor to think seemed more than justified. His ride yesterday had done much to clear his head, but having Francine alone in the maze with him last night had only served to muddle it again. She was so… *Magnificent* seemed to be the only word he could find to do her justice. He could still feel her pressed against him as he ran back to the manor, her hands clasped around his neck, her fingers teasing the curls at his nape. It had steeled every muscle in his body then and sent a shiver through him now.

He closed his eyes and inhaled deeply. He could still sense her, the lavender and rain. She was so sweet, succulent. He wanted to taste her, breathe her essence, feel her flesh prickle with awareness as his fingers gently caressed her. He knew from the reactions he'd already witnessed how she would respond to him. How her breath would be nothing more than a sigh. He stood, fighting another rush of blood. This was not good. He couldn't prowl around the manor like an unsatisfied rake, and he knew if he stayed here that's exactly what he would end up doing. For Francine's sake, and his own, he had to leave.

Three hours later, Francine was surrounded by soft pastel muslins; lush, heavy velvets in burgundy and deep blue; prickly, stiff tulle; dark, serviceable broadcloth; vibrant, slippery satins; heavy patterned brocades; and several other exquisite fabrics covered in pearls, beads, and lace. The volume of the fabrics overwhelmed her, as did the speed with which the dressmaker spun them around her body, making measurements and notes and then moving on to the next. "Laura, that pink is horrible with her complexion. Try the deeper silk," Madame Basire said.

"Yes, ma'am," her assistant replied, dropping the bolt of fabric into a pile and reaching for a deep blue Italian silk and a black corded trim.

Mrs. Weston stood. "No, that color is too bold, Madame. His Grace would never agree, and you know it isn't proper for a miss," she said sternly.

Francine groaned. *Proper, proper, proper! I am so sick of proper.* She had never felt so trapped by her inability to speak. Madame Basire grasped the divine silk, wrapping it around Francine's middle as she watched the end flutter gracefully to the floor. Francine grinned at the way it drifted about her ankles. She glanced at Mrs. Weston, who was refusing to return her pleading look.

"Fine," Mrs. Weston said after a moment. "But just the one. Please also allow for a riding habit. A deep green or blue would be appropriate for that."

Francine gave her an excited smile and Mrs. Weston signed *you're welcome.*

Monsieur Gautier Larrabee opened the letter from Lord Hepplewort, expecting confirmation of his daughter's consummated marriage and instructions for the final payment as reward for his patience. What he found, however, was a rambling missive ending with his daughter being held by a duke at his remote English estate and the payment of his funds being retained by Hepplewort until she was restored to him.

"*Merde!*" he exclaimed, then called to his wife. "*Eglantine! Me venir maintenant!*" She rushed to his side, hearing the anger in his voice. "*Il faut que nous allions à l'Angleterre, notre fille manqué,*" he said briskly.

Eglantine gasped. "*Elle manqué? Mon Dieu!*" she said, stunned to learn her daughter was missing.

"*Oui, c'est vrai, cette lettre est d'elle fiancé. Nous devons aller immédiatement,*" he responded.

"*Bien sûr, mon mari,*" she agreed. They packed and left for England without hesitation.


Francine walked to the window while Madame Basire and her assistant spoke with Mrs. Weston about her requirements. She leaned against the windowsill, looking over the drive in front of the manor. A sleek black carriage pulled by four beautiful black horses waited majestically. She motioned to Mrs. Weston to come to the window, then pointed down to the carriage.

"They are magnificent, aren't they? Look, there's Samson," Mrs. Weston said as she gestured to the steed now being tied at the back of the carriage. "Why the barouche?" she mused aloud. "Oh," she said, sounding distressed. They watched a footman place a trunk in the boot. Mrs. Weston's brow creased and she looked to the outer door. Roxleigh was giving directions to Ferry.

*He's leaving*, Francine thought as she latched onto Mrs. Weston's arm.

"I'll be back shortly," Mrs. Weston said, pulling Francine's fingers loose. She patted her arm and strode to the fireplace. A few moments later, she reappeared at the front entry next to Ferry.

Francine watched with a heavy dose of concern. She guessed from the trunk that the duke was going somewhere for an extended time, and though she knew she shouldn't, she felt a great deal of disappointment. After last night she was hoping they'd be able to spend some time together, even though they were still separated by his damned propriety. She wished she knew when he would return.

Her brows creased and she leaned against the window, desperately trying to catch a glimpse of his face when he turned to climb inside the carriage. She could see him pointing and speaking directly to Mrs. Weston, and she knew he was admonishing her for being what he thought was careless.

Mrs. Weston straightened her back and nodded, her hands clutched in front of her. The footman said something to Roxleigh and Francine caught his profile as he turned to acknowledge him. Her breath raced against the glass.

Roxleigh paused, then lifted his face and looked directly at her.

She held his gaze, neither of them giving any hint of emotion as they studied each other. She placed both hands in front of her face, fingers spread, palms toward her. She pulled her hands downward sharply and, when she looked back up, he was stepping into the carriage. She felt a pull deep within her chest. He moved the window curtain aside momentarily and Mrs. Weston nodded, then glanced toward Francine in the window. The outriders and Ferry mounted the carriage and rode swiftly away from the manor.

Mrs. Weston returned to the room before Francine had a chance to move away from the window. "He'll return soon, miss. He has business in London that he's neglected and he needs to attend to," she said, taking Francine's hands in her own. "He'll return," she whispered again.

Francine smiled, but the sadness she felt at watching the carriage rolling swiftly through the far gates refused to abate. She turned back to the room to find she had an audience.

Lord Hepplewort paced in the small bedroom at the Running Iron Inn, his jowly face turning beet red and sweat dripping from his straggly grayish hair. He shook as he raged, his paunchy belly threatening to burst the buttons on his satin brocade waistcoat, sending them dangerously through the air like arrows to lambs. Madeleine's betrothed, Lord Hepplewort, possessed a deportment that matched his manner measure for measure.

Upon taking a foreign bride, the earl was required by tradition to show his betrothed her new country with a carriage tour that would end with the marriage at the chapel on his estate. To that end, on Madeleine's seventeenth birthday he'd retrieved her from the convent in France where she'd led a peaceful and completely sheltered life. They'd proceeded by ship to the northern port of Newcastle upon Tyne, and from there to the northernmost edge of the United Kingdom in Scotland, close to the lands of the Duke of Roxleigh.

He refused to return home without his bride, yet there was no way for him to retrieve her from Eildon Manor. He knew of the duke and his stalwart reputation. He would have to retrieve his bride later. She must have begged for shelter, provided some ridiculous tale about who she was, or that she had been mishandled or kidnapped or something of the sort. As her father's property until marriage, certainly the duke would have no choice but to return her.

He knew Roxleigh wasn't one to dismiss the law, and by contract, she belonged with him. The problem would be explaining why he was on the duke's land without permission. He was sure to be brought on charges of poaching for having his dogs out, and how would he explain them chasing her? Hepplewort fumed. No, it was all too difficult; he would have to wait until she was returned to her father. The man would certainly hold to the contract that had made him a rich man, especially with half the money awaiting confirmation of her chastity upon their marriage.

He'd sent a message to France the day after the incident to notify Monsieur Larrabee that he expected to complete the bargain upon her return, and in the meantime he'd proceed to his estate in Shropshire. Perhaps he could pluck another fresh apple on the way home, sweet and tart, to have a little fun with as he had the one he found outside of Kelso. He went to tell his footman of the plans.

Madame Basire broke the silence with a hearty laugh, drawing all the attention in the room to her. She was studying Francine and Mrs. Weston. "Oh my," she said, waving her hand in front of her face like a fan. "It seems the most eligible duke in the kingdom has an admirer."

"I'll thank you not to perpetuate such a rumor if you wish to stay in His Grace's good temper," Mrs. Weston admonished.

"Well, Mrs. Weston, if my lips were loose my business would have suffered ages ago," Madame Basire said happily.

The housekeeper nodded. "Are we finished?"

Madame Basire thought for a moment. "I need a few more measurements for her foundations."

"Of course."

Madame Basire whispered a few directions to her assistant, who nodded, then measured Francine a bit more and made some notes in Madame's book. When they finished, they gathered the bolts of fabric and trimmings in a flurry of colors and sent the footmen to load her carriage.

Francine turned to the settee in front of the fireplace, and clapping her hands to get their attention, she motioned to the garments they'd left.

Madame Basire smiled. "I cannot leave a beautiful peach as you without a stitch! These may not fit perfectly, but they'll do until I return. I've also left some drawers and nightgowns, a few stockings and a corset. That's fine with you, Mrs. Weston, yes?"

"I've no doubt His Grace will appreciate the courtesy. I will be sure to let him know upon his return," Mrs. Weston said.

"Well, we will *all* await his swift return, won't we?" Madame Basire placed her hand gently on Francine's and, with a wink, a devilish grin, and a rustle of skirts and fabric, she was gone.

Francine stood in awe of the brazen woman, then turned to the garments she'd left behind. She reached out, feeling the soft muslin in pale hues with delicate trimmings. The drawers were a bit strange to her. She realized with a frown that the cheeky panties and boy shorts she was fond of would not be available.

The drawers were long, thin, bloomer-like pants with ribbons that tied at her hips. She looked from the drawers and stockings to the corset, petticoats, and dresses, and realized what a production being "proper" was. She lifted one leg of the drawers and saw the crotch shift, and thinking they were torn she looked closer, seeing both edges trimmed with a delicate lace. She rather suddenly understood the purpose for the slit in the drawers was that she wasn't supposed to remove them when she used the bathroom.

She ran her fingers over the delicate lace then tucked them through the slit with a shudder. *This is considered proper? There is nothing between the ground and me.* She sighed heavily as Mrs. Weston approached.

"Well, now. Let's get you out of the manor. Since His Grace has taken his leave I've arranged for afternoon tea over the gardens. I thought a small celebration of your lack of restrictions would lift your spirits, yes?" A sparkle lit her eye.

Francine nodded happily and started yanking at her nightgown. Mrs. Weston laughed at her excitement and picked up the sturdy whalebone corset, holding it up over her chemise to lace it tightly in the back. Francine gasped as the housekeeper tightened it, jerking the laces tighter. Francine put her hands on the corset, feeling the stiff, restricting bodice as it molded her torso to its shape. She breathed slowly to keep from passing out.

Mrs. Weston buckled a bustle at her waist, then picked up a large petticoat and swung it over Francine's head, fastening it over the bustle. The heavy skirts of the cotton petticoat were gathered meticulously at the back of the garment, leaving a long, clean silhouette in the front. Several layers of skirts were attached under the petticoat to give it the proper fullness. Francine groaned, thinking she must have just gained fifty pounds.

Mrs. Weston helped her into a shirtwaist and fastened the numerous pearl buttons at the sleeves. The tailored shirt was covered with pin tucks that fitted her waist. After the shirt was fastened, Mrs. Weston tossed the lavender skirt over her head, pulling it down in place. The skirt was flat-fronted with large gathers of ruffles in the back, covering the petticoat perfectly. It didn't add much weight to the overall ensemble, which she was glad about, wishing she could skip all the foundation garments and simply wear the lavender skirt alone. She was finally ready for her independence. *Funny. My freedom comes with such physical restrictions.*

"Beautiful!" Mrs. Weston exclaimed. "Now let's see to that cup of tea, shall we?" Francine followed Mrs. Weston from the room.

"Never you worry Miss, he shall return."

*Yes, but will I still be here?*

R

# FOUND
## PART TWO

# NINE

D r. Walcott rose shortly before sunset. He was surprised he'd been able to slumber for so long with the girl in the state she was. The thought that she hadn't made it through the day, and they'd chosen to let him sleep, disturbed him.

He washed at the basin quickly before rushing out. Nobody was about—*not a good sign*. He knocked gently and entered.

Her parents sat in the dim room in chairs at the end of the small bed. She was covered with so many linens that in her stillness they resembled a death shroud. He shuddered as he walked toward the bed, nodding to her parents as he passed. Her mother's face was drawn and puffy, her father's empty gaze on the small window.

Dr. Walcott grasped her wrist and, feeling the flutter of her heartbeat, he finally took a breath. He started looking over her bandages. They all seemed to be holding well, staying in place and not drying out. He stroked the hair back from her forehead, whispering, "Good girl, Lilly, we all know you are a strong, brave girl."

He started once again with her face, checking each wound and adding salve, before replacing the linen. They propped her forward on pillows to relieve the pressure on her back for a while, then turned her to the other side. It was unnerving that she didn't react to their handling of her, but he surmised that the laudanum they'd poured down her throat was helping to keep her insensate. He had no intention of stopping the medication just yet. He wasn't sure if it was because he thought she couldn't stand the pain, or because they wouldn't be able to stand her cries that would surely follow.

He spent a second night by her side, taking breaks only for the necessaries.

Gideon made the long trip to London primarily by rail, but as the lines were under construction, he detoured through the country by carriage whenever necessary. He was not anxious to get to Roxleigh

House on Grosvenor Square. Not because the house itself wasn't appealing, but because it was in London, a social mecca amidst squalor.

The town house, though, was a small sanctuary surrounded by the bustle. While most of the houses on Grosvenor were five to seven bays in width and three stories with an attic, Roxleigh House held nine bays with four stories. It was the crown jewel on the square with its Georgian architecture and dramatic columns rising the full height of the façade.

Like Eildon Manor, the bedrooms and sitting rooms at the front rose with the sun, and the common rooms and ballroom gazed upon the sunset over a large, private garden between the rear terrace and Blackburne's Mews, where his outriders and cattle were housed.

He bounded up the front steps and across the shallow portico into the house, exhaling the moment his foot crossed the threshold at the heavy door. Sanders attended him straightaway as Ferry assisted the footmen with Gideon's accoutrements.

"A guest awaits you in the study, Your Grace," Sanders said as Gideon handed off his greatcoat and hat.

He stopped cold, presenting Sanders with a severe gaze. "My outriders were sent ahead to direct that my arrival be held in confidence. Who would be here at this hour?"

"His lordship, Your Grace," Sanders replied without wavering.

"Of course," Gideon ground out.

His younger brother would have noticed Roxleigh House being lit and warmed, even in the dead of night, from his own town house across the square. His brother held to the hours of a rake, sleeping through the morning and into the waning light so he could attend society parties in the evenings and entertain women deep into the night.

"Shall I have Cook prepare a repast?" Sanders asked.

"No, Sanders, that will be all." Gideon slapped his gloves on his thigh.

"Yes, Your Grace."

Gideon handed off the gloves and Sanders withdrew. Steeling himself, he strode toward the study where a liveried footman swung the door wide. "And to what do we owe the honor?" his jaw tightened as he walked directly to the tantalus on the sideboard for a snifter of brandy.

He was not prepared to face his brother just yet. He had assumed he would have at least the night to rest and consider. His brother was the Lord Peregrine Trumbull, Viscount of Roxleigh in name, but a rake of the worst order by action.

"Your Grace," Perry said wryly. "I did not receive advance notice of your arrival, even though your household has. Surely an oversight."

"*Surely*, my lord, a terrible oversight," Gideon replied, shaking his head in mock confusion.

"Humph. So, to what do *we* owe the honor?" Perry asked.

Gideon sat in one of his plush wingback chairs next to the fireplace as Perry poured his own snifter and followed, dropping into the chair across from him.

"I have matters that need tending. As you are well aware." Gideon examined the face that could have served as a younger mirror of his own. He studied Perry, attempting to determine a suitable tack to follow.

"Indeed, Your *Grace*, as I've been aware for months. Yet I did not expect you for some time, as you prefer to leave most of these things to gather for one visit," he said while Gideon glared.

"Yes, of course," Gideon said, shifting his gaze to the fire, then back as he swirled the brandy. "I— I had need to take my leave," he said quietly, measuring his brother's reaction. He wasn't disappointed, as Perry's jaw dropped.

"From Eildon? You cannot be serious. You cannot bear to leave that reclusive estate, regardless of the condition of your affairs. What on earth could possibly drive you away?" Perry rolled the brandy over a candle flame to warm it.

Gideon considered where to start and how much to reveal. He ultimately decided on full disclosure, because if anyone could help him with this conundrum, it was surely the one man in the world who knew him better than he knew himself.

Gideon leaned forward, resting his elbows on his knees as he palmed the balloon of brandy. "Well," he began, "her name is Francine, and she is a—a paradox."

Nearly an hour and another snifter of brandy later Gideon's tale was complete. He turned to stoke the fire that had burned down in the grate.

Perry leaned casually in the chair, legs straight, ankles crossed, brandy chilling between his fingers. With his mouth agape and his eyes wide and twinkling, he'd sat uncharacteristically quiet while Gideon finished.

"What?"

Perry rubbed his jaw with his thumb. "I, uh. Hmm. I— Well, I believed it would be a while yet."

"For what?" Gideon asked, staring at his snifter as he swirled the liquor in the bowl.

Perry chuckled.

Gideon glared at his younger brother from beneath his eyelashes.

"Good God, man! You really don't see it?"

"What— That I am besotted with this female? That has naught to do with love. I simply have no idea why she draws me the way she does."

"Yes, well. Perhaps it's not love then, but merely lust." Perry drew the last word across his tongue as he considered. "I must travel to Eildon Hill," he said, hitting the arm of the chair.

"No! You'll arrive at Eildon soon enough. The last thing I need is a pompous ass trouncing around the manor, declaring his ill-gotten knowledge to everyone. Besides, there is no audience, so you would

find it discouraging."

Perry smiled. "True, I do prefer to flaunt your misdeeds in front of others, when it benefits me."

Actually, to his benefit, Perry had never undermined his authority. He was a jovial man who was audacious and entertaining, but his honesty always managed to land on the mark. Gideon needed him. He needed, right now, his opinion.

"Perry."

"Yes?" he replied carefully, feeling the tension coursing from Gideon.

"How much do you remember of Mother?" Gideon stood and leaned against the mantel.

Perry grew silent, then set his snifter aside and stood before his brother. "Is that what has you panicked?"

Gideon added a warning note to his gaze so Perry understood he would not tolerate any glibness.

Perry cleared his throat. "Gideon. You suffered much more than I when we were young. You protected me from much of the reality and didn't speak on the circumstances thenceforth. I'm not sure that I'm able to aid you with anything you must feel about our mother. What I do remember of her is that she was the very light and air to me. The embodiment of love and spirit."

Gideon searched his brother's green eyes earnestly and knew his words were genuine. "Yes, she was that," he agreed, choking on the last word. He cleared his throat. "Do you remember the end?" he whispered, looking away.

"No, Gideon. I only know what others tried to explain, which wasn't much to a seven-year-old boy. I understand that she was ill and had to be taken away, but her illness didn't show itself to me—at least not in ways I could understand at the time. To me, her illness manifested itself as a playmate, someone I related to easily. Beyond that, well, I've no idea."

"You were well protected."

"I was…by you."

"Yes, I—I still do not know whether that was in your favor or not."

"I believe it was. And I would have it no other way, other than to share your burden, to ease your pain in any way I would have been able," Perry said.

The corner of Gideon's mouth turned up slightly in acknowledgment before he went on. "She was very truly ill. I only wish there was something else I could have done." They had never spoken of her. Not like this. The only words shared previously between them before were inconsequential.

"You were twelve. What could you possibly have done?" Perry examined him, then his spine straightened. "Wait— Is that what this girl is? An attempt at redemption?"

"No!" Gideon argued, then paused to consider. "Maybe. I don't honestly know. All I know is that I cannot relegate another person to *that* fate. I know that after our mother was taken to Bedlam, she was never the same and— Well, and she never did come home," he finished quietly.

Perry looked into Gideon's eyes, wishing only that his offer to share the burden could somehow be managed. He studied his brother; he was slightly taller with traces of worry and age in his face, but beyond that they could have been twins. Perry knew his sometimes flippant and irreverent humor toward life was as unlike Gideon's singular intensity as any perspective could be, and it was because of their divided experiences as boys.

Perry placed his hands on his brother's shoulders, giving him a stout shake and forcing him to meet his eyes. "This isn't the same," he said. "In *this* instance, in *this* moment, in *this* place, you have to judge the situation without regard for the past. If she is a danger to you or anyone else—including herself—then something must be done. You cannot expect poor Westy to handle her if she's a loon."

Gideon's eyes blazed momentarily before Perry tightened the grip on his shoulders and continued. "Listen to me, just hear me out," he said. "It doesn't sound like that's the case. She may be flighty, but she doesn't seem to be unhinged, and I trust that Westy would ably judge her state before allowing this woman to remain in your home. You know how much that old woman loves you," he finished with a wink and a weak attempt at lightening the mood.

Gideon looked at the floor. Mrs. Weston was the strong sensible mother to him that his own mother was never able to be. When his mother was taken and father irreparably broken, Mrs. Weston served in her stead. He trusted her, probably just as much as he trusted Perry.

Perry cocked a wicked grin. "So, tell me more about these ankles that have you all ensorcelled." He waved one hand about and winked.

Gideon laughed and knocked his hand away, downing the rest of his brandy. "Not tonight, you irreverent rake. I have traveled far too long. I'm going to sleep."

"Fine. Tomorrow, then. We'll break our fast at six-thirty, shall we?" Perry didn't wait for a response, shouting for Sanders as he walked confidently toward the door.

Gideon shook his head, knowing full well there was no avoiding his beloved brother now that he'd come to London. But then the entire point of his trip was to see him. To attempt to gain some insight into his current predicament. His intention upon leaving Eildon may have been to get away, but somewhere in his mind he knew why he was coming here. Placing the snifters on the sideboard, Gideon went directly to his bedchamber, a weight lifted.

Meggie was in a terrible way after Stapleton read the missive from Dr. Walcott. Francine heard her weeping in the garden after Mrs. Weston set Francine up for tea on the back terrace, and she went to find her. It took a while for Meggie to calm down enough to speak, but after a bit of silent pleading on Francine's part she told her what had happened to her sister. Francine sat with her, holding her hand and comforting her until she quieted.

Mrs. Weston found them on the bench before the labyrinth and quietly watched Francine's attentions as Meggie sobbed. Francine held the poor girl's shaking frame to her as though, if she let Meggie go, she would fall to pieces on the lawn around her.

When Mrs. Weston walked over to them Meggie stood abruptly, holding out the communication Dr. Walcott had sent.

"Oh my, we must get you home, Meggie. Come, I'll have Davis ready one of His Grace's carriages."

"Oh no, ma'am, I cannot! If His Grace were to find out—"

"If His Grace were to find out I sent you home afoot, he would have my neck stretched. Davis will take you so you can tend to your family straight away."

Meggie whimpered nervously and turned to follow Mrs. Weston. "Yes, ma'am."

Francine followed as far as the table on the terrace. She felt horrible for Meggie, and for her sister. From the letter, she wasn't sure if she should pray for a recovery or a quick end. It just didn't seem like something anyone would wish to recover from, or suffer through.

Her stomach turned. She sat back and drew her knees up, holding back tears for the girl she knew, and for the one she didn't. Her mind turned to her own situation. What was she doing here? She suddenly felt very lost and alone and didn't know if her life up to the accident had been the dream or the reality. Unfortunately, she had a great deal of time on her hands lately, and it was time she truly considered what was happening.

She certainly felt as though she was present where she was. Of course, if it wasn't a dream that left only the improbable as an option: it meant her father's journals weren't lunatic ramblings. It meant the unnamed lineage in her father's journals was her own. It meant she had taken the place of one of her ancestors.

Francine supped in her room even though she was presentable enough for the dining room. If her foray into the garden the other night had upset the duke so greatly that it sent him away, she wasn't willing to push any more boundaries regardless that Mrs. Weston said it would be acceptable. He was right; she didn't know the first thing about manners here. Wherever here was, she was going to have to relearn how to behave. How had it come to be that her foremost thought was to please him—or was it more to avoid his ire?

She pecked at her dismal supper for a while before giving up and heading for the only other room he had ever allowed her to enter, the library. She poked and prodded around the bookshelves, looking for a hidden gem. She wandered past the drafting table and spied a few old books in the corner. She pulled them out and shuffled through them. *The Girl's Own Book, Children's Manners and Morals*, and *Ladies' Book of Etiquette: Fashion and Manual of Politeness*.

She thumbed through the books, thinking about how these titles would compare to more current titles like *Skinny Bitch* or *My Horizontal Life*. She shook her head—"current" wasn't exactly the correct term. She decided the Cliff's Notes on etiquette might come in handy and she settled on the third book, then headed to her suite where Mrs. Weston would have her evening cup of tea and a warm compress for her throat.

She hadn't spoken all day and didn't want to tempt fate because she was feeling better. Logically, though it was painful, she knew she'd merely strained her vocal chords, probably from screaming. It was certainly worse than when she screamed her way through the last *U2* concert, and they seemed to get so worked up every time she opened her mouth, she figured it wouldn't hurt to allow them this primitive care.

She wanted to be able to speak, to apologize to the duke for her behavior, to explain that it hadn't been Mrs. Weston's fault that she was out in the garden. She wanted to tell him— What? *Everything*. She wanted desperately to tell him everything; how her parents died, why she didn't speak French, how much she would appreciate a comfortable t-shirt and a pair of underwear. *God. Underwear.* She'd never felt this need to communicate with anyone since her parents were killed. Tonight, though, she wanted some peace. Her mind, body, and soul were overtaxed.

"Gideon," Francine said, awakened by the weight of his knee parting her legs and pressing her into the soft, thick mattress beneath. "You've come back," she whispered.

"I have," he said, the words rumbling forth. "Say it again," he

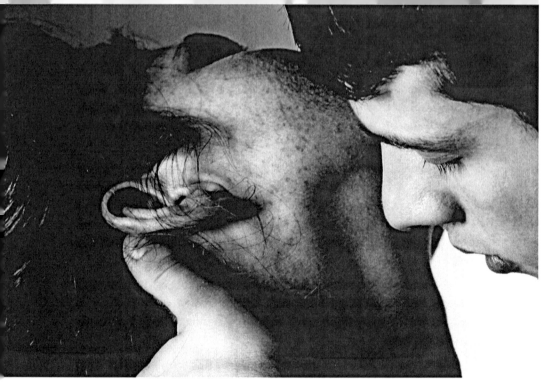

commanded, his hands on either side of her head as he lowered himself over her, favoring her with slow, sweeping kisses.

"Gideon," she breathed into him as he took advantage, allowing his tongue to taste her, then search her depths.

He broke from her, igniting the skin on her cheek with the edge of his teeth.

"Gideon," she cried as he slid his mouth down her chin to her throat. The sensations sunk past her senses and into the channels of her heartbeat. He slowly parted his lips over her pulse, touching the tremor with his tongue and sucking. He kissed his way beneath her chin, her head falling back as he lifted her to his mouth. She melted, the fire in her veins flooding her chest, setting it alight.

Her moan was a low guttural sound that escaped her before she could capture it, and the vibration against his lips stoked his passion. Her hands fluttered, then came to his broad shoulders as he gathered her nightgown to her hip, skimming across her naked flesh. The heat of his fingertips burned as his hand slid from her thigh to hip, then to the steady rise of her breast.

His mouth returned to hers, brushing her, warming her, preparing her, nipping and licking and tasting until she yielded to him fully and he took, sweeping, plunging, surging and driving her.

He spread his fingers at her nape, curving her smooth, white neck toward his mouth. Lifting her from the pillow, he let her hair spread between his fingers as his other hand searched her soft curves and circled her nipple with his thumb.

She arched into his chest when he sat back on his knees, pulling her onto his lap. He took advantage of her squeal to cover her mouth and reach deep within, then placed heated kisses on the outline of her lips. He turned and sat on the edge of the bed, spreading her thighs and draping her over his lap, letting her warmth stroke his erection as she moved.

She could feel the strength of his passion pulsing against her, and she slowly, cautiously started moving, feeling the intensity of his kiss rising with the intensity of his need. She threw her head back, her hands tangled in his hair.

He wrapped his arms around her waist like iron shackles then felt her tense as he moved his hands up, holding her shoulders and pulling her against his rigid strength. She cried out and he teased her nipples through her gown with his teeth.

"Your Grace," she said.

"Say my name," he responded with a moan, pulling her hard against him.

"Your Grace!" she said more sternly.

He looked up at her questioningly.

"Lord Trumbull has arrived, Your Grace," she said, frowning down into his face.

"The— Who?" he asked, confused.

"Your brother, Your Grace." The lips were hers, but the voice was Ferry's.

Gideon's hands fell to his sides as Francine dissolved before his eyes and he found himself lying naked and alone in his bed, tangled in his sheets with a painful cockstand.

"Bloody hell!" Gideon yelled, twisting himself further in the sheet that barely covered his naked form.

Ferry finished laying out his clothes and filled the basin next to the bed with hot water. "I'll be outside, Your Grace."

Gideon grunted his reply, not wanting to move.

Perry had hardly slept after leaving his brother's town house the previous day. Waking before dawn, unable to spend another minute in bed, he bathed and dressed, taking as much time as he could to avoid being too early.

Gideon had found a girl who rendered him insensible. After all the years of his brother taking care of him, their mother, and ultimately their sire and the business of the dukedom, Gideon deserved this bit of happiness.

Perry's only concern was where she'd come from; they knew naught but her name. *No matter,* he thought, *if she isn't marriageable, Rox can certainly take her as a mistress.* He left his own town house which was smaller and not at all prominent on the square as Roxleigh House. That they held two properties in this exclusive bit of London said as much as their joined titles. He arrived at his brother's just as the sun peeked over the horizon behind him, earlier than warranted, but the servants were certainly up and he could wait.

He stood at the entrance, smiling up at Sanders' disgruntled gaze. If he hadn't known the man for years, he would certainly be filled with terror at the glare dispatched against him. Sanders stood as tall as both he and Gideon, if not slightly taller, and held an ominous countenance, his long wrinkly face perched atop the tall, lanky figure like a pebble precariously balanced on a toothpick.

"Lord Trumbull," he drawled, opening the door wide.

"Sanders, old boy! Beautiful day, is it not?" He walked into the entry.

"Is't? I wasn't aware we had ended the night—as of yet," Sanders said, clearly enunciating each word.

Perry laughed at the irreverence, handing off his greatcoat and hat. "Wake my slumbering brother, won't you? There is much to be done, for he must return to Eildon Hill as soon as possible."

"Truly?" Sanders asked, with one stiff, bushy eyebrow raised. "I understood His Grace to be staying in residence for several days."

"Oh no, no, no. We will be off as soon as Sunday, if I have any say."

"Yes, my lord." Sanders strode smoothly from the entrance, leaving Perry to find himself a place to hover until Gideon awakened. He walked to the breakfast room, where a footman was preparing a pot of coffee. They soon heard what sounded like a captured tiger upstairs.

The well-trained footman's eyes widened, but he showed no other outward sign that he had heard anything. Perry simply smiled to himself as he settled at the table and the footman rushed over with a cup.

"Milk and sugar, thank you."

Gideon groaned, then rolled over in the bed and growled. Then he let out a veritable roar and kicked his way out of the tangle of sheets around his legs. He sat at the edge of the bed, trying to remember the last time he'd had such a vivid dream. He couldn't, not like this. He could still feel her silky skin across him, the very scent of her caught in his breath. He shivered.

"Ferry!" he boomed, as he looked down at his naked body. The door opened swiftly.

"Yes, Your Grace?"

"*Cold* water," Gideon bit out.

"Yes, Your Grace."

The door closed and Gideon fell back to the bed.

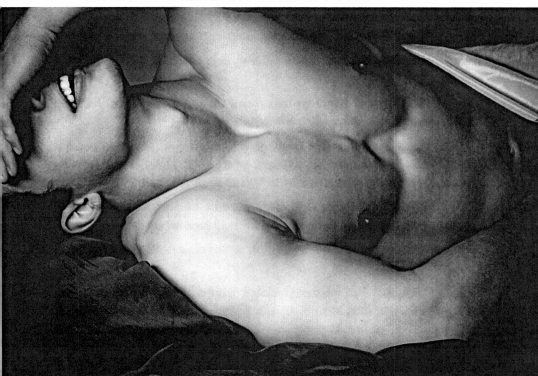

Moments later, Ferry returned with an ewer of cold water that he left next to the basin. "Will there be anything else, Your Grace?" he asked.

"My brother."

"Yes, Your Grace?"

"My brother is to be drawn and quartered. Please inform him directly."

"Yes, Your Grace." Ferry closed the door and went down to the ground floor to notify Lord Trumbull of his pending execution.


Perry laughed heartily at the news.

"That is fantastic! I must have interrupted him with a woman," he pondered aloud, glancing at Ferry.

Ferry gave no quarter.

Perry threw his head back and laughed again.

Ferry left the younger man to his musings and returned to attend His Grace.

He stood outside the door until he heard his name. Roxleigh sat with a warm towel over his face to soften his night beard. "Lord Trumbull is in the breakfast room," Ferry said as he walked to the dresser and prepared the spicy soap His Grace used for his shave. "He is aware of the sentence and appears to look forward to the execution."

"He would," Gideon said curtly.


Francine tossed in her dream, the sheets wrapped around her ankles and her nightgown twisted around her thighs. She gasped and bolted upright in the bed, almost slipping off to the floor in the tangled sheets.

Mrs. Weston woke with a start. "Miss Francine, are you all right?" she asked, tottering over to her.

Francine nodded, her face flushing wildly.

"Oh miss, have you taken a chill? You are a might bit flushed. Let me fetch some cool water."

Francine nodded and smiled.

As Mrs. Weston turned around, Francine's hands fluttered to her face, fanning herself to try to cool her heated skin. *Where had that dream come from?* She colored deeper at the thought of it, of him, and started kicking at the sheets that bound her ankles. She felt a tightness in her belly.

The dream she woke from had been so real she couldn't bear to try to stand, so she lay back against the pillows and waited for the feelings to subside. Instead of waning they only grew in intensity, her heart racing and her breathing quickening as her mind wandered.

Mrs. Weston brought the cool water and Francine drank deeply, then splashed some on her face and sighed as the heat caused it to evaporate. She set the glass down on the stand next to the bed and willed her body to calm.

Mrs. Weston looked at her with concerned eyes. "Are you sure you're all right, miss?"

Francine nodded.

"I'll ready a nice calming bath, how does that sound?"

Francine nodded again. She had a feeling that Mrs. Weston could have recommended she walk on burning cinders and she would have nodded still. But a bath did sound nice, and she hoped it would help calm the nerves that seemed to be beyond frayed. She lay there pondering her interrupted dream as Mrs. Weston fussed about.


Sanders met Gideon at the base of the stairs. "We have prepared for your swift departure, Your Grace," he said.

"Have you now? And what, pray tell, compelled you to make such arrangements?"

"Lord Trumbull instructed as such," Sanders replied.

Gideon stood on the bottom step of the staircase, giving him the ominous position of looking down on Sanders with a cold eye. "So in truth, nothing has been prepared."

"Quite, Your Grace, in truth," the butler answered.

"Good man." Gideon went to greet his brother.

"I hear I'm departing swiftly," Gideon said when he entered the breakfast room.

"I hear I'm to be drawn and quartered," Perry countered.

"Touché."

"Yes, quite. However, you *are* going to depart rather quickly. I've no doubt we can tie up any business you may have, with haste, so you can relax through the weekend, attend a soirée, and be off at first light Tuesday." Perry smiled. "We must get you back to this girl," he said, leaning forward.

"Francine," Gideon said with a swift glance. "What soirée?" he then added gruffly.

"Oh, you caught that, did you? Yes— Well, it's more of a minor presage to the Season at the estate of the Earl of Digby."

"Digby. They have a town house here on the square, do they not?"

"Yes. But the ball will be held at the Grand Prout Estate, just east of London," Perry said.

"Oh, I see. And now it's a ball. What happened to soirée?" Gideon grumbled.

"Well, you know the English. They only like to mimic the French for so long, and soirées have become quite blasé." Perry grinned.

"In a matter of moments, in fact," Gideon replied flatly.

"As well, our cousins will be in attendance, saving us the rounds. Bad enough *I* wasn't notified. If they were to learn of your objectionable handling of this visit, there would be no end to the discourse."

"Cousins." Gideon grunted. "How many of them?"

"Insofar as I can see, all of them."

Gideon sighed heavily. "I suppose this is to become a production, ably managed by your hand."

Perry cocked an eyebrow and nodded with a grin. "At any rate, we should break our fast and be on our way. I sent ahead to the solicitor, and you are expected precisely at eight."

"You are handling me, Perry. I don't like to be handled." Gideon's voice was low and steady.

"Am I? I hadn't realized." His brother gave an innocent lift of his shoulders. "I had only hoped to be accommodating and get you back where you belong, out in the middle of nowhere."

Gideon smiled and sat at the head of the table, motioning to the footmen to serve breakfast. This side of his younger brother was intriguing and somewhat amusing, as always. He might have to see what kind of trouble Perry led him to.

Meggie woke early to see Lilly. She'd arrived late the night before, but didn't want to disturb what rest she thought her sister might be getting. She'd been exhausted from the trip and went straight to bed, deciding she would visit her at first light. She dressed quickly and went to Lilly's room where nothing—not the letter, which she had tried to read countless times on the way home, nor any spoken words, nor anything else--could have prepared her for what she saw.

The thin light filtered through the drapes by the bed, illuminating Dr. Walcott as he hunched over Lilly's feet, lifting and checking and rubbing and rewrapping the long strips of linen. He looked as haggard as Meggie felt.

Her sister was as still as the grave while he ministered. He straightened, then slowly pulled a sheet up to her chin, being very careful not to drag it across her skin but to let it gently waft down over her, soft as a feather.

He turned toward Meggie and she knew she must be a sight, standing in the doorway, pale as a ghost, streams of tears pouring down her cheeks, her hands tied in white and red knots of tension.

He sighed and walked to her, pulling her into the hallway and closing the door quietly. "Meggie, I am so sorry you have to see this."

"How is she? Will she be all right?"

"I don't know anything more than I wrote in the letter. There isn't much else we can do for her. I rewrap her bandages every day, making sure her blood is not poisoned and her skin is not becoming taut to where it would crack when she moves."

"It's no matter," she said, straightening her spine and looking him square in the eyes. "I'll see to it. Just tell me what need be done. Send the other women home. She is my sister and I will tend her."

"Of course," he replied. He gave her explicit instructions as to how to administer both the laudanum and a beef broth to prevent Lilly from wasting away, as well as how to lean her body up and move her about so she wouldn't get pressure sores. It took almost an hour to go over all the instructions.

Meggie nodded, and as she started to walk into the room to attend to Lilly he asked about Francine. "She is well, sir. She is up and about—the dressmaker came yesterday, or was it the day before? I'm not sure, but she left her with a few samples, so Miss Francine can get about. Mrs. Weston stays with her at all times, and she still doesn't speak. Mrs. Weston has followed your directions carefully."

Dr. Walcott frowned. "Is she acting— Is she behaving normally? I mean, she isn't doing anything dangerous, or terribly unsound?"

Meggie thought for a moment about the night Francine ran off to the garden, and then about her care and attention when Meggie received the letter about Lilly. "She's not perfect, sir, but she doesn't seem injured beyond her voice being done."

"I should go check on her, but I fear I can't leave Lilly right now," Dr. Walcott said.

Meggie nodded. "His Grace was called to London. Mrs. Weston bid me let you know so you would understand why he hasn't come here. He doesn't yet know the injured girl was Lilly, and he's not aware of the extent." She waved her hand toward the bedroom where her sister was.

"I will be sure to send an account to him, and to Mrs. Weston, so she will not worry unnecessarily. I will take my leave. Remember, if anything changes, you are to wake me. No exceptions," he said. "Thank you, Meggie."

"Yes, sir, Dr. Walcott. I will."

# TEN

"His Grace, Gideon Trumbull, Duke of Roxleigh," the assistant announced as he opened the door to the solicitor's office. Perry entered behind Gideon and smiled at the assistant, who then said, with slightly less effect, "And Lord Peregrine Trumbull, Viscount Roxleigh."

Perry rubbed his chin with his thumb and followed his brother over to the stately desk as the man behind it stood in deference to them. *Well, to the duke, anyway,* he thought wryly.

"Please, sit," said the small bespectacled man, motioning to the chairs on the opposite side. "To what do I owe the honor?"

"A terrible bit of honor floating around these days," Perry said under his breath as the brothers exchanged humored glances.

"Let's get on with this," Gideon replied sternly.

"Yes, let us."

"I will be signing over the title and management papers for Westcreek Park to the viscountcy," Gideon said without preamble. "I understand you have the documents."

Perry stared. "What the bloody hell are you talking about?"

Gideon turned to the solicitor. "A moment, if you please?"

"Of course," he replied, standing to leave his office.

"What the devil are you up to, Gideon? I do not fancy a jest," Perry said once the door closed.

"This is no jest. It's time you overtook management of the estate—"

"I do not need an estate to hold a courtesy title," Perry interrupted sorely.

"I am aware of that, but you are not my employee and should not be treated as such. I discussed it with Father before he passed. He filed the original documents requesting the severance of Westcreek from the entailed properties, with transference to the esteemed viscountcy." He paused. "Just as he petitioned that the title pass to you, instead of me."

Perry stared at his older brother, his jaw clenched and his teeth bared. "Why wasn't I informed of this?"

"I wasn't sure the severance of Westcreek from the titled properties would be accepted by the House of Lords. I was only notified a few months ago of the sanction, and this has been my first opportunity to see it through. As you did not know about it, I decided it wasn't a pressing issue, but the time has come now. Westcreek is yours."

"And if I refuse?" Perry drawled.

"You will not," Gideon answered definitively, then knocked on the door to alert the solicitor.

Perry seethed at his brother's heavy-handedness as the solicitor completed the documents.

As they walked out to the street, Perry turned to Gideon and held out his hand. Gideon ignored it, pulling his brother into a rough embrace and clapping him on the back.

"You earned that title, as you earned your place in Her Majesty's Royal Navy. Now, not another word," Gideon said as he pushed him into the carriage.

"Yes, Your Grace," Perry answered with a crooked grin.

They continued their rounds, finalizing accounts no longer needed and bringing others current, leaving Gideon with no task to occupy his brain but to think of Francine.


Meggie carefully rolled her sister from one side to the other, singing to her, smoothing what was left of her hair, making sure her bandages did not dry. She talked about her work at Eildon Hill, about His Grace and how he was planning to change the manor and the gardens. She spoke of the extended gathering that he had planned for the end of summer and how they would need extra help. She explained to her sister how she thought maybe Mrs. Weston would hire Lilly then, because she would surely be able.

Meggie fussed over her as she told her about Francine. She told her about how she'd lost her the other night and feared for her job, and how the master's horses, which also killed a hound in the chaos, had injured Francine and how she was still unable to talk. At this Lilly seemed to struggle through her unconsciousness. Her hand shot out and grasped at Meggie, who screamed.

Dr. Walcott stormed through the door. "Meggie?"

"Oh, Dr. Walcott, quick, she is waking!"

Dr. Walcott walked to her side, looking at Lilly.

"Calm down, Lilly, everything will be fine," he said. "Meggie, the laudanum."

Lilly shook her head. "No," she whispered. She clenched her eyes, and a tear squeezed out onto her cheek.

Meggie blotted it away quickly before the salt of the tear caused pain in her sister's wounds.

Lilly looked up into Meggie's eyes. "The man, he was—" She cringed. "He was horrible," she cried, her voice breaking.

"Please, Lilly, not now. Rest a bit, please," Meggie begged, sitting carefully at the edge of the bed.

Lilly shook her head, wincing again. "No. Listen, please. He said things. He was angry with his betrothed. She ran from him, through the wood. He said—" She gasped, clutching at Meggie's hand.

"Please, Lilly, stop," she pleaded, her eyes welling up with tears as she watched her sister struggling.

Lilly shook her head again as she looked into Meggie's eyes. "He said even his hounds could not retrieve her," she whispered.

Meggie's hand flew to her mouth. "No!" she cried.

Lilly wept silently.

"No, it cannot be the same man," Meggie said.

The doctor looked from Lilly to Meggie.

"I'll send a messenger to His Grace immediately," Dr. Walcott said.

Meggie could only nod as he strode from the room. Lilly turned her head into the pillow, falling into a restless sleep.

R

# ELEVEN

Francine walked in the gardens. She knew that Roxleigh had told her specifically not to return alone, but she chose to ignore his admonishment because she needed to feel close to him. She was drawn to where they'd spoken. She walked slowly through the rose arbor, gently stroking the white buds, remembering how they had glowed that night in the moonlight.

She smiled. There was no way to retrace her footsteps; she'd been running headlong in the darkness and today she was strolling lucidly, the garden bright and warm with a gentle breeze. She inspected the hedgerows: their perfect vertical faces of lush green foliage, growing up from thick twisting roots.

Delicate flowers were also woven throughout the hedge—on one wall pink, the next yellow or blue, then back to pink. She followed the walls of pink petals to what she thought was a dead end. Then, turning around, she followed another hedge to the end of the row. She rounded the corner and found herself in the center of the maze, staring into the cool, blue pool at the base of the fountain.

She sat at the edge and pushed her slippers off. Surely now, alone in the middle of the maze, she could dare to put her feet in the water. She smiled and swung her legs over the side, lifting her skirts to keep them from getting wet.

She kicked her feet out, remembering the summers she'd spent with her mom at Congress pool. It's where she'd learned to swim and, when older, she'd joined the swim team. The smell of remembered chlorine and cut grass filled her senses, bringing her back to her former, future life.

When her parents were killed in the accident, she'd lost everything. She was unceremoniously dumped in one foster home, then another, and yet another. It was the last home where she'd met Ava, the girl who taught her to sign.

Ava had always striven for acceptance from her peers in any way she could because of her disability. She hadn't grown up with a decent role model. The two girls looked to each other as adolescents forging their way through middle and high school, trying to either join the popular crowd or stay off their radar, but always, always watching.

It seemed to them that the only way into the elite circle was to have a popular boyfriend, and the way to get a boyfriend was to sleep with someone. Although Ava became quite successful in her quest, Francine never did. She rode on Ava's deflowered skirt-tails, pretending she knew about sex and was willing to participate, but still a virgin and terrified they would find out. She'd wished there was a way to just get rid of her virginity; for her it was like the scarlet letter. *Virgin*, she signed, though no one was in the maze.

The way she felt back in high school had persisted long after. She was never one of the cool kids, never belonged. She thought of Roxleigh—he was definitely in the clique, but not because he wanted to be. He was quiet and brooding, the one everyone was afraid to cut out of the group.

Francine shook off the memories and stood in the fountain, walking around the base as she held her skirts. Her skin pricked as she thought about the circumstances. Her mind wanted to panic, but her body felt content. She'd never felt at peace in her own skin before. She was always unnerved—prepared to be moved.

The nature of foster care was so unsettling that she'd become accustomed to the *feeling* of being unsettled. No matter that she'd been thrown into a different culture and time, she was starting to feel more comfortable here than she had anywhere since losing her parents. Between the man she barely knew who somehow provided an overwhelming sense of security, and the servant woman who was more of a mother than any of her too-busy foster mothers had been, Francine felt safe. Finally, safe.

Francine jumped, nearly toppling into the fountain at the sound of a human roar that traveled over the tops of the hedgerows. She closed her eyes. *Please don't be Gideon, please don't be Gideon.* Stepping out of the fountain, she slid her damp feet back into her slippers as her heart raced. Turning in the direction of the voice, she breathed slowly to calm the heart that rattled painfully against the inside of her ribs. She listened and heard more admonishing curses. She walked to one of the entrances leading back into the maze, creeping cautiously toward the sound.

"Blast it all!" Amberly Shaw yelled as he walked into yet another dead end. He was generally quite astute when it came to navigating new places, even other mazes he'd found himself in, but this one was different. It wasn't patterned from an easily recognizable geometric shape; in fact, the hedgerows held no real pattern within the perimeter whatsoever.

"Insanity!" he cursed, turning about once again to retrace his steps. He leaned back, turning his face toward the waning sun. The hedgerows loomed high above, leaving no chance for him to climb his way out. He couldn't even logically fathom how the groundskeeper managed them so beautifully.

He had to find a way through or be stuck here until Roxleigh returned; and if he was found here, the duke would surely lose all confidence in him, having been bested by fancy shrubbery. He let out a deep-throated yell as he stumbled into yet another dead end. He went to lean against the hedge wall but was pricked, sending him back upright.

He'd only decided to examine the maze in the gardens as part of the estate mapping he'd been hired to complete, and now he realized the duke's concerns were more than valid. He felt as though he might explode, more from embarrassment than anything. He couldn't imagine trying to explain his way out of this predicament. Of course, that was supposing he found his way *out* to begin with. He'd thought it would be an interesting challenge and the day was perfect for a long walk in the garden, but now the delicate petals peeking out from the hedgerow mocked him, as did the thorns hidden behind the mask of green leaves. It was in that moment he determined that the best course of action was to level the site. He was sure the duke wouldn't mind.

He cornered again to find another dead end and, turning back, came face to face with what he believed could only be an angel. Her gown was long and full with delicate detailing covering the bodice— the sort of gown which would definitely inhibit any kind of cleaning, scrubbing, or cooking required of a maid. "Who are you?" he asked.

The girl looked at him without a word, her eyes wide and unblinking.

This was decidedly not her duke. *Her duke*—what made her think that? *Gideon—no, Roxleigh. This was not Roxleigh. Definitely not Roxleigh.* She shook her head to clear her thoughts.

This man wore chocolate brown trousers that were pulled snug to his boots and a light blue shirt and dark blue waistcoat with a brown jacket. She thought about how even Roxleigh's attire seemed severe in comparison. This man was traditionally attractive, though currently a bit disheveled, his dark blond hair sun-streaked and a bit unkempt, some of the curls falling over his forehead. She noticed his eyes, such a light blue they looked almost grey, ringed with a deeper blue halo. They were honest and trusting, and she smiled.

He spoke again, rousing her from the analysis. "Pardon, miss," he said. He straightened his jacket and swept his unruly curls back in place. He seemed flustered. "Uh, begging your pardon, miss, I am Amberly Shaw. I'm here to map the gardens and manor for the Duke of Roxleigh. I wasn't aware there were any other guests here in the maze, or at the manor, for that matter."

She didn't reply; instead, she patted her throat gently with one hand and lifted her other in a fist, circling it over her heart and mouthing *I'm sorry.*

A hint of amazement flashed in his eyes, and he responded with a sign of his own.

She examined his gestures, similar to what she knew but too fast for her to keep up with.

She gently touched his hands to still them, but he drew back at the contact.

Francine shook her head and tried to explain. Slowly she signed that she could hear, she just couldn't speak.

He nodded. "I apologize, miss. I assumed you were deaf."

She smiled and spelled her name. But he didn't understand. She realized the alphabet had to be different. She turned and stood next to him, using her finger to spell her name on her palm.

"Miss Francine?" he asked, and she nodded. "It is an honor to make your acquaintance, Miss Francine. Are you a guest?"

She nodded again, still smiling. She pointed to him and then motioned with both hands, as though she were holding something between them, and then let it fall.

"Am I lost?" he asked. He considered his response. He could admit defeat and be rescued by a woman, or he could feign intelligence only to have her discover his idiocy for herself soon enough. He chuckled. "Yes, quite. I am quite lost," he said, looking down and kicking the toe of his boot in the grass.

She smiled broadly at his admission. She pointed at him, made two fists and held them together, sweeping them in a circle away from her body, then questioning him with her eyes, she pointed to herself.

He sighed heavily. "Yes, please rescue me," he said under his breath, then louder: "Yes, I would very much like to accompany you."

She smiled as he proffered his arm, and took it, then paused and turned toward him. She held one hand up like a tunnel and pushed her other hand through it, then pulled it back out, looking at him.

"Good question. Is there something inside the maze I should see?" he asked.

She nodded vigorously.

"Well then, by all means, let us go in, and then we shall go out."

She took his arm again and led him to the fountain.

Mrs. Weston took the note from the runner, expecting only to learn that Meggie had arrived safely in Kelso. What she discovered, however, chilled her to the bone. She pointed at the messenger, then at the ground to stay him. "You have one more errand," she said, and he nodded, waiting at the service entrance for her to return.

When Francine stopped at the clearing in the center of the maze, Shaw's jaw dropped. "This is magnificent," he said. "I've quite changed my mind about leveling the area. Thank you for bringing me here."

She nodded to him stiffly, wondering what he was getting on about as she rested at the edge of the fountain.

"I had no idea there would be such beauty here. It truly is a peaceful area among the chaos of the labyrinth. It's simple genius, really, to build a sort of oasis within that horrible maze. The perfect juxtaposition of chaos and beauty— Oh. I do go on. Apologies. It's a habit of mine to find explanations for types of architecture, of course, but I needn't bore you with my opinions."

Francine waved him along and headed toward the fountain to sit at the edge again, letting her mind return to Roxleigh. Shaw was right about the way it was planned. It seemed the manor was a reflection of his personality, difficult on the outside with so much more on the inside if you took the time to find it. But which would come first? It was the old chicken and the egg analogy, of course. Here the manor quite obviously came first, but did the chaos of the manor truly help to shape him as a man? That seemed a bit of a jump.

Shaw followed her to the fountain but remained standing. "You have been here for a while?"

*No*, she signed, then felt the wrinkle in her brow that mother-number-two always warned her would stick one day.

"Are you a friend of the family?"

She shook her head and slowly signed that she was here as a guest, because of her injury. It felt good to have an actual conversation that wasn't stunted by coughing fits, pain, and yelling. She sighed. It was ironic; she was in a country where the people spoke English, but she couldn't speak, and the language that they did share was still desperately in need of some translation. She'd no idea when she would talk again. The last tear in her throat had been so painful that she still winced when she swallowed. She shrugged, quite literally at a loss for words.

"Well, I certainly hope you are recovered quickly, and I'm sure the duke will be a gracious host in the meantime." He shifted as he thought about said esteemed host. He really couldn't allow a bad word to reach Roxleigh, and this situation was wholly inappropriate. "Shouldn't we be heading back to the manor?"

She stood and took his arm, leading him from the maze with little difficulty, which, when she glanced at the set of his jaw, she could tell irked him.

They arrived at the back terrace just as Mrs. Weston walked out from the breakfast room. "Oh, miss, wherever have you been? Carole said you were in the garden, but she lost sight of you."

"I'm afraid the fault is entirely mine, Mrs. Weston. I must beg your pardon. I was lost in the maze, and Miss Francine came to my rescue."

Mrs. Weston looked at them in shock. "But, miss, how do you know the maze?"

Francine smiled one of her broad, inviting smiles and winked at her.

"You are a bunch of surprises, aren't you? Well then, supper'll be served in a bit. Would you like to go ready yourselves?"

Francine nodded and released Mr. Shaw with a curtsey.

Shaw responded with a bow and then signed a quick thanks for the tour and rescue.

Francine returned the *Thank you* and walked up the staircase to the private parlor.


Mrs. Weston turned to Mr. Shaw as Francine walked away. "Mr. Shaw, what was that you did there?"

"The sign, you mean?"

She nodded.

"Oh, well, I was surprised to meet someone who knew sign language, though I believe what she knows is French, or possibly American. I don't think it could be the German variation," he mused, more to himself than Mrs. Weston.

"Sign language?" she questioned.

"Why yes, she is quite fluent," he said. "As am I. I learned it because my younger sister Anna is deaf, though I understand Miss Francine is not."

"Yes, she is quite able to speak. I mean she has spoken, but she is injured and should not be talking."

"I see," he replied distractedly. He wasn't sure, but her tone seemed a bit admonishing, and he felt the need to be very careful where Miss Francine was concerned.

Mrs. Weston continued. "I hope your rooms are to your satisfaction?"

"I had not actually made it up there yet. I allowed the footmen to take my things, as I wanted to look over the grounds before supper.

Then I was lost, Miss Francine found me and, well, here we are." He opened his arms in a wide gesture.

"I will show you to your room and send up Aldon to assist you before supper." She was still inspecting him.

"That won't be necessary. I can attend myself," he said as he gathered his hands before him. "But I thank you for your attention."

"Of course, sir, this way," she said, and he followed. Shaw reached for the packet Roxleigh had left on the grand table as they passed, headed toward the grand staircase to the first floor.

# TWELVE

Gideon examined the cravat then nodded to Ferry, who turned to leave. This was to be a bit of business he wasn't too interested in conducting. His intention in attending the season was merely to procure a bride. It was his duty, and his Queen had made it clear it was his time. She wasn't interested in the dukedom slipping to some other branch of the Trumbull lineage, one without as much care for her position.

But now—what now? What were his intentions toward the woman left in his home? He was drawn to her, that much was without contention, but could he act on such without knowledge of her family? He placed both hands against the wall on either side of the large oval mirror and dropped his head. Surely she would remember more soon, but would he like what she said? What if she were already taken, already married? No, she seemed too missish at times for that. And yet she was bold, which harkened of a woman with experience, one also not suited to him.

He straightened and checked his cravat once more. The fact remained he was trained on her for the time being. Until such a time as her fitness for his suit would be disavowed, she was his goal, and this ball—this was merely for his brother's twisted sense of humor. But he was game—for the moment being.

Gideon descended the staircase to find Sanders staring his brother down grimly in the front entry. Perry paid no heed to the vicious gaze and walked over with a smile.

"Are you sure of this, Perry?"

"Of course I am. Just imagine: the Duke and Viscount Roxleigh unexpectedly arriving for the Dowager Countess of Greensborough's spring ball. Every tongue, gossip or proper, will be wagging on the morrow," he finished with a flourish.

"Since when are proper tongues not the ones who carry the gossip?"

Perry laughed, clapping his brother on the shoulder as they walked to the door. Sanders handed Gideon his hat, gloves, and greatcoat, and they left.

The carriage ride to the Marylebone terrace house of the dowager countess was fairly short, and Gideon hoped they would be able to enter without presentation. Both dressed in formal black and white cutaways, the two of them were a sight. No, there really wasn't much hope of them attending the ball unnoticed, or unmolested.

*The rake and the recluse. How charming,* Gideon thought.

They were the two most ineligible bachelors in all of England, yet the mamas still tried. Every time he went out, the debutantes batted their eyes as their mothers placed them in his path, like animal traps snapping at his feet.

The carriage ground to a halt at the entry. Gideon exhaled slowly when he heard a commotion outside—presumably, the other guests had seen the crest on the carriage door and were alerting the dowager countess. He glared at his brother.

"Was it not your intention to attend the Season?" Perry asked with a grin.

"Of course it was, but as with all things miserable, I was attempting to delay the commencement."

"Indeed, as with everything, such as signing over estates, visiting relatives—"

Gideon stopped his brother with another cutting stare.

"Let us be done with this," he ground out.

"Yes, let us," Perry said with a magnificent grin. "I cannot *wait* to see if you are still able to dance."

"I never said anything about dancing."

"Of course you didn't. However, that doesn't mean it's not going to happen. After all, it wouldn't be *proper* to attend a ball and simply ignore all the ladies who will be vying for your attentions."

"Of course it wouldn't," Gideon muttered, descending the carriage steps.

The dowager countess abandoned her guests to greet the brothers at the front entry. She was stunning regardless of her advanced age, and still moved like a woman of fifty. "Your Grace, my lord, an unexpected treat. Welcome to Greensborough House. Will you be in London long, Your Grace?" she asked as she curtseyed and lifted her hand.

"No, my lady, I return to Eildon soon." He bent slightly at the waist.

"How unfortunate for all of us. I had heard you would be attending more of the Season. Will you make it to the Grand Prout Estate for the Digby affair?" she asked, obviously fishing; his attendance at her ball and none other would truly be a success.

He smiled, happy to disappoint. "Yes, of course. Actually, we already sent notice."

Perry glared at his brother's callous comment, obviously meant to quell the countess' preening. "Forgive His Grace's insolence, my lady. We all know that only the very best affairs are worthy of attendance, especially when one arrives without notice as we have tonight." She turned to him and smiled politely.

Gideon closed his eyes. He really needed to work on his manners. He cleared his throat. "My lady, may I escort you into the ballroom?" he asked, and it seemed all indiscretions were immediately forgotten.

Lady Greensborough smiled and adjusted her skirts with a flourish, then straightened her frame. After a moment of hesitation she placed her hand carefully on his arm, as though he might bite, and nodded to the butler.

The ballroom doors opened and the butler gained the attention of the guests with three loud whacks of the baton on the floor. "His Grace the Duke of Roxleigh," the butler announced. And then, with slightly less enthusiasm, "The Right Honorable, the Viscount Roxleigh."

As they descended the stair, Gideon noticed minor movements from various quarters and leaned toward Perry.

"Cousins," he said quietly.

"Cousins," Perry agreed.

They reached the base of the stair and were immediately swarmed by gentlemen looking for polite conversation.

Gideon dropped his arm, prepared to bid a good evening to the dowager countess, when she turned to him.

"Your Grace, this ball is in honor of my granddaughter, Lady

Alice Gracin, for her coming out. Perhaps you would favor her with a dance?"

Gideon smiled stiffly. "Of course, my lady, only introduce me before the dance."

She glanced around the ballroom, finally catching sight of a willowy girl in a white gown, her russet hair piled on top of her head in a mass of vibrant curls. She gestured to her. "I shall find you before the first dance." He nodded, then turned back to his brother.

Perry winked at Gideon and smiled the charming, wide-mouthed smile that made him such a successful rake.

"Why did you bring me here?" he growled under his breath.

"For the entertainment value, of course."

"Mine or theirs?" Gideon nodded toward the crowd.

"I'm not quite sure yet," Perry answered, eyeing his brother carefully.

Gideon growled again, silencing the gaggle of gentlemen who were pooling around them, and walked off.

The group stared after him, then all eyes turned on Perry, who laughed deeply, shaking his head. His brother's ferocious reputation was intact.

Gideon made it only a few paces before realizing his error. If he'd stayed within the group of men he might have been safe. As it was, he was now surrounded by a much dodgier crowd. He looked from one face to the next, unconsciously counting. "Where are Jerrod, Maebh, Grayson, and Poppy?" he asked. "They're certain to be disappointed when they learn they've missed this opportunity." He turned to his right in time to see Perry approaching with a splendid smile.

His brother bowed and the group returned the favor, all eyes shifting to Gideon expectantly as he also bowed. His cousins were numerous, as his sire had two brothers and two sisters who were likewise accountable to the Crown. He turned to his left and nodded to Thorne and Isadore Calder. Thorne was Marquess of Canford and future Duke of St. Cyr, and his sister was one of the most eligible young ladies in Britain. Jerrod, Thorne's twin brother, was one of the missing.

"And Jerrod is?" Gideon asked.

"Jerrod is…Jerrod," Isadore said simply. Her smooth blonde hair was pulled in a severe chignon with little flourish for decoration. Her sparkling grey eyes reflected the colors of the ballroom—sometimes blue, sometimes green, occasionally dark but more oft light.

He smiled and took her hand, sweeping a kiss across the back before looking up to her brother, whose visage was as hers, with a nod. Their mother, Auberry Trumbull, now Calder, Duchess of St. Cyr, was the eldest of his grandsire's brood. The next in line was his own sire, followed closely by the delicate Lady Brianna Wyntor, Marchioness of Cheshire, whose two strapping sons, Wilder and Quintin, now stood just left of Perry. Those brothers were among the youngest of the cousins.

"Rox!" came an impatient female voice from in front, pulling his attention.

"My precious Saorise, have I been remiss?" He smiled and leaned over her hand, gazing into jeweled eyes much the hue of his own. He stood, wincing at the great mane of riotous red curls that swept down her back and drew attention to her like bees to honey. He remembered countless hours of her screaming as her mama, Bridger Trumbull's wild Irish bride Fallon, tried to force it to behave—to no avail. Obviously her mane had won out in the end, to the delight of many and the consternation of many more. But Saorise, pixie though she was in stature, was well protected within the circle and none would hear any talk of her improper locks.

"Yes, you have ignored me too long. Mama said we weren't to visit this summer until Season's end. How will I survive?" she complained.

He grinned at the sweetest of his cousin, one who held a special place in his heart. "I have something special planned for the end of this Season. Have no fear, my precious Saorise, you will have your time with my Friesians."

She beamed a smile as light as the air, contented. Her sister Maebh stood silently next to her, watching Gideon carefully. Her smooth ginger locks were pulled up in an intricate twist on her crown.

"And you, Roxleigh, what brings you tonight?" Quintin asked.

"Well, I do, of course," Perry cut in.

Gideon grimaced, then nodded once.

The dowager countess pressed into the exceptional circle no one else dared breach, curtseying and catching Gideon's attention.

He stiffened; the time had come for him to pay his penance for his earlier insolence.

"If you will excuse me, I am expected to dance," he said with a brilliant smile.

Every one of his cousins inclined their heads in surprise as they watched him move away.


Lady Alice Gracin stood amidst a group of young girls who had just been introduced to the ton. They surveyed the room, looking for the eligible peers their mothers had listed and forced them to memorize in order of rank and respectability. There were two footnotes to the list. The first was the Duke of Roxleigh, who held one of the most powerful titles in the kingdom but was also known to be an angry recluse, stern and unforgiving, who rarely traveled away from his estate. His brother the viscount was the other footnote. A devoted rake, he had no intention of ever marrying, instead openly dedicating his life to the pursuits of pleasure and ruination of innocents the country over.

She gasped when they were both announced at her come-out. Looking up to her grandmother at the entrance, her breath caught. They were stunning—tall, dark hair, and perfectly turned out. She shuddered, putting her arm around her friend Bethany to steady herself. "Oh my, but aren't they a vision," Lady Alice said.

"A vision is all they are, Alice. Remember what our mamas said. The first is impossible, the second impermissible!"

Alice frowned. Of course they were, but that was irrelevant. How could either of the amazingly beautiful brothers be an acceptable match for her, with her gangly freckled limbs, fiery tangle of curls, and sea-foam green eyes? She was most categorically an unconventional sight.

She smiled as she saw the duke conversing with his cousins, the wild Irish sisters Saorise and Maebh included. It was due to Saorise's unconventional mane of bright curls that hers were currently left unnoticed. She continued to survey the room with Bethany, picking out the other bachelors.

Her eyes paused on the duke's flock again, noting how the crowed parted about him, much like an immovable boulder among rapids. Her grandmother approached the group and spoke with him. Alice's jaw dropped and she squeaked, her nails digging into Bethany's arm.

"Alice!" Bethany yelled. "That hurts!" But Bethany saw the terrified look in her friend's eyes and followed her gaze, directly into the face of the Duke of Impossible.

Alice was pinned by his annoyed expression.

*I should have known better than to entertain my brother's fancy,* Gideon thought as he crossed the room with the dowager on his arm. *Now I'm to be displayed as a lamb to slaughter. Dancing. There'll be hell to pay after this.* He wished he could turn down the dowager's request, but his stomach was already in knots from the improper way he'd spoken with her at the door. Social functions of the *ton* always managed to bring out the worst in him, as if his demeanor wasn't bad enough. *She looks terrified. Good. She will take the first dance and then leave me be. Nothing like a silent turn around the ballroom to scare the women away.*

He had to admit that her ladyship was brilliant; one dance with him and every gentleman here would request a dance with the girl. *What did Lady Greensborough say her name was? Bloody hell!* He stopped a few yards in front of her as the crowd seemed to part between them like the Red Sea. She seemed frozen in fear. Finally, her friend whispered in her ear then pinched her, bringing her around.

"Your Grace, may I present you my granddaughter, Lady Alice Gracin. Lady Alice; His Grace, the Duke of Roxleigh." The dowager then nodded to the orchestra on the second landing.

"Y-Your Grace," Lady Alice stammered, curtseying deeply as he bowed. Much to his dismay, the musicians began a waltz. He shook his head. The dowager countess had orchestrated the display very well, regardless that she hadn't known he was attending. He wondered whom he had displaced for the dance. He proffered his hand and Lady Alice took it reflexively. He swept her out of the crowd and onto the empty dance floor.

Gideon looked down at the small girl in his arms. She was shaking terribly and he suddenly felt like a buffoon, realizing from her expression that this wasn't exactly what she would have wished.

"Lady Alice, do you need to sit down?" he asked, aware that his question might be entirely too forward.

She glanced up at him with wide eyes, shaking her head quickly.

He laughed. They were quite un-matched. The pile of curls on

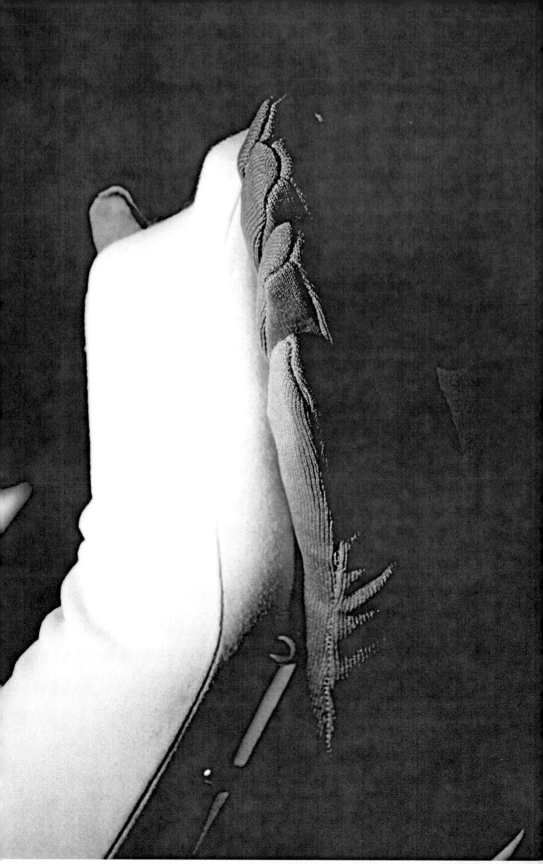

her head only came to his shoulder. They must be a spectacle. "Are you enjoying the Season?" he tried again.

She shook her head.

He frowned, realizing he needed a question that could not be answered with a mere shake of her head. "Why not?" he asked finally. He felt her body tense.

"I— Well, this is my first ball, so it is difficult to have enjoyed it when it has only just begun."

"I see," he said. *I am an imbecile.*

Then she spoke again. "You and Lord Trumbull are quite, um…" She bit her lip. "Well, I don't believe anyone was expecting you," she finished.

"No, I don't believe they were. And yet here I am, dancing with you." He led her through the corner, her skirts sweeping the floor behind her.

She glanced up at him again. "My mother will be furious."

He thought for a moment. Her mother…furious? But he was the Duke of Roxleigh, and he was fairly certain he didn't know the Countess of Greensborough. "Why is that?" he asked.

"It is just that I seem to have lost all of my senses suddenly by dancing with you. I beg your pardon, Your Grace, it is only that you and your brother, I mean, Your Grace and Lord Trumbull are quite—" She paused.

"Yes I suppose we are…quite," he said, with a gleaming flash of perfect white teeth.

"Oh!" she cried, losing a step. He caught her carefully and they continued, no one the wiser except perhaps her mother, whom he'd picked out from the crowd by the hawk-like gaze she held on them.

Lady Alice was actually a delightful young lady. Much too young and missish for him, of course, but he wasn't available regardless—not that anyone here would have any idea of that—and the thought steeled him.

"My mother. Oh, dear," Lady Alice said.

He glanced back over to where the mother stood and saw her drawn-up face; she was frowning at the way her daughter was clambering around the floor in an attempt to keep up with him.

"Oh, dear," he repeated with the same emphasis, followed by a grin. "Straighten your back and steady your shoulders," he commanded.

She complied.

"Stiffen your arms…more. Much better, but lift your chin. Very nice. Now take a deep breath and let *me* lead," he said gently.

She acquiesced.

On the next turn of the floor he glanced at the mother, who was starting to smile proudly, nudging the guest beside her and pointing.

"Very well, young lady. I believe we have fooled them all," he said in a triumphant tone.

Lady Alice smiled.

The waltz ended and Gideon bestowed a regal bow on his partner, sending a blush soaring to her hairline. The entire ballroom started buzzing. "Would you like some refreshment?"

She nodded.

"Excellent. Perhaps you could gather your chaperone and meet me on the terrace."

"Of course, Your Grace." She curtseyed, a little off-kilter.

He turned to the refreshment table.


Alice's friends descended on her like a flock of vultures, all speaking at once.

"Yes—no—no—wonderful—charming—no—what? Of *course* not!" She tried to answer all the questions as they followed her toward her mama. She informed her that they were to attend the duke on the terrace and her mother beamed, following at a discreet distance.

Bethany walked with Alice to the exit, their arms entwined. "I thought he was impermissible," she said, leaning toward Alice with bright eyes.

"Not quite impermissible—impossible." Alice shrugged, smiling.


Gideon nodded to the Countess of Greensborough as he passed her on the terrace, appreciating that she at least maintained a respectable distance. "Well, I believe you have a victory," he said to Lady Alice with a smile a few moments later as he handed her the lemonade.

"Yes, Your Grace, thank you. I truly thought I was done for, and I had only just begun."

"After this turn you will be quite successful in landing yourself an acceptable peer, and your mother should enjoy a successful Season for you. That is obviously what she wants." He nodded toward her mother, who was watching and attempting to listen to their conversation, from much closer than she'd been before.

Lady Alice sipped her lemonade. "Since we seem to be speaking freely, Your Grace, I should tell you that I'm not interested in landing you as a husband. Or any other blue blood, for that matter."

She looked back to her mother, then leaned toward him, whispering. "You see, Your Grace, I am already promised to someone. He only has to prove himself before he approaches Papa."

Gideon cocked a brow.

"He is not of the peerage, so they certainly won't be too keen on the notion," she added.

"Why are you telling me this?"

Lady Alice bit her lip. "I— I am not sure. I suppose because you were so, well— I'm just not interested in you," she finished with a nod.

"Defending your own honor? I cannot blame you, I suppose. I have acted somewhat boorish this evening." He swirled his lemonade. "I'm guessing your family doesn't know about your betrothed."

Dismay crossed her features. "You would not— You will not say anything? Will you?"

"I have no interest in betraying your trust. It occurs to me that whichever gentleman you tip your cap for will be fortunate. I only hope that he is as deserving of such a sweet girl as you."

She blushed at the bold compliment, then noticed her mother was anxiously pacing, surely wanting to return Alice to the ball to take advantage of the duke's good graces. "Actually, Your Grace, he is— As you will find..."

He was just about to ask what she was on about when her mother interrupted, rather ungracefully. "Pardon, Your Grace, but my daughter should return. I have no doubt her dance card would be filled by now, had she not been out here on the terrace."

Gideon gave her a cutting stare. *Her dance card. Right. So be it. He wasn't her quarry, but the woman was using him to field them.*

"Alice," he said, using only her Christian name without permission, "might I entreat you for another dance this evening?"

She smiled at his dismissal of her mother and curtseyed.

"Of course, Your Grace, I would be most honored," she said, handing him the card.

He listed his name for another waltz, then, with a wry grin and casting a sideways glance at her overbearing mother, he wrote his brother's name in no less than two places and proceeded to sprinkle his cousins throughout.

Handing it back to Alice, he leaned in. "Lady Alice, there is someone you must make the acquaintance of." *Preferably before the next dance begins.*

She returned the grin and took his arm. He led her back to the ballroom while her mother shuffled to keep up.

They strode across the cavernous room, sidestepping the gentlemen who placed themselves in her path and losing her mother in the sea of guests. He scanned the ballroom for his brother, finally catching sight of him as he walked in from the terrace behind a suitably rumpled chit.

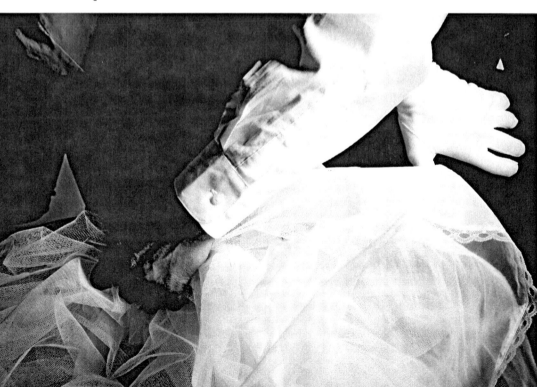

Gideon grunted and walked directly toward him. "Trumbull," he said, "may I present Lady Alice Gracin."

Perry lifted his brows as he finished straightening his waistcoat.

"Lady Alice, I present to you Lord Peregrine Trumbull, Viscount Roxleigh."

She curtseyed and proffered her hand to Perry, who smiled the brilliant smile that was known to make women swoon, and kissed her hand while she giggled behind hers.

*Rake*, Gideon thought.


Perry glanced at his brother while his mind raced to figure out what Gideon was about; his brother knew he never dabbled with innocents. Perry smiled crookedly at the vision in his mind.

"Lady Alice, I am most honored to make your acquaintance."

Gideon leaned in and whispered to his brother as a waltz started, then: "Well, Trumbull, according to the lady's dance card, this is *your* waltz."

Perry laughed, holding his hand out to her. "So it is," he said jovially, then swept her out to the floor.

She smiled. "What did he whisper to you, my lord, if I might ask?"

"Ah, my lady, I'm not entirely sure I should answer. I will tell you that my brother has no patience for overbearing women such as your mother, and that we are to endeavor to keep you busy...*all night*." He waggled his brows.

She blushed wildly, much to his delight.

He laughed. "Have no fear, sweet, your innocence is quite safe. I was merely referring to the ball."

Alice searched through the crowed to find Gideon conversing with their cousins. They all turned to watch the pair of them dance, and Gideon winked at her. Perry laughed, and she tensed in his arms. He looked around to find her mother scowling at them.

"Your mother." he said, with a nod in her direction.

Her eyes widened, then her jaw tensed, apparently attempting to quell a much-too-satisfied smile. She understood. Looking up into

Perry's face with a laugh, she said, "Why, Lord Trumbull, I never expected to find myself a champion tonight, much less two."

"Or five, I'd imagine." He grinned. "You are charming! My brother does pick them well."

At the request of the dowager, Gideon made his way to the library. He knew not what she was about, only that he wasn't keen to disappoint her again.

Two royal guards met him at the door and he felt his back straighten without a thought. By the grace of God, Queen Victoria. His breath stilled—even his lungs were nervous. He felt eyes on him, though he could swear nobody had even so much as twitched. Damn bloody good at what they did. He pointed to the door, and they made no motion to help him or stop him, so he reached for it—slowly.

"Roxleigh, what by heavens has kept you? Dear boy, it seems I've been waiting for ages."

"Your Majesty." He bowed as far as his waistcoat allowed, then pressed further.

"Stand up, let me look on you. I see. Well, keeping you up north does something for your complexion. It appears we have more sunshine up there than here."

"Your Majesty " His fingers twisted behind his back.

"Well, I've come to remind you. I cannot wait forever, and that cousin of yours is much too eager and much too close for my taste."

"Yes, Your Majesty, I believe I might have a ready solution that quite, well, quite came by way of accident."

"I hear you do not know who she is." He started to shake his head, then was struck with the thought that nobody knew of Francine outside of his household.

"Minor obstacle."

"One that must be remedied. You of all people cannot simply marry. You are Roxleigh."

"Yes, Your Majesty, I understand." He cast his eyes downward—perhaps for a moment to think, he wasn't sure. But in that moment she moved toward him faster than any person of her age had right to do.

"I see. So it's like that, is it?"

"Apologies, Your Majesty. Like what?" His palms were sweating inside his gloves and her hand came out to lift his chin.

"You love her."

There went his lungs again. Undoubtedly he would have permanent damage from lack of oxygen. Terribly inconvenient.

"Do not attempt to cozen me, Roxleigh. I can see it plain as day. You seem to forget—"

"I have not forgotten, Your Majesty. I beg pardon, nobody could possibly forget His Royal Highness. As always, you have my deepest sympathies." He watched her eyes; she seemed so deep in thought that he felt like an intruder. After a time, she whispered and he had to lean toward her to hear the quiet words.

"Make her yours, Roxleigh. Whatever it takes, then hold on to her for as long as you possibly can." She nodded and swept out of the room without another word.


The rest of the night was spent with his cousins, who laughed and danced through the evening, endeavoring to entertain Lady Gracin, protect Lady Saorise, and enliven Lady Isadore and Lady Maebh. The ladies never wanted for a partner, as the gentleman were on constant call.

For the first time ever, Gideon was actually disappointed to leave a societal ball. On their way out he made sure to invite the dowager countess to his house party at the end of the summer.

"I only wanted to provide you with advanced notice. The formal invitation will follow, of course," he said.

"Of course, Your Grace," she replied, "and I shall be honored to attend."

"The honor will be mine, my lady, particularly if you bring your charming granddaughter."

"Why, Your Grace, I most certainly will."

And with that the dashing brothers departed.

R

# THIRTEEN

"One more stop I think, Grover," Gideon said two days later, eliciting a groan from Perry. They had spent all of Friday before the ball making the rounds of London and most of Saturday as well. He dealt his brother a vicious glance and Perry feigned retreat across the carriage. "Take us to Knightsbridge. I have business at Harrods."

"Yes, Your Grace," the coachman replied.

Perry gave his brother a sideways glance. "You *never* have business at Harrods," he grumbled.

"I do today." Gideon smiled, drawing a hearty laugh from Perry.

They spent the afternoon perusing the monstrous store. Perry glared at Gideon, who was examining a silver comb. "Visiting shops should not be such a chore for one as well appointed as you," Gideon murmured.

"I do none of my own purchasing, brother. This escapade is akin to having teeth yanked. I will, however, endure further for your benefit," he said, then paused. "If you deem it necessary."

"I do so deem it," Gideon replied, with a sly half-smile.

"You are gathering some rather extravagant gifts, Gideon. Does this mean you have made a decision about your guest?" Perry fingered the matched silver brush on the counter. Gideon put the comb down and picked it up.

"Well, I can't truly make a decision until I know more about her, but in all honesty I plan to do what it takes to care for her."

"That sounds rather formal."

Gideon motioned at the set. "To be delivered to Roxleigh House." He turned to Perry. "Formal it might be, but it is also as it should be."

Perry nodded and followed as Gideon moved toward the front entry and the carriage.

Perry couldn't help but chuckle. "So, dear brother, what fresh hell have we to visit next?" he asked as they took their seats in the carriage.

Gideon shifted uncomfortably. "I need a dress shop," he mumbled.

Perry dropped his walking cane, his jaw agape and eyes bulging. This time, Gideon was the one to chuckle.

The brothers entered the Iron Duke Taproom, laughing. "But will she like it?" Gideon asked.

"Ah, but she must. She has no choice," Perry responded. They took a small table close to the front and a barmaid came over, sitting on Perry's outstretched thigh. "Ah, Lucy, and how are you this fine evening?"

Gideon watched as Perry surveyed her curves with his hands and his eyes.

"The night's much better since ye've come 'round, milord," she said, glancing across the table at Gideon. "An' who might yer 'ansom friend be?" she asked, tittering.

"Wouldn't you know, Lucy, this is my elder brother, the *Duke* of Roxleigh."

"Well, well, Yer Grayce." She drew the title over her tongue like she was wrapping tobacco. "P'raps the two a ye're lookin' fer some entertainment?" she asked wickedly, leaning hard on the table and pushing her cleavage toward him.

He glared at Perry, who laughed dismissively. "Unfortunately, my sweet, Roxleigh here is already quite taken with another buxom beauty."

Gideon winced. He didn't want others thinking of Francine's bosom, buxom or no, even if his brother was merely goading him.

"Oh, ye know I dun mind tha, milord. I'll no' take 'im, I'll jus borra Yer Grayce fer a tiddle," she said, pausing to look at Perry and sweeping her hand down his jaw. "As long as ye're game to join."

Gideon's glare intensified as Perry's eyes widened.

"Thank you for the invitation, precious, but we must decline such a—" He paused to appreciate her bosom. "—generous offer." He smiled. "Ale?"

"Aye, milord," she said.

Lucy sauntered off to the tap while heaving a sultry gaze over her shoulder at Gideon, who was still attempting to bore a hole into his brother's head with his stare.

"Oh, come on, Giddy, it's all in fun."

"Do *not* call me that," Gideon forced through clenched teeth.

Perry waved his hands in surrender. "Fine then, I beg off, you win. Let us simply drink our fill."

Gideon nodded, looking down at the worn patterns on the pub table. "So she will like it?" he asked suddenly.

Perry chuckled. "She would be absurd not to."

Gideon smiled, leaning back against the wall behind his bench, feeling heartily satisfied as Lucy returned and plopped two pints on the table in front of them.

"Monday night we attend the ball and Tuesday return to Eildon," Perry said. "This has been a good day, Rox. One more day like this and you'll have shattered all of my previous notions of what a stodgy boor you are. I cannot wait to reintroduce this new gentleman to society," he finished with a flourish of his gloved hand.

Gideon grumbled.

"And with that, the new man is gone." Perry's flippancy brought the smile back to Gideon's face.

"We shall see, after tomorrow, which of me you will be dragging to the next godforsaken function."

"One thing I will say about this girl, she's done much to ameliorate your overall demeanor. Last night's ball was a great deal of fun."

"She is not a girl, but a woman," Gideon said, then shrugged. "And I am not so sure about that."

"Which part are you unsure of?"

Gideon sat back with his ale, ignoring the question. "So... Have you?" He motioned toward Lucy as he took a drink of his ale.

"Have I? Oh... Lucy? No, not... No. She's had a bit too much fun for my taste."

Gideon nodded. "And what about the other bit?" He watched his brother's expression, waiting for his comprehension.

Perry grinned widely. "Well, not in the way she offered—I've certainly never rubbed cocks with another. Now an abundance of breasts, that's something I have done."

Gideon shook his head. Perry laughed and waggled his brows, tipping his ale to his brother, then back.


Amberly Shaw took the paperwork with him to breakfast. He wanted to delve into all aspects of the manor, and, more than anything, he wanted to impress the duke when he returned. He knew if he could complete this appointment successfully he would be well on his way to making a respected name for himself. Not to mention the estate party the duke was planning for the end of summer; if his name were associated with the project, it would be a great boon to his reputation.

He took breakfast on the back terrace overlooking the gardens that he'd lost himself in only the day before. He was enchanted. Beyond the landscape, the air this far north in England was pure and clean, begging one to breathe deeply with every step outside, and the light was indescribably beautiful—gentle and colorful and not the least bit harsh or difficult on the eyes.

Shaw learned that one of the other hills held the ruins of an old Roman fort known as Trimontium, and he hoped to be able to explore the site before his return to London. He took another deep breath, leaning his head back and looking up at the bright blue, cloudless sky. He wasn't getting a bit of work done here. He sat up, finishing his breakfast as quickly as possible before walking to the heart of the manor to find the library.

He spent most of his time at the old drafting table, studying the rough plans Roxleigh had drawn up. With the help of Aldon, one of the footmen, he made needed measurements and completed a sketch of the grounds and primary floors. He examined a missing section in the sketch at the center of the north wing, behind the families' suites. He must have missed one of the passages or servant suites, and would have to return later to measure it.

While the manor was a frustrating web of confusing passages with adjoining suites and rooms, it was not quite as difficult as the hedgerow labyrinth. Shaw marveled at how easily Miss Francine had navigated it. She must have discovered the key. Even the most complex of labyrinths had a key; a perfect example was the Heatherton Maze, where two rights for every left would take you to the center.

Even from the balcony it wasn't possible to see more than the first two rows that made up the maze, because they loomed over the interior hedgerows, blocking any pattern from sight. He would have to ask Miss Francine about the key the next time he saw her, though she was doing a very good job of keeping to herself. She had probably realized how inappropriate their visit had been and was avoiding him until a chaperone was available.

He leaned away from the table. The more involved he became in Eildon, the more mysteries appeared. He decided to quit the assessment until another day and rose to return to his suite, but his jacket caught on something.

He bent and inspected the brass hook, then pulled it. The top of the drafting table popped up, and he moved his sketches and plans aside, then lifted the desk top. Inside were stacks of plans that, upon closer inspection, proved to detail the manor and several of the larger outbuildings.

He sat back down at the drafting table and started comparing the plans and making notes.

When Gideon and Perry finally returned to the town house Sunday night, Sanders met them with a silver salver bearing a letter. Gideon exchanged his greatcoat and top hat for the letter, and Sanders turned to Perry, his arm outstretched.

"Thank you, Sanders, but I won't be staying."

Sanders turned from the entrance.

Gideon opened the letter, expecting a simple update from Mrs. Weston, but the message brought him up stiffly. He handed the note to Perry. "I have to leave. Ferry!" He ran up the stairs.

"Rox, wait," Perry called as he followed, scanning the letter.

"It's Meggie from Eildon. Her sister was attacked outside of Kelso and apparently there's reason to believe that the man who did it was after Francine. I have to get back. She could be in danger."

Perry ran back down the stairs, then paused to turn and point at his brother. "I will pack and inform my staff. Do not leave without me," he said, then ran from Roxleigh House.

The brothers were under way within the hour.

# FOURTEEN

Francine woke suddenly in the night at the sound of a carriage. She jumped from the bed and ran to the window. The outriders descended from the carriage, opening the door for the dark figure that stepped down. "Roxleigh," she sighed. Her heart jumped when she saw another man exit the carriage. *There are two of them.*

She pressed against the window to get a better view. The first man was definitely not Roxleigh—his movements were too fluid, too smooth. The man on the right, the one who had just stepped down, *this* was her duke.

She shook her head. He wasn't hers. She shouldn't feel so possessive of him. Roxleigh straightened and turned to look directly at her window, forcing her back a step into the shadows. Considering his obsession with proper behavior, upsetting him before he even walked back into the manor seemed a bad idea.

The first man said something when Roxleigh looked up. She watched him nod in response. Then, with a great flourish, the stranger turned toward her and bowed, a broad grin lighting his face.

Roxleigh scowled and said something else, making the man chuckle.

There was no doubt that they knew she was watching. The other man stood up straight, still smiling, and put his arm on Roxleigh's stoic shoulder. They were similar, but even the subtle differences in manner and expression were apparent from where she stood.

She sighed but didn't move back to the window, knowing that if they were able to see anything of her now it would only be her nightgown. When the stranger moved to enter the manor, she moved forward and placed one hand flat against the pane to welcome Roxleigh home.

The night air was electric, as if a great storm loomed on the horizon. She could feel the static gathering, looking to release the charge. Her body tensed as she stepped back again, willing herself to bed even though her nerves were on edge. She curled up in a tight ball against the chilly sheets, drawing them around her, trying to create a cocoon to hold her warmth. She smiled as she drifted asleep, feeling safer than she had since he'd left.

The tender gesture of her hand on the window caused Gideon's stomach to tighten and his resolve to melt—he wanted nothing more than to be with her. At the same moment his brother turned to look at him, and he dropped his gaze from her chamber window, following. "Good God, man, must you act like a dandy?" he grumbled, marching past him.

Perry followed Gideon up the grand staircase as Stapleton appeared. "Your Grace, we had not received word."

"There's no need to fuss. We are to retire, as should you. There will be no further disturbance."

"We, Your Grace?" Stapleton asked before he noticed Perry. "My lord Trumbull, I did not— I will have your rooms readied immediately," he said, turning on his heel and shuffling into the darkness of the first floor as yet another sleepy face appeared.

"Your Grace," Mrs. Weston said with a sleepy smile. "Oh, *my lord!* Welcome home," she said excitedly, pushing past Gideon to embrace Perry. He squeezed her hard, lifting her from her feet.

"Oh, I see how easily I'm to be displaced." Gideon folded his arms as he waited.

"My lord... Peregrine, you need to unhand me!"

"Why yes, of course I do, but it's been so long since I've had the chance to unsettle you, I couldn't resist."

Mrs. Weston pulled away from him, straightening her robe. She adored Perry. He was such a wonderfully happy soul, and he brought an air of lightness with him whenever he visited. She realized that as much lightness as he brought, his older brother carried just as much tension. She sobered.

"Your Grace, I haven't said anything to Miss Francine. We've kept a close eye on her, but I didn't think you'd want me to be the one to tell her."

"I take it the entire household is aware?"

"Indeed, Your Grace, I thought it necessary the staff know of any danger."

"Certainly. Thank you for your astute assessment, and for notifying me so quickly. As always, you are an irreplaceable asset."

Perry burst out laughing and Gideon rolled his eyes, then turned toward his suite.

Mrs. Weston admonished Perry for his insolence with a stern look and a light smack on the shoulder. He stifled his laughter, accepting her reprimand with a smile. "So, Westy, do tell me of this mystery woman. Everything. Leave nothing out."

"Well, I don't see how that would do much good right now, do you? Tis the middle of the night!"

"Nonetheless, I want every detail. I imagine Gideon may need a few strong pushes in the right direction," he said as Mrs. Weston stared at him with wide eyes.

"Perry, you do not think—"

"No, Westy, I do not... *I know*," he replied, giving her the grandest smile he could muster.

Mrs. Weston drew her hands together, clapping with excitement. "Well in that case, I've slept entirely too much lately, anyway. Let us go chat." She headed toward the kitchen. "How about some kippers and milk?" she said with a wink.

"Kippers, yes," he replied with a flash of teeth, "but big boys drink whiskey," He returned the wink.

Mrs. Weston smacked his shoulder. "You are an irrepressible rogue."


Francine rose as soon as Mrs. Weston entered. She had slept soundly, and looked forward to seeing Roxleigh in ways she couldn't explain. Her skin was tight over her muscles, she could feel every breath she took down to her toes, and every shift of fabric and air around her made her jump.

"Up already, Miss Francine?" Mrs. Weston asked as she filled the tub. "His Grace returned last night." Francine perked up, listening intently. "Lord Trumbull, his brother, accompanied him."

Of course, he has a brother.

"His younger brother," Mrs. Weston clarified. "Lord Trumbull spends his time at his bachelor house in London. It's not often he makes his way home. Actually, I don't think I've seen Trumbull in some two long years," she said wistfully.

The housekeeper poured vanilla and lavender into the tub. "Oh, I do go on. I beg your pardon, miss, I just adore the boys. Known them for the whole of their lives, you see. But it isn't right for me to go on," she said, shaking her head.

Francine smiled, walking over to the tub and sliding in, as Mrs. Weston turned to take the kettles out of the bedroom. Francine sighed as she sank, disappearing below the surface.

"I am impressed with what you've drawn up so far, Mr. Shaw. You must be off in the north wing, however, because you haven't missed any rooms or passages. It's not an issue—as dark as some of the passages are, they could have easily been misread. I will assist you so we can verify them properly." Gideon looked up. "I trust you arrived safely and found your suite accommodating?"

"Of course, Your Grace, you are most considerate, and I would very much appreciate your assistance with verifying the measurements."

"I am curious about the hedgerow sketch. You have a general idea of the perimeter shape, as well as the fountain. Were you able to navigate the maze yourself?"

"No, Your Grace, at least not well. In fact—" He paused and shifted. "To my disgrace I lost myself quite effectively, which has never happened. Even without a key I'm generally quite spatially adept, but since I also seem to have created space in your manor that doesn't exist, I choose to believe it is the manor itself which is attempting to bamboozle me."

Gideon let out a laugh. "So if Eildon Manor is bamboozling you, how did you find your way out?"

"Miss Francine, actually."

Gideon stilled. "And how is that?"

"Well, Your Grace, she must know the key. She found me in the maze, took me to see the fountain, then brought me back out again without so much as one incorrect turn."

Gideon felt his muscles tense through his abdomen. What Shaw said wasn't possible, as there was no key. Gideon himself had memorized the maze out of sheer determination.

"I apologize for any appearance of impropriety," Mr. Shaw said, attempting to break the silence. "It was only out of fear of being marooned in the labyrinth that I accompanied Miss Francine. I should have requested we leave directly, but she was charming and I— I beg pardon for the transgression."

"I understand how you could be taken with her. She is… exceptional. I appreciate your candor and hold no fault against you. I trust any meetings with my charge have since been properly chaperoned?"

"Actually, I haven't seen her since. I've been quite busy with the measurements and plans, and I imagine she had no interest in rescuing the likes of me again, even though the conversation was refreshing."

"You spoke with her?"

Shaw nodded. "My sister is profoundly deaf, Your Grace, and she studies at the Braidwood Academy for the Deaf and Dumb in Hackney. I endeavored to learn the language for her and, although it's terribly unfashionable, I enjoy it."

Gideon was dumbstruck. He thought of the motions she'd made with her hands. He'd thought she was just trying to convey something; he hadn't realized she was actually using language. He should have known better. "So this"—he motioned with his hand—"means what, thank you?"

"Yes, Your Grace." Shaw seemed to ease a bit.

"And this, what does this mean?" he asked as he lifted his hands and imitated the sign she'd made from the window when he quit the estate.

Mr. Shaw paused. "I believe it means to convey a deep sadness, Your Grace."

Gideon thought for a moment. "I'd like to learn a few more phrases, if you have the time."

"Of course, Your Grace."


Francine rested at a small table on the terrace overlooking the gardens. The cloudless sky was a clear, bright blue, almost lilac. She enjoyed the peacefulness here, but longed for some distraction. When would she see him? She'd missed the duke at breakfast, and Mrs. Weston said he was currently meeting with Mr. Shaw. Then, of course, there was the brother. When would she meet him?

"Well, hello," Perry greeted her.

Francine's heart skipped a beat as she looked up the staircase that went to the upstairs parlor to find an impeccably dressed, younger version of Roxleigh leaning arrogantly against the balustrade. She waved at him nervously with just the tips of her fingers as she braced herself. This man wasn't like his brother, she could see that much from the way he carried himself. This man was the quarterback, the prom king, Mr.

Popular, the ever-elusive crush who didn't know you existed, and here he was with her, giving her all of his attention.

He spoke quietly. "No doubt you are Miss Francine, my brother's… houseguest."

She studied him warily from beneath her eyelashes and he returned a grin so blatantly satisfied it curled her toes.

"I am most honored to make your acquaintance." He descended the final stair and bowed before her, one leg thrust forward, sweeping his arm to the side with great fanfare. "I am Lord Peregrine Trumbull, Viscount Roxleigh. *You* may call me Perry," he said, with a twinkle in his eye. He straightened, and as an afterthought then added, "*When* you are able to call me, that is." The sound of his words came more from his chest than his throat. *Like Gideon. Gideon.* The name sounded strong and safe in her her mind.

"I understand your voice is injured. I am terribly sorry, as it does leave you at quite a disadvantage, particularly since I love to talk." He approached the table.

Francine smiled bashfully. The quarterbacks of the world had never paid much attention to her before, and she felt terribly overwhelmed with this one.

"It's true, he does love the sound of his own voice," Gideon said. Francine stood abruptly, toppling her chair. The defensive lineman had arrived.

She was quite effectively pinned to the spot as she looked from one man to the other; they were both dressed in crisp white shirts with black trousers that pulled sharply to the bridge of their black shoes. Though the viscount was finished with a dove grey cravat and waistcoat, whereas Gideon appeared to have foregone them both at some point.

"Please, Miss Francine, sit. I insist you finish your tea. For your voice," Gideon said as he righted her chair. "Please," he implored again, looking into her eyes.

Francine's breath hitched as she gazed back at him. She sat down and he lifted the teapot, warming her tea, while she motioned to the chairs at the table for the brothers to join her. She felt quite like Alice at the Mad Hatter's tea party. Perry was grinning like the Cheshire Cat and— She wasn't sure who Gideon was. Perhaps the handsome prince Lewis Carroll forgot to include. *Such an oversight,* she thought with her own Cheshire grin, before it occurred to her that Mrs. Weston was much like the easily startled White Rabbit, always running off as if she were late.

Gideon and Perry—no, Trumbull; she didn't feel right using his name. And how odd was that?—exchanged glances, pulling two chairs next to each other opposite Francine as she reached to pour tea. She frowned, realizing only one cup had been brought out, and glanced up apologetically. She wanted to pull her feet up on the edge of her chair and hide behind her knees. She was generally beset by the sight of one Gideon, but two— Now she felt downright conquered.

She stared, wide-eyed, into her cup of tea as they watched. She willed her legs to steady and her feet to remain on the ground, pretending to blow across the tea to cool it. She cupped it with both hands while attempting to hide behind the tiny piece of china. What she wouldn't give for one of her giant lattés from St. Mark coffee house. Certainly there was more of a cup to hide behind.

She glanced from one man to the other. Trumbull was focused on her eyes, but Gideon was focused on her—*mouth.* She squeaked and placed the teacup on the table with an audible clink. *This must be what it feels like to stand before a firing squad. Something has got to give or I'm going to pass out. Are they oblivious to their effect?* She twisted her skirts in her hands.

Gideon's concerned gaze and Trumbull's curious stare held her fast. She could tell that Trumbull was, in fact, not oblivious to their effect on her as his grin kicked up on one side of his mouth. She started to tremble.

"Miss Francine, I beg your pardon, as I wasn't here to introduce you to my brother," Gideon said.

"Why on earth must you beg pardon for that?" Trumbull asked.

"It's not as though the girl needs protection from me. As it is, she's probably the safest girl in all of England where I'm concerned," he said with a laugh.

Gideon grimaced and cast him a sideways glance.

Francine smiled, then reached across the table to pat his hand gently. She saw her error when a flash of discomfiture crossed Gideon's features. She pulled her hand back and signed *I'm sorry.*

Gideon shook his head. "No, no, wait," he said, reaching for her. She looked up to the deep, emerald pools of his eyes that held the most sincere of gazes.

"What is the meaning of this?" Mrs. Weston screeched as she appeared on the terrace. The brothers stood quickly and penitently, like two boys caught in the mud before Sunday school.

Francine watched as Mrs. Weston turned on them. "What are you two rakes doing out here with Miss Francine? It's a bit like an inquest! The two of you should be ashamed," she admonished. "You," she said in her most stern mother-voice, pointing at Trumbull. "Your breakfast grows cold. You get in to the table, and leave the miss be."

"Why, yes, of course, Westy. I do apologize for such untoward behavior with regard to your charge," he said jovially, with a slight bow.

Mrs. Weston only twitched her head toward the breakfast room with a wink, then with hands on hips she turned on Gideon. "As for you," she said, lifting her chin as she looked at him. "I have some goods to fetch from town since we've more guests than planned." Gideon's brow creased. "You watch over Miss Francine while I am away," she said with a stout nod.

Gideon was taken aback. Had he just gone from being a scolded scoundrel to a suitable chaperone in the space of a minute? He was the Duke of Roxleigh, and Mrs. Weston had managed to shame him into feeling like a young child.

He straightened, squaring his shoulders and clasping his hands behind his back. He widened his stance a bit and stared down at his housekeeper.

Mrs. Weston froze, averting her eyes. Grabbing at her apron and twisting it, she continued, stuttering, "I will t-t-take my leave, Your

Grace." She backed away quickly then pushed through the door.

Gideon turned to Francine, whose eyes were round as she watched Mrs. Weston scurry away. She glanced back to him, and he slowly relaxed his posture.

He took a deep breath and smiled. He pulled his chair over in front of Francine and sat down, gazing at her. "I have something to say to you." He took his right fist and put it to his chest, making a circle over his heart.

Her jaw dropped, and she shook her head.

Gideon raised his hand to stop her. "I'm not finished. When I left, you made me aware you were upset. I could feel the intent in my bones and I am most remorseful that I didn't trust my understanding. I did not stay. I understand now."

Unshed tears glistened in her eyes, they that were the sweetest pools of light, iridescent blue. He looked down and saw her hands shaking. He reached out, taking them in his. "I am so sorry," he whispered, and with that her tears spilled.

They sat in silence for a while as he stroked her hands, wiped the tears from her face, and tucked an errant lock behind her ear. She trembled with his every touch.

*She must be an innocent to react to a man's touch in this manner.* He drew back slightly, then lifted her chin so she looked into his face. Putting the fingers of his right hand together and touching his chin, he moved his hand in a circle around his face, his fingers spreading wide as his hand passed his forehead. *Beautiful.*

He stood, pulling her with him, and strode toward the maze. "So," he said, turning to her at the entrance, "I understand you've discovered the key to my maze."

She looked at him dubiously.

"Mr. Shaw informed me of your service to him in delivering him from certain danger," he said wryly.

Francine's eyes lit up and she lifted her skirts, moving swiftly toward the labyrinth. He was surprised when, after several determined turns, they arrived at the fountain. She dropped her skirts and turned to look up at him.

"How did you— I mean, when did you learn, or who— I. Humph."

He stood with one hand on his hip and the other reaching toward her. Her presence calmed his addled brain. "Where did you learn the key?" he asked, bewildered.

She smiled and reached for his hand, but he pulled away as though he were ice, and she fire.

*This was a mistake.* "We really shouldn't—" He started. But then she pleaded with her eyes. "It…isn't proper," he said nervously, trying to deflect her questioning glance, even though he desperately wanted to talk with her. She took a step toward him and he backed away a pace. She stopped and looked at him, shaking her head, then pushed her lip out in a pout. *That was another mistake*, he thought with a sigh.

She held her hand out to him and he winced as he yielded, placing his in hers, feeling the cool touch on his heated palm.

He breathed deeply and she moved to stand beside him.

She held his hand up in front of them like a blackboard and traced the letter A into his palm.

His breath caught, a shiver coursing his spine from the tingle her small finger caused, tracing over his skin.

She then made the sign for the letter A.

His mouth turned up at the corner in understanding. Then he lifted his other hand and signed the letter A in return.

She smiled her broad smile and they went on exchanging the written letters of the alphabet for the silent ones until Francine, with a mischievous grin, decided to quiz him and spelled a word.

"Francine."

A giant grin brightened her face and she jumped at him, wrapping her arms around his neck and kissing him on the cheek. The movement startled him and he stumbled back from the force of her crashing against him, coming up against the high edge of the fountain, his arms flung wide.

She let go, sliding down, but he caught her up against his chest with one hand spread at the small of her back, not letting her move. Her body was drawn taut against his, her toes barely touching the ground between his feet, his strong thighs embracing her soft ones.

She spelled a second word.

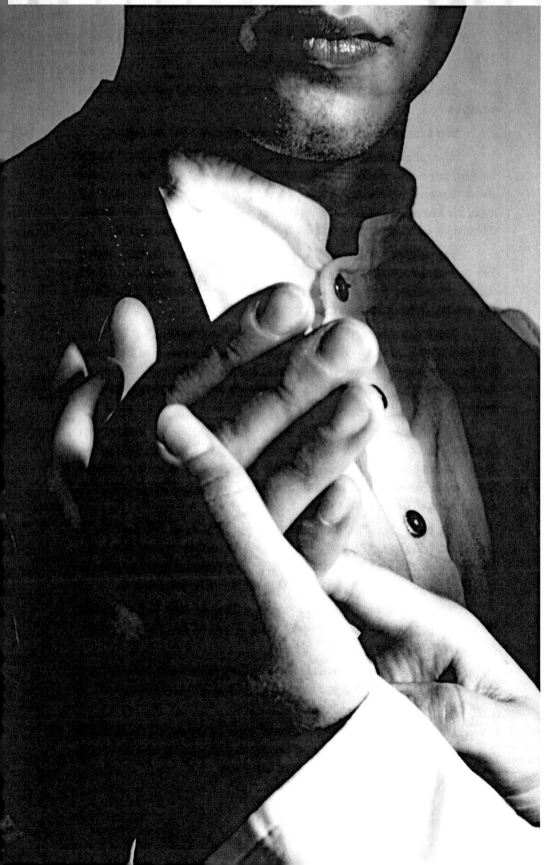

His composure shattered. "Gideon," he ground out in a throaty whisper.

She looked up into his face and this time, *her* breath caught.

The quiet sound was his undoing and he raised his hand to the back of her neck, placing his thumb at the hollow below her ear as he slowly lowered his mouth to hers, covering her sweet, soft lips with his own. He kissed and nibbled, making her gasp. The moment her mouth opened he took advantage, tasting her, dipping his tongue gently.

He stroked her jaw with his thumb from her ear to chin, urging her mouth to open wider for him. Desperately in need, he delved further, searching for the spring that fed her sweetness. She sighed into his mouth, driving his heartbeat faster and harder.

His hand moved from the small of her back to the cleft between her shoulder blades, feeling the shudder travel her spine in his wake. He bent his knees, allowing her to catch her feet on the ground, and he curved his back, giving his arms more length to surround and envelop her.

Her hands fell from his neck, down his back, and across the breadth of his muscles. He felt them respond to her: tightening, strengthening, stretching, and rolling beneath his skin. Her hands fluttered to his waist and he straightened as the heat of her palms sank through his shirt, into his sides.

He broke away with a guttural moan. His head fell back as he pulled her hips to him tightly, his manhood pushing against her belly. She wriggled and he hissed in a breath, gazing down at her through the veil of his thick eyelashes, trying to control his rampant passion.

"Don't." He held her hips firmly, trying to stop her wiggling. "Stop moving, or neither of us will make it out of this maze anytime soon," he said gruffly.

Her skin flushed, a heated blush rolling from her toes to the top of her head. He couldn't bring himself to release her as the heat soaked into his hands.

"Just a moment, I—" He broke off, gasping for air. He looked into her eyes and watched the fever of her blush blossoming over her face, forcing another rush of blood toward his groin.

Francine froze, her arms held between their chests. His eyes smoldered, like the ebb of a fire. Her hips were still pulled solidly against him, and she could feel his turgid shaft against her. Her eyes grew wider as she felt it move against her belly and she drew in a breath as their bodies melded. She let it out slowly, hoping that the wild beating of her heart would never subside, and she sank into the feeling.

"Just…let me," he whispered again, lowering his head over hers and sliding his other hand around her waist, effectively melting her nerves and removing the last of her inhibitions. He held her fast against his muscular form as his mouth met hers again and she fell against him, her hands pressing into his chest while her knees went weak.

"Oh my," she breathed against his lips, without a sound.

He laughed, sobered by her enervation. He leaned more comfortably against the fountain, pushing one of his thickly muscled thighs between her legs. He had one arm wrapped around her waist and he smoothed the other hand up her abdomen, resting it against her rib cage just below her breast. He was telling himself he shouldn't, but his hand wasn't listening, and neither was she.

Francine pushed forward, gently forcing the roundness of her breast into his palm.

He stroked her nipple with the pad of his thumb through the thickness of her dress, feeling the peak harden between the whalebone stays of the corset.

Francine rested her head against his chest, breathing heavily, and he caught a fresh rush of her scent, lavender and rain.

He moved his hand around to her nape, softly stroking the hollow beneath her ear again. She let her head fall backward into that hand and he kissed her with more fervor.

Suddenly brazen, Francine dropped her hands to his hips, her thumbs caressing the matching ridges of muscle that framed his hardness like an arrow, from his hip to his loins, as she pressed herself down on his thigh. She felt a jolt of passion from the contact with his rigid thigh and she threw her head back, arching into his chest.

The adamantine length of his body clenched violently in response.

She heard a low growl that started in his chest and moved upward as he swiftly stood and moved her away from him.

As soon as there was a measurable space between them, he clasped her worried face in his strong, warm hands. "Are you all right?" he asked, slowly tracing her cheeks and eyebrows with his thumbs.

She grasped his wrists with her own small hands and nodded. She was unsure what had happened. Everything had been fine and then—then he just stopped.

He gave her a gentle smile. "I'm sorry, but we cannot do this." He closed his eyes as he ran his thumb over her pouting lip. "I mean to say that I want you, every part of you, but it's not right. Not until we learn where you came from, and where you are supposed to be." He paused. "I will not be your ruination."

She broke away from him, shaking her head. She started to sign *What if,* but her hand dropped and she looked down, unable to finish.

"What if…we never learn?"

She nodded, her eyes stinging with the threat of tears. She'd never imagined she would be refused when she finally tried to give it up.

"I have to try," he said slowly. "I simply must. It's the proper thing to do."

*But we'll never learn because I don't belong here,* she thought, frustration tensing her features. She shook her head in resignation, feeling more lost than she ever had.

He pulled her back into his embrace, stroking her face and hair, imploring her to calm. "Francine, look at me," he said.

She gazed into his fiery green eyes and something inside her shifted, filling a void like a puzzle piece.

"I am not known to be a patient man. I will *not* look forever."

She studied his face, reading the honesty in the depths of his emerald eyes, and it eased her mind. She could trust in him. She nodded once, then smiled.

He chuckled, grasping one of her hands in his and bringing it to his lips. He was so taken with her. At no point in his life had there ever been a moment where he felt this complete.

"Now. Tell me how you solved my maze," he said.

She signed.

"I— wait, what?"

She shook her head with an exasperated expression. Taking his hand, she pulled him to one of the exits and pointed at the flowers woven into the wall of the hedge. He shrugged.

She led him down the row to a juncture, pausing to look at the different walls and rows before pulling him toward another row. She pointed again to the tiny flowers that dotted the walls of the hedgerow. He looked, seeing the same small yellow flowers she had pointed at the last time. *It cannot possibly be that simple,* he thought, as understanding sank in. She ran ahead to the next juncture, picking out the row covered with yellow flowers. The answer was so uncomplicated it was genius.

"You followed the flowers— I must need to work on my vowels."

She took his hand and they followed the yellow flowers out, exiting on the south side of the maze facing the stables.

"You are magnificent."

She smiled.

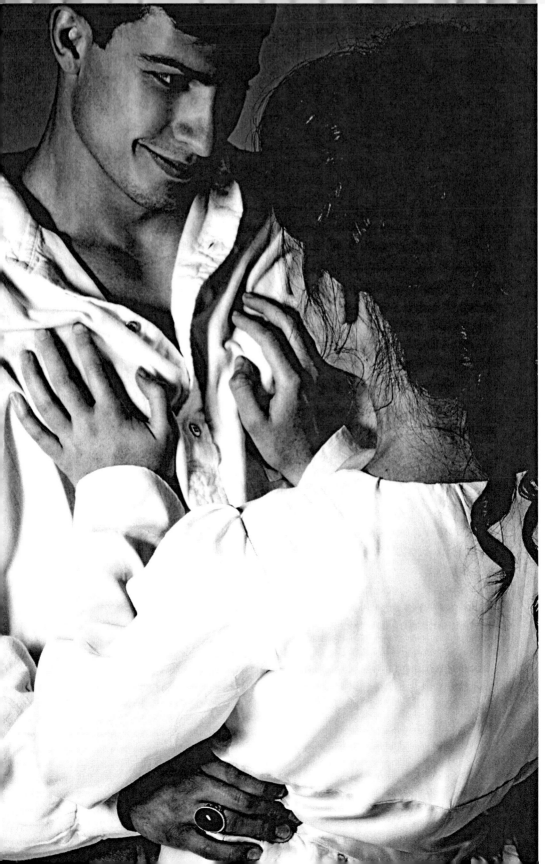

# FIFTEEN

Gideon and Francine strolled back to the manor. She showed him some simple signs like *sunrise, sunset, supper, mother, brother, good, bad, horse, eat,* and a few others. When they arrived at the threshold of the great entrance he paused.

"Thank you for a wonderful morning," he said, reaching for her hand. "I would be honored if you would accompany me to a formal supper this evening," he whispered, pulling her hand to his lips and placing a kiss in the palm. He meant the indecent gesture to carry all of his hopes to her.

Her mouth dropped open slightly as she watched him.

He couldn't quite place the expression on her face. "What?" he asked, afraid he had gone one step too far.

She shook her head, suddenly worried. She didn't want to insult him, but the food was terrible and she didn't want to fake her way through a formal dinner with him watching. Francine pulled her hand away, considering how to turn down an offer she didn't want to decline.

*Worry*, he thought. *Worry and—fear?* He frowned. He needed to change his tactic. "It's only that Chef has returned from a trip to France to retrieve some wines and recipes for an extended house gathering I'm planning at the end of the Season. She needs to try the recipes on as many people as possible so she can finalize the menu, and of course my brother and Mr. Shaw will attend with—"

He stopped as a smile broke across her features like the dawn. He grinned triumphantly, but he wasn't sure whether to be happy that she was going to join him for supper, or sad that she didn't want to join *him* for supper. He shook his head as she nodded hers. "Well, it is settled. Until then."

She nodded, still smiling.

*Until tonight*, he signed slowly. He took her hand again, gently touching his lips to her wrist.

She tilted her head as the heat from his kiss spread like wildfire through her veins. She gasped, and he looked into her eyes with a half-cocked grin. Her heart bolted.

He stood tall, putting his hands behind his back as he lifted his chin. She touched her wrist where his kiss had seared her exposed flesh, then turned to the stairs, ascending slowly as he watched.

Mr. Shaw appeared at the crest of the staircase and gave a curt bow when she stopped before him. "Miss Francine, how lovely to see you again."

She smiled and signed, *Thank you, nice to see you as well. How are the plans?*

"Very well, I believe. Will we see you at supper this evening?"

*Yes, I'm excited. I wasn't aware the regular chef was away. I was worried.*

He laughed, understanding most of her remarks, certainly the important parts.

She signed goodbye and turned for her room. Mr. Shaw looked down the stairs into the angry eyes of a wellborn duke. The sight had him retreating before he realized it.

Roxleigh bounded up the grand staircase toward Mr. Shaw. When he gained the landing he watched Francine as she disappeared into the guest suite, then he turned on him. "What was that?" he asked.

"I beg pardon, Your Grace. I was coming to meet you, as we had planned. I merely held a polite conversation."

Roxleigh looked through him and Shaw looked back. "Your Grace. I am, most certainly, overstepping my bounds in saying this. However, I would like to make my position plain. I appreciate honesty and feel that you must as well. I am betrothed to a young lady in London. It is a love match. I have no ulterior motives when speaking with your Miss Francine, other than to treat her with courtesy."

Roxleigh's shoulders relaxed.

"If I may say, Your Grace, she seems to be a wonderful girl. You are quite fortunate, and I believe so is she. I hope that in the future I will do nothing to disrespect you."

"There are few men who would dare speak to me in such a manner," Roxleigh replied. "I appreciate your candor. It is difficult at times to know whom to trust or believe, particularly with a title that demands certain proprieties." Roxleigh studied him for another moment, then his countenance changed with the blink of an eye. "Shall we investigate your measurements?"

Shaw let out a long breath he wasn't aware he'd been holding. "Of course." The tension dissolved entirely and the two men walked to the panel between the two main family suites.

They spent the rest of the afternoon measuring, checking, and re-measuring, trying to find the discrepancy to no avail. There was unquestionably a void in the manor that could not be reached from any of the known entries or passageways. Unfortunately, it was getting late. Even if they hadn't needed more light, they couldn't explore further if they were to be ready in time for supper.

Perry woke from his nap to a banging behind the fireplace in his suite. He hadn't seen his brother all day, even as hard as he endeavored to intercept his path within the manor. He wasn't going to enter the maze, that was certain; first, because he wasn't sure what Gideon would do if he happened upon his brother behaving in an improper manner with his young, beautiful guest—he imagined it would be similar to coming upon a lion in its den—and second, because he had no desire to find himself lost in that bloody hellhole of a maze ever again. Once as a child was quite enough.

He stood, straightening his disheveled clothes, and left his suite only to find Gideon speaking quite excitedly with whom he assumed was the architect.

Gideon stopped when he caught sight of Perry. "Look at this! Here, look at this," Gideon said, striding over to him. "There is a disparity."

"Measure it again," Perry replied dismissively.

"No, no, we *have* measured it. Checked it three and four times on some walls. There is an inconsistency," Gideon said, as close to beaming as Perry had ever seen him. It was a bit discomfiting.

Perry stared at his over-excited brother like he was a bit off, but he couldn't help but to catch a bit of the excitement oozing from him.

"Are you mad?"

"Possibly, but in this there is no error."

"Don't you mean there is an error? That's incredible. How could we have never discovered this? Running about as children, you would think—"

"You would," Gideon said, "but we never— We need to find the way in." The first dinner bell rang, and he grunted. "But, of course, it is too late."

"We shall find it tomorrow," Perry said definitively.

"Tomorrow," Gideon replied with a nod.

Shaw watched, his arms crossed over his chest, rocking on his heels as he enjoyed the jovial display.

Perry clapped his brother strongly on the shoulder. "Damn, I knew Marcus was a bit off, but this is beyond expectation."

"Yes, quite." Gideon looked at him with a broad smile, then turned to Shaw.

"Blast it all, I forgot. Shaw, this is my brother. You will call him Trumbull."

Shaw took the viscount's proffered hand. "At your service, my lord."

"Please, not at all. You have managed to make this visit infinitely more enjoyable than I thought possible. I am in your debt." Perry placed his other hand on his chest and inclined his head slightly.

Shaw smiled. "Well, gentlemen, I must go dress for supper. I understand we have a special guest, and I am covered in dust."

"Of course," Gideon said, panic dawning over his stern features. "I must take my leave as well, for quite the same reason. Trumbull, Miss Francine will be joining us for supper."

"So I take it. This should provide an even better distraction than the missing suites."

Gideon scowled at the thought of dinner with his brother and Francine and stormed off.

"Roxleigh!" Perry boomed, but the only response he got was a stiff wave behind Gideon's head without so much as a turn or pause.

Shaw was aghast at the effective handling Roxleigh had succumbed to. He smiled and looked at Trumbull, who turned on him in surprise.

"You still here?" Trumbull gave him a knowing glance. "Good God, man, we shall get along fine, just fine," he said, then went to his suite to ready for supper.

Shaw watched him go, pondering the show that had just taken place before him. He was quite aware that an outsider such as himself had probably never been privy to such cavorting between these two extremely powerful men, and he was genuinely taken with the honesty of their actions.


Francine could not stop smiling. She'd thought there had been no way to improve upon the night in the garden from last week, not until this very moment. She walked through the entry, the sitting room, and into the bedchamber, where she stopped cold.

She turned to leave the room, thinking she'd somehow ended up in the wrong suite. But Mrs. Weston walked over and took her hand, pulling her to the settee, which was covered in beautiful bundles of silks and satins.

"Come, miss, look at this!" she exclaimed as she picked up a package and handed it to her, directing her to a chair.

"What— What is all this?" Francine mouthed, waving her hand at the packages.

"This is a gift from His Grace."

"No, I can't," she whispered, shaking her head and pushing the box back at Mrs. Weston.

She gasped. "Oh no, miss, you must not. I mean, perhaps you misunderstand. His Grace is quite taken with you, and if you refuse the gifts, he will be quite em—" She broke off and cleared her throat. "You mustn't."

Francine reached out slowly, taking the box from her hands as she nodded.

She pulled the green satin ribbon free from the package, unwrapping the lavender folds of paper. She was left holding a large bristled hairbrush with a silver back and handle.

Francine gazed at the brush, turning it over in her hands. It was beautiful, and quite a thoughtful gift. She looked up at Mrs. Weston with wide eyes and Mrs. Weston handed her another package, then unfurled a large cream-colored brocade throw over her lap.

An hour later, the floor was littered with wrappings and ribbons, and Francine was truly and thoroughly overwhelmed, but Mrs. Weston wasn't finished with the duke's surprises. She smiled as she rang for Carole to bring the slipper tub so she could ready Francine for supper.

Gideon entered his suite. Ferry had already filled his tub and had kettles heating over the fire to warm it, in case he was delayed. Ferry was best at thinking ahead and keeping his distance, which was why Gideon appreciated his service, but right now he wanted to actually speak with him. "Ferry."

His valet appeared from behind the fireplace. "Your Grace."

"Ferry, have you spoken with Carole or Mrs. Weston?"

"Your Grace, Miss Francine was suitably beset."

Gideon wanted to know what, precisely, she thought of his gifts, but understood there was no more to be given. He grunted. "That is all."

Ferry nodded and left as Gideon readied for his soak.

Francine rose from the tub, into the soft towel Mrs. Weston held, and walked to the dressing table. She sat, running her fingers over the beautiful brush, small silver trinket box, and hair combs that Gideon had brought back for her. He had also given her a brocade blanket, an opera cape, some gloves, and a mantle, which just looked like a shorter cape to her.

Mrs. Weston said the gifts were all very personal, the kind of gifts a proper gentleman would purchase only for his wife if he followed the dictates of society, but she rationalized that Francine had nothing and His Grace was merely seeing to her comfort.

They both knew there was no need for the items to be so ornate and expensive.

Mrs. Weston smoothed and pulled Francine's hair into a sweeping pile of curls on top of her head, leaving a few strands down to frame her face. She used the decorative combs to secure it, then went to the wardrobe and pulled out a magnificent ivory dress with violet pinstripes. It had a great bustled train of giant bows and gathered flounces, and was trimmed with violet satin ribbons that were layered over and over until they swept the floor with their folds.

Francine's breath caught as she advanced, gently caressing the fabric between her fingers as she looked at Mrs. Weston, who beamed.

She laid the garment on the bed and Francine stood, suffering Mrs. Weston's ministrations like a flag caught in the wind. She tied her into her drawers, laced up the corset, and layered on piles of crinoline and petticoats. Then Mrs. Weston turned her and fastened more than fifty buttons up the front of the dress, which was cut very low across her bosom. The sleeves were long and fitted with multiple buttons at the wrists. Mrs. Weston buttoned every one, then tucked a violet silk scarf across the neckline.

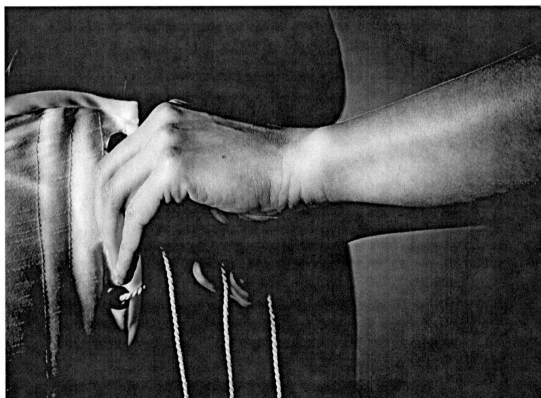

Francine examined herself in the mirror, turning round and round, marveling at the fit and precision with which the gown's ensemble was constructed. She glanced at Mrs. Weston, lifting her hands and shrugging her shoulders.

Mrs. Weston simply shook her head. "I have no idea, miss. I never would have imagined it, but somehow those boys managed. Oh!" Mrs. Weston rushed to the dresser.

As Francine stood looking in the mirror, Mrs. Weston came up behind her and reached high over her curls. She lowered a necklace, clasping it at her nape.

Francine gasped. *No!* she tried to say, her eyes wide, shaking her head. It was the most stunning piece of jewelry she'd ever seen, intricately filigreed silver strands delicately woven into a vine with tiny flowers created from different colored stones. The centerpiece was a flower with five matched petals of deep purple at the outer edges, which then faded into a brilliant yellow as they met at the matched yellow center stone. If she'd been able to use her voice, she would have been rendered speechless.

Mrs. Weston turned to her, seeing the panicked look in her eyes. "Now, Miss Francine, this piece is only being loaned to you for the night, so you mustn't fret."

Francine exhaled, relieved. That necklace was entirely too much.

"I believe it's time for supper," Mrs. Weston said.

Francine nodded, checking herself in the mirror one last time before strolling out of the room. Her arms looked impossibly long and slender, resting at her corseted waist. *Breathe*, she thought. She was becoming more accustomed to wearing a corset, but she did have to constantly remember to pace herself so she wasn't overcome by lack of air.

The duke, Lord Trumbull, and Mr. Shaw met in the study before dinner for a glass of Gideon's fine Raynal Cognac. They were enjoying a discussion on the possibilities behind having hidden rooms within the manor. Shaw believed it was some sort of safe room in case the manor were to be attacked, while Perry believed it was just another odd way for Marcus to spy on the inhabitants.

Gideon believed the private rooms were actually built for his mother, but he was interrupted by Stapleton before he could share his thoughts. "Miss Francine."

The three men looked at each other and, setting their glasses on the sideboard, they walked toward the entry and gathered at the base of the stairs. Gideon stood in front, watching as Francine gracefully descended. Her cheeks were rosy and her smile demure.

Gideon was taken. He knew then and there, watching her move toward him, that he was hers, and she would be his. No matter the outcome of his search for her history, he was done and undone. She was his end.

Perry laughed and whispered, "Breathe, Rox," with a nudge, and Gideon inhaled, shaking his head slowly in disbelief and acceptance.


Francine stopped close to the bottom of the staircase and paused to take it all in: Gideon's smooth black trousers, crisp white shirt and black neck cloth, black dinner jacket and green silk waistcoat that mirrored his eyes. Shaw and Trumbull were also turned out very nicely. How was she so lucky as to be accompanied to dinner by three perfectly smashing gentlemen? She thought for a moment about the strangeness of it all.

There really should have been some other women involved, and she felt a twinge of awkward selfishness before she felt Gideon's fingers grasping hers gently, lifting her hand so he could rest his lips on her wrist. She gazed down at his shiny dark locks, remembered the satiny smoothness of them against her cheek, her hand, her chest. She flushed violently and glanced away.

Gideon caught the blush spreading across the tops of her cheeks, and lower, across her breasts. He locked on her eyes, willing her to look down at him. "Do you approve?" he asked quietly.

She nodded, resting her hand on the necklace and signing *beautiful* as she met his gaze.

"I thought the color was appropriate. The petals are made of a stone called Ametrine—found only in Bolivia." He turned and placed her hand on his arm.

Trumbull and Mr. Shaw exchanged uncomfortable glances, as though they had walked in on something they definitely shouldn't have.

As Francine took Gideon's arm, she glanced up to the first floor balcony to see Mrs. Weston, Carole, Ferry, and several others gathered in the shadows, unnoticed. Stapleton walked over to the giant doors of the main dining hall and swept them open, then stood silently as they entered, followed by Trumbull and Shaw.

The hall was light and airy, with large western-facing windows that let in the last vestiges of sunset as it blazed across the horizon. The room was luxuriously appointed with grand mahogany pieces and inlaid paneling. The table was dressed with an ivory cover and silver candelabras that countered the soft glow from the large chandeliers hanging above the long table.

Gideon decreed they should all be seated together at one end since they needed to discuss dinner, per Chef's request, and if they were properly spaced out there would be no way for them to communicate. Gideon was, of course, at the head of the table, and his brother was seated to his right. Mr. Shaw sat next to him with Francine on Gideon's left.

Gideon asked about every dish and made notes for Chef, determinedly sticking to the greater purpose of Chef's need to work on the menu for the summer gathering. They drank fine red wines from Bordeaux and sampled spicy thin soups along with savory thick ones. Glazed asparagus spears followed, drizzled with a tangy yellow sauce, and finally braised lamb shanks in a burgundy sauce with mushrooms, carrots, and caramelized onions and scallops swimming in beurre blanc.

When the main courses were complete, the footmen presented trays of confections: fluffy, buttery lemon pastries with berries of every color and poached pears in a red wine sauce with crème patisserie. The sweets were complemented with a glass of sweet, thick white wine.

Francine filled her belly. She ate well; she ate everything. She ate until she was full and then she ate some more. She leaned back and thought she actually heard her stays creak under the pressure. She glanced quickly around the table to make sure nobody had noticed, then giggled to herself.

Trumbull looked at her, then his brother. "Haven't you been feeding your guest, Rox?"

She glanced at Trumbull, a smile gaining strength on her lips as she turned her gaze to Gideon, who placed his fork on the table. "Well, I imagine she has suffered more of the sous-chef's cooking than the rest of us have," he said, looking back to her. "Has my kitchen been lacking?"

She shook her head vigorously, giving Shaw a sideways smile.

Gideon laughed, bringing his fist to the table, making the settings and silver jump. "I beg your pardon, I should have made other arrangements. I don't pay much mind to the gruel we're required to deal with when Chef is away because I know she'll take care of us when she returns. I should have explained. No wonder you were frightened of my invitation to supper!" He laughed harder, pushing the half-eaten pear closer to Francine. "Please pay them no mind. Eat all you want. We are among friends, are we not?"

Trumbull and Mr. Shaw picked up their own silver, drawing their plates closer to themselves in agreement.

Gideon studied the red stain on Francine's lips from the juice. His mouth watered when he thought of tasting the brandied pears on her.

She finished off the pear then leaned back again, appearing quite comfortably sated.

"I see you approve of Chef's latest creations?" His mouth had gone dry and his voice cracked a bit.

She nodded wildly, pointing at the empty plate.

"Ah, so poached pear is a favorite?"

She smiled again.

"Then we shall have poached pears with every meal, if you wish," he said, tapping gently on the edge of her plate.

She shook her head then rested her hand on the back of his. He looked down, feeling the tingling sensation burning through his skin, snaking its way up his forearm inside his veins. His heart skipped and he withdrew, suddenly aware of all eyes on him. She glanced from one face to the next apologetically, both Perry and Shaw apparently stifling a chuckle.

Gideon cleared his throat. "Usually the ladies retire to the parlor to gossip, and the gentlemen join me in my study for an after-dinner port and cigar, but since you are the only lady in attendance, I don't wish to abandon you. Shall we all retire to the grand terrace over the gardens?" He wanted to see her in the moonlight. He wanted to ferret her to the edge of the darkness and taste the pears. He couldn't take his eyes, or his mind, from her mouth.

Francine stood, drawing the men from their chairs. She looked at Mr. Shaw, entreating him with her eyes. He smiled and nodded.

She signed to him.

Gideon picked out dinner, sunset, and bed—he thought.

Shaw began to speak, but Gideon lifted his hand to stop him without taking his gaze from her. He would not communicate with her through someone else.

He advanced on Francine and her hand disappeared into his large palm. "Thank you for the wonderful company at dinner. I am glad you enjoyed it, and though I'm sure we would all like to spend more time in your presence, we completely understand your regrets."

She smiled her broad smile as he brought her hand to his lips and once again pressed his mouth to her wrist, a scandalously long kiss, and bid her good night. The gentlemen followed her to the great entrance and as Gideon paused behind her, Shaw and Perry exchanged a glance and strode toward the back of the manor.

Francine became dizzy, knowing he was watching as she ascended the staircase, but she kept going nonetheless, willing the grace from her stature and gait. When she reached the landing, she paused and took the deepest breath she could, then turned to see him smiling up at her. She closed her eyes to capture the memory and swiftly headed toward her room.

Gideon remained a few moments after she disappeared, wanting her to return to him, though he knew she could not, she would not, and even if she did, he knew he would be required to return her untouched. He felt his loins suffuse with heat and he willed his mind to other thoughts. He bent over, resting his hands on his knees, and breathed deeply for a moment.

"Roxleigh!" Perry shouted through the open doorway, and then, a few moments later, "Gideon!"

He grunted and turned to join them.

"Roxleigh tells me you are enamored as well, Shaw," Perry said as they sat at a table on the terrace together.

"Well, you certainly don't hesitate to strike up a conversation," Shaw replied with a grin. "And yes I am, quite."

Perry considered his reply. "Most men wouldn't care to flaunt that in polite company," he said, reaching for the small humidor Stapleton had brought to the terrace with the port.

"I don't see how this evening could be any further from polite company than it already is. I also don't see how being polite about love would do me much good. The fact is that I'm besotted. There's no way around that. And from the looks of it, His Grace is headed toward the same fate, and there's not much hope for saving him from it, not that either of us would. You appear to be quite as thrilled at the prospect as he is, at any rate," Shaw observed, sitting in the chair across from Perry.

"I suppose I am. I suppose further that I do not believe anyone to be more deserving of it, though since we have no idea yet who this girl is, I can only hope for a good outcome. I believe my brother has already decided that propriety be damned should he learn something of our miss that will not mend well with the dukedom." He lit a cigar and rolled it between his fingers as he thought. "Actually, I doubt he would give the *ton* a second thought should he do something they disapproved of, and of course he has my support in any case. Not that he needs it." He paused. "Where the bloody hell has he gone off to, anyway? He certainly shouldn't send the gossips to post so soon. Roxleigh!" He waited impatiently. "Gideon!" Shaw raised his eyebrows at his use of his brother's Christian name.

"We shall get along smashingly," Shaw said as he lit his cigar.

Perry looked at him. "Yes, quite," he replied with a grin and a chuckle.

"Yes, what?" Gideon asked, striding to sit in the chair between the men on the terrace, then resting with his legs stretched out before him.

Both men simply shook their heads, sipping port.

Gideon looked at his brother from underneath his eyelashes, a glint of retribution pulling a low chortle from his brother's throat. The gentlemen sat silently, drawing on their cigars and sipping the rich, sweet, red wine.

Stapleton walked toward Gideon, proffering a salver with a card, and he took it.

"It's a bit late to be entertaining visitors, is it not?" Perry drawled. Gideon glanced from him to Shaw pointedly, then Perry added, "You know what I mean."

Gideon's smile faded as he read the name on the card.

*Monsieur Gautier Larrabee.*

# SIXTEEN

ideon stood abruptly, turning to Stapleton. "Show him to the green parlor," he ordered, concentrating on the card. " Y e s , Your Grace." Stapleton bowed and turned to leave.

"What is it?" Perry asked, taking the card from Gideon. "Who is Monsieur Larrabee?" He paused. "Gideon!"

"What? Oh, I'm not entirely sure, but I believe that was the surname Francine gave."

"It cannot be that easy. Do you think it's her family? It cannot be."

"There's only one way to find out."

Shaw stood. "Gentlemen, I shall leave you to the mystery, as I am definitely not needed in this foray. I bid you both good evening."

Gideon inclined his head. "Of course, Shaw, until the morrow."

"I am coming with you," Perry grunted at Gideon as he followed.

Monsieur and Madame Larrabee sat patiently on the settee in the parlor. "What if he knows nothing of Madeleine?" Mme. Larrabee asked in French.

"I have no doubt they are aware of the location of our daughter. Lord Hepplewort was clear: she was lost on this estate. He would know where she is," M. Larrabee said as the butler opened the door.

The Larrabees looked at each other. They certainly weren't prepared to deal with a duke, much less with two British peers. They stood, M. Larrabee bowing and Mme. Larrabee curtseying.

"It's rather late for a social call," Gideon greeted rather gruffly. Perry quietly cleared his throat.

"I believe that you have, *eu, ma fille,* my daughter," M. Larrabee replied in a thick French accent.

"And what, pray tell, gives you that idea?" Gideon asked.

"*Monsieur, eu,* Your Grace, I receive a letter from Lord Hepplewort concerning *ma fille*. She was taken from him—on your land," M. Larrabee said.

Perry stepped in front of Gideon as he felt the tension course through his brother at the statement. "Pardon me, *monsieur*, but you may do well to not levy accusations straight away."

M. Larrabee shook his head. "Of course. I apologize, my English is not so well. I did not mean to offend Your Grace. I received a letter—"

"Perhaps if you show us this letter," Perry cut in.

"*Mais oui, un moment, s'il vous plait,*" M. Larrabee replied, looking through his coat pockets, then presenting it.

Perry smiled, taking the missive and turning to Gideon. "You need to compose yourself, brother. You have no idea what these people are about yet," he said under his breath while he unfolded the paper and held it up. The letter rambled on about the point without ever reaching it, but at the end it clearly accused the Duke of Roxleigh of holding captive one *Madeleine* Larrabee.

Gideon tensed, his eyes grew dark, and his mouth drew white with anger against his teeth.

"*Un moment, s'il vous plait?*" Perry said to M. and Mme. Larrabee as he pushed his brother from the parlor, then dragged him to the study on the other side of the great entrance. He called for Stapleton, then turned to Gideon. "Gideon, listen to me."

Gideon looked at him with eyes full of anger.

"We can deal with this Hepplewort chap later. Right now we need to clear up a few things with this man and Francine—if that is her name."

Gideon jolted, all of his muscles taut like a crossbow preparing to fire, and his brother retreated a step.

"Gideon, listen! She had a terrible accident, she doesn't remember anything, or hasn't said what she does remember. If this is her father, finding him is what you intended to do to begin with, is it not? The search ends here, we can clear this up right now, and you will be free to marry Francine. Is that not what you want?"

"But the letter—"

"The letter be damned! If you received that letter, you would assume the worst as well and immediately go looking for your child. Good God, man! Have some sense here! That man's daughter is missing, and some damned swine accused you—*you!* He is behaving rather politely, I dare say. If it were you in his position, I believe you would have stormed the gates without any polite formalities, *n'est-ce pas?*"

Gideon relaxed a bit, pushing his brother back. "Except that apparently this *Madeleine* is already betrothed. We need Francine," he said. "And we should ask Shaw to join us. He's better able to communicate with her than I."

At that moment Stapleton walked in. "Your Grace?"

Gideon turned to the butler. "Stapleton, bid Mrs. Weston to ready Miss Francine to greet our guests and ask for Mr. Shaw to join us as well. Also, please send in some tea."

"Yes, Your Grace."

"Good to have you back," Perry said, clapping Gideon on the shoulder. "Shall we see to the guests?"

"So be it."


They walked back into the green parlor and the Larrabees stood. "Monsieur, madame, I must beg pardon for my previous demeanor. I do not take kindly to being accused of absconding with innocents," Gideon said.

"Of course, Your Grace. I understand your reaction, as you must understand mine."

"I do, and let me assure you there is no one being held against their will here at Eildon Hill or at any of my estates, nor has there been at any time. There is a woman here who answers to the name Francine. She was injured in an accident with my curricle and horse team just over a fortnight past. We have been caring for her while she recovers, but have no idea where she came from or why she was on my land."

"It is possible that she is our Madeleine," M. Larrabee said in a hopeful whisper.

"I imagine anything is possible, yet I hesitate because she does not seem to acknowledge any past involving a family or a fiancé. I have asked for her to be brought to greet you, then we shall see."

M. Larrabee looked at the duke, finally understanding he

was merely a victim of circumstance. "Your Grace, I appreciate your hospitality and consideration."

Carole entered the parlor with a tray of tea.

"I expect you are tired after a long trip. Please, sit." Gideon motioned to the settee as he and Perry took the two chairs across from them.

"I must warn you, Francine isn't able to speak. She hurt her throat in the accident, and it hasn't improved entirely. Of course, she's been able to communicate using sign language. I'm assuming now that it's the French derivation." he said, watching them. It eased him a bit that they didn't seem to understand. "I happen to have an architect working on the manor who is also adept with sign language. I have asked him to join us, though I suppose if she is your daughter, you would also be familiar with it."

They both looked confused.

Stapleton opened the door to the parlor and Francine walked in.

M. and Mme. Larrabee both stood, then Mme. Larrabee ran to Francine, hugging her tightly, before Gideon and Perry even had a chance to stand upright.

Perry instinctively put his hand out to grasp Gideon's arm, but he was too late; his brother was already across the room, next to Francine.

"*Ah, ma fille précieuse? Est-tu bien? Le Duc, il dit que tu ne peux pas parler, c'est vrai? Madeleine? Mon petit chou?*" Mme. Larrabee went on in rapid-fire French. "*Monsieur! Qu'est cet?*" the woman asked, looking at Gideon.

Gideon watched Francine's eyes as the small woman fussed. "Madame, I must insist you unhand her," he said firmly when he saw panic reach Francine's eyes. She looked quite terrified, and Gideon felt instantly protective. "Madame, Monsieur Larrabee, sit down!" Gideon ordered.

M. Larrabee rushed to his wife and took her into his arms to comfort her.

"You can see she doesn't recognize either of you. There is no need to terrify her." Gideon put his hand on Francine's back to steady her.

"Let us be seated, and have some tea, and attempt to discuss this rationally," Perry said, ever the diplomat, motioning to the chairs.

M. Larrabee walked to the settee with his arms around his wife, easing her down. She was weeping and trying to convince him of something in French.

"*Je sais, je sais, s'il te plait mari, un moment. S'il te plait,*" M. Larrabee said. She nodded as he handed her a handkerchief and she blotted her eyes, attempting to quell her tears.

Gideon steered Francine to the chair next to his. He wanted to be closer to her, to hold her hand, but if this did turn out to be her father then there was no sense in enraging his feelings of propriety by handling his daughter in an untoward fashion. It made his skin ache and his heart wrench to be unable to comfort her.

Perry could see the effect of the situation on his brother and decidedly took over the conversation to move attention from Gideon and Francine before any inappropriate conduct could be insinuated.

"Monsieur Larrabee, are we to understand that you believe Francine to be your missing daughter Madeleine?" he asked.


Francine's heart sank. She shook her head violently and stood from the chair, but Gideon grasped her wrist and pulled her back before she could speak. He placed her hand on the arm of his chair, hoping to offer some bit of reassurance that he wouldn't let them remove her, particularly if she were unwilling.

She looked at her hand, then up to Gideon's eyes, which bid her hold his gaze. She forgot the rest of the room, losing herself in the iridescent depths.

Perry drew the attention back to him. "Monsier Larrabee?"

"Yes, my lord, this is our Madeleine," he said, gesturing toward her. "Our *fille*, our Madeleine, she was betrothed to Lord Hepplewort when she was of ten years. He came to France one month past to bring her to England to be married. If you ask what our daughter looks like, our answer is this girl. I would swear an oath on the Bible that this is our Madeleine."

Every word he spoke drove her heart faster, but at that moment Stapleton announced Mr. Shaw and everyone turned.

"Your Grace, my lord," Shaw said, looking from one to the other.

Gideon stood and spoke quietly to Mr. Shaw, who then took the chair next to Francine and began signing.

The Larrabees watched the silent exchange, astounded, as Gideon looked on intently.

"Where did your daughter learn to speak with the deaf?" he asked quite bluntly.

M. Larrabee stood. "She did not, she does not. I do not know what this is. This is our Madeleine, but I do not know this," he said with a dismissive wave.

Francine's eyes narrowed and she folded her arms across her chest.

Gideon wasn't sure what to think.

Shaw stood and, leaning toward Gideon, began to quietly explain to him what Francine had said. But M. Larrabee interrupted.

"If she has said something, we have every right to know it."

Gideon looked at him, then nodded at Shaw, who sighed and began to explain.

"Mr. and Mrs. Larrabee? Miss Francine has said that she does not know you," he said.

"Is that all?" M. Larrabee asked.

Shaw glanced at Gideon, who nodded. "She was quite empathetic." Shaw paused. "More specifically, she said she doesn't recognize you at all, in any fashion. She feels no sort of connection with either of you. She doesn't speak French and she doesn't know who you are or what you want, and will not go anywhere with you."

M. Larrabee looked directly at Gideon. "I would like to speak with Your Grace in private."

Perry started to shake his head, but Gideon waved him off. "Go find Marcus," he said, holding his brother's attention.

Shaw was confused, then seeing the crooked smile on Perry's face, comprehension dawned. Then Gideon turned to him.

"Mr. Shaw, would you mind attending the ladies?"

Shaw nodded and glanced between the women, who were examining each other carefully as though each wished to know their opponent before waging battle.

Gideon looked at M. Larrabee and motioned to the door. "My study is this way. We can speak privately there." M. Larrabee nodded, following Gideon from the room.

As soon as they were out of sight, Perry followed.

Francine looked at Mme. Larrabee. She held a certain familiarity for her; her face held a reminiscent countenance that she couldn't quite place, like a long lost relative you have only seen in old photographs. Before her panic could set in, she placed her hand on Mr. Shaw's to get his attention.

He looked at her as she began to sign. "Madame Larrabee, Francine says she is saddened by your grief. She wishes she could help somehow. She doesn't remember much before the accident, but she remembers her name, and feels as though if you were her mother, no matter what had happened, she would feel something when she saw you. But she has felt nothing, just as she has felt nothing for any—" Mr. Shaw stopped when she did, gesturing for her to continue, but she didn't. Mme. Larrabee looked at her.

"Nothing for what, *ma fille?*" Mme. Larrabee asked.

Francine shook her head, not wanting to finish the thought. She did feel something after the accident—she felt a very distinct pull toward one person: Gideon. She was desperately drawn to him, as if a memory of him had been born with her. She was irrevocably his, no matter where she had come from or where she was going. That bond could not be broken.

It must be what had drawn her from her own time, brought her here. She was suddenly terrified that she might be taken away by the Larrabees, more so than before, when she'd worried that she would awaken from this life to be spirited back to Denver and the 21st century, where she had come from.

She looked at Shaw, shaking her head, and Shaw nodded. "I beg your pardon, madame. She is quite tired, and still recovering."

"*Je comprends, eu,* I understand. I only want her to find comfort, eu, to find herself. I believe *dans ma cœur, eu,* in my heart, that she will remember," she said as she gazed at Francine. "Your name is Madeleine Adelais Larrabee. You are born *le cinq Février mille huit cent soixante-deux.* You are the second of our *quatre belles filles,*" she said as she held up four fingers, pointing at the second. Then, pointing at the first finger, she continued. "*Votre sœur* Aisling is the *plus vielle*, and Amélie and Maryse are at home in *Lisieux, prés du Port de Havre*. Your fiancé is Lord Hepplewort, the Earl of Shropshire, and he also looks for you. He will expect us to arrive with you soon."

Francine's heart beat rapidly. Something about that name sent it pounding against the inside of her ribcage. Her hand stole to her chest, pressing back against the heavy beats. *Madeleine*, she thought, *Madeleine Adelais*. She was the girl from the portrait. Shaw glanced at her and she started signing rapidly: *I have no sisters, there are no sisters, I have no family, please don't listen, don't believe her*. Her hands shook, and her breath quickened. Francine panicked.

"Madame, please. I must beg of you to stop. I must protest. She is obviously distraught," Shaw said, catching only part of what she tried to tell him.

Francine sat quietly, her mind racing. She didn't have sisters. Her parents were dead. They carried her family's name—Larrabee—and the only other facts of significance were the rambling words of her father's thesis. She shook her head, looking down. He had been right all along and it was one thing to believe something in theory, quite another to believe it in truth.

Gideon walked into his study, motioning to the sideboard. "Can I offer you a brandy, Monsieur Larrabee? I believe this situation warrants. I happen to have an exceptional 1864 Raynal Cognac," he said as he poured himself a snifter of the fine French brandy. He turned to Larrabee, who smiled and nodded. Gideon handed it to him and poured a second, then walked to the chairs in front of the grate, gesturing for Larrabee to sit. "What is it you would like to discuss?" he asked.

Larrabee warmed the brandy, swirling it in the glass between his palms. "Perhaps I should explain, more clearly, my position on this situation. My daughters are raised most of their lives in convent, for *garantie leur chasteté et leur innocence*. You understand? I make a promise to the betrothed, and in return, they make *une promesse, eu*, a pledge to my family, for our dedication."

Gideon was beginning to understand. Larrabee sold his daughters' maidenhead for profit. He stifled a groan. *Grotesque*, Gideon thought as he cleared his throat and steadied his features.

"It is not different from your girls here being chaste for marriage," Larrabee said defensively.

"Except for a few details. My understanding of your practice is that there is a complete lack of explanation, none whatsoever, to the young girl of what will happen to her. She's not even instructed in basic anatomy. Girls raised in this manner are led much as lambs to slaughter. I imagine it would be a terrifying position to be in," Gideon said coldly, rolling the balloon between his palms to avoid crushing it with his fingers.

Larrabee glared at him. "The difference is not important," he ground out. "But the fear of her duty may be causing my daughter to be untruthful. The fact remains that she owes the obligation to her family. *Les femmes ne sont rien mais des machines pour produire des enfants*," he spat.

Gideon tensed as he understood why M. Larrabee felt it necessary to talk to him privately. "There is no reason to quote Napoleon to me, on this land, under these circumstances."

"Napoleon understood the place of women."

"And Napoleon has been put in his place."

Larrabee's eyes widened and Gideon stared into the brandy, endeavoring to calm his temper before responding again. *Was she so terrified by the prospect of marital relations that she bolted and is now lying about who she is? What then of her behavior in the maze today?* He shook his head and narrowed his eyes at Larrabee.

"Regardless, if Francine is in fact your Madeleine and she felt *threatened* by what Lord Hepplewort said or did, then she is still to be protected. No peer of the realm should behave in such a cowardly fashion. If he had prepared his fiancée appropriately, she would have no need to run scared. He either intentionally terrified the girl, or he did something unconscionable, otherwise your scenario is unfounded. In either case, she still needs protection." He took a deep breath. Holding Larrabee's gaze, he continued, enunciating every word carefully. "I will not stand for barbaric behavior. It is one thing to demand chastity and claim one's wife's maidenhead. It is entirely another to terrify an innocent."

Larrabee put the snifter on a side table and stood. "*Non, monsieur,* actually you do not have a choice in the matter. As Madeleine is my

property until married, you have no right to say anything about the way I treat her. As for her future husband, you would need to speak with him. However, as of this moment she belong to me." He turned for the door.

"Larrabee." Gideon's jaw tensed as he concentrated on the light from the fire filtering through the swirling brandy, willing the motion to calm his nerves. "There is one thing I can do," he said.

There was a loud thump against the wall behind the fireplace and Larrabee stopped, looking at it.

"It's nothing. The manor is old. Possibly a bothersome squirrel in the chimney," Gideon said.

Larrabee turned on him. "What exactly do you propose?"

Perry fell out of the passageway and into the great entrance, calling to Stapleton.

"Yes, milord?"

"Get Roxleigh out of there," he said, pointing at the study.

"Pardon, milord?"

"Get him. I don't care how. Tell him the kitchen is on fire, tell him his horses are out, tell him I jumped from the roof, tell him anything, *just get him out of there!*" he yelled.

Stapleton knocked once before entering. "Your Grace, I must implore you, your attentions are required on a matter that is most urgent?" he said in a confused tone.

Gideon glanced up, raising one eyebrow, then looked at Larrabee. "I beg your pardon, monsieur, I shall return momentarily. I am sure there is something that indeed requires my immediate attention or my man would have waited for a more opportune moment."

Larrabee nodded and Gideon rose, handing his brandy to Stapleton as he passed, giving him a look that promised retribution. As he walked from the room he thought he heard Larrabee say, "Perhaps squirrels."

Gideon stormed into the hallway, knowing full well who was going to suffer the interruption. "Peregrine!" he boomed. Everyone within earshot jumped at the sound as it echoed through the great entrance. Perry turned away from the door to the green parlor, striding quickly to meet Gideon beside Marcus' table. "*What* do you *need*?" Gideon asked angrily.

"Are you about to do what I think you are about to do?" Perry asked.

"That depends. What exactly do you think I am about to do?"

"Oh, hmm, let me think. Could you be considering purchasing a bride?"

"Don't be vulgar."

"Don't give me cause, brother. You *cannot* be part of this ridiculous farce! You cannot be involved. You must think of the dukedom. This is an absolutely impossible situation, but *you* cannot be part of it."

Gideon's face fell. He looked down and shook his head, putting his hand to his forehead and massaging his temples. "I cannot in good conscience allow this man to proceed with this arrangement," he said quietly.

"Yet *you* cannot become involved in a scandal like this, either."

"I understand that, Perry, but if I allow him to take her I may never see her again. If she leaves with them tonight, I just cannot—" Gideon stopped.

Perry watched his brother's countenance break. "You cannot be part of this situation," he said again, taking his brother's shoulders. "But I can." He turned and stormed into the study with Gideon close at his heels. Perry didn't give Gideon a chance to stop him, but strode directly to M. Larrabee.

"Monsieur Larrabee, I am here to break your arrangement with Lord Hepplewort. I will make reparation with him. Furthermore, I would request you break your arrangements for any other daughters as well. I will provide payment to you and serve as guardian. They will come to England and I will provide for their education, and a proper dowry, and will provide them a *proper* marriage," he said definitively.

Gideon's jaw dropped.

# SEVENTEEN

arrabee looked dumbfounded. "My lord, you cannot—"

"I most certainly can, and I most certainly will," Perry cut in.

"But the girls are already promised—"

"Not for long. You cannot possibly think there is a better arrangement. You will receive the money you have requested, the girls will be well taken care of, and the bescumbered sods you sold them to will be left wanting. I cannot think of a better solution."

Larrabee fumed. "I must speak with my wife, *privately*." His glare rested on Gideon, who realized Larrabee never had believed in bothersome squirrels. He nodded and called again for Stapleton.

"Your Grace?" he said, sounding slightly exasperated.

"Stapleton, please take Monsieur Larrabee to the green parlor and retrieve Miss Francine and Mr. Shaw. Then bid as Mr. Larrabee requests, until further notice."

"Yes, Your Grace," he said as moved to the doorway. M. Larrabee nodded to the brothers and followed. Moments later, Francine rushed in. She shook off Shaw and dodged Perry, going straight to the arms of Gideon.

"What the devil is going on?" Shaw exclaimed. "Larrabee has Stapleton standing guard outside the parlor like a gargoyle. Larrabee told him to bang on the door if any of us dare leave the study."

Perry smiled.

Gideon wanted to know how Francine was, frustrated by their break in communication. He looked at Shaw, who relayed the conversation they had with Mme. Larrabee while the brothers were in the study.

Perry caught on the number of daughters included in the tale and not much else. "Four?" he choked.

"Well, presumably the eldest is already married," Gideon said with a grin.

"Roxleigh, you—uh. I cannot… When I—" Perry grabbed the two snifters of brandy that had been abandoned on the sideboard and drank one right after the other, then turned and reached for a glass and the bottle of whiskey. He raised the bottle by the neck without turning to the others and gave it a decisive shake.

"No, thank you," they replied.

Shaw turned to look at Gideon. "Dare I ask?"

Gideon chuckled, shaking his head. He was thoroughly amazed by his younger brother's actions on this night. He was also still drawn as tight as a hunter's bow, awaiting the results of the conference between the Larrabees, but he felt he was as close to a settlement as he could be.

Mrs. Weston walked into the study. "Your Grace, I wondered if I could help—" She broke off as her eyes came to rest on Miss Francine, who was standing in the duke's firm hold. Her eyes were closed, her hands held up against his lapels, breathing quietly as he slowly patterned a circle on her back with his hand.

He nodded, placing his other hand under Francine's chin, lifting her face to his. "I want you to rest."

She shook her head angrily. "No!" she tried, holding her throat as she whimpered from the burn, trembling from head to toe in anger.

He caught her cheek, stroking it with his thumb. "Francine,

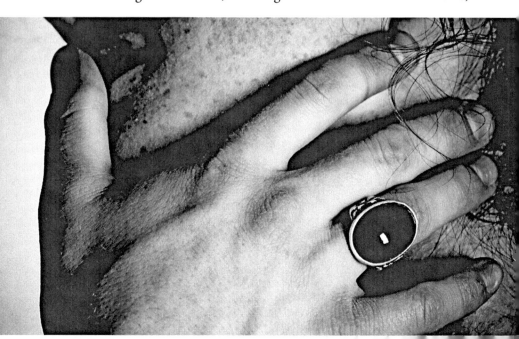

please calm yourself. Don't damage your voice further, I implore you. I will see to this," he whispered tenderly so only she could hear. "Please, go with Mrs. Weston. We will speak on the morrow. Believe me when I say nobody will disturb you, and you will not be leaving this manor. I promise you I will protect you, only trust in me."

She nodded. He could see she was overcome by frustration, but his gentle words had soothed her. He held her face, looking into her eyes, and Mrs. Weston moved to her.

Francine fought the departure, her gaze fierce, and Gideon took her hands.

"Please," he said again, placing kisses in both of her palms, "please go with Mrs. Weston and let me take care of this for you."

She allowed Mrs. Weston to lead her from the room, not taking her eyes from his until she was gone.

"Shaw," Gideon said, still watching the doorway. "I feel I owe an explanation."

"No, Your Grace, you most certainly do not owe me anything."

Gideon turned and smiled. "My gratitude for that. However, it is hardly possible that you do not want for one."

Mr. Shaw smiled in return. "You have me there, Your Grace, but please, do not include me in your affairs out of some sense of guilt or—"

Gideon cut him off with a wave. "No, no, not guilt. An explanation is due. It would suffer to save my reputation, as I have no idea what strange ideas must be battling in your mind."

"There are a few, Your Grace, but none seem plausible, considering the fact that your reputation for honesty and your sense of propriety and justice are infallible."

Gideon laughed. "I am far from infallible, but I do appreciate the thought. Lord." Gideon sighed heavily. "Let us sit." Shaw nodded and followed him to the chairs.

Perry was sprawled across a settee with three fingers of whiskey still in his glass and the half-empty bottle in his other hand. Gideon and Shaw sat across from him.

"How are you feeling, brother?" Gideon asked carefully.

"Not drunk enough yet— Still feeling, thank you," Perry replied with a raise of his glass.

"I see," Gideon said, then turned to Shaw, who looked astounded. "I believe it is my brother's reputation that may be further in need of repair than mine at this juncture." He then set out to explain the events that had transpired before Shaw was brought over.

Francine was shaking like a carriage on a washboard road. She curled up in bed, holding herself tightly, attempting to subdue the tremors. That woman downstairs was certain she was her daughter. Francine could see in every inch of her demeanor that she believed it to be true. Francine knew deep inside that she was right, even though in some small sense she wasn't.

She looked like herself, except her hair was long and brown, and of course she wasn't really herself, was she? She wasn't in her hometown, she wasn't in her apartment, she wasn't riding in a cab on the way to work, she wasn't even in the 21st century. She exhaled sharply. She was this woman's daughter. She sat up. *The woman downstairs is my mother.*

She shook her head, driving away the thought. The woman downstairs had seemed cold and distant after that first startling outburst. If they had at one time been irrefutably connected, wouldn't her body feel some physical twinge when they came together again? She didn't feel the slightest sense of recognition, and shouldn't she? She hoped that the connection between a mother and a daughter wasn't so easily disrupted.

She remembered the feeling every time she had returned home to see her mom; she would feel a small tear in her belly until she was warmly embraced by her, repairing the damage of separation. She still felt that tear, so the woman downstairs could not be her mother.

Her mother had been so safe, so warm, the epitome of what motherhood should be. She knew she probably embellished her memories as they pertained to her parents, since she'd been so young when they were killed, but that didn't matter. The underlying feelings, the basic sense of connection, was still there. She already had a mother, and that woman was not Mme. Larrabee, regardless of heritage and ancestry.

She felt dangerously adrift, and she needed something tangible. She had no control over herself, her future—anything. She couldn't even decide what she was eating for lunch—it was simply made for her like it had been when she was a ward of the court. But she had become used to having complete control of her life since leaving the system. Nobody told her what to do, and if they tried, she fought against it and generally won. She sighed and huddled on the bed. She hated being handled. *I can handle myself. Or maybe—maybe I can't.* How could one small person become so irretrievably lost, and why did it have to be her?

Stapleton jumped when the door to the parlor opened.

"You may retrieve His Grace," was all M. Larrabee said.

Stapleton bowed and walked back across the great entrance to the study. "Your Grace, Monsieur Larrabee has requested your presence in the parlor." Stapleton held the door for the gentlemen.

Shaw was sitting in the chair nonplussed. Gideon stood, clapped him on the shoulder, then reached out to his brother.

"Blargh!" Perry spat as he was yanked unceremoniously to his feet.

"You are a mess. You could have waited until after their decision to get soused, could you not?"

"Four," was all the reply Perry gave.

"Time to pay the executioner," Gideon jeered at him. "Come, Shaw, you won't want to miss this."

Shaw nodded in agreement and helped Gideon straighten his brother's jacket.

Mme. Larrabee looked at the three men with a great deal of satisfaction when they entered. The look eased Gideon quite a bit. He walked directly to M. Larrabee and stood tall, his shoulders squared, his hands clasped behind his back, causing M. Larrabee to step back a pace. Perry came to stand beside Gideon, attempting the same stature, but coming up just a bit shy, as foxed as he was.

"We have decided to accept your offer, with a few caveats of our own," Larrabee said. Gideon and Perry gave him twin cautionary looks, causing him to back up another pace and clear his throat.

Mme. Larrabee nudged at his back. "First," he began, "we expect to be apprised of our daughters' progress. We do not wish to be removed entirely from their lives."

"And second?" Gideon asked with a glare.

"Second, *you* must inform the suitors that the girls are no longer available, and make reparations directly, making sure they will not seek remuneration from us."

"And?" Gideon prompted again, expecting a laundry list of petty requests.

Larrabee stood straight and looked into Gideon's eyes. "*C'est tout.*" His hand cut the air in a gesture of finality.

Mme. Larrabee hit her husband on the shoulder.

"Yes?" Gideon encouraged.

"Yes, Your Grace, *eu*, we would request a room *pour la nuit.* It is quite late and we have traveled a great distance. If you have accommodation, may we rest?"

Gideon thought for a moment. He couldn't very well kick them out without a word. He would—after all—be their son-in-law, though they weren't aware of it. Misguided as they were to their daughters' upbringing, he would not begrudge them shelter.

"Stapleton will show you to a guest suite. Of course, in consideration, and because we have not yet formalized this arrangement, I would request that you do not leave the suite unaccompanied. I will have a footman attend you, and please be aware that should you leave the suite at any time, I *will* be informed."

"Of course, Your Grace. We will abide by your graciousness and hospitality."

Gideon nodded. "We can make the arrangements on the morrow. I have a man in town who can draw the necessary guardianship paperwork."

Perry groaned, drawing the attention of everyone in the room. "Excuse me, I believe the lamb is not sitting well. I must bid you all good-night," he said, then practically scampered from the room.

Gideon called for Stapleton, and the crowd retired.

Gideon disrobed and crawled directly into his bed, throwing the heavy counterpane aside as he stretched and settled the many sheets over his body. He was too exhausted to even bother dressing in his cotton sleeping trousers. He had no plans to leave his room until the following morning.

He snuffed the last candle over his headboard and was settled on his stomach for some much needed sleep when he heard first the outer door, then the sitting-room door, and finally his bedchamber door open and close quietly. He lifted up on his elbows, expecting to hear Ferry traipsing across his room. Then, realizing Ferry would have come from behind the fireplace, his breath caught.

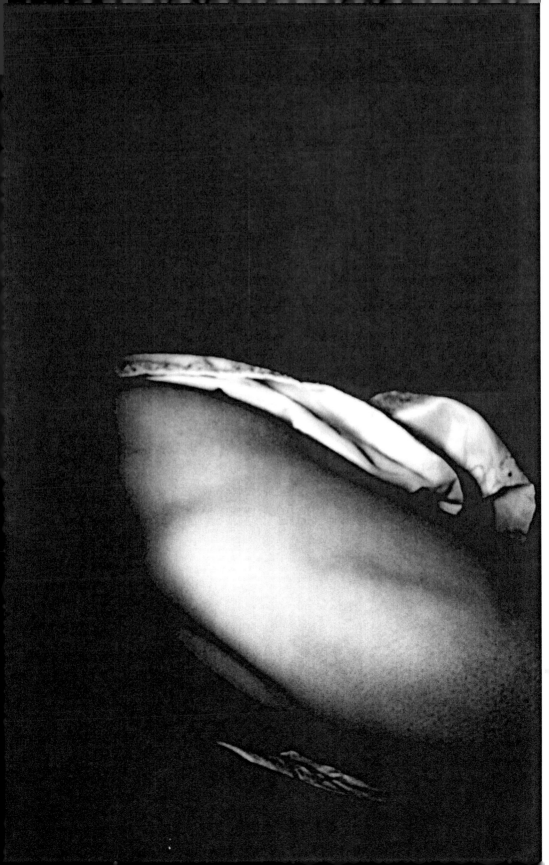

# TAKEN
## PART THREE

# EIGHTEEN

"**G**ideon," Francine whispered, and with that one small word he was rock hard. He jerked up, trying to discern her figure in the darkness. He heard her trip on something, a tiny cry escaping her lips. He moved to help her, then realized he was trapped in the bed by his nakedness. His breath hissed as he inhaled.

"Gideon," she whispered again, "are you still up?"

He shook his head. Still? *Not still. Again—yes, but not still.* "Yes," he grumbled. "What are you doing here?"

"I couldn't sleep. I had to see you," she whispered so softly he could hardly hear her.

Leaning forward, he grasped her hand, trying to stop it from moving across his body as he felt her fingers passing over the blankets, coming dangerously close to the evidence of his arousal. "You shouldn't be speaking, and you shouldn't be here," he said.

"And yet, I am."

"You *defi nitely* should not be in *here*," he said, attempting to

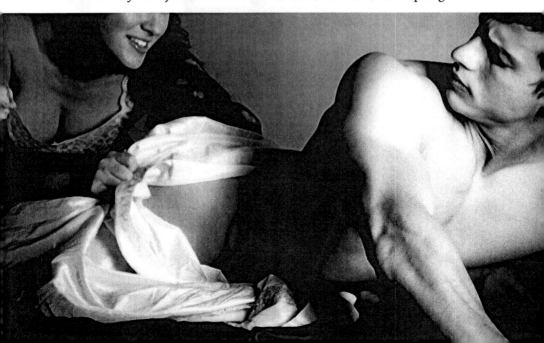

convince her again that she should leave. "Mrs. Weston will have an apoplexy when she discovers—" He drew in a resolute breath as he felt her other hand on his chest and the weight of her body on the bed.

He let go of her wrist as she moved toward him. "Lord take it, Francine, you must leave, you simply *must*. This is terribly untoward, you cannot—" He was cut off again by her hand, this time against his mouth. He thought his cock would burst from the pressure pulsating violently to his loins. He groaned, and her lips caught the noise before it had a chance to escape, her tongue teasing timidly.

He reached up in the dark to find her shoulder to push her away, but her arm wasn't where he guessed it would be, and he ended up with the soft mound of her breast cradled in his hand. She gasped and pressed her lips harder against his as he opened his mouth to her.

The woman above him was not acting like an innocent. He marveled at the thought as he momentarily yielded to her pleasures. Larrabee said he hadn't received confirmation of the consummation of her marriage; Gideon had assumed that meant that she wasn't yet married, but what if she was? What if Hepplewort had already claimed her? Gideon could never marry her, and she had been lost to him before this began—but for tonight, if she was married and he made love to her, he would cuckold that bastard for terrifying his innocent wife.

"Stop thinking," she whispered.

"Hush." Gideon found a new source of passion. His thumb circled the hard point of her breast through the fabric of her nightgown as her breath wilted in a sigh. He rolled her beneath him in one swift move, twisting the blankets about them, placing one of his thighs between her soft legs. He spread her below him and she whimpered. He shifted achingly slowly, settling his heavier points into her supple curves. With one hand on her hip he moved the other to her nape, gently caressing the hollow below her ear with his thumb.

She opened her mouth to him and he took, plunging into her, tasting the satiny inside of her lips and the slick underside of her tongue, feeling a powerful shudder wrack her body from her head to her toes. He suckled her lower lip, tasting the essence of the drunken pears from tonight's dinner, which even now lingered. He drew her lip between his, teasing it with his tongue before letting it go then licking and nipping at the other. He felt her hands on his back, the pressure of her touch making him aware of his muscles twisting beneath his naked skin.

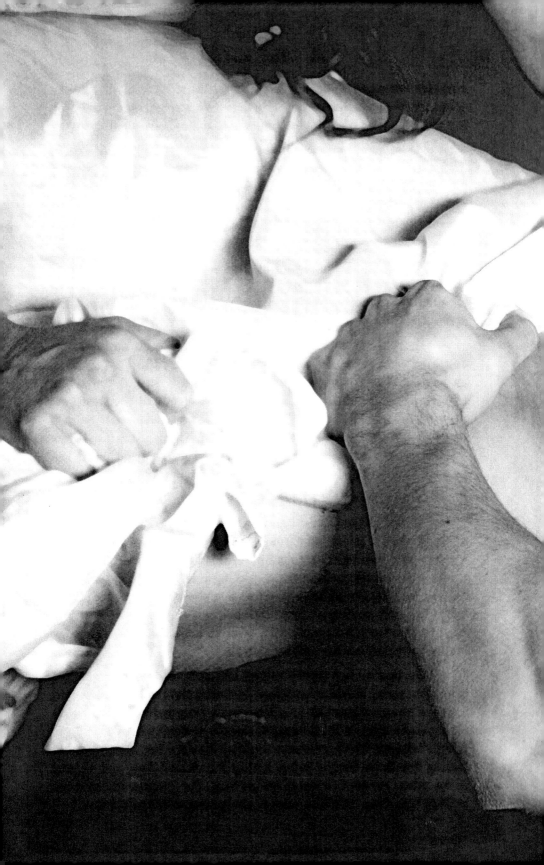

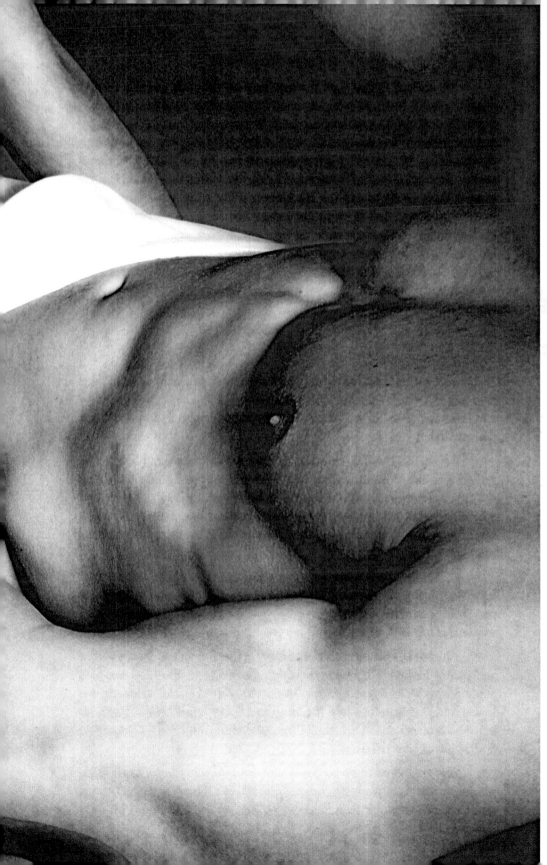

He shifted against her, the hardness of his body settling further into her pliable form. Moving his hand from her hip, he skimmed across her belly and up the center of her body between her breasts, pausing to feel the flutter of her heart as she arched into him, digging her nails into his shoulders. He winced and leaned up on one elbow, keeping his hand on her chest as he looked down into the darkness that enveloped her. He wanted desperately to see her. He imagined her silky skin shimmering in the moonlight, and the thought caused him to press his hips into her involuntarily. *Blasted curtains!* he thought, with a deep-seated moan. He preferred to sleep in total darkness, not waking until Ferry came to open the folds to the morning light. He never thought the darkness would bestow him such disadvantage.

Grasping both sides of her head as he balanced over her, he took her mouth again.

Her mind centered on the hard shaft that stroked her sensitized skin through the fabric. As Gideon moved he kissed her cheeks, eyelids, and forehead, drawing a path of heat over her face with a long slow burn that made her gasp for air.

He pushed his fingers into her hair, holding her head back as he trailed kiss after kiss down her jaw. With his tongue he lit a fire down the curve of her neck until he found the hollow at the base of her throat, where he rested his lips, quietly groaning against her, pausing for what seemed an interminable expanse of moments. His entire body tensed in check.

"Francine, I am very much past the point where I can rationalize," he growled, the vibration of his baritone resonating through his chest and sinking into hers, firming her nipples. "You either need to find your way out of my bed, or I will find my way into you."

She felt the blood rush to her head at the delivery of that sentence and nearly balked. His strength, which currently surrounded her, was evident and a bit overwhelming. She felt every muscle wrapping his bones and pressing into her, the length of every band held at bay over her. She had never felt so fragile in all her life. But then— *Doesn't he realize this is why I'm here?*

Her response was to bend the leg not caught beneath him, wrapping it around his waist, urging him on. His hardness inched closer and closer to where it was made to be, and every increment brought the cadence of her heart to a stronger rhythm. *This is it,* she thought. *Finally, tonight, right now, this is it.* The warmth of his breath against her neck loosened the muscles of her throat, forcing a sound of carnal ecstasy to escape her lips.

She moaned that final plea and his senses unraveled. Rising above her, he kicked their legs free of the blankets and reached down with one hand, dragging the hem of her nightgown up until his knuckles rested against her exposed knee. He breathed deeply of the scent caught in the hollow of her neck.

His hand traced her knee to the crease that led around the back, into the softest skin of her leg. He trailed his calloused fingers up her thigh, drawing her leg up slowly as the nightgown slid on his forearm.

"Gideon," she said, almost *sotto voce.* It drove him.

"Again," he said gruffly. "Say my name. Again."

"Ahh, Gideon!" It left her lips in a cry that caught as he reached the crease just below the soft roundness of her buttocks.

He pushed his fingers between her legs and she was wet—*for him.* Drenched in passion *for him.* He held a triumphant smile in the darkness as she gasped again and her hands flew to his shoulders, pressing him back slightly, sobering him as another, smaller cry escaped her lips. With great difficulty he raised himself on his elbow, releasing her hair and bringing his hand away from her womanhood.

She clenched his shoulders. "No, please, please, please, Gideon. Don't stop," she breathed. She gasped sharply as he carefully placed his hand on the side of her hip and stroked the juncture between leg and belly with his thumb. Her body started to tremble at his pause and withdrawal.

Gideon thought about what he'd learned this night, how she must be terrified of moments like this. How Hepplewort must have taken her by force and how difficult it must have been for her to soften and come to him. "Francine. Sweet, lovely Francine. We should not—"

"No more," her voice wavered as she whispered. "I am only scared, because—just—don't stop," she begged. "I want you, Gideon. I want to feel you inside of me, filling me."

He was shocked. She ignited a fire that no power on Earth could repress. He felt unbound from his senses, his emotions grazing the surface of his skin, raw and unprotected. His head dropped to her chest as he uttered an agonized sound, his brain wrestling with her fears and his conscience. Slowly, surely, he moved his hand to the triangle of curls at the base of her belly and smoothed them with his fingertips. He felt her thighs open to him instinctively. He turned his head and took one nipple into his mouth, wetting the fabric of her gown with his tongue, teasing with his teeth.

She jerked at the shock of the wet heat, the sensations racing from her breast to her belly, concentrating inside with a tingling pressure that threatened to burst. She opened her eyes wide, straining to see his head bowed over her body through the inky darkness, but she couldn't. She reached for his disarrayed locks and immediately tangled her fingers, stroking and pulling and pushing, urging his mouth over her breast. He moved to the other, where an equally powerful shock sent her hips thrusting forward into his hand.

His mouth teased at her nipple, gathering the intoxicating threads of energy. She felt his fingers unfurl and shift as his palm flattened against her, and she pushed back. Never in her life had she been closer to another human being. Never in her life had she been so naked, her emotions laid bare. The darkness intensified rather than softened. She felt her entire being on display for him, as though he were reaching in to stroke her very soul.

He slipped farther into her curls, searching to find that which lay protected within. The first touch sent another jolt to her belly as he gently encircled the crux with his thumb, caressing and teasing mercilessly. Her heartbeat quickened against the lips pressed to her chest as his hand slid even farther down, until one finger slowly smoothed through the soft folds, leaving his thumb to stroke the delicate nub.

*Oh God. Oh God.* She could feel the callouses, the hard flesh, the bend of his finger. She closed her eyes and felt. Simply felt. The texture of his hand was so different from everything of her. He moved slowly, practiced, almost perfectly, so steady it was maddening. She squirmed, only to have him restrain her with his weight.

Gideon moaned at the hot wetness enfolding his finger. *How can she still be a virgin?* Even though he couldn't see, he closed his eyes to concentrate on his other senses. Letting his hands speak to him. *If Hepplewort had his way, certainly she would have been loosened.* He shook his head, panting heavily against the warmth of her flushed skin. *Perhaps she is merely tense from fear.* He stroked her, feeling her saturate with desire until he reached the precipice which he could not sustain without taking her.

"Please." she said. The word came on a breath.

Soaring down the peak like an eagle in flight, the last vestiges of propriety left his consciousness. He quickly moved his other thigh between hers and spread his legs, pushing her open for him. In the same moment he swept her nightgown up over her head, tugging it free from her arms and flinging it across the room.

He placed one hand at her nape, the other coming to the small of her back. Carefully tilting her pelvis for his intrusion, he kissed her throat with searching, open kisses, breathing deeply as he attempted to control the forward thrust of his hips. Every muscle in his body trembled as he reined his advance.

He felt the head of his manhood encompassed by her folds, and his lips drew back across his teeth, sending a hiss of breath against her neck. His mouth parted against her neck as though to bite her, but he never pressed the sharp edge of his teeth, only the pliable pressure of his lips as he drew against her.

He moved forward slowly—then felt an undeniable resistance. Through the haze of his desire he gradually comprehended the meaning of the barrier and froze in pained abeyance as the reality of the matter set in. He shook his head. His eyes opened wide as he lifted above her, trying desperately to see her through the veil of blackness.

Her eyes flew wide as he began the advance, the pressure intense as her body stretched to accept him. Then she felt the sudden twinge that threatened a searing pain, followed by his nearly imperceptible retreat. *No... No, no, no.* She reached down, grasping his hips. Digging her nails into his buttocks, she urged him forward. "Please," she begged.

He froze. His breath quickened, his entire body tensed, and her nails dragged over his flesh as he pulled back from her, causing Francine to cry out a great sob of defeat.

He rested his hardened member between the soft folds of her

womanhood, holding her as she whimpered and attempted to pull away from him, suddenly ashamed. But he held her fast and moved against her slowly, gently, steadying her jagged nerves. Tears welled in her eyes and he crushed his lips to hers. "I'm sorry. I cannot, I simply cannot. I am very sorry. Please, Francine, my sweet, you must understand— Just let me," he panted softly.

She felt the tension gathering again as he moved, and she sank back into the bed, attempting to push him away yet holding on. He slid his hand between their sweat-streaked bodies, one deft finger sinking into her warmth. *Just let him what? Why did he stop? Is it because I'm a virgin? Did he expect more from me? Was I doing something wrong? Am I not good enough?* She shook the web of confused thoughts from her mind, concentrating on the feel of his hand between her legs and his mouth on her own.

He kissed ardent apologies into her lips as his fingers stroked through the petal soft skin, afraid to trespass further, his thumb steadily encircling her center. He started moving against her and her body settled into a rhythm with his, the tempo hastening. Her tangled fingers in his hair nudged his mouth over her breasts and he obliged, disturbing the precarious balance that still held her body in check.

He descended upon one nipple, grasping it between his teeth as he flicked the bud with his tongue. Her body quickened when he drew it into his mouth. He felt the pulsing flesh below tightening, attempting to draw him in.

She relaxed into him, concentrating solely on his hand on her. His mouth on her breast. The hardness of his erection against her pelvis. The taut arm against her side. The heavy thigh between hers. The steady pulse of his attentions, building.

Her senses seemed to break loose from their tethers, wrenching her muscles in spasms as she thrust against him, stroking his erection with her body. He groaned loudly as the pressure between them drew his release without permission, and he spilled his seed across the flesh of her belly.

He collapsed, capturing her cries with his mouth, sealing their breath together in a finishing kiss. He rolled to the side, pulling her with him in a tangled mass of limbs, neither able to move out of the haze of their euphoria. His hands gently roamed the landscape of her body as she drifted quietly, consoled by the power of something she'd never expected.

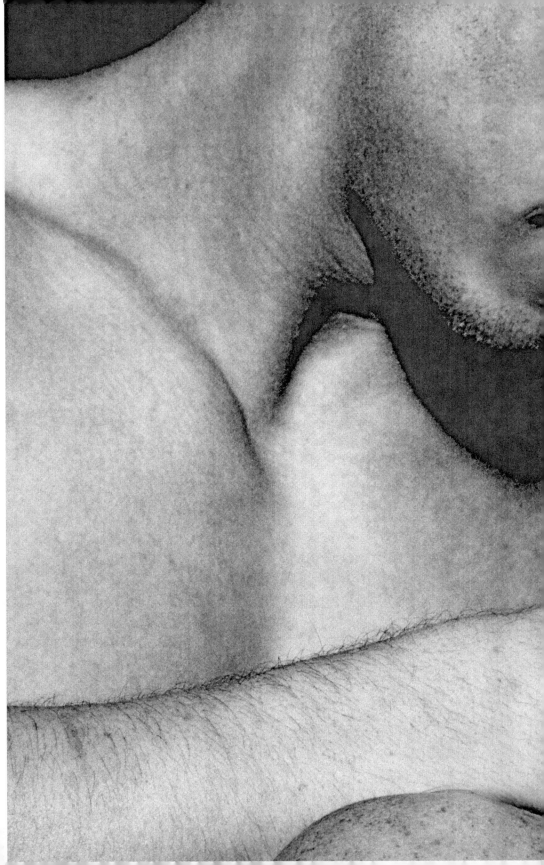

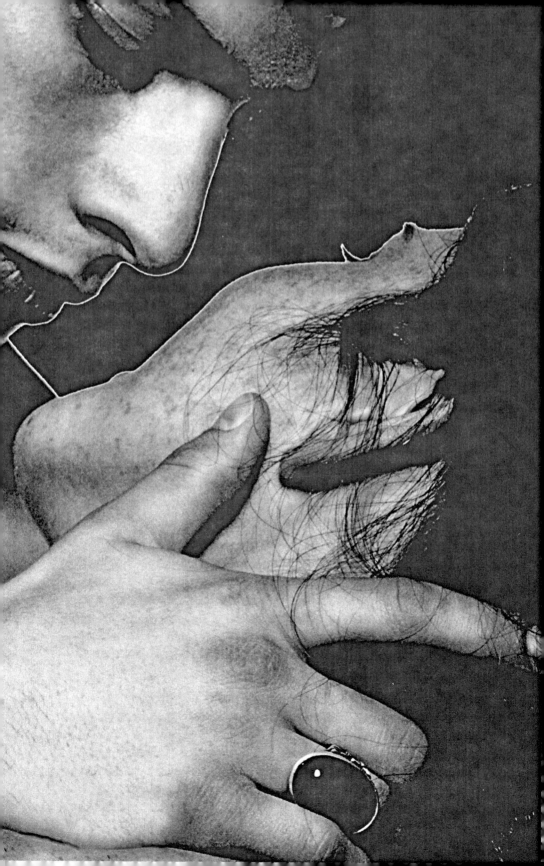

# NINETEEN

Francine lazed in her bed, thinking of the previous night. She'd tried to sleep, but it hadn't worked. She didn't want to be taken away from Eildon Hill, from her duke, from everything she currently knew. He had promised he wouldn't allow it, but she'd heard promises before. It was always the last foster home, the last family court hearing, the last school, the last time she'd ever say goodbye to someone she cared for. The final goodbye she'd promised to herself, over and over again.

Her mind kept returning to the desperation of her situation. She realized she had to do something, but didn't know what that something was.

She'd slept in the curve of Gideon's body and woke in the still darkness to the sound of his breathing. Wiggling out of his strong, protective arms as quietly as she could, she'd reached for the robe she'd left at the end of his bed. She had no idea where her nightgown was, but figured it didn't matter much and, wrapping the robe around herself tightly, she'd crept back to her room.

She hadn't wanted to say goodbye again so she went to him, but he'd been so damnably honorable. Back home, a twenty-year-old virgin was a rarity. Not that she hadn't *tried* to be done with her virginity; she'd just never had the opportunity—men seemed to shy away from her. Until now, until *this* man, and she was suddenly thankful that she had this gift to give him. She hadn't realized what a treasure it was until *he* refused to take it, and she'd tried to give it not just willingly, but almost by force. She massaged her tender throat as she pondered.

Where she was from, being chaste wasn't accepted and didn't generally last. Promise rings were given up as prayers were returned without being granted. Chastity was prudish, and men didn't like prudes. But this man had treasured her innocence. He wasn't ruled by human instinct. He ruled his actions, and his sense of morality was so powerfully a part of him that she couldn't sway him, even with the seduction of her body against his. He carried his passion close to the surface, but didn't let it break.

His fervor last night had been different—so strong, almost ferocious. She finally understood what it was he was restraining when around her. It wasn't that he was stuffy or stiff, it was that he held himself in check. And the evidence of his true passion she had now witnessed. She'd seen how his emotions could carry to a fevered pitch.

Francine had no idea how long this adventure was to last, whether she would be here for another day, another minute, another second. She marveled at the thought; according to her father's assumptions, this was it. This man, Gideon, would be her end, as he was her beginning. She had traveled through time to find the man who was born for her, and she him. No wonder she'd never felt like she belonged anywhere; she hadn't found where she belonged until now.

She knew his touch, his intimate embrace, but there was so much more to learn. He'd given her something she'd never felt, but even with that knowledge she sensed that what she yearned for was so much more powerful, more thorough, more important. She sighed, and her skin flushed at the memory. *My duke.* She couldn't wait to see him again.

Gideon woke at the sudden beam of light breaking the darkness of his room. He reached out to the pillow next to him, but it was empty. She was gone—or had she ever really been there to begin with? He moved across the bed and winced as the sheet shifted across his backside—the scratches she left behind were no dream. He closed his eyes and sighed. Ferry had dealt with his peculiar behaviors enough lately, and now Gideon was going to have to dress without him.

Well, mostly without him. Ferry wouldn't take kindly to not being able to fuss over him. The valet was proud and it showed in his work. Gideon had always been well-dressed, perfectly pressed and appointed—until recently. He heard water splashing into the tub and grumbled. "Ferry, leave me to my bath. I shall call for you when I am ready to shave."

"Yes, Your…" The statement faded as Ferry bent to retrieve a candlestick wrapped in a piece of white fabric. His eyes widened as the nightgown unfurled in his hand, then dropped it back to the floor dismissively. "…Grace," he finished. He placed the candlestick back on the side table and left.

Gideon heard him stride determinedly from the suite—which was odd, as Ferry was respectfully silent when he moved—and cursed under his breath. He wondered what Ferry had seen, certainly not the marks on his person—yet. *Perhaps the marks aren't that bad,* he thought. He stood, twisting to look at his backside in the glass. No. They weren't bad. They were *horrible.* Big, angry, red welts, four on each cheek. He turned away and walked to the tub. He'd need to have his pants on before Ferry returned to his room. He looked over his shoulder again, saw the smaller half-moon scratches on his shoulders, and realized he would need to have a shirt on as well. *Good Lord. The woman has talons, not nails.*

This was a right damnable turn of events, as Ferry would object to shaving him with a shirt in place. Gideon sank in the tub, hissing through his teeth as the heat sank into his scored flesh. *Damnable situation,* he thought, shaking his head. She overpowered him. Not physically, of course, but his mind felt addled whenever she was around. He had no idea how he had managed to refuse her last night. His entire body ached from trying to control his movements. As he leaned back in the tub, it dawned on him. His eyes snapped open.

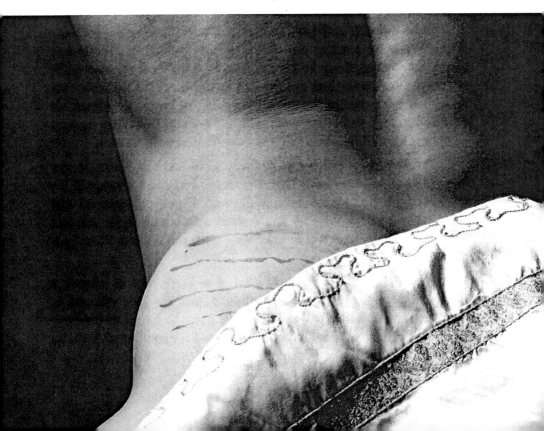

"Ferry!" And he was there—silently. "You may shave me," Gideon said as he settled in.

"Now, Your Grace? In the bath?"

"Yes, get on with it. I am quite sore from—from *riding* yesterday. I wish to soak for quite a while. If you are to shave me today it will be now—"

Ferry stiffened and Gideon looked at him with a warning glance.

"Or not at all," he finished.

The blood drained from Ferry's face and he brought the wet, warm towel from the bucket over the fire and wrapped it around Gideon's face before moving to the dresser to retrieve the soap and shaving tools. He shaped the blade with the strop and added a bit of oil to the sandalwood soap, then moved back to Gideon.

When he finished shaving him, Ferry left the room until Gideon allowed him back in to fuss over him again, but only after he'd pulled on a pair of trousers and a crisp white shirt. Ferry huffed when he was called back to find Gideon nearly dressed of his own accord. He went straight to the wardrobe and pulled out a cravat, waistcoat, and jacket.

Afterward Gideon descended the stairs, rubbing his jaw against what was possibly the closest shave of his life. He went to his study so he could make notes before the meeting with the solicitor. M. and Mme. Larrabee would both attend, as would he and Perry, then the Larrabees would depart for France to send the other girls back.

Shaw also rose early, his mind quite active after the excitement of the day before. He couldn't stop thinking about the missing area on the first floor. He walked into one of the passages near the suites and began examining the walls for evidence of catches that would release a hidden panel. He'd been in the passageway for an hour when he heard a voice in the main hallway and went out to see who else was about that might be interested in the search.

"My lord, you certainly are up early," Shaw said when he found Perry heading toward the staircase.

"Me? You are the one ferreting around in the back passages at an ungodly hour," Perry said.

"Oh, I beg pardon, my lord. Did I wake you?"

"I beg you, please call me Trumbull, and no, you didn't wake me. I cannot imagine anyone could still be sleeping at this point, especially me, as I am to be guardian to four young ladies from France." He clapped Shaw on the shoulder. "Sleep is a commodity I can no longer afford."

Shaw grinned. "Remember, *Trumbull*," he said with a nod, "we believe the oldest is already married off and of course, Francine— Well, I think we all know Francine will not be under your care for long."

Perry grunted as he turned toward the stairs. "Still. Until then, she and two other chits are to be under my guardianship, and that is not a fate I would wish upon the worst sort of person."

"Which are you referring to?" Shaw asked irreverently. "The fate of the guardian, or the ward?"

Perry glared back at him. "Either one, I would say."

"Which is why it was left to you, I suppose."

Perry looked at him curiously.

"I mean to say that most would not be aware of the precarious nature of the situation. You are well suited, simply for your knowledge. And who better than you, to—to know how to protect innocents from the rakes of London?" Shaw finished with a smile

Perry growled.

"Careful there, Trumbull," Shaw said cautiously. "You don't want to be mistaken for His Grace, do you?"

The comment sobered Perry and he turned, considering Shaw's statement. "That does not interest me," he said, a cavalier smile breaking his severe expression. "Shall we break our fast together?"

"Of course," Shaw replied. "Of course."

Halfway down the stairs, Perry heard his name again and looked down into the great entrance. "Ah, Rox. Ready for breakfast?"

"Yes," he replied distractedly. "I have made arrangements for us to travel to town with the Larrabees to draw up the paperwork for your guardianship. I would like to get this taken care of as soon as possible." Shaw was silent as they reached the bottom of the stairs and Gideon stopped in front of him. "Shaw, would you mind terribly continuing your work here in my absence?"

"Not at all, Your Grace."

"It's settled, then. We'll leave after breakfast and return when the papers are drawn and—"

Gideon was cut off by the sound of Stapleton opening the front door. The three turned to see several footmen carrying stacks of packages, followed by a beautifully attired woman in a blazing red silk dress that looked like wildfire as she moved. Her dark brown hair was piled loosely on top of her head and adorned with sparkling jewels. A second impeccably dressed young lady accompanied her.

Stapleton took her calling card on the salver and walked over to Gideon. "Your Grace."

He took the card and read it. *Madame Basire.*

"Ah, the dressmaker. How fortuitous. Stapleton, please notify Mrs. Weston immediately. Have you seen the Larrabees yet today?"

"In fact, Your Grace, I have not. Though their suite is still guarded, so it is my assumption that they remain inside."

*Good. I was somewhat definitive about them leaving the suite.* "See to them," he said to Stapleton. "They should break their fast soon, so we can be about our business."

"Of course, Your Grace."

Gideon walked over to greet Madame Basire.

"Madame Basire. Do you usually call so early?"

She winced at his curt greeting while, out of the corner of his eyes, Gideon saw Perry and Shaw depart quickly toward the breakfast room.

The dressmaker examined him. "Why, Your Grace, when the wardrobe of a young lady is in question, I would call in the dead of night." Her smile warmed her features.

"Well, by all means then, carry on."

"As you wish, Your Grace." Madame Basire curtseyed. When she looked up her gaze shifted from Gideon, and he turned to find Mrs. Weston approaching.

"Your Grace, this could occupy Miss Francine for most of the day," the housekeeper said. "Will you have need of her?"

"Of course not, Mrs. Weston. Please see to whatever she needs." He was moderately disappointed that Francine would be occupied for the day, regardless that he was to be away from the manor as well.

"Yes, Your Grace." She curtseyed, then turned to the dressmaker. "This way, Madame," she said, leading the parade of packages upstairs.

Mrs. Weston left Madame Basire and her entourage in the sitting room outside Francine's bedchamber and went in to prepare her. She found her already up, with her chemise and drawers on, sitting in one of the velvet chairs reading *Moby Dick*.

"Oh, miss, I do have a surprise for you! Madame Basire has arrived, and she has armloads of packages! You cannot imagine!" Mrs. Weston walked to the windows, drawing all the curtains aside. She returned to the sitting room to gather Madame Basire, her assistant, and all of her trappings as Francine stood.


Perry and Shaw sat in the breakfast room, allowing the footmen to serve them. "So, Mr. Shaw, tell me of this girl in London you are to marry."

Shaw looked out at the gardens, his eyes glazing as he considered the request. He smiled. "She is unspeakably lovely," he said quietly.

"That seems an unwieldy name for a girl, does it not?" Perry asked with a grin.

Shaw laughed. "It would be, but— Well, in truth, we are not formally betrothed as yet. She is the daughter of an earl and our match would obviously not be approved, so I really do not bandy her name about. I would prefer to be able to approach her father without any idle gossip preceding me."

"I see. I suppose I do bear a resemblance to the worst sort of gossip," Perry said teasingly. He had never really considered the fact that lack of title would be a stumbling block to a match, since he was of the peerage and never had need to consider it. Well, that and the fact that he was a rake of the first order, and even the *discussion* of marriage turned his stomach.

Shaw looked at him. "Actually, no, you do not at all, my lord. I beg your pardon if I inferred that you did. I only meant that I hope to make a respectable name for myself, beginning with my work here at Eildon Hill Park, before I approach the earl. To that end, I have not spoken of her."

Perry nodded. "Would the work here be enough, do you think?"

"I'm not sure," Shaw said.

Perry was quite sure that regardless of Shaw's work at Eildon Hill, an earl would not consent to his daughter being wed to a professional man. "But you still haven't answered my question. *Who* is this girl who has you smitten?"

Shaw gave him a devilish glare. "In truth, she only recently came out into Society, only a sennight prior. Her grandmother, the Dowager Countess of Greens—"

He stopped as Perry dropped his fork and started laughing so boldly that Shaw considered he'd lost his senses.

Gideon entered the breakfast room and glanced at his brother, who was caught in a fit of laughter. He sat at the small table as the footman brought trays of eggs, ham, potatoes, and a large glass of fresh orange juice. Another footman followed with a sauceboat filled with the same thick, yellow sauce that Chef had served the night before with the asparagus.

The footman gestured to his plate and Gideon nodded. "Apparently we are still being used for Chef's studies," he said as he looked from Shaw to Perry.

"I have managed to learn something interesting about our Mr. Shaw here."

"Is that so?" Gideon raised a brow. "Why don't you enlighten me?"

"Do you remember our darling dancing partner from the Greensborough affair?"

"Of course. How could I possibly forget such a treasure?"

Perry gazed at Gideon expectantly.

Gideon looked at Shaw as a napkin was placed in his lap, then at his brother, but Perry simply grinned like the cat that had eaten not just the canary, but the hamster and the goldfish as well. A smile broke across Gideon's face as he turned to Shaw. "*You* are the professional man our Lady Alice is enamored with?" he asked.

Shaw froze and Perry and Gideon both laughed. "This is quite unexpected! Now I understand! She told me I would like you," Gideon said, rather unceremoniously waggling his fork at Shaw. "She knows you are here. Of course." He shook his head and looked at his brother.

"Yes, she does," Shaw replied.

Gideon thought for a moment. "I believe we will need to go over the plans when I return to London, so *you will* need to accompany us," he said. "We should be leaving in about four days, as soon as Grover and Gentry return from Newcastle upon Tyne. We will be meeting the boat with Trumbull's wards in London, and since the Season has begun, there will be at least one ball we can attend—perhaps more." Gideon glanced at Perry again. "No doubt that overbearing mother of hers will be parading her around, still looking for a suitor."

Shaw grimaced. "Your Grace, I am not invited to the distinguished parties of the *ton*."

Gideon waved the statement away. "Mr. Shaw, no one would dare turn away a guest of *mine*."

He smiled. *This could be entertaining.*

Perry grinned.

"Trumbull, did you inform Shaw of our noble efforts with his betrothed?" Gideon asked.

His brother shook his head, laughing at Shaw's annoyed glance. "Actually, I hadn't made it quite so far."

Shaw frowned at them. "Well? Why don't you enlighten me?"

Gideon nodded and motioned to Perry, who embellished the story quite admirably.


Francine had no idea that fittings were so exhausting and decided right then and there that off-the-rack clothing was like manna from Heaven. She lost track of how many gowns she wore and imagined the poor girl who was doing the last of the alterations over in the window light was cursing her under her breath, even though outwardly she was perfectly sweet and composed.

Mrs. Weston took the finished gowns and hung them in the wardrobe. When they were done, Francine looked at Madame Basire and smiled to thank her.

"Madame Basire, I thank you for your efficiency," Mrs. Weston said. "The gowns are beautiful and I am sure the duke will be pleased."

Madame Basire waved her gloved hand at her assistant. "Not at all, Mrs. Weston. I was more than happy to oblige." Then she left in another flurry of fabric and skirts.

After nearly four hours of debates and changes in terms, M. Larrabee and Perry, with their respective interested parties, Mme. Larrabee and the duke, came to a final agreement of the guardianship. Mme and M. Larrabee would remain in town while Perry and Gideon hired a governess to return with the Larrabees.

Perry scrutinized his copy of the agreement as the carriage started back to Eildon. He was now the official guardian for Madeleine, who was listed as being nineteen years of age, as well as Amélie, sixteen, and Maryse, fourteen. There was an older fourth sister, Aisling, and it was of little consolation to him that she was already wed. "Fourteen," Perry said. "Do you *remember* fourteen?"

"I remember *you* at fourteen," Gideon replied.

"Exactly my point. This is not going to be effortless. I shall endeavor to never let them out of my sight. There are hellions everywhere looking to grow into the reputation I have built. Look, there. Four of them, just wandering the countryside," he said, pointing out the carriage window.

Gideon laughed. "Well, it is good you have a well-protected estate where you can hide them away."

Perry glared at his brother. The stare was beginning to lose its effect after being overused the past two days, and Gideon merely laughed at him again.

"Stapleton," Gideon said as his man held the door for the brothers. "Is the dressmaker still here?"

"No, Your Grace, she quit the estate nearly half an hour ago."

"Good, send Mrs. Weston to the study."

"Yes, Your Grace."

In the study, Perry walked directly to the sideboard and poured himself a whiskey, making Gideon smile as he walked to his desk.

"You really shouldn't turn into a souse before the young ladies have a chance to become inured to your presence. They might be quite put off," Gideon said.

Perry looked at his brother. "I have no plans of becoming a souse, as you so eloquently put it, but you cannot possibly fault a celebratory gesture to my new position." He tipped his glass toward Gideon for effect.

"Celebratory." Gideon paused. "Then, if you deem it, so be it."

Perry grunted and lifted the glass to his mouth. "Fox hunting and old port, ships at sea," he said, and downed the whiskey.

Gideon scowled. "Blast it all, Perry, you cannot toast the Royal Navy and leave me sitting here like a buffoon."

Perry refilled his glass to two fingers full and poured another glass for Gideon, then walked over to sit across from his brother. They clinked and toasted.

"Your Grace?" Mrs. Weston questioned as she entered the study.

"Ah, Westy, how are you this afternoon?" Perry asked.

"Quite well, my lord, as you must be." She nodded toward the glass of whiskey before turning to look at Gideon. "Your Grace, you requested me?"

"Yes, Mrs. Weston. We have need of a governess, rather expediently. Do you know of any?"

"Actually, Your Grace, I know Miss Faversham is recently returned from the estate of Lord Tanvers. His youngest daughter came out this Season, and they no longer require her tutoring. She should be back to Kelso by now."

"Please send Grover and Gentry for her straight away," Gideon said. "Have them stop by Meggie's house and check on her family, and send some food along."

"Yes, Your Grace. They will be much obliged."

Perry glanced up suddenly. "Were you going to run this past me, Rox? After all, these young ladies are my wards."

Gideon held out his hand, motioning for him to proceed, and Perry stood before Mrs. Weston placing his glass on the desk. "What are Miss—" He paused and waved his hand at Mrs. Weston.

"Faversham," she replied.

"Yes. What are Miss Faversham's references?"

"She was with Lord Tanvers' family for these last eight years, my lord. I should think that would be sufficient reference?"

"Of course. Do carry on."

She smiled and left the study as he sat back down.

"Really, Perry, how was that information different from what I obtained?" Gideon asked with a sigh.

"It was different because *I* obtained it," Perry said stiffly. "You cannot possibly think that you will be watching over every move I make with respect to my wards. The ladies are *my* responsibility... You cannot oversee it. It would not be—" He paused, looking his brother in the eyes. "Proper," Perry finished, narrowing his gaze and silently daring his brother to argue. Gideon studied him, then nodded with a half smile.

"On that subject, Rox, there will be no impropriety where Miss Francine is concerned," Perry added. "She is legally bound to me. Simply because you are my brother does not mean any liberties are extended to you. I am sure you have no intentions of ruining my ward. I just find it important to make sure there is no misunderstanding."

Gideon straightened, considering his younger brother with an increasing amount of respect. He had been concerned about signing over Westcreek Park, but any reservations he still held had just been shattered. This Perry was a changed man, an honorable man. He looked away, feeling a sweep of red crossing his cheeks and the bridge of his nose as he thought about his actions the previous night.

Perry scrutinized his demeanor. "Roxleigh… It has come to my attention that perhaps you have behaved in an untoward fashion with one of my charges."

Gideon glared at him. "Has it?" he asked through clenched teeth.

"It has," Perry continued carefully. "And while I am fully in support of your courting my ward, I feel I must remind you that until you are wedded, there will be no more improper behavior."

Gideon lifted his brows. Had his brother just called him out? He was rendered speechless. He could not form a thought, much less a decent sentence. He nodded once as Perry stared pointedly at him. He cleared his throat.

"My lord, I would appreciate the opportunity to court your ward, Miss Francine Larrabee," he said respectfully.

Perry stood with a wry smile. "Well, as I am not guardian over any such chit, may I offer another from my *bountiful* selection?" he asked, waggling his eyebrows rakishly.

Gideon laughed. He was mistaken; Perry hadn't changed all that much. "Of course, dear brother. Shall I leave it to your expertise to choose a suitable young lady for me?"

"By all means, though I suppose we should follow the lines of convention and that puts *Madeleine* as the first available. She should be coming out this Season. Perhaps you would endeavor to throw a ball in her honor at Roxleigh House?" Perry asked with a devious grin.

Gideon smiled in return. "Well, my lord, you are well acquainted with the business table. I will agree to the venture, but we must first discuss the dowry. If it is found to be lacking, well—" Gideon shrugged.

Perry laughed. "Good God, man, I may have received extra coaching at the business table, but your expertise still outranks me by far. Do remind me to always be on your side of a negotiation, will you?"

"After this one, we shall be," Gideon said. They laughed, and Perry downed his whiskey.

"What plans have you now?" Perry asked.

"I plan to ride, and I would like to ask Lady *Madeleine*—" He said her name with a great deal of effect, looking Perry squarely in the eye. "—to accompany me. By your leave, of course."

"Yes, of course. Carole will serve as chaperone," Perry replied with a smile.

"Agreed." Gideon sighed. "Lady Francine. Sounds nice, does it not?"

"Yes, well, it shouldn't be too difficult to get used to. Though I don't entirely understand the reasoning behind it, since the French peerage was abolished more than twenty years ago."

"Let the House of Lords sort it out. An unrelated ward would not be recognized with a title, but most wards are unrecognized by-blows of the peerage, and granting them title would only give them a foothold their families do not want them to have," Gideon said. "I prefer Miss Francine to be addressed as the Lady Francine."

"Thank you for the lesson." Perry shrugged. "Still the very least of my worries where these wards are concerned. I will see you after? I have something to see to."

Gideon nodded. "As long as what you are seeing to involves none of my maids," he said as he walked around his desk, patting his brother on the shoulder.

Perry groaned as they left the study. "No, Your Grace, you have drawn a line there that I quite shudder to cross."

# TWENTY

M rs. Weston packed a large basket of food with the help of Chef. She sent it along with Grover and Gentry to Kelso with a letter requesting the presence of Miss Faversham, then she went to Francine's suite.

Francine was finishing her lunch in front of the fire and intently studying the section on peerage and titles in her book of manners.

"Well, miss, you have already had such a busy day, and now you've been invited to go riding with His Grace. That is, if you are up to it?" Mrs. Weston asked.

Francine stood, her eyes sparkling as she nodded her head vigorously.

Mrs. Weston laughed and went to the wardrobe to pull out the peacock blue riding habit. The stunning color mirrored Francine's eyes, as vibrant in hue as her eyes were pale. The habit consisted of skirts and crisp white shirt with a beautifully tailored jacket that had black velvet-covered buttons crossing from one hip to the opposite shoulder and at the sleeves from the elbow to wrist. The matching top hat included a silk veil to protect her from the sun, also held in place by black velvet buttons.

Mrs. Weston helped Francine into the habit and then, seeing her confusion at the lop-sided skirts, pointed to her hip. "See this large button?" she asked. Francine nodded. "You pull the skirts up here and button it. That'll keep it from dragging the ground while you walk. Now, when you're mounted you undo it, so as to cover your legs properly. See here?" She billowed the skirt out around Francine's legs. "It'll cover you and the horse. You look so elegant, Miss Francine," she said, sighing.

Mrs. Weston pulled up the skirts and fastened them to the button, then steered Francine to the dressing table and fussed over her hair until it hung in a long, thick plait down her back with a few loose tendrils curled around her face.

Francine smiled. She actually liked what she saw. She ran her hand down her neck, from her chin to the little hollow that Gideon liked, and a shiver ran down her spine. Was it just last night that he had refused her? Heat infused her cheeks. Rather suddenly, she was afraid to face him. She had not seen him since his refusal, and wasn't entirely sure how he would react toward her. Or, frankly, how she might react toward him. Then she thought about his intentions.

*I had my list all wrong. It isn't job, house, husband, children, dog, fish, happiness. The list is much simpler.* Mrs. Weston pinned the top hat on and handed her a pair of riding gloves, then hurried her out the door. Francine looked down the stairs at the man who waited for her, and as his eyes caught hers she revised the list: *Gideon...happiness.* She smiled.

Gideon waited in the great entrance for Francine in his doeskin riding breeches and favorite old topboots. He paced, circling the grand table and adjusting his gloves.

Carole entered with a curtsey.

"Good afternoon, Carole. I understand you do well on a horse," he said, attempting to pass the time as they waited.

"Yes, Your Grace, my da insists we learn. Though I do not have the proper skirts for it, begging pardon, Your Grace," she said shyly.

He waved her off. Her lack of proper skirts was the least of his worries.

They both looked up when they heard footsteps, and Gideon's breath caught.

"Oh, my, but she's a vision!" Carole said under her breath.

Gideon swallowed audibly, his mouth suddenly quite dry.

Francine paused at the top of the steps, the habit traveling her body in perfect curves and sweeps, hugging every turn with perfection.

Carole looked at him. "Oh, I forgot to tell you, but Mrs. Weston bade me pack some treats for the ride, in case you get hungry, Your Grace."

"Truly," he whispered. "Well, that is fine, er, good. I mean that is good, yes, that will do fine," he managed. He walked to the base of the stairs and held out his hand.

Francine jumped slightly as a jolt of electricity coursed between them.

He bent, kissing the back of her wrist between the sleeve and her glove, then turned, placing her hand on his sleeve as he led her to the stable.


"Did you ride much in France?" Gideon asked Francine.

She glanced at him curiously, then realized he now believed her to be Madeleine, and why shouldn't he? The last name, the Larrabees' reaction to her—of course he would believe them. If her father's journals were right, she was now Madeleine Larrabee, and Madeleine was Francine. Quite unexpectedly, she was okay with it. She shook her head and lifted her hands in question.

*No*, Gideon thought to himself, *even if she remembered anything of France, horseback was probably just as forbidden to her as any other pursuits that might endanger her maidenhead.* He scowled, then paled, remembering that he had, in fact, endangered her maidenhead. He looked away, lifting one hand to his brow to cover his expression as they walked to the paddock. Three Friesians stood saddled and warming in the sunshine.

"Davis!" Gideon called as he opened the paddock. Samson walked straight to Gideon as Davis led the two mares. "Lady Francine, you remember my steed, Samson, and this is Delilah," he said, taking her rein. "Carole, Davis has saddled Kalliope for you."

Carole curtseyed and moved to help Davis with the animals, but he shooed her away.

She jumped up on Kalliope without hesitation as Francine watched; the maid had a regular saddle, and her skirts bunched up around her as she sat astride.

Francine smiled, looking at the strange contraption on Delilah, wishing she could ride like Carole. The basic saddle was there, but near the top was a large, curved horn that pointed skyward, and below it another that pointed down toward the stirrup. It was confusing, and she wasn't sure where to place her legs.

Gideon walked over and handed Samson's rein to Davis before returning to Francine. She stroked the mare's neck as she looked at him. "Here," he said, turning Delilah's head to her. "Touch her here, on the muzzle." He lifted her hand and pinched the fingertips of her glove, pulling it carefully from her hand.

She reached out and stroked Delilah's nose. "Oh my," she whispered. "I've never felt anything as soft as this pony's nose."

"Shh," he admonished her speaking with a smile. "And yes, there is nothing softer than—than a pony's nose. Let me help you," he said, wrapping his hands about her waist. She smiled as he turned her to face him and lifted her handily to the saddle. "May I?" He motioned to her leg.

She nodded and held onto his sturdy shoulders to keep from sliding off the far side of the horse. He placed her right knee around the upper pommel, then feeling her left leg through her skirts, he gently slid her other knee below the lower pommel. He placed her boot in the stirrup as he adjusted the length, jerking on the saddle below her skirts. Drawing back, he examined her for a minute and she stared at him, waiting for his next move.

He cleared his throat and tapped the button at her hip. "Oh," she whispered, looking down and undoing the button. He watched as a light pink blush colored the crests of her cheeks and nose.

She smiled sheepishly as she loosened her skirts and he pulled them from beneath her, letting them billow around the horse so Francine could sit snugly in the saddle. She smiled again as she put her glove back on. He handed her the rein before walking to Samson and deftly jumping astride the steed.

Gideon clicked his tongue and Samson and Delilah walked toward the meadow side by side, Carole guiding Kalliope behind.

Francine was nervous at first. She'd always had very good balance and body control, but she felt quite vulnerable atop this large animal with no experience in how to ride. She also felt a bit off-kilter on the sidesaddle. It was awkward. She'd ridden on carousels and merry-go-rounds, even on motorcycles, and astride seemed much more comfortable.

Gideon's instruction was gentle and helpful as he explained about the horses: how to push them forward, how to direct them and to hold. She hadn't realized that riding had more to do with the pressure of her legs on the horse than the rein. He spoke a bit about the Friesians, their English history, and their origins in the Netherlands. It sounded like he loved them very much. His eyes crinkled at the corners and his mouth broadened into a grand smile, and she enjoyed seeing his face lit with excitement. He obviously carried a great deal of pride in his animals.

Francine watched the horses communicate: the sounds they made, the way they behaved with each other. Samson liked to lead Delilah, even if by just a nose, and if she passed him he would snort and take a quick step to correct her. She appeared to ignore him, but Francine could see the way the muscles in her neck tensed when he pulled ahead of her, and Francine knew that Delilah was anything but oblivious.

Francine was aware of Gideon watching her and her face flushed warmly. She felt so removed from the person she had been before. She'd spent so much of her life ignoring anything that made her feel, and keeping herself busy, that now she was overwhelmed with the feelings she allowed herself. She sighed, looking around the meadow.

"What are you thinking, my lady?"

Her forehead creased; why would the duke call her "my lady"? Her book on manners was quite clear about the rank of peers, and she certainly didn't qualify. She'd read *A Tale of Two Cities* in high school, and, though she hadn't thought it the most significant book at the time, she did remember that the French Revolution had done away with the aristocracy. She should reread it. It might be an interesting story if she weren't being forced to analyze it for credit.

She shook her head as her mind wandered and made a mental note to look for it in the library. *When was it published?* Her brows pulled together. No, she'd seen other Dickens books in the library. It must be old enough. She thought about it more. She wasn't so much concerned about *where* she was—that much was obvious—but she had no definitive idea about *when* she was. From the size of her bustles, she would guess the Victorian era, but that still left quite a large bit of time. She frowned and sighed, glancing up at the approaching forest.

"Francine?" Gideon asked. "What is it?"

She shifted her gaze to the duke when he called her, pulling her out of her literary reverie. She smiled, and he visibly tensed. She tried to devise a strategy for discovering the year. Years were printed on newspapers, business documents, books, checks, bank statements, and birth certificates. She didn't have access to any of these except books, but that wasn't going to help since knowing when a book was published wouldn't tell her how long it had been around.

"I wish I could know...what you are thinking," he said slowly. "It looks frightfully puzzling, and therefore must be terribly interesting."

She considered how she could ferret out the information she wanted and was grateful that he waited patiently while she formed her plan. Then she snapped her fingers and signed, *February 5*, but hesitated afterward as she realized the year was an issue. A serious issue. She shook her head and pointed to herself, then pointed at him. He had one brow cocked and his mouth hung open. She laughed and signed again: *My birthday is February 5*. She pointed at him again, her brows raised.

He gave a little chuckle. "Oh, I see. Do you wish to get me a gift?"

She shrugged her shoulders, imploring him with her eyes.

"I was born the twenty-sixth day of February in the year eighteen-hundred and fifty-one."

She felt shock crawl across her face. She truly was in the latter part of the 19th century.


Gideon watched her, leaning his elbows on his pommel to effectively stop the horses. "That would make me nine and twenty, my lady. Certainly an acceptable age, is it not?"

She nodded violently, nearly displacing her hat and knocking herself off-balance. Her arms shot out, and Gideon laughed as he quickly nudged Samson closer and reached over to her outstretched arm.

She lowered her arms and looked at him, into him, begging forgiveness with her eyes.

"You are forgiven, *my lady*," he whispered.

She signed my lady and shrugged.

He nodded. "You are now officially the ward of my brother. We determined it was in your best interest that we procure you a place here in England that would release you from the agreement your parents made with Lord Hepplewort."

She appeared stunned, and he waited for her to consider the situation. Her features flashed emotions of confusion and rage, then finally settled on annoyance. Her brows knit together, her mouth opened slightly, her eyes narrowed, and her jaw lifted.

He shifted his seat. "It was done in reaction to the events last night. I wanted to protect you. It was obvious you didn't want to be taken away, and once I learned about the arrangement with Hepplewort and the plans he had, I simply could not—" He was cut off when she abruptly turned Delilah and rode away.

Samson bristled and stomped. "Settle," he said firmly, stroking the Friesian's neck and patting him on the shoulder. "Just give her a minute," he added, more to himself than the horse.

Francine didn't want Gideon inspecting her, as he seemed so fond of doing. She didn't necessarily mind that he knew what she was feeling, but right now she wanted to think. She glanced over her shoulder to make sure he wasn't following. *He's manipulating me, right?* He had created a guardianship agreement with her so-called parents without even consulting her. Then again, the alternative was being returned to people she had never met. She shook her head. While being tossed about at the whim of others was commonplace in her previous life, it was no longer something she wished to tolerate, but this—this was clearly different.

She thought she understood why it would be his brother. He was close to his brother and Gideon couldn't do it himself if they had a relationship, but—why couldn't he ask? Nobody ever asked her permission for anything. Her brain, so fond of playing good cop/bad cop, thought: *Of course they didn't. It's freakin' 1880!* She looked back at him again through narrowed eyes. Gideon was behaving with much more patience than his cocky steed. She could see Samson was annoyed that Delilah had wandered off without him, and she grinned.

Maybe he didn't intend his actions to come across as such high-handed gestures. He'd been raised in a different era, a different world entirely. It was wrong, inappropriate, and impossible, but the reality was that she was in his time, not the other way around. There was a point at which she would reach her limit of handling, but this was not going to be it. She could see his reasoning, understood his behavior, and frankly, she liked the way he attempted to protect her. Nobody had ever done that. They feigned protection well, but never actually achieved it. She turned Delilah and met his gaze.

She had the most beautifully broad smile. It opened her face and brightened her eyes. Even her ears seemed to smile at him. He took a couple of short breaths, trying to release the tension that had gathered in his gut. *How could this be the same woman who crawled into my bed in the middle of the night, demanding I ruin her?* He shifted his gaze. *Perhaps her boldness requires the dark of night.* He shook his head and looked back toward her, returning his own grand but wary smile.

He nudged Samson, who was more than ready to regain his lead. They approached Francine and Delilah, the horses rubbing their muzzles together before Gideon turned Samson and they began walking back toward the wood. "I...am sorry if we behaved too expeditiously. I believed—*believe* we acted in the best interests of both you and your sisters."

Her brows drew together and he shook his head.

"That is the other thing. We also arranged guardianship for your sisters. Once we learned M. Larrabee, your, uh, father, was selling his daughters, we couldn't possibly leave them to him."

She nodded, though she knew there was something he wasn't saying. *Did he say they were sold? The Larrabees were odd, she would give him that. She certainly didn't want to go anywhere with them, or the man they said she belonged to, but to take two other girls away from their family as well?*

They reached the edge of the clearing, where the tall grass rose to meet the shade trees that protected the forest from the meadow. He jumped down and walked around Samson to help Francine.

His hands reached up, settling on her waist. She lifted her right knee from the pommel and shifted in the saddle, pulling her boot from the stirrup. Placing her hands on his shoulders, she rested her weight on him as he moved closer.

He let her slide down between his unyielding frame and Delilah, who didn't budge. Holding her at eye level, he leaned forward slightly.

*He's going to kiss me. Here in broad daylight, in this field, with Carole as a chaperone, he is going to kiss me.* She gasped and the breath she took in her mouth was his, warm and spicy like unsweetened cinnamon. *How scandalously improper.* Delilah shifted her weight, pushing them together abruptly, and their lips met in a searing kiss. He let her toes touch the ground as his arms bracketed her shoulders, putting his hands on Delilah's saddle to steady the mare behind Francine and hold her to him. Her lips parted from the pressure, and he accepted the invitation by exploring inside, sliding across the roof of her mouth with the tip of his tongue.

Her mouth opened wider as the sensation spread through her like tiny fingers, and he captured her groan, venturing deeper, tasting every part of her.

Carole politely cleared her throat from the other side of the three horses as she spread a rug below a tree and unpacked the basket Mrs. Weston had prepared. She had included fruits from the orangery with some crème fraîche, a few cuts of cold ham roasted in honey, some crusty sourdough, and a bottle of Lindisfarne Honey Mead. Carole looked at the bottle and blanched. Mrs. Weston certainly knew it was traditionally served at wedding brunches and for honeymoons. She peered behind her. All she could see below the horses were skirts tangled around legs. She stood and cleared her throat again.

"I think mayhap I should gather some berries. P'raps Chef would care to use them for a pie. Would you mind too much, Your Grace?"

Delilah shifted away from them sharply, breaking his grasp on the saddle. He clutched Francine before she could fall away and kissed

along the edge of her jaw. He heard Carole, but she sounded so far away from where they stood. He continued kissing his way down Francine's neck, unbuttoning her jacket slowly as he moved. She let out a deep breath and threw her head back to give him access as she held his shoulders.

She could no longer think. His fingers trailed down her hip from the line of velvet-covered buttons, pulling her skirts up as he nuzzled and kissed the delicate underside of her jaw.

He put his hand on her lower back and stood straight, looking into her eyes. They were light, glassy, and heavy-lidded. He blew gently across her face and her eyelashes fluttered, clearing her vision and bringing her around. He cupped her chin with his large gloved hand and handed her the button loop from her skirt.

"Oh," she whispered, "is that what you were doing down there?"

He gave her a warning gaze when she spoke, and she smiled as she buttoned up her skirt. He proffered his arm and she wrapped her hands around his elbow as they walked past the horses.

"Thank you, Carole. Have fun looking for berries, but do not go far."

"Yes, Your Grace," she answered with a small curtsey, then ducked past the trunk of a large tree.


Perry left the study to track down Shaw and inquire if he was interested in a treasure hunt, which he was. Perry had never really inspected the passageways, due to the fact that he simply didn't like them. They were dark and he assumed there wasn't anything to be seen. He was wrong. Small transom windows let in a modicum of light, allowing for safe passage, but without the additional lights one couldn't see the walls. They lit the sconces that lined the passage and had Stapleton bring extra candelabras to make the area as bright as possible.

"This woodwork is exquisite," Shaw said. "Some of these panels are inlaid with dozens of types of wood. Look here. This is a twilight setting—stars, clouds, and moon, and this one is sunrise."

Perry studied the panel. "How do you know this one isn't sunset?"

"It's on the east wall."

*He is serious,* Perry thought. As he looked at the other side of the

passage from that panel, he found a similar picture and began to believe him. "So what is the opposite of twilight?"

"Dawn," Shaw answered simply.

Perry started to consider the panels with a new respect. The tonal variations of the woodwork actually supported Shaw's assumptions.

Each panel was framed with intricate molding, which the men inspected meticulously for any movement. About halfway down the passageway, with Perry on the east wall and Shaw on the west, Perry heard a click. He stopped and turned to Shaw, bumping into him as he stared at the slightly moved panel.

"Should we? I mean, should we wait for Roxleigh?" Shaw asked.

"Like hell!" Perry carefully placed both hands on the panel. He pushed gently at first, checking the borders of the door around the frame. He glanced at Shaw, who appeared eager to follow, and Perry pushed the panel harder, the hinges groaning against the intrusion. He stepped carefully over the threshold. There were windows somewhere in the room because he could see light, but couldn't tell what it was filtering through—some sort of fabric?

He looked back to make sure Shaw was still following and then grasped one of the translucent panels. Dust wafted down around him as he felt the soft, undulating cloth.

"It must be silk chiffon," Shaw said. "That would cost a fortune. Look at all of it."

Perry gazed at him questioningly.

"Well, even wealthy men have limits, or they should at any rate. This is an extravagant type of purchase. These walls must be thirty feet high, which makes the use of silk chiffon an exorbitant expense."

Perry thought about it as he walked through the panels, deeper into the room toward the light. "Shaw, look at this," he said excitedly.

"Now *that* is what I would call beyond reasonable."

"I would have to agree."

They walked toward the bathtub, and Perry reached for the faucet.

"I wouldn't try that," Shaw said, shaking his head. "You have no idea of the source, do you? It could be an old well, or an empty cistern.

We should attempt to trace the lines before using them. I wouldn't want to cause irreparable damage."

Perry grunted and turned to the windows, where the shutters were pulled away, like giant boxes with small openings to allow a bit of light. They served to funnel the light, letting it spill from the top and illuminating the fabric panels.

Perry walked past, examining the shutters. He came to the one at the end, which looked damaged, and he took a hold of the shudder. As he opened it, the hinges on the side of the giant shutter gave way with a loud creak. It shook as it broke away from the wall, crashing to the floor, taking several of the sheer fabric panels with it. He and Shaw covered their faces, turning from the cloud of dust rising around them.

Shaw peered back at the large piece of wood on the floor. "I think perhaps we should limit our explorations of the room until we can properly judge its safety."

"Perhaps that is wise," Perry replied with a cough. He walked over to the now-uncovered window and looked out to the northern side of the meadow. "It's rather ingenious, really. I suppose none of us walked around counting the windows, and it appears as if the boxes would have prevented us from seeing inside to wonder what this room was."

"Yes. Though the way they directed the light would be more effective if the windows were clean. There's not much light coming through them now. Shall we, perhaps, go out to the garden and see if we can locate the windows from below?" Shaw asked.

Perry shook his head and smiled. "Where is your sense of adventure?" He chuckled, then heard another groan of wood from somewhere in the room. "Ah, on second thought, let's do go out. I will have Stapleton make arrangements to clean and uncover the remaining windows."

Francine straightened her skirts as Gideon sat with his back up against the trunk of a tree. He reached for the wine and read the label, then smiled. Picking up the wine goblets and filling them about half-full, he handed Francine a glass and lifted his to hers. "A willing foe and sea room," he said. They touched glasses, and she looked at him, befuddled, as she drank. He laughed. "Royal Navy toast...and it is Friday."

She shook her head, still not quite understanding the reference.

*Navy, huh? How very Officer and a Gentleman,* she thought with a smile.

He reached into the basket and pulled out a small bundle of ripe strawberries. He started to remove his riding gloves, but she grasped his hands, loosening them finger by finger before she pulled them off and massaged his palms. He picked up one of the berries and, dipping it in the crème fraîche, lifted it to her lips. She bit into the plump fruit, sighing at the fresh, sweet flavor.

*Navy?* she signed as he fed her another strawberry.

He nodded. "Both Perry and I served in the Royal Navy. It isn't expected of the peerage to serve, and even when done the heir stays at home for safety. My brother had something to prove. I followed. As it happened he was well suited to the sea, while there was little use for me there. There's not much to tell beyond that. It gave me a sense of belonging, a desire for that type of camaraderie. Brought Perry and me closer."

*How?* she signed.

He smiled. "Before the Navy, I thought of him only as a child. A spoiled, impossible child who couldn't take care of himself. He proved to be a taut hand, moving up ranks quickly, working hard, commanding his own vessel. It was quite a feat, considering his age. Actually, he only returned recently. I have been back since Darius, my sire, passed. Nearly four years," he said as he looked away, his features darkening. "My father wasn't close to us. I believe he loved my mother uncontrollably, and when she fell ill he was destroyed. He withdrew, unable to accept the circumstances. Though I don't know the truth of it, as we never spoke of anything of consequence. This is all conjecture on my part. I suppose trying to reconcile that missing part of my life. Perhaps that was partly why we both abandoned him." He turned back and smiled at her, but it didn't reach beyond his lips. She placed her hand on his, and they sat quietly.

He reached up and grasped a tendril of her hair, smoothing it between his fingers. "Tis a warm, rich color," he said softly.

She smiled. *Mother-number-three always said it was the color of Kansas wheat at harvest,* she signed.

His fingers stilled as he looked at her. "Kansas—in the colonies? What would you be doing there?"

Her chin dropped and turned away as she realized her error.

Then, thinking about his statement, she became defensive. "I was never there, but I believe they prefer to be referred to as the United States of America," she whispered sternly.

"I beg your pardon, my lady," he said with a chuckle. "Kansas wheat must be a sight. I would have likened it more to a blonde than your brunette color," he said as he smiled wryly.

*Centuries pass and still the grudge?* she signed.

"It's a family grudge, far be it for me to let it lie. What of this 'mother-number-three'? Did the nuns in the convent not have names?"

She laughed, trying hard to stifle it, to no avail. *Well,* she signed finally, *they do all dress alike.*

His head fell back as booming laughter broke loose from his chest. It sent a shiver through her. He reached for another strawberry and she signed, *I have sisters?* He poured a little more honey mead into her glass, dropping the strawberry to the bottom, and told her about the eldest sister and the two younger ones that were also now wards of his brother. She could tell he didn't go into everything they had learned about M. Larrabee and her betrothed, Lord Hepplewort.

Carole walked back into the meadow with a small basket filled with dark berries, and Gideon and Francine stood. The servant swept up the remains of the picnic in the blanket, securing it to her saddle as he checked the horses.

Francine waited patiently with Delilah, but Gideon took the mare by the rein and led her to Kalliope, fastening her to the back of the saddle.

Francine looked up at him, confused.

"We shouldn't test you overmuch. That was quite a ride." He held his hand out to her.

She walked over and he swept her up astride Samson, then in one lithe movement he mounted the horse behind her. She drew in a sharp breath as his body settled closely to her, his chest pushing against her back and the feel of him sending a chill across her skin.

He reached around her, grasping the rein and turning the horse toward the stables as Carole followed.

He pushed Samson into a trot, bouncing them gently together, creating a warm friction. Then he leaned into her as he urged Samson to a gallop. Francine sank back into his sinewy frame, resting her hands on his thighs, reveling at the smooth movement of the muscles beneath his skin. She closed her eyes and breathed slowly, feeling the rush of air as it hit her face and stole her breath. His muscles tensed and hardened behind her, moving with her.

She sighed. It was heavenly.

He slowed the horse to a walk.

She could have easily been lulled to sleep. She reached up, stroking his defined jaw, then put her hands on the pommel. "Hepplewhatsit," she whispered, before she realized she'd spoken aloud.

"Shh," he said. "I already warned you about speaking." He paused. "Hepplewort."

"Betrothed?" she whispered against his jaw.

"You really are tempting a dragon, my lady," he said, laughing. "Yes, betrothed. I believe you tried to get away from him, and he set his hounds—" He stopped and she looked up, trying to see his face.

"No!" His face paled. "Lilly," he whispered. "Why did I not see this? We need to get back to the manor." He took off for the paddock, yelling for Davis. Her hands tightened on his thighs as they ran and she couldn't help but to smile, even with the concern she'd heard laced through his voice.

"Yes, Your Grace," Davis answered, running from the stable toward the field. Gideon halted a few feet away, jumping down and pulling Francine with him.

"Watch for Carole, she's just over the rise."

"Yes, Your Grace."

"As soon as Carole gets here, I want you to ready the carriage."

"Your Grace, Grover and Gentry have the carriage to Kelso, but they should be returning soon. Should I prepare your curricle?"

"Damn it all!" Gideon cursed. His voice overwhelmed the meadow and Davis jumped at the sound. "No, thank you, Davis. It's much too far for the curricle and I don't yet trust the mares."

Francine paled. She had never seen him so angry, but she wasn't as much terrified as she was worried for him. She tried to reach for him, but he was unaware.

"Let me know as soon as they arrive, and switch the horses if they need rest," he said finally.

"Yes, Your Grace," Davis replied shakily as he took Samson. Gideon turned and strode toward the manor, tugging Francine behind him as she squealed in surprise.

Perry and Shaw followed the passage down to the kitchen and called for Stapleton.

"Stapleton, in the passage behind the family suites we have opened a room." Perry saw Stapleton frown, but went on. "I have left the panel open. I would appreciate it if, carefully, you could have some men remove the window covers and clean the windows. Perhaps you could also have the fabric panels removed for cleaning, though I'm not sure they are in good enough condition to retain. I suppose the servants will figure that out when they pull them down."

Stapleton nodded and left the kitchen.

Perry saw Chef glaring at the filthy intruders in her workspace, so he and Shaw turned and also left the kitchen.

They strolled outside and gazed up at the manor. "It should have been obvious. Look how dark they are," Shaw said.

"Yes, but they are also above the orangery, out of the way of a more direct line of sight." Perry wanted a better view and turned to walk farther away from the manor, then stopped. Gideon was pulling Francine briskly behind him, his face carved in anger. Perry frowned, then ran into the manor to meet him, leaving Shaw staring after.

# TWENTY-ONE

"There's probably no way to prove it was him," Perry said wearily. "Rox—"

"What?" Gideon asked, looking up at his brother from the other side of the desk.

"I said... We probably won't be able to prove it was him," Perry repeated to his brother, who was quite obviously not paying attention.

"Yes, I know. I was just trying to think of something. Anything. He shouldn't be able to get away with what he did to Lilly and Francine. I won't let him."

"Gideon. We have to find out where Hepplewort is. Francine doesn't remember anything, and what Lilly does— It puts them both in a great deal of danger. Lilly should be protected. If we could find him—"

"We have to meet with him, Perry. Or have you forgotten that you are required to break his contract with Larrabee?"

Perry appeared stunned. "Must you remind me? I was having such a nice afternoon." He rubbed his hand back and forth across his jaw. "Rox, there is something else." He paused, considering the timing, but then he shrugged. "I have something you should see."

"Does it have something to do with your current dishevelment?"

Perry scowled as he stood, motioning for Gideon to follow. They walked into the first floor passageway, which was still well lit.

Gideon looked at the walls. "What the devil? I never—" He glanced at Perry.

"I don't think any of us did. It is quite beautiful." He ran his fingertips over the smooth patterns in the wood as he walked. They reached the open panel and Gideon stopped his brother with one hand on his shoulder.

"Wait—please."

Perry nodded. "Of course."

Gideon stepped over the threshold into the room, drawing his breath in sharply. The smell of the dust barely masked a scent which pulled memories from his head like the icy water that crashes over rapids. His mind spun through the recollections at a devil's pace. His mother's embrace, her soft secure arms, the clear green of her eyes, the way she always rescued him— He suddenly remembered all of it. Including when she hadn't been able to rescue him anymore.

"I thought it was a dream," he said quietly. He reached up to the panels, walking through the maze as the dust drifted like snow around him. Going to the bathtub, he sat at the edge and turned it on. The pipes shook, and a loud groan tore through the manor walls like the wheels of a freight train sliding on a rusty track.

Perry rushed toward him. "Rox, Shaw said we—"

Gideon waved his hand, cutting him off. Water poured from the pipe, brown and muddy at first, then clean and clear. He put his hand under it and looked up to his brother.

"I have been here before." He turned and shut the water off. "This was our mother's room."

Perry stared around the room in awe. "Tell me," he replied, sitting at the edge of the tub next to him. Gideon opened his mouth to start as Mrs. Weston rushed into the room.

"Oh, Your Grace, my lord, we heard a terrible noise belowstairs."

Gideon looked at her apprehensively. "You knew of this room."

"Aye, Your Grace, at one time. But it has been naught but a memory for many years. Your father, may he rest in peace, ordered it left. He built it for her, of course. And when she was taken... Well." She looked down as she twisted her hands in her skirts. "He could not bear to remember," she whispered in a faltering tone.

Gideon turned his gaze away. "Why was she taken?"

"Oh, Your Grace, you know the ans—"

"No, Weston, why exactly was she taken? She survived in the manor just fine, then one day she was gone. I want to know why my father didn't want to put her up anymore."

"No, Your Grace. It wasn't like that." Mrs. Weston paused, her eyes reddened from falling dust and threatening tears. "It was spring when she—left. She was so lovely in the spring. Ribbons in her hair, with fresh flowers from the gardens." Mrs. Weston smiled, reminiscing. "I loved her, you know. She was like kin to me, as are the two of you."

Gideon looked around and grabbed a cushioned chair, pulling it in front of the bathtub so Mrs. Weston could sit.

"Oh, no, Your Grace, I'm al—" He pointed at the chair with a lifted brow and she sat down. She sighed. "The window, the broken one. She used to open it and stand in the wind. She loved the breeze as it came up off the meadow. I would come to find her here, standing next to that window. Then that day, she crawled up into the window and was leaning...out."

The brothers looked at each other, their faces mirrored images of tension. Mrs. Weston wept. "I do not know what happened, Your Grace. I was watching the breeze coming in, and the next thing I knew your father ran in and pulled her down," she said as she cried. "She was distraught. She didn't understand why he was upset. She wailed all night, for he blocked the panel so she couldn't come in here. She wasn't ever the same."

Perry leaned forward. "Did she— Was she trying to kill herself?" he asked, the sound scarcely more than a breath.

"I don't know, my lord. I wouldn't think it. But your father, he believed it. And after that day, after he kept her out of here, she did try. So she was taken to Bedlam, Your Grace. He said it was to protect her from herself," she whispered, looking directly at Gideon. Then she looked down, the wet lines of tears dividing her dust-covered face. They heard a sound behind her and Gideon stood, spying a figure through the silk fabrics.

"Francine," he said as she pulled aside a panel.

Her mouth dropped open to form words, but no sound came out as they all waited. Tears streaked her dusty cheeks as the particles in the air irritated her eyes, making the color glow with a chimerical blue fire.

"I am so sorry," she whispered.

He strolled toward her, and her face lifted to meet his when he stood in front of her. He took her face in his palms, smearing the lines of tears and pulling her to him. She put her hands around his waist, splayed across his lower back, and she leaned her head into his chest, tucking under his chin, breathing quietly as his hands held her tightly to him. "I'm so sorry," she said again, unable to find better words.

"Shh." He gently massaged her back with his wide hand. He took her face in his hands again and placed a kiss on her forehead, then turned to Perry and Mrs. Weston.

"You should go," Perry said. "We shall be out in a moment."

Gideon nodded, leading Francine from the room.

"Westy. This wasn't your fault," Perry said.

"Oh, my lord, I believe I know that. But I think, if I had been there—if I had protected her. I do not know, my lord. I just wish—" Perry put his hands on her shoulders and she peered up at him. "I am so sorry, my lord."

"There is nothing to be sorry for." He could see that she was entirely overtaxed. He stood and pulled her close for an embrace as he tried to think of a way to push the mood back toward the light and airy, away from the dark and dismal.

They quit the chamber, but Perry stopped her as she was headed downstairs. "Westy, I can't bear to see you so worked up. Roxleigh has you running around here on pins and needles after his lady."

She glanced back at him. "Tis true, my lord. He has given me charge of her. To see to her needs, and to make sure she is safe."

"I do not want you to be responsible for her anymore."

"Oh, my lord, have I—"

"No, Westy, nothing like that. I believe you have done a wonderful job attending her. I don't like that you are over worried. I have watched Lady Francine, and I believe she is perfectly able to do as she pleases. Carole can attend her when necessary."

Mrs. Weston turned away from him, wringing her hands. "My lord, I do like to attend her."

He nodded. "Let me be clear then. You may tend her, for so long as you wish, but you answer to me now. Not to him. In all of her concerns, I am her guardian. That's how it will be done. Is that understood?"

"Yes, my lord. What will I tell His Grace?"

"You won't tell him anything. I will deal with him."

"Yes, my lord." Mrs. Weston curtseyed and moved to go belowstairs.

Perry returned to the chamber and looked around. He'd no

memories of the soft, billowy panels. No memory of the tiled bathtub, the large cushioned bed covered with brightly colored pillows and inches of dust. The muted vibrancy of the dyes begged a beautiful memory that would not come. Had she ever brought him here? Or was it only Gideon who was part of her world?

Gideon escorted Francine into the private parlor and motioned for her to sit. He rang for Carole to chaperone; his brother's newfound sense of responsibility and honor wasn't something he meant to test anytime soon. Not that he believed he and Perry would find themselves at opposing ends of a rapier, but that his brother's pride wasn't something he wished to damage. When Carole arrived, Francine was on the settee and Gideon across from her in one of the chairs. He read to her from *Wuthering Heights.*

"Your Grace?" Carole said when he paused. "Grover and Gentry have returned from Kelso with the new governess. They only just arrived. I believe Davis is seeing to the carriage as you had requested."

"Thank you, Carole. Please see to Lady Francine." She nodded with a curtsey and he stood, turning back to Francine. "I must beg my leave. I need to interview the governess. I hope to see you for supper."

Francine frowned. He reached for her hand and bowed as he kissed her wrist. "Good afternoon, my lady."

Gideon walked out of the parlor and straight into his brother, who was just leaving the passageway.

"Francine?" Perry asked.

"She is in the parlor with Carole. She's fine, just a bit surprised."

"You never told her of our mother?"

"No. When would I have had the time?" Gideon changed the subject. "The carriage is here, but it's a bit late to return to Kelso. We should interview the governess. Stapleton has her in the green parlor."

"You mean the spring parlor, do you not?" Perry corrected, trying to lighten the mood.

Gideon glanced at him as they descended the stairs. "What?"

"Look at it. Everything about it says spring."

"Bedding a designer?"

Perry laughed. "I would equate it more like courting disaster, which would be why the whole thing is over. Though I did get quite a nice sitting room out of it."

Gideon smiled. Perry felt his brother's disquiet and clapped him on the shoulder.

"Spring parlor, then?" Gideon asked with another half smile.

"By all means."


Miss Emily Faversham waited in a soft green chair. She thought the parlor was wonderfully appointed in various hues of green: deep emerald, flower petal, grass, and moss, all surrounded by hues of cream and ivory. It reminded her of spring, with the thinly striped damask fabrics in cream and mint, bordered by emerald trims and pearl beading. The curtains were also quite lovely—the heavy emerald velvet drapes were pulled back, leaving light and airy cream alternating with flower-petal green panels of silk georgette to filter the sunlight into the room. She stood and paced in front of the windows, and then she sat, only to rise and pace again.

Her last appointment with the Tanvers had ended quite abruptly. She had expected at least to attend the youngest of the girls through her first Season, but they'd sent her home to Kelso. And just as unexpectedly, she was retrieved by the Duke of Roxleigh for a position. She had no idea for what position he would need her. The notorious recluse had no children or bride to bear them, unless his wife was even more reclusive, which was entirely doubtful. *Someone* would know of his marriage. Emily sat on the damask striped settee, holding an emerald green brocade pillow to her chest.

She didn't want to be a nursemaid, or lady's maid, or anything other than a governess. She loved to teach. She'd considered that her love of knowledge was what had ended her tenure with the Tanvers, but the girls had always sworn allegiance to her. They promised never to tell of their extensive lessons that most young women weren't allowed, history and government among the most inappropriate of them. Sadly, a knowledgeable woman wasn't a marriageable woman. And an unmarriageable woman was of no use to a blue blood, who only needed daughters to make good matches with other peers, thereby increasing the father's rank and pull.

The butler opened the door and she jumped off the settee and curtseyed deeply. "Your Grace, my lord, I am Miss Emily Faversham. You requested me?" she asked, her voice faltering slightly at the end.

"Miss Faversham, thank you for agreeing to come on such short notice. Please." Roxleigh motioned to the settee. She sat back down as the brothers moved to the chairs across from her. She was quite stunned by their presence and demeanor. In point of fact, she would have been stunned if it had been only one of them, but the force of them twofold had her perfectly speechless. They exuded power, grace, and propriety. There was a long silence as they made no effort to hide the fact that they were looking her over quite thoroughly. She blushed at the inspection, then her wits quite abruptly returned and she spoke.

"Would you like me to stand and turn so you can have a better look?" she asked a bit indignantly.

Roxleigh and Trumbull exchanged a swift glance and Roxleigh nodded to him.

"I see," she said. "So have I passed your test, then?"

Trumbull smiled. "Well, Miss Faversham, we are not interested in employing someone who is weak of mind." He looked directly in her eyes and added, "Or spirit. Generally people of lower station are unable to stand their ground with us, particularly when we both are involved. I refuse to hire a governess who would cower to either of us. Because of my—somewhat legendary pursuits. a less than stalwart governess might call my new wards' respectability into question. It is something I wish to avoid entirely."

She looked from one brother to the other. "There is not a chance anyone in the *ton* would believe I would allow for any such impropriety. So am I to be your employee then, my lord? I wasn't aware you had a ward."

Trumbull shook his head. "Not yet, and there are three."

"Oh!" Emily realized she was still clutching the green pillow from the settee and set it aside.

"Certainly you can handle three young ladies, can you not?" Roxleigh asked.

"Of course I can, Your Grace. I was just surprised by the… suddenness of it. And the quantity. I mean no offense, of course, my lord, but—"

"But I see you understand now the importance of a respectable and strong governess for my wards."

"Why, yes, my lord. Quite."

"And you won't allow my brother to ruin a single girl, will you, Miss Faversham?" Roxleigh asked.

She looked at him, affronted. "Your Grace, I say!"

"Or *my* brother?" Trumbull asked sardonically.

"My lord! This is quite an unpleasant line of questioning. I assumed you would want to know of my skills as an instructor, my manners and ability to teach deportment and morals, not that I will be able to control the behavior of a rake and a recluse such as the likes of you both!" She sharply raised her chin.

Trumbull and Roxleigh looked at her, then Trumbull smiled at Roxleigh, quite obviously satisfied with the set-down. "Miss Faversham. We are very interested in your ability to teach. However, if you were unable to undertake this situation with the amount of respectability I require, then your intelligence is of no import. It is of the greatest consequence that you behave beyond reproach when it comes to the question of the young ladies' reputations under my guardianship. Is that understood?"

"Yes, my lord. Very well understood." She straightened her skirts. "As I believe we have thoroughly covered that particular subject, I must insist upon informing you why I believe I was sent from the Tanvers household." She twisted her fingers nervously.

"Sent away?" Roxleigh asked, leaning forward. "Mrs. Weston said they had come of an age that you were no longer required. This is not true?" There was a clear edge of disappointment in his voice.

"Not exactly, Your Grace." She cleared her throat and looked directly at him. "I chose, without the permission of Lord Tanvers—" She cleared her throat again and willed herself to continue. "—to instruct the young ladies in the same fashion as the young men." The duke gazed at her as if he was still waiting for her explanation. She glanced at Trumbull, who looked quite the same and, once again, cleared her throat. "They— they did not tell me that this is why I was sent home. However, there could be no other explanation. I was expecting to attend the youngest of the ladies through her first Season."

The room was silent.

"What exactly does it mean, that you instructed them the same as the young men?" Roxleigh asked, his brows pursed in concern.

"I gave them lessons in history and government, Your Grace, as well as the required lessons in deportment, languages, literature, and the like."

Roxleigh looked at Trumbull. "Women are not taught these things?"

Trumbull laughed. "No, Your Grace, most women are not."

"That explains much," Roxleigh said, more to himself than anyone else. "I thought the Society chits were merely playing at being ridiculous. I had no idea they actually are."

Trumbull chuckled. "I wouldn't exactly put it that way. How could you not know that women were not taught the same as men?"

Emily cleared her throat, rousing the brothers from their discussion. "May I assume then that my teachings will be accepted under your supervision, my lord?" she asked, hopeful.

Trumbull appeared to think for a moment, exchanging glances with Roxleigh before holding her gaze. "I find your lessons to be acceptable," he said, then looked back at Roxleigh. "We will simply explain that, since the young ladies are from France, we felt they needed lessons that would give them knowledge of their new country." He shrugged.

"Or we educate them and Society be damned. I answer to no one."

Trumbull smiled at his brother's statement and Emily felt her eyes widen.

She shook her head quickly. "They are French?"

"Yes, Miss Faversham, they are. The eldest is here now. You will meet her shortly. In the morning you will accompany her parents to France to retrieve the other girls, after which you will meet us in London. Of course, the eldest, Lady Francine—" The duke smiled as he said her name. "—will not need lessons, as she seems quite intelligent, so you may merely be required to chaperone for her."

"I'm to France? In the morning? Was that an official offer, then?"

Roxleigh looked at Trumbull, who nodded.

"Then I accept. However, I must warn you: if my rules with regards to the ladies are not followed resolutely, I will leave your employ rather than be found lacking in my own respect for propriety. Is that understood?" She looked first to Trumbull then to Roxleigh, who nodded. "Well, then. Perhaps I could see my room so I may freshen up from the trip, and I could meet *your* young lady," she said to Roxleigh.

He looked at her questioningly. "I beg your pardon?" She noted that he seemed slightly annoyed.

She stood. "May I speak freely?"

Roxleigh lifted his chin cautiously and she cleared her throat again.

"I believe I understand your situation at this point, Your Grace, and mean no disrespect to you. As long as you bring no disrespect to my name, I have no qualms with serving as Lady Francine's chaperone, as needed. I can see in your eyes your most honorable intentions to this young lady and wish you the best. Simply keep in mind my duty to *you* extends to *Society*."

Roxleigh stood as well, looking down on her. "You have my word, as Duke of Roxleigh, that your reputation is in no danger here, Miss Faversham."

She smiled, then turned to Trumbull. "My room?"

"Of course." Trumbull jumped from the chair, but Roxleigh waved him off as he walked to the pull to call for Stapleton.

"Tell me about them?" she asked, looking at Trumbull with a smile.

"Oh, well, Lady Francine is nineteen. Then there are Amélie—something—and Maryse, who are sixteen and fourteen, I believe." He added apologetically, "We haven't yet met."

She frowned. "You haven't met?"

"Yes, well, this is all quite sudden, within days. One day, actually," he said, chuckling as he held her gaze. "And I am not at all used to this situation and having not yet met them, I— I find it difficult to relate to them as actual, um, as people yet. So, I beg your pardon."

She stared at him, suddenly realizing that the situation she had agreed to was much more complex than she'd first thought. She wondered if perhaps the rakish brother would make an advance and she'd be allowed to leave her position. *I can only hope*, she thought as the butler entered the parlor to show her to her room.

Roxleigh spoke as he followed her out. "Miss Faversham, it has been my pleasure. I do hope we haven't terrified you too greatly, and would ask that you join us for supper tonight, if you are able."

She looked at the duke and nodded, then followed Stapleton up the stairs.

Perry walked out of the parlor. "You had better be on your best behavior around that one, Rox. I have no doubt she will find you wanting at some point, at which time she won't hesitate to cut you down to your knees."

"Yes, Perry," he said with a grin, "she will do fine."

Francine was in the private parlor with Carole, reading *The Divine Comedy* and trying to relax before supper. It wasn't working very well. Her mind kept returning to that room. How beautiful it must have been when it was fresh and new. She would have loved a room just like that— warm, inviting, safe.

Francine now understood why Mrs. Weston had been so upset with her when she found her in the window that day. What Gideon must have felt, to know his mother was out there and he was helpless to do anything. She couldn't imagine losing her mother like he had—watching the struggle, yet powerless. She had long since closed herself off from the types of relationships required for those feelings, because the pain was more than she wanted to deal with. Her mother and father had been gone for more than a decade, and she was far too removed to even try to imagine such a closeness. She thought about losing Gideon and her heart wrenched. She wasn't sure she ever wanted to feel that kind of pain again.

She needed to get him alone. She wished the ceremony surrounding propriety wasn't so strict and awkward. She felt compelled to try to understand the feelings he held for his mother and his father. He had a way of making her feel, like she never had. Before, a sunrise was only light, but when he was near it was more. It was the miraculous exchange of darkness for illumination. If he spoke of his parents, maybe she would begin to understand that depth of emotion—maybe she would be able to experience it for herself.

Gideon and Perry waited patiently in the great entrance as Shaw emerged from the library. Gideon nodded to him. "Good evening, Shaw."

"Your Grace, I have been in the library researching the manor. I found the old plans in the drafting table. I realize you have probably seen them before, but we should have known of this room long before now. I understand the plumbing works?" Shaw asked with a cutting glance toward Perry.

"It wasn't me." Perry raised his hands and pointed at Gideon.

Shaw chuckled and nodded. "My belief is that the water comes from an underground cistern fed by a deep well, most likely the same cistern that feeds the fountain in the maze." He looked at Gideon. "I believe running water throughout the manor is a distinct possibility if you are interested in considering that. Perhaps just for the family suites, kitchen, and main guest suites. Not sure. We should discuss that more. They did have a system set up for heating the water to that room, though it is in disrepair. I am quite surprised they ran water to a first floor room but not the kitchens. The kitchen would need a pump to bring the water out of the well, but the cistern would feed the water throughout the manor faster. We could also heat the water in the tubs. Not to mention, standing showers." He paused and finally noticed Gideon and Perry gawking. "What?"

Perry smiled at him.

"You are entirely too efficient," Gideon said. "I had no idea there was anything in that drafting table. I would be very interested in the plans you found. As far as your ideas for water, I like them. Continue with what you are working on. For the present, supper and some mindless conversation would be well-ordered, so come up with something to discuss that has nothing to do with business, the missing room, guardianship, or anything else of great import."

"I see. I will, um, consider my options."

Gideon smiled as they all turned toward the stairs to find Francine and Miss Faversham descending, arm in arm.

Perry leaned over to Gideon. "Lots of trouble," he said quietly.

Gideon sighed. His tension had eased at the sight of Francine, but his brother's ribbing caused him to tense. He reached for Francine's hand as she stopped at the bottom stair and he kissed her wrist. He heard Miss Faversham clear her throat and he straightened swiftly to smile at her. "Miss Faversham, I trust your accommodations are agreeable?"

"Yes, Your Grace, they are perfectly suitable for the night."

"Good."

"I have packed for the trip. I trust the rest of my things can be taken with your party to London?"

"Of course."

"And what of Lady Francine while I am away?"

"Carole has been acting as chaperone and will continue in your absence. You are more than welcome to give her your own explicit instructions if you wish."

"I appreciate that, Your Grace. I would like to speak with her after supper."

"As you will. I'll have Stapleton make the arrangements. Shall we?" He turned for the dining room as Stapleton swept the doors open.

Gideon stood at the head of the table with Perry on his right. He looked to Miss Faversham, who nodded and placed Francine on his left, as she was the next highest rank in the room. Shaw was seated next to Perry and Miss Faversham next to Francine.

Shaw managed to come up with several topics of conversation of minor import, from the style of dresses worn at the opera to the differences between barouches, phaetons and curricles, and why the duke owned all three, as well as recently published books and plays.

It seemed Gideon and Francine were drawn together by an intangible force. Their hands often brushed as they both reached for seasonings or silver. By the end of supper, they were both wound so tight from the momentary encounters that retreat was the only option.

Gideon retired to the library with the men to peruse the hidden plans, and Francine followed Miss Faversham to the warm and inviting evening parlor.

As she looked around, Francine realized it was the first time she'd been in this room. It was more masculine than the other parlor, decorated in a rich burgundy with gold trim. The gold was simple striping and piping, not tassels and gilding. Several more settees and chairs occupied the room since it was an evening parlor and used for entertaining.

The women sat together on one of the settees by the fire and Miss Faversham told Francine more of her previous position.

Francine interjected minimally, whispering. She felt her voice getting stronger, but she didn't wish to take any chances on damaging it further, so she was trying to abide by Gideon's wishes and not speak as much as possible.

"I do hope your voice is recovered when I reach London," Miss Faversham said. "I want to learn more about you. I wish I could use the sign language I have seen you using. It is wonderful—perhaps you could teach me some when I return?"

Francine smiled and nodded, also wishing she could speak, but a bit thankful because it protected her from saying something wrong, like *I learned sign language from a girl with no home, from Five Points in Denver.* Without much conversation, they decided to turn in. Miss Faversham would be leaving early and needed rest, and Francine wanted to relax and read some more in the private parlor.

"He's more myself than I am. Whatever our souls are made of, his and mine are the same, and Linton's is as different as a moonbeam from lightning, or frost from fire." Francine read the passage from *Wuthering Heights* aloud. She put the book down on the small table next to the settee, closing her eyes and absorbing the prose.

"You are more myself that I am," Gideon said, the words rumbling forth in that baritone Francine loved so well. She stood and looked at the entryway. "Whatever our souls are made of, yours—" The words reverberated through his torso. "—and mine—" He paused, looking into her eyes. "—are the same." His voice came from deep within his core, raspy and coarse. It burnished her soul. She gasped, feeling his voice beneath her skin, firing every nerve. He silently shut the parlor door, engaged the bolt, and walked toward her.

"Gideon," she whispered.

"Francine, I am going to kiss you."

She looked up at him. His hair was messy from the day, falling over one smoldering green eye.

"Ah, Gideon." She whispered his name again, letting it float softly from her lips.

The tension inside him broke loose and his mouth descended to hers, their lips meeting in strength and softness, his begging hers to open to him as she sucked and licked his lips. He massaged the hollow beneath her ear with his thumb and she sighed. He took advantage, delving into her offer with his tongue. He tasted of sweet red port and undone passion.

She shut her eyes tightly, allowing his supplication.

His lips released her but their gazes held as he gently lowered her to the settee. She stared up at him, her long dark lashes distorting the room like a screen. Something about his countenance had her heart rushing to keep up. He sat at the other end of the small settee and leaned back against the corner with one knee bent, lazily resting on the seat beside her.

"Lay your hands on me," he whispered, his voice low.

Her eyes widened and she reached out to his knee, her hand shaking like the top of an overheated teakettle.

"No," he said quietly, and she drew her hand back. He reached out, grasping her wrist to lead her as he spread his thighs. "On your knees."

She moved slowly to the floor in front of him, a bit frightened by the forceful demand. He released her wrist, stretched his arms wide along the back of the settee as he watched her, waiting.

She finally reached up, unraveling the delicate folds of his neck cloth before sitting back.

He nodded.

She unbuttoned his silk waistcoat, spreading it wide across his abdomen, the heat of her hands sinking through the cotton of his shirt. He hissed, drawing breath through his teeth, and leaned his head back on the settee.

"Keep going," he growled.

Her forearm inadvertently brushed the rise of his manhood. She gasped at the thick hardness she felt through the fabric of his trousers.

"Oh, lord," he inhaled sharply. She smoothed her hands up the front of his shirt and started undoing it, slowly revealing his warm, smooth chest in the flickering candlelight.

She pushed the shirt open, teasing his nipples with her thumbs, and he tensed with a groan. Her manner instantly shifted to brazen. She ran her hands down the inside of his shirt, tracing the ridges of his muscles as she spread the shirt wider, pulling it from his trousers.

His breath came faster as she leaned forward and circled his navel, then placed a kiss in its depth, smoothing the soft black dusting of hair that encircled it and trailed into his trousers.

She gazed up at his face. His head was thrown back over the edge of the settee, his mouth open, his breath fast and heavy. She traced that patch of skin on his stomach, tucking her fingers beneath his trousers to

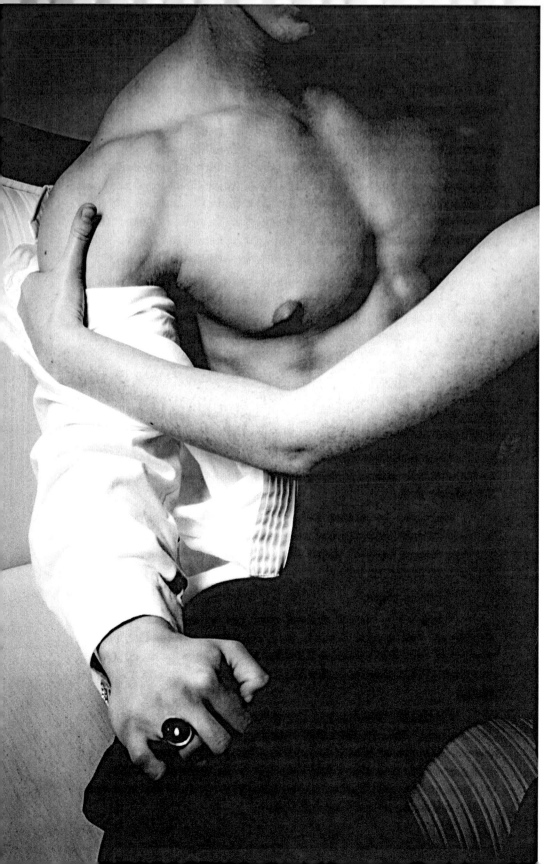

feel the wet tip of his erection. She gasped at the unexpected moisture and his hips jerked.

He gripped her wrist and pulled her hands back then leaned forward, his hot mouth on her neck as he pushed her down on the thick, plush carpet beneath them. He knelt over her, one hand on her neck and the other running up her leg, tickling the sensitive skin behind her knee, moving her skirts higher. His lips kissed a trail of heat down her chest to the bodice of her dress, biting at her nipple through her garments. He ran his thumb over her kiss-swollen lips and pushed it in her mouth. She drew on it, sucking hard on his salty taste as she watched him.

He lifted her skirts and tore at the opening to her drawers, splitting them to the waist. His finger slipped into her hot, wet sheath. Again she was ready for him. She arched up, releasing his thumb with her gasp. Massaging her gently, he kissed her soft belly through the tear in her drawers.

She breathed deeply as he kissed, and kissed, and kissed, knowing what would happen next. He ventured lower and lower, until his mouth was buried in the crest of her privacy, his heavy breathing creating a cool, tingling sensation over her aroused flesh and her heart sang.

There really was no other explanation for it. The feel of his mouth on her—*on her*—was so arousing her entire body was humming with the little shocks of it.

He teased her hidden nub with his tongue and she tangled her hands in his hair. Drawing her knees up and arching her back, she angled her hips toward him. He tasted slowly, his tongue delving deeper and deeper until it slipped inside.

"Gideon, please."

"Hush." His breath fanned over her exposed flesh and she shuddered. His tongue plunged and his finger circled. She felt the tendrils of electricity coursing from her toes to her belly, the tightening and relaxing, her muscles increasing their cadence, marching toward her center.

He slid his knuckle into her as he suckled the little nub of flesh and she came undone, the waves coursing through her body, wracking her violently against him as he held onto her, pushing her climax higher and higher. He rose above her, listening to her sighs and looking into her passion-flustered features as she inhaled powerfully and repeatedly before collapsing on the floor below him.

*I am never going to recover from this man.* This wasn't anything like she had read in the romance novels that mother-number-two had, or the movies she and her foster sister watched on cable in the middle of the night.

This was so much more.

This was everything.


He stroked her legs then straightened her skirts as he sat back and willed his overexcited body to calm. He watched her for innumerable moments, realizing he was going to remain in a turgid state until long after he was away from her. He shook his head and pulled her limp, sated body into his arms, holding her as tight as possible against himself to minimize any movement between them. He stood with her and walked to the parlor door, opening it quietly and slipping through. He carried her to her suite, setting her on the bed.

She reached up, smoothing her hand over his jaw.

He smiled down at her and loosened her dress, kissing her lips. "Francine," he said, placing a finger over her mouth to keep her silent. "I have to go before we are discovered. I should never have come to you tonight. I—should not have. We really do need a chaperone." He shook his head with a quiet laugh.

She smiled as she leaned back into the bank of downy pillows, speechless as she watched him disappear back into the passage.

He returned to his room, entirely disheveled but not caring in the least. *The question is no longer when will I see her next, but can I survive one day, one hour, or one minute without her? And I simply cannot.* He hadn't meant to do seduce her. He'd only wanted to see her once more before going to bed, but when he heard her reading in the parlor he was drawn in. He hadn't meant to, he kept telling himself—but the look she gave him…

Well, he'd felt entirely unnerved. He groaned loudly. He had to find some control, or at least some semblance of it. He stripped what was left of his clothing, unceremoniously leaving it on the floor at the foot of his bed. Falling to the pillows, he rolled under the sheets and tried to sleep.

# TWENTY-TWO

he next morning, the Larrabees arrived at Eildon Hill early to gather the governess and outriders. Then they loaded the carriage and left.

Stapleton ordered footmen to remove the box shutters, curtains, and panels from the duchess' room. Mrs. Weston had the fabrics in the laundry house, carefully trying to clean them so they could be re-hung. There was a lightness to the work. Scrubbing away the years of dust and debris cleansed the room and her memories. She wanted to see it again the way it had been, when everyone was amazed by it.

Mrs. Weston also felt that Gideon should at least see the room back together before deciding whether to destroy it. She certainly hoped he would save the chamber, since his father, Darius, had designed it for his mother, wanting a calm, beautiful area for her to relax and read and spend time with her beloved boys. He had spent a fortune on the decorations and the installation of the tub and running water.

With the curtains and panels down and the windows cleaned, the barren room appeared cavernous. There was a large, low bed against one wall with an overstuffed horsehair mattress and countless pillows. Behind the velvet drapes that had lined the walls were bookshelves filled with small trinkets and keepsakes that Mrs. Weston planned to give to the brothers.

There were hundreds of small items they'd collected: pressed leaves, stones, and bricks from the ruins on the property that they'd given their mama as gifts. The housekeeper picked up a heavy stone that Gideon had carried back to Melisande, all the way from the ruins, when he was only five. Mrs. Weston took both hands to lift it from the shelf and she laughed, remembering him inching his way up the grand staircase one step at a time to give it to his mother, just to see her face.

There were also crystal animals, enameled boxes, dried flowers, and several pieces of jewelry that had been gifts from Darius. He never came home empty-handed from a trip. No matter where he went, he found something for the duchess, even if he was simply gone out to the stable to check on the horses. Mrs. Weston collected the items carefully so the walls and bookshelves could be cleaned.

"Oh, Your Grace, I am so sorry if I failed you," she said to the room as she sat at the edge of the tub, looking around. "Your sons are amazing men. I so wish you could see them, how they've grown. I see your spirit in both of them, even though I've had to look harder when it comes to Gideon. But lately, I see you more and more." She sighed.

"There you are, Westy. Hiding out in here?" Perry asked as he entered.

"No, my lord, only gathering your mama's things for you. They need to clean the walls and such, and I wanted to make sure everything she kept was safe."

"I see. So what have you?" She pointed to the baskets and he looked inside. "We collected these things for her?" He twirled a dry leaf in his fingers. "She kept everything?"

"Melisande adored the two of you, my lord. She kept everything you gave her."

He reached into the box and pulled out a small, black river stone with a white grain across the surface. He rubbed it between his fingers as he sat next to her.

"Did she bring me here?"

Her heart broke, seeing the lost little boy in the face of this powerful man. "Yes, my lord. The bed there," she said, nodding to the mattress. "She wanted it low so you could play on it safely, nap here while she read."

He looked down at the stone. "I don't remember," he said softly.

She patted his arm. "You were but a babe, Perry. You can't expect to remember these things. It was so long ago, and you were so tiny."

"I remember her scent. I remember the feel of warmth. I remember the slick of the stone in my palm, but I cannot bring a vision to my mind's eye." He stood and picked up the box of nature's trinkets. "I'll just…take this to my suite. You can let Rox know."

Mrs. Weston nodded. She stood and pulled a thick leather-bound book from the shelf, placing it in the basket before carrying it out of the room to give to Ferry.

Gideon and Shaw sat at the old drafting table in the library, going over the original plans for the manor and the plans that his father had used when he built the room for his mother. According to the date, the room was done about three years before Gideon was born. There was a passage they hadn't found yet which led from the room directly to the master bedchamber. It appeared to open up behind his wardrobe. The paneled room had always belonged to the duchess' suite but, before his father's renovation, only had fifteen-foot ceilings like the rest of the first floor. Darius had opened up the structure, removing another set of guest suites from the second floor to create the space. Shaw could see the alteration was structurally sound; they had reinforced the walls in the room with interior buttresses that were hidden by the velvet drapes.

"I believe we should restore the room as it was," Shaw said, looking at Gideon. He could see the duke's face tense, relax, and tense again, the indecision drifting back and forth across his features. "The space isn't accessible from the main areas of the house, and there isn't a way to make it accessible because it's tucked behind the family suites. There isn't really anything else to do with it, other than restore it, perhaps update it, and return it to the lady of the manor. As it was meant to be."

Gideon nodded sharply. "Make it so, Shaw. If the fabrics are not salvageable, refer to Lady Francine for direction. The room is hers. If she has questions about it, refer her to Mrs. Weston. She was here when it was built." Gideon stood to leave. "I need to prepare for London. We'll be leaving in a few days. I must make ready everyone for my absence as we will be gone at least a fortnight, possibly twice that. You should make sure you have everything you need: measurements, samples, sketches, whatever."

"Of course, Your Grace."

Gideon turned on him. "Roxleigh," he said stiffly. "I told you to address me as Roxleigh."

"Roxleigh." Shaw paused as he looked into his serious countenance. "Eildon Manor is on the brink of an amazing restoration. The room, Lady Francine's chamber, will be the crown jewel. This is a good thing."

Gideon nodded and turned again, leaving the library.

Perry walked down the main stairs to find Gideon leaving the library in a daze. "Rox, are you ready to go to Kelso?"

Gideon shook his head, clearing his thoughts. "No, I… I shall have the phaeton brought around soon, then we'll be off."

"Gideon?"

"I'm fine, I just… There's been much to consider, you understand."

"Yes, I do. Why don't we ride instead?" he suggested.

Gideon stared at him for a moment, then nodded.


They arrived in Kelso early that afternoon, bringing more baskets of food from Mrs. Weston. Meggie and Lilly's parents were shocked to find the duke and viscount at their home. The duke was attentive to his lands, but never made unannounced house calls. The girls' mother rushed about the tiny house attempting to make it more presentable, even though Gideon told her not to. She looked like a woman on the brink of disaster.

"She obviously needs a distraction, Rox," Perry murmured to his brother.

Gideon nodded and handed her the packs of food that had been strapped to the horses. She took them gratefully and rushed to the kitchen. Dr. Walcott came into the main room looking a fright. He sat in a chair across from the brothers.

"How is Lilly?" Gideon asked as her father, Byron Steele, walked into the room.

"She's better," Dr. Walcott answered. "I believe she'll recover. The superficial wounds are healing nicely, leaving only the deep wounds to worry over. She's not been taken with another fever and she survived the first, so she must be getting stronger."

"My Lilly's a strong girl, Yer Grace. She fells the crops wit the boys wit ne'er a worry."

Gideon nodded, looking up at Mr. Steele. "Sir, actually, the reason I'm here is that we believe we know who did this."

Mr. Steele collapsed in a chair, his mouth gaping.

"Have you heard of a Lord Hepplewort?" Perry asked.

Dr. Walcott shook his head, but Mr. Steele looked down at the floor.

"Steele?" Gideon asked.

He glanced up. "Yer Grace. I b'lieve a Lord Hepplewort stayed at the inn. He were here 'round time Lilly were found. He did this to me girl?"

Gideon nodded. "We believe so. As you must understand, there isn't much that can be done through the law, though I want you to know that I will make sure he doesn't get away with his actions. Even if he cannot be publicly punished for what he has done to your child."

Mr. Steele nodded, then looked back at the floor.

Gideon continued. "My greatest concern is that he may feel threatened and return to hurt her, or any of your family. This is why I am asking that if she remembers anything, she tells no one but you and me. The last thing we want is for him to seek out revenge. He's obviously unbalanced."

"Yer Grace, me family's in yer debt. Everything ye've done. I canna thank ye."

Gideon stood. He reached for Mr. Steele's hand and shook it. "There's no need to thank me, Steele. I do what's right." He turned to leave.

The door to the sitting room opened and Meggie walked in. "Yer Grace, I'm so sorry I abandoned my duties. Tis thoughtful of ye to visit my family."

"Meggie." He shook his head. "How are you and your sister?"

"Better, Yer Grace. Better every day. How is Miss Francine?"

Dr. Walcott stood.

"She's well, Meggie, thank you. Her voice seems to be recovering. Mrs. Weston has taken very good care of her. Followed your instructions to the letter," Gideon said with a nod to Dr. Walcott.

"I'm glad to hear it, Yer Grace. I hope to return soon."

"Your position at the manor is safe. You may stay with your family for as long as they need you. Do not return a moment sooner, or I will send you home. Do you understand?"

She curtseyed. "Yes, Yer Grace." She turned to go back to her sister.

Gideon caught Steele's eye. "There is one other reason we came by today. We'll be off for London soon and won't return for at least a fortnight. If you have need of anything, you will send word to Mrs. Weston. She has instructions and will contact me if needed. If anyone sees this Hepplewort, anywhere, I want to know. I won't see your family damaged further, Steele. You will leave this to me, is that clear?"

"Of course, Yer Grace. We will send word without hesitation."

As Dr. Walcott followed them out to the horses Gideon paused. "I appreciate you caring for Lilly so carefully. I will cover your expenses. Simply send the bill."

"Your Grace, I wasn't expecting—"

"I know you weren't, but you've had to stay here, missing your regular appointments. You must be compensated, and I will take care of it."

Dr. Walcott nodded as he reached out and shook the duke's hand, then the brothers mounted their horses and headed back toward Eildon.

"Gideon."

"Yes."

"You are too quiet."

"Yes."

"One word answers aren't arguing your case."

"No."

Perry grunted and stopped the horse. "Rox."

"Yes?" he said, bringing Samson about.

"To the clearing?" Perry asked with a devilish taunt.

Gideon looked at him and his stoic façade melted into a challenging glare.

"To the clearing," he growled, leaning hard into Samson and turning him as Perry flanked him on Zeus.

They raced through thick meadows, across streams, and into the wood behind Eildon Hill. The paths were tight and the brothers fought for advantage through the trees, gaining and then falling behind with every gnarled root.

Gideon leaned back and threw his arms in the air, letting out a roar of vigorous, raucous laughter as he vaulted through the break into the clearing with Perry just behind him.

Samson nickered and stomped, aware of his victory, and Gideon leaned over, patting the steed's neck.

Perry jumped from his mount. "Are there any beasts in your stable that can best that animal?" he asked, gently rubbing the horse's nose.

"No."

"So, in truth, I never had a chance?"

Gideon laughed, his eyes flashing as he shook his head. "No."

"Still one word answers, brother?" Perry said wryly.

"Not a chance," Gideon said, holding up one finger for each word to count them. He leaped from Samson, feeling much invigorated as he strode toward the large, flat rock that sank into the edge of the pool. He pulled his old Hessians off and threw them aside, along with the rest of his clothing. He stood on the rock naked as the day, then dove into the cool water.

Perry watched him curiously as he hit the water, then disrobed and followed.

Gideon launched himself up from the water at the opposite edge of the pool, drawing a strong breath and looking back for his brother, who was nowhere to be seen. The water ran from his form as he stood perfectly still. He waited, patiently scrutinizing the surface for any breaks in tension. He saw a small ripple, followed by several air bubbles breaking the surface to his left, and he realized Perry was already there. Before he could adjust his stance Gideon was submerged in the pool again.

Perry burst through the surface with a triumphant yell, holding his arms out as he gave his battle cry.

Gideon gained his feet on the slippery bottom and stood up, glaring at his little brother. But instead of retaliating he pushed away, swimming calmly back to the flat rock.

Perry examined his brother as Gideon pulled himself up to the rock. He grabbed his shirt and lay back in the sun. "Rox?" Perry swam toward him.

Gideon lifted his head up with a grin. "Yes?"

Perry grunted at the single word answer. "What happened to your, uh, posterior?"

"My wha—" Gideon's face fell and his head sank back to the rock. "Oh, that."

"I don't suppose those marks have anything to do with my ward?" Perry asked as he walked up the bank, reaching for his own shirt.

Gideon groaned as sat up. "Well. I suppose there's no hiding it."

"Not stark naked in broad daylight, no," Perry answered snidely.

"*She* came to *me*."

"She…came to you?"

"Why are you surprised? Am I not a handsome fellow?"

Perry snorted. "Of course, but truly, Rox, I haven't seen much of this firebrand you claim to have fallen for since I've been here. Are you sure there aren't two women here, somewhere?"

Gideon glared at him. "Quite sure."

"When did this happen?" Perry yanked his trousers up his wet legs.

"The night the Larrabees arrived," Gideon said. Perry looked at him, stunned. "After everyone retired, she came to my room."

"How the hell did she make it to your bed? Honestly, it should have been easy to stop her, don't you think?"

"Let me think. First, I wasn't properly dressed to rise—to my feet—and remove her from my chambers. Second, I wasn't about to call for Ferry and have him do it. Third, it was completely dark."

"You do sleep in a room as dark as a crypt."

"And fourth, she's a woman, and I am quite—eh, quite—"

"Yes?" Perry asked with a smile.

Gideon rolled his eyes. "I cannot refuse this woman. I did, eventually. I did not ruin her, though not without some forceful opposition."

Perry's jaw fell, as did the boot he was holding. "She did that, because you were—"

Gideon nodded, then finished the sentence. "Refusing her."

"Good God, man, couldn't you have refused her *before* it got to that point? I mean, what must that have done? I've been refused once at such a time, and it doesn't exactly go well. Quite uncomfortable, I must say, I mean *horrible*, really. Is it like that for women? Obviously she was strongly opposed to being left…"

"Intact?"

"Yes. Intact." Perry thought momentarily. "No, not intact. *Frustrated*." He enunciated the last word very slowly as he stared down at the boot and then reached to pick it up.

"That I left her intact does not necessarily mean I left her— unfulfilled. It wasn't just her mouth I kissed."

Perry looked at him agape. "Indeed! Good God, man."

Gideon smiled like an unrepentant schoolboy.

Perry cleared his throat. "I am torn. On the one hand, conquests have never been a—"

"*She* is not a conquest," Gideon cut in roughly, but Perry waved him off.

"No, no, let me finish. On the one hand, I'm your brother and this type of discussion is suitable indeed. On the other hand, I am *her* guardian and you should be admonished. To be blunt, I believe I should call you out. But in truth I simply want to shake your hand. How have you mastered her so well that she comes to your room and demands you ruin her? The virgins I meet are all so tedious and frightened." Perry grimaced. "Really, not much sport at all."

Gideon glanced at him as he pulled his trousers back on. "I'm not so sure that she is the one who's been mastered," he said quietly. "I stopped because I found she was intact. I stopped—to protect her. I was unsure. The way she acted, the way she came to me, I thought she'd already been ruined. I thought Hepplewort had taken her maidenhead, and I had the thought to cuckold the bastard. But I realized I was terribly mistaken—and I *couldn't* ruin her. I am the one who is mastered." He inspected one of his topboots.

Perry sat beside him on the rock. "I don't think that's the case, either, Rox. Honestly, to see the two of you, it's mesmerizing. It makes me want something more." Perry paused. "Which is preposterous, because I've been having entirely too much fun in London keeping up with the rumors of my virility."

"Rumors?" Gideon said through his teeth

"All right, so they aren't entirely rumors. That is, there is truth to them. The point is," he said, looking at his brother, "I happen to enjoy that particular freedom. *A great deal.* I find it unimaginable to want to be with one person for the rest of my days, but then, when I am in the company of the two of you, that notion seems real, and entirely too... palatable."

Gideon smiled warily. "I have reached the point at which I don't know what I would do, were I to lose her. It is a very real pain that I have in my chest when I consider what could happen."

Perry leaned over to Gideon, elbowing him. "So, how did Ferry like your battle scars?"

Gideon laughed. "Do you know that dealing with him was my greatest fear that morning? To figure out how I was to get away with him *not* seeing them? They aren't too horrible now, are they?" he asked, wrenching his neck to try to see his shoulders.

"No, not too terrible," Perry answered. "Though your backside is still a bit shocking."

"You can't imagine how uncomfortable I was that day. And there was so much sitting that had to be done. You know, I believe Ferry has decided I've lost my wits. I have him shave me while I bathe."

Perry laughed. "Ferry should have no say in the marks on your person. You shouldn't go to such trouble. He is the most dedicated man I've ever met. No doubt he has seen past your ruse as it is and he's *choosing* to protect you."

Gideon grunted.

"Really, Rox, I can't even hire a valet. They are all so entirely inclined to gossip, my reputation as a rake would be ruined. Now, if I had Ferry..."

"Never."

Perry laughed, clapping his brother on the shoulder.

"What of you and the wards?" Gideon asked, changing the subject.

Perry's face fell, his demeanor changing instantly. "I don't know about this, Rox. I'm not sure I will survive. How am I supposed to champion two young girls while I spend my nights running around London, determined to be the ruination of the very same?"

"Maybe you *have* reached the point where you will change."

Perry shook his head. "I don't want to. Not yet. I was very much looking forward to this Season. With you there to gossip about and terrify the prospects, I was sure to have a most triumphant year in under their skirts."

"Yes, well, I won't be there," Roxleigh said. "And must you be so crass?"

"I mean it all in good humor. Need I remind you that *I* am not the one with red welts across my backside from raucous coupling?"

"I wouldn't call it raucous. Or coupling...quite."

"Oh no? How would you characterize it, then?"

Gideon thought about the night of passion, how she had taken him, and how, in turn, he had taken—or at first attempted to take—her. "Actually, raucous would be...sufficient."

"I should say so, and bravo for it."

Perry stood, putting his jacket back on and turning to the horses as Gideon finished dressing. "To the manor?" Perry asked as he gave Gideon another devious grin, then launched himself astride Zeus.

Gideon grabbed his other boot, yanking at it, then grabbed his jacket and ran at Samson. He jumped on the horse, which was already moving toward the forest path in anticipation. "To the manor!" Gideon yelled after him.

On Wednesday morning the barouche was loaded with a team of four, plus Samson and Delilah in tow, and then they were on their way to London. Gideon decided to make the trip primarily by carriage, as parts of the northern rail lines were under repair. The outriders preceded them, making sure their stays at the local inns were announced, holding rooms ahead of their arrival, and ensuring the innkeepers cleaned and prepared the staff to attend the duke's traveling party.

There were moments that Francine enjoyed, particularly the afternoons when Gideon would allow her to ride Delilah with him ahead of the carriage while he rode Samson. Carole sat up front at Grover's side to chaperone. Mostly they rode in silence, simply enjoying the countryside and one another's presence.

Francine did try conversation since her voice was growing stronger, but Gideon continued to frown upon her attempts, explaining that he wanted her voice fully recovered. She taught him more signs, and their leisurely ride provided the ability to use their hands in communication.

Gideon had really become quite adept at signing. She decided Shaw must have been privately tutoring him, because he knew things she hadn't taught her. It excited her. Signs were meant to be fairly inherent, but some of them could be a bit odd. She made up a game, like Twenty Questions, to teach him the more complex signs. *He's a fast learner,* she thought, *and quite talented with his hands.* She blushed and turned away. *But I already knew that.*

Perry decided to ride with Gideon one morning, taking one of the outrider's horses and relegating the servant to a perch on the carriage.

"Perry, I've decided, after talking with Shaw and Mrs. Weston, and I suppose I am asking you, but I would like— Well."

Perry glared at him. "Out with it, man."

Gideon cleared his throat. "I would like to restore the duchess' chamber for Francine."

"Of course, I would have it no other way," Perry answered without pause.

Gideon was a bit surprised. "You—you wouldn't—"

"Of course not. I've no actual memories of that room, but others, including you, *do.* And I believe it would serve to provide a place to remember her happiness. I think it's needed. Have you discussed this with Francine yet?"

Gideon shook his head. "Not yet, but I do plan to speak with her soon."

"You might want to do that, as it occurs to me she might not appreciate you making plans without her."

"I— Yes, of course, but I believe we have an understanding."

"Gideon, if there is one thing I know about women, it's that there is no understanding to be had, unless you have spoken of it explicitly."

"Yes, she is…different. I want everything done properly. There's one other thing."

"Yes?"

"I would like to give her the sapphires," he said quietly.

Perry stopped his mount. Gideon pulled up short, allowing the carriage to gain some ground on them. "I've never actually seen them," Perry said. "Father spoke of them, but I never— Mrs. Weston found them in her room?"

Gideon nodded.

"I would like to see them, Rox. I was so preoccupied with the box of trinkets that I never looked at the rest of it. By all means, give them to Francine. They should be hers, but I would like to see them first."

"Of course. Actually, I need to have them cleaned and repaired. Perhaps you could take them for me?"

"Sure. There are what, four pieces?"

"Were." Gideon paused. "She didn't find the bracelet. Only the other three."

"No matter. I'll see to it."

The carriage gained on them and the brothers nudged their mounts ahead once again.

"The rubies should be taken in as well. I realize you won't have use of them for some time, but… Well, you could be prepared."

Perry's eyes narrowed but never shifted from the road ahead. "As you wish."

Gideon grinned.

They arrived at Roxleigh House on Grosvenor late Sunday after leaving Shaw at his flat so he could work undisturbed. The brothers considered having Francine and Carole stay at Perry's town house, but it was smaller, and not at all set up for company. The guest rooms were sparsely appointed: they had beds, but no linens, and no other furniture. The women would have to stay in Gideon's town house until other arrangements were made. The footmen unloaded the carriage, hauling trunks and cases to several different suites.

Francine stood in front of the home, excited for her next adventure. She'd always wanted to visit London. Granted, she hadn't considered Victorian era London, but she thought it romantic. To see monuments like Big Ben when it was relatively new as well as Westminster Abbey, and Buckingham Palace, not to mention the infamous Tower of London. The popularity of Queen Victoria would be ever on the rise, and there were many exciting celebrations, as well as tragedies, on the horizon.

She stared at the grand façade of the town house. It dwarfed the others nearby; she could see it was the biggest on the square. She wondered if any of these homes were still standing, and felt a twinge of sadness. She tried to recall more of London's history. She was hopeful the more she saw the more she'd remember, but she'd been a business major—not a history major—and hadn't learned much more than the required world history. She once again wished she'd paid more attention in school.

She walked into the entry, smiling at the long row of servants as Gideon spoke with them. Ferry traveled with him, as did Grover, Smyth, and Riband, who'd stepped in as outrider while Gentry was away to retrieve the sisters. Francine appreciated having familiar faces around.

Gideon was speaking with a man who, she assumed by his dress and demeanor, must be butler of this residence. He seemed very severe, and she hoped she wouldn't offend him. She had studied her book of manners, but nothing was simple. There were so many rules, and she didn't think it would be a good idea to cross him. She suddenly missed Mrs. Weston a great deal.

Gideon approached her with a concerned look on his face. "Is everything all right, my lady?"

She nodded and glanced at the butler.

Gideon followed her gaze. "Oh, Sanders. He is an ominous presence but dedicated. Don't let him frighten you."

She looked into Gideon's warm gaze and relaxed a bit as he continued. "As late as it is, Cook has prepared a small supper. It can be served in the main dining room, if you would care to join me." He looked at Carole. "Of course, you could also join us, as chaperone."

Carole blushed and looked down. Francine knew Carole was

a lower servant, certain never to be more than a lady's maid, and her station required that she be both unheard and unseen. Francine could see she wasn't comfortable being pushed into this situation.

Francine glanced at him. "Your Grace," she whispered.

His skin reacted to her voice, immediately flushing with the anticipation of her words. "Please don't strain yourself."

"I'm doing fine," she whispered. "I think, after such a long trip, dinner in my room would be better. While I would very much appreciate your company, I am tired, and a formal dinner really doesn't sound very enticing."

He nodded, placing a finger across her lips to silence her.

She glanced at Sanders, who was peering down his long, straight nose at her proximity to the duke with a disapproving glint in his eye. She cleared her throat and spoke softly enough that she believed nobody else would hear her.

"Thank you for understanding, Gideon." She kissed the finger at her lips and smiled up at him.

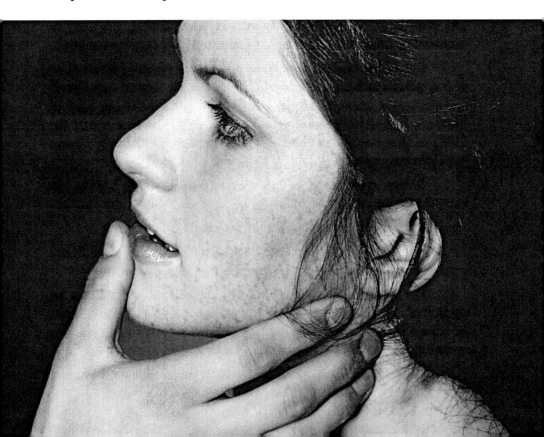

"Not at all, my lady. I look forward to seeing you tomorrow," he said, and she proffered her hand. He took it firmly, gently kissing the exposed flesh of her wrist between her sleeve and her glove.

She sighed silently, her skin prickling as he straightened and turned, barking orders to no one in particular.

"Send a tray for Lady Francine—and Carole—to her room."

Carole curtseyed and they turned to follow one of the housemaids upstairs as Gideon continued to command. "I shall also take my supper in my suite. Trumbull?" He searched for his brother. "Trumbull!" he yelled. "Where the devil's he gone off to?" he said under his breath.

"Here, Your Grace," Perry replied, walking from the study. "You yelled?"

Gideon rolled his eyes as the servants scattered. "I trust the handling of your ward is thus far satisfactory?"

"Of course." Perry grinned. "Mind if I join you for supper? I'm fairly certain that my household won't have anything prepared since they weren't expecting me, and I'm usually not *in* for supper at any rate. They're far more adept at breakfasts and luncheons." He studied his fingernails.

Gideon grimaced. "Not at all. Sanders!" he bellowed before realizing the butler was just behind him.

"Supper for two in the study, Your Grace?"

Gideon nodded.

"Yes, Your Grace."

Gideon's skin tingled and he looked up the stairs just in time to see Francine disappear around the corner to the first floor suites. He and Perry retired to the study, Gideon filling two snifters with brandy and sitting at his desk. "How long are we to put off the inevitable?" Gideon asked, warming the brandy between his palms.

Perry looked up at him in confusion.

"Hepplewort," Gideon ground out.

"Ah, yes. *That.*" He sighed heavily. "That bit of ugliness can stay put off forever, as far as I'm concerned."

Gideon lifted a brow. "I see. So you want me to post the banns and have Hepplewort learn of it from a Society rag and bring a public claim?"

Perry grunted. "We haven't yet discussed it and no, I don't suppose I do. I imagine we should leave before the week is out. But I need some time in London first. We should at least get our bearings before wandering off again."

"Bearings." Gideon chuckled. "Agreed. But not too long."

Francine rose early, hoping for a chance to wander London playing tourist. She had breakfast on the rear terrace over the gardens, wishing someone would join her, but nobody came. She walked back to her room after breakfast to retrieve a book, thinking she would take it outside. The town house was different from Eildon; it was lonely. Trumbull, of course, was at his own town house across the square, and Shaw was on the other end of London, working. She was alone save the servants, who were ghosts, and Gideon, who was nowhere to be seen. The servants were detached, more professional. They only seemed to be there when she needed them, and they weren't the least bit comforting.

She grabbed *Dante's Inferno*, thinking it was a good day to peruse the multiple circles of Hell, and she walked out across the large terrace and descended the wide steps to the garden bench on the lawn below.

"Where have you been all morning?" came the familiar baritone just as she'd given up hope. Carole strolled behind Gideon, then stopped to stand close to the French doors.

*Me?* she signed.

He nodded, pointing at her.

She smiled—she couldn't help it, but she did her best to twist it into a stern glare. *I have been here. Where have you been?*

He smiled in return, descending the steps. *I'm sorry, I had some documents. But now I am all yours. What would you like to do?*

She beamed. *Will you show me London? I've never been.*

Carole shifted from one foot to the other, looking around uncomfortably.

*I would love to show you London,* he replied, then held his hand out to her.

She took it, rising from the garden bench.

He turned. "Carole, will you prepare a luncheon basket? Perhaps we can picnic in Hyde Park."

Carole nodded and skittered through the doors, happily released from her discomfort.

Francine laughed. They hadn't behaved in an indecent manner, but Carole always seemed so nervous.

They took the town carriage to Marylebone, across the Thames to Westminster Abbey, then to Charing Cross near Whitechapel.

"Whitechapel." Her eyes grew wide as they passed through the bustling inner city sprawl. "Jack the Ripper." *Glad I didn't wake up as a prostitute.*

"What did you say?" Gideon questioned as he watched her.

"Nothing," she whispered. *Do you know 221b Baker Street?* she signed, looking at him hopefully.

Gideon shook his head and knocked on the roof, bringing the carriage to a halt. "Grover, are you familiar with 221b Baker?" he called out the window when Grover leaned down.

"Pardon, Your Grace, I believe Baker Street numbers don't pass the first 'undred, but we can drive it on the return to Roxleigh House."

Gideon turned back to her and she smiled as she shifted her gaze to look out the window.

He waved the carriage on, wanting to know everything she was thinking, but loving the mystery of her expressions.

Carole shrank into the opposite corner of the carriage, determinedly watching out the windows. She wished she were at Eildon, at the town house…anywhere but here. The duke and Lady Francine were so powerfully connected, she could feel them communicating without raising a hand, or parting their lips. It seemed very untoward and she understood, explicitly, the duke's need for a chaperone. She could only hope they would marry soon, and leave her be.

# TWENTY-THREE

With the Duke of Roxleigh in residence the ton came in droves to visit. Gideon stayed true to his reputation and did not respond to the callers. The rumor mill buzzed, since this was already the most anticipated London Season in years. Gideon's interest in finding a bride had generated most of the gossip, but the fact that he had yet to attend a second Society function and appeared to be off the market had the *ton* in a right frenzy.

After the Greensborough ball, the rumors were thick with presumptions about Lady Alice Gracin, who had been occupied throughout the night of her coming out with the Duke of Roxleigh and Viscount Roxleigh. That they both disappeared shortly thereafter, without a word, staunched the stories and stumped the gossips. Even Perry's rakish cohorts had no idea where he'd gone off to, or why. Nobody knew what to think and everyone was rife with anticipation for their return.

Gideon and Francine spent the mornings and evenings together—dining, reading, and riding. He didn't linger over her wrist, and she didn't gather herself close to whisper, both behaving as perfect models of propriety around the servants, much to Perry's approval.

Francine was disheartened by the recovery of her voice, since she was now able to speak at a more easily heard level and the intimacy gained from whispering was becoming lost to her. She often reverted to sign language to recapture the closeness she missed with the duke, but even that private conversation, within the boundaries of a public setting, was still frowned upon by many.

"It is time we made our way to Hepplewort's estate," Gideon ground out from behind his desk.

"Indeed," Perry answered.

Francine knocked at the door of the study. Gideon and Perry had been holed up in there all morning, and she was bored. The brothers rose as she entered.

"Lady Francine, what can we do for you today?" Perry gave her a smile and a quick bow.

She shook her head. "I just came to say hello." she said quietly.

"Your voice is getting stronger," Perry said, and she smiled and nodded.

She walked over to the desk and settled in the chair next to Perry as Gideon sat back in his large desk chair, watching.

"We were just discussing some business that we must attend to," he said.

"Business?" she asked, tilting her head.

"Yes, we'll be leaving late tonight," Gideon said, noting how her expression fell. "But we'll return before your sisters arrive," he added quickly.

"Then we can move to Westcreek Park, where you'll no doubt be more comfortable," Perry said, expecting her to be excited.

"Of course, once you move out there you'll have to redecorate," Gideon said. "The guest suites haven't been used for some time."

*They've been used,* Perry thought. *But not for proper guests.* "Indeed, it will give them something to do."

Francine watched as they conversed like she wasn't even there. She frowned.

"Perhaps you could have them plan a dinner or small gathering," Gideon said.

She was growing more and more frustrated. She'd been rather self-sufficient until she wound up here, and she hadn't minded the care everyone had taken with her, but it was starting to get on her nerves that nobody seemed to consider that she might have an opinion. Her face drew taut, her mouth pursed, and her fists clenched.

"Do not manage me further, gentlemen, I'm sick of it. What I would appreciate is a full explanation of all these plans you've made without asking me." Her voice was clear as a bell, and her speech carried a gently lilting accent she didn't remember acquiring. She cleared her throat, smiling at the lack of pain. Her muscles didn't react by tightening. She felt her neck, but there was no swelling.

Gideon smiled. *She even sounds beautiful.* Her voice was rich and full, not meager and squeaky, no longer fouled by the tension and swelling that had distorted it. "Of course, Lady Francine, I beg your pardon. Everything's happened so quickly since your family arrived at Eildon, I'm not sure of what we've managed to tell you and what we haven't."

"Well, then," she said. "Start at the beginning."

Gideon nodded and exchanged a wary glance with Perry. They discussed the events of the Larrabees' visit and the arrangements they'd made, most of which she already knew. It was the unpleasant details that she didn't. When they finished, Francine sat with her hands folded in her lap, concentrating rather resolutely on something.

The men waited patiently.

With a confused look, she said, "So this Lord Heppewhatsit—"

"Hepple*wort*," Gideon corrected.

"Yes. He...*purchased* me?" Her eyebrows knitted together.

They both nodded.

"And the two girls, they were also bartered away?"

Again they nodded.

"That's horrific. I wouldn't wish that on my worst enemy."

Gideon looked at her with grave concern. "You still don't remember anything about Lord Hepplewort, or your family, or any of this?"

"No," she replied swiftly. "It's as though you are telling me of someone else's life. I feel no connection to any of the people you are talking about, other than a desire to help the girls." She looked at Perry. "Which you've already done, so thank you." She thought about it a bit longer. "When will they arrive? It's been a couple of weeks since they left for France, yes?"

"Almost a fortnight, yes. They should be arriving here in London within the week, which is why it's so important that we go to Hepplewort now."

"Oh." She glanced at Gideon. "And how long will the trip be?"

"Only two days, maybe three. I should hope. We believe he's in residence in Shropshire, which is most of a day's drive, but we've two other stops on the return."

*Two days,* she thought. *I can wait two days.*

"I will endeavor to make it two," Gideon said with a warm smile.

Perry glared at him over the rim of his snifter.

Francine saw the glance and cleared her throat. "And, when you return, I'll be living with Lord Trumbull?"

"No," Gideon cut in, before his brother could answer. Gideon grimaced apologetically. "I mean... You shall be living in his home, as he is your guardian, but you will not be living together."

"Of course." She nodded with a smile. "Lord Trumbull, we are moving to Westcreek?"

Perry exchanged another glance with Gideon before answering. "Until the sisters arrive, we will stay in London. Then we should go to Westcreek Park, which is not far outside London. That's where you and your sisters will live until each of you is old enough to enter Society and find a suitable husband."

Francine darted her eyes to Gideon. He grinned.

"Don't worry, I've several suitors who are waiting to call on you," Perry said smartly, then sighed. "But I've already given His Grace permission to court you," he added, as if it was an afterthought.

She blushed and turned her face away. It all seemed a bit outlandish, but in the end she was dating her duke. She would be close to him and she would not be forced to leave.

*This is exactly what I want, isn't it? Nobody bothered to ask me, but that doesn't change the answer, does it?* She sighed heavily, suddenly more resigned than overjoyed.

Perry turned to Gideon. "Have you decided on the parties Francine will attend?" She looked up once again, curious, as they seemed to be starting another conversation around her.

"No. I thought I would leave that to your inimitable knowledge and discretion. However, Francine's first ball *should* be her coming out, which I will host here at Roxleigh House." He inclined his head toward Francine. "If that suits you?"

Her tension melted and she smiled. "Yes, I think so. What exactly do you do at a coming out?"

"It is your formal introduction to Society," Gideon said. "Before the ball, you aren't allowed to *be* in proper Society. But it is mostly an event for socializing among the *ton*. The events tend to be a spectacle. There will be dancing, possibly a dinner, and many young girls attempting to capture the eye of an eligible peer."

"Like you?" she asked.

"Not like me," he said with a smile. "As you've already caught my eye, and my—"

Perry cleared his throat in warning.

She blushed. "Dancing?"

Gideon nodded. "Oh yes, there will be much dancing. Waltzes mostly," he replied, and she smiled, trying to hide her panic. "Francine?"

"Yes?" she said cautiously.

"Is there something else?" he asked, a hint of suspicion coloring his tone.

She shook her head as she blushed again. "No. No, it's nothing. I, uh, I should find Carole," she said quickly as she stood, drawing the brothers from their chairs, then turned and left.

"What is it?" Perry asked after the door closed.

"I'm not sure, but I intend to find out. In the meantime, let's get this nasty bit of business done with, shall we?"


"This is bound to be the ugliest business I've ever had need to attend to," Gideon said as he stood looking out the window across the gardens of Hepplewort's estate. Perry walked around the room, inspecting the decorations. The appointments were appalling, entirely over-styled and serving only one purpose: to demonstrate Hepplewort's wealth. Every piece of exposed wood was gilded, and every hem and edge was trimmed with fringe or tassels.

"Well, we are certainly in the proper room for a bit of ugliness." Perry frowned as he flicked a tassel that dangled off the satin-upholstered divan. "And what exactly is this thing? It cannot be comfortable to sit upon without a backrest," he said with a sneer.

Gideon turned. "Oh, come now, Perry, I'm sure you could find something to use it for." The corner of his mouth turned up in a smile.

Perry grinned. "Indeed. Then perhaps it should be in a bedchamber. However, the fabric looks a bit slippery for *that*."

The door opened, and the brothers stood shoulder to shoulder across from the entry to greet the earl. Gideon straightened his shoulders, clasping his hands behind his back and standing tall. Perry followed suit and they watched intently as Lord Hepplewort entered the room. He wore an old, thick, brown brocade jacket, the sleeves torn from duress, and his trousers and shirt looked as though they had been slept in.

Hepplewort instantly realized who they were. "Gentlemen, where is my bride?" he asked without preamble. He plopped himself down on an olive-green, satin wing-back chair dripping with gold tassels, then motioned to the chairs across from him.

Gideon sat, allowing Perry to take the lead.

Perry chose to stand, directly in front of Hepplewort. "My lord. I am Lord Peregrine Trumbull, Viscount Roxleigh and this is His Gra—"

Hepplewort cut him off with a dismissive wave. "I am aware of who you *both* are. What I am interested in is your business here, as you don't appear to have returned my betrothed," he snapped.

Gideon raised a brow, looking up to his brother as he waited for his retort.

"My lord. We have a business matter to discuss concerning Miss Francine Larrabee," Perry said resolutely.

Hepplewort frowned. "Who is *Francine* Larrabee?"

"I beg pardon, *Madeleine* Larrabee," Perry said quickly.

Hepplewort stood. "Yes, Madeleine. What have you done with my fiancée?" The color in his cheeks rose from his collar like a steam pot. His nose barely reached the top button of Perry's waistcoat at full height. "Out with it, then."

Gideon stood and moved next to his brother. "Lord Hepplewort, if you let my brother finish, that's precisely what we are here to discuss."

The sight of the two large, foreboding men seemed to sober Hepplewort, and he backed up a pace.

Gideon thrust a bundle of papers at Hepplewort as Perry spoke. "You will find in these documents that M. and Mme. Larrabee have entrusted me as guardian for their three youngest daughters, Miss

Madeleine Larrabee included. All previous agreements are hereby dissolved. I have brought reparations. What you already paid for Madeleine, plus five percent."

Hepplewort began to shake, his jowls vibrating. "What interest have you in my— Why would you? What is the meaning of this?" he spat.

"This is a simple guardianship. Her father agreed to allow me to act as guardian in his stead, to finish their education in a *proper* manner, and to provide them a dowry for a *suitable* match."

"But— Why?"

Gideon started to answer, but Perry stopped him with a hand on his arm. "Because it is the right thing to do," he said simply.

Hepplewort launched himself at Perry but Gideon moved in front of him, taking Hepplewort up by the collar. The squat, corpulent man sank into his clothes, his flesh gathering at his chins as Gideon lifted him.

"You will compose yourself," Gideon said, furious. "This matter isn't the only one with which we have issue. I recommend you control your mouth or I will send for the constable and see to it that you are taken to the Dana," he threatened, his gaze narrowed on the man.

Hepplewort stared at him from overwrought, bloodshot eyes, trying to quickly determine the duke's true intent.

"This is your copy of the agreement," Perry said, stuffing it in Hepplewort's jacket pocket. "You may have your solicitor look it over, though he will undoubtedly find it infallible."

Gideon lessened his grip on Hepplewort, slowly lowering him to his feet. "You have no more business with Larrabee. Any and all contact should be directed specifically to Lord Trumbull—or better, to his solicitor."

Hepplewort jerked loose and backed away, straightening his jacket and shirt and smoothing his unruly tufts of hair. Looking from Perry to Gideon, he scowled. "This matter is *not* finished," he spat, causing Gideon to flinch as if his very saliva was toxic. "She is mine. You cannot keep her from me."

Perry advanced on him, forcing him backward until he fell into his chair. "This matter *is* finished, and she *will* be kept from you. You will not, under any circumstance, endeavor to interact with *any* of my wards, at *any* time, for *any* reason. Have I made myself perfectly clear?" he asked as he leaned over the plop of a man.

Hepplewort sputtered throatily as he shriveled further into the gaudy armchair. "I have a contract with Larrabee—"

Gideon cut him off. "As you recall, *that* contract was unfinished. You were not yet wed, and you did not complete the payment as agreed. Since there was no wedding, no consummation, and the payment was not made in full, we are returning your original expenses and canceling that contract on behalf of Larrabee. There is *nothing more* to be *done.*"

Hepplewort lifted his shaking hand and pointed at Gideon. "You! You stole my bride! You held her hostage! You have done this to me!"

"You have done this to yourself. Our business here is concluded. Might I recommend you do not attempt to obtain another wife by similar means?" Gideon boomed.

Hepplewort shrank. The force of Gideon's statement and the power of his voice had stayed him entirely. He appeared to gather his wits. "Of course, Your Grace. My—my behavior today has been irrational. I did not sleep well last night. I'm not accustomed to rising this early. I, I—" He stuttered as he attempted to find other excuses to lob at the brothers.

Perry and Gideon relaxed slightly. "My lord," Perry said, "I understand how this news would be unwelcome, and perhaps we should have handled it another way. I believe we both wanted to notify you as promptly as possible, considering the letter you sent to M. Larrabee concerning Madeleine. We should not have made the assumption that this was merely a business matter, and for *that alone* I beg your pardon."

Gideon had no interest in smoothing things over with the earl, and kept his opinions to himself.

"I appreciate your candor, my lord. I suppose I shall send the document to my solicitor and that will be the end of it. However, I will reserve judgment until I hear from him."

The brothers looked at each other and left.


"There's something I have no interest in ever doing again," Perry said as the carriage was underway.

"Yes, well, unfortunately, we have two more such visits yet to make on our return."

Perry leaned back, putting his hat over his eyes, stretching his long legs out in front of him with his feet on the opposite seat as he tried to relax before the next stop.

"I am not content with leaving the situation unfinished," Gideon said.

"Neither am I, Rox, but until Francine is safely married to you, we cannot pressure him further. You must be patient."

"Who is the next sod?"

Perry looked at the paperwork. "Ringolsby."

"Good God, I have had drinks with the man."

"Well then, perhaps I shall leave this one to you," Perry said with a grin.

Gideon growled and leaned back in the squabs next to his brother, feeling rather unsettled and weary.


Francine lazed about the town house for the next two days, reading her books and wandering around. She finished *Dante's Inferno* and studied her book of manners. She found the rules of the peerage particularly fascinating. She had no idea Gideon, as the duke's progeny, had been bound by such a definitive set of rules. She could certainly empathize more in relation to his constraints, and had a greater respect for his will and morals than she had before. She finally understood what he meant when he spoke of the importance of propriety. *But it still doesn't necessarily mean I am going to follow it.*

She considered the things he'd said, the actions he took while they were in the maze, and she blushed. *No wonder he got a hard-on from an exposed ankle,* she thought with a wicked blush.

She tried to find new places to read, as if the change in setting would help to pass the time, but running into Sanders always unsettled her. Her favorite spot was the gardens, because the stodgy old butler seemed to shrink from the light like a three-day-old petunia.

She wanted to explore Gideon's study, or his bedroom. She wanted to touch his things, look through his drawers, smell his shirts. She sat up straight from the bench in the garden, then bolted without thinking. She ran up the stairs to his suite, looking around carefully; there was nobody in sight. She ducked into his bedchamber and pulled the door closed behind her.

She turned and took quick stock of the room—chairs, tables, *bed*. *A massive bed.* Her breath caught and she forced her gaze to continue. Closet. She smiled and ran to it, throwing the doors wide. She ran her hand over the row of jackets and shirts, all perfectly straight, well-spaced, and neat. She pulled one of the crisp white shirts down from the rod, trying to shift the other shirts to conceal the missing garment.

Francine held the shirt to her face and inhaled deeply, but was disappointed. She frowned. The cloth didn't hold his scent, of course, since he hadn't yet worn it. She shrugged and turned.

"Hello."

She dropped the shirt.

"Gideon, I—"

He laughed. "Francine, if you are in need of clothing, you have only to ask Carole. She would be more than happy to accommodate you."

"I, um, no. I just—" She squeaked as he approached her.

"You just what?"

She stared up at him, looming over her, and took a deep breath to steady her nerves, but instead she found what she'd been looking for and smiled. She pushed his jacket off though he began to protest, and she quelled the sound with one finger across his mouth. She unbuttoned his waistcoat and loosened his cravat before unbuttoning his shirt and pulling it from his trousers and over his head. She took the shirt and held it to her face, breathing deeply of his scent. Sandalwood, spice, and a touch of salt. She smiled broadly and picked up the clean shirt and pushed it toward him.

"Thank you," she said as she rushed from his room, leaving him standing there, shirtless.

Francine was sitting in the garden reading when Gideon walked out. "There you are," she said.

"Sorry for the delay. I only wanted to, uh, freshen up."

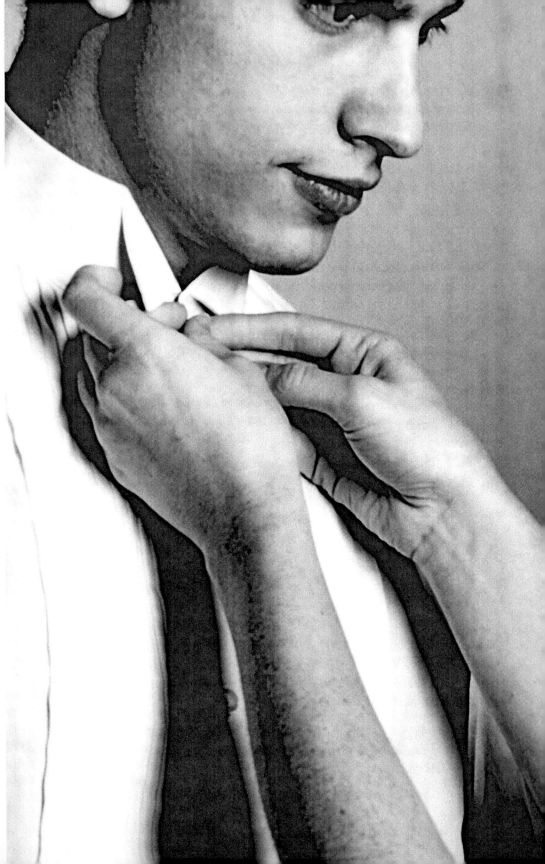

She smiled up at him brilliantly, then noticed the others behind him.

Perry was followed by two young ladies she could only assume to be the sisters. They rushed to her, squealing and hugging and jumping, a veritable vibration of energy.

Francine stood to greet them with a touch of panic. The sisters were obviously speaking French, but she didn't understand a word of it. She thought back to her high school French class. *One more thing I should have paid better attention to.*

"*Un moment, un moment, s'il vous plait?*" She tried to calm them. She searched her memory, trying to remember the names that Gideon had mentioned, but couldn't. She shook her head, looking to him for help.

He walked swiftly to her side. "Amélie, Maryse, *assez-y-vous.*"

Sitting immediately, they folded their hands in their laps and stared up at the duke. *Like twin robots.* If Francine looked shocked, her expression paled in comparison to Trumbull's, which was one of pure terror. She relaxed instantly as she gazed at him, laughing and drawing all the attention to herself, which she immediately regretted.

She covered her mouth with her hand.

Gideon glanced at his brother and grunted. "Well, Trumbull. How are you now? Are you sure the dukedom could not handle this bit of scandal?"

Perry shook his head. "No doubt in my mind that it could. I was entirely wrong. Let's draw the papers and handle the situation without delay."

Gideon shook with laughter and clapped him on the shoulder. Hard.

The two sisters sat on the bench in the garden, looking from one person to the next as they spoke. They were so tiny and well behaved. Francine could tell they had no intention of breaking into the conversation. They were two very well-trained, well-dressed young girls. They looked like a couple of dainty cupcakes—pastel satin dresses covered in white ruffles and frills, with lacy roses and ribbon bows. She immediately thought of Marie Antoinette, without the powdered wig. She looked into their faces and saw something she hadn't seen since the night her mother died. Well, no, since she'd met Mme. Larrabee.

Recognition. She sat back on the bench.

It wasn't the type of recognition you experience when you know someone, but a kind of recognition of self. They looked like her. They had her missing blonde hair and light-colored eyes, though the smaller one had bluer eyes and the larger one greener.

"Do you— Do you speak any English?" she asked breathlessly.

The little twin faces swept to her in unison and their chirping voices choired, "Yes, of course." This was followed by countless giggles.

Francine looked to Gideon, shaking her head, and she knew he saw the same thing that she did.

"Maryse," she said carefully, not looking at either of the girls.

"Madeleine," Maryse said, in a tiny French voice.

"Francine, please. Amélie." The other girl smiled at her. "I'm sorry, I don't remember— anything. But I do hope we can be friends."

"Oh, we understand, don't we, Maryse?" Amélie said.

"But, of course! And we will be great—"

"Friends. Just like we always have been."

"Yes, like we always have been. Someday you will—"

"Remember everything. Someday."

"Until then, we will be—"

"Friends, the closest of—"

"Friends," Maryse finished.

Francine was suddenly jealous, and a bit sad at the way the girls finished each other's sentences. *What an amazing thing, to be so close to someone as to know exactly what they are thinking and saying.* She felt Gideon's gaze on her and she smiled slightly. She reached for his hand and he grasped hers, squeezing it warmly before releasing her.

Perry stepped forward. "Lady Francine, perhaps you would like to show the sisters to their room? Miss Faversham went up to unpack her things. I thought you might appreciate a little time together."

Francine nodded. Standing, she turned to Perry. "They need clothes."

Perry lifted a brow and she motioned to them.

"Do you think this will get any better the more trunks that are opened?"

Perry examined the two girls, who were whispering to each other on the bench. He had no argument as he look at the shiny, puffy, frilly, obnoxious attire. "I imagine a few simple dresses would be appropriate for the country. You and Miss Faversham can determine what they need and we'll see to it before we leave for the estate. I won't attend you on this shopping trip. My brother has recently become fond of shopping, so he'll take the four of you. I've no doubt he'll enjoy it."

Gideon shot his brother a glare, but Perry didn't act the least bit repentant.

The girls stood as Miss Faversham walked out to the garden unexpectedly. Amélie and Maryse walked over and stood safely behind her. She looked at Francine, who smiled back but made no move to follow.

Gideon leaned over her, whispering in her ear, and Francine nodded, then left the brothers. They watched as Miss Faversham led the three ladies back into the house.

Francine paused at the doorway and glanced back over her shoulder at Gideon.

He examined the way her long neck turned. Admired the soft skin at her nape dusted with curls that escaped her upswept locks.

Her eyelashes fluttered as she looked down, inhaling.

He walked two steps closer and took a deep breath: lavender and rain. Just the hint of her sent his blood to his gut and forced him to suck in air.

A smile pulled up the corner of her mouth as she met his gaze, then she turned and went inside.

Gideon groaned and rubbed his temples.

Perry stood silently.

"How long does this courting have to last?" Gideon ground out.

"You should at least let her come out to Society before sweeping her away. I've no doubt that if we announced a ball for *this* evening, carriages would line the streets to get a peek inside your house."

"The ball will be Friday. Is that enough time?"

"Friday is more than sufficient to double the turn out," Perry said, grinning at his brother's state.

Gideon's gaze imparted the only issue of importance in this entire affair: that Francine be his, as expediently as possible.


Roxleigh House buzzed all week with preparation. The simple ballroom in the town house was scrubbed floor to ceiling, the inlaid wood polished meticulously, the leaded glass windows cleaned, and the marble columns and the attached terrace over the gardens scoured.

Francine looked forward to the ball, but she was also extremely nervous. She had never danced, at least not formally. *The Chicken Dance* certainly doesn't count, she thought as she wandered the halls looking for Miss Faversham. She found her in the upstairs parlor with the sisters.

"Good afternoon, Lady Francine."

"Good afternoon."

"Is something troubling you, my lady?"

"Oh, please, *please* call me Francine." Miss Faversham nodded and took her hand, pulling her to the window seat.

Francine fidgeted. "I— uh, the ball," she said quietly so the sisters wouldn't hear.

Miss Faversham placed her hands over Francine's to steady them.

"It's just, I—I've no idea how to dance." She stared at her hands.

Miss Faversham smiled brightly. "Is that all?"

Francine looked at her, then nodded.

"Do not fear, sweet girl. I'll make arrangements."

# TWENTY-FOUR

ater that day, Miss Faversham found Francine reading in the parlor. "I've arranged for your dance lesson, my la—Francine. If you don't mind, Carole will accompany you to the ballroom, and please put your gloves on. "

Francine put the book down and stood. She took the gloves that Miss Favershamm handed her, then followed Carole to the ballroom. As she crossed the threshold, her skin prickled. She took a deep breath and turned to the French doors that led to the garden. They were open slightly, letting in a breeze that drifted past Gideon, drawing with it his familiar scent. She inhaled deeply and smiled.

Carole walked to the French doors, nodding as she passed him, and went out to the terrace as he moved toward Francine.

Her body reacted to him without permission. Her skin awakened, her heart raced, her eyes glistened. As she went to meet him, the fabric of her dress created goose bumps on her arms and her skirts created a stir of air that she felt swirling around her ankles and up her legs.

He moved impossibly slow, like a jaguar stalking its prey. She held still, reminding herself to breathe.

She didn't shift except for her eyes, which watched him as he began to circle her.

"I understand you need dance lessons before the ball tomorrow."

"Mmm-hmm." Her hands trembled.

He savored the energy between them. Stopping just behind her, he reached out and said, "I can help you with that."

The air between them shifted.

She closed her eyes and inhaled, lifting her hand slowly, waiting to feel his hand on hers. Unexpectedly, she felt pressure on her belly as he drew her back into his sturdy form. She felt his chest rise as he breathed, nuzzling into her hair. Her head fell back against his shoulder and she covered his large hand with hers.

"Shall we begin?" he breathed into her ear.

"Mmm-hmm."

He smiled and spun her around. "This," he began as he pulled her tight against him, "is too close."

She felt herself blush as she stared over his shoulder.

"You'll have the gossips in a right state if we dance without the proper distance between us." He loosened his grasp as the silent dance began.

She wasn't entirely sure how she was to survive the lesson, much less the ball.

"Close your eyes."

She did.

Her breath caught as the memory of their first kiss assailed her. His hands tightened, and he placed his feet next to hers, the sides touching. He pulled her hand, leading her around the floor slowly while he whispered directions.

"Keep your feet against mine." He lifted one of his boots, pulling her slippered foot along with it as if they were tethered. He counted the steps. "One, two, three, one, two, three. That's right."

She relaxed into his hold, allowing him to lead her, and before long they were swirling around the ballroom and she was laughing at the twinge in her belly from the swift movement.

"It is merely another form of communication without words, something you are already good at," he said quietly.

Francine opened her eyes and immediately missed a step.

Gideon caught her, pulling her back into the waltz without missing a beat.

"So this is why everyone loves to dance," she whispered.

He smiled, and she closed her eyes again and concentrated on the feel of him beneath her hands. She could feel him along the entire length of her body. The way his thigh parted her legs through her skirts when he moved toward her, the feel of his muscles twisting below his clothes. Her entire being was suffused in reaction to his closeness.

She felt his chest against her corset and her lips parted. His strong thigh brushed against her leg and she drew a breath, releasing her hold on him. She felt her insides unravel like a ball of yarn. She held her chest, trying to calm her breathing.

"My sweet, are you all right?"

"No, I am most decidedly not all right," she said. "You walk into a room and I'm overwhelmed by your scent. I walk past the study and I can feel you inside. I'm within reach of you and my skin is sensitive to the point that the very air around me makes me tremble. When you look at me, your eyes burnish my soul. I can feel you touching me, within and without, and you don't even have to move. I know how your body feels. Your calloused hands, the strong muscles that shift under your skin against mine. The way you touch me. Here, and—here." She gestured to her neck, then swept her hand down her neck. "The way your lips conform to mine, willing my mouth to your bidding. I am overcome, overwhelmed, saturated. I feel you surrounding me, and I want nothing more than to feel you inside of me, as one with me. *No*, I am most decidedly *not* all right."

He was obviously satisfied by his effect on her, and she laughed, blushing as her hand flew to her face.

"No, don't," he said. "Don't ever hide yourself from me. Not ever."

She dropped her hand and he caught it in his. He brought it to his mouth, kissing her palm.

She bit her bottom lip and a low groan escaped him.

His hand went to her jaw and he tilted her face, kissing her with all the heat and desire of a man drawn deeply into love.

Her hands stole around his waist, feeling his muscles tense wherever she touched him, and she closed her eyes, fighting against the swoon.

He pulled away from her and she gasped for air.

She rested her hand on his chest and felt his heart skip a beat under her touch. She slowly slid her hand down, aware of his body's unchecked reaction to her, and was mesmerized at the effect of her touch on him.

"And this is what you do to me." He pushed her hand farther down, to the ridge of his trousers. "I can scarcely sit in a room with you. I can't have a polite conversation for fear my thoughts of you will color my words. My body yearns for you, my heart beats for you, my being strains for you. You have me undone."

She placed both hands on the narrow of his waist and looked up at him, realizing how close his words came to capturing her heart. She heard the French doors open at the end of the ballroom and he pulled her back into a formal stance, sweeping her into the waltz as Carole entered, but she couldn't keep up with him. She struggled to breathe, and the spinning caught in her brain and her world started to slide.

*Love. He loves me. I can't do this, because love only ever leads to…* *to—*

She faltered and he caught her. "I am not this weak. I don't know who I am anymore," she yelled, "but I am not this weak!" She pushed away from him. "You have me at a disadvantage, sir! This is not who I am!" She turned and strode from the ballroom, leaving him stunned, his arms held in midair. Carole ran past him and the rush of her skirts was enough to knock him off kilter as she followed Francine.

Francine hurried into her room, pulling clothes from her wardrobe and throwing them aside. She was furious. Damned skirts. She walked back out to the hallway and ran into Ferry. "I need a shirt and some pants."

He stared at her.

"Shirt and pants, trousers, whatever." She waited. "Now," she said.

Ferry looked around and spotted Gideon at the base of the stairs.

Gideon nodded, and Ferry looked back to Francine.

"Just a moment, please, my lady." He turned toward Gideon's room, then soon returned to the hallway carrying a pile of clothing.

Francine took the bundle and nodded. "Thank you." She glanced down at Gideon. "I'm going for a ride. You have ten minutes to ready the horses, and do not use that infernal sidesaddle." Without waiting for his opinion, she went straight to her room.

Her heart was racing, her palms were clammy, and she shook from head to toe. She yelled for Carole, but the maid didn't answer. "Where did she get off to?" she wondered as she walked back into the hallway. "Ferry!" she yelled, and the two men at the top of the stairs jumped in unison.

Ferry glanced to Gideon and Gideon jerked his head toward her.

The valet smiled nervously and followed her into her room.

"Help me with this corset, please," she growled.

Ferry paled and walked directly back out of the room as she watched, disgruntled.

A few moments later the door opened and Carole entered.

"Where did you go? Help me with this."

"Of course, milady, I beg yer pardon. I went to prepare some tea. I thought ye might need somethin' fer yer nerves."

*That's great. I am in the midst of a nervous breakdown, and the proper response is to prepare some tea.*

Carole helped her change into the shirt and trousers, but they wouldn't stay up. Carole studied her. "One moment, please, my lady." She scurried from the room, then returned swiftly with a pair of braces and fastened them to the trousers. The waistband sagged from the points of her hips around to the center of the back between the buttons. Carole gathered Francine's long hair into a tight knot at her nape and secured it with pins, then she pulled out some riding boots, fastening them for her. "Is there anythin' else I can do for you, milady?"

"No, thank you, Carole. And I won't be needing a chaperone."

Gideon watched as Francine emerged from her room, meeting him at the head of the stairs. She had no corset on, and her breasts grazed the inside of his borrowed shirt, which hung loosely from her smaller frame. The sight of her naked breasts, the taut nipples, grazing the inside of his crisp white shirt stirred his passion.

She looked into his eyes, checking for any hint of censure, but he simply turned and went down the stairs.

Sanders stood at the front door with his face drawn and sour. He handed Gideon his riding coat and hat, which Gideon turned and placed on Francine. She was engulfed in both, but suffered the indignation in exchange for the freedom she searched for. They walked outside, where Samson and Delilah were attended by the groom. Gideon checked the saddles and moved to help Francine with the mare, but she'd already put her foot in the stirrup and grabbed the pommel, lifting herself astride the saddle without hesitation. He looked up at her and adjusted the stirrups to fit without a word.

Francine glanced across the square and smiled, feeling the horse shifting beneath her weight. This saddle was so much more comfortable

than that contraption she had been forced to use before.

Gideon silently mounted Samson.

Francine drove Delilah across the road to the park. Then, holding the pommel with one hand and leaning forward, she urged Delilah to run. The mare needed no further direction as she sprinted for the center of the park.

Gideon followed at a much slower pace, staying close enough only to keep an eye on her.

She raced across the park, the wind hitting her in the face, her loose curls stinging as they whipped around under the brim of his hat. Sitting back in the saddle, she slowed Delilah, letting loose a peal of laughter that Gideon could hear from halfway across the park. She stopped, bringing Delilah around to face him. She smiled invitingly as Samson walked up to Delilah and they nuzzled.

Gideon regarded her cautiously.

"Now, that's more like it," she said, grinning from ear to ear.

"I believe you may have given Ferry an apoplexy."

She laughed, looking down at Delilah and stroking her neck. "You will have to apologize for me. I'm quite sure if I approach him, it may only aggravate the situation."

Gideon chuckled. "You may be correct. Francine, I—"

She waved her hand. "Don't. This has nothing to do with you. I mean, it does, but— I don't know. It's been a month, and I just recently realized that I'm not myself. I've changed, and not necessarily for the better." She shifted in the saddle

"Francine," he tried again.

"No, don't. Let me finish. I've never in my life felt the way I do when I'm with you. But I also haven't felt like myself. I wonder, if I would feel differently if I felt like myself, or—" She sighed heavily, shaking her head.

"Francine, whatever you need, I'm here."

"I understand that. I've heard it before and still been abandoned, but with you it seems different. I hope you can bear with me as I become more accustomed to my new position in this world. I pray that your feelings for me continue. I pray that you see me."

He smiled. "I believe I do see you, and I am still here."

"I used to be smart. I used to be passionate. I used to be strong. I used to be a lot of things, and then I came to be here, and I don't know who I am anymore." She looked up at him. "I love you."

She turned Delilah and drove her back to the center of the park.

Gideon was confused. He had no idea what to say or do. He thought about the first day, the way the raging woman had keened his senses and fired his passion. He realized that her reaction that day was the spark that had started his fervor. Until then, he had merely been moving through life with perfunctory actions. With that one yell, the scream, the way she advanced on him, he was awakened. Enlivened.

He stared at her now. She wasn't afraid of him and she didn't require anything of him. She wasn't bent on a title and lands. Here she was, in stolen trousers riding through the Grosvenor Square Gardens, and she had never looked more beautiful.

"Francine," he called.

She spun Delilah to him, and the smile on her face lit her expression like a flash bulb, catching his attention.

He pulled Samson closer to her as they faced each other, their legs caught between the two horses. He kicked her toe out of the stirrup, placing his boot in its place and, as she started to object the heavy-handed gesture, he pulled the horses together and jerked her off balance. He took her waist and tugged her toward him, catching her face with his hand. She glared at him, but he paid no heed. His mouth met hers, quelling her protest. She sank toward him as he held Delilah steadfast against Samson with that one strong thigh, his boot solid in her stirrup.

He grabbed her, pulling her across his lap onto Samson, and held her fast to him, driving his tongue deep into her mouth, tasting her, stealing her breath.

She succumbed to his possession fully, wrapping her hands around his waist, her heat sinking into his thin shirt and jolting his muscles. He loosened his hold, suddenly remembering where they were, and drew her back. She held on tight, grabbing his shirt in her fists, refusing to give.

"If you want *me*, you get *me*, and that includes *all* the eccentricities that make up who I am. I will not be conventional. I will not conform to Society's expectations, and I *refuse* to shrink into the background. You will take all of me—or none of me." She paused, her eyes blazing in the afternoon light. "Decide," she said, deftly kicking his boot from Delilah's stirrup, holding the pommel on her saddle as she slid from Samson and back to Delilah with a great show of dexterity. She turned the horse and pushed her into a gallop toward his town house, leaving Gideon gawking at her from the park.

Francine jumped from Delilah, handed the reins to the waiting groom, and ran into the town house, straight to the study. She saw Trumbull talking with Shaw and ignored them as she strode to the sideboard. She poured three fingers of brandy in a glass and downed it, the liquor scorching her throat as it slid down. She refilled the glass and turned toward Trumbull.

He stared at her, wide-eyed.

Shaw looked from Francine to Trumbull and back.

She leaned against the sideboard and set her glass down, then removed Gideon's hat and let her hair tumble from the pins around her shoulders. She took the coat off and threw it across the back of a chair, revealing her slight figure in gentleman's clothes.

Trumbull choked and Shaw gasped, staring at her like a hypnotized snake.

"Trumbull," she said resolutely.

He looked like a cat suddenly trapped by a mouse. "Yes, my lady?" he croaked.

"I have no need of a chaperone. I will no longer conform to your Society's rules and regulations. I will attend the ball you've been planning, but after that the *ton* be damned. I don't give a *shit* what anyone thinks of me. I never have, and I'm not going to start now. I expect you to teach the sisters to be strong and independent or I will have something to say about it, and *you* will hear me. I will not move to Westcreek with you. I'll be staying here with Gideon—if he'll still have me—or I'll be finding my own way." She met his gaze evenly. "Any questions?"

He cleared his throat and motioned with his hands, pointing at her and waving them about as if he were going to break into some meaningful remonstration, but the words did not erupt. He finally rested his hands on his hips and shrugged. "So be it," he said.

She smiled triumphantly and strode from the room.

"This is not going to go over well," Perry said.

Shaw glanced at him. "Where is Roxleigh, anyway? I was supposed to meet him here."

"As was I. It would appear that she left him in the park, or buried him in a ditch, or sold him to gypsies, or something of that nature. Whatever the case, she is no longer my responsibility, obviously, and he never has been."

Shaw studied the gaping door and chuckled, shaking his head. "I would not wish such a woman on anyone," he said, "and yet you encourage this match with your brother?"

"Oh, I do, Shaw, I do. You see, I've been wondering since the moment I met that shrinking violet exactly what my brother saw in her that had him so besotted. She was quiet, charming, intelligent, sweet, beautiful—a perfect companion." He paused, and Shaw gazed at him in confusion. "It is only now, at this moment, having finally seen her fire that I understand. She is magnificent. Truly his equal, of *that* I've no doubt. No regular chit would survive him. Whether or not *he* survives *her*? Well, that's another situation entirely, and I wish him the best of luck."

"What about Society?"

"You heard her, just as clearly as I did. Society be damned."

Shaw and Perry sat back down in front of the desk in silence. "How long do we wait before sending out a search party?" Shaw asked.

"Oh, I imagine at least another hour. I'm sure he'll return as soon as he's done licking his wounds." Perry chuckled. "Besides, if she gave him any of what she gave us, I've no interest in seeing him soon. If at all. In fact, would you be interested in continuing our previous conversation at the pub? I suddenly have need to leave Roxleigh House." He stood.

Shaw nodded, following behind.


Gideon took a few turns around the park quickly, slowly, quickly again. It didn't matter to his muddled head. He'd no idea what had started her fit. He had no idea what would finish it. What he did know was that he was just as scared by the power of his emotions as she appeared to be. He wasn't sure of her past but he knew his fear began somewhere with his father. She had to know he would never do what his father had to his mother.

That's when it struck him, and he knew one thing and one thing alone...

He headed back to the town house. He saw Perry and Shaw skittering down the road and wondered what fabulous episode he'd missed. He leaned on Samson, driving him forward as he called out to the two men. They stopped and looked at him and then at each other.

"No rescue needed," Perry said.

"What about for us?" Shaw mumbled.

Perry continued striding toward the pub, which was only a few blocks off of the square. Gideon left Samson with the groom and ran to catch up with them.

"I thought we were meeting in the study," he said.

Shaw and Perry exchanged a glance. "Well, yes, but as it turns out, you were late," Perry said.

"Yes, *you* were late and Lady Francine, well, she showed up," Shaw said.

"Yes, quite," said Perry.

Gideon laughed. "Yes, I suppose she did. And what, pray tell, did she have to say?"

Perry stopped. "Well, it seems she is not happy with our living arrangements."

"What does that mean?"

They started walking again. "She informed me that she will not be moving to Westcreek, whether she stays with you, or goes out on her own."

"On her...what?"

Shaw winced and moved to the other side of Perry.

Perry smiled as Shaw began to explain. "I believe she meant that she wasn't sure if you were still interested in her, and, if not, she would not stay with you or...something to that effect."

"Why would she... Oh." Gideon shook his head as her reasoning dawned on him.

Shaw opened the door to the pub and they walked in to a round of cheers and welcoming salutations. It appeared that Perry had been missed, and when the crowd caught sight of Gideon walking in behind him, the din grew to a thunderous level. The crowd fell upon the brothers, herding them to the bar amidst the chaos.

"Damn, Trumbull, where the hell did you get off to?" someone yelled across the pub.

Perry smiled. "Oh, here and there."

"Oh sure, I bet here an there, an e'rywhere as well, I'd say," someone else shouted as raucous laughter burst from the others.

Perry smiled.

"We've had a terrible spell wit ye gone. Nobody has tales like ye, milord," an older man called out.

Gideon shook his head and, reaching for the pint of ale slammed to the bar, he walked to a quieter corner across the room.

Shaw grabbed the next pint and followed.

They sat facing one another, leaning over their ale.

Shaw gestured toward Perry. "He is quite…"

"Yes, he is quite. Actually, that is the most common description I get for him—'quite'—which is effective, since there really are no words for the wonder that is my brother." Gideon laughed.

Shaw smiled. "You two are close."

"Closer than we've ever been, in fact."

"Indeed? I would never have guessed you weren't close."

Perry slammed a pint on the table between the two of them and sat down with a grunt. "Did I really do this every night?"

Gideon laughed. "Not every night, just the nights when there wasn't a Society function."

Perry glared at him. "Rox."

"Yes, Perry."

"Your Grace, you cut me to the quick."

"Have I, my lord?"

"Quite."

Shaw burst out in laughter and they both looked at him. "Oh, I beg your pardon! It's just, it seemed funny. I mean you were only just described as, well, 'quite,'" he said with a shrug.

"Quite what?" Perry asked.

"That's it, just…quite."

Perry glared from Shaw to Gideon, then grunted.

"Shaw, have you managed to spend any time with Lady Alice since our return to London?" Gideon asked.

"No, unfortunately not. I've been too busy with the arrangements for Eildon, so I really haven't had an opportunity. I can only hope that changes soon." Shaw downed the pint and set it on the table.

"No matter. She'll attend the ball Friday, and we'll see to it that you are there to accommodate her." Gideon said with a smile.

Shaw lifted a new pint that the barmaid brought. "And what of you and Lady Francine? She is introduced to the *ton* Friday and then what? How long will you wait before coming up to scratch?"

Gideon glared at him. "What did you say?" he asked, surprised by Shaw's bravado.

That was all it took for Shaw to back down. "I— I meant, how long will you wait before you ask her to be your wife?" He studied the bottom of his second empty pint.

"Rox, stop scaring him, and Shaw—this conversation requires more ale," Perry said as he waved at the barmaid again, who came over and pushed him away from the table to sit on his lap.

"Milord, welcome home. I've missed ye a fair bit. Why've ye been gone fer so long?" Lucy drawled.

"Oh, precious, I had to see to some business far, far away."

"Ah, milord, an this business—it has to do wit yer brother the Grace here, don't it?"

"Why, yes, sweet Lucy, it does. Now, why don't you find us three more pints, and don't be a stranger. We may need more than that."

"O' course, milord, an 'tis the 'more than' that I'm happy to oblige ye wit." She stood and leaned over the table, conveniently placing her voluptuous breasts in Perry and Shaw's faces as she reached for the empty tankards.

Perry smiled as Shaw stared forward and Gideon snorted.

After she walked away, Shaw looked at him. "So, you are *friends* with Lucy?"

"Not as friendly as she would like to be. But she does try. There's no harm."

Lucy returned with three fresh pints, sloshing the ale over her hand. "Oh, sorry, gents," she said as she licked her hand and winked at Shaw, dipping one finger in her mouth and pulling it out slowly as she leaned toward him. Then she turned and sauntered away through the thick of the crowd.

Gideon cleared his throat. "How long do you think I should wait with Francine?" he asked.

Perry looked at him, momentarily stunned. "What? Oh, well, she should attend at least one ball after the coming out, and then you should court her publicly, of course. Perhaps a month, and then you can post the banns."

Gideon grunted. "A month?"

Perry shook his head. "Perhaps not. It now poses several logistical problems, considering that she doesn't want to be moved to Westcreek with me. Society be damned or not, I'm not interested in explaining any of this to her." He pointed at Gideon with a threatening glare.

Gideon gave a smirk and nodded, then they both watched for a while as Shaw flirted with the buxom Lucy, downing his third pint a bit quickly before taking another.

"Sso. What exactly iss the plan?" Shaw asked, slurring each S like a snake.

"Pardon?" Perry said.

"Well, you guyss always sseem to have a plan, but you n-n-never let anyone know…what the plan isss. So I's juss wondering. You know, what wass the plan?"

"Oh," Gideon said. "I understand, he wants to know what the plan is. How we are planning on getting him wed to our Lady Alice. Is that right, Shaw?"

"Quite," he said, with a crooked smile as Gideon and Perry began to multiply.

"You are well into your cups already, aren't you?" Gideon asked.

"Quite," he said again, laughing at the two dukes sitting across from him.

"Well, in that case, our *plan* is to have you ruin Lady Alice. It seems the most uncomplicated way to get it done, barring knighthood," Perry said.

Gideon cut Perry a glare, then watched Shaw's expression change from happiness to concern, then to fear.

Shaw glanced from one brother to the other. "I'm to need more drink," he said in a broken voice.

"What are you worried about?" Gideon asked.

"Oh, worried? I juss, I worry that I'll ne'er ssee 'er again. I worry that the lasst time I ssaw 'er, wass the lasst time I'll ever ssee 'er. I worry that she will be bartered away into a marriage of convieniensse. I worry that I'm not good enough for her."

Gideon nodded and Perry shook his head.

Shaw laughed. "You two are funny. Indeed, you," he started, pointing at Gideon, "you sscare the pisss out of me. I am sssoo glad that you weren't there when I got to Eildon. I was ssick the entire trip there, and then to find you gone, I felt sso much better." He smiled, his eyes wide. "Of course, then for *both* of you to show up together, I almost wished for it to have been just you. But you are funny. Very funny, but sc-scary."

Shaw downed the tankard and reached for the new one Lucy set down. He turned to thank her and his nose ended up firmly rooted in her bosom. He opened his mouth in a gasp and promptly shut it, pulling back suddenly and toppling off the bench to the floor.

Lucy grinned as Gideon peered under the table. "One more all around, please, Lucy," Perry said as he grabbed Shaw's arm and yanked him back up.

# TWENTY-FIVE

he ball started at eight o'clock on Friday evening, with Francine's presentation scheduled for precisely nine o'clock. The sisters fussed over Francine most of the afternoon. As was tradition for a coming-out, they dressed her in a perfectly tailored white satin ball gown with the gentlest of colors in the trim. She was a vision of paleness.

Carole fixed Francine's long tresses on top of her head, leaving ringlets hanging down around her face and shoulders, then she quit the room. Francine walked over to the cheval mirror and inspected herself. The ball gown had a fitted bodice that led to a flat-fronted skirt with a large ribbon-festooned bustle in the back. She wore a pair of gold gloves that went all the way to her shoulders, just beneath the cap sleeves. The gloves offset the paleness of the gown, highlighting the way she held her arms loosely in front of her.

She stared at herself in the long mirror, neither happy nor sad, simply nervous for the ball to begin.

She walked over to the front window of her chamber, watching the carriages pull up. Row after row of beautifully appointed ladies and gentlemen descended, entering the town house with smiles of excitement lighting their features. They were here for a show and a story, and they expected it from her.

Francine jumped when Carole knocked at the door and entered. "You look beautiful, milady."

"Yes, I suppose so, Carole. Thank you," Francine replied dryly.

"His Grace has sent something for you to wear tonight."

Carole held the most beautiful necklace, stunning in its simplicity. A set of clear stones led toward the blue heart-shaped center stone. The necklace was short and when Carole fastened it, the sapphire rested just above the hollow at the base of Francine's throat, filling it with blue fire.

"I suppose this is another loan?"

"No, milady. His Grace bid me tell ye 'tis a gift."

"Ugh!" she exclaimed. "This will never do."

Carole shook her head. "No, milady, I don't s'pose it will," Carole said with a smile as she moved to the wardrobe.

Gideon waited at the bottom of the stairs for his brother to be announced, one of the last guests to arrive, but Perry walked in without pause and descended the three small steps to the ballroom as Sanders quickly rattled off his title. The brothers made their way over to Shaw, who stood with a group of gentlemen at the back of the room.

Gideon ably sidestepped the majority of his pursuers, but much to his chagrin he couldn't avoid the cousins. He smiled. "Isadore, Saorise, Maebh, Quintin, Calder, Jerrod, Wilder, Poppy." "How wonderful to see you all here tonight. I assume your mothers are present?"

Calder smiled. "You know, if you had agreed to receive them this week, or arranged for a family dinner, the task at hand might be less tremendous."

"Where is Grayson?" Perry asked as he dragged Shaw into the gathering.

"Grayson is...Grayson," Calder replied.

Gideon grunted. "I haven't seen him since his return and ascension as the Duke of Warrick."

Poppy smiled, but her eyes were sad. "I would so much like for you to speak with him, Rox. He always did look up to you," she said sweetly, her dark locks bobbing about her cheeks.

Gideon took her hand and kissed her cheek. "Your wish is my command," he said with a smile.

Poppy beamed. "I don't know why everyone is so fearful of you."

Gideon growled. "Well, let's just keep this our little secret." He winked.

Poppy giggled and Calder elbowed Gideon. "Actually, I was being regaled by a group of gents who were enamored with the infamous railway deal that you brokered in less than a day, especially after so many others had unsuccessfully tried for more than a fortnight. Quite an impressive bit of work in your off-time."

Gideon scowled. "It only takes simple reasoning to bring multiple parties together for the benefit of the outcome. They were all being quite ridiculous, after all. The newer engines can travel upwards of seventy miles-per-hour, yet the track they travel can only manage the heat and pressure of a fully loaded locomotive at thirty. It is entirely logical that the track be replaced, providing a more efficient transport across country. The cost and loss of income from the downed lines will be offset within months of replacement by the more efficient and more oft traveled line. Any argument against the improvements was ludicrous."

Shaw's eyes went round. "I— Well."

"Once everyone agreed with me, the only major obstacle was the process of figuring out which lines needed to be closed and when, to interrupt service north as little as possible, which wasn't much—"

"Shaw, I must introduce you to the family before Gideon's business mind carries the night away entirely," Perry interrupted. "There are a wealth of run-down properties in need of an architect to update them."

"An architect? That is fortuitous!" Calder exclaimed.

"He won't be available at least until the fall," Gideon grumbled.

"You always have been so possessive. I am Lord Thorne Calder, Mr. Show. Marquess of Canford and cousin to these two boors. No doubt when they are finished with you, you will have a look at my estate."

Shaw smiled. "Of course, my lord, with haste."

Perry introduced the rest of his cousins, who all eyed Shaw curiously, then Shaw turned back to Perry.

"Trumbull, have you—"

He was cut off by the wave of Perry's hand. "I spotted her when I walked in. Are you telling me you haven't seen her yet?"

"No."

"Well, we shall change that. Gideon, how soon will they be announcing Lady Francine?"

"It should be any minute. Actually, it should have already been done. I gave Carole the necklace just before we came down, and she said she was prepared."

"Is that a peace offering?" Perry asked with a sly grin, taking a cutting stare from Gideon.

His cousins shifted in expectation of a row.

Perry nodded. "The musicians look to be getting antsy." He glanced up to the first floor balcony that encircled the ballroom. "Well, it won't hurt to go find our Lady Alice then, will it?"

Gideon shook his head as someone stumbled into him and he turned, a heavy growl rumbling from his chest.

"I beg your pardon, Your Grace, I seem to have tripped. I beg your pardon," the man said.

"You already said that," Gideon grumbled at the stricken man. Perry elbowed his brother's side to warn him of his manners as the man skittered away.

"Good God, man, I thought you were going to make the best of this evening,"

Gideon looked at him. "I was. It's just that I haven't spoken with her since yesterday and I—" He was cut off by the three loud whacks of the baton on the floor.

"The Lady Francine Larrabee," Sanders announced.

Gideon's breath caught as he turned, flanked by his cousins and brother, to see her.

A collective gasp emanated from the ballroom as the *ton* caught sight of the stunning woman in the entry. Her hair was long, piled loosely on top of her head, with ripples of curls cascading down her back and past her waist in ringlets that glistened like burnished bronze. Her face glowed, her chin tipped up with confidence while her bright blue eyes searched for him. She wore a peacock-blue silk gown that was cut very low across her breasts. The dress was tailored perfectly, accentuating her ripe bosom but barely covering it. The front was gathered below the waist, the skirt layered and drawn up in a bustle that cascaded back like a waterfall. The dress flowed like the wings of a butterfly when she moved.

Draped around her smooth throat was the necklace he had sent her, the brilliant sapphire in the center.

"Rox," Perry said. Gideon's mouth had gone dry. "Good God, man. Roxleigh!" he said again, pushing him toward the stairs. "You can't leave her standing alone. Get *over* there!"

Gideon strode across the empty dance floor toward her as his cousins swarmed Perry with questions.

Gideon stopped at the base of the steps. "My lady, you look—ravishing," he said softly. She smiled down at him. "This is not at all what we expected," he said with a grin. "As I am sure you are aware." He took her gloved hand in his and kissed her wrist, lingering just a moment too long.

She continued smiling at him as he nodded to the musicians. They listened to the murmur of the crowd spread through the ballroom in gaining waves. He swept her in a large circle around the empty dance floor, finally pulling her in and placing his other hand high on her back as the music started. She lifted her arm and let it rest atop the length of his, placing her slippers just next to his sleek black shoes.

Gideon was beaming, and it took her breath away. The man was a vision any day, but with his formal black and white dress and this smile, he was astonishing.

"To what do I owe *this* honor?" he asked, inspecting her dress with hungry eyes as he spoke.

She caught his gaze and parted her lips, hesitating before she answered. "Well, Your Grace, the necklace you sent for me to wear simply didn't match the other gown."

"Indeed?" His eyebrows lifted.

"Indeed," she echoed with a small nod. "It's breathtaking." She ran her hand over the stone.

"Breathtaking," he repeated as he assessed her.

"Yes, entirely too beautiful. The dress ruined it. The color was wrong. The trim was gold, which clashed. I couldn't possibly snub the Duke of Roxleigh. After all, he was so gracious as to host this ball for me. I would appear entirely ungrateful. There would be a scene."

"Mmm. Entirely."

"I don't suppose you've heard of him? The Duke of Roxleigh? He is a terrible boor, so I'm told. He is a mean, unsightly recluse and quite obnoxiously proper."

"Truly?"

"Oh, yes, and I wouldn't want to cross him, you see. That would be a terrible mistake."

"I must agree there," he said. "What does this duke look like?"

Her breath caught. "Well, stunning, really."

"Really? When you said he was unsightly, I pictured an old, awful, filthy—"

"Oh, no, no," she said. "That's part of the trap. He is absolutely handsome. At least, you know, as long as he doesn't remove his shirt. But with his clothes on—dark hair, bottomless green eyes, perfectly tailored formal suit, perfectly shined black shoes." Her eyes traveled his lean, powerful figure, coming to rest on his chest. "Perfectly fashioned tie." She looked up into his striking green eyes and her breath caught again. "Stunning," she whispered as he spun her through the ballroom, aware that every pair of eyes was on her, including his.

"Francine." She gazed into his smoldering eyes. "Francine," he breathed.

"You already said that," she whispered.

"Yes, of course. I— Francine," he said again as she giggled. "Francine, would you do me the honor—"

She tripped over his foot and he caught her up against himself and the rest of the ballroom disappeared on a hush. He dropped to one knee before her, knowing that he needed to beg her permission. "Francine, would you do me the honor of becoming my wife?" he asked as he looked into her eyes.

Around them, the ballroom broke loose with chatter. Even the Duke of Roxleigh, reclusive and foreboding as he was, was expected to follow the line of decent behavior—and this was *not* it, Francine realized.

"Yes," she breathed, overcome by the emotion she found in the depths of his green eyes, and suddenly, she trusted him, no matter the consequences. "Yes…yes! Yes, Gideon, yes!" she called out as the ballroom fell silent again, the music stopping. He leaned back and laughed joyously as she grasped his lapels and urged him to his feet, searching his face.

"Francine," he said with a husky voice. "I love you."

Thinking quickly, Perry caught the attention of the musicians and waved to them to start the music again. Then he moved across the dance floor toward Lady Alice Gracin and bowed perfunctorily, sweeping her out to the dance floor as her mother attempted to protest.

Meanwhile, Gideon pulled Francine back into the waltz.

Perry eyed Shaw, who was scowling at him, and carefully passed Lady Alice off, then swept the young girl next to her out to the dance floor without missing a step. "And who might you be?" Perry asked the small brunette in his arms. She stared up wordlessly as his cousins followed suit, taking the closest available partners and escorting them onto the floor to finish the waltz.

Gideon walked out of the ballroom to the terrace and straight into

the lion's den.

"Hell and damn, Rox! Are you trying to ruin yourself...and me? And Francine?" Perry yelled, advancing on his brother.

Gideon smiled. "You have nothing to fear from this," he said. "I just saved her reputation, didn't you hear? She has agreed to be my wife."

"Oh, I heard. Everybody heard. Everyone," Perry said, turning away to pace.

"Well, that makes it easier, doesn't it?"

"What about any of this has been easy? I'm starting to think I preferred you as a recluse," he said through clenched teeth.

"Careful, brother, people will mistake you for me, or me for you." Gideon tried to smile, but he was stonewalled. "I see. So I suppose congratulations would be too much to ask."

Perry stopped in front of his brother and sighed. He held his hand out. "I congratulate you and your betrothed. I assume that the surprises at this point will wane?"

"Perhaps. Though I believe I'll look into a special license. I would like to wed as soon as possible. Of course, we can always go to Gretna Green. It isn't far from Eildon." Gideon paused, a smile breaking across his features. "We could leave London. We could go home." He shook his brother's hand vigorously as his excitement grew.

"Your Grace," Francine said as she walked out to the terrace.

"My lady, I must congratulate you on such a successful match."

Francine hugged Perry tightly. His eyes widened. He grunted, immediately aware that he was superfluous, and bowed to her before returning to the ballroom, where he surveyed the crowd.

"You never stay where I leave you, do you?" Gideon asked.

"Am I supposed to?" she asked sweetly.

He shook his head with a laugh as she walked over to him. "How is this to work if you do not do as I request of you?"

"Very well, I should think." Her approach signaled an increasing cadence in his heart. His veins suffused with heat from her proximity, and he squared his shoulders to ward off the onslaught of emotion.

She pulled one glove off and touched his gloved hand, turning it over and rubbing a circle into his palm through the thin grey fabric. His heart raced and his pulse quickened as she pinched the tip of each finger to loosen the glove. "What are you—"

"Shh," she whispered, slowly pulling the glove off, then tracing the skin between his fingers with the tip of hers.

He groaned at the gentle touch and a shiver traced up his arm, making him jerk away.

She frowned. "I'm sorry, I didn't mean to offend," she said quietly, holding his glove out to him.

He took it as he stretched his fingers, releasing the charges that surged beneath his skin.

"I'm not offended. Quite the opposite, in fact." He turned, taking her arm and pulling her swiftly across the garden. He stopped beneath a large willow tree, the curtain of branches sweeping the garden floor.

They didn't touch, they didn't speak. His eyes grazed over her strong yet delicate figure, sweeping her curves, making her muscles tense with his glances.

The gown itself meant nothing. He realized that whatever the condition of her clothing, he was equally drawn to her, amazed by her, in love with her.

She sighed heavily. "Kiss me," she said, and he reached out with his bare hand, cupping her face and drawing her to him. Slower than sunrise he leaned down to her, brushing his mouth across hers, breathing her scent, as he warmed her lips for his kiss.

She held still, suffering his teasing ministrations as her senses flared in the agony of her patience.

His hand traveled to her nape, spreading her hair then clenching it between his fingers.

She allowed him to control her. Parting her lips, she felt his tongue caress her, his mouth hovering. He stroked her tenderly, compelling her mouth to open wider to him.

She marveled at the way he responded to her, and the way her body responded to him without permission. She lifted her hand and placed it on his hip, feeling the muscles across his abdomen tense. She inhaled through her mouth, tasting his breath, that familiar unsweetened cinnamon. She smiled under his lips and felt him smile back before he opened his hand on the back of her head and forced her mouth to his, stoking her passion.

Her mouth went dry as she thought of the feeling of his hardness, covered with satiny skin. She brushed her hand across the front of his trousers, her knuckles grazing his erection through the fabric, and his muscles reacted, his hand pulling her hips against his, melding them together. She was drawn completely against him, shoulder to toe.

She arched her back and the corset strained, her breasts swelling over the bust line of her dress, filling the delicate scarf that attempted to control them.

Gideon broke the kiss and leaned his shoulders back, forcing his turgid shaft against her belly though her skirts. He pulled the silk scarf away from her chest, sending traces of electricity shooting to her core.

She gasped, unable to move her head out of his firm hold as he bent to trace warm kisses across the swollen ridge of softness, delving his tongue into the tight crease between her breasts and tasting the sweet and salty honey of her skin.

He moved across her breast to her arm, placing kisses at the edge of her sleeve. He reached up and tugged on it, freeing the nipple that was tucked just below the bodice's trim, and drew it into his mouth.

She cried out and he quickly covered her mouth with his, catching her pleasured gasp between his lips.

His kisses slowed, calming rather than frustrating her desire. He released her, and she turned, adjusting her bodice. He held out the scarf, which she attempted to take, but he refused to release it, forcing her to turn back to him. He lifted the scarf to her bosom, laying it neatly across the crest and tucking it into her bodice.

"I do believe we should return to the ball, my lady. The *ton* will be concerned with your absence," he admonished, smiling. "Let me have a look at you." He straightened her gloves, and her skirt, gently untangling her hair and combing through the long curls. He studied her kiss-swollen lips and smiled again, brushing his thumb across the surface. "There isn't much to be done about this."

She blushed, tucking her fingers into the front of his trousers and pulling him toward her. "Or this," she said gruffly, stroking the tip of his erection through the fabric with her thumb.

He grumbled. "All in due time."

"*I* believe the time is overdue," she replied, and he grasped her shoulders and moved her away from him, breaking her hold on his waistband.

She examined his strong form, the muscles beneath his formal suit flexing as he straightened his waistcoat and jacket, adjusted his trousers, pulled the jacket closed, then allowed his eyes to travel over her once more. "I will commission a portrait of you in this very dress. I never want to forget how you look tonight."

*Madeleine.*

It was the dress and the necklace from the portrait of Madeleine, but it wasn't Madeleine. It had been her all along. "Your Grace, I would request you have it made a miniature, so that you could keep it close to your heart," she said quietly, accepting the truth of the realization as she spoke.

He smiled. "And so it shall be." He replaced his glove and offered his arm. "A miniature. I like that idea very much."

She laughed. "Whose idea was it to go for a walk in the garden?"

They ducked out from beneath the canopy of the willow tree and walked back to the terrace, only to find Perry pacing by the entry.

Perry's eyes widened at the sight of his ward, who was quite obviously tousled. Gideon laughed and leaned toward Francine.

"Perhaps you should go to your suite and have Carole help you…" He gestured toward her hair and bodice. She moved quickly for the stairs.

"Really?" Perry growled. "Really?"

Gideon lifted a brow. "It wasn't my fault."

"We have work to do," Perry said as he walked over to his brother and straightened his neck cloth and lapels. "In your absence, Shaw has been abandoned to a room of insensitive girls and mothers who aren't interested in his lack of title."

"Are you saying Shaw is no match for the Countess of Greensborough? Well, we'll see who triumphs in this affair." Gideon strode into the ballroom and surveyed the crowd.

He growled when he spotted the countess and, sidestepping her smartly, he bowed before Lady Alice. He took her hand and kissed her knuckles. "Lady Alice, it has been entirely too long. Are you enjoying the ball?"

She curtseyed and looked up at him. "Why, yes, of course, Your Grace. It has been…quite entertaining thus far."

He smiled, motioning to the dance floor as a waltz started, and she nodded. He led her in a broad half-circle before pulling her close to dance.

"You look quite lovely tonight," he said, inspecting the moss-green gown that complemented her pale skin and fiery curls perfectly.

"I thank you, Your Grace, for that thoughtful comment. But won't your fiancée be upset to find you dancing with me?"

"Not at all. She'll understand when she learns of my ulterior motives."

"Ulterior motives?" she asked nervously. "And what would those be?"

"Lady Alice, I endeavored to bring your betrothed to visit you all the way from Eildon Hill, yet here you are playing coy with me."

She smiled. "I'm afraid one dance is all I'm bound to get." She sighed. "My mother won't let him near my dance card."

"That is something easily overcome."

"Have my champions returned?"

"Yes, my lady, they have—in force." Gideon bowed as the dance ended. "In fact, there are a few you'll need introductions to."

She curtseyed to thank him for the dance and politely handed him her dance card. He filled in more than a few lines. He would enjoy another dance, and Perry would enjoy at least two, and of course Shaw. He thought for another moment, then filled in the balance of her card. Her mother glared at him, and her grandmother smiled, pinching her daughter-in-law's arm.

"I see your grandmother looks pleased," Gideon said.

Lady Alice nodded and placed her hand on his forearm, allowing him to escort her to her grandmother.

Gideon bowed before the countess then the dowager countess, taking her hand for a greeting. "My lady, I am so glad you could join us this night."

The dowager countess smiled. "Well, of course, Your Grace. I certainly wouldn't have missed this for anything," she said, turning that smile on her granddaughter. "Is His Grace making an effort to keep you busy again, my dear?"

"Yes, Grandmother, he is."

The dowager glanced at Gideon, then dismissed her daughter and granddaughter with nothing more than a nod.

"Your Grace, are you aware that my daughter has been diligently working to attain my granddaughter a suitable peer?"

Gideon assessed her expression. "I assumed as much," he answered, preparing for a lecture.

"Are you further aware your attempts are quite effectively thwarting those efforts?"

He attempted to quell a devious smile as he nodded. The dowager looked at him as if to measure the contents of his soul. "I hear you have an architect working at Eildon Hill?"

"I do, my lady. A Mr. Amberly Shaw. He is quite impressive. I believe he shall be most successful. Have you made his acquaintance?"

"Yes, I have, and I am quite impressed with him as well. I've no doubt with *your* help he'll be even more successful," she said with a grin. "I happen to be quite impressed with your lady—your fiancée—as well, Your Grace."

Gideon smiled. "Thank you, my lady, I do appreciate the kind words. I believe your granddaughter's dance card is in need of the attention of my cousins, if you do not mind?"

"By all means, Your Grace. If you'll excuse me."

Gideon bowed, then watched her glide across the ballroom. He realized Francine was standing just behind him, talking with a group of older ladies. He listened and found she seemed to be getting along famously, their scandalous dance and his proposal hardly damaging her future.

The women lauded her for her success in taming the reclusive beast and bringing him up to scratch without the benefit of a true dowry to promote the match. She simply smiled and nodded, skating along gently on the words of their jovial banter. They were completely taken with her.

Gideon laughed, and Francine's arms tingled. She put one hand behind her and he caught it behind him, gently caressing a circle into her palm. The ladies whispered among themselves for a moment until she excused herself, turning to her duke.

Without a word he swept her once again to the dance floor. He pulled her around in grand arcs, her skirts floating through the air behind her. She tilted her head back, feeling the heady rush of the swift music.

As the music waned, Gideon's vision grazed the crowd, resting on a face he found both familiar and unsettling. He tensed, instantly drawing Francine into his protective stance as she looked up with concern.

He pulled her into the throng, calling for Perry as he kept an eye on the man. But as he searched for his brother he momentarily lost sight of his target. His body tightened under Francine's hands, and she stopped him.

"What is it?"

"Hepplewort."

"He doesn't belong here." She looked around. "Or does he?"

Gideon located Perry, who'd been dancing with Lady Alice. Perry's smile faded the moment Gideon caught his attention and nodded toward Hepplewort. Perry scowled and went after the earl.


"Attendance at this event is by invitation only, my lord. You have none," Perry said without preamble.

The short, rotund man looked up into Perry's face. "I have business with you, actually. Why don't you have your brother meet us in his parlor?"

"Why don't you call on the duke and myself at an appropriate hour, if you indeed have business that requires our attention?"

"Oh, I think the duke will be quite interested in this."

Perry waved to Sanders and asked him to escort Hepplewort to the blue parlor and to wait with him.


"Francine, I would like you to go up to your room while we *dispose* of this man." Gideon watched her eyes narrow at his request. "Can you do that for me?"

She nodded and he knew that simple agreement took a great deal of effort on her part. She followed him out of the ballroom.

Gideon waited as she ascended the staircase, then turned to Perry. The brothers walked into the parlor. "What business have you brought to my house, tonight of all nights?" Gideon asked as he strode directly to Hepplewort.

The earl stood. "I took your advice, Your Grace. I had my solicitor look over the paperwork, and we found an error. It seems that your agreement is just as incomplete as mine. Until one of us actually completes the terms of either, neither is binding. I only thought it appropriate to inform you in an expedient manner."

Gideon's blood boiled as Hepplewort continued. "The fact is that should *I* marry Madeleine, and consummate said marriage, *my* contract with the Larrabees would then be complete, legal, and binding. Unless, of course, you can procure a proper marriage for her to a peer before I am able to retrieve her."

Gideon stared at him, grinding his teeth as his brain worked to find a solution to get the grotesque man out of his town house and away from Francine permanently.

"Actually, Hepplewort, you must have come late to the ball," Perry said, stepping next to Gideon. "Because if you had been here earlier, you would have been witness to the fact that I *have* actually made an agreement with a peer to take Lady Madeleine off my hands. We have already discussed the dowry and terms."

"Who is it?" Hepplewort spat at the brothers.

At that moment the door to the parlor slammed open and Francine walked in with Sanders trailing behind. "Why, my lord, it happens to be this gentleman here, the Duke of Roxleigh." Her eyes blazed as they cut through Hepplewort, taking his measure. Her expression turned to one of disgust as her gaze traveled over him.

Hepplewort stared back at her, his eyes bulging, his skin turning beet-red and sticky with sweat.

"I apologize that we haven't sent out formal announcements yet, since we are only just betrothed, but as it happens, I am, in fact, promised to the duke. There is no need for you to continue this farce," she said. "You need to leave me alone."

"You are mine!" Hepplewort sputtered, clenching his fists at his sides. "You were *promised* to me!"

Francine's lips pulled tight across her teeth as she walked forward and slapped the small man as hard as she could, knocking him off kilter. "You son of a bitch!"

The brothers looked at her in shock as Hepplewort grasped his cheek, his eyes flaring. Gideon and Perry both reached for Francine, quickly tucking her behind them.

"You stupid little—" Hepplewort started, but Gideon grabbed him by the arm and dragged him toward the portico doors that exited directly to the front of the town house.

Hepplewort glared at him. "She is mine," he squealed, pointing at her.

"That is quite enough."

"You haven't ruined her. I can tell by your demeanor, and as long as she is intact, she is still mine," Hepplewort said as he tripped toward the door.

"Our business has concluded. You are leaving and you will *not* return. In the future, should I see you anywhere near the lady in question, I will notify the constable and have you removed. Is that perfectly clear?"

Hepplewort yelled, kicking and screaming. "You cannot do this! You cannot keep her from me! She is mine! She is *mine!*"

Gideon pushed him out the door, then nodded to Smyth, who was waiting nearby.

Hepplewort charged back up the steps but Gideon's man placed his hand on the butt of a pistol to warn him. "Thank you for attending, my lord. Have a wonderful evening." Smyth waved to Hepplewort's driver, and the carriage pulled up in front of the town house.

Gentry opened the door for him, then pushed him to the carriage floor. "Have a nice evening, my lord. Return home safely," he said, shutting the door and securing the latch with his own cravat before Hepplewort could right himself.

Gentry looked up at Hepplewort's oversized driver. "If you value your job, then you value the life of your master. If he stays in London another minute, he'll not live to see the dawn. Are we understood?" he asked, handing the coachman a purse of coin.

The enormous driver took the money and nodded. Swiftly pulling the ribbons, he sent the horse team flying down the street. They heard Hepplewort yell as he was knocked off his feet again when the carriage lurched forward. The men smiled stiffly as they walked back into the town house.

Gideon moved toward Francine, who stood staring after the carriage through the open doorway. "What exactly does he mean that this isn't over? How could it not be over?" Her voice was panicked as she looked at him.

He glanced at Perry, who turned to wait inside.

"Francine, he honestly believes that as long as your maidenhead is intact, he can still lay claim to you."

The blood drained from her face. "What?"

"I've no idea how much you heard, but he truly believes that you belong to him. Even our betrothal has not—and will not—stop him."

She took a deep breath, trying to steady her ragged nerves. "Well, being forced out of London should do the trick," she said indignantly. "How is it that men believe they can own women?" she asked, straightening her spine and shifting her weight away from him. "I don't see how any of this is logical. He is antiquated and ridiculous." She looked out the doorway again as Gideon's men walked up.

"I'm sorry that you've had to go through this," Gideon said.

She glanced at him, then turned from the entry to return to the ball, but it wasn't quite the same.

Hours later, she walked around the entry hall with Gideon at her side, bidding farewell to the people she'd met and thanking them for attending. Gideon appreciated her diplomacy, marveling at what a wonderful and genuine person she was. She invited people to tea, she invited others to supper, and even more to the house party at the end of the summer. She gave a final wave and started up the stairs to her room leaving Gideon in the foyer. She paused at the landing and caught his eye. She nodded at Perry and Shaw who stood next to him, then disappeared into the depths of the first floor balcony.

"That was quite an eventful evening, Your Grace," Shaw said with a grin.

"Indeed, Rox, I haven't had such an enjoyable time at a ball in years," Perry added.

Gideon turned on the men, forcing them to back up a step, then he grinned broadly.

"Well, gentlemen, I do nothing in small measures, after all." He shook their hands before they took their leave.

Gideon saw the last carriage roll away from the house and nodded to Sanders, who clapped his hands and called for the team of footmen and maids to begin the cleaning. Gideon took the stairs two at a time, went straight to his suite, and collapsed on the bed.

# TWENTY-SIX

Gideon awoke the next morning more than slightly disgruntled. He thought for sure Francine would have been emboldened by their tryst in the garden, but perhaps the words of her former betrothed had stayed her. When he finally drifted off, his sleep was undisturbed. He rose and dressed for their morning ride, then found Francine in her borrowed riding clothes, already astride Delilah, patiently waiting.

He stopped short, thinking Sanders must be having a fit with Francine in front of Roxleigh House like this. He smiled as he pulled on his riding gloves, and she smiled back before taking off across the park. Samson bristled, his eyes wide, stamping his hoof impatiently as Gideon vaulted onto his back and gave chase.

Although she was a natural rider, she was still quite inexperienced. He didn't want to tempt fate, so he held Samson carefully in check to avoid spooking Delilah.

They dodged around the park and he reveled in the way her strong laughter carried. She finally rested, leaning back in her saddle and walking the mare. When Gideon pulled Samson abreast of Delilah, Francine smiled coyly at him.

"I'll be taking the sisters shopping this afternoon," she said.

Gideon deliberated momentarily. He had become so accustomed to barking out orders and seeing them followed that interacting with Francine was oddly difficult. He knew, however, that she wouldn't allow him leave to treat her commonly.

"All right," he said slowly. He felt like he was being forced to relearn how to interact. "But I would appreciate it, for my sake, if you would take the carriage and outriders, considering the events of last night."

She smiled; he breathed.

"Hepplewort must be miles from here by now. You and Trumbull were quite specific when you removed him, and so was I."

"Yes. However, he didn't seem convinced by the first meeting we had that he was to keep his distance, so I am not entirely sure that he'll take heed this time." He didn't like the idea of Francine away from him with Hepplewort on the loose, but he didn't see much choice. He hoped that Hepplewort was at his estate, taking the time to gather his wits and realize his errors. In the meantime, getting Francine safely married was of the utmost importance.

"I was hoping we could talk about the wedding," he said.

She turned to him. "Thank you. For letting me take the sisters out." She spoke as if she hadn't heard him.

He laughed, considering there was nothing he could have said or done to stop their excursion. "Francine," he said. "The wedding?"

"Well. What do you have in mind?"

He regarded her intently. *This has to be a trick. Doesn't every female dream of planning their wedding?* He pulled Samson up, sitting straight in the saddle. *No, she wouldn't, would she? For someone with her past, a wedding would be a sign of bondage and nothing more.* The realization saddened him and his voice lowered. "You agreed to marry me," he said dejectedly.

"Yes, I did."

"Why?"

"Because—because I love you."

"Yes, and I you. But why do you want to be my *wife*?" he asked in a dishearteningly serious tone.

"I— I don't know." Francine turned away, not wanting to feel the emotions mirrored in his deep gaze. She hadn't really thought about it. *Why is he asking this?* She urged Delilah forward. She'd never considered the subject of marriage beyond the obligatory ten-year plan. It was only another check on the list: graduate high school, check; finish college, check; get a good job, check.

*Find a man,* she thought as she turned again, looking back at him. *Check.* She smiled.

"Every inch of me wants to be with you. I can feel you in my bones, within and without. My skin aches for your touch, when you are nearby and far away. I suppose that is why," she said as she glanced down. She took a deep breath. "It is as if you are another layer of my soul, perhaps a missing part of the whole of me."

He leaned forward in his saddle to hear her clearly, nudging Samson alongside Delilah. He'd never expected to find someone who wanted to marry him for no tangible reason. He'd believed that he'd be relegated to a loveless marriage with a blue-blooded chit who would bear him issue. Previously, his only desire for finding a wife centered on his need to have sons, just as his desire for physical intimacy would lead him to find a mistress, and any need he had for intelligent conversation would be appeased with a visit from his brother or business associates. How he'd come to believe that all these needs would be better served by one person was beyond comprehension for him. Except…that one person was Francine, and that was what made the difference.

"There is no reason for us not to be *to-ge-ther*," she said, smiling without meeting his eyes.

"I agree. Indeed, I expected you to come to me last night after— well—last night." He loosened the rein and leaned his elbows on the pommel.

She laughed and reached out, running her fingers through his inky black hair, pushing it back from his brow. "You've no idea how difficult it was for me to not come to you."

"Why, then?" he asked, straightening in the saddle and forcing Samson to shift beneath him.

She placed her hand under his chin and searched his eyes. "I figured you deserved a respite from my rather indecent behavior," she said in her best proper voice. She dropped her hand and slid from Delilah.

He jumped from Samson and ran to her, catching her up against him. "I want no such respite," he said. "I want you. There is no way about it. Do not withhold yourself from me. Not ever. Do not assume anything about my wishes. If you are unsure of something, you have only to ask. Is that understood?"

"Yes." He took her up, kissing her face fervently. "Gideon," she groaned, then: "Gideon," she said again, laughing.

She tried to turn her face away from his kisses. It struck her then that he had refused to—*What had he called it? Ruin her.* He'd refused to ruin her.

"Gideon, I am not the one who has been withholding." She looked up at him from the shade of her long eyelashes, taunting him. He smiled and held her face in his hands.

"We are leaving on the morrow. We are going directly to Gretna Green, which isn't far from Eildon. We will be married immediately, and then I am taking you home—for our wedding night."

"Still so *proper*," she said teasingly, though with a hint of disappointment. "If the issue is that I must be ruined, then be done with it. Ruin me, Gideon," she pleaded in a throaty voice.

He groaned and gripped her shoulders as he studied her. "This isn't something that can be done twice, Francine. I have waited and now want it to be perfect."

"There is *no such thing* as perfect. Waiting for perfect is waiting forever," she said, then tried to move away.

"I used to think that before I met you. But for you I want everything to be perfect. Because of you I understand all the fuss that women make over the wedding ceremony. And it is *for you* that I will endeavor to make that happen," he said as he smoothed his hands down her back, causing a shiver to streak her spine.

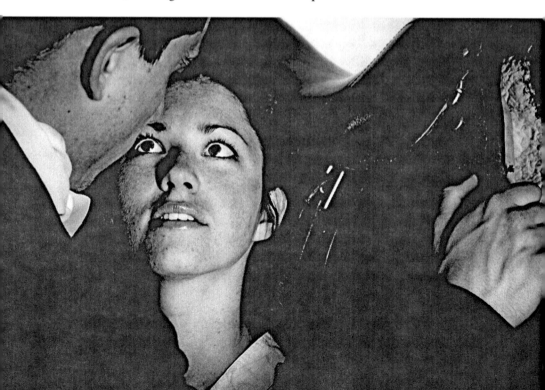

"Perfection?" she asked breathlessly, staring at the full, soft lips that threatened her mastery.

"Yes," he whispered. "Perfection."

"But, Gideon," she complained, in no more than a whisper, her resolve melting under his scrutiny. "You are such a tease."

"We only do this once, Francine." He gave her a cunning look. "How is this going to work if you don't *listen* to me?"

Her gaze jumped to his, feeling the sudden shift in his demeanor. "Just fine, I should think," she said, glaring at him through a smile. He relented with a silent chuckle.

"Please let me do this one thing, Francine. Let me do *this* right."

"Right, for the sake of Society, propriety, posterity..."

"*Propriety be damned*," he cut in gruffly. "I want this for *you*."

That was the only thing he could have said to sway her, and there it was. She inhaled sharply, looking into his eyes and remembering how it had felt to have him treasure her innocence. "I love you, Gideon." He stroked his thumb over her mouth, sealing the words in.

"And I you." The words were a prelude to his kiss.

They took their time returning to the manor, walking side by side as they led the horses. They strode into the dining room for breakfast to find Perry, Shaw, Miss Faversham, Amélie, and Maryse already sitting and chatting. The men realized at second glance that the smaller gentleman with Gideon was actually a gentlemanly-clad Francine and stood.

She smiled back at them demurely and greeted the sisters, walking over to sit with them. They enjoyed breakfast, the men discussing the pending departures and the ladies discussing their shopping trip.

The sisters laughed and finished their breakfast quickly, wanting to set out. Nobody had ever taken them shopping. They were not allowed to go into town, much less into crowded boutiques and shops full of other people. They tittered away in French as everyone looked on in wonderment at their pure, unaffected behavior.

The ladies started at Harrods. Francine enjoyed perusing the displays, but it didn't look much like the giant conglomeration that she had seen in the news. She assumed this was the original building, by the way it had overtaken several neighboring structures. Inside was a veritable labyrinth of merchandise from home furnishings to groceries and ready-to-wear clothing. She smiled as they moved from department to department. She had never really been much for shopping in her other life, but could see how it could become an obsession for some, especially in a place that seemed such a magical patchwork as this.

Keeping track of the sisters was like wrangling cats. One would see something and the other would rush over, only to have a newer and shinier item catch her eye, leading her off in the opposite direction.

Francine was excited to find clothes that didn't need so much primping and preparation, not to mention assistance. She and Miss Faversham helped the girls choose some comfortable ready-to-wear dresses—simple, easy frocks for the country. She picked out doeskin riding trousers, shirts, jackets, hats, gloves, and boots to match, for all of them.

They purchased everything they could possibly need and then some, having everything sent to Roxleigh House.

They eventually left Harrods and returned to the bustling London streets. "I need a bookstore," Francine said suddenly. They continued walking, avoiding the horse patties and dodging delivery people who were oblivious to their finery. Halfway down the block, Francine spotted a large bookstore. The sun was shining and the only clouds in the sky were from the coal burning fires at the factories.

Grover moved to follow in the carriage, but Francine waved him off. The street was so crowded with hacks and other carriages, it would be easier for them to walk back.

"We're only going to that bookstore," she said, pointing it out. "There's no need to follow."

The men nodded but kept a close eye on the ladies as they wandered their way to the shop. As they approached the bookstore, the sisters looked around, a bit disgruntled, and Francine glanced at Miss Faversham.

"Would you mind? Maybe you could take them to the shop across the street? I won't be long," she said.

Miss Faversham nodded and Francine thanked her. She heard a muffled squeal and turned, smiling at the sisters.

A bell rang at the door as she entered and a small, bespectacled man greeted her from behind a small counter. "Well, miss, what can I help you find today?"

"Can you show me where the most recent publications are?" He walked around the counter and led her to a shelf beside the front window.

"These are the newest periodicals and news sheets. The books are here on this shelf," he said as he inspected some of the titles.

"Thank you," she said, nodding. "Are you familiar with Sir Arthur Conan Doyle?"

He looked puzzled. "No, I regret I'm not, though I can add the name to my notes and—"

"No, no. No, please, don't trouble yourself." She began pulling books from the stacks and soon carried an armload to the counter.

"Here, miss," he said, reaching out. "Will this be everything?"

"Yes, thank you. Will you have this sent to Roxleigh House?"

"Oh," he said, then smiled at her. "Why yes, my *lady*," he said deferentially. "I had no idea."

"Pardon?"

"My lady," he said as he walked back around the counter to the front table, picking up a sheet of paper and handing it to her.

She thanked him and he bowed to her. She walked outside reading. *Mrs. Witwick's Society Page*, the title printed in fancy letters across the top. Francine giggled, thinking how much she missed the *New York Time's "Page Six."* She read the headline: "The Rake and the Recluse entertain Society with a spectacular soirée."

Reading those words was the last thing she did.


Miss Faversham brought the sisters to the carriage to wait for Francine, and wait she did, for what seemed entirely too long of a time.

"I shall be right back," she said to the sisters. "I'm going to go into the booksellers." She stepped out of the carriage and asked Grover and Gentry if they had seen Francine.

"No, ma'am," Grover answered. "We saw 'er enter the bookstore, but I don't think she's come out yet."

Gentry nodded his head in agreement.

"I will go check. I'm sure she just got caught up in the stacks. Please watch over the girls, Grover."

"I'll go with ye," Gentry said.

The bell on the door chimed as they entered and a man walked out of the stacks.

"Well, well," he said. "Two beautiful young ladies in one day. How did I happen to be so lucky?"

Miss Faversham smiled. "Is the other young lady back there?"

The man stopped, a furrow appearing on his brow. "The lady? No, she left more than an hour ago."

Miss Faversham's heart lurched and Gentry pushed past her. "Are you quite sure?" he asked gruffly. "An hour past?"

"Why yes," the man said, concern lining his features. "I only just finished wrapping her purchases. The boy should be by any minute to take them to His Grace's town house." He held one of the packages up.

Miss Faversham clutched Gentry's sleeve to steady herself.

"Do you know where she went after she left?" he asked.

"Well." The man gestured to the street. "She walked out reading *Witwick's*, and—and I do not know after that," he said, looking back to Gentry. "I went to the back to wrap her books. She must be close by, miss," he added, glancing at Miss Faversham.

Her face paled.

Gentry grumbled, taking the packages and turning to the door.

"Is there a problem?" the bookseller asked carefully.

"I don't know," she said.

Gentry turned back as they walked from the store. "If you see her, you will hold her, and you will notify His Grace immediately."

"Of course, sir," the man said quickly. "Post-haste." The door shut, the bell ringing above the bookseller as he stood looking after them.

Miss Faversham strode ahead of Gentry, searching up and down the street, the sounds of the city muted in her mind as it raced for clues. As they walked toward the carriage, she saw a copy of *Mrs. Witwick's Society Page* in the gutter. She reached for it and looked around again, handing it to Gentry.

He whistled for Grover, who drove the horses to them briskly with Smyth yelling to clear a lane.

"She's gone," he said to Smyth, handing him the bundled packages. "Take them to the house immediately and inform His Grace. I'm going to look around. I'll return shortly."

Smyth nodded and helped Miss Faversham into the carriage before jumping up to the rear step. Grover snapped the ribbons, racing toward Roxleigh House.

Hepplewort had waited in the carriage, shaking with anticipation from his slobbery jowls to his knocking knees. He sweated profusely, the stains gathering on his silk shirt and brocade jacket and making stiff, uncomfortable splotches on his clothing around the neck and armpits. He wiped his brow with his arm, streaking his sleeve.

He'd waited all week to find her away from the people that seemed to hang around constantly. He was so desperate and frustrated that he'd even tried to retrieve her from Roxleigh House the night before, but was thwarted. Then he caught her leaving the town house that morning, but that damned duke was close to follow. He cringed at the memory of their intimate ride.

When he saw her walk to the bookstore alone, the other three girls heading across the street, he squealed with excitement, then realized his error and hid from the window as she turned in his direction. He'd clasped his chest, breathing deeply as she entered the shop.

He sent his man to retrieve her as he watched. It all looked so easy; Morgan came up behind her like a lost lover hugging his beloved and no one paid heed, turning away from the improper spectacle. This beloved, however, went limp when her mouth was covered, not by a kiss, but a rag soaked in ether. He'd pushed her into the carriage, placing her on the seat next to Hepplewort, and then mounted the rear carriage step as the driver pulled away from the bookstore and drove them out of town.

Hepplewort had tied her hands and feet, placing a scarf in her mouth to keep her quiet should she awaken. It was several hours before he allowed her to come around fully, covering her nose with the ether-soaked rag whenever she stirred, making her his unwitting plaything.

His pudgy hands roamed her body while she was unconscious. He scratched at her bodice, lifted her skirts slowly, stroked the bridge of her nose, tickled her ears, and massaged her pink lips while giving her an open-mouthed glare, his eyes glossy and his tongue licking the drool from his lip.

"Get my brother!" Gideon yelled at Smyth, who ran from the house and mounted his horse, bolting across the square. Gideon turned on Miss Faversham. "Explain to me precisely what occurred." Miss Faversham stood tall, trying to remain composed as she told him everything she knew.

The front door swung open and Perry stormed in, followed by Smyth. "Are the horses ready?" Perry asked.

"No." He gestured toward Smyth to run to the stable to help ready them. "It's been nearly two hours. It has to be Hepplewort. I should have known better." Gideon cursed. "I never should have let her—"

"Let her what, Gideon?" Perry said, taking his shoulders. "If you try to control her, you lose her. There is nothing you could have done differently. Let's not waste time on what we cannot change."

Gideon scowled and the servants scattered like mice for their holes.

Perry turned to Gentry, who had just entered after pulling up in an old rented hack.

Gentry shook his head at Gideon's hopeful glance.

"Help Smyth ready the horses, all six," Perry said. He looked to Gideon. "We can catch him. He must be bound for his estate—"

"Gretna Green," Gideon cut in. "His intentions are to complete the contract."

Perry shook his head.

"He couldn't obtain a special license now. He'd need to take her to Gretna Green."

"I don't know, Rox—"

"Think about it. He's entirely predictable. He refused to ruin her, he waited to take her, but he wouldn't go through all of this only to screw it up at the end. He must marry her before he claims her, and…" Gideon clenched his jaw.

"And what?"

"And I have to *believe* that she's all right," Gideon said as his voice faded.

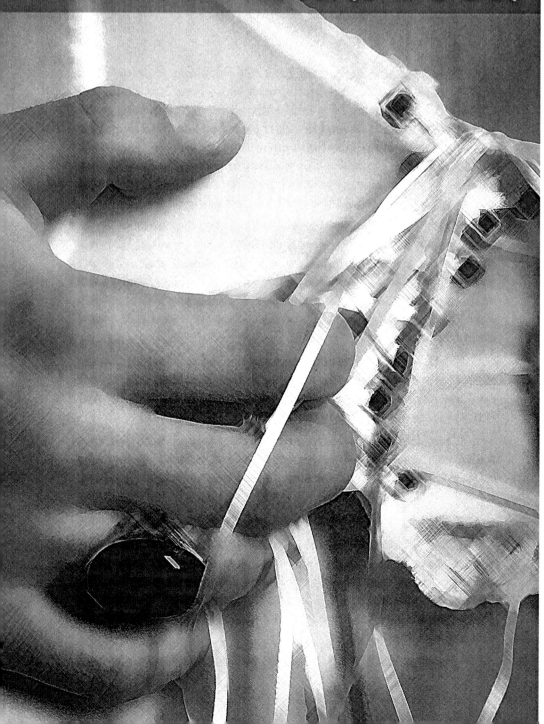

# RUINATION
## PART FOUR

# TWENTY-SEVEN

rancine was dizzy. Her head felt thick and it pounded as though a child were beating on it with a shoe. Her mouth was full of cotton and fire and her throat burned all the way to the pit of her stomach. It seemed like days passed as her mind fought for purchase, in and out of consciousness, willing the webs to clear so she could awaken. She groaned against the band in her mouth, but her hands wouldn't move and her eyes wouldn't open. She tried to remember what had happened, but couldn't remember anything beyond the ball.

She clenched her eyes, trying to clear the thickness that lay in front of them. It was like the time she'd tried on her grandfather's coke-bottle spectacles—she couldn't see. She also couldn't move and she couldn't speak, but she could feel, and what she felt was a clammy hand drifting up her leg toward her hip, underneath her skirts. The movement jerked her body awake abruptly and she kicked out, then heard a howl and a rain of curses.

She felt for the edge of the seat and pushed up. She pulled at the piece of fabric in her mouth, dragging it down and then rubbing her eyes. She realized her hands weren't just working in tandem, but that they were actually attached to each other.

"Sonofabitch!" she screamed, looking around until her eyes settled on the angry troll cowering in the seat across from her. The carriage bounced hard and she thought they were moving swiftly down a deeply rutted country road.

"You worthless fuckwit! What the *hell* are you doing?"

He straightened his jacket. "What does it look like I'm doing, you ingrate? I'm claiming what's mine, what always has been mine. I've waited more than ten years for your tutelage to be complete. You think I'll sit aside and let some damnable duke ruin you?" he yelled. He shook from his core, his loose skin flailing around his face like that of a drooling bloodhound.

Francine tore angrily at the binds on her wrists. Her skin scraped

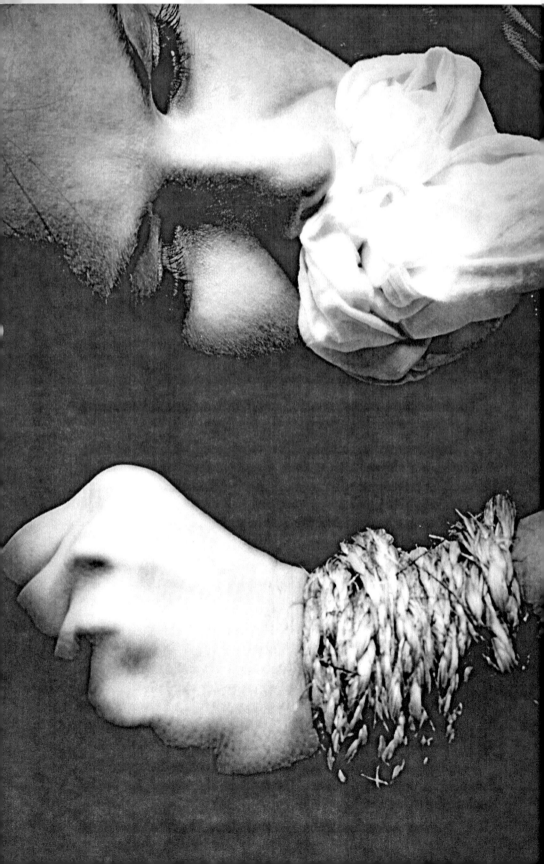

against the hard ropes as she twisted and pulled, making them raw and bloodied, but she wouldn't give in to her bondage.

Hepplewort watched her. His eyes widened with heat and she shuddered, her vision blurring from the anger coursing through her. She couldn't remember what to do. The self-defense class she'd taken didn't include being tied up and trapped in a carriage. She kicked at him, pushing her back against the wall to steady herself as she lashed out.

He was like a rat trapped in a cage with a pissed off cat. The binds didn't immobilize her; they only inhibited her movement, making her more violent. She kept kicking.

Hepplewort screamed, the noise pealing from his throat, making him sound like an frightened thirteen-year-old girl.

The carriage ground to a stop and the door swung open. Hepplewort fumbled his way out and a man so large and unwieldy that he had to squeeze through the carriage door entered, one arm and leg at a time, silencing her struggles with a glare. He pressed in next to her and Hepplewort rejoined them.

Hepplewort stared at her, then reached out and slapped her, slamming her face into the side of the carriage. She winced, her bound hands flying to her cheek.

"I guess you won't be trying that again," he said with a triumphant snort.

She felt a hot, sticky rush of blood to her lip and sat still, crushed against the side of the carriage by the brute next to her. She started running various escape scenarios through her mind, closing her eyes tightly as each vision failed.

The carriage ride was long and arduous. Every bump in the road–of which there were many–threw her alternately into the side of the carriage or into the structure of man to her left. She drifted into sleep occasionally, even as she tried to fight it off, but every movement of the carriage set her body aware and her mind reeling, wondering where Gideon was.

Sometime late the next day she saw a large, patchwork manor come into view as the carriage rocked and the curtains swung open and shut. It loomed on the horizon, surrounded by a great open field. The manor appeared to be a misshapen assembly of outbuildings that extended and built upon the main house in multiple architectural styles without regard for the existing structure.

They rolled up the long drive toward the ugly manor and she looked for signs of anyone who could help her. She didn't see any houses or a town nearby. Her heart sank when she realized that this was their destination, in the middle of nowhere.

The carriage lurched to a stop in front of the dark entrance and the giant of a man squeezed out, dragging Francine behind him before tossing her over his shoulder. She squealed as he carried her up the steps after Hepplewort.

The butler opened the door. "Your mother is in the parlor."

Hepplewort turned to the large man. "Take her to her room. Do not leave her alone." He watched as Francine bobbed against the man's back limply and then turned to the parlor.

He found his mother sitting straight-backed on the divan, her hands in her lap as she peered down her pointy beak at her son. Her dark grey hair was drawn to the back of her head in a severe knot. It pulled at her wrinkly features, giving her a cat-like appearance.

"Is she here?" came the shrill voice, buried under years of stern complaints.

He walked over, sat on the divan next to her, and patted her hands.

She jerked away from him, continuing to stare.

"Yes, Mother, she is here."

"Good. Did you send for the priest?"

"Yes, mother."

"*Where* is she?"

"I had Morgan take her to her room. No reason for her to be uncomfortable."

His mother stood. "I expect you to finish this, Fergus. I expect her to be heavy with my grandchild within a fortnight."

He stared after her. "Yes, of course, Mother."

She straightened her dark woolen dress. "Well, it is due time," she spat at him, and then she left him in the parlor.

Gideon, Perry, Gentry, and Smyth left within the hour with six horses, only pausing for rest for themselves and the animals when necessary. With several legs of the main northern rail down as they replaced the old rails with steel, and the available detours so far from the mark, the men stayed close to the railways by horse and jumped trains wherever possible, taking the horses aboard, which afforded at least some rest for everyone but Gideon.

By the time they reached Roxleighshire, he was a hot-tempered mess. His hair stood on end from the weather and the rides, and his hands were painful and stiff. They went straightaway to Eildon for fresh mounts. Gentry and Smyth turned the horses in as Gideon took for the manor, Perry close at his heels.

They hoped they were ahead of Hepplewort. He had to be in a carriage the whole trip, as there was no way he could travel by rail because he would have Francine with him, and she would be none too happy which would draw some sort of suspicion. Gideon hoped they had passed him somewhere, or that Hepplewort had taken a longer route to get to Gretna Green—perhaps along the coast, where he would be less known. Gideon was still determined in his thinking that Hepplewort would insist upon marriage before touching Francine, and the only way to do that expediently was to go to Gretna Green in Scotland.

Mrs. Weston ran to Gideon, surprised to see him. "Oh, Your Grace, what are you doing here?" she asked as he stormed through the entry, kicking aside crates of supplies and tools for the work that had begun on the manor.

"Your Grace?" she questioned, noting each brother's expression. "Where's Lady Francine?" She glanced around the men out the door.

"We need food, Westy." Gideon stopped in a weary stance, resting his hands on his hips.

"What's happened?" she asked, her hand fiddling with the buttons at her neck.

He shook his head and headed for his study.

"That is it!" she boomed. "Gideon, get back here!" she yelled in her best mother-in-charge voice. Something about it stopped Gideon in his tracks the same way it had when he'd run amok as a child.

Gideon turned with painstaking care, his jaw clenched, not wanting to actually voice the words to her. "Hepplewort has Francine," he choked out.

"Oh no, no, what are you doing here if he has her? Gideon! Why are you here? His estate is in Shropshire!" She advanced on him.

Perry tried to explain. "Without a license—"

Mrs. Weston shook her head. "No!" she railed. "*That man* told Lilly about Francine, he told her what he planned for her, while he— he—" She shook the memories from her head. "No! No! You do not understand! Lilly said they were to be married at his estate as soon as they returned. He already has the license. There is no reason for him to take her to Gretna Green. He only has to get a priest to carry out the license!"

Perry's breath caught in his chest.

"No. Oh God, no." Gideon stood in the doorway to his study, stricken and pale, his arms hanging limply. "What have I done?"

Mrs. Weston went to him, stretching to rest her hands on his shoulders.

"Your Grace. I'll see to the food. We'll get you out of here."

The brute threw Francine unceremoniously on the gilded four-poster bed, then overtook one of the chairs at the other side of the room.

Francine glanced around. The room was decorated in hues of

garish orange trimmed with gold braids, filigree, and paint. It made her even more dizzy and nauseated. Any bare wood appeared painted with a thick coat of glaring white enamel.

She looked down, the rough-hewn rope splintered, digging and tearing at her raw flesh. Her skirts were ripped and tangled around her, her stockings torn and slipping, and her ankles were bloody and painful as if full of glass shards, and sore from the same roughly-made ropes.

She caught the man's eye on the other side of the room. "What's your name?"

He only stared at her.

"Please, *please* help me. If you help me, the Duke of Roxleigh will be forever in your debt," she begged quietly.

The brute did not give.

She stretched out on the bed, trying to straighten her tensed muscles after the cramped ride.

He only continued to stare and soon a small, pointy woman walked into the room.

The man stood, looking intently at the floor, and the woman waved at him, sending him out. She paused, listening for the door to close behind her, then slid toward the bed.

Francine watched carefully. "Please, help me," she implored from atop the thick covers.

The woman stopped near the edge of the bed and peered down her nose.

"Do not address me as if you are of my station," she drawled. If Hepplewort was the embodiment of sloth and gluttony, this woman's demeanor bespoke wrath. Her beady black eyes bore into Francine, unnerving her, and she shrank.

"You," the woman said in clear disgust while reaching out and grabbing Francine's skirt before she could move away, "are a filthy mess. Have you no pride? You are betrothed to my son, the Lord Fergus Darburgh, Earl of Hepplewort. Consider that in your actions. Your one purpose in being born was to bear the future Earl of Hepplewort. If you cannot do that, you serve no purpose at all. Do you understand?" The woman turned, not waiting for Francine's response. "Morgan!"

The behemoth thumped back into the room, his gaze downcast.

His entire being oozed simplicity, and his quiet actions scared her. It was the air of violence, pure and unadulterated, that chilled her to the bone.

The woman spoke at Francine over her shoulder, not wasting any effort by turning around. "If you behave, we will remove the binds. If you make one errant move, Morgan will stop you." She nodded to the man, who moved to the bed and cut the ropes.

Francine didn't move.

"Good," the woman said, shifting her gaze back to the doorway. "I'll send the girl in to attend you. You are filthy. Unworthy." Without hurry she slipped from the room, and a few moments later a mouse of a maid entered.

She bade Francine follow as she walked into an attached room covered in light green tiles. In the corner rested a square basin on the floor, and Francine looked closer, seeing the piping that rose above it. A shower, Francine thought. She would have smiled, but her body and her mind wouldn't allow it.

The maid unhooked her dress and corset, letting them fall to the floor. Then she carefully removed her stockings, peeling them away from the injuries to her ankles. She shook her head. "I'll get some salve fer ye, miss. As soon as we get ye clean," she whispered.

Francine turned to smile at her, then shrieked when she saw that Morgan had followed them. "Get out!"

The maid quickly hushed her. "Please, miss, ye don't want the lady back in 'ere. Please," she begged.

Francine convulsed, but her stomach was empty. She let the girl lead her to the shower and stood silently while she was washed. She clenched her eyes shut and thought of Gideon, willing him to her. The uncomfortable shower dribbled on and when she opened her eyes, Morgan was still the only man there.

The girl toweled her off and brought her back to the bedchamber.

Francine stood still again, her eyes closed, trying to pretend the brute wasn't inspecting her with a threatening disregard as she was dressed in a chalky white dress. It was simple and tight, fitted over a painful corset and a giant caged crinoline with heavy woolen underskirts. Her breasts were compressed flat, her lungs crushed within her ribcage. The skirts itched horribly and weighed her down, but she bore them.

The maid pulled Francine's hair into a tight bun on top of her head and secured it, covering it with a white linen mobcap. She left her for a few minutes then returned with a jar of brown goo that she smoothed on Francine's wrists and ankles before wrapping them with strips of linen.

The mother scrutinized Francine. "This is to be my successor, the Countess of Hepplewort?" She frowned at the white bandages around her wrists. "These are terribly unsightly," she said to the maid as she yanked and pulled and pushed at Francine's dress.

"I beg pardon, my lady, I thought to heal them with salve."

"It will do for now."

The girl curtseyed and left the parlor expediently as the woman motioned to the divan.

Francine didn't think she could be any more uncomfortable, but she was wrong. She walked over and sat down carefully, feeling the metal bands of her crinoline biting her legs. The dress and corsets didn't give an inch. It felt as if her lungs were being forced up under her collarbone, into her throat, and her stomach was crushing her heart physically, as the woman attempted to do the same to her hope. She stifled a cry, feeling her face flush from the pressure. She clasped her hands together in her lap and the woman handed her a small basket with an embroidery hoop and thread.

She sat across from Francine in a chair and picked up another basket, staring at her as Francine toyed with the hoop.

"I expected you to be well trained. What is the difficulty?"

Francine shook her head.

"Do what you can," the mother said disapprovingly.

Francine steadied her hands and set about figuring out how to embroider. She bided her time, the dutiful fiancée, waiting for the moment when she could flee. Every time she looked at Morgan he glared back. She was no match for him. She tried to think of something to say to the woman, to find some common ground that might weaken her terrifying resolve, but nothing would come. She wasn't even sure she *could* speak, as contracted as her torso was.

After what seemed an eternity of forced silence, punctuated

only by the minute pinpricks of the embroidery needle, the door to the parlor swung open.

"Supper," called the butler.

Morgan, who had been sitting in the corner, stood to follow Hepplewort's mother and Francine from the room.

Francine carefully studied her surroundings and the movements of her captors—which doors required keys, which ones led outside, which windows she'd seen open.

She'd watched Gideon tighten the saddles on his horses, not to mention all the Clint Eastwood westerns she'd watched when she couldn't sleep. She didn't think it would be too difficult to get one on a horse, but she wouldn't have much time to do it. She suddenly wished she had participated in Westernaires as mother-number-two had wanted her to, but she'd been too stubborn and angry—an immovable attitude that eventually got her sent to yet another home.

She sat at the end of the table, trying to catch her breath after the short walk from the parlor. Hepplewort was positioned at the other end, but he wasn't seated in the first position. His mother was. Hepplewort sat to her left which, Francine knew—thanks to the book of manners she had been studying—to be a blatant put-down since his mother's immediate right was left unoccupied. He wasn't worthy either, but it didn't serve to make her feel better.

She stared down at the soup they placed before her and a shiver ran the course of her spine as she slowly began to spoon it to her mouth.

She felt as though she sat in a vacuum, the only sounds the clinking of her silverware on the dish. Francine was so far away she could hardly hear the conversation between them, and she considered that she might be better for it. They paid no attention to her, except when she needed a reprimand because the spoon hit the side of her cup or scraped the bottom of her bowl.

"Lady Madeleine," the mother would shout at her, "you should endeavor to be silent."

Hepplewort smiled a crooked, rotten grin when the talk turned to the young maids in town who were looking for positions within the household, and Francine tensed.

She watched as they supped on beef in a thick sauce and vegetable soup with crusty breads and fruit compote. Then she stared into her bowl, watching the different patterns made in the surface of her liquid.

"Look at her, Fergus. She isn't the least bit appreciative of what we've done for her. She can't carry herself, gasps for air at every turn. She'll be bedridden when she is with my heir. Ridiculous. This isn't the girl we were promised," the mother complained.

Hepplewort remained silent.

After supper Morgan escorted her to her room, then stayed and watched as the small maid undressed her. The corset and dress she'd been forced into provided so little room that she'd lost her breath again halfway up the stairs, and the removal of the corset and sudden rush of air made her head spin, reminding her of the day she came to be here. Her eyes stung as the maid pulled a flannel nightgown over her head.

She noted that Morgan seemed to be getting tired, and hoped that she could outlast him and make a run for it in the night. She would never make it far in that corset, but the nightgown certainly held possibility.

The mother walked into the room with another maid, who was carrying a serving tray with a small teapot. She gestured for her to pour Francine a cup of tea and waited, watching while she drank it, not saying a word before leaving with a nod to Morgan.

Francine lay in the bed, alone in the dark, waiting for the giant to nod off so she could sneak out, but her chance never came. She couldn't keep her eyes open no matter how hard she tried. As she fought her way against a deep sleep, the thought occurred to her. Her eyes jerked open in one last vain attempt before the room disappeared.


The next morning Francine stirred, her thoughts finishing where they had been interrupted. Drugged. She grunted, shaking her head and glancing around the room. Morgan stood and rang the bell.

The maid came in the room and helped Francine stumble to the shower for her morning ablutions as Morgan followed.

Francine wasn't sure how much she could take of this before she passively let them beat her to death. She allowed the girl to dress her in another white gown of the same fashion as before: breathtakingly tight and uncomfortable. The diminutive maid fixed her hair and pushed her toward the door as Morgan—yet again—stood to follow.

Panic set in unexpectedly and Francine bolted for the staircase like a wild rabbit. She was clutching her chest, yanking on the top of the tightly laced corset before she made it ten steps, and within fifteen Morgan had her about the waist. His sweaty palms burned through her dress and his malodorous exhalation engulfed her face. She wanted to hold her breath against the stench, but as she gasped for air she gagged on it and her lungs gave up. She passed out cold.

She was awakened by a stinging slap across her face. "Do you need to be bound again?" the voice screeched.

Francine opened her eyes slowly to find the drawn-up face of the mother staring down at her from beside the bed. She skittered away but the woman caught her ankle, digging her nails into the injured flesh under the linen, tearing at the loose skin surrounding the deep gashes.

Francine cried out in agony, the searing pain shooting up her leg and spine. She lashed out at the woman, trying to stop the seizure of her leg, but it only caused the grip to tighten. She wailed and screamed, assailing the sickening woman, not understanding why she couldn't unlatch her. "Why? Why, why!"

"Why? Why, you ask? Because we paid for you. You are here as his betrothed, to be his subservient wife and acquiesce to his bidding, and to bear my grandson, who will assume the earldom when he dies."

Francine shrank into the bedcovers as she stared at her.

"You have no other purpose," his mother said simply as she gave her leg one final shake, then turned her loose. "You would do well to learn your place more expediently, you arrogant girl."

Francine nodded at the woman as she sank farther into the golden-embroidered counterpane in shock. The mother moved away from the bed, saying something to Morgan. Francine curled up, grasping her knees to her already compressed torso as she tried to conquer the heaving, dry sobs that wracked her body. She looked up from the bed at the shower room and saw her lady's maid, her face red and tear-streaked, cowering in the doorway. The maid shook her head quickly and ducked out of sight.

The door to her room slammed and she rolled over to see Morgan approaching the bed. His hands reached out to her as he leaned over the bed and she screamed, all her breath leaving her body as she lost consciousness.

She started to come around with the sound of a voice. "Oh, milady," the maid whispered. "I beg ye, please, don't let them hurt ye. Ye would'na believe some o' the goings on 'ere. Please, milady, are ye all right?"

Francine stared at her, still unable to breathe fully.

The maid shifted slightly, allowing Francine to see Morgan standing behind her. A warning.

Francine reached down to her ankle and winced at the flash of pain. When she pulled her hand back, it was bloody. Her head fell to the pillow as the girl tended to her, using a cool rag on her face, smearing more of the thick brown salve around her ankle, trying again to care for her wounds.

Francine wasn't requested at supper that night; she spent the rest of the day tied into her corset, trying desperately to recover from lack of air.

The mother returned much later with the cup of tea. Francine drank it quickly, against the threat of pain and possibly hopeful of the respite, as the mother glared at her and Morgan wrapped his hand stiffly around her leg. The mother left without a word and the maid stood her up, took the dress off, and loosed the corset. Air rushed into her lungs with such force she grabbed for anything to hold her upright. The maid pulled the nightgown down over her head and helped her up into the bed. She barely had time to lie down on the pillow before she succumbed to the drugs.

Francine shifted under the counterpane the next morning, the puddle of drool under her chin cold. She sat up halfway, looking around the room as she shook her head against the heaviness. Morgan was asleep in a chair at the end of the bed. *Asleep.* The thought startled her to her senses. She stood, then began creeping toward the door. She opened it softly, but heard voices.

"Mother, the priest should be here soon. We only need to keep her occupied until then."

"We are not here to entertain her, you buffoon. This situation is perfectly abhorrent. You are so inept you couldn't control your own bride without me. I cannot believe my issue has become such an incompetent oaf. The earl is turning in his grave." The words rolled across the old woman's thin lips like a riptide.

"I am not incompetent. I *will* handle her. You *will* see," came Hepplewort's voice, small and whiny like a badly tuned violin.

Francine heard a pair of footsteps coming toward her room and ran over to the bed, jumping under the counterpane as she tried to calm her nerves and her heartbeat.

"Morgan, you are dismissed," Hepplewort yelled.

Francine sat up.

Hepplewort turned and advanced on her like a spider to a fly and she felt equally trapped, shrinking back into the bed. A slow grin broke across his face as she considered her options. Perhaps she could sway him—after all, she did have something that he wanted rather desperately.

"My lord, it is rather untoward of you to visit my bedchamber before we are properly wed." She forced a smile.

"Yes, well, I was of a mood."

"A mood? Couldn't your *mood* bring you back later?"

"You will find that I am much more genial in the mornings, when I haven't dealt with certain tasks all day."

She thought quickly. "Your mother can be quite—" She paused, gathering her strength to continue. "—*meddlesome*, my lord," she finished, letting the words roll from her lips like an endearment. Her stomach physically turned in her gut, nausea rising toward her throat.

Hepplewort heard the stomach complaint. "You must be starved after yesterday. Mother believes you should be more slender, that it would make you more compliant. I, however, believe much the opposite. I will arrange for something," he said as he rang the bell for her maid, then gave her instructions when she appeared.

The maid glanced around him with a concerned gaze before rushing from the room.

He turned back to Francine and she smiled demurely. "My lord, you are thoughtful. Should I dress to break our fast?"

His eyes glazed over her like molasses in March, sticking in all the wrong places.

"Or perhaps you prefer this flannel nightgown?" she asked quickly, trying to break his inspection.

He cleared his throat, glancing up into her eyes.

"Madeleine." The name slithered off his tongue. "I would prefer you live in a nightgown at all hours, but not that one. Mother, of course, has your wedding trousseau, and after we are married you will be attired much more to my liking." He licked the spittle from his lip.

He turned to the wardrobe, throwing aside several fluffy white dresses before finding a simple country sheath. It was fitted at the bosom with an empire waist, the folds of fabric falling from the breast and dusting the floor with a delicate ruffle.

She was excited. It was more Regency than Victorian and, while entirely out of fashion in this age, the style didn't allow for a corset. The tightly fitted skirt would keep her legs together so she wouldn't be able to walk a full stride, much less run, but at least she would be able to breathe.

She considered his indecisive stare as he stood before the wardrobe and decided to tip the scales. She sighed and rose to her feet. "Why, my lord, what a beautiful gown! It is quite reminiscent of an earlier time, when life was much simpler and women, including mothers, knew their places." She walked toward him slowly.

"Yes...yes," he said with longing.

She reached out, smoothing the fabric and inadvertently—with purpose—she brushed her knuckles across his hand.

"Exactly my thought. Women weren't as…independent as they are these days." His eyes darted to her. He smiled and handed her the gown. "Please, put this on," he said, with a sickening sweetness.

She took it and glanced around the room.

"No, no, dear, right here. I may not have yet paid for the goods, but I certainly can browse." His jowls pulled up in a grotesque version of a smile.

She covered her mouth with her hand, fluttering her eyelids at him.

"But, my lord—"

He frowned. "Why should Morgan and the maid be allowed to see but I can't?" he whined.

She sensed she was losing his interest. "Of course, my lord," she said, and grasped the nightgown at the waist to pull it up. She paused when her face was hidden to breathe deeply and tried to gather the courage to expose her body to him. She had to trust that he would stick to his morals, misguided and revolting as they might be.

She slid the gown over her head and reached for the dress.

"Wait—" He held his hand up. "You are a vision," he drawled.

"My lord, the maid will be returning."

"Yes, of course." He snatched the gown from her hands and moved closer, gathering up the fabric. He smelled sickly sweet and she cringed. He tried to slide the dress over her head, but his jacket was too tight and she was too tall.

She crouched slightly and let him pull the dress down, running his knuckles across her skin as he yanked at the hem. She shuddered as his face drew close to the front of her body, his sour breath pelting her skin while it reacted to his touch. She held her breath, but the very air surrounding him was sour, making her gag.

"Thank you," she said as genially as possible, glad that he didn't notice her convulsing.

A knock sounded at the door. "Enter," he grumbled.

The maid walked in with a large tray, her eyes wide with panic. She set the tray on a table next to the two overstuffed wingback chairs by the fireplace and moved to Francine, watching Hepplewort from the corner of her eye.

"Milord, shall I assist milady?"

He nodded and moved to the tray, picking up a piece of ham with his portly fingers, tearing it apart in his stained, crooked teeth. His chin was covered with grease as he reached for another slice, not waiting to finish the first.

The girl fastened the placket of buttons at Francine's back and went to the wardrobe, pulling out stockings, garters, and drawers. She helped Francine dress, doing her utmost to keep her covered from Hepplewort's stare, then she reached for a pair of brown calfskin ankle boots. Blocking his sight with her small body, she carefully pulled them over Francine's feet and fastened the buttons up the sides slowly, trying to avoid too much pain from the rope cuts.

The girl patted the toe of the boots. "There ye are, miss. These're comfortable slippers, but if you and milord choose to go outside the manor to view the gardens, ye should be careful in the deep grass, and ye certainly shouldn't venture into the wood without better shoes. The wildflowers are bloomin', milord." She glanced up with pleading eyes, pulling Francine's hem down tightly over her toes. "The ones by the northern gardens."

Francine nodded in thanks while Hepplewort smiled at the lascivious thoughts of the two girls dancing through his head. "Hmmm. We'll see what Mother has to say," he hedged.

Francine pouted, running her hand over his brocade lapel. "Your mother doesn't want us to do anything until we are married. How are we to get to know each other if we are to be kept apart, or together only here in the manor under her vigilant eye?"

His eyes bulged and he swallowed hard.

Francine moved closer to Hepplewort, cautious to keep her boots from view. "I would love to see your estate, my lord. I imagine you have beautiful lands and gardens. I daresay you must be quite adept with a phaeton as well, judging from the way you carry yourself." She smiled, the picture of innocence.

"You!" he snapped at the maid. "Have the groom prepare the phaeton, and make sure there's a basket included for luncheon. It's a lovely day for a picnic, and I do need to keep my fiancée occupied until the priest arrives." He turned to Francine. "I could show you the estate," he continued with a devious grin.

The girl nodded and curtseyed, hesitating momentarily before leaving them alone again.

"Well then. Let us break our fast and then you can show me your grand…estate." She paused before enunciating the last word with a wide grin and as much of a sparkle as her soul would allow.

He gulped audibly and she pushed him to sit at the tray, falling immediately back into the role of innocent. She allowed him to feed her, pandering to his foibles. By the end of the meal he was sure to make their private excursion a reality, which she was glad of, but also terrified because she had lit a fire in him that she had no intention of stoking. She could only hope she could manage to get away before she was burned.

He escorted her downstairs, past the parlor where the mother was working on her basket of embroidery, and toward the front door. The butler walked up to him but Hepplewort waved him off. The butler looked down his nose at the short man and turned, striding toward the parlor as they left.

"How charming you are, my lord, and thoughtful to include a picnic," she said, trying to hurry his movements.

He smiled up at her as she climbed into the phaeton, placing his hand on her rump, feigning assistance.

"Fergus! What is this?"

Francine froze like a deer in headlights.

"Mother."

Francine gripped his sleeve.

"What are you doing?" she spat. "Where is Morgan?"

Hepplewort looked at his mother, surreptitiously removing his hand from Francine's rear end. "I imagine he's asleep in his room, since he was charged with standing vigil over my betrothed last night. As for what we are doing, I am going to show Madeleine around the estate."

The wrinkled old woman's eyes blazed. "You will do no such thing, you incessant twit," she said as saliva sprang from her mouth.

Francine backed away, into the seat of the phaeton.

"Perhaps a picnic in the meadow," Hepplewort sputtered.

"Sometimes I wonder where you came from. You quite obviously do not have my intelligence, or the earl's. If I didn't know better, I would say you belonged on the land, not in *charge* of it."

Francine glanced down at Heppelwort and sighed to remind him of her presence, then she reached out and gently stroked the back of his sweaty red neck.

He reacted to the touch and straightened. "We shall return in time to dress for supper. Good day, Mother." He bowed perfunctorily and turned to climb into the phaeton.

Francine patted his hand in encouragement as he struggled to get aboard. Then she grabbed his moist chubby hand and yanked him up.

Slitting her eyes, the mother grumbled and stormed into the house.

Francine jerked around when Hepplewort took the ribbons and drove the horses to the field. Next obstacle, she thought. Looking around, she decided to ask about the estate. Hopefully he would continue to behave like a stooge.

"Where exactly are we?"

"The estate?" he asked, and she nodded. "Well, we are in Shropshire, which is northwest of London most of a day by carriage. The road is rough and difficult, so it must be traveled slowly. Since the railroad connected us to London, it's gone much without repairs."

"Railroad?" She hadn't really considered the railroad. If she could find any tracks, she could follow them to London, and from there it shouldn't be too difficult to find the duke. *Gideon*, she thought. *Where are you?*

Gideon rode toward the sunset like the devil was on him. Hepplewort's estate was more than halfway back to London, and he could only hope there was some sort of delay in his plan. How could he have been so foolish? *He* had insisted they go to Gretna Green. He hadn't even considered that Hepplewort would already have a license.

"Gideon!" Perry yelled. "You cannot treat the animal like this! You must let it rest!" Gideon drove the horse harder, until he felt Perry next to him, reaching for Samson's bridle. "Gideon!" Perry shouted.

Gideon yelled, not an easy expiration of air but a guttural, all encompassing, gut-wrenching cry that emanated from his very core.

Perry put his hand on his brother's arm as they slowed. "We'll find her."

"I know we'll find her. I know we will," he replied. "But I don't know if it will be soon enough. You didn't see her, Perry. You didn't see her bloodied and bruised. You didn't see what he caused."

"I know, brother—"

"You can't know."

"Gideon." Perry tried to stave off the words that would only work to worsen his brother's agitated state. He took one of Gideon's shoulders, forcing him to meet his gaze. "We are going to take this leg by rail. We should arrive in Shropshire early on the morrow. His estate won't prove much of a ride beyond that."

Gideon nodded and the brothers walked the horses, coming to the station at the edge of county Westmoreland and handing them off to his men so they could see them boarded and cared for. They arranged passage and boarded the train, Perry keeping a close eye on his brother. He remembered this Gideon all too well. This was the boy who couldn't help his mother, who had grown into the man who'd lost everyone he cared for.

Francine knew she could take Hepplewort, but she needed him out of the carriage. She didn't remember the accident with Gideon's curricle, but it had been described to her in detail and she wasn't interested in a repeat performance. They came to rest at the far edge of the meadow. Hepplewort threw the heavy brown rugs down so he could spread them on the ground and then he slid from the phaeton, motioning for her to follow.

She jumped down, careful to keep her boots covered by the hem of her skirt, and walked around the phaeton, inspecting the horses' attachments as she pretended to stroke and speak with them. She would at least need to disable the carriage. She already knew she couldn't take it because of the state of the road, and she needed speed. Horseback was the only way.

Hepplewort placed the basket on the blankets and motioned to Francine to sit down. She kneeled, tucking her boots underneath her. He looked at the basket, expecting her to serve him, and she smiled, pulling it closer even though they had only just had breakfast. They had some fruit, cheese, meat, and a bit of a red wine.

She felt his hand on her booted ankle beneath her skirt. "What—"

She panicked when she saw the confused look on his face and reached in the basket, pulling out the block of cheese to throw at him. As she grabbed the cheese the handle of a knife jabbed at her wrist and she yanked it out, too. She jumped to her feet.

He reached for her and she kicked. He squealed and retreated from her range. She moved toward the horses, which shifted uneasily at her brisk movement. Hepplewort's eyes bulged and his mouth gaped, catching flies as he tried to get his rotund ass off the ground.

She turned on him with the knife as he approached. She kicked him hard in the knee then punched him in the face, sending him back to the ground.

"You bitch!" He gasped for breath.

"You sick, twisted monster! Did you really believe I could enjoy *your* company? You perverted, unkempt, slimy, rotten—swine!"

"Mother was right," he squealed.

"Screw you!"

He had never been set down so soundly, and by a woman no less. His jaw flapped, begging for purchase on a retort, but found none.

She patted one of the horses gently to calm it, then unbuckled the large belt that held the arms of the phaeton to the horse's back. Hepplewort crawled over and grabbed her boot and she turned, kicking at him again.

"Get off of me!" She caught his fingers under her boot and stomped hard, then kicked him in the face. There was a resounding crunch, and he rolled over on his back, yelping and twisting like a snake run over by a carriage as blood poured from his nose.

Francine spun back to the horse, yanking at the ribbons and trying to unhook them from the leather straps of the phaeton, but she couldn't. Her mind raced. She glanced back at Hepplewort to make sure he wasn't coming at her again, but he was still rolling around, blubbering and holding his face in his hands.

"You broke my nose! You broke it!"

She shook her head and looked over the back of the horse at the manor to see Morgan astride a giant brown horse and moving straight for her. She panicked as she pulled on the ribbons, using the knife to saw through them, releasing one of the horses. She led it to the side of the phaeton and crawled up onto the seat, hiking up her narrow skirt. She leapt onto the white horse, letting the knife slip from her hands to the grass as she held on for dear life.

"Oh, God, please help me, what was I thinking." She grasped the cut ribbons in one hand and a fistful of the horse's mane in her other to help steady her, clicking her tongue as she leaned forward. She glanced back once to see Morgan approaching rapidly and Hepplewort running toward the manor, and she cried out, losing her balance. She steadied herself on the horse and leaned forward again like she had seen Gideon do every time he broke for the forest at Eildon.

Her mind raced and her breath caught as she attempted to steer the animal toward the wood. She heard too many hoofbeats, pounding the ground hard like a thunderstorm. She thought it sounded like a whole team was after her, and when she heard the deep panting of a horse coming up next to her she yelled as loud as her voice would allow, belting out the sound from deep within, letting it carry through her and fill the meadow. She thought she heard someone calling her name and she leaned harder, gripping the horse tightly between her thighs.

She closed her eyes momentarily, trying to think through the deafening sound of the approaching hooves before opening them again and concentrating on the land ahead.

She could hear the other horse gaining but wouldn't look back to see how close it was. She was determined to keep her focus on where she was going, because she didn't want to lose her balance again. She kicked at the horse, driving it as hard as she dared, listening, praying the hoofbeats and heavy breaths would break off.

The four men raced down the drive that led onto Hepplewort's estate at a breakneck pace. They could see the manor just above the rise. Gideon's heart pounded in his chest, matching the sound of the hooves on the ground. He looked across the meadow and saw movement, then, hearing a scream, he bolted toward it, the other men following.

He saw a phaeton with only one horse, and Hepplewort running haphazardly toward the manor. He scanned the horizon for Francine and caught sight of her on the back of the other carriage horse, steering it toward the forest. His breath stopped—no way was there a saddle on that beast. Another movement caught his eye and he saw a giant of a man on horseback chasing her through the field. His gut lurched to see the brute gaining on her handily. He pointed at Hepplewort and yelled "Gentry!" and Gentry immediately left his side to go after the man.

Gideon and Perry came up behind the brute, flanking him. The sound of hoofbeats multiplied, shaking the ground as they traversed the meadow. Perry and Gideon pushed their horses, with Smyth behind them, until they overtook him. They both reached out, grabbing the man's shoulders as they slowed their horses. They pulled him from the saddle and sent him to the ground in front of Smyth's horse, which jumped over the mass, narrowly missing his head when it landed. The giant rolled to a stop in a cloud of dust.

Perry turned back to help Smyth collect him.

"Francine!"

She tried to be frightened, but realized her mind wouldn't let her. She knew that voice. As sure as if she'd been speaking it her whole life, she knew that voice. She loosened her death grip on the reins and tried to sit back to slow the horse, but it was determined to continue the run like a train with no brakes.

"Gideon!" she screamed, "I can't stop! Please, please help me!" The forest loomed ahead of her and she panicked. Gideon came up alongside her, moving Samson as close as possible.

He reached around her waist. "Just lean to me. I have you, trust me."

She closed her eyes and leaned, letting go of the cut ribbons as she reached for his shoulders.

Gideon dragged her from the horse with one strong arm, sitting back to slow his steed. The white carriage horse disappeared beyond the break as Gideon pulled her across his lap.

She cried, she screamed, she kissed, she grabbed, and she felt as she had never felt so much in all her years. "Where have you been?" she gasped, turning her face into his rigid neck. "Where have you been?" Her mouth pressed into the hollow at the base of his neck, her lips on the strong pulse, the salty taste.

"I have been looking for you."

"He took me from the bookstore. He brought me here, and his mother—"

"Hush, my sweet Francine."

"There is also a very large man, he, he— Morgan, that other man, the giant is *there*. He is— We can't—"

"We took care of him."

She stopped and breathed of him, grasping his shirt tightly in her hands.

He walked the horse, rubbing a small circle into her back to calm her breathing. He tried to think of a way to ask the most important question, but before he could she looked up to him.

"He hadn't a chance, Gideon. I am yours." She turned her head into his chest. She had nothing more to say. She only wanted to take in his scent, the very essence of him, to keep it in her soul and her memory and never let it out. "Gideon, something must be done."

He rested his chin on her head. "Now is not the time. *This* is not the place," he said gruffly.

"Gideon." She turned her face up. "The only perfection I need"—she kissed the soft underside of his jaw—"is the man you are, and what you carry with you every day."

Gideon grunted, then held her tightly to his chest, lost deep in thought.


Perry caught up with Lord Hepplewort, whose face was bloodied and battered as he ran toward the manor screaming, with Gentry giving chase. Perry kicked him to the ground with his boot to shut him up, then jumped from the horse and pulled Hepplewort up by his jacket, leaving his feet dangling and toes barely touching the ground.

"You repellent sack of used up man-flesh," Perry said, letting the man fall back to the ground. "Get up and walk. You disgust me."

Hepplewort grunted, rising and turning quietly for the manor, flanked by the three very large, very angry, very armed men.

Perry examined his face. "Did Fra— Madeleine do that to your face, man?" he asked jovially.

Hepplewort ignored him and kept walking.

"Must kill yer pride to be thrashed by a woman, yeah?" Gentry added.

Hepplewort grunted again and continued limping toward the manor as the men carried on around him.

"She's no woman," he countered, unable to control his mouth.

Gentry jumped toward him with a deep growl and Hepplewort squeaked, covering his head with his hands.

"You had best watch your words and tone as it pertains to the future Duchess of Roxleigh," Perry said easily. "If she heard you, she might break something else," he added with a wry grin.

Perry looked over his shoulder at the large man they had tied to the saddle of a horse, to make sure he was still unconscious, and saw Gideon turning his horse toward the break in the wood with Francine in front of him. He grinned from ear to ear. "About that contract of yours, Hepple…wort. I believe it may soon be void."

Hepplewort scowled. "*That* is *not* possible," he huffed.

Perry glanced back over his shoulder. All he could see was the phaeton with its one remaining horse. "Oh, I believe you'll find it is possible," he said, chuckling as he pushed Hepplewort forward.

The men moved at a leisurely pace toward the manor, partly to give Gideon time to catch up and partly because Hepplewort was a stunted little man with a newly acquired limp.

Francine's breathing slowed and she opened her eyes to find them headed into the wood where she could see a meadow beyond dappled with sunlight and covered in a thick blanket of wildflowers.

She held him tighter as they came to a stop in the shade, just inside the safety of the trees. "Gideon?"

"Francine," he said gently as the sun broke from behind a cloud, creating a halo of light behind him, "you are absolutely correct. Hepplewort will not stop looking for you, this much we know. He will not give up, not until his contract is void."

"And? It isn't likely we will find a priest in the meadow or the forest between here and that manor," she said, pointing back toward the estate.

"No, I don't suppose we will." He neatly lowered her to the ground and jumped from the horse.

Her gaze followed him. "Then what do you have in mind?"

"My lady," he said, standing in front of her, so close that the heat from his body permeated her gown. "My intention—" He paused as his breath quickened and his baritone deepened in his chest. "—is to ruin you."

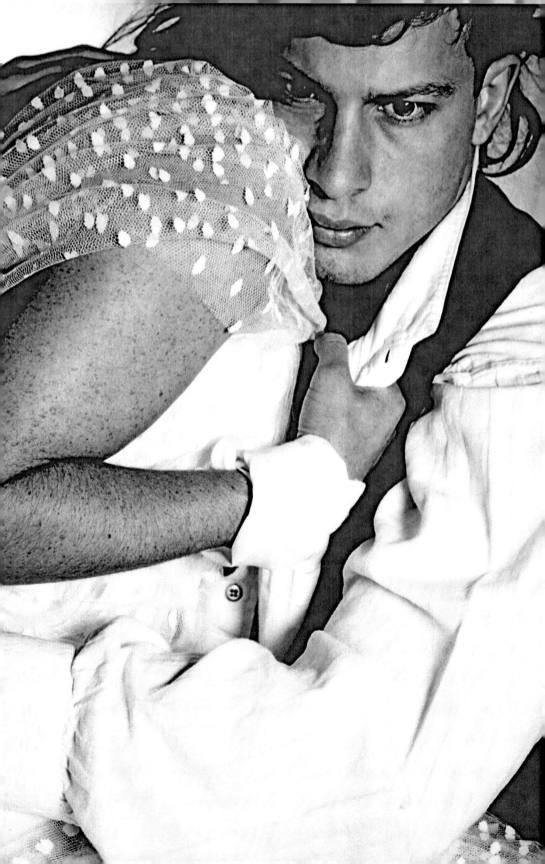

# TWENTY-EIGHT

Gideon's hands cradled her chin, weaving into the hair at her nape as his head lowered, drawing her mouth to his.

When their lips met her heart fell back into the panicked cadence it had been used to with his touch. She looked up into his eyes. He took her about the waist and drew her away from the horse to the wavering shade of the meadow.

"You c-can't," she stuttered.

"I can," he countered.

"You wouldn't."

"I will." He kneeled before her on the blanket of flowers, running his hands under her skirts, up her legs, unfastening the ties that held her stockings in place and unbuttoning her boots.

She gasped, trying to push her skirt back down. "Gideon! I didn't exactly mean—"

"No," he replied, "I don't think you did. However, here we are."

"What about— What about propriety?" she begged.

He glanced up at her, rolling the other stocking smoothly down her leg. *"Propriety be damned,"* he said with a devilish grin.

Her skin prickled at the sincerity of his words and she had no more reservations. *This is it,* she thought, and her head spun.

He ducked back under her skirt to find the ties of her drawers, one hand carefully reaching into the slit, testing her warmth.

Surprised by his touch, she cried out, her knees buckling as her drawers slid down to her ankles. He caught her against himself, delivering her trembling figure to the earth beneath him.

They created a bed of flowers with the weight of their bodies. Surrounded by the field of green, lavender, blue, yellow, and pink, they laid together in the peaceful meadow bordered by the tumult of the world.

"Gideon, what if—"

He cut her off with a strong, fervent kiss. Covering her body with his own, his hands rampaged over her dress, searching for the ties and buttons that bound her.

He reached beneath her and sank his fingers into the button placket and, giving it a solid tug, he tore open the back of her dress, pulling it down from her shoulders. She was completely bared to him as he lifted up on his elbows with a sharp breath and gazed at her heaving breasts. "I like this dress," he declared. "I really, *really* like this dress," he added breathlessly.

Her skin flushed pink and she giggled at his untoward demeanor. He bowed his head to one nipple, teasing it to ripeness with his mouth before blowing a gentle breeze across it, forcing the pale tip into a hard point and creating the epicenter of a wave that reached out in spirals to her nerves, wakening every one. She laced her fingers in his hair.

Gideon pushed one strong thigh between her legs, but couldn't force them apart because of the constraints of the sheath dress. He grumbled at the impediment and moved to her other nipple as he reached down, pulling the skirt up to her waist and smoothing his heavy palm across her exposed belly.

He rose again to her face, kissing her lips till they pinked and swelled beneath his bruising mouth.

She struggled for air and he broke the kiss.

"Francine?" he questioned.

She lifted her hands, fumbling as she undid his shirt to bare his muscled chest. His breath caught, sending ripples toward his center. She traced the lines of his ribs, remembering the first time they had come this far together. This time she was able to see where they led. She followed the twin creases that framed his hips and ducked below his waistband. This time he didn't stop her. She felt for the fastenings inside the front of his trousers and her fingers brushed the crest of his arousal. This time he urged her on with a groan as he stiffened above her.

"Did I— Did I hurt you?" she asked quietly, her brow knitted.

He shook his head and lowered his face next to hers. "Touch me," he whispered in her ear, tickling the edge with his tongue.

She felt for the small clips inside the placket, trying to slow her breathing and steady her hands. She loosed them, spreading the front of his trousers wide, freeing his erection. Her eyes widened as she gazed from his manhood to his face and back.

"Gideon," she said nervously, her hands clutching the opened placket of his trousers.

"No. God, no— Francine, don't stop."

Brazenly she wrapped both hands around the silken shaft, amazed by the sensation of pure softness encasing unyielding hardness. She moved her hands, stroking.

He groaned and shook, crying out with a rasping moan and she stopped, unsure of what she should be doing or, for that matter, what she should do next.

He clenched his eyes momentarily then looked down at her. The sun passed through a thin cloud, adding shadow and light to the emotions that rolled across her face. The breeze rustled the leaves and the tall wildflowers and grasses whispered the secrets of the peacefully hidden meadow to the lovers as birds sang in the distance. They lay among the tall grasses, protected from the outside world by the wall of colorful wildflowers.

He pulled her skirts up higher, spreading her legs with his knees as he pressed into her womanhood with his calloused hand, gently stroking the curls and dipping his finger into her warmth.

Her breath escaped her lips in small exhalations. She was so wet, so warm, like a hot spring begging to be entered and enjoyed.

"Francine. For whatever pain I cause you, I will make it up to you a thousandfold. This, I promise you."

She felt a panic rise and clutched his shoulders as he positioned himself.

"Please don't look away, Francine."

She gazed into his hooded eyes, seeing the green of his irises deepen in passion.

"May I?" he asked.

"Yes, Gideon, only you," she whispered. She watched intently as his face tensed and he advanced on her slowly. The pressure felt hopelessly tight and her body retreated involuntarily. She cried out and dug her heels into the ground,, trying to push away. He sensed her panic and held her steady.

"Gentle, sweet. Gentle," he said tenderly. He reached between their barely coupled bodies and massaged the little nub above her opening as just the tip of his manhood was enveloped by her folds.

She felt a building of tension, a gathering of nerves. Every feeling she had came together deep inside her belly, pulsing stronger and stronger as he moved forward slowly and she came closer and closer to the edge. All of her anger, all of her worry, all of her pain and suffering collected, until her fingers and toes went numb, as though he meant to erase all of it and replace it with his touch.

He moved his hips, stroking just outside her with the head of his arousal, methodically matching the cadence with his hand as they explored each other's eyes.

She was incomparably beautiful. Her eyes blazed like liquid fire, urging him on.

A knot formed in his gut as he considered how he treasured her, how he feared the pain he was to bestow. He shut his eyes momentarily to clear his thoughts, then looked into hers again, feeling her body's response to his heated ministrations. He tensed, willing himself to wait just one more moment.

"Come off for me, Francine," he breathed.

She was marching toward an unseen cliff, the pressure building until it could not be held in abeyance any longer, and she cried out, her arms flying out to the flowered blanket beneath her. He grasped her hips with both hands and drove into her in one swift, powerful motion.

He groaned from the pain of her unyielding flesh as he forced his way through the taut barrier. He felt her innocence tear around his intrusion at the onset of her climax. She writhed beneath him, trying to escape. The searing pain and impossible fullness melded with the pulsating rhythm of her ecstasy, and he could see the depths of her as her eyes opened wide and a tear escaped, rolling down her cheek as he held her steady.

He paused and kissed it away, then dropped his head to her shoulder as her arms flew to his, urging him on. His hips, unrestrained, drove harder, deeper, feeling her body opening further. He was carried along on wave upon wave of her undulating passion as it threatened to crest and break around him again. He felt the circles of tension coursing around his manhood as he moved methodically within her, and she let out another impassioned cry. With one finishing thrust he cried out, his body convulsing as he arched up on his hands above her, his seed flooding her womb.

The pulsing dissipated and he collapsed, breathing heavily as he caught her gaze. He moved one hand to his face, his fingers together pointing to his chin, then swept them in a circle, spreading his fingers wide as they passed his forehead. *Beautiful.*

She smiled her broad smile, now infused with a sultry curiosity, and he pulled her to him as he rolled to his side, smiling like he never had before. She threw one leg over both of his, the feeling of his trousers on her bare skin sending tingling ripples coursing up her body.

"Ah, Gideon," she said breathlessly as she nestled into his chest.

"I love you," he said quietly.

"And I you, Gideon," she replied.


Gideon stood, turning to fasten his trousers as she watched, then he pulled Francine carefully to her feet. He held her face between his strong hands. "How are you?"

She felt something inside her had changed with their joining, something had shifted, and she tried to look up at him but couldn't bring herself to meet his eyes.

"I'm…all right…I think." She lifted the hem of her dress, inspecting the rusty stains at the edge. "A bit surprised. I mean, you are rather, uh. I'm not sure how… I don't know that I can discuss this with you." She pressed the side of her face into his chest.

He lifted her chin with one finger, turning her face to his, waiting patiently for her to meet his eyes. He kissed her eyelids, sinking his hands into her silken hair as her arms wrapped around his waist and she leaned into him.

She smiled, relaxing into his solid form. "Gideon, I expected the pain. I did not expect—the rest. You are… well. It felt very, um… full." She bit her lower lip in uncertainty, waiting for his response. "Will it always be like this?" she asked.

He urged her to look at him again, his expression guilty and penitent. "I am so sorry to have caused you this pain," he whispered, his voice wavering. She was mesmerizing, a paradox that she was so brilliant and yet so innocent. This new facet of her personality, this shy wonderment, sobered him, enervated him.

She reached up, placing her hands on his wrists and stroking his forearms as he held her neck.

"No, Gideon, I am glad it was you to have caused it. Don't apologize for that, I won't allow it. Every emotion I have with that intensity should come from you, and only you."

He breathed in sharply and leveled a bruising kiss on her mouth, pushing his fingers into the tousled hair at the back of her neck, pulling her tightly toward him. He raised his head slightly, stroking her nape.

"This should never again be painful, and if it is, you must tell me. But I can say that any discomfort you feel will lessen as your body becomes more accustomed to mine."

She nodded, blushing.

Then he saw her delicate hands and the white bands covering her wrists. He unwrapped them cautiously. His eyes darkened at the angry red welts and he held both of her hands gingerly, turning them over. "He did this to you."

"Well, he tied me up, yes, but it was my struggle to free myself that actually did this."

He glanced into her eyes. "*He* did this to you," he repeated in a voice that promised vengeance. He kneeled, reaching for her boots, and saw the bands on her ankles that covered more rope burns and cuts. He winced. "We should leave these loose."

She nodded and he shook his head, fighting a wave of fury. He needed to remain calm while he handled her.

He stood and straightened her dress as best as he was able, examining the grass stains patterned across the back and smoothing his hands over her body before finally looking at her with a quiet laugh.

"What?" she asked indignantly.

"Well, the effect is complete. You look quite thoroughly ravished, sated… spent." His voice lowered with each word. Then, standing before her, he pulled her into his arms. "Ruined," he said in his deepest voice as she gasped and her knees buckled.

"Oh, God, Gideon, what have you done to me?"

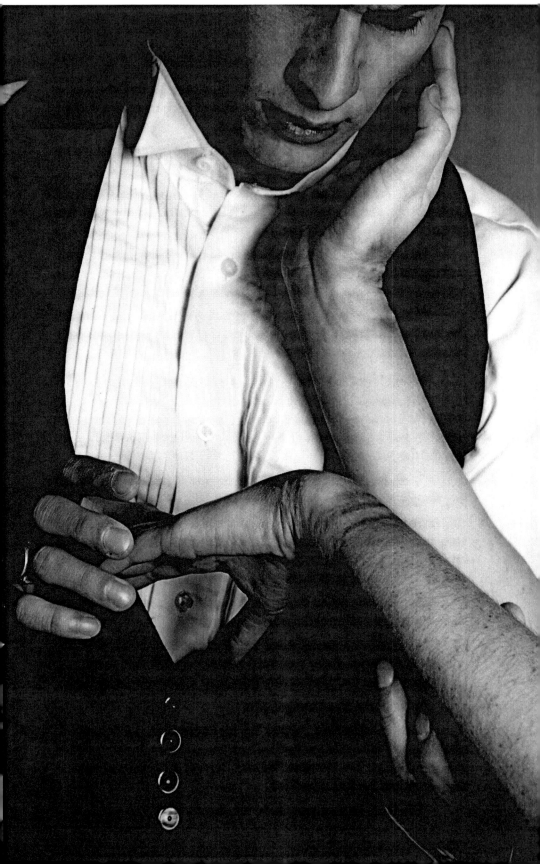

"Quite the same thing you have done to me, I imagine, and something nobody else has ever done before, and only *I* will do again." He gave her a victorious smile. "Though hopefully we will find better venues than gardens and fields, and…" He trailed off as he noticed her swift blush.

He caressed her lips with his own, kissing her gently. "Unfortunately, it is time to go see a man about a contract." She stiffened as he took her in his arms, then tried to sooth her sudden wariness. "Today is the day we finish this."

He turned toward Samson and mounted, then pulled her up across his lap in front of him, protecting her from the saddle as she rested on his strong thighs. She leaned into him and wrapped her arms around his waist as he sheltered her and steered Samson toward the manor.

Hepplewort's mother watched from the parlor window, trying to assess the situation. When the men came close enough, she called to the butler to attend her and went to the entry.

Perry pushed Hepplewort again and the man faltered, falling up the steps as he went. "I believe you misplaced something," Perry ground out, flanked by Smyth and Gentry. "We found this toad trespassing."

Hepplewort's mother walked out of the manor behind the butler, her brow furrowed, her eyes narrowed, her mouth set deeply in a scowl. "My son has done no such thing." Her lips blanched as they pulled tight across her teeth. She peered down at him.

Perry smiled charmingly.

"Oh, my lady, I believe you'll find that your son has done not only that, but he is also guilty of kidnapping, assault, and—" He paused, looking down at the earl. "—screaming like a little girl." He grinned. "Not to mention that he got his nose broken by a woman. Not a crime, of course, but notable nonetheless."

His mother's beady eyes bulged as Hepplewort hid his face in his hands.

Gentry and Smyth laughed and Perry's chest shook.

She stared down at Perry, who glared back at her, daring her to speak.

"Where is my son's betrothed?" she asked sourly.

"To my knowledge there is no such person," Perry said, looking over his shoulder again. There he saw Gideon and Francine making their way toward the manor.

The old woman followed his gaze. "Here she comes now, and you will find my son has acted well within the binds of his contract. You will leave her here. She belongs to me," she said definitively.

Perry bristled, but knew her rant would be short lived. "We shall see."

Hepplewort glanced up from his seat on the top step to see Francine pulled across Gideon's lap on the horse and he stood, sputtering indignantly. "What the devil is he doing—"

"Sit down," Smyth and Gentry said in sturdy unison.

Perry raised a brow at Hepplewort's mother as Gideon came to a stop in front of the manor.

He let Francine down carefully, then jumped from the bay and advanced on Hepplewort.

Hepplewort skittered backward on the stair, bumping into the butler, who kicked at him with a grunt. Perry and Gentry reached for the angry duke, holding him back.

Gideon broke free and Smyth moved to help, standing in front of him as the others held his arms. Gideon took a deep breath and turned.

"It took you a while to catch up," Perry said, and Gideon smiled, shaking his brother's hand. Perry laughed and embraced him, clapping him on the back. He then turned to Francine, who was keeping the back of her torn dress to the horse in a poor attempt to not look entirely disheveled.

She smiled at Perry sweetly and he bowed. "My lady, my sister, the future Duchess of Roxleigh. It is so wonderful to see you again, even in this rumpled manner," he said with a sly grin.

She blushed deeply and glared at Gideon, who lifted his hands with a show of penitence. "I had to have an accomplice."

She blushed even deeper.

Gideon moved to stand just behind her and placed a hand on her waist. He tried to refasten some of the buttons on her dress but only one had survived him. He shrugged, pulling her hair behind her shoulders and smoothing it down her back.

She turned slightly and looked up at him, smiling. Then she turned on Hepplewort, thinking about his return to the manor. *It must have been comical, really. A squat, corpulent, broken man hobbling toward his manor, flanked by three tall, handsome, stately men. It must have been the longest walk of shame on record.* She laughed to herself, then saw that horrible woman staring down at her in judgment, and her eyes blazed. With a look of pure rage and hatred, Francine advanced on Heppleworth without warning.

Gideon reached to grab her first but she was too fast for him. Perry and Gentry managed to catch her arms but her forward momentum drew her feet out from under her, and her foot caught Hepplewort hard in the jaw.

His head snapped to the side and blood splattered across his mother's skirt as he fell sideways on the stairs, quite thoroughly done in.

Her temper flared again when the men released her arms and she pointed in his bloodied face. "You will *never* have me. You never *did* have me," she screamed. "I was *never* yours, and I *never* will be."

Hepplewort flinched at the power of her voice. Then she turned on his mother.

Gentry and Smyth looked to Gideon for instruction but he merely nodded, a large smile growing across his features. The woman tried to hide behind the butler, who appeared shocked and more than uncomfortable, and who also soon moved out of the way.

"I am ruined," Francine said, standing tall, holding her hands out wide for inspection, tilting her chin up. "From my forehead to my toes, thoroughly ravished. This man," she said, gesturing at Gideon, "lay me down in your field, and he ruined me. He took my—my maidenhead, and claimed my body as his, and I allowed him."

Francine waited as the awful woman examined her. She knew her mouth was swollen, her hair tangled, and her dress was torn and covered with grass and other stains. Hepplewort's mother merely grunted, and Francine spoke again. "My womb is for his children, my mouth is for his pleasure, my body is for his use alone," she said proudly.

The mother stepped back, cringing in disgust. The gentlemen shifted uncomfortably, looking around for something to inspect.

"And," Francine continued, "with any luck, I am already with his child." She smiled as she turned toward Gideon.

"So you see," Gideon said, approaching Francine carefully, his mind reeling from her statements, "the contract your son had with Larrabee is void, unfulfilled. There is no way for him to claim her maidenhead, as I already have. And since I've ruined this woman, there is nothing left for me to do but marry her, make an honest woman of her, and hope that my heir is increasing safely within her even now."

Gideon shifted his gaze to the wrinkly woman. He wrapped one arm gently around Francine's waist, his hand on her stomach as he leaned his temple to touch hers. He smiled up at Hepplewort's mother, and she paled. Her features went slack and she fell to the ground like a sack of dirty laundry before anyone could move to catch her.

Hepplewort looked up at the butler. "Well?"

The butler picked up the crumpled woman and carried her inside.

Francine whispered to Gideon and he stepped forward. "Francine had a lady's maid here. Send her out."

Hepplewort sneered. "I think you have plundered my estate plenty for today."

Gideon let go of Francine and took another step toward the earl with a menacing growl.

Hepplewort crawled backward, yelling through the door of the manor. "Blasted girl! Damnable chit! Come here!"

The petite maid walked out of the manor, pale and terrified, looking from the face of one gentleman to the next. "Yes, milord?" she said with an obedient curtsey.

He waved his hand at Gideon.

She stood on the third step, but was so diminutive she still had to look up to meet his eyes.

"There is a position available in my household," he began to say, but the girl turned away from him and ran back into the house.

Gideon and his companions leaned sideways, peering through the open door as she vaulted up the interior staircase, taking two at a time.

"My, but she's spry for a tiny gel," Smyth mumbled. He shrugged his shoulders when Gideon looked at him. "I guess she don't want the position, Yer Grace."

Gideon turned back to the manor and a few moments later he saw the girl running back down the stairs with a small sack and a blanket. He grinned.

"Well then, I guess we're off. One more thing, Hepplewort. Your behavior will be reported to the House of Lords, as well as the London Society pages and all the gossip sheets. If you know what is best, you won't step foot off this estate again. Ever."

Hepplewort seemed to understand his sincerity. He shriveled and looked down as Gideon advanced on him. "I know you, I know the things you've done, and if you think for one minute that you can continue, you're sorely mistaken. Consider yourself never to be heard from again, by anyone, *anywhere*. Is that understood?" Gideon stood over the man as he cowered on the stairs. He wanted desperately to take revenge for Lilly, but this was not the time.

Hepplewort nodded and dragged himself into the house, half walking and half crawling. He kicked the door shut behind him, leaving Morgan tied to the horse out front.

Francine smiled at the tiny maid whose face shone brighter than the sun.

"Oh, milady! Ye're my hero! Ye've rescued me and I canna thank ye enough!"

Francine laughed and hugged her. "It was you who rescued me. I couldn't possibly leave without knowing the name of the girl who buttoned me into such fine boots."

"Yes, milady, I thought as them boots might come in handy. I'm called Melinda."

"Well, that is a beautiful name. Shall we?"

Melinda smiled and handed her the blanket. "I thought mayhap ye could use this."

Francine grinned and Gideon wrapped the soft blanket around her. She turned to him as he once again jumped up to his horse and pulled her cautiously across his lap.

Perry, Smyth, and Gentry followed suit.

Smyth grunted and put his hand down to Melinda and she grasped it, the strong man pulling her tiny figure up astride the horse in front of him with ease.

"Oh my," she exclaimed as she wiggled in her seat, "but this is a big animal."

Smyth's jaw dropped as he paled and they all laughed, turning to leave.

Francine wrapped her arms around her duke, her Gideon, and closed her eyes. She wasn't afraid anymore. She was with him. She had been numb for so long and because of him she could now feel. She'd traveled through space and time and found the love of an eternity. She was content knowing that she belonged in his arms and she knew, somewhere deep inside, that she wasn't going anywhere.

# TWENTY-NINE

Riding nearly straight through to London they arrived late, surprising Gideon's household. The staff had not expected them back since they believed he'd return to Eildon after retrieving Francine from Gretna Green.

Sanders yelled for the servants to make up rooms since Perry insisted on staying at Roxleigh House in case a reprisal from Hepplewort came, but Gideon stopped the butler's orders. "The main guest suite is already prepared. Lord Trumbull can sleep there. We'll all retire immediately. There's no need to fuss about in the dead of night."

"Your Grace, the lady needs a place to rest as well. If Trum—"

"She will stay with me. There will be no discussion on the matter," Gideon said as he pulled her close.

"Your Grace—"

"That will be all, Sanders," Gideon said. "You are overstepping your bounds. I will not endure another word. Show our new maid, Melinda, to a room on your way to the third floor."

Sanders straightened and walked slowly toward his quarters without a sound. Gideon shooed the rest of the servants away and they went skittering for the darkness like a disbanded troupe of chattering mice.

"Gideon," Perry said.

"Not you as well," he said, looking at his brother with a distinct lack of patience.

"Let me have my say," Perry said. "I understand your need, and for tonight I believe we can turn a blind eye, but on the morrow she should return to the guest suite, and behavior should return to some semblance of propriety. I understand this situation is rather out of the norm, so I give you leave—"

"You give me leave?" Gideon boomed as he released Francine and approached his brother.

Gentry reached for his master's arm but Gideon shook him off without effort.

"Rox," Perry said, attempting to quell the angered duke. "We are all on the same side here. Nobody is going to deny you—*tonight*. We all need rest," he continued slowly, "and I understand that you need to know she is safe and the best way to do that is to have her close. I, as her guardian, *give you leave*," Perry pronounced each word carefully, "to see to that."

Francine reached out to Gideon, and her small hand on his shirtsleeve brought him back to her in that moment. "Gideon," she whispered before covering her mouth and looking from Perry to Gentry apologetically. "Your Grace, we should rest, we should all rest. We can talk in the morning, but for now, please, let's rest."

He nodded, wrapping his arms around her frame. He looked at Perry and nodded, then shook his hand and Gentry's before taking Francine to his suite.

Perry watched as they ascended the stairs. "Her safety here in this household will be your sole responsibility until we return to Eildon," he said, looking at Gentry. "But for tonight, she is as safe as she could possibly be, so you should get as much sleep as feasible."

Gentry bowed. "Yes, milord," he said, before turning and melting into the darkness.

Perry ran his hands through his disheveled hair, disrupting it further as he heaved a sigh and walked up the stairs toward the guest suite. He shook his head as he closed the door behind him, taking in the scent of his ward and his brother's betrothed. *Lavender and rain*, he thought, scoffing. "I hate lavender and rain," he mumbled. *Two days from a proper bath and she still held that scent. As if it wasn't the oil but her very essence.* He grumbled as he fell to the counterpane and kicked his boots off without a further thought to undressing. He was well asleep within moments.


The next morning, Ferry walked into the duke's bedchamber, swept the heavy drapes open, and turned.

Gideon heard his approach and flung the counterpane over Francine. "That will be all, Ferry," he called out from the shelter of the bed.

Ferry looked at the overlarge mound on the bed and strode quickly for the door. "I beg pardon, Your Grace," he said as he left. Shutting the door behind him, he grumbled. *Someone could have warned me*, he thought as he leaned back against the door, trying to catch his breath.

Gideon looked down at Francine as she stirred beneath the tent of blankets. She was still quite disheveled, but lovely as ever. He had undressed her and placed her in his bed, watching as she drifted off to sleep. He sat in a chair next to the bed, not wanting to close his eyes for fear that he was in the throes of madness and she would disappear the moment he turned away. His heart beat stronger and his chest filled with pressure as he watched, until he could no longer stand to be so far away. He'd put out the light and crawled into bed, molding her to his form.

Gideon threw the counterpane aside, his gaze roving over her. He didn't believe she was ready for a second encounter with him, though he could feel to the depths of his soul that he was, and just the thought stirred him. He groaned and rolled from the bed, tucking her in carefully. He donned his robe and walked to the door of his chamber and opened it swiftly. Ferry fell back into the room in shock.

"I beg pardon, Your Grace, I didn't expect—"

Gideon waved him off. "Have a bath prepared here for Lady

Francine and run mine in the bathing room," he said quietly. "Have one of the maids attend her. The new girl, Melinda."

Ferry nodded and walked away.

They bathed and dressed in separate rooms, but she stayed in his chamber as he finished readying for the day.

"I do wish we could have simply returned to Eildon," Francine said as Gideon straightened his shirt and pulled his waistcoat off the stand next to his bed.

He looked up at her, and the waistcoat fell back to the stand. "Truly?"

"Of course, why do you ask?"

"I guess I thought you enjoyed London." He walked over to her.

"Well, yes. I thought London was nice for a visit. But I have come to love Eildon. It's peaceful and beautiful, and the light is different. It's clear, and the air is clean and sweet, not foul. It just feels different, and I really miss Mrs. Weston," she said with a smile.

He took her up in his arms and kissed her. "You cannot know how that pleases me, and I shall endeavor to return us *home* as soon as possible. Within a sennight should be reasonable. I'll make sure Shaw is finished with his work, and there will be the ball to celebrate the posting of the banns in six days, and—"

"I thought that was going to be in a week," she said, moving to the fireplace.

"Actually, now I think on it, five days is plenty of time to make arrangements. Then we will leave directly."

She laughed and picked up the paper slipped under the door, reading the headline: *Dashing Duke saves blushing bride from Evil Earl with lascivious lovemaking.* Francine laughed and glanced back at Gideon. "Oh my," she said, her hand hovering in front of her mouth.

He read the paper over her shoulder. She imagined him turning beet-red with steam shooting from his ears, but instead she was greeted with a devilish grin as he grabbed her by the waist, turning her to him and leveling a passionate kiss on her lips.

"Gideon!" she exclaimed as she broke free.

He laughed as he nuzzled her, pulling her back into his strong arms. "Well, my sweet, I wouldn't want to make a liar out of the author, and we cannot hide from the gossips. The way I see it, this is fantastic press considering what it *could* have been. The ball in *four* days will be the most sought after event in the *ton*, not to mention the wedding ceremony and banquet back at Eildon. Wouldn't you agree?"

"Oh, I see. Now it's four days? Gideon, honestly, I don't care about all this ceremony, you know that."

"I know, but you can't argue with the fact that you have become the most celebrated *ruined* woman in all of London."

"No, *you* can't argue with that. After all, you were determined not to ruin me for the sake of my reputation, and this turn has you gloating. I will *never* live this down."

"Of course you will. In a fortnight we shall be old news. After all, we are far removed from Society at Eildon, and they much prefer the fodder they can keep an eye on."

She smacked playfully at the arms around her waist and moved to leave the bedroom, but he held her steadfast against him.

"Gideon, I have plans to make. You are a most demanding gentleman. I have less than four days now to plan—"

He cut her off, leaning in to kiss the edge of her ear.

"God, Francine, I am reaching my limit. I had hoped to give you time to recover before—" He sighed heavily and released her with great difficulty, clenching and unclenching his hands.

She turned on him. "The last thing I want from you is time, or distance. The time I want is with you, touching me, and the distance—none."

"Well," he said, his passion loosed by her words, "I don't believe an hour will slow down your progress too terribly." He moved toward her again.

"An hour?" she replied breathlessly, leaning her head back as she sank against him.

He shrugged. "Well, maybe a bit longer."

She exhaled, the air drifting across his ear and sending a shiver down his spine, awakening his senses and his need. His hands traveled her form, investigating the rise and fall of her chest with every breath, the goosebumps that rose under his calloused fingers as he drifted over her soft skin. He measured the heartbeat in her neck with his kisses, softly licking and nipping, feeling the tempo increase beneath his smiles.

He drew her back to the bed and sat at the edge, undoing all the ties, buttons, stays, fastens, laces, and binds that kept her from him.

She turned under his attentions, her eyes wide with nerves as her trappings all fell away, landing in a pool of soft, multicolored fabrics at her feet. One hand fluttered to her chest and the other below her waist and he reached for them, pulling them aside slowly.

"I told you never to hide yourself from me." He lifted her hands, kissing the marks on her wrists, then placed them on his shirt. "Undress me," he said in a voice which was no more than a pleading whisper. He shook from the effort to slow his movements.

She blushed violently and pulled him up from the bed.

He smiled as he bent his head to her. The kiss warmed, drove, opened, and revived her.

She pulled at his waistband, feeling for the clasp hidden inside, and his hips jerked forward. The tension from his rising erection slowed her progress. Her fingers moved nimbly down the placket and his breath quickened against her hair. Feeling his muscles tightening, she released him and looked up into his face anxiously.

He smiled, patient.

She pushed his shirt off his shoulders and he held his hands up as she unhooked the sleeves and tossed the linen to a chair. Her gaze drifted over him before finally resting on his face, searching his expression. Her first time had been in a field of flowers, under the dappled sunlight, like a dream. Now she was here, in his bedchamber—*his bedchamber*, she thought.

He smiled as she hooked her thumbs in his waistband and pushed his trousers down. He sat again at the edge of the bed and kicked his shoes off while she pulled each pant leg by the ankle, then tossed them aside.

The she was looking at the bed behind him, through him, around him, but never quite at him.

He stood again and closed the gap between them.

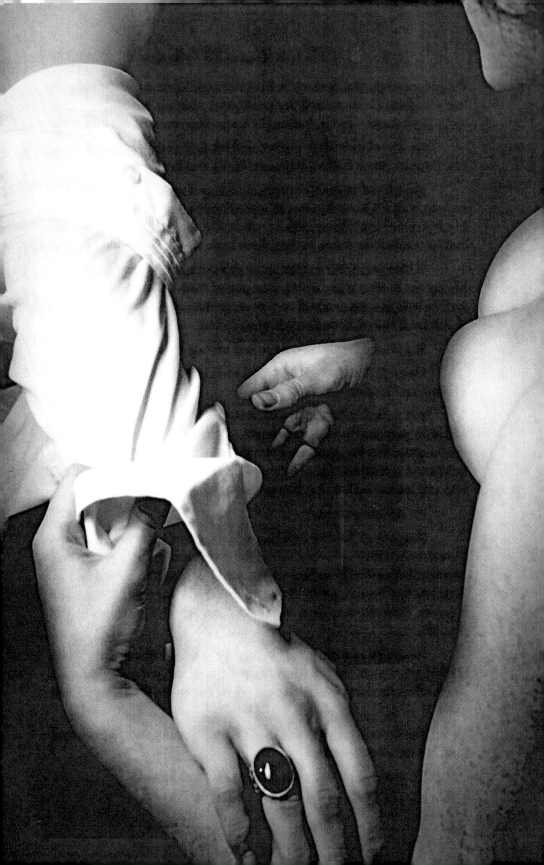

She shut her eyes, concentrating on the feel of her naked skin against the full, bare length of his. The slightest move sent shivers through his muscles. Her nipples rose to tight peaks as they grazed his chest, and trails of pinpricks spread like wildfire beneath the surface of her skin. Her breath hitched as his fingers traced up the backs of her arms from wrists to shoulders, straightening her spine as they progressed, at last raising her face to meet his kiss.

"Gideon," she breathed nervously. She looked up into his eyes. "Gideon, I...I am..."

He quieted her by brushing his lips back and forth across hers. "You have naught to fear from me. We will be slow," he whispered, kissing her lower lip, his hands reaching around her waist. "And I gentle." He drew her up against him carefully, aligning their bodies to fit together as he turned. He lifted her then, placing her in the center of the large bed, and stood proudly, allowing her perusal.

She watched his breath come and go, his strong arms held at his sides. She could see his willful restraint and it reinforced her desire. She implored him to join her with her eyes, and the bed sank from his weight as he mounted the bed. He crawled over her, kissing his way up from her toes, drawing soft whimpers from her. He lowered himself over her, matched part for part

"You're trembling," he whispered.

"I— I'm just nervous. I guess. I mean. Ahhh."

"What can I do?" He lifted her hair and spread it across the pillows around her, smoothing it out.

"Just touch me," she whispered. "Just keep touching me and don't stop, not ever. Not for a moment."

"That," he said softly in her ear, "I can do." He spread her legs beneath him with one knee. He caressed her nipple, causing her to arch into him. His hand skimmed down her side to her knee, lifting and wrapping her leg around his waist.

"Gideon, slowly. Please, slowly," she whispered as she was opened to him. She pushed at his shoulders and he shifted over her, making her skin tingle. Her fingers tensed against him as he entered her with painstaking caution. She felt herself stretching to accommodate him and she squirmed. The feel of his skin sliding across hers, his spicy scent, salty taste, the sound of his exertion as he breathed, and the warmth of his breath drifted across her senses.

Gideon groaned as he felt her ease around him, and his momentum increased.

She watched his expressions change, feeling the network of electrical webs spreading then condensing. Her mouth opened wide as she inhaled, over and over, trying to gain more oxygen, her moans turning to screams as the quickening enveloped her.

Gideon urged her on, holding steady and deep, feeling her pulsing flesh drawing his release. He shuddered, his hips thrusting as he cried out, their hearts racing in matched cadence. He rolled swiftly to his back, pulling her with him.

She squeaked at the rushed movement and collapsed on him. He smoothed her hair back from her face, spreading it across her back, then lifted it and blew a stream of air across her warmed skin, drawing goosebumps and making her sigh.

"You have me spent. How do you do that so easily?"

He smiled. "It's not me, but you. You bring this out of me."

She smiled shyly, studying him from beneath her long eyelashes. "You simply can't keep doing this to me."

He held her tightly. "I can, and I will. And what's more, you will enjoy every minute of it." He placed a kiss at the tip of her upturned nose.

"Yes, Your Grace," she whispered, her fingers at her kiss-swollen lips.

Gideon walked into his study to find Perry and Shaw deep in conversation. "Gentlemen," he acknowledged, reading the story from *Miss Witwick's Society Pages* again. He laughed and handed the paper to Perry as he sat as his desk. "You may have to send these to us at Eildon after we leave. I'm finding them quite enjoyable."

Perry stared at his brother, agog.

"Come now, Perry, did you expect me to return to my awful manner so quickly?"

"I really hadn't considered it." Perry shifted in his chair and glanced at the paper. "Dashing Duke, heh? Where are they getting this?

Why am I not mentioned? Dashing… I'm the younger, handsomer brother. Dastardly Duke would be more like it, or perhaps Asinine, Arrogant Aristocrat? Hmm, mayhap I should write for Miss Witwick, Your Devastatingly Dashing Dukeness."

Shaw choked on his tea, trying not to laugh as Gideon gave his brother the familiar warning glare.

"There he is! The Dastardly Duke returns," Perry said with a grin.

"Shaw," Gideon said, ignoring his brother, "are you prepared to return to Eildon and transform the place into the masterpiece we all know it will be?"

"Yes, of course, Your Gr— Roxleigh," he finished after Gideon cut him the same warning glance. "I have arranged for all the shipments: fabric, furniture, wood, and other appointments. They are now scheduled to arrive about the same time we will. We have only a month left before the gathering, which has recently become a wedding celebration. Mrs. Weston has assured me that there are enough locals to complete the work, and anything else we may need should be simple to obtain."

Gideon nodded. "Is the current work on schedule?"

"Yes, I received an update less than a sennight ago."

"That's good. I must apologize, though—I wasn't expecting to return to Eildon so precipitously. I expected that we would be attending a few more social events before returning home. We didn't get far in our quest with the lovely Lady Alice."

"Actually, I wasn't expecting to see her until midsummer, so the fact that I have, and that I was able to spend a wonderful evening *attempting* to be in her company, was certainly worth the effort and the journey."

Gideon smiled. "Perry, are you ready to move to Westcreek?"

"In truth, Rox, I do not believe I am. In fact, I was hoping to impose on you a bit. Westcreek hasn't been inhabited for some time, and since the most talented architect in London is otherwise occupied by the Distinguished Duke of Dashingness, I won't be able to make any changes for at least two months."

Gideon looked at him with a grin. "Not going to drop it, are you?"

"Not a chance, your Deliberately Debonair Dukeness," Perry answered as Shaw covered his face with one hand to hide a smile.

"Don't encourage him, Shaw," Gideon grunted as he turned again to his brother. "Your intention isn't to saddle me with your charges, is it? Have you rethought your agreement so soon?"

Perry waved him off. "I rethought my agreement with the Intrepid In-laws the moment I offered it, and every five minutes thereafter. I assume that the life of the Valorous Viscount is to change greatly, for better or worse, but I won't be the sacrificial lamb for your happiness. That, dear brother, was your job, and though you have vacated the position, I am not keen on acquiring it."

Gideon glared. "No, I wouldn't wish that on you, Your Valiant Viscountness. Of course, the sisters can come with us, as can you, at any time. I'll speak with Francine, but I don't believe she'll mind. I suppose she wants to get to know them, and we have had a bit of fun recently, haven't we? However, I must insist the alliterations come to an end."

"If you insist," Perry said with a deliberate frown.

Shaw laughed. "So, the Boorish Blue Blood becomes the Dashing Duke," he said quietly, drawing surprised laughter from the brothers.

"Well done," Perry said, clapping Shaw on the back as Gideon smiled inwardly behind his scowl.


Francine went to the parlor that afternoon to look over the guest lists and menus for the upcoming ball. She wasn't at all prepared to plan such a lavish evening, but she had insisted, wanting a project, and since Gideon had given her all the information she needed, she was determined to shine.

When the sisters came in, followed by Miss Faversham, she was happy for the reprieve.

"I thought you might like some help with the preparations," Miss Faversham said.

"Oh yes, I would definitely like some help." The ladies sat in the parlor, planning the ball and dinner all that afternoon. The sisters were actually quite adept at making arrangements; she guessed that was part of their education. By the time supper rolled around, they had the majority of the plans complete and the guest list finalized, and the ladies all went to dress for the formal supper that Gideon had arranged in the dining room.

Gideon, Perry, and Shaw gathered in the study before dinner while Francine, Amélie, Maryse, and Miss Faversham gathered in the blue parlor. Sanders knocked and opened the door. "The Dowager Countess of Greensborough and Lady Alice Gracin," he announced.

Francine stood and greeted them, her arms outstretched. "My lady, how wonderful it is to see you again, Lady Alice, how have you been?" She hugged her, kissing her cheeks.

"Very well, Lady Francine, and you? I am certain the gossip pages are greatly embellishing your tale, but I imagine it was harrowing none the less," Lady Alice said.

Francine led the women further into the room and motioned for them to sit. "Well, yes, it was quite an adventure. Miss Witwick actually did a good job with the report. Though I've no idea where she got her information."

"I was very interested to receive your invitation, Lady Francine. To what do we owe this honor?" the dowager said.

Francine smiled. "Well, I believe we have a common goal. Gide— uh, His Grace recently told me of a project that he and Trumbull have championed. I believe you are both acquainted with a Mr. Amberly Shaw?" Francine didn't think it possible, but Lady Alice's expression grew even brighter—so bright, in fact, that Francine flinched.

Sanders knocked at the door again. "Supper is served," he said, then turned and waited for the ladies to follow. They filed out of the parlor in order of rank as the gentlemen walked out of the study laughing.

Gideon saw them and stopped with a conspiratorial grin. "Well, Perry, it looks as though our Lady Alice has yet another champion." He glanced at the brandy Perry had refused to relinquish to the sideboard.

Perry looked up as Shaw leaned around the two men. Shaw caught sight of Lady Alice and his mouth went dry.

Francine ran over to Gideon, launching herself at him and pulling herself up on his broad shoulders to plant a kiss on his cheek.

"Why stop there, my lady?" he whispered as he caught her to his chest. "You have already moved in such an untoward fashion," he said with a grin.

He laughed, losing himself in her eyes until Perry elbowed him gently. Everyone had stopped, uncomfortably bearing witness to the quiet conversation.

He cleared his throat and straightened his jacket. "I beg your pardon. All the excitement of the past week seems to have altered our sensibilities."

The dowager countess looked at Gideon with a smile. "Well, thank God for that."

Perry choked on his brandy and Gideon smacked him hard between the shoulder blades.

Perry turned to Shaw. "The dowager countess is wonderful, don't you think?"

Shaw was staring intently at Lady Alice. He smiled and glanced at Perry out of the corner of his eye. "What?"

"The dowager," Perry repeated.

Shaw looked at him, confused, then slowly realized what he had missed. "Oh right, the dowager... I...yes?" he offered, unsure of the correct response.

Perry laughed. "Preoccupied with something, Shaw?"

A moment passed.

"Sha-aw?" Perry sing-songed, trying to catch his attention.

"My lor— I... er, no?" he tried to answer, but Perry was already shaking his head and moving toward the women to greet them.

Relying on what she could remember from her book of manners, Francine arranged the guests in order of rank. Gideon nodded and moved to enter the dining hall, only to have the dowager stop the parade and rearrange everyone to her liking. She sat at Gideon's left with Lady Alice next to her. Perry sat next to Francine, at Gideon's right, with Miss Faversham and the sisters next to him, leaving Shaw next to Lady Alice.

Gideon gave an approving nod to the dowager.

"We are among friends here," she said smartly, "and we seem to have nudged propriety for the evening. Let us not get too carried away, but you will have posted your banns by week-out."

Gideon nodded to the footmen, who began placing plate after plate of delicacies in front of the guests.

Francine cleared her throat. "Now, you must all tell us what you think, as I believe many of these dishes will end up on the menu at the ball."

Gideon sat back in his chair. "Actually, I have a surprise. Chef had need of another run to France for wine and truffles—you know how very particular she can be. She will be in London within two days and she will be preparing the dinner."

Francine's eyes lit up. "Really?"

"Mmm, yes, really," he answered happily, using her words and swallowing a sip of wine.

Francine turned to the countess. "Just wait," she said excitedly, "the food Chef makes, oh— It's divine. I've never had anything like it. Your Grace?"

He guessed her thoughts and smiled. "Yes she traveled to Angers, and will be bringing home a large selection of pears."

Francine clapped her hands together and jumped from her seat, grabbing Gideon around the neck and planting a big kiss right on his mouth. "Oh, you remembered! You wonderful, wonderful man! You are so good to me." The entire room was silenced and she looked around penitently giggling happily.

He unhooked her arms, shaking his head. "Perhaps I should have waited until later to tell you of these plans," he said with a great smile.

The dowager laughed gently. "No, no, Your Grace, I believe we are all the better for this display. I wouldn't have had it any other way. Please, what else can you inform your betrothed of?"

"I beg your pardon, my lady," Francine said, "it's just that Chef makes the most wonderful dessert—with pears and brandy, is it? Or maybe it's wine, I don't know. It's so amazing. Oh, Your Grace, I can't believe you. How did you arrange this?"

"I have my ways."

Francine smiled and sat back in her chair.

"I guess we don't need to discuss the dinner in depth." She

sighed. She had tried so hard to be a proper hostess that night and so far had been thwarted on all counts by good news. She smiled to herself, looking at her hands folded in her lap.

Gideon reached over and squeezed them, and her smile broadened.

Lady Alice didn't notice the performance one bit. Her eyes were trained on Mr. Shaw, as were his on her.

The sisters watched the others with curiosity—the lovers, the smitten, and the newly introduced—intently learning the behaviors and intimations only two intangibly connected people could share.

The Dowager Countess of Greensborough sat back as the sisters giggled and gossiped and she watched with the knowledge only a lifetime could bring. She loved the expressions of wonder, excitement, and love because nothing was new to her anymore. She had lived and loved and lost. Now her only hope was to capture some of the excitement from her young friends. She wanted to see her granddaughter fall deeply, helplessly, and irrevocably in love. She wanted to see the new babies born and raised. She observed from a visage lined with all that laughter, love, and loss as the sisters examined the same couples from the other end of a lifetime.

Mr. Shaw sat stiffly next to Lady Alice. He tried desperately not to draw attention to the fact that he was beyond smitten with the dowager countess' granddaughter. The dowager smiled as Alice teased and Shaw blushed, looking around to see who had noticed. He was such a gentleman, even though he wasn't of the gentry, and the thought saddened her. *Curse Society,* she thought, turning away in annoyance. She saw Roxleigh and Lady Francine conversing with the same jovial banter, their teasing colored with the undertones of an intimate couple. The countess blushed, remembering her husband, how it had felt to know what he wanted. How desperately she missed his warm touch.

She looked across the table at Trumbull, who spoke with Miss Faversham about his wards. She could see that Miss Faversham would be in for a difficult time with that one. It was obvious he was still intent on his rakish behavior, but that he had no idea he was currently unleashing his powers on her, and quite to her disadvantage. She smiled again, thinking that there were very few women in London, probably in all of England, who would match him and tame his roguish behavior—certainly nobody in this year's crop of innocents, or the next few that she could bring to mind. That man would be a chore, but then, her beloved husband had been the same.

She looked back to Lady Francine and Roxleigh and her brow creased. She had always thought that Roxleigh would be the difficult one. She smiled as they glanced up at her.

"Is everything to your liking, my lady?" Gideon asked.

"Why, yes, Your Grace."

"I beg you, call me Roxleigh," he said with a smile.

"Of course, Roxleigh. How soon after the ball will you be leaving for Eildon?"

"Very soon after," Francine said. "You will visit us there, yes?"

"As you see fit. I shall accompany Lady Alice to the house party. His Grace, hmm, Roxleigh has already graciously invited us to stay."

"Lady Alice," Francine started as she looked down the table, then cleared her throat to gain the attention of the young lady with the vibrant red hair. "Lady Alice?" she said again, questioningly.

Lady Alice looked up, startled. "Yes, my lady? I do beg your pardon. Mr. Shaw was telling me of the work at the manor," she said with a timid smile.

"Well, I certainly wouldn't want to interrupt. Please carry on," Francine said happily. She glanced at the dowager countess, who mirrored her pleasure at the couple's interaction. "Well, I would like to thank everyone for coming tonight. I look forward to seeing you all at the ball, then back at Eildon."

Francine hoped Shaw and Lady Alice would have an easier go of it than she and Gideon had. Her eyebrows knit together. No, she wouldn't have changed anything that had happened, not for the world. If one small thing had gone differently she may not be sitting here now, with this great company, at the right hand of her duke.

# THIRTY

rs. Weston ran out to greet the approaching carriages. She loved Francine dearly, this girl who had happened into their lives and changed them all for the better. She could hardly wait to get a good look at her, just to be sure she was all right.

"Oh, my lady," she gasped as Francine descended the carriage on the hand of Gideon. Mrs. Weston pushed the duke aside hastily and reached her arms out to hold her.

Francine smiled and sank into her welcoming arms.

"Oh, Lady Francine, is it true then? You are well?"

Francine gave her the warmest possible smile. "Yes, Mrs. Weston, I am," she said in a bright, clear voice.

Mrs. Weston hugged Francine again and laughed as Gideon stood and watched, grinning. Mrs. Weston turned to him. "You have done well, Your Grace," she said boldly.

Perry's carriage pulled up behind them as all the servants started shuffling outside to welcome them home and see to their effects.

Mrs. Weston backed away from them with a curtsey. Francine could see her eyes misting with emotion and she leaned into Gideon, looking up at him. He looked more peaceful than she had ever seen him. She rested one hand on his chest, feeling his breath moving, his heartbeat steady and strong. She closed her eyes and sighed as he placed one of his large, warm hands over her small one.

Francine glanced at the manor in time to see Meggie walk from the entry, followed by a smaller girl. She walked over to the maid, taking her hands. "Meggie, it's so good to see you again," she said before she turned to the other girl. "You must be Lilly."

The smaller girl nodded with a smile and a curtsey.

"I'm so glad you are better and I'm glad you've come to Eildon. If there's anything you need, please don't hesitate to let me know,"

Francine said.

Lilly blushed wildly, looking at the ground as the girls curtseyed.

Gideon walked up behind Francine and whispered in her ear. "You are the most wonderful woman in the world, but Lilly is not accustomed to this sort of behavior. You might want to let her get used to you before suggesting such bold things," he said quietly.

Francine examined the girl. She could see tiny crisscrossing scars covering her skin, and she unconsciously touched her own wrists where Hepplewort had injured her. She turned to Gideon; there was nothing she could do, nothing she could say, to change what had happened.

He saw Francine's silent panic and Lilly's discomfiture and he swept Francine into his arms, carrying her across the threshold. The movement made Francine's head snap back and she laughed.

"Oh, Your Grace, we aren't married yet!"

"Where my actions are concerned, we are." he whispered in her ear. "This is your home, you are my duchess, and from what I understand, your room is ready." He carried her up the grand staircase and to the right—away from her room.

She reached out, looking behind him. Her brow creased. He opened the panel to the passageway behind his suites and carefully squeezed through without letting her go. Then he walked down the passage to the entry on his left.

He stood her before him and smiled at her confused expression.

"You said my room is ready. Why are we here?"

"This room belongs to the duchess. That would be you, my sweet," he whispered.

Her eyes grew wide and she turned slowly, looking around. She grasped his hand and they moved across the threshold.

The walls were paneled with a light-colored wood, brightening the entire room. They walked past the pale silk panels, which had been re-hung, toward the far wall where the bath sat. It was big enough for two and then some, the edge wide enough to sit comfortably.

It had been cleaned meticulously, the white tiles brightened and showcasing the hand painted flowers, the brass hardware polished to a mirror finish. It was surrounded by more of the flowing silk panels, creating an ethereal, semi-private feeling.

The large mattress had been removed, and a grand four-poster bed that matched the walls was centered on the left, flanked by a wardrobe and dressing table. The bed was covered with a large, colorful counterpane and soft, oversized pillows that looked as though they were made of the remnants of the velvet panels that had once hung on the walls.

He walked over to a polished brass wall sconce and lifted the glass cover, striking a match against the base and lighting it.

"You've had gas run?"

"Yes, it was one of the projects I wanted to have completed while we were away. Argand gas lamps now light the main rooms. They also ran water to the bathing rooms and main suites," he said, very pleased with the results. The update should have been done decades ago, but the dukedom hadn't the money to make such extensive upgrades.

"So would the duchess' room be attached to the duke's room?"

"Of course." He turned the water on to run a bath and took her hand, pulling her toward the windows. "I had all the window boxes removed. Shaw said you preferred well-lit rooms, so we decided there was no need for them. The furniture was custom built for you," he added as he ran a hand over the settee and matching chairs. "There are pockets in all the dust ruffles, for you to keep your books from the floor."

She eyed him suspiciously. "Is that why Shaw was asking me all those random questions in London?"

"Oh, there was nothing random about the questions," Gideon said. "Do you know how difficult it was to convince the woodworkers to forgo a deep stain on all the wood?" He shook his head.

Gideon led her back the length of the room then paused. He looked down at her as he reached up to a piece of molding and twisted it.

She heard a sturdy click within the wall and the panel popped open. He pulled her through the short passageway and pushed on the wall at the other end. They entered his bedchamber, right next to his rather large bed. She sighed as she looked around the room. "It's rather like my room, only *much* larger."

"You mean it is rather like the main guest suite, don't you? My duchess will not live in a room so far from mine. In fact, my wife will share my bed every night," he said, wrapping his arms around her.

She breathed deeply, taking in the scent of his room, infused with sandalwood and salt.

"Ferry!" he called out as he released her, and Ferry was there like a breath.

"Yes, Your Grace?"

"Please see to the bath I have drawn in my lady's chamber."

"Of course, Your Grace." Ferry walked to the tunnel behind them and pulled the panel closed.

Francine explored his chamber. It was the epitome of what she would consider masculine: dark wood, deep colors, thick fabrics, and scant ornamentation. Beautiful in its simplicity. She found the small table next to the main entry and ran a finger across it with a quiet laugh.

"What?" he asked as he walked up behind her.

"Well, I believe this would be the table I stubbed my toe on," she said with a blush.

"You stubbed your toe? When woul— Oh." He gave her quite the grandest smile she had ever seen.

"Did you have this room redecorated as well?"

"No, I wanted to wait for you before redecorating *our bedchamber*."

She drew in a sharp breath at the words.

He cleared his throat, and she looked up at him.

"Gideon?"

"Mmm hmm?"

"Why is there a bed in the other room if we are to *share* a bedroom?"

He grinned brightly. "Are you unhappy with the appointments in your chamber?"

She shook her head as he smiled teasingly.

"Well, my lady, we aren't yet wed, and though we have shared much together, we will need to continue to have separate bedchambers until our wedding night."

"For propriety's sake?"

"For propriety's sake. However, with our rooms being ever so discreetly joined, if we were to—"

"Share a bed?"

"Yes, share a bed. No one would be the—"

"Wiser?" When she finished his sentence again, he drew her up, kissing her eyelashes, her cheekbones, her earlobes, and her chin. Then he kissed her lips, drawing her moans into his mouth.

His night beard gently chafed her skin, making her flush. Her breathing hitched and he touched the reddened skin.

"Gideon?"

"Yes, Francine?"

"Would you— Would you mind helping me with my bath? I'm not familiar with the pipes, and I fear I may do something wrong."

"Of course, my love," he answered as he kissed her, pushing her backward through the passageway to her room.

She saw that Ferry had lit the argand lamps throughout her chamber and cracked the windows, stirring the flames in the lamps, and the sheer panels, creating a dreamlike vision before her. She breathed deeply of the warm, scented bath water and looked up at Gideon.

"Lavender and rain," he whispered, tickling her ear with his warm breath.

He undressed her slowly, removing her gloves by pinching gently at the fingertips, then sliding them slowly from her hands. He unbuttoned her soft muslin dress, letting it fall to the floor in a puddle of blue. Then her corset, her chemise, slippers, stockings, and drawers.

She stood before him, completely naked but for the blush that raced wickedly across her figure from head to toe, infusing her body with heat. This time she didn't hide herself.

He left her hair piled on top of her head and pulled her toward the bath, sitting on the edge as she stepped over.

Her pink-kissed mouth dropped open in a sigh as she sank her toes into the warm water. She sat back in the large bath, examining the bars of soap and fancy glass bottles of oils on the edge. *I had all of these wonderful things in my apartment, but never the time.* She stretched and soothed her travel-wearied muscles, sore from the journey home. *Home. This is my home.* She smiled and there were no doubts, no regrets, and no harried thoughts about waking from a dream or being transported back to her small furnished apartment in Denver. She was home; out of all the many rooms where she had spent wakeful nights, this was the first place she had ever truly belonged.

She looked up at him through her half-lidded eyes, silently imploring him to join her, but he merely sat on the edge, watching her move under the water. She had become accustomed to being attended during her bath, but this was different and so much more exciting. "Come on in, the water's fine," she said bravely.

Gideon cleared his throat, feeling it tighten. "Ferry is waiting in my suite." He watched her deliberate movements, his words suddenly catching as his mouth went dry. *But I would like nothing more than to stay right here and watch.* "I am in desperate need of a proper shave since I refused him this morning at the inn," he explained, never taking his eyes off her figure.

Her lower lip jutted out to tease him. The pout caught him off-guard and he moaned deep within his chest.

"Bring me the razor," she said.

He sobered and looked at her. "Have you any experience shaving a man?" he asked with a touch of poorly veiled trepidation.

"Tell Ferry *I* require a sharp razor."

She shifted under the water, creating ripples of movement on the surface, each miniscule tide hitting the side of the tub where he rested, hypnotizing him, and just like that he was transfixed.

She giggled at his hundred-yard stare and the small sound roused him slightly.

"Go on," she urged.

He stood and walked awkwardly to his suite without a word, returning a few minutes later while shaking his head. "He refused to give up my usual shaving kit," he said as he approached the bath. "He sent an older one that he packs when we are away from Eildon, and I had to promise that he would be allowed to shave me before supper." He stopped a safe distance from the bath.

"So I can keep this razor?" she asked as she held her hand out.

He shrugged and set it on the edge of the bath before she trapped his gaze. He was once again transfixed, his bright green eyes roving over her body.

"Did he sharpen it for me?"

Gideon nodded, his eyes wide as the new moon. "What exactly are you going to do?" he asked in a hushed voice, his mouth gone dry again.

She pulled the straight razor from the kit, carefully opening the blade.

"You don't seem to understand how particular my valet is," he started, trying to clear his throat. "You realize, of course, the ideas running through his head. The last time he came up against you, you demanded he remove your corset after requesting he retrieve some of my clothing for you to wear." The last bit of his sentence broke off as she gestured invitingly toward the bathtub.

She was smiling at the memory. "We simply cannot afford to lose him. You should increase his wages to ensure his compliance."

"After that particular incident I had to double them," Gideon said with a wide smile, relaxing a bit as he took the last step toward the bathtub and sat down on the edge.

Francine lifted one leg out of the water, placing her foot high on his leg, near his hip. He started to protest, but as her toes moved against him the sensation made him more accepting.

"You don't mind me getting you a little wet, do you?" she asked in a sultry voice. Not waiting for a response, she lifted the razor. "Don't move," Francine warned as she pointed the sharp edge of the razor at him. "I haven't ever used one of these before, but considering they've shaved a great many faces over the years, I should be able to manage." Then, with the greatest care, she began to shave her leg. With each pass she smoothed her skin with some of the oil-infused water from the bath, letting it run over her velvety leg.

He didn't move an inch. Every stroke she made affected him greatly. His mouth watered, his skin flushed, his jaw clenched, the hair on his neck stood on end. He could barely breathe, and his hands held on to the edge of the tub to quell the dizziness that threatened to overtake him. Gideon stared intently as she ministered to that long leg.

The gaslights glistened off the water as she passed over the pale flesh with the razor, giving the impression of flames dancing across her wet skin. Her sweet sighs escaped her lips at the trickle of the water over her newly shaven leg. She exhaled one last time, resting her head back on the edge of the bath, moving her leg slowly in and out of the water, breaking the surface tension. The rivulets streamed down her leg, only to drip back to the water's surface to create more ripples. She glanced up at Gideon to find his face pale and shocked.

"I don't— I…I don't understand," he stammered. "I never— Where did you—"

"Gideon." She raised her leg out of the bath and placed it across his dampened lap while sinking back into the water. "Touch me," she said in a throaty, seductive voice.

He pulled his hands from the edge of the bath and reached for her. The idea of attending her bath was arousing enough, but a woman using a razor was so foreign to him that he wasn't sure what to think or do.

He laid one finger on her leg, testing the skin as though it might burn. She bent her knee, moving her leg to fill his palms with the soft silkiness, drawing a deep guttural moan from his chest.

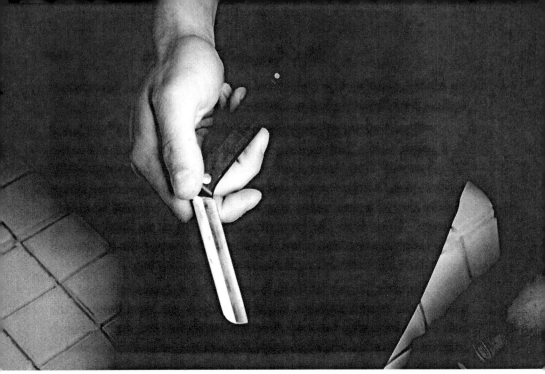

"So soft," he whispered. His smile grew as he remained transfixed on the length of her leg. He smoothed his palms over it tenderly, relishing the feel of her skin against his sturdy, calloused hand.

Francine was taken by his awestruck perusal. Her powerful duke was lost, speechless and befuddled. She smiled at the thought that she had tamed this important, beautiful, and incredible man. And beyond that, she'd shocked him, awakened something in him nobody knew existed.

He drew in a breath and nudged her leg back into the water as he reached for the other. She turned her body to rest on her hip. He shifted at the edge, pulling his knee up as she laid her warm wet leg across his, her foot resting at the joint of his hip. He reached for the razor in her hand, willing her to trust him.

She complied, forcing herself to hold perfectly still as he lifted her leg from his lap and wrapped his long fingers around her ankle. He pointed the razor at her. "Don't move. I haven't ever used one of these myself, but as they've done the job on my face hundreds of times it can't be all that difficult." He winked as she giggled, then started shaving in cautious, lingering strokes. He set his mind to the chore, replicating her gestures, alternately drawing the blade across her skin then rinsing her leg with the bath water, letting it run the length of her, causing her skin to flush.

His actions drew roused sighs from her parted lips, each stroke soothing her nerves as he deftly completed his task. When he finished, he lowered her leg back to his and released her ankle, letting her foot lay against his strengthening arousal as he closed the blade with a deep exhalation and set the razor aside. He caressed the smooth leg, running his fingers up and down its length.

She sat up in the bath and drained the water, then rinsed and refilled the tub. She reached for his neck cloth, her movements opening her body under the water for his hungry gaze. He wasn't sure he could manage much more of this tease. His hands moved to grip the tub again, and she reached for his waistcoat and shirt, undoing them and pressing them open across his chest. The water from her hands streamed the length of his torso, soaking the fabric of his waistband. His stomach tightened.

His breath came faster, matching the rhythm of her pulse, and she grabbed him by the shirt, yanking him into the bath on top of her with a great splash amid her wild laughter. The dousing soaked the floor and sobered him. He rose to his knees between her outstretched legs, giving her an admonishing glare. He inspected her, open like the petals of an iris before him, her breasts rippling the water as she giggled.

Francine leaned forward and peeled off his shirt and waistcoat, kissing a stray ribbon of water at his navel before throwing the clothes to the tiled floor. She moved to his trousers, where the water had pulled the fabric tight against the contours of his body.

He stood in the bathtub, removing his soggy shoes and tossing them down on top of the other wet clothes that puddled on the floor.

She shifted to her knees and peeled his trousers down his taut, muscular legs, forcing them inside out as her breath came up against his naked arousal, making his lungs seize. She could almost hear his heart rioting inside his ribcage, pounding as she inspected the gleaming, wet erection poised in front of her. She could see the fluttering heartbeat that suffused it, making it grow.

He was transfixed like a moth to a flame, trying to hold his position as close as possible to the heat. *Let's see if I can shatter his composure.* Mesmerized, she leaned in, placing a gentle kiss at the crease where the silken shaft rose to meet the head.

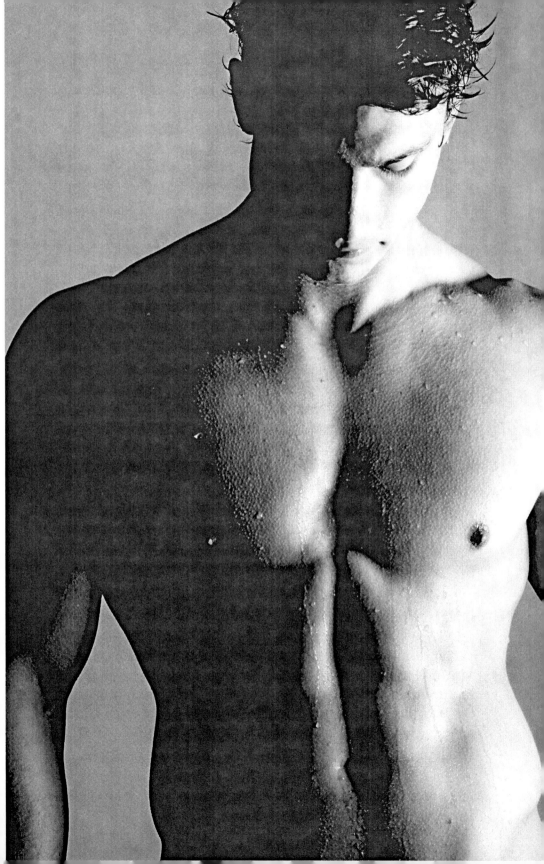

His jaw opened then clenched, and he held as still as Michelangelo's muse as he looked down at her. Spurred on by his supplication, she gave a slow lick along the crease with the very tip of her tongue, then kissed her way down the base, wrapping her hands around his hips. She placed her palms in the half-moon indents in the sides of his buttocks while his breathing grew more and more audible, his impassioned groans meeting her attentions.

He grabbed Francine's shoulders, digging his fingers into her flesh. He was torn. He wanted to hold her in place, but his need to possess her overpowered his want. He pulled her up from the bath and drew her mouth to his for a bruising kiss. His hands moved to the back of her head to hold it steady as he massaged the edge of her jaw with his thumbs, teasing her mouth open wider. He delved into the offering, tasting, licking, and exploring her.

He kicked his feet free of his sodden trousers then stepped from the bath, lifting her with him, forgoing the plush towel that waited. He kissed and stroked her wet body, rushing toward the bed.

She tripped in his hurry and he pulled her up, wrapping her legs about his waist as they tumbled to the mattress. He smoothed his hands over her wet legs as he shifted her beneath him, feeling the softness rushing against him, amazed at how supple and smooth she felt as she encircled his hips and drew him to her.

He was pliable, and she moved him, physically, emotionally, and spiritually. They created heat together, his hair-dusted skin caressing her silky legs.

She rolled him to his back with a leg on each side of his waist. As they lay on the bed he yielded to her, allowing her to roam his body, exploring him with her fingers, her tongue, her lips. Without ever coming together fully, they discovered each other, testing the limits of their patience and arousal. His breath was heavy and full as she teased him.

He tried to caress her, but she pushed his hands away with a warning glance. His mouth dropped open and he groaned.

She released her hair, letting it drift over his skin like a silken curtain. She used her fingers to measure every length, every girth, every nook and cranny of his flesh as she crawled over and around him. "Francine." She tested the feel of her nipples and lips against his bare chest, grazing his night bearded jaw and mouth, traveling back down his carved torso and stopping at his arousal.

He tried to catch parts of her with his mouth as they passed across his face, groaning at his failures. "Francine, I can't take—" He cried out, his eyes clenched tightly against the inundation of his senses as she kissed, touched, and tasted all off him. "Francine— Oh God, Francine," he grumbled as she wriggled, hovering over him.

He twisted below her and she gently reminded him to stay put, holding down his wrists with her hands. His hips thrust involuntarily as she leaned into him, matching her body to his, testing him with her hands, her mouth, and her breasts.

"Francine," he roared, his passion unleashed. He pulled her tight against him, her hair spreading across them like a shiny web. His chest heaved, his muscles tensed uncontrollably, and he was spent.

She watched the strain in his features wash away as she rose above him. He reached up and brushed his lips against hers, then kissed her with all the passion of a man undone before letting his head fall back to the pillow. She lay upon him, the burning heat sealed between them, and moved her hands over his exposed skin. She looked up to his relaxed features and rested her head on his chest, savoring the minute adjustments they made as they fit curves into valleys, slowly stretching cramped muscles, moving closer and tighter together.

She couldn't pull a lucid thought from her brain for the longest time. At last, she smiled. She had mastered him, disallowed his mastery of her, forced him to her bidding, and given him an unanswered pleasure. *So beautiful.* She glanced up at his chin as he slumbered. She smiled and shifted slightly, feeling the pulse of his manhood stir, growing between their bodies.

"My turn," he said hoarsely. She felt the reverberation of his voice in his chest, rousing her nipples to firm peaks. She closed her eyes, waiting for his bidding.

He caressed her slowly, his hands searching her body for hidden points of tenderness and regions of undisclosed arousal.

He gathered her hair, only to let it fall again to her back like rain. She moved and he grunted a caution for her to succumb to his explorations as he had hers. She relaxed upon him, more content than she had ever felt.

Her breath came slow and steady as though she slept. He gathered her hair up again then rolled her underneath him, straddling her waist and spreading her hair carefully across the pillows like a fan.

She tried to touch him and chirped a tiny complaint when he pushed his hands into her palms, lacing their fingers together. He pressed them back into the bed at her shoulders, then let go, and she trembled at the effort of holding her arms away from him as he arched over her.

"Watch me," he said, holding her gaze for an instant. She obeyed as he kissed her nipples with wet, open kisses, weighing each breast with his hands then gently blowing across the tip, watching her skin tighten and flush. She saw them become roused beneath his touch and her heart stuttered at the feeling.

He roamed down her body, enjoying every inch as she opened to him. He touched her toes, then kissed the fading marks on each ankle and spent extra time gently caressing her soft, new-shaven legs.

The sweet whimpers that escaped her lips drove him mad, and he followed the patterns of her blush with his fingertips. He smiled at the display of color, the likes of which he had never before been witness to.

He encircled her belly button with his tongue, leaving a kiss in its depths as he moved over her. Her body shifted to meet the kisses he placed at the edge of her hips, eliciting a quiet cry from her. She grasped the pillows around her as he shifted up, tracing the line of her jaw with his nose, tasting the pulse on both sides of her neck and kissing the hollow of her throat, then tending again carefully to her breasts.

He ran his fingers into her hair, gripping her head and holding her neck for his mouth.

"Ah Gideon, Gideon. Oh God, please, Gideon," she pleaded with him as he nipped and licked at her skin, his breath fanning over her strong and hot, and neither one of them could stand to be kept apart any longer.

He shifted, parting her knees and advancing slowly, his turgid shaft gaining entry as he pulled her legs around his waist. He lifted her up to his lap, impaling himself inside her as she held tightly to his shoulders.

His muscles vibrated with the tension of keeping his body still. He resisted the urge to withdraw himself and drive into her hard and strong. Instead he waited with his jaw clenched as he tried to extend the moment. He spread his knees, watching, waiting.

She tilted her hips against him, electric fingers spreading through her body and rejoining in her core, pulsing hard and close as she cried out his name. She concentrated on where they joined, the feeling of him inside her stretching and pushing. She tightened, feeling every hard inch of him, then released slowly.

His eyes flew wide and he groaned, his head falling back. "My God, Francine, where—"

She shifted and tensed around him again, lifting slightly as she did. Then she relaxed and sank again, his body shaking beneath her. She repeated and repeated the motion until she felt her own response, her body clenching and pulling at him, and she cried out in release as she came down on him fully.

He exploded without further stimulation and seized her, wrapping one arm around her waist and pulling her to him as he pulsed within her.

Her arms and head fell back and he suckled one flushed nipple. A passion-cry, the likes of which he'd never heard, tore from her as he felt her body surge around him again, and he held her tight. It was something he had never in his life experienced.

They collapsed to the bed on the piles of pillows, entangled in a sweaty mass of limbs, each gasping for air. He was heavy upon her, and she relished the weight of his body and the feel of his arousal still buried and hard. He moved with an impossible slowness of power, looking for the one prevailing spot that would cause her body to react.

Her breath caught and her eyes flew open, trapping his gaze as she cried out again, the passion strengthening. She pushed at his shoulders, the sensations too intense, but he pulled her tight against him as she fought. His arms were underneath her, holding her steady, refusing to let her give as he moved relentlessly within and without.

"Gideon," she gasped.

"Don't fight me, sweet. Come off for me again, Francine," he said gruffly. "Again." His hands slid up her back and he tangled his fingers in her hair, holding her to him as her body pulsed.

Her breath hitched and she cried his name as her climax broke and his followed. Tears streaked her cheeks while he continued holding her, allowing the insurmountable emotions to slowly subside. The moments passed languidly as he soothed her with caressing words and movements, both meant to pacify and quiet.

Shaw and Perry inspected the gaslights that had been installed in the main rooms and unoccupied suites, then the water baths. They returned to the library to look at the next step in the plans. The remaining guest rooms would be moved around, the walls shifted.

"If you look here," Shaw said, pointing to the guest suites, "and then look at the grid, you can see that with the movement of just a few walls, the manor will finally be orderly."

Perry nodded. "What was your question for me, then?"

"Well, these are all set up as guest suites. I wanted to ask about the sisters. I can easily change the plans to modify this last suite into a joined bedchamber, much like a marriage suite, and then I could add one more bathing room between the two here. I only thought to ask since you all came here instead of returning to Westcreek."

Perry studied the plans. "I'm not quite sure. We should discuss this with Rox. Hopefully he'll be at supper. I'm sure the combined suite would serve well for a nursery in the future, since I'm assuming that this is to be the governess suite?" He pointed to the paper.

"Yes, exactly."

"Good. Now, we have a few hours until supper. I heard you were interested in the ruins. Have you been yet?"

"No, actually, I haven't had the time."

Perry glanced at him. "Shall we?"

Shaw smiled and nodded.

Perry informed Mrs. Weston that he and Shaw would be taking luncheon to Trimontium, and Mrs. Weston recommended taking the sisters and Miss Faversham.

"How are you getting on with the sisters?" Shaw asked.

"Famously," Perry grunted.

Shaw looked at him carefully, trying to assess his mood. "Not quite settled in your responsibilities to the two girls, eh?"

"Three." Perry gave Shaw a stern look, reminding him of his responsibility to Francine. "And no, not entirely."

"I beg your pardon, Trumbull, I just assumed from the way Roxleigh and Francine have been since we returned that—" Perry cut him off with a glare and Shaw paused. "I beg your pardon. Well, then. Are we off?"

Perry groaned. "The sooner to have it done with, I imagine."

"Yes, quite."

Eventually Gideon moved their tangled limbs, then lay next to her spread-eagle, endeavoring to dissipate the intense heat of their coupling. In time he rose from the bed to run another bath and she rolled to her belly to study him. He moved efficiently for a tall, broad man, agile and expedient, but his gestures hinted of something else—grace and caution.

She ran her hand under the tangled web of hair at her neck, pulling it off her back and shoulders to cool her body.

"I don't think we will make it to luncheon," she said. He looked over at her, realizing she had been watching him, and the very idea piqued his interest.

"No, I don't suppose we will," he agreed, then paused. "Do you approve?" He swept his hand the length of his body.

Her face suffused with heat as she gave him an exhausted

smile, not taking her eyes off of him.

"And you, Your Grace? Do you approve?" She rolled to her back with a long sigh, her head lolling off the bed. He walked to her silently, stopping at the edge.

She was taken aback at the sight of him hovering above her, large and naked, and tried to move away. But he caught her and reached for her knee, tickling it with circles. "You are a wicked thing. Wherever did you learn such a trick?" he asked as he ran his hands up and down her smooth legs. Her eyes grew wide as she examined him.

"I'm…not sure, I…just love the feel of a cleanly shaven face. *Your* cleanly shaven face," she quickly amended. "I wanted you to know how it felt to be me, touching you," she added, smiling sweetly.

"But if I could only return the favor," he said, tracing his fingers over her as he knelt beside the bed.

"You have bestowed many favors on me, Gideon," she said, her breath catching. "If you only knew."

His hands skimmed over her torso.

"Oh, God, Gideon, please stop, I cannot—" She gasped, her skin still oversensitive from the heights he had taken her to.

He smiled, kissing her. His hands left her body, holding her head for him as he kissed her upside down, then he deepened the kiss, reaching up to trace her nipples. He stood, lifting her from the bed and carrying her to the bath, carefully stepping over the edge as they sank into the warm water together.

They rested at opposite ends, gazing at one another, his lucid green eyes searching hers, their souls communicating effortlessly as they rested. The bath was the perfect length for two lovers. If she sat up straight, her legs would reach perfectly from one end to the other, her toes outstretched. So when they sat together, her legs between his, her toes played, tickled, and roamed his body. They lazed for long moments, her body calming, her strength returning.

Never in her life would she have expected something like this. Little girls grew up playing at things, expecting certain things. They played house, married their teddy bears, lived happily ever after. Her dreams had been shattered long before most, but she'd still never had an inkling of the depths of emotion she could experience. She would stay here forever, and she was confident in that. She knew to the tips of her toes that she was born to be with this one man. And that he'd only been waiting for her to arrive.

"What is it?" he asked quietly.

"I just, I can't remember a time before you at this point. And I can't imagine having to give you up, or having to leave, or—"

"There is no need for that."

"I know, I'm just amazed by the truth of it. Aren't you? I mean, we met because you ran me over in your carriage! When does that ever happen?"

He winced at the memory. "Once in a lifetime, if that."

He poured in just a touch of oil as she stretched for the bar of soap. She lathered her hands, building the froth around her fingers, then reached over and laid her hands on his broad, velvety chest. He slid his feet behind her, pulling her closer.

She lathered her hands again and he bowed his head to her as she massaged his scalp, making spiky little nests of frothy, black locks. He tilted his head, enjoying her treatment. "Nice mohawk," she said with a grin.

"What?" he asked, his eyes tightly closed.

She shook her head and giggled as he grabbed her ankles and moved her feet over his legs, past his waist and down under the water. He shook his hair out and she giggled at his boyish manner. Then he dunked his head beneath the water.

When he broke the surface he inhaled deeply, rivulets running down his face before he wiped it to clear the bubbles from his eyes. He smiled at her and drew her toward him, forcing her head into the bathtub, saturating her hair.

She laughed when he pulled her up, water sloshing to the floor as he spun her around on her rump and pressed his chest against her back. He reached for her soap and cleansed layer upon layer of sodden hair.

"You have so much hair. It weighs near a ton. Do you have headaches?"

She laughed and shook her head. "Not at all. I suppose you just get used to the weight."

He sat back, pushing her forward to submerge her hair again. He ran his fingers through the long, thick tresses and leaned over her, surprising her with a wet kiss to her spine. He pulled her up and twisted her hair up around her crown as she rested against him, her eyes closed, her body spent, fully relaxed in his embrace.

"Gideon." His name floated from her lips like a prayer. The answering growl was not the answer she had expected.

He yanked the plug, releasing the bathwater. When it got low enough and the cool air sent gooseflesh across their bodies, he twisted the faucet and refilled the bath with fresh, warm water.

"We might make it to supper," he said, smoothing her hair from her face. As if in response her stomach grumbled. She covered it with her hand and smiled up at him, her cheek laid against his chest.

She turned, curling her knees up and wrapping her arms around his waist under the water as she nuzzled into him. He ran his hands over her skin, massaging her sore muscles. The water in the bath cooled again and he released it, then lifted her and held her close as he stepped from the tub. He wrapped her in a fresh, thick cotton towel, then gathered up his saturated clothing and rang for Mrs. Weston.

"I will miss you terribly while I'm away."

She stilled. "Where are you going?" she asked as she watched him back away.

"To my chamber, to ready for supper, of course."

She advanced on him and punched him playfully in the shoulder. "Don't do that."

He laughed and took her up in his arms, pressing an impassioned kiss to her lips. "Never again," he said against her mouth. "Never again." He let her down and ran for the door to his room as he heard Mrs. Weston shuffling through the passageway.

Since Ferry wasn't nearby Gideon went to his wardrobe for clothes. He opened the door and sifted through the shirts, jackets, and trousers. When he bent to pull a pair of shoes from the lower shelf he saw the basket of trinkets Mrs. Weston had brought to his room. He took it over to his bed and laid everything out. There were several books he thought Francine would like, and he wanted to give them to her.

He sifted through the pile, coming to a thick leather volume that didn't quite lay closed. He let it fall open, only to find a small flower pressed between the pages, next to a handwritten note. *My Gideon picked this flower in the hedgerow, he insisted it be placed in my hair. He is such a dear boy. 14 April 1859.*

He turned the page. It was his mother's diary. He read a few pages, noting how her diction seemed vaguely familiar, yet out of place. She wrote about strange things that must have been dreams.

He closed it, feeling much like an intruder. Perhaps someday he would read it all. Unlock the mysteries. Today was not the day. He placed the book next to his bed and returned to dressing.


Gideon returned to Francine's chamber to find Mrs. Weston tending to her hair. They were laughing, and he stood behind the panels and watched with an admiring gaze. Mrs. Weston wrapped Francine's long hair up in a knot with curling tendrils falling loosely around her face, then began weaving fresh wildflowers throughout.

Francine caught sight of him in the mirror of the dressing table and smiled. Mrs. Weston placed one last pin in her hair then turned to leave, giving Gideon a grin and a sharp pat on the shoulder.

"My lady," Gideon said to Francine, inspecting the pale pink gown she wore for supper. "You look lovely."

She smiled and stood, moving to embrace him. "Gideon, I love you."

"Yes, I believe you do. Are you ready for supper?"

She shook her head. "No, my beautiful, sexy, powerful, amazing, *wonderful* man. I am *not* ready for supper."

"No?" he asked, his brow falling in concern.

"No, definitely not, because you walked in here and I'm all dressed and done up and my hair is fixed. And look," she said, leaning her head toward him, "Westy had Meggie fetch flowers for my hair. Fresh flowers. Can you believe it?"

"Well, as I can see it, I suppose I can believe it," he said carefully.

She grunted. "Don't you see?"

"No, my dear, I beg your pardon, but—"

"Oh well, here it is. You are here, ready to take me to supper. But I am just not ready for supper. I mean, I'm dressed, but I just don't *feel* right. I feel like we are on our honeymoon and should be locked away somewhere. Away from people, left to *explore* each other undisturbed, but we aren't because we're not on our honeymoon, we are here, and we are running around secretly, and all I want is to kiss you in public, to hold your hand as we walk in the garden, to let everyone know, to let everyone see how much I love you."

"Honeymoon?"

"Honeymoon. You know, you get married and then you leave for your honeymoon directly after and you have a chance to spend time together, doing—well, *everything*," she said, her eyebrows raised.

"Ah, yes. Well, that is also traditionally preceded by the betrothed couple being kept apart for an entire month before the wedding. Is that also something you are interested in?"

"No— No, not so much. I just haven't wrapped my brain around this situation, and I can see how a honeymoon would be a benefit. It would give me time—" She stepped closer to him, brushing against him. "—to become at ease—" She brought her hands up to his hips. "—with being able to touch you, discover you. I just want to be able to learn you, without having to worry about what everyone else *thinks* about it," she finished as she blushed and looked away. "There are so many things I would like to do with you, but they are all so… improper."

He smiled down at her, touching a finger to her chin and lifting her head to meet his gaze. "I would like nothing more than to be locked away with you for the rest of our days—"

"Well, then." She stared into his eyes, silently imploring him to kiss her. "What exactly are you waiting for? Take me, lock me away," she whispered as he lowered his mouth to hers.

He lifted his head after kissing her soundly. "Hmm. You do look like a proper lady, but you sound—"

"Yes?"

"Well, you sound a bit like a strumpet." He shifted one hand to hold the back of her head while the other stroked her neck tenderly.

"Do I?"

He released her and walked around her, inspecting her gown. She wore one of the ready-to-wear dresses she had purchased at Harrods.

He surveyed the simple design, noting the lack of corset.

"And what of *your* rather unseemly behavior?" she asked. "I mean, here you are in *my* bedchamber, not to mention the rather unconventional way you relieved me of my virginity," she added with a wicked grin.

He smiled. "I do find it humorous that my sense of propriety has rubbed off on you, while your sense of recklessness has managed to invade me." He stopped behind her and wrapped his arms around her waist, gathering her long skirts up into his hands. His breath caught and he groaned as he bent his legs, his thighs surrounding hers as he stroked the smooth exposed skin at the tops of her stockings. He loosened the ties at her sides, letting her drawers fall to the floor.

Her mouth dropped open. "I have never been quite so reckless as when I am with you. Have you nothing to say for that?" She felt him grin against her neck.

"Talking is overrated. Let me instead show you." She felt the strength of his voice rumbling through his chest and into her soul.

He shifted his hands, trailing his fingers up the backs of her thighs to her buttocks, then grasping her hips and pulling her back against his arousal.

"Gideon," she protested weakly.

The myriad of ways his name escaped her lips astounded him.

At times a curse, a prayer, a request. But it was here, the supplication, the want pervaded that word, that gave him chills.

He moved one hand around her hip, cupping the curls at the juncture of her thighs. He massaged her gently, sending one dexterous finger deep into her womanhood and, despite her surprised cry, he found her ready for him.

The discovery made him groan as she arched her back, the valley of her buttocks stroking his length. He moved her toward the bed and she stepped out of her drawers. He placed her hands around one of the bedposts, just above her head.

"Hold on." He trailed kisses along the back of her neck, from one ear to the other.

Her surrender pushed him over the edge, and he loosened his trousers and leaned back. Bending his knees, he tilted her hips. Then, in one strong, upward movement he impaled her, grasping both of her hips as he pulled her down tightly against him, shifting slowly, teasing her gently, grinding their joined bodies together.

She felt the crisp fabric of his grey trousers rubbing the backs of her bare legs, and the friction raising gooseflesh on her thighs. Her breath quickened.

She tilted her hips back and forth against him, his shaft burrowing deeper in her as she tensed and released.

He lifted his hands to her breasts, teasing her nipples through the soft cotton of her dress, relishing the feel of her body with no corset to confine her. He groaned, the sound rumbling against her, and she arched her back again, forcing their bodies together. His rhythm increased, his breath coming fierce against her back between her shoulder blades as the heat from his hands sank through the gown's fabric, warming her ribcage. The feel of his breath dragged a shudder first down her spine, then from each of her limbs, coming together then spreading and gaining force as it coursed through her veins.

He ran his hands down her ribcage to her thighs, gently working her, and her passion unfurled, crashing violently through her body in waves of breaking tension. He wrapped his arms around her torso, pulling her tight against his body as she kept her hands clamped around the bedpost, holding them upright. She clenched around him, her muscles drawing him further inside and his release deeper, closer to her womb.

They stilled. He bent his knees and slowly withdrew from her. She mewled a complaint. Her acclimation to his intrusion was becoming more insistent. She was beginning to prefer the feel of him within her, as opposed to without. He fastened his trousers quickly and turned her to him, taking her hands and massaging the red impressions from the bedpost with his thumbs while he kissed her.

She collapsed against him and he lifted her, sitting on the bed with her in his lap. She wrapped her arms around his neck and rested her head against his cheek.

His breathing slowed, the passion fog clearing slowly, and he held on to her without complaint, even as the flowers in her hair tickled his skin.

"I will ring for Mrs. Weston. We will dine here."

"But what abou—"

"We will dine here." He tightened his hold.

"Gideon, I need to breathe."

"Sorry, I—" He relaxed a bit, but did not loose her. "I still fear I will let you go, only to find you gone once again." He was suddenly tense with the realization of how much he could not bear to lose her again. The fear infested him, spreading like tendrils through his mind until he couldn't quite concentrate on anything else.

"Gideon, I need to know you are safe as well. I'm happy to dine wherever you wish."

He knew that wasn't what she meant. He knew she was conceding because she felt the sudden terror as it bolted through him. He wasn't familiar with having his deepest emotions laid bare, out where others could touch them, poke at them, but at the moment he didn't much care.

He hid his face in her hair, taking in the very scent of her. "We will dine here."

And so they did.

The next morning, Mrs. Weston and Ferry walked upstairs through the passages from the kitchens after sharing breakfast. "I'm glad to have them back, are you not, Ferry? Well, I guess you travel with His Grace, so for you it's a bit different. But I haven't seen hide nor hair for entirely too long," she said with a laugh.

Ferry smiled as they reached the main hallway where they would part.

"I expect I'll be seeing you in a bit," she said, then called "Good morning" as she walked into Francine's room with a grand smile. She hummed a quiet summer song while she threw the drapes open across the windows and strolled toward the bed.

"Francine?" she cried out. She panicked as she looked around the room. "Oh, what will I tell him… What will I say?" she fretted. "She's gone again."

She bolted from the room and nearly ran into Ferry, who was striding briskly down the passageway. "Ferry," she cried, "is His Grace yet awake? Lady Francine is gone!"

Ferry took the stout woman by the shoulders and looked into her eyes. He was pale as a ghost, his face drawn. "She is *not* gone," he said simply.

"What are you about, Ferry? She's not in her bed, she's not in her room, she's gone!" she yelled at him, her panic quickly rising.

"Shh." Ferry shook her shoulders. "Milady is *not* missing, Mrs. Weston. She is…unavailable, but she is *not*…" He cleared his throat and squeezed his eyes shut momentarily. "She is with His Grace," he ground out through clenched teeth, the last word a shocking pitch, then stormed off down the steps.

Mrs. Weston flinched and stared after him for a moment. Ferry was indeed a man of few words, and she had never once heard him raise his voice. Her jaw dropped. "Oh," she said quietly, finally understanding. She followed him.

She caught up to him in the servants' hall, pouring a cup of tea. "Ferry, you know His Grace and Lady Francine intend to marry."

"Intentions and actions are two entirely separate matters, madam, as you well know. If that were my child up there, I would call him out at once and demand reparations."

"For what? He's already come to scratch," Mrs. Weston said, desperately trying to defend the duke.

Ferry stood. "There are actions that are acceptable for a married couple, and there are— There is no excuse for subjecting a household staff to such impertinent behaviors. I cannot carry out my duties if I have no idea when and where I can be, and at what times, and I certainly don't appreciate walking in on— Well. You can inform His Grace that I am taking the day. I will return, but I would appreciate knowing exactly how to complete my tasks to his approval. I will not be held lacking." He turned and walked out.

Mrs. Weston frowned. She would have to speak with Gideon. For now, she needed to figure out the same as what Ferry was concerned with—how to go about her duties without knowing when and where she could be.

As she climbed back up the stairs she ran headlong into Perry, who was leaving his suite for breakfast. He lifted her in his arms as though they would waltz, even gave one good spin, but she didn't smile. "What ails you?"

She looked away, then back up at him with a huff as she hung there in his arms. "Lady Francine wasn't in her bed and I thought she was gone again, but Ferry found her." She paused. "And he was quite upset. Now he's gone off."

"Will he return?" he asked as he set her down.

She straightened her skirts and nodded.

"I will speak with Gideon. He should be more aware of his actions as they pertain to Lady Francine, and I will see to it that he doesn't offend his staff, lest he lose them." He grinned. "However, Ferry would be a grand addition to *my* personal staff," he said delightedly.

Mrs. Weston smacked his shoulder and laughed. "If Ferry can't manage this situation, he would not fare well in your employ," she said before walking down the hall to attend to her duties.

He smiled a broad smile, but it faded quickly once Mrs. Weston left.

At eight o'clock precisely supper was served. Gideon and Francine hadn't been social since they returned to Eildon Hill, so when the two entered the dining room at five after, everyone was stunned.

Perry nodded to the footmen, who shifted plates and trays around to accommodate the late arrivals.

Shaw talked about the work on the manor and the work yet to be done.

Gideon agreed with the idea of the children's suites, but might have agreed to just about anything as his mind was actually on Francine's shaven legs underneath her silken skirts. He had seen from the way she walked down the steps that she enjoyed the smooth fabric caressing her bare legs, and his mind wandered at every opportunity. He stared intently at Francine and she blushed. He smiled, then cast his gaze about the room to let her settle.

She gave him a vengeful grin and slipped her foot out of her shoe. She furtively raised her foot, tracing Gideon's leg up to his thigh. She watched his face, saw how his eyes widened almost imperceptibly as her foot lifted higher and higher still. She smiled triumphantly.

Perry noticed the comfort levels of their guests dropping and turned to Francine. "My lady," he began softly, but she didn't turn. "Francine," he said stiffly.

Startled, Francine jumped, digging her toes in and drawing a tense expression across Gideon's face.

"Am I interrupting something?" Perry asked gruffly as Francine turned away. "Because we could all quit the dining room and leave you to it."

"Trumbull!" Gideon boomed, standing and knocking his chair over. "You will not speak in such a common tone toward Lady Francine. Is that understood?" Nothing about the words was questioning, yet he waited for a reply.

Perry pushed his chair back slowly, then stood. "I beg your pardon, Your Grace, if you find my words overly common. Perhaps you could explain the nature of your behavior as it pertains to my ward here at the supper table?"

"There is nothing I need explain to you or anyone else within the confines of my manor."

"Oh, but there is, especially when you behave in such an inappropriate fashion in proper company."

"And you believe this conversation is rather more proper?" Gideon ground out.

Perry thought for a moment, then bowed with deference. "I beg pardon, Your Grace, my lady. I seem to have forgotten *my* senses. I will take my leave." He threw his linen on his plate, then turned and walked determinedly from the room without a backward glance while the rest of the supper party watched uncomfortably.

Francine glanced at Gideon, silently pleading with him to follow. When he didn't, she kicked him in the leg. "Go!"

It seemed to break his reverie and he rushed out.


He found Perry in the study, pouring a glass of whiskey. "What was that?" Gideon yelled, slamming the door behind him.

Perry shook his head, downed the glass of whiskey, and poured another.

"You've no right…" Gideon started, letting the words trail away when Perry cut him off with a glare.

"Don't I?" he asked. "Really? All your stalwart morals and rules of propriety, and I don't have the right to protest when *my* ward behaves in an untoward fashion? Indeed."

"Who are you? And what have you done with the brother who has spent years complaining and harassing me for my stringent sense of propriety?"

"Gideon, we have all looked away from your behavior in consideration of the ordeal that Hepplewort forced upon Francine, but there is a point at which you must return to the present and conduct yourself in an acceptable manner."

Gideon took Perry by the lapels, looking him in the eye. "I finally loosen a bit, and you come down on me like the Maharaja

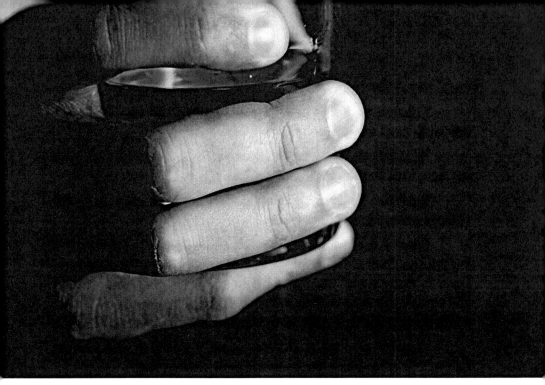

demanding my blood for indiscretions," he railed. He released him with a push, spilling Perry's whiskey as he turned away.

Perry wiped his hand and set the glass on the sideboard. He shook his head. "I have— I've goaded you for years, but I never thought for a moment that you would actually—" He turned and walked toward the tall windows that looked out over the south meadow, the land now dusted with moonlight. "You are supposed to be the strong one, the dependable one. And now that you've changed, where does that leave me?" He turned to Gideon, who remained near the entry. "I have never been interested in donning that particular cap. Yet here I am, saddled with two French chits—and not at all the way I prefer—until I can marry them off." His shoulders fell and he rested his hands on the desk. "You don't seem to understand," he mumbled. "This isn't the bullet I expected to take for you." He collapsed in the chair behind the large, paperwork-laden desk.

Gideon watched silently, then moved to the sideboard to pour a fresh whiskey. He took a sip before walking to the desk. "I should have known better. I didn't think that you would become just as resolute in your beliefs as I am." He set the glass of whiskey on the desk in front of Perry. "And you're right. You have turned your way of life over entirely, for the sake of my propriety and in the name of the dukedom, and I have been callous with that action."

Perry glanced up, surprise registered in the set of his brow at his brother's self-admonition.

Gideon sat down. "My affairs are not your responsibility and I have taken your efforts for granted."

Perry shook his head, drinking the whiskey. "The tables have turned a bit, haven't they? Only two months ago I was the one with a gentle foot in my lap at dinner," he said with a wry smile. "Yes, brother, it was *that* obvious."

Gideon dealt him a warning glare.

"I just— I cannot fathom the responsibility you have with your title," Perry said. "Mine is only courtesy, or at least it was until you signed over Westcreek. But even that isn't much of a responsibility. These two girls have me in a bind. Every time I look at them they giggle, and I should be enjoying it, not terrified of it. But they are my *responsibility*, Gideon, not my pleasure. I suppose I wouldn't feel so desperately obligated if I didn't know what they had been promised to, but— Rox, I cannot comprehend this, I cannot wrap my mind around it." Perry shook his head. He appeared entirely defeated, and something in Gideon's chest broke loose.

"Go back to London," he said quietly.

Perry looked up and his jaw dropped. "What?"

"Go back to London. I hadn't even considered where your head was in all of this, but it obviously isn't where it should be. I won't force anything on you, even under the guise of it being your demand. Go back to London," Gideon commanded. "Go live your life. The girls are safe here. Shaw will see to Westcreek. Eventually, you will take your place."

"But the house party and your wedding, I should be—"

"I don't expect you to," Gideon said. "I *want*, more than anything, for you to be here for my wedding. But not like this, Perry. If what you need is to get back to London, back to your life, I understand. Just as I need to be here. We are brothers, but as much as we are alike, we are just as different, and I need for you to be sound."

Gideon watched as Perry relaxed incrementally and sat back in his chair. He looked stunned.

"Go back to London. I am not the only one deserving of happiness. Do what it is that you do, and then return. Hopefully before the wedding, but if not, *know* that I understand," Gideon said with great emphasis.

Perry nodded and looked away. "Still the strong dependable one," he murmured quietly.

"And you are still the brave and loyal one," Gideon said. The brothers stood from opposite sides of the desk then both went to the end, meeting in a strong embrace.

Moments later, Perry left without another word.


The guests in the dining hall remained silent and pensive, waiting to be apprised of the situation by one of the brothers. Gideon returned only after hearing the carriage depart. His movements were deliberate as he perused the guests, from Shaw to the sisters. They all looked hopeful that he would enlighten them without prompt, but he didn't. He waited, giving his brother time to get away from Eildon.

"My dear brother, though a bit brusque, was absolutely correct in the observations he made. I have taken leave of propriety as of late, and while none of you would dare blame me, my behavior has been deplorable. For that I beg your pardon. Especially you," he said as he looked at Francine. "It was my greatest endeavor to protect you from the scalding opinions of Society. My improper conduct has done just the opposite. I will make an effort to do better."

Francine reached for his hand but he stopped her, putting his hands behind his back and standing tall.

"Trumbull has quit Eildon. He returns to London, to his position in Society."

Francine looked around the room apologetically, knowing Gideon was right. The weight of the reality of this world seemed to sink into her bones at that moment. She stood, drawing the other guests from their seats as she realized the power of propriety and marveled at it.

"I must also apologize," Francine started, sending Gideon a warning glance before he could interrupt her. "I realize my arrival has turned this household upside down, and while I understand that I'm welcome here, there are things I still need to learn." She smiled up at him then, and her eyes sparkled like the heavens at twilight. "I will endeavor to do better for you, for all of you. Because you are the only family I have ever really had."

Gideon nodded, then returned to his chair. They finished supper swiftly and quietly. When they ascended the grand staircase afterward, he made a show of leaving her at the passageway before going to his suite.

It seemed hours before he heard the panel open next to the bed and felt her warm body crawl under the counterpane next to his. They lay facing each other, just staring for the longest time.

"Roxleigh?" she began.

"Lady Francine," he said with a touch of annoyance, and she grimaced. "That is not a name I wish to hear you address me by in our bed."

She lifted a finger to his mouth. "Hush, please. I need to talk to you about something, and I'm trying to work up the nerve." She searched the darkness for his eyes, trying to decipher his mood.

He relaxed into the bed and waited.

"I've been thinking. I love the idea that in this bed you are all mine, to do with as I please. That I don't share you with anyone, in this way. I believe our knowledge of each other will be more powerful, because it will be kept in confidence."

"I agree, but—"

"Please wait, there is one more thing. I realize it may be a bit late for this discussion. However, I grew up having the issues of *safe sex and birth control* beat into my head and—"

"What? What are you talking about? Birth control? You mean preventing a—a babe? Are you not wanting to bear me children?" Gideon asked in a heartrending tone.

"Yes— I mean, no— I mean... yes," she stammered, reaching for him.

He sat up in the bed and lit the candlestick on a side table. "I don't understand. When you spoke to Hepplew—"

"Wait. Birth control is to prevent pregnancy, yes. And I do want to have your children, I just— Tonight you promised that we would be more proper, and we haven't discussed this at all. I just don't know what you want. If I'm already pregnant, awesome. It would be an incredible blessing. But if not, is there any such thing as birth control here?" She tensed and sat up as well, drawing her knees to her chin. "I mean the old pull 'n pray isn't exactly—".

"Stop," he broke in gruffly, the blood rushing from his head. "Just, please stop, you aren't making any sense. If you were to become preg— uh, with child it would be exactly that, a blessing. And the *ton* would have no choice but to accept the babe as we are to be married long before it would arrive in this world. As for birth—that is, what you speak of, yes. Of course there are methods, though I've no idea about the one you referred to. What was it? Pull and what?"

"Pull 'n pray," she whispered quickly. "Gideon, I didn't mean to offend. I only thought that as a sexually active couple we should have this discussion, particularly as we are to uphold the appearance of propriety before we become husband and wife."

Gideon's jaw dropped and he moved across the bed. "I beg your pardon, I am not accustomed to this. I realize I am no stranger to being *sexually active*, as you so eloquently put it, but my mistress always handled that end of our affair. That is not to say that I am ignorant, either, and if you wish to practice—" He gestured for her to remind him of the term she had used.

She blushed wildly. "*Safe sex,*" she whispered, peering at him from under the safety of her eyelashes.

"Yes, *safe sex,*" he repeated awkwardly, "before we are man and wife, then I have no issue with obtaining *French letters*, or whatever you would be most comfortable with." He looked down, quite a bit flustered by the subject of their conversation.

She giggled through her blush and reached out to him. "Your Grace," she said in her thickest English inflection, trying to lighten the mood, "the fact that you would hinder the creation of your issue at my behest is quite endearing to me."

He looked up at her, his mouth drawn in shock, his eyes open with awe. "I— So you do wish to bear my children," he said clearly.

"Yes, Gideon, as many as you will give me."

"And this—this idea has all come about because of decorum?"

"Yes, Gideon. There is no other reason, as well as there being no other option."

He looked at her questioningly.

"I have no intention of keeping from your bed until our wedding, as I've no doubt of your intentions to visit mine."

He nodded. "You, milady, are quite the most unnerving innocent—no—*woman* I have ever bedded, and yes," he said as she started to protest, "I do mean that as a compliment. For a chaste creature you certainly have a wide range of vocabulary at your control." He slanted her a wicked grin. "What else have *you* to teach *me*?" he asked, turning and crawling across the bed toward her.

"Nothing, Your Grace. I am but your humble apprentice," she said breathlessly as she watched his feline approach.

"Well then, shall we continue?"

She stilled, caught by his smoldering gaze. "Oh, I— well, yes, I— I suppose." Her composure melted into the warm sheets beneath them.

"And you have no objection to being laid with my issue this very night?" he asked in a rumbling voice.

Her breath hitched as he lowered over her, settling between her legs, his hips pressing her into the bed with his weight, his heavy frame encompassing her soft body. "Oh, well, no. Not if that's your desire. No objections, none whatsoever," she whispered as his demanding lips descended on hers.

Mrs. Weston and Ferry stood between the panel entry to the duke's suite and the passageway to the duchesses' suite. They had heard of the ruckus last night from the footmen who had attended supper. Mrs. Weston nervously wrung her hands as Ferry shifted.

"Well," she said. "I expect it is time to wake milady," she said in a long breath.

Ferry grunted a nod.

Mrs. Weston moved slowly down the passageway to wake Francine while Ferry waited another moment before pushing through to the duke's suite.

Mrs. Weston entered Francine's room, as hopeful as she could be, to find Francine snuggled in her bed sleeping soundly. By herself. She released a relieved sigh and set about running a bath and letting in the morning light as she hummed quietly.

From that moment on, Francine thought the tenor at Eildon more relaxed and welcoming. It was an easier place to be. Her realization that propriety wasn't just something garnered for the sake of others' senses, but to protect the secrets only two lovers should share, had eased her mind and her actions.

As for Gideon, he had no problem falling back to his most proper behavior during the day while he waited eagerly for the nights, when Francine would tiptoe into his room and he could let down his guard, showing her exactly how he felt. Withholding during the daytime only made their passion deeper and stronger, and the intimacy they shared became that much more powerful because it was private.

# THIRTY-ONE

Hundreds of workers toiled day and night, remodeling and redecorating Eildon Manor over the next month. It buzzed like a hive bursting at the seams. The sisters enjoyed helping Francine choose colors for every room, particularly their own. Maryse liked purple and lavender hues with dark stained wood, while Amélie preferred the reds and pinks with whitewashed wood. Francine loved that they were learning so much about themselves.

She decided the master suite's walls were perfect, but the colors needed just a bit of updating. Instead of the deep midnight blues and burgundies of the original upholstery, which was ornamented with the Trumbull family crest in gold thread, the new fabrics were a deep sea blue—just a few shades lighter. It brightened the room while remaining true to the original masculine feeling which Francine adored and wanted to preserve.

The wedding approached without causing much apprehension—it was just a date in her book. After all, what more could she want? The ceremony would come and go and they would continue on as they had. Well, for the most part. She looked forward to ending the charade of separate bedrooms, but beyond that she was already fairly content. They weren't able to spend a great deal of time together. She was busy orchestrating the hive while Gideon tied up contracts as Perry forwarded them to him. He didn't forward much else, and Gideon hoped he was better than he had been upon his departure.

Working with Chef, Gideon planned wonderful rendezvous in the evenings— suppers in the orangery with glazed duck, on the rooftop with cut pork in a spicy sweet sauce; on the terrace he fed her roast beef in a wine and mushroom sauce, and tonight in the center of the maze, they dined on whitefish and scallops prepared in a creamy lemon-butter sauce.

The suppers had been Mrs. Weston's idea, something she remembered his father doing for Melisande. Each ended with a new variation of drunken pears that Gideon spooned into her mouth, leaving Francine sated. The first was mulled wine, then brandy and sugar, another with honey mead and cinnamon, and the next with cream and Corps de Loup wine from the Rhone Valley.

Francine was swayed with each new creation from Chef, and Gideon laughed at her indecision.

"Well, if Chef would stop experimenting, we would have a menu!" she protested as she sat across from him on the rug spread next to the fountain.

"My dear, stopping Chef from experimenting is like stopping you from—euh…"

"Well?"

"Well," he returned, mocking her tone, "from anything."

Francine sat back and gazed up at the fountain. "Hmm." Her eyes darted over to Gideon from beneath the shade of her eyelashes.

"What are you up to?"

"Do you remember the first night we were here?"

"How could I ever forget that night? It changed my life and future, and yours as well." He raised his glass of wine to her.

"It did." She stood, walking over to the fountain and sitting at the edge, sweeping her skirts up to her knees. He saw her bare legs, her feet naked in her slippers.

"You knew we were having supper here." She nodded and his eyes narrowed. "Who told you?"

"I plead the fifth," she said wryly.

"Pardon, what?"

She blushed and covered her mouth, her head spinning from the drunken pears. "I, um— I'll never reveal my source?"

"Only one source, eh?" he said, eyeing her suspiciously. He rose from the rug. "And did you say never?"

She shook her head, dipping her feet into the fountain, the cool water running off her legs. She laughed suddenly.

"What is it?" he asked as he leaned against the fountain.

"You said I didn't have morals." Her eyes burned into him.

"You certainly didn't seem to, at least none that I was familiar with."

"Oh? And has your opinion of me changed so drastically?"

"It must have been very difficult for you, as you were unable to converse through speech. Was it not?"

"Yes, it was difficult. I felt entirely trapped, in this time, in this dream."

"What— what do you mean?"

She looked at him and shook her head. "Oh, I don't, I don't— I meant…" She sighed heavily. "I don't know what I meant. I think I meant that I didn't know where I was, because what I *did* remember of my past did not mesh with what I knew to be happening. It was all very confusing," she said hesitantly.

"So you do remember some things from your past?"

"No. Well, I don't know. I have dreams, but they are convoluted, strange, and impossible. I couldn't even begin to explain them. It's as if I lived an entire life away from here, this time, this place, this man that I love." She rested her hand on his chest.

"Do you wish to go back?"

"Never."

"You didn't hesitate."

"There is no reason to. Though I worked terribly hard for everything I had, I was never sure it was what I wanted and now I know. I am here with you. Right here, right now, and there is nothing that I want for, from those dreams, that could bring me to wish to return. Not a bit. Not in any way."

Gideon smiled. "If you do—" He paused. "If you change your mind, I want you to tell me. I would do anything for you. You understand that, yes? You never need fear telling me something. I am not my sire. I will never judge you, nor send you away, no matter how strange your dreams."

"I do know, Gideon. I know, and that is why I love you. This is my home, where I belong. Everything that came before only prepared me for my life here, helped me to navigate this life, helped me to reach you. If anything had happened differently, I don't think I could have gotten to you. I wouldn't have interested you. Everything happens for a reason—kismet."

"Kismet," he grunted, sliding his shoes off and pulling the edges of his trousers up above his knees. He yanked his socks off, then spun around on the edge of the fountain and sank his feet below the surface, shocked at the cool feeling of the water. She smiled and stood, splashing him. He growled and ran at her, grabbing her up and spinning her around in his arms.

"Francine, my love, my life, my heart. My soul. I love you. Today, tomorrow, yesterday…forever," he whispered.

"And I you, Gideon."

He leaned back with a laugh and she wriggled from his hold, gathering her skirts up as she ran to the other side of the fountain.

Later that night, as they lay together, Francine told Gideon a fantastic tale about a girl from the future and how she came to be where she belonged. Gideon studied Francine as she spoke, his gaze jumping to the book on his bedside table as he considered her.

It was the sound of Francine's speech that made him think of it. That was the familiarity he'd found while reading the diary. His mother sounded like Francine, the words and phrases so similar. He understood this should be very difficult to believe. He trusted Francine with every fiber of his being and thought he finally understood why so many things seemed out of place. It was a fantastic tale, a sensational tale. And Gideon, true to his word and his honor, forced himself to believe every word as he held her tightly to him. He had an entire lifetime with her to figure this out, to learn all about this other life, and to find out how his mother fit in. He would share this with her, but not until he was sure of certain things himself.

By the Sunday before the wedding Eildon Hill stood tall and proud, restored and rebuilt to better than its original glory, shining at the top of the hill. The darkest of corners were now bathed in light. The confusing passages were reworked and opened. The wood panels were all polished brightly and the fabrics cleaned and re-hung or replaced with brighter, more translucent draperies, letting the remarkable light of the north drift through the manor instead of being shut out.

That week the wedding guests arrived in droves. As Gideon had planned so efficiently, the northern line from London was complete and his guests arrived in style and speed, all thoroughly impressed with the new rail lines. Stately carriages brought guests from the new station at Roxleighshire to Eildon Hill Park, and the footmen carried their things from the carriages to their accommodations. The first and second floor guest suites were filled to capacity with visitors who'd been invited to stay through the ceremony.

Arriving guests expected to be greeted by Gideon, and when they weren't they assumed he had returned to acting the reclusive duke they'd rarely met in London. Francine greeted them in the spring parlor, welcoming them to Eildon, informing them of events and distractions and letting them know when suppers and luncheons would be served. Just as Gideon had predicted, Society had moved on from news of their betrothal to easier and more convenient fodder, leaving them to their own distant world far from the *ton*.

Unfortunately, for the first two days of the estate party Gideon only encouraged those whispered rumors by being further reclusive. It wasn't the least bit intentional, but it did create conversation. The truth was that he would have liked to greet the guests with Francine, but he had to complete last minute documents that Perry had forwarded. He wanted no such interruptions after the wedding.

The last time Perry left the manor, his lightness of mood hadn't left with him, but some of the old darkness had. Gideon was surprised to find he truly missed his brother's company. He felt them to be on closer footing than ever before. His mood had lifted considerably, bringing it closer to Perry's notable demeanor. He leaned back in his chair with the missive his brother had enclosed with the latest documents.

*Rox,*

*The London tradesmen seem to have forgotten themselves; they believe you to be concentrating more on your coming troth than your duties to Queen and Country.*

We should endeavour to remind them

that you remain the Duke of Roxleigh

and, regardless of current dealings,

they should be wary.

The enclosed missives should serve

to alleviate these disruptions.


Much has happened from the moment

*I quit the estate.*

*I endeavor to return as expediently as possible.*

*There is much to discuss.*

*I promise to send word.*

*Love to Francine, Westy, and the girls.*

*P.*

Gideon read the letter again for any hints of Perry's thoughts, but found none. He took the stack of papers Perry had dispatched from the solicitors and settled in for several hours.

Mrs. Weston roamed the manor, making sure guests were settled and that everyone who was hungry made their way to the back terrace overlooking the gardens for the buffet Chef had set up. There were trays covered with fresh fruits from the orangery, sliced vegetables from the gardens, and cut meats accompanied by thick, savory, and sweet sauces and biscuits.

Davis was busy putting up horses and carriages; Meggie, Carole, and Melinda showed the lady's maids around their ladies' suites; and Ferry and Aldon familiarized the visiting valets and footmen. The manor hadn't seen such activity since the time of Marcus.

Francine walked out to the terrace to find the Dowager Countess of Greensborough and Lady Alice. She waved them over, kissing their cheeks.

"Oh, Lady Greensborough, I've missed you. How did you sneak past me?" Francine asked.

"Well, I'm not quite sure, my lady. We have missed you as well, and your devilish counterpart. Where is he, anyway?"

"He's working, of course. He'll join the party soon, I think."

They linked arms and walked toward the gardens.

"My lady?" Francine asked the countess. "Was the earl a kind gentleman? Or was he a boor?"

Lady Alice coughed and the countess laughed, patting Francine's hand.

Francine glanced at the countess, realizing how unseemly her statement was. "Oh, I didn't mean—"

The countess waved off her apology with a smile. "Please don't, I understand what you're asking. My late husband, Phineas, God rest him, was a wonderful husband and a wonderful man, though we were not originally a love match as you and Roxleigh. I was promised to the earl at a very young age. Love was entirely unheard of back then as a reason for marriage, but we did love each other, which made it magic. I suppose that's why I do my best by my adorable Alice here. She reminds me of myself, once I realized the earl was actually the man I would have chosen for a husband, had I a choice." She smiled at her granddaughter, then at Francine.

"My lady—" Francine started again.

"Do call me Gelema, dear. I am terribly tired of my title. Without my husband to accompany it, it simply doesn't mean much."

"And you *will* call me Francine," she said as she smiled back. "Gelema, I am so glad to have met you."

As they rounded the terrace three women, the first aged closer to Gelema and the other two younger than Francine, walked toward them briskly.

"Lady Greensborough," she said to Gelema then, "My lady," she said down her nose to Francine.

Gelema smiled curtly at the Countess of Rigsby as she leaned into Francine. "Pay this wretch no mind. She is lucky for her title and unhappy in its bearing. There is no doubt she's jealous of you. Not to mention that these two girls just came out for the Season, rushed actually, with the sole purpose of meeting your duke," she said with a nudge.

"Well, then we must all become friends, if only to annoy the Lady Rigsby."

Gelema smiled.

"Why has the duke been kept hidden from his guests?" Lady Rigsby asked haughtily.

"Why, Lady Rigsby, he isn't hidden," Francine said. "He merely has business to attend now, so that he will be free to enjoy the events to come."

The woman wrinkled her nose and snorted. Then introduced her nieces.

Francine smiled and turned to the girl named Maitland. "Were you at the duke's ball in London? You look familiar."

"Why yes, my lady." She curtseyed. "Actually, I had the honor of a waltz with Lord Trumbull that night, immediately following your betrothal," she said with a timid smile.

"Yes, of course. Lord Trumbull was endeavoring to be my champion. I'm told he's an amazing dancer."

"Yes, my lady, he was, quite," Maitland replied shyly.

The Countess of Rigsby grunted. "A scandal is what that was. Highly inappropriate. He wasn't introduced and he didn't bow. He merely swept her out to the floor with no preamble. Highly untoward." She grunted again.

Francine smiled broadly and leaned toward the small brunette girl with the big brown eyes. "Quite romantic, if you ask me."

The girl's face lit up brightly and she nodded, though only after making sure her aunt wasn't paying attention.

"Well, I do hope you ladies enjoy your stay here at Eildon Hill. There are ruins if you are interested. I haven't even been yet. Perhaps the ladies would like to picnic? I could bring the sisters—you should meet them."

The countess, uncaring of the younger girls' acceptance, turned on Francine. "Considering the state of your propriety, I don't believe *my* charges will be accompanying you anywhere without a chaperone," she spat.

Francine frowned and turned away momentarily. She knew of the distaste of some of the *ton*, but hadn't yet been verbally assaulted by anyone. Her heart sank.

Gelema leveled a strong eye on the haughty woman. "I will be attending the ladies, as will the sisters' governess. That should carry enough propriety for anyone, wouldn't you say, Ernestine?" she drawled.

"Yes, I— Yes, of course."

"This afternoon then, my lady?" Francine asked.

"Fine. Ladies, you should rest so you have your energy," she said. The younger ladies curtseyed and followed the cranky older woman into the manor.

"What was *that* about?" Francine asked once they had gone.

Gelema laughed. "Well, I imagine the fact that this extended gathering has called all the eligible peers away from the London Season, and the fact that Lady Rigsby was required to follow them for her charges, has got her drawers in a twist."

Francine glanced at the dowager countess as Lady Alice paled from the boldness of the comment and they all laughed, then returned to the manor.


When they strolled through the great entrance Francine was drawn to the doors of the study. Placing her hand on the seam, she smiled brightly.

"Gideon," she whispered to herself.

The door opened swiftly and he was there like a memory recalls déjà vu. Her hand pressed against his chest before she realized and she looked up at him.

The countess, knowing, and Lady Alice, curious, watched the exchange carefully.  Gelema could see the way he looked down at Francine—his eyes passionate and intent. She remembered that look from her earl and she took a sudden silent breath and turned her head away, a tear at the corner of her eye.

Gideon watched her as Francine turned, remembering they were not alone. He walked to Lady Alice, bowing over her hand and making her blush, then he bowed before the dowager countess, taking her hand.

She laughed, leaning her head back and covering her mouth as she tried to disengage the duke, but he refused.

He peered up at her with a devilish grin. "My lady, you are a treasure. Your family has no idea what a precious gem you are, do they?"

"Oh, Your Grace, I believe *some* of them know, others perhaps not as much."

He released her hand, smiling broadly. "My beautiful wife—Hmm. My beautiful *fiancée* has no true family to speak of, you know. I wonder…if you wouldn't mind acting on her behalf at times. She is quite taken with you. You could visit anytime you wished, and remain for as long as it pleased. I've no doubt Lady Francine would enjoy your company to no end."

"Well, Your Grace, that is quite an invitation. I'm simply overwhelmed and happily accept the offer, if it pleases your *fiancée*."

They turned to Francine, who blushed from the sudden scrutiny. "Your Grace, my lady, the offer is beyond my wildest dreams." She looked up to Gideon. "You have once again seen into my heart and discovered a need I had not realized was there. Thank you."

He bowed, kissing her wrist and turning back to the study.

"Gideon?"

"Yes, my sweet."

"Any news of Trumbull?"

He shook his head, his gaze falling.

"And what of you?"

"Not much longer, my love, then I am all yours." He gave her a half smile as he backed into the study, pushing the doors closed.

"Well, Francine, I must say it is difficult to be around him. He is quite charming and so very handsome," Gelema said. "He does remind me of my Phineas." They turned for the staircase.

Francine frowned. "I wouldn't want the attention to cause you pain, my lady."

"Oh no, dear sweet child, not like that. It's difficult to remember him at times. Distance turns our memories against us, you see. Seeing your duke brings them back, and though I am grieved by the earl's passing, I am enlivened by the return of the memories."

"I don't believe the world truly understands what you have there, my lady," Alice said suddenly, turning to Francine at the top of the grand staircase.

"No, they don't, do they? I suppose nobody ever took the time to look. His true nature is only just beneath the surface."

"And what a surface it is!" Alice said.

Gelema and Francine's eyes went wide and the three laughed in a raucous, unladylike fashion as Gelema swatted Alice on the arm in admonition.

Alice blushed, then glanced at Francine repentantly. "I was referring to his notorious demeanor, Lady Francine, honest."

"Mmm hmm…" Francine said coyly. "Oh! There is something I would like to share with both of you."

The countess smiled and nodded and they followed her.

They entered her private chamber.

"Well, it has been a while since last I saw this room. His Grace did this for you?"

Francine looked at the countess. "You've been here before?" she asked, following Gelema over to the large comfortable chairs close to the windows.

The countess nodded. "Melisande was a dear friend." Then to Alice: "The former Duchess of Roxleigh was a precious soul. Strong and willful, exquisitely beautiful. Her hair was dark as night, and she had deep green eyes to match her sons."

"Does Roxleigh know you were acquainted?"

"I'm not certain. He was still so very young when his sire stopped allowing us to visit Eildon. I expect he knows Phineas and Darius were friends, but—" The countess sighed, looking out over the meadows.

"I wish you would tell him about his mother. That's something I cannot give him, a pain I cannot touch in his eyes."

"I will. Someday we will reconcile his memory with mine. It was a tragedy what happened. I believe his father was pulled in the wrong direction, when all he wanted was to help his wife."

"Tell me what happened."

"No," the countess said brusquely. "I won't cross that bridge with you, not before I cross it with Roxleigh. What happened with Melisande is something you should learn from him, not I. One day we will all discuss it. Until then, know that these are not secrets kept to damage you, but to prevent pain and to offer healing—when the time is right."

Francine took her hand. She wanted to return the carefree

expression to Gelema that she'd worn before coming to this room, which still held so many shadows for her.

The ladies sat for a while, gazing out the grand windows at the estate. "I suppose we should ready for our excursion," Francine said, breaking the reverie.

"Of course." Gelema took her granddaughter by the elbow. "Let's away, and allow our hostess to ready. We shall meet you at the grand entrance soon."

Francine laughed and carried on gaily despite the looks and grumbles she endured from many guests for wearing trousers and riding astride. She didn't pay them any mind, but the younger girls shifted uncomfortably, wanting to be more like her, not wanting to care about what others thought. She was thankful that the Countess of Rigsby wasn't joining them.

It turned out that Miss Faversham was quite adept with a small carriage, and once they got far enough away from the manor the group of women had a wonderful time chatting and defying propriety by using first names, talking about body parts, illnesses, marriage, and love. They enjoyed themselves so much that the sun began to sink in the sky before they realized they needed to return to the manor to ready for supper.

Francine rode ahead of the carriage stuffed with women to alert Davis, but when she arrived at the stables she found Gideon waiting for her.

"My lady, we have missed our ride the past few days. Would it be terribly improper for me to ask a favor?"

"And what would that be, Your Grace?"

"I would ask to accompany you now on a ride," Gideon said.

Francine nodded as Delilah shifted under her. "And what of our guests?"

Gideon thought for a moment then spied the returning phaeton, covered in giggling women. He was taken aback by the amount of happiness exuding from the vehicle and he smiled, walking over to attend them. One by one, the ladies took his hand and dismounted the carriage with a curtsey to their host. The last to step down was the dowager countess. He kissed her hand and held her attention.

"My lady, would you mind entertaining our guests at supper?"

She studied him, struck by the question. "That depends, Your Grace. Am I personally required to see that each and every guest enjoys themselves?"

"No, my lady. Simply act in my stead as host and certainly endeavor to enjoy yourself. I merely wish to attend to my betrothed. I have ignored her a bit much as of late."

She looked at Francine, who was still astride Delilah, and the corner of her mouth turned up. "Your Grace, I would be happy to direct the entertainment on your behalf tonight, if—"

"Yes, my lady?"

"*If* it is what my dear friend Francine desires of me."

He smiled and looked to Francine.

"Yes, Gelema, that is what I desire," Francine answered, as stoically as she could.

"So be it. Shall I send for a chaperone?" she shouted over her shoulder as she walked toward the manor, then before either could answer, she added wickedly, "All right then, have a wonderful evening."

Gideon smiled and turned toward Francine. He removed her boot from the stirrup and jumped astride Delilah behind her, taking the reins and turning the mare for the meadow. Francine let out a peal of laughter that caused all the guests outside of the manor to pause.

The next morning Gideon joined the festivities, mostly unbound from the requirements of the business of his title. He joined the hunting party early, then luncheon on the back terrace. He sat with Francine, who was at this point inseparable from the dowager countess and Lady Alice.

Mr. Shaw walked out to the terrace and Gideon called him over. They whispered and Shaw smiled, taking Gideon's seat as the duke stood and bid good day to his guests.

Gideon walked to Francine, kissing her wrist and then turning to the countess. "My lady, won't you accompany me for a walk? I heard you were interested in my hedgerow maze and, since I've forbidden anyone from entering it, I would like to give you a tour."

The countess stood. "Yes, Your Grace, I would very much enjoy that."

Gideon gave Shaw a pointed look, then placed her hand on his arm and covered it with his, leading her into the maze.

When they reached the center the countess walked to the fountain with a grand smile. "It is as beautiful as I remember it."

"I knew the earl, God rest his soul, was friends with my father. How well did you know my mother?" he asked, leaning on the edge of the fountain.

"Your Grace—"

"Please, call me Roxleigh."

"Roxleigh. I believe I knew her as well as any friend could have. She loved you very much, but that goes without saying."

"I was not the most wonderful son, I'm afraid," he said quietly.

"You weren't given much of a chance. A boy cannot protect his mother from things that are beyond a child's control."

He shook his head.

She took his hand in hers, as a mother would her son. "Listen to me. Your father had no idea how to help her. He was told her illness was curable. How could he not try?"

"What was it that needed curing?" he asked, looking at his hand in hers.

"It was a great and powerful sadness. It would overtake her mind, her body, even her soul, sometimes for weeks. She would lock herself in her chamber, refusing visitors, refusing Darius, refusing even you," she said. "It was heartrending." Her voice wavered. Until that week, she hadn't spoken of her friend in many years, and the memories flooded her like the tears to her eyes.

Gideon's eyes glowed fiercely with threatened emotion. "Why was she taken away, if her only crime was sadness?"

"Mrs. Weston found Melisande standing on the windowsill, wailing. They believed she meant to take her life. Darius would have let her continue, protected here at Eildon, of that I am sure, but when she became so distraught that she nearly died, he was afraid for her. He was told they would help her. He was told she would be safe, and she would return home."

"But she didn't," Gideon said, his voice distant.

"No, she didn't. I visited her there until Darius disallowed me. He didn't want anyone to remember her that way, in that horrible place. Once she was there, the beautiful Melisande I knew never returned."

"Thank you. I have always wondered why. I only ever remembered her smiling face, and, once it was gone, my father's anger."

"You mustn't blame him. Without her he was lost. And when he could not bring her from the sadness, it broke him. I see him in you more and more. He was such a passionate man. You love much like your father did."

"Why didn't you come to me sooner?"

"Do you think you were ready before now?"

He shook his head.

"I didn't believe anything I said could help you."

"And now?"

"And now, you are the man everyone wishes you to be. The man you were born to be, the man Francine deserves, looking forward to the life you deserve. Much like your father—however, that is due in large part to your duchess."

"Future duchess," he corrected.

She smiled. "Of course. I see the two of you together and know that it was meant to be. You must always trust in her, always." She pulled something out of the small reticule on her arm. "Melisande gave this to me as a gift for my wedding." She looked at him. "I would like for Francine to have it."

He nodded, running his fingers over the sapphires. "I would like that as well, my lady." He handed it back to her. He glanced up, hearing a giggle from behind one of the hedgerows, and the distraction brought about a sudden change in both their attitudes.

"I believe our little plan has come to a crossroads," he said with a smile.

She looked at him questioningly.

"I must go find Francine. You will need to find your way out of my hedgerow. However, I have some rules to guide you. Should you wish to leave directly, follow the small white flowers to the entrance at the back terrace. If you would like, however, to take a… _detour,_" he said hastily when they heard the giggling again, "you might run into someone you know. Should you wish to find them—together—you should follow the blue flowers. A word of caution, however. Once you find them, there will be no turning back."

Gelema lifted a brow. "I see. I believe I shall have to consider a moment, Your Grace."

"Roxleigh," he said with a warning edge. He smiled, bowing and kissing her hand, then took off through the hedgerow at a dead run toward the manor and Francine.

The guests on the terrace gawked as he ran, taking the steps to the private balcony two and three at a time. When he reached the top, he swung the French doors open wide and, seeing her on the settee with her legs curled up beneath her, he walked over, pulled her up into his arms, and kissed her senseless, his mouth bruising her soft lips with his fervency.

She dropped her book to the floor and lifted her hand to his face, gently holding him. She tried to pull away, but he chased her with his mouth, delving deeper, tasting her, memorizing her.

The sisters were on the settee across from where Francine had sat, their expressions shocked, staring. Miss Faversham roused herself from the trance he'd cast and went to the couple, shooing them out of the room.

Francine eventually broke away from him in a spill of giggles.

"Francine Larrabee, I love you. With all my heart and all my soul. I cannot survive a minute without you."

Francine's head fell back, her hands still holding his face. She ran her forefingers across his eyelids, traced the edges of his ears with her ring fingers, and stroked his powerful jaw with her thumbs. "Ah, Gideon, and I you."

He carried her to her chamber and placed her in one of the chairs by the window. Sitting across from her, he told her about his mother. He also told her of the journal, and what he now believed to be true. He promised to share it with her.

Francine cried. She cried for his mother and for hers, she cried for their fathers, and his brother, and she cried for the small, broken children that they had been and, when her tears stopped, it was finished. They stood together in her room, looking out over the meadow, holding each other silently, strong and safe in the knowledge that no matter what happened, they would be together.

The dowager countess waited in the clearing, pondering. Taking her glove off, she wetted her hand in the fountain and walked around, inspecting the hedgerows and contemplating her next move. "I have always liked blue," she said to herself. "Of course, white—purity, chastity—always a good color choice."

She stopped in front of one opening, then turned and walked directly to the other. She heard giggling and whispering from within the tall boundaries of the rows, but she didn't follow it. Instead she followed the tiny blooms as she'd been instructed by Gideon. As she rounded a corner she came face-to-face with her granddaughter. She looked at Lady Alice questioningly, and then looked back at the row where she'd come from, confused. She heard her squeal and glanced back to her. "Alice? What's the meaning of this?"

Alice stood perfectly still.

"Alice?" She approached her slowly. Her granddaughter's skirts rustled. The dowager countess lifted the corner of Alice's skirt to find Amberly Shaw crouching on the ground underneath.

Alice blushed violently, as did Shaw.

"My lady," he squeaked, looking up. "It is not what you think."

"Are you certain?"

He stood and brushed his trousers off. "I believe I have been set up."

"Is that so?"

"Yes, I— I was trying to fix the band on Lady Alice's slipper," he said, handing it to the countess. "There was no action on my part that was dishonorable. It is just that Lady Alice's foot, well, it is quite sensitive, I find, and she kept wiggling away and I—"

"I say, Mr. Shaw, I do not need a graphic description of your plundering of my granddaughter."

"My what? No, my lady, you misunderstand! It was entirely innocent!" he protested.

"Was it, Mr. Shaw? From my perspective you have compromised my granddaughter, and there is only one thing to be done."

He looked down at the slipper in her hands then up at her penitently. "There is?" he croaked.

"There is," she said sternly. "You must make an honest woman of her," the countess said resolutely, handing back the slipper.

The shock in his eyes was evident to the dowager and she shook her head.

"I will not have my granddaughter's good name dragged through the gutter of Society. You will marry her."

Shaw was dazed. "I will?"

"Yes, you will. Post haste, I must say. Gretna Green isn't far from here. I'll not wait for the rumors. No doubt they are already spreading!"

"Yes…my lady," he said, more as a question than response.

"Come." She led the couple from the maze, a grand smile breaking.

Alice squealed and wrapped her arms around Shaw, kissing him all over his face.

He held onto her as he followed the dowager countess and, by the time they reached the manor, he was smiling as well.

R

# THIRTY-TWO

Francine's wedding day arrived after a week of fanfare. She wasn't to see Gideon today; the plans had already been set in motion. He left early for another hunt, and the hunters would have luncheon in the dining room while the women had their meal on the terrace. Every guest at Eildon was prepared to keep the duke and his bride separated for the entire day.

The only thing Francine knew about the ceremony was that instead of a Saturday morning wedding, as was customary, they would have a Friday evening wedding, followed by a full night of dancing and dining. Twenty cases of sweet, thick, Lindisfarne honey mead awaited the traditional toast that sent the newlyweds off to honeymoon. She'd no idea what Gideon had planned, but as with every dinner he'd orchestrated with Chef—on the balcony, in the maze, on the roof—she couldn't wait to find out.

The entire household rested that afternoon, so as to be ready for the night's festivities, and after that Francine was not allowed out of her room.

Mrs. Weston fussed over her while Gelema, Alice, Maryse, and Amélie helped. The gown was a beautiful, creamy white silk, the skirts long and full, creating a train that flowed out behind Francine like moth's wings. The bodice was cut low and close, with a silk georgette scarf across the neckline. It was trimmed in blue, as Roxleigh had asked that she wear her sapphire necklace for him. He had also sent her a matched set of sapphire earrings that had belonged to his mother. The gesture touched her deeply, and she felt like a princess as the ladies fussed, meticulously pinning her hair up and securing a long, flowing net at her crown.

"Ah, milady, you're a vision," Mrs. Weston said, clasping her hands together as tears welled in her eyes. She smiled and turned to help the sisters who crouched behind Francine, giggling, as they straightened the folds of her skirts. They flounced the fabric so it would breathe and move with her.

Francine hugged Mrs. Weston. "I love you as I would love a mother. You are so dear and precious to me."

Mrs. Weston's tears fell.

Gelema took Francine's wrist and clasped a sapphire and diamond bracelet around her long glove.

Francine looked down. "Oh my, Gelema, I simply cannot—"

"This too was Melisande's. She gave it to me as a wedding gift. I already spoke with Roxleigh, and I am giving it to you with his blessing. The set will once again be complete."

Francine's eyes stung and she stared into the gaslights on the wall, trying to stave off the threatening tears. *I need to at least make it to the altar before becoming a sobbing mess.*

Gelema took her arms and kissed her cheeks as a loud knock came at the door.

"Is everybody decent?" came Perry's booming baritone.

"Perry," Francine screamed as she ran across the room toward him, snapping her train from the hands of her sisters.

He stepped around the last panel between them, and his breath caught in his chest.

She launched herself at him, wrapping her arms around his neck and kissing his cheek. "Oh Perry, I am so glad to see you! Are you well? Does Gideon know?"

He laughed and lowered her to the ground. "There is rarely anything that happens at Eildon without his knowledge, though I may just have one surprise that has slipped his notice," he said with a smile, taking her hand in his and kissing her knuckles.

She watched him carefully, his hand on hers, then gasped. "Perry!" she yelled, drawing the attention of the room, "is that a wedding band?"

He grinned devilishly, then bowed. "My lady, there will be much time to chat. For now, as your guardian, it would be my honor to escort you to pledge your troth." He put his gloves on and held out his arm.

Francine smiled and took it.

"Ladies, you have just enough time to find your seats," he said with a wink.

The countess gathered her skirts, rushing past Francine with a kiss as she headed out of the passage with Lady Alice and Mrs. Weston. Maryse and Amélie were left behind to tend the train.

Francine assumed that the ceremony would be in the ballroom, so when they turned down the passageway in the opposite direction she was confused. She saw the beginning of the sunset breaking through the transom window, the brightest streaks of light across the horizon just threatening to unleash their vibrant glory.

Perry led her down the hall and through another passage, then down a set of stairs that she thought led to the passages behind the dining room.

She shook her head. They were on the wrong side of the manor, but Perry simply smiled down at her. When he opened the passage, they were standing at the front of the manor just beyond the great entrance. The grand table had been moved out and hundreds of chairs were filled with guests who began to stand, turning to look at her as the door opened.

She smiled at her sisters as they billowed her skirts behind her, then she took a deep breath and crossed the threshold.

There were chains of lavender hanging from the doorways, lining the aisle of chairs, and wrapping around the balustrade that led up to the first floor and—and her duke. She exhaled when she saw him at the top of the grand staircase, waiting for her, inconceivably handsome, gazing down upon her.

He wore a perfectly pressed black suit, a crisp white shirt and neck cloth, and a sapphire blue waistcoat that matched the trim on her gown. He also wore his royal blue garter sash adorned with medals, garter stars, and badges denoting and honoring his heritage and position as a peer of the realm.

It struck her then, looking upon his decorated chest, how very important this man was to the kingdom. Without being led or looking for permission, like the first time they'd met, she was drawn forward.

Perry steadied her as they climbed to the landing. He stood momentarily between Gideon and his bride. Bowing and kissing her hand, he turned to his brother and embraced him, then moved to stand next to him. Her sisters followed quietly, standing next to her.

As the ceremony began, the golden streaks of sunset blazed through the high windows above the family parlor into the great entrance, catching the crystal of the giant chandelier and emblazoning the walls in rainbows of color. The beams of light caught on her jewels and his, forcing her eyelids to flutter.

Francine was overcome. Her hands trembled and Gideon turned to her, holding them tightly before pledging his troth. She looked into his deep green eyes which were swimming with emotion, and repeated everything said. She slowly removed his gloves, then he hers, and their bare skin sparked at their first touch as husband and wife.

**Gideon grasped Francine's left hand in his and slid a perfect,** deep blue sapphire onto her finger—the fourth piece of the matched set she wore—and her eyes grew wide and filled with tears.

She looked up at him in time to hear the priest say "*Husband* and wife." It was then her tears fell.

The ripple of words rushed through the crowd at the impropriety of the proclamation, and Gideon stepped closer to her, his bejeweled sash pressing against her as he bent, running his hand up her nape into her hair, gently pulling her head back to meet him. He smiled, his lips descending to hers. He kissed her, pulling her closer still, for a scandalously long time.

Even for a married couple.

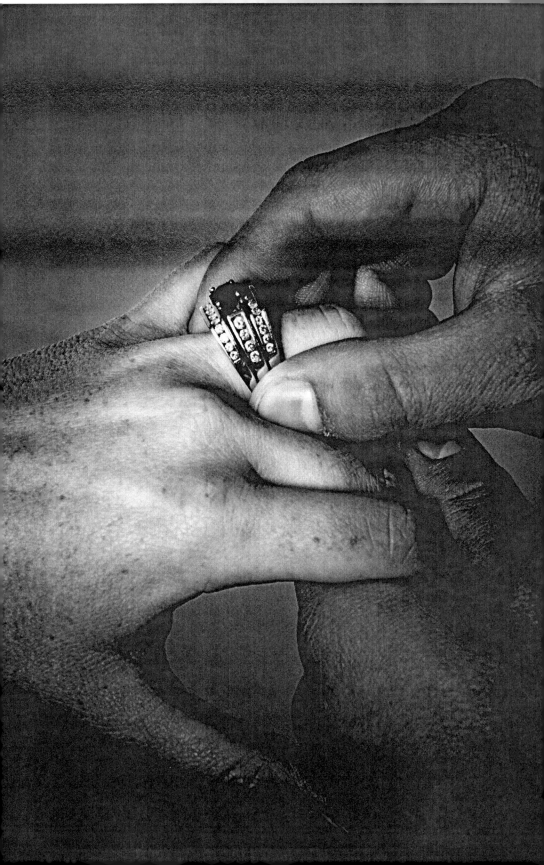

R

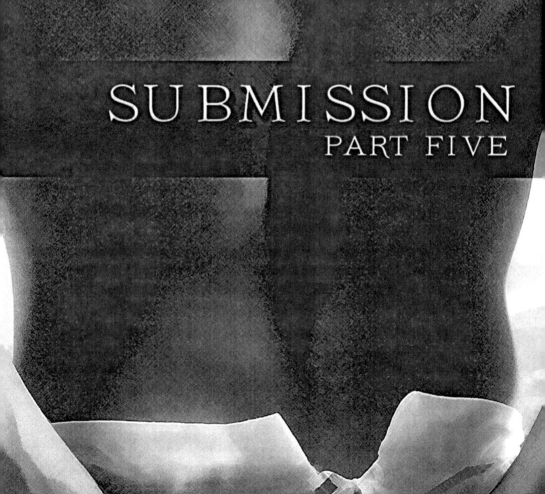

# SUBMISSION
## PART FIVE

# THIRTY-THREE

erry left his brother's house under a moonless sky without a backward glance— like a coward. The past month had sent his life into a spiral and he was unable to right himself. In the space of a Season his brother, Gideon, the Duke of Roxleigh, had gone from recluse to fiancé, and Perry had gone from rake to guardian for three young French ladies.

He sat in the dark, tossed to and fro in the seat as it traversed the country ruts, and pondered. Guardian. Respectable.

He shook his head and leaned back into the squabs of his landau as it rolled away from the seat of the dukedom. He stretched his long legs across to the opposite seat, folded his arms, lowered his chin, and let his lids close. The carriage lulled him and he slumbered heavily.

Half asleep, Perry felt a tingling sensation and his foot twitched. He snorted, pressing his head further into the plush paneling. When the sensation skimmed his knee he kicked and moved his boot to the floor, pulling at his trousers to stop the nerves that spread through his leg. When it returned, farther up his thigh, he stomped his foot to rouse the sleeping limb and arrest the incessant tingling.

Then he felt what was quite clearly a feather-light touch against his shoulder, so he relaxed his eyelids, allowing a narrow view from beneath his thick eyelashes. He searched the shadowy depths without moving. When he saw a hand move toward him he snatched it, wrapping his fingers tightly around the wrist and pulling it across his body.

It was then he knew two things without a doubt: first, that there was a woman in his carriage—for the slide of a woman's bosom across his chest was all too familiar—and second, that she trembled. Whether from fear, anger, or passion—of that much he was unsure. But his gut told him fear.

She slipped to the floor with a squeak and a thud as he sat up and lowered his other foot. He felt her hand press weakly against his knee as his eyes attempted to adjust and he stared intently, willing his vision to clear the thick darkness between them. Without taking his eyes from where the intruder's face should be, he banged a closed fist against the roof, then yelled, "Gardner!"

They ground to a halt and he heard the coachman jump down. The door opened swiftly and Perry backed out—without releasing the delicate wrist.

"Light."

Gardner took the lantern from the forward bracket and handed it to him. Perry reached through the open door, casting the flickering glow throughout the carriage, bathing a small bundle huddled on the floor.

"Please, milord, I beg ye." Her voice was tiny, her arm stretched out above her head as he held firm. He lowered the lantern to see who was piled on the floor of his carriage but she ducked, turning her head away.

"Please, milord."

"Turn your face to me or I will drag you from this carriage and abandon you in the field."

The mound of fabric shifted, then shivered, and the girl rose like a flower opening to the errant sun, her pale skin reflecting what light was available and increasing it as she stepped down, following the luminescence. She cowered before Perry and slowly looked up.

Her pale, fear-stricken face implored his concern without permission.

"Lilly." His breath caught.

# THIRTY-FOUR

Her features were small but for her large, wide-set cinnamon eyes. Her lips were a soft pink, almost the same color as the blush that carried up her cheeks, and her nose turned up at the end just a touch. Her soft brown hair framed pale skin, but his recognition came from what crossed it. Tiny, pale, pink scars traveled her cheeks, forehead, chin, down her neck...

"Aye, milord," she said, dropping her gaze. His own gaze flashed back to her face.

"I— You do not understand. I return to London. You should be at Eildon...with your sister." He released her wrist, running his hand down his greatcoat as though to erase the memory of his handling.

She tilted her head back and his eyes narrowed as she studied him. She'd no doubt survived much worse than the glare of a rogue, of that much he was certain, but her particular assessment of him caused a tightness in his muscles. He shifted to release the tension. "That will be quite enough," he said, adjusting his stance and pulling his greatcoat closed, hiding too slowly his manifest eagerness at her inspection.

She paled when he moved, as though she were suddenly aware of her untoward appraisal, and her gaze caught the ground as she fell to her knees, tangling her fingers in his long cape. "I beg you, milord, take me to London. I canna stay here. I left Meggie word, so she'll not be worried. I need to go. Everyone's so nice here. I need to get away from all the— They all care too much, milord. I beg you, I'll outride if I must...if you'll have me."

If there was one thing he understood about people's feelings, it was that they were difficult to hide and there were some—like pity— that were impossible to stomach. The sky lit with a strike of lightning and thunder followed close behind, signaling the men there was no time to dawdle.

"Outriding is not necessary. I require you to ride with me so you can explain exactly how it is you came to be in my carriage without my—or my driver and outrider's—knowledge." He gave a stern glance to Kerrigan, his trusted man. "At any rate, there's not much of a threat that I would ruin you."

Perry heard each word as he spoke, the devil on his shoulder laughing at him, but was simply powerless to stop the advance. He flinched when he heard her swift intake of breath, and his men grunted uncomfortably behind him.

"I—I did not mean— No. I meant that I intend to sleep." He handed her rather unceremoniously back into the carriage, then followed her up, lighting the interior lantern before allowing Kerrigan to shut the door.

Perry took the seat across from her, careful not to look on her with an inch of pity. "Tell me then, what is your intention?"

"I heard you and His Grace," she started in a small voice.

He shook his head and she cleared her throat.

"I was sent to clean His Grace's study. When the two of you came in, I hid. All that yelling—I was afraid. I am sorry for that. I tried not to listen, but when he told you to get to London, I decided 'twas my chance to go as well." She twisted her hands in her skirts.

Perry rubbed his chin as he held her gaze, his thumb stroking the rough edge of his jaw.

"I—I arranged to leave a note for Meggie. I didn't want her to be worried, and I packed a bag and snuck in here. I was hidin' under the seat here, see." She ducked her head and waved her arms toward the space below the seat she was sitting on. "I can squeeze in fairly well, and 'tis dark…" Her voice faded.

He shifted his gaze to her hem when she motioned below the seat, then returned it to her face as her skirts adjusted to cover the ankle he wasn't aware he'd considered. As a man dedicated to the pursuits of pleasure, he was well aware of every tic of his body. He knew what every fleeting thought, shiver, twitch, and clench was leading him toward.

At the moment, he was attempting to decipher a peculiar twitch in the region of his thigh. Or more like his hip. Perhaps somewhere between the two. It was an awkward discomfort that made him want to stand and stretch his muscles. Or press his hand to it, to relieve the tension. He was quite sure moving his hand anywhere near that region would not impress.

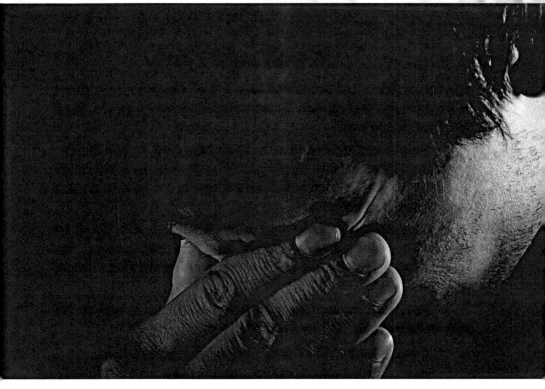

Along with the twitch was an overwhelming need to wrap her up in his arms and glower at any approaching ruffians. He pinched the bridge of his nose.

"I will take you to London, but I insist you stay with me. I will not allow you freedom— My brother would have me flayed. You will have a position within my household and at that point, we will return to the strictures of Society that are to be somewhat disregarded to manage this trip."

"Yes, milord," she said quietly, but he saw the smile she attempted to suppress.

He examined her. He had never paid much mind to servants; they brushed past him to retrieve whatever it was he needed—save a select few of the most buxom females—but beyond that there was never much consideration. This small woman was quite fetching, really, quiet and sweet, with a precious little mouth that was ripe for kissing, and something more. The twitch became incessant and he clenched his jaw.

He knew why she was damaged, and shuddering at the thought, he realized that must be the reason for this overwhelming need to protect her. He also knew that due to one vile man, she had much to overcome. As for the constant reminder of the scars that crisscrossed her flesh, he recognized that she couldn't even have a conversation without someone taking notice. *I suppose the questioning stares of strangers would be of more comfort to her than the pitiable looks of those who knew. I would certainly prefer it that way.*

He turned his head toward the carriage wall. He had no intention of using this particular servant girl. She'd dealt with enough, considering that Hepplewort had nearly killed her in sport, leaving her for dead and covered with reminders. He clenched his jaw and forced that image from his mind, but the fact that he'd recognized her appealing features was definitely a step in the right direction—back to his former self. He chuckled. His brother's shenanigans had definitely put a kink in his rakish lifestyle. Perry put his feet up on the seat next to Lilly. Giving her a quick nod, he attempted to go back to sleep.

Clearly dismissed, Lilly sank into the bench, willing the pounding of her heart to subside as she settled in. He was strikingly tall in comparison to her, yet she was a mere breath above a child's height even at the age of eighteen. Her nose had met the top button of his deep purple waistcoat as she looked him over brazenly.

She knew it to be true that he was recognized as a rake all through England, and most of Scotland, even though she was unsure just what that meant. Her parents only said it meant he was someone to stay away from. A man with no true moral compass.

It was also true he was handsome; not merely an off-the-shelf type of eye catcher, but absolutely turn-your-head-and-lose-your-breath stunning. Her fingers itched to touch the rough edge of his jaw, the soft curl just behind his ear. His nose had a slight bend to the left—probably from some discretionary fight, as she couldn't imagine a man who could overtake him to land such a hit; and a faded scar on his right cheekbone. His lips were thick and full as his tongue darted out to wet them—as though his mouth had gone suddenly dry.

He straightened a bit and a lock of inky black hair fell over one of his wide green eyes. It startled her—as she thought he'd been sleeping—and she shuddered, abruptly remembering her place and the fact that she was at his mercy. And under his gaze. She drew in a breath as she felt a tumble in her belly. At some point she was going to have to be more careful around him. His eyes narrowed on her then closed, and she let out the breath she didn't know she'd held.

With that exhale came the thought that she was well and truly on her way to London. Away from all the well-meaning people who would

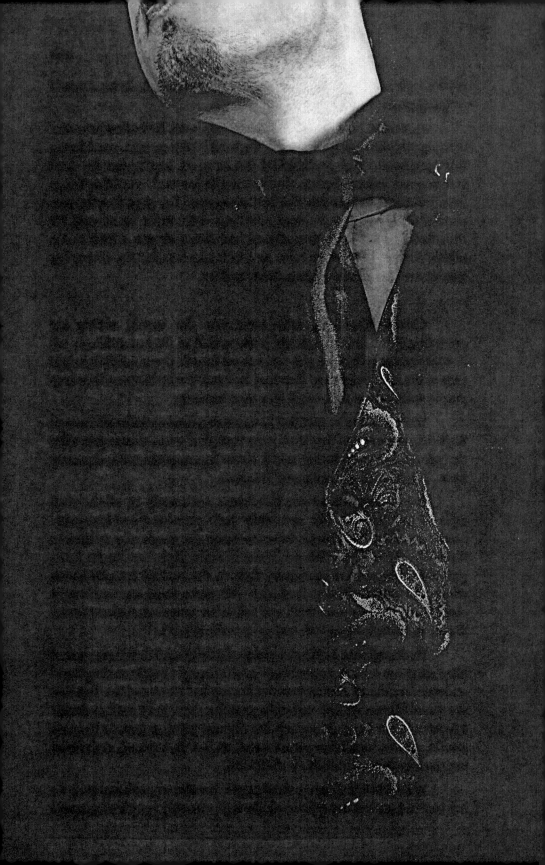

still end up suffocating her. She loved her family, her sister in particular, for everything they had done for her since her injury, but she could no longer stomach the attention. She wanted to get back to where she'd been before all of that.

She had never been one to be handled. She could keep up with both of her older brothers. She rode with them, practiced shot with them, built barns and troughs with them. She was simply one of the boys, just as Meggie had been. But ever since the incident it had been different.

She was protected. Not let out of anyone's sight. Daniel wouldn't have her—he wouldn't so much as look at her, had stopped coming to the house after what happened, wouldn't sit with her in church, didn't say even one word to her. She closed her eyes and said a prayer for him.

What that man had done was taken her future and smashed it like crystal upon a stone. The remnants remained scattered, and she couldn't very well chase after each one and put them back together. She could see the rainbows of her former dreams cast about her, but couldn't quite reach one before it disappeared. She wanted that tumble in her belly to lead her to love, not to fear.

She looked across the carriage to the viscount. He was not Daniel; he was much more than him. Daniel was all muted colors and soft lines. He was comfortable, safe. She had known him all her life and knew he was to be her future. He'd spent more time with her family than his own when not caring for his animals, and the fact that they would be married was simply accepted.

But when everything changed... She closed her eyes and considered. She had decided to leave Kelso for a position at Eildon, hopeful that away from her home she might be treated normally. It didn't happen that way, though, because they all knew about her since Meggie was already an underservant to the duke. It was hard not to know who she was, anyway, with the tell-tale scars. She wanted to disappear, and when she'd found her chance by stowing away in this carriage, she'd taken it.

She opened her eyes on the viscount. She had seen the brothers when she was a child, as her mother had brought her to visit her father when he was in charge of the Eildon stables. Lord Trumbull was always a sight. Tall and broad, loud and brash, while his brother always loomed, quiet, watching. The viscount wasn't all that much older than she, but as children it was enough. He had once taken her for a ride across the fields, and she still remembered the way he moved with the horse, the thrill of that ride. From that day she had refused to wear skirts or ride like a proper girl, much to her parents' disappointment.

Lilly's gaze followed the lines of his trousers to the hands held securely in his lap. Even at rest he seemed fully aware of his surroundings.

She felt her eyelids growing heavy and she shifted in the seat, trying to get comfortable. Her legs were much too short to stretch across like his, so she turned and curled her feet beneath her, leaning into the corner. She hadn't even fallen fully asleep before she was tossed across the carriage at him. He woke with a start when she landed across his lap.

"I beg pardon," she squeaked as she pushed away from his hard chest and fell to the floor once again. What was it about contact with this man that made her feel so insufficient?

"I do hope you'll not be ending up on the floor every time the carriage stops," he grunted, reaching for her.

"Pardon, milord," she said again, steadying herself.

"You really must stop that, I've no doubt the reason you've ended up on the floor is not by your doing."

The carriage door jerked open and a sheet of rain came in. Perry watched Kerrigan's face harden when he saw Lilly at his feet, before she scampered back to her corner of the cabin.

Perry cursed. "What now?" he asked stiffly, straining to hear the outrider over the din.

"My lord, the road is out. We should turn back te Gretna," Kerrigan said.

Perry nodded and the door closed. The carriage swayed then lurched as they turned around in the muddy road, jolting across the heavy ruts and tossing Lilly like a ragdoll as Perry held on. When the circuit was complete he pressed the heels of his hands to his eyes in an attempt to relieve the sudden pressure. The way this was going, there was no chance Lilly's reputation would survive this night intact.

Once at the inn, Perry left his men with the carriage and pointed to some cases for the inn's boy to bring inside. He pulled Lilly through

the entry behind him. He scanned the rough crowd as she latched onto the back of his greatcoat. He could feel her trembling through the heavy fabric.

The innkeeper approached, rubbing his hands together as if in anticipation of polishing the coin he was to receive.

"Two rooms," Perry said as Lilly buried her face in the crook behind his arm.

"O' course, milaird, the best o' them for you and your lady," he said with a crooked smile.

Perry grunted as he looked over the dregs in the great room. "We shall sup in my room, if you would be so good as to send up a tray, and see to my men."

The innkeeper handed him two heavy brass keys as he pointed out the hallway at the top of the main staircase. Perry took the keys and reached back, pulling Lilly along so closely she stumbled.

He unlocked the first door and entered the room. He released Lilly and left her at the threshold, timid as a mouse, as he removed his gloves and hat and watched her… waiting.

She didn't move.

"My dear Lilly, it will not do for you to stand in the doorway for the rest of the night. I should like to at least have the privacy it brings," Perry said as he tossed his greatcoat aside.

"Yes, milord," she said with a curtsey. "I just, I never… I—" She shuffled a bit and Perry walked over, taking her by the shoulders and moving her to the side so he could reach behind her and shut the door firmly.

She stared up at him with wide, terrified eyes.

"I am not entirely sure why you look on me as though I intend you harm," he said. And then, because he was quite obviously a cad and not at all a gentleman, he cursed.

Loudly.

He clenched his eyes and turned abruptly, shaking his head at the second callous slip of his tongue. Considering she was already sufficiently and tragically ruined—and not by her choice or his doing— he felt like an ass for doing a damn fine job of reminding her of the injury.

"I can assure you, your modesty is safe with me." He walked across the room, rubbing his temples. He wasn't accustomed to the addressing of innocents. His conversational skills were more suited to the pub, the whorehouse, and the bedchamber. The strain of this conversation was bringing on a headache.

"Milord, I trust you. His Grace is most honorable and I know that of course you'd be much the—"

She stopped, considering how everyone talked about the brothers and how alike they were—by sight alone. His Grace was honorable, that much was true, but his lordship, this man— She choked back a sob. She'd no idea what a true London rake was, and her meager flattery wasn't bound to sway his intentions—if he held any.

If the viscount set himself on her, she had no hope of getting out of his room unscathed, regardless of his declaration to the contrary. Her breath hitched and she spoke quietly. "Milord, I'll do whatever 'tis needed of me for you to take me to London." She clenched her eyes in fear as she raised her hands in front of her.

Lilly felt a breeze as Perry turned on her and made the distance between them naught in a mere two pounding steps. "Damnation, Lilly, I've no intention of—of whatever it is you think my intention is. I recognize I've a reputation, but I'll have you know every participant in the establishment of that reputation was not only willing but enthusiastic and much appreciative," he ground out through clenched teeth. "The only reason you are currently in my chamber is because the crowd below watched every move you made once we entered this godforsaken inn."

His voice calmed slightly as he shook his head, then he took her chin and forced her to meet his eyes. "I have no idea the extent to which Hepplewort damaged your mind and your body. But I promise you this… The only thing to be damaged in this room is my pride. You are perfectly safe. With me. Tonight."

He dropped her chin and she melted at his feet in a pile of grey woolen fabric. "Mi—milord, I beg you, please— Forget what I say. Please, I only—I never— The things he said to me, the things he expected…" She sobbed: heavy, wracking, movements that tore her breath from her lungs with every heaving shift. "Milord, please, I beg you, I'd no right to speak, I— Please, m-milord, please forget what I said." She grabbed the

legs of his trousers, leaning her forehead against his knees as she cried.

"Well I, for one, expect nothing, and all will be forgotten, just as soon as you get off the floor. You have spent entirely too much time at my feet." He reached down and lifted her gently. She pushed at the lapels of his jacket, the shock of his hands on her burning through her memories. Then she breathed and caught the heady scent of him, the rain, the starch in his collar, something beneath that. It calmed her and she suddenly buried her head in his chest. She sank against him and he lifted her—lest she end on the floor again—and carried her to the bed. He laid her down, managing the release of her hold on his jacket before turning back to one of the well-worn chairs in front of the large fireplace.

He watched her pull her feet up, her knees tucked into her chest as her breathing slowed and she calmed. Perry was held in shock as he realized he'd no idea how to handle this girl. She looked terribly uncomfortable in her traveling clothes, and he had a momentary wish to remove them, but there was no chance of that happening.

"Would you like a bath?" She looked at him warily as he continued. "I could— I will use the other room, while you bathe. If you like, I will have a bath brought up and have you tended to."

Her eyes went wide at the suggestion. He knew she'd been well taken care of after she was injured; she knew what it meant to be tended. This offer from him, however, was much too personal, and he understood the depth of his error only after he had offered.

She nodded her head almost so slowly that he didn't recognize her acquiescence. He stood quietly, thankful that she simply agreed, probably only to be done with him for a time, and he went to the door to find the innkeeper coming up the stairs with a large tray. Perry swept the door wide, allowing the man to enter.

"I would ask that you have someone see to my traveling partner. Prepare her a bath and provide her with night clothes, as I believe her things are well sodden. I will take a bath in the next room."

The innkeeper placed the large tray on the table. "Should I wait til ye've had time to sup?" Perry nodded. "I'll start the kettles on the fire and have my girls tend your miss soon." He bowed and left.

"Come. Eat. You must be starved. I know the usual order of

things, but we left before our supper was finished so you certainly had not yet eaten."

She looked out from under a veil of long brown eyelashes and her stomach growled in a rather unseemly command of its own. Perry laughed and pulled the old wooden chair out from the table, waiting for her.

She rose from the bed and walked toward him, then gave a small curtsey. "Milord—"

He waved her off. "No more of this. You are apologetic, I am apologetic, we are both pardoned, let us eat." He motioned to the seat of the chair with an inviting smile. His comfortable rakish demeanor was setting off everything inside her. She wasn't charmed as she should be and it right put him off. Not that he wanted her charmed, but pliant would be acceptable. Easier. She seemed an immoveable force.

Lilly removed her traveling cape and folded it across the chair, then turned and sat, silent as he pushed her up to the table and started piling food on a plate. He glanced at her when he placed it in front of her, finding that she looked like she might at any moment cast up her accounts. He paused, attempting to discern what he'd done this time.

"Milord. I'm not proper company. You canna serve me, I canna—" She started to stand, tears welling in her big eyes.

"I can and you will." He picked up the full plate and handed her the empty. "I'll allow you to serve yourself, but you'll not move from my table or I'll consider that a cut direct." If she wouldn't acquiesce to his traditional style of convincing, he would try being more blunt.

She was studying him. He wondered if she would decide it better to deal with her own reservations about propriety or to offend him. She exhaled slowly. "As you wish."

He smiled and she returned it slowly as he sat at the table across from her and pulled a napkin across his lap. She quietly filled her plate, then—though he'd have believed it impossible—even more quietly she started to eat. Her movements were delicate, fluid. Her mouth opened over and over again to accept the food she'd chosen.

His mouth went dry and he found it difficult to swallow even the juiciest bit of fruit as he watched. He placed his fork on the table next to the plate and forced his gaze to the window.

As he'd pulled the napkin across his lap his smile shifted to triumph, and she understood at that moment what a rake was. Irresistible, irreverent, incorrigible and impossible, it was no wonder women were so drawn to them. Then she ate, and he watched. No matter how quiet she endeavored to be, his eyes were always on her, inspecting her.

When the innkeeper's girls pushed the slipper tub into the room, the viscount wiped the corners of his mouth with his napkin then stood, clutching it in one hand. "I shall take my leave."

He pushed the chair to the table. One of the girls smiled at him, and he asked for his portmanteau to be brought to the other room before bowing to Lilly. "Miss." His mouth hung there, as if he intended to say something else, but then he snapped it shut and stood straight, turning for the door with his napkin still in hand.

Perry entered the room next to hers and heaved a breath, leaning over with his hands on his knees. He felt like a rutting schoolboy, hard as a rock from a soft breeze. "What the bloody hell," he grumbled, throwing the napkin across the room. It fluttered, then wafted to the floor quite unsatisfactorily.

He stood, dragging his fingers through his already disheveled locks before undoing his white neck cloth while he walked to the tub. He tossed the neck cloth away as well, the long piece of fabric catching on one of the bed posts. He felt a sort of relief wash over him; he was at least finally able to let his guard down now that he was away from Lilly.

She was damaged. *Damaged.* There was no accounting for his attraction to her. It was uncalled for, inappropriate, unseemly, simply wrong. Regardless, she was certainly able to get his ire up, as well as other things. Perry turned when the door opened without a knock, and one of the inn girls walked in with his bag.

"Milord, I've been sent to *tend* ye," she said, dropping the heavy bag and approaching him with a wicked grin.

His jaw dropped and his eyebrows shot up. He was used to women throwing themselves at him, but this was rather unexpected. He didn't particularly remember paying this one any heed; he wasn't even sure if she'd been in the other room at all. *How inconvenient.*

She reached up and unbuttoned his waistcoat and shirt as he

gawked. She looked at him questioningly, her brows knit together. "If I am not to your liking, milord, I can leave you be."

He smiled, not sure whether to turn her out or accept the invitation as she reached for his trousers.

"Oh, I see," she said with a bit of disappointment, then she turned. "No matter. I'll ready your bath, milord."

He looked down. Had it not been only moments ago he was fighting an erection? Perry shook his head. This was a right horrible turn. He watched her move around the room, her round bottom swaying beneath the layers of heavy skirts, her bosom ripening over the wide collar of her shirt, which was gathered up with ribbons at the shoulders. He concentrated…hard. One little pull and the whole thing would unravel before him, her sweet perky breasts spilling into his greedy upturned hands. He looked down again and—nothing. *Nothing*!

He shook his head and stripped clothing went soaring about the room like kites as the woman looked on in shock, then he sank into the tub like an ungrateful toddler. He dozed as he listened to her moving about, no doubt picking up his strewn clothing. Then he felt her hands on his scalp and he leaned forward, allowing her access. When she finished he leaned back and slipped beneath the water, shaking the soap from his hair before resting his head against the edge of the tub.

He moaned softly as he thought back to the carriage. The way Lilly's gaze had raked over him, assessing his countenance like a stern governess…or a wanton mistress. She'd looked up at him with eyes like hot buttered cinnamon melting on toast.

He shifted in the tub, sloshing a bit of water over the edge. He heard a distant squeal, but continued his reverie. The corner of her mouth pulled up in a teasing smile as she reached for him, pushing her hand below his waistband and—

He jolted, sitting up in the tub and surveying his surroundings. The woman stood, wet from neck to knee, her white shirt clinging to her bosom as her eyes begged him to understand.

"What, uh—"

"Milord, you seemed to be, euh, interested—" She motioned to his nether region.

"I beg your pardon, I was…not. I mean to say that I was perhaps daydreaming and…well, and I was—not," he said carefully.

She turned to leave and he stood in the tub, water pouring from his rigid body. "Wait," he said gruffly. She turned back and he watched as she assessed his figure; warm, wet, and hard from stem to stern. She sighed and smiled.

*I've done this before. I've used a willing girl to sate my need,* he thought as she approached. He closed his eyes and pictured her: sweet, soft, quiet, submissive. And he continued picturing her as he felt the warmth of this woman's mouth envelop him, evoking a groan as he wove his hands through her hair.

Lilly sat curled up in the bath, her translucent chemise adhering like paper to her skin. She'd tried to explain to the girl that she wasn't above her station and she wasn't supposed to be tended to, but the girl wouldn't listen.

"I was told to tend you, and if you think for a minute I'm set to be whipped for disobeying your laird, you can forget it," she said sternly in her thick Irish brogue. The girl grimaced as she stared at Lilly's face and she shied away. Lilly felt thankful for the veil of water that seemed to obscure the rest of her body from her notice.

*How can ladies stand this? 'Tis horrible being fussed over, I canna stand her hands on me. 'Tis no wonder why I was born to my family; I was not meant for this.* She closed her eyes and reluctantly allowed the ministrations. She felt like there were hands all over her, even though the girl was only washing her hair.

Lilly felt something sharp graze her shoulder and she screamed like a hawk taking flight for its quarry. She stood in the bath, then tumbled backward out of the tub. She scampered for the other side of the room.

"Miss? What did I—"

The girl was cut off by the door behind her slamming open, and she moved aside.

"Lilly," Perry bellowed, the sound careening from his belly like a freight train. He stood in the doorway, a lion preparing to attack, surveying. He had naught on but a robe, and water pooled at his bare feet. He saw Lilly across the room, huddled behind a chair.

"What the bloody damn hell happened?" he roared as he crossed the room in three strides. He grabbed the counterpane from the bed as he passed and swung it like a cape, covering Lilly's bare shoulders before he lifted her petite frame and carried her to the bed.

"Milord, I beg pardon," the inn's maid said. "I was only trying to get the tangles out. I don't know what happened." Tears threatened to overrun her cheeks.

"Go— Just go." He tried to put Lilly on the bed. "Have my case brought over," he said over his shoulder as she rushed from the room. Lilly wouldn't release him, and he soon discovered that his robe had come undone, his nakedness sure to be revealed if he forced her to let go. He turned and sat on the edge of the bed, holding her in his lap. *This is a right unsavory turn of events.*

Perry swept his hand in steady circles over Lilly's back, calming her until the innkeeper entered with his case. "Milord, I—"

Perry cut him off with a wave. "No, that will be all. It wasn't the girl. She did no harm. Just see to my men."

The innkeeper nodded and pulled the door closed, yanking at it to fit it back in the frame. Perry heard his footsteps plodding down the hall and he turned to the bundle in his lap.

"Lilly," he said gently. "Oh, sweet Lilly." He pulled the counterpane away from her face, trying to find her in the thick folds. He saw one eye, then the other, looking up at him from the small hole he'd made. He chuckled quietly. "You look quite like a mouse."

She closed her eyes. "I'm sorry," she replied, then opened them again. "I'm so sorry."

He shook his head. "There is no need for you to apologize— Is there?" Suddenly he wasn't sure what had transpired. Then remembered exactly what he'd been doing next door. "We certainly have made a mess of this place, have we not? Next time my carriage pulls up they will tell us they are full, I am assured of that."

She smiled brightly, and it lit the dim room. He was awed; he'd never seen such a brilliant smile. The scars faded a bit when she smiled, and her eyes sparkled as she wiggled.

"Lilly, wait. Hold on now," he cautioned. "You need to let me… uh, just—stop for a second and let me…" He placed her on her feet facing away from him and stood to retie the belt, then he cleared his throat. He pulled her back to the bed and sat her down as he looked around the room. "I suppose she hadn't yet brought you the nightgown I requested?"

She shook her head.

"No, of course not," he grumbled. He went to his portmanteau and pulled out a clean white shirt and pushed it toward the little hand that grasped the edge of the thick counterpane.

She took it, the blanket slipping just a touch before she caught it back up.

Perry looked around the room again, then moved toward the dressing screen in the corner. "I'll just go—" He motioned to the screen as he pulled a pair of under drawers from his bag and stumbled behind it. He stared into the dark corner, one hand on each wall, and breathed as deeply as his rattled nerves would allow. He shook his head and pulled the drawers on under the robe, wishing, for once, that he'd packed pajamas, but he always thought them an unnecessary bother.

He leaned one shoulder against the wall as he listened to her small sighs and grunts as she tried to get the shirt on. He turned and peered around the screen. The tented counterpane in the middle of the bed shook and moved as though there were a wrestling match beneath it. He smiled as he saw the soggy chemise tossed out to the floor with a wet thwack, then the wrestling match continued.

The blanket stilled and he turned quickly, averting his gaze. She cleared her throat and he looked around again, finding her on the bed, her hair a mess, his white shirt engulfing her petite frame, the counterpane pooling around her legs. He swallowed hard, struggling to remember who she was and who he was.

He walked slowly to the chair next to the fireplace. "So, would you like to tell me what caused the ruckus?"

Her smile faded instantly. "I'm not accustomed to being… tended. I mean, beyond—" She waved her hand in a circle. "The girl would not listen. She insisted on washing me, and I just—" She cleared her throat. "She scratched me. I—it, um… the sharp—" She stopped, looking up.

Perry wanted to reach out and hold her, protect her, but he forced himself to remain still, watching as her mind wrestled. He tried to show his understanding, hoping his patient expression would calm her.

"I was walkin' home from the dairy after Mama sent me to fetch milk. Of course, what else would I do at the dairy?" she said nervously, twisting her hands in the blankets. "He offered to bring me home. I refused. I didn't know him. It wouldn't be proper." She inspected her hands for a while, then spoke again, so softly he could hardly hear her. "I thought that he'd left, but he'd waited. He grabbed me by my hair and rode on." She stroked the long strands and looked out the window. "He took me to the wood…"

Perry followed her gaze, saw the night deepen its folds across the countryside, the pinpricks in the blanket of night twinkling their innocence over the meadow behind the inn. She took a deep breath and turned back to him.

He looked on her with care, diligently controlling his expression. He had been informed of her injuries in general terms. He understood how they were likely caused, he could see the scars left behind, but he wasn't aware that Lilly had ever told anyone exactly what had happened. He didn't want to hear it, didn't want to be the keeper of this knowledge, but he didn't want to stop her, either, because he could see she needed this. He could feel it in his bones.

Perry sat back in the chair, his legs crossed at the ankles and stretched out before him, his hands clasped at his waist, eyes on her; waiting, hypnotizing, imploring, demanding—patiently. The next breath she took seemed to take all the air from the room, and his own lungs stilled.

"He pulled me into the forest. I screamed, but nobody heard. At least, I thought I'd screamed." She looked up at him for a moment. "I remember screaming, I do. I remember it—but nobody came." She glanced down as her breath hitched, and she picked at a loose thread on the blanket, then simply said, "I tripped, fell. He took me."

Perry moved then, his discomfort of mind too great for his body. Leaning forward, he rested his elbows on his knees and lowered his head to his clenched hands. She waited. He looked up slowly. The next rushed from her.

"He, mmm, he used the crop when I would not do as he said. I tried to fight him, you see, but he dinna like that, or, mayhap he did because— Well." Her eyes filled with tears and her voice trembled as her chin shook. "Do men like that?" she asked earnestly.

He could feel the strain in his features, knew he attempted to shake his head. Didn't believe he was successful.

She shrugged and looked back to her hands which were busy unraveling the edge of the counterpane. "There was a picnic there. Where he had stopped. He took a bottle from the basket and broke it against a tree. He—ah…" She trembled violently, gathering her knees up and hiding her face for a moment. "I tried to get away, I did, please believe me, I tried. But he dragged me back, pushed my face into the ground as he—"

Perry stood. He felt his muscles twitching with the tension, his feet not following his command to remain still as he strode across the room and sat on the bed next to her. He reached out, his hands hovering mere inches above her, then they grazed her arms as she jerked away.

He was afraid to touch her, afraid to hold her, but needed desperately to comfort her somehow, to make her feel safe. He had tried to be patient, but he couldn't listen to this. He couldn't hear this, not from her. His brain finally snapped back into control and he gathered her trembling form into his arms.

She jumped at his touch and tried to push away but he held her, controlling her fighting limbs as he held her gently but securely, whispering tenderly. He wasn't sure it was the correct thing to do, to resist her fight, but it was what felt proper.

"Hush, Lilly. You were so brave. You did scream and you fought, and it was not your fault. You were good, you were strong, you tried, it was not you. It was him, that horrible wretch of a man. It was all him."

He took her face between his palms and looked into her watery brown eyes. He felt her struggle to remain still. "You carry no fault for this. He carries it, all of it." He closed his eyes, suddenly realizing how Gideon had felt when he'd figured out what Hepplewort had done to Francine. Hepplewort hadn't even completed the task with her; Lilly, on the other hand, had suffered the brunt of that man's anger because of that loss.

"I shall never know the love of a man," she whispered.

Perry studied her face, counting the small scars that crossed her cheeks. He ran a finger over each one.

"Show me," she whispered.

He leaned back. "What?"

"Show me, please— Show me what it means to be loved, to be cherished. Help me forget that…man. Help me," she pleaded. "I can feel him all over me, touching me." Her hands moved over her body anxiously. "I can feel him surrounding me, the way he felt on me, *inside me*—" The last she nearly screamed as her body shook violently and she begged through her tears.

Perry shook his head. "I cannot do that, I— You need to find someone else. You *will* find someone…"

"I'll never find someone so long as any touch makes me jump, so long as the closeness of another person frightens me. You see how I fight, and I don't mean to, not with you. I'll never be all right, not until someone shows me what it *means* to be all right. Please, please show me. You are practiced, you know how to make a girl feel important. You can help me. I believe you can teach me how to feel…right again," she beseeched quietly.

"Lilly, I cannot, I— I have never had a relationship of import. I have never taught a soul a thing. I cannot be the one you need, you must find—"

She shook her head stiffly. "No, I want you to show me, I trust you. This is no relationship. That should make it easier, because I don't expect anything from you but a tender touch, a caress, a bit of care. 'Tis why it must be you, because you can do that, without expecting it to be anything else—"

Lilly looked into his green eyes and could see the tumult, the thoughts wrestling between what was right and what was proper.

# THIRTY-FIVE

Perry was disheartened by her final words, that he could take her without expecting anything from her, that he could show her what love felt like without actually giving his heart, or taking hers. She was right, of course, he knew this, but with Lilly it wasn't what he wanted.

He wanted more for her, he wanted better for her, someone who would care for her, love her, take her to wife. She deserved more. More than him.

His hand went to his face, rubbed his eyes, closed them tight against the sting of the truth as he held her at a distance. If only for one night he could shake off the invisible binds that held him from her, this small damaged woman he had no right to touch, no right to care for. How had it come to this in one night, that he was irrevocably drawn to protect and honor her wishes? He opened his eyes, lit with the fire of his pain, and lowered his mouth to hers gently.

Her eyes fluttered shut.

He brushed his lips across hers to warm them for a stronger kiss.

She flinched.

He shook his head. "Lilly, this is impossible. You ask the impossible. You will find someone to help you through this, but it won't be me. It can't be me. I'm sorry. I understand your pain— at least I believe I understand what it is you wish for. But I simply cannot do what you asking of me.

She pulled away then, turning and lying down on the bed. She gave him her back and nothing more. His hand reached out to her, only to stop a mere breath away from touching her. He should go.

He stood and moved to the door, hoping she would be all right alone in this room. Because there was no way he could stay here with her and not hate himself the next day.

# THIRTY-SIX

Perry didn't sleep a wink that night; instead, his ear was practically pressed to the wall for fear she would have night terrors. She didn't, by the grace of God, and he was dressed and prepared to travel on at first light. He met his men in the stable yard as they were hooking up the landau.

"This simply will not do." He looked to Kerrigan. "We need to take the train. Traveling with Lilly simply will not work."

"I believe the line from London is finished through Carlisle, the next train should depart in the morning. We can take the train from there. I'll send a wire to prepare a private coach and make arrangements for the team and carriage."

Perry nodded and turned back to the inn to find Lilly at the window of her room, gazing down from above like an angel wrapped in white. "I'll go— Eh, I'll go get our charge prepared to travel."

"Milord—"

Perry turned and put his hands up. "What? Tell me how this is to be handled. I am managing by a thread."

"Milord. I only meant to say we shall be ready to quit the inn at half past."

Perry's mind emptied. He blinked, attempting to restart his thoughts to no avail.

"Milord. Half past."

He shook his head and pivoted toward the inn.

Lilly met him at the door, smoothing her gloves over her knuckles, the drab woolen traveling dress she'd worn yesterday like a curtain in front of their previous ease. "Milord, how can I help?"

"You are my guest, you are not my servant. My men can handle the arrangements. We will travel on to Carlisle where we will take the train to London. We will arrive late tonight if the train leaves on time. "

She nodded and took up her bag.

Perry handed her up to the carriage. "The next train won't leave Carlisle until the morning, so we will spend the day in the country, staying the night and leaving early tomorrow."

She didn't respond as he took the seat across from her. The carriage swayed as his men boarded. When it lurched, he leaned down to take her foot. She pulled away and he gave her a warning glance.

"Trust me," was all he said, from the approximate vicinity of her knees. His skin warmed where he held her. He ran his fingers down her leg, then grasped her ankle when she tried to pull back, lifting her leg up across to his knees. Removing her ankle boot, he massaged her foot. She jerked, but he held fast. "There is more to intimacy than the sexual act," he murmured. "There is more to learn, beyond how to be with a man in a state of undress. Anyone can learn that easily."

She watched his long fingers wrap around the bridge of her foot, massaging, working, tensing, relaxing. She had never been touched in such a manner. She slowly loosened into his hold, concentrating on the feel of his hands on her.

She finally leaned back into the squabs and looked out the window, settling in for the ride to the station.

The rest of their journey would be completed by rail, and the prospect of a train ride excited her. As per His Grace's plans, the final leg of the rail line replacement was underway and would be complete within the next two weeks, before his house party. It was all the talk back at Eildon.

She took a deep breath and felt him replace her boot, fastening the hooks then carefully setting it on the floor. He reached for the other. She watched him move, willed herself to sit peacefully, but her nerves jumped nonetheless and her foot jerked. She shook her head and closed her eyes when he looked up to her with a half smile, holding her foot solidly to prevent her kicking him in the jaw.

He wrapped his warm hands around her leg through her skirts, chasing the tremors away as he stroked. She breathed deeply and slowly. Concentrating on the pressure from his hold, the sweep of her skirts against her over-sensitized calf, the lulling sway of the carriage, the bright warm sun through the wide curtains in the box. She closed her eyes and gave her senses rein.

The fact that she fell asleep easily under his ministrations confirmed that she had not slept the night before, just as he hadn't, thereby explaining the lack of night terrors he was sure she suffered. He pulled her across the carriage, tucking her against his side and pulling her legs across his. He studied her features, how the tension slowly softened. The carriage rolled along, avoiding the large ruts from the previous night's storm. Occasionally her features would strain and he would caress her hand, carefully releasing the tension, allowing her deeper sleep.

*How am I to survive this?*

They pulled through a gate into a high meadow to break their journey and take lunch. Perry jumped down from the landau and lowered Lilly to her feet, then pulled a rug from the boot, taking it and the basket of repast to a nearby great oak. He spread the rug as his men saw to the horses and set to their own feast at the back of the carriage.

Satisfied, Perry looked over to Lilly, who seemed torn between joining his men and staying where she was. Perry grunted. How could it be she had nary a thought for joining him after all they had shared?

"Lilly, you cannot possibly feast with my men. You will have to suffice with my company for luncheon. I do beg your pardon for not having separate arrangements for you. I should have considered your position. The men will not think on it, for there is no other choice," he said, loud enough for everyone to hear.

She walked slowly to his side, then knelt on the opposite edge of the rug. He hadn't fully realized how difficult their separation of status would be, or how it might pain her to cross those boundaries.

"Please take as you will, there is enough for an army here," he said, pushing the basket toward her. "Are you enjoying the journey as yet?"

"Very much, milord. I haven't ever been this far south, of course, never more south than Roxleighshire, really."

He watched her take a stem of grapes, savoring each one, then poured her a glass of sweet wine. "Tell me of your family."

"You know Meggie, my sister. There's Keegan and Patrick, my brothers, and of course Ma and Pa. Just us six there. But the people in Kelso are terribly close, as we all take care of each other. Well, we have to, since we're so far from the rest. I mean, not so far as London, mayhap, but we prefer to be afar, ye see."

"It must be something in the water up in the north country, as my brother tends to that same affliction."

"His Grace must be the most wonderful man there is up north, milord. He sees to us all without complaint. We're ever so distant from the seat, but still he takes care of us as need be. I hear tell of many a landowner that has no countenance for support to the lands not directly in his grasp."

"He is quite dedicated to his entailments, of which Kelso is undoubtedly one, regardless of its removal from the seat of the dukedom. His Grace sees no difference in status between the entailments of the dukedom and the entailments of his earldoms and viscountcies. That, in truth, is what makes him possibly the greatest duke in Britain." He paused, sipping his wine. "Of course, I do carry a partiality," he added with a grin.

Lilly giggled, and the sweet sound of her laughter broadened his smile. He let it drift over his skin like silk and cast it to memory, pledging himself to force the sweet notes from her as often as he was able.

"Milord." The word was tense and he knew what was next.

"Lilly, do not."

"Please, sir, you do not know how difficult it is for me to even ask this of you. A viscount, for heaven's sake! I'm nobody, and you're a viscount. I shouldn't even be speaking with you, much less…" Her voice trailed off. "This cannot be too much to ask, your reputation—"

He rubbed his eyes. "Is not based on the ruination of innocents."

"I'm no innocent."

"But you are, in every sense of the word save one. You are. We cannot be together. It would not be right."

She shook her head. "Have you ever wondered about the aristocracy? How God chooses one man to be born a duke and the next in a gutter?"

"I cannot say as how I had ever thought on this until I met you."

"And now?"

"Now I wonder how I could have been so fortunate. Touched by God to be a leader among men, and what have I done with that as yet?"

"You served in the Royal Navy, milord. You served Queen and Country."

"Then returned only to serve myself." His jaw clenched and he twisted away from her.

His coachman, Gardner, walked up to gather the basket. "Milord, 'tis time we got on," he said, startling Lilly to her feet with a squeal.

Perry stood and caught her as she swooned, dismissing his man with a wave. "Lilly, sweet Lilly," he said, smiling gently as he bundled her back down to the rug with him.

She shook terribly, but calmed within the circle of his arms. He lifted her chin, gazing down into her upturned face as she slowly lifted her lids to gaze deeply into his eyes. He gasped, feeling her stare deep within. Something about her stilled his soul, paused his searching, calmed his confusions.

Before he knew what he was about, his mouth had covered hers, their eyes still locked, and he was watching, waiting. Then his mouth shifted over hers and she yielded. His eyes closed and his hand tensed behind her neck, holding her to him. Her fingers quivered their way to his lapels, then drifted up, lacing at his nape, her thumbs gently caressing his jaw as her eyes closed.

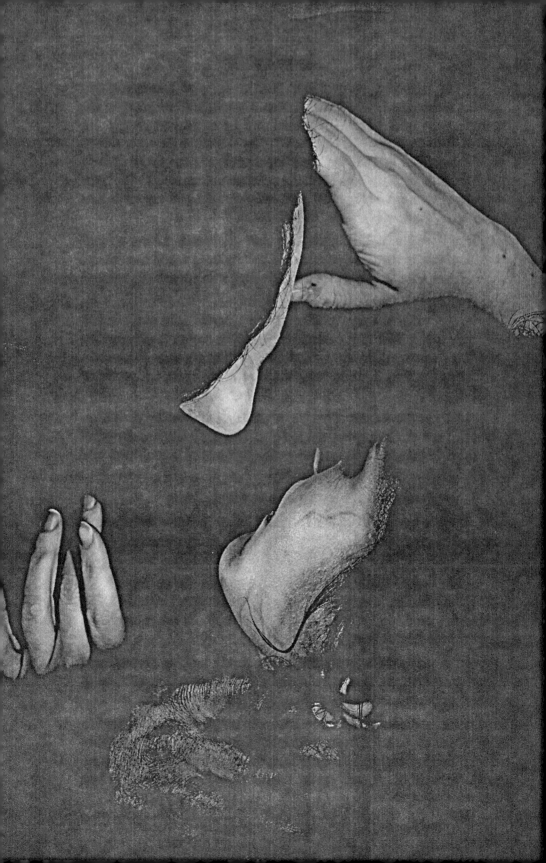

The sigh that escaped her became trapped between them, serving to harness his rampant passion. He soothed her, gentling his ministrations until her hands loosed and he could break away. He looked up to see the boots of his men as they shifted on the other side of the carriage. He could tell they were impatient by the way they dug their heels in, disrupting the soil. He made a mental note to speak with them later. They wouldn't like him using one of their own, and any servant in his house or Gideon's qualified on that point.

They arrived in Carlisle late that afternoon, taking several rooms as the inn was nearly deserted. The next train would leave in the morning, and the keep was happy to be busied with guests and prepared a feast with Perry's accord.

That night as they withdrew, Perry escorted Lilly as far as her door. He watched his men enter their respective rooms, then turned to her. "My dear sweet Lilly, my room is just adjacent to yours. These walls are sturdy, but thin. The slightest sound and I will be here, if you have need of me."

He saw the corners of her lips lift without her looking up at him. "Not that sort of need, sweet, not tonight." Her smile faded as she lifted her chin. "Remember, there are other things you need learn. This is one of them. You need to learn to be alone."

She shook her head, imploring him with her eyes.

"Once we reach London there will be no chance of being alone for you in my household. This will be our last opportunity for this lesson."

She looked warily around his tall form, into the open doorway. The room was dim, lit only by the fire and one lamp next to the bed. She placed her hands on his arms, and he became pliable at her touch, his immoveable form shifting at her bidding.

He watched her enter the room, slowly looking around, and regret tensed his gut. She turned, hand on the door as she smiled up at him, then she pressed the door closed before him.

He reached out to the doorjamb and leaned forward, resting his forehead as the bolt slid home, protecting her from the outside world—from him. He breathed harshly, willing the door to open to him, to no avail. He heard heavy steps on the stairs and he turned, sweeping into his room.

He retired in his shirt and trousers, his concern for the woman in his trust making him restless. At some point he drifted off, unaware he was dreaming of her until he heard the shriek through the wall behind his head. He vaulted from the bed and went through her door in a rain of shattered wood. Scanning the room, he found her curled beneath the bed, shaking the frame above her.

"Lilly." He walked to the bed, but she didn't move. He started to kneel as the keep ran to the door. "Apologies, I will make reparations." The keep turned and left, grumbling the whole way. Perry kneeled beside the large bed then laid down on the floor, reaching out to take her small hand in his.

"Sweet, sweet Lilly," he sang softly under the bed toward her. "Lilly, my Lilly, you are all right. Everything is fine, I am here, please, sweet Lilly, come out," he whispered. He saw her shift, and her face lifted to his, her eyes reflecting the light from the fire. He heard boots behind him and knew it was Kerrigan. He waved him off without looking and heard him retreat to just outside the open door. Her hand tensed and he tugged, gently pulling her out and rolling to his back, lifting her body across his. She clung desperately and he paused to hold and comfort her.

Slowly he rose, first sitting up and shifting her, then standing to his feet. He carried her back to his room, as the door to hers was irretrievably broken. He nodded to Kerrigan as he passed. The man went into her room and gathered her things, then followed.

"Milord, p'raps—" Kerrigan started.

Perry laid her out carefully on his bed and tucked her in before he turned around.

"Perhaps what, Kerrigan? Perhaps she needs the rumor of two men in her chamber? Perhaps she should be watched by you, easily as strange to her as I? Perhaps what, Kerrigan?"

Kerrigan shifted uncomfortably, not finding an answer as Perry approached. He took Kerrigan's shoulders and commanded his gaze. "Perhaps, Kerrigan, you worry too much. I've done nothing but protect her thus far, and I'll do nothing she doesn't ask of me in the future. She'll be perfectly safe under my watch, and not a soul would dare argue her respectability with me," Perry said. "I do, however, appreciate your concern, but for tonight let us try to rest as best we are able."

Kerrigan smiled stiffly. Looking over Perry's shoulder at the girl now sleeping, he grunted then turned, pulling the door shut behind him and returning to his room.

Perry moved to Lilly, brushing the hair back from her face and watching her expressions. Content that she was settled at least for a while, he moved a chair next to the bed, putting his feet up and sinking in as far as he could. Sleep was most definitely a necessity at this point. Beyond that, there wasn't much outside this room he needed.

R

# THIRTY-SEVEN

The next morning they boarded the train—carriage, horses, and all. Perry took an entire car for his party. It consisted of several berths. He steered Lilly toward the largest forward berth, which took up nearly a third of the railcar, and let his men settle in the others. The berth had a single bed, a seating area near the windows, and a dining table. He thought it quite luxurious and considered looking into having a railcar outfitted for himself.

He led her to the seats by the window, which were beautifully appointed in a velvet brocade, soft and plush enough to sink into. He rather enjoyed the rails. He considered that he would travel to Eildon more often, as his brother would begin the begetting of heirs and he would most definitely need to be present to ensure they were not raised to be thoroughly stodgy boors as Gideon had been.

He liked the idea of being an uncle. The bad uncle who always brought sweets and toys and the like. The favorite uncle. Not that there would be another. His first gift would be a beautiful grey hunter. It would quite clash with the chattel in Rox's stable. The thought of it made Perry grin.

The sway of the train, the graceful speed with which it moved, was erotic. It swayed the body as opposed to jerking it around like one was in a carriage. It passed over the country easily, as a knife through butter. The newer rails and stronger engines were an incredible improvement, the trains moving faster and smoother from station to station. He knew Gideon had planned a private car to travel back and forth to London more efficiently, and he certainly could outdo him. His car would have a large bed, right in the center, surrounded by windows. He grinned wickedly at the thought, then looked to the woman his mind had placed lounging on that beautiful bed.

She stood once they were moving steadily, her hands pressed up against the glass as the countryside swept past them. Her eyes were wide, her mouth an amazed smile. Her breath came against the chilled window in little puffs of condensation. His vision exploded in his mind, the excitement on her face bringing him an altogether different kind of joy. He followed the line of her jaw, past the shoulder of her traveling cloak, to the long fitted sleeves of her blouse. The lines of her clothing were so much simpler than the current fashions of the *ton*. It was rather refreshing.

She wore a full skirt, no fancy bustles, though it appeared from the roundness of the skirt that there was something going on under there, other than just her legs. He groaned and turned away. This woman had him tied in knots.

In general he took pleasure in one woman, then moved on. Or several women at a time. In different ways. He'd had mistresses who he'd kept for longer periods, but he always tired of them, eventually looking for someone new.

How was it that this woman had captured so much of his attention in so short a time? He couldn't form the face of a single of his former mistresses in his mind; she had effectively chased them all away.

He turned when she shook his arm. "Look! Look there, do you see them?" Perry stood and leaned around her, looking out the window to where she pointed. A group of red deer grazed at the edge of the forest. "Do you hunt?" she asked.

"I do, in fact. I have been practicing with a bow recently." He placed his arms on the frame of the window, near the level of her shoulders, and saw the swift puff of breath on the window that signaled her awareness. "The huntsmen at Westcreek swear it to be the most efficient and least cruel way to down a buck." His words stirred the loose curls at her neck.

Her smile wavered. "My father would never let me attend a hunt." She glanced back to the window. "Will the rails come to Kelso?"

"I believe the plans call for an eastern leg to run from Roxleighshire, close to Kelso, then on to Berwick-Upon-Tweed."

She nodded, her eyes taking on a faraway cast.

"You will not have time to miss them," he said. "You will be too busy with your new life in London."

"Thank you."

He let the train rock him as he considered his situation. This wasn't bound to turn out well, no matter how it was handled. He should take her to Gideon's town house and leave her there with instructions to contact his brother and notify him of his new town maid. He couldn't.

He knew what it was to be a rake and, at this moment, the definition was simple. Selfish. He wouldn't take her to Roxleigh House because he wanted her with him. He wanted to continue these lessons. He wanted to see how much she could learn, and how well she would master his teachings.

He had a feeling she would prove to be an excellent student.

He was a rake, and it appeared he had not changed that much after all. He wanted her. So she was to stay with him.

# THIRTY-EIGHT

"I concede."

Her heart stopped as the words drifted across her shoulder, and she turned slowly toward him, her side coming to rest against his solid chest. He should have moved to give her room. It would have been the proper thing to do. He didn't. He did what a rake would do: he crowded her infinitely more by flexing the muscles that caged her to the window. "You...what?"

"I concede, I yield, I will do as you wish." His voice was so low she felt it in the breath that sang across her ear, through the vibration of the words where she was drawn up against him.

She felt his breath quicken then, the tempo with which his chest expanded and released picking up. She glanced around the berth, as if there would be witnesses to this. As if he were not so experienced that he knew the precise location of each of his men without looking, not to mention every other passenger, porter, conductor, and engineer. Rather quickly, she realized the reason she could feel his breath come and go so easily was because hers was completely still. She huffed it out, then tried to convince her lungs to take in more air—she needed it desperately. She heard the choking sound come from her throat as she watched his eyes widen, and his lips parted when she finally took a breath. She could not take her eyes from them.

"Unless..."

"Unless?" She felt as though she might simply faint.

"Unless you have changed your mind?"

He sounded almost hopeful, but a line marred his perfect expression just between his brows. She fought her nerves, which at the moment were clearly working against her. *Say something, anything. Nod, smile, acquiesce. Somehow. Move!* Her head jerked.

"You have, then? Changed your mind, I mean?"

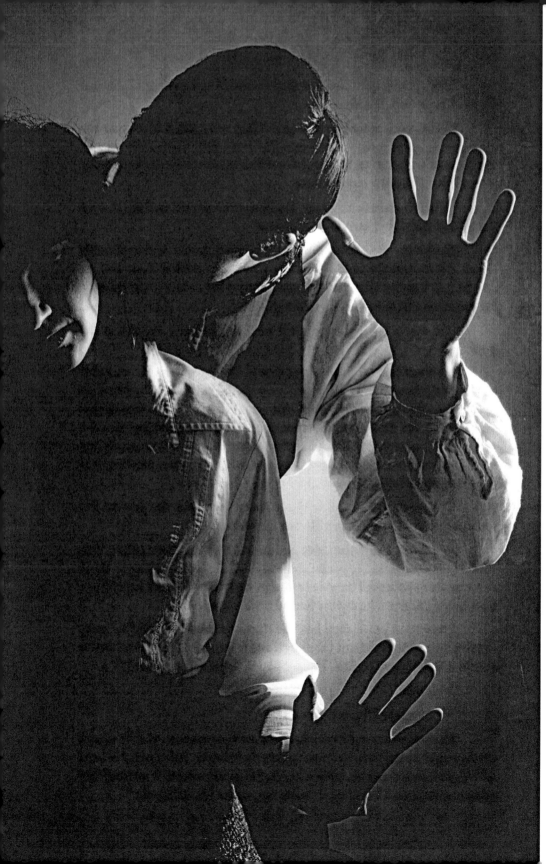

"No!" Thank goodness for that sound. "No, I have not. I haven't changed my mind. Thank you."

His lips caught up in a slow grin. They were silent. She turned to the window, quick jerky movements that were forced from her by will. The sway of the train on the tracks and the sound of the distant engine were all that filled the empty space.

"When?" she asked. There was almost no sound and she cleared her throat. But didn't turn to look at him.

She felt the shift in his muscles, his breath hotter and impossibly closer, his mouth descending to her neck. She melted then and he caught her, but her muscles stiffened, fought his capture. He released her to the seat then followed her down.

"I'm sorry, I— I don't appear to have complete control at the moment."

He knew he had to progress slowly. To make sure she wouldn't become frightened. After all, it was only the simple things that had set her off thus far. This—any part of this—could terrify her and send her into a panic. He reined in his fervor and kissed along her jaw, but she jerked away, so he slowly moved his hand around her back to steady her. Her entire body tensed at the pressure, and when his other hand went to her knee she kicked him—solidly.

"I'm sorry," she said, a blush spreading from the top of her forehead down her face like a closing curtain.

He set her away from him and stood, looking down at her. This wasn't going to work. He paced the length of the berth, trying to think of a way that she would be able to accept his kisses without fear. When he reached the door, he swiftly locked it then turned.

Every time he touched her, she shook or shuddered, jerked away or lashed out. He could not take her if she feared him. He would not be able to bring himself to that. He stopped in front of her. "Stand."

She stood.

"Undress me," he said quietly.

She looked up at him with a confused expression, and he closed his eyes against the pain and fear he saw in her eyes. He shook his head and looked down at her, taking her hand gently where it grasped her traveling cloak and bringing it to the buttons of his waistcoat.

"If this is what you want…undress me," he said. He left her hand there and dropped his, watching, waiting. She tightened her fingers on the top button and twisted slowly, the button popping free.

She worked her way down the row of buttons while he shrugged out of his jacket and loosened his neck cloth. She continued with the buttons of his shirt, then reached up and held both sides of the shirt and waistcoat. She pushed them open slowly, revealing inch by inch his heavily muscled chest.

She gazed at it, now bare and warm. She could feel the heat of him. She could see the pulse at the crest of his ribcage, there at the very base of his neck. Lilly inhaled, quelling her nerves, then thought he smelled of strength. She had no idea what that meant, but knew that it calmed her.

He didn't move, only allowed her inspection. She swallowed. He was so different from anything she'd ever encountered. Perfectly sculpted, restrained, patient.

She reached out and touched the smooth hair dusting his chest. At this she saw his arms move, and she pulled back.

"Wait— Don't." He held his hands together behind his back.

She stepped forward again, reaching up and tracing the patterns of his muscles, the lines of his ribs on each side, the gathering of muscles below. They twitched under her searching fingers, and he lifted his hand to stop her momentarily. She glanced up, worried.

"I'm sorry," he whispered. "I am a bit sensitive there, and the way you are touching me is—"

She started to turn away but he stopped her again, placing her hands back on his chest. She waited, patiently, trying to catch her breath, then followed her hands down his chest with her gaze, halting when they reached the waistband of his trousers. She could see the ridge of him through the fabric and she froze. Her breath hitched and he put his hand over hers. She looked up at him.

"You do not seem to understand that you have all the power here. I have none. I am at your mercy. You will see, even as a woman, that you can control me." His eyes glowed with the fire of his restrained need. His hand moved to the clasp at her throat, releasing her cape and letting it fall behind her.

She flinched at the sudden movement and the raw edge in his gaze, amazed by the difference between the inner passion she could see all too clearly and his outward demeanor. He raised his eyebrows, then pulled his shirt from the waistband and let it fall to the floor with his waistcoat. He clasped his hands behind his back, silently urging her on. His chest broadened in this stance, appearing more powerful, and she felt the command emanating from him, his questioning gaze demanding her touch. His control, though he professed none, was palpable—and she balked.

She stepped back, and he let out a long breath as she spoke. "Mayhap— Mayhap this was a mistake, mayhap you're right," she said quietly, then turned away from him.

Her touch, her exploring gaze, were part of the most impassioned exchange he had ever experienced with another person in his life. Unfortunately, she had persuaded both his mind and body and neither was interested in being dissuaded now. His thoughts raced as he tried to find a way to convince her, to gain her trust. He groaned and sank to his knees behind her, his head down, waiting patiently. He swore to himself that if she walked away now that would be it. He would move to another berth and not return.

She turned, and his head came up slightly. He saw the shock cross her features when she found him on his knees. He was still so large that his nose came to just beneath her breast. His warm breath moved the shirt against her abdomen, and she inhaled sharply. He closed his eyes, the floor shifting as they took a bend in the track. She took the step back to him and he felt her hand skim through the thickness of his hair, pulling his head back slightly, then his body forward. He leaned into her, his chin grazing between her breasts, and she jumped at the touch but did not release him.

He leaned back on his heels and opened his eyes, looking down at first so as not to scare her off again, trying desperately to control the desire that must be so obvious. He needed to be able to look on her without disquieting her. His gaze moved up her body. He counted the buttons on her shirtwaist, the stitches in the placket, and the threads in the fabric, slowing his gaze as he came to her bare neck, where the twin pulses rushed at each side. He swallowed hard and waited.

He made his look one of pleading permission, and it was

apparently exactly what she needed. She tugged his hair, pulling him back so that his eyes caught hers, and she gave it, running her thumb over his open mouth. Then she stepped back, sitting at the edge of the seat. "Milord," she said with a breath. He wasn't sure if it was meant to call him, or simply an exclamation.

"Perry," he said. "If we are to do this, you will call me Perry."

"I— I cannot," she stuttered.

He grumbled and she shrank away from him. He was immediately penitent. "Call me what you will," he whispered.

Her back straightened a bit. "I am afraid."

He sank onto his heels again. He reached out and stroked her bare leg. Taking her foot carefully in his hands, holding her steady when it jerked, he unhooked her boot and let it fall, then massaged her foot through her heavy woolen stockings. She sighed and he moved to her other leg, paying it the same attention. His mind played over the scene she had depicted, of that atrocious beast dragging her into the forest and forcing her body to his wicked intent. He closed his eyes. He wanted Hepplewort dead. He was amazed Gideon had left him breathing.

He looked up at her. "Lilly," he said, releasing her foot and standing before her. "We do not—"

She hushed him, her gaze trapped on his loins. She twisted her hands in her skirts as she looked to his eyes suddenly. "He was the first. I had never—" She gestured toward him. "Even my brothers, I'd never— I, I had never seen even—" She swallowed, her throat tensing as he watched her.

He understood. She was an innocent—in her mind, anyway. What Hepplewort had done to her in that forest didn't change the hopes and dreams she'd had growing up. Hepplewort had violently derailed them but no longer. Now Perry was purposed with setting her back on track. He loosened his trousers and pushed them off, then stood before her in his under drawers. He heard her sharp intake of breath.

He lifted her hands and placed them on his waist, ever waiting her decision. Her face flushed hotly, then she shut her eyes, tucking her chin into her shoulder. Her fingers found the buttons that held the drawers in place and, with a deep breath, she tightened her closed eyes and pulled at them bit by bit. When the waist was loose, she held the edges of the opening to keep the drawers in place while she attempted to control her breathing.

She swallowed, her fists clenched over the ties, her knuckles white with strain as she struggled. He stroked one hand with his finger. "The reality is not as fearsome as the memory which is fueled by your imagination," he murmured.

She nodded briskly and her hands relaxed, dropping the ties and letting the drawers slide low on his hips. She felt for his waist, her eyes still closed. Her fingertips dipped into his bellybutton and he vibrated with a silent chuckle. She followed the smooth, soft trail of hair and tucked the tips of her fingers in his waistband, pulling forward so the ties loosened and his drawers slid away. She let go, though her hands hovered there, not wanting to continue but refusing to retreat.

The sight of her closed eyes and her small hands hovering just above his freed erection was enough to stand his nerves on end. His mouth went dry and he moved slightly, pushing the head into her palm, as her other hand found his belly again, as though to stay him.

She drew in a breath. "Soft," she whispered. Her hand closed slowly around the tip, her thumb smoothing across the skin as she opened her eyes. They grew wide, then wider still.

He clenched his jaw, willing his body to submit.

He felt her retreat and groaned a complaint. "Lilly, you cannot possibly understand how difficult this is for me as well. I am not familiar with allowing this sort of perusal. I wasn't aware how much of a trial it would be to tolerate your simple touch."

She drew her hands away. "I beg pardon, milord, I—"

"No, you misunderstand. This is not an unbearable discomfiture, it is merely different from my customary role in the bedchamber." Her sweet mouth was so close to his cock that he had to look away to staunch his desire to plunder. "You cannot understand what I feel just yet, as you are still too much an innocent." He paused, then added, "But you will."

He pulled her up from the seat and drew her close. His head lowered and their breath mingled as he studied her through his lashes, making sure she was with him, and not back in that forest. His hands moved down her arms, tracing along the backs, all the way to her hands—energy coursing between them. He took her hands and drew them around his waist, leaving them to rest on his backside before continuing his gentle perusal of her mouth and body.

She held her mouth open and he knew she was unsure what to do, so he danced around her lips with his tongue, exploring, teaching, and searching her. He showed her how different touches felt, how his tongue on hers could send a chill down her spine. How his lips against hers made them swell eagerly.

She spread her fingers over the hard muscle of his buttocks, the tension swaying and ebbing as he moved with her. His hands roamed lower and he traced the line of her backside, his thumbs finding the twin dimples at the base of her spine through the fabric of her shirt. He caressed, pulled her closer still, all the while keeping her attention on his mouth, her lips, his hips, her hands, vigilantly watching, making sure.

He moved carefully, one hand holding her round bottom in place, the other cautiously circling around her hip, caressing through her skirts. Then his fingers went to work. He loosened every catch, every tie, all the binds that wrapped her, and let it all fall away before she even knew what he had done.

"You would be a very efficient lady's maid."

His eyes found hers, the smile in them bright. "Would you believe that position has been offered to me once before?" She blushed and he caught her chin. "I refused then, but I'll not refuse you. From here on out, I'll never refuse you a thing." His other hand had shifted to the buttons of her shirtwaist, making quick work of them before it met the same fate as her other clothes.

She shivered against him, he naked as the day, she in her chemise and woolen stockings.

He took her waist, his thumb pressing slowly as his fingers rested on her hip, imploring her permission. She was perfectly made. He could feel her points between her curves, each one just where it should be.

He reached between them, and he saw her eyelids flutter. He retreated, caressing circles into her flesh under the fabric as his other hand strayed up her back and into the short locks at her nape. He massaged the back of her head as he held her face, turning her to kiss her cheeks, her jawline, over her forehead, down her neck and beneath her ear. He grazed her ribs, then caressed a pebbled nipple through her chemise.

She gasped and he took advantage, quelling her startle with the soothing sweep of his tongue at her lips. He stroked and calmed her with gentle movements, hypnotizing her with patience, diligence. His hardness stroked her thigh and she shied away, but he pulled her closer, neck to knee, securing her in his embrace. He felt her lean into him, her stiff form melting, melding, sinking, and then he was there.

His hand slid carefully to the vee of her thighs, resting in the curls under her chemise before she could retreat. She sighed, but he held her in place, watching, ever watching. His hand fell lower, and he couldn't help but smile triumphantly against her neck when he found her hot, wet…for him. He shifted to her side and lifted her. Kicking his feet free of his drawers, he moved her to the bed.

He arranged her carefully on the pile of pillows, then turned to his portmanteau for a lambskin cap, letting her watch as he moved purposefully around the room before slowly crawling across the bed toward her. He held her gaze, still watching her eyes, which were drunk with him. He could see it; she was his to do with as he wished. Her countenance bespoke acceptance, agreement, restrained consent.

He smiled to himself as he untied the neck of her chemise and took her hands, placing them on his body to give them something to do besides interfere with his progress. She traced his shoulder, then his chest, smiling when his nipple tightened under her thumb.

She pushed against him as if to test her power and he stopped—capturing her gaze. He waited patiently for her fingers to soften and her eyes to close, then he moved over her, pulling the chemise down. She was perfect and he was suddenly aware that nobody had ever trespassed here. His gaze floated down her ripe breasts with the palest peach nipples. Her belly was taut and untouched by harm and he couldn't resist running his hand across it, raising goose bumps in his wake. Then he looked at the soft silken hair that lay below, guiding him toward her treasure, and his eyes caught on a horror.

He jerked his head away to hide his shocked expression, but she'd noticed his hesitation and rolled to her side beneath him, pulling the chemise safely around her deeply scarred thighs, a sob surprising both of them as her eyes tightened.

He reached out, running his hand the length of her arm, drawing her eyes to his, silently expressing his sincerest apologies. He turned her to her back again and lowered himself over her, sealing her secrets between their bodies as he leaned down and kissed her thoroughly, slowly stoking the fire that had grown suddenly cold. She wrapped her arms around him, and they settled in to explore each other with lips and tongue. Then he leaned back and watched her, waiting until she decided.

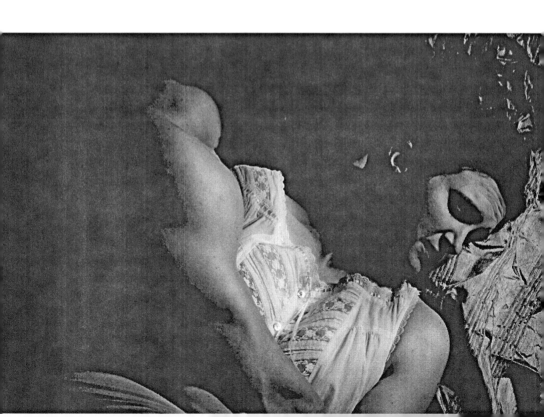

Lilly felt the conflict in him, in the shift of his muscle, and she looked up to examine his face, the strong lines and tense expression. She watched as his muscles twitched then relaxed, his pupils dilating incrementally. The sunlight played across him, brightening his eyes and outlining the green of his irises. She could almost see herself reflected in the deep centers. She moved closer, bringing her mouth up to his, gently kissing him.

Part of her wanted to stop. Perhaps to wait, try some other time. But she had already come so far. She thought if she quit now, she would never gather the courage to make it to this point again, and he...he would never agree.

He was patient, letting her explore and taste him. Her tiny soft kisses traveled his mouth, then up to his eyes, brushing lightly over his wet eyelashes. He returned the favor by fluttering light kisses over every scar on her face, treating each one with reverence and care.

She shifted beneath him and felt his hands tighten, his pulse quicken beneath her palms as she pulled him tight against her, pushing her hips against his aroused strength.

He gave himself over to her. He was not practiced in the art of submission; in fact, he preferred the dominant role at all times. He only now realized how difficult the submissive bent could be, particularly for someone like him. He breathed slowly, forcing his nerves to settle, commanding himself to give in.          She lifted up, kissing his chest and neck. His hands clenched tightly on her hips as he concentrated on the feel of her mouth on him. His hands went around her, pulling her close as she twisted and tried to pull away. But though part of her seemed to refuse, her legs spread beneath him, cradling him, and he pulled the chemise from between them, the heat of their bodies melding. He kissed her face, around her jaw, and he studied her again, watching to make sure she was still present in the moment.

She shifted against his manhood, which pulsed against her thigh. She gasped into his mouth as he descended again. He reached down and lifted first one leg then the other, bending them at the knee to adjust the tilt of her pelvis. She wrapped her legs around his strong thighs, her feet resting behind his knees as he moved toward her. He rose slightly on his elbows, looking into her eyes.

"Lilly, I—" He had no idea the kind of pain this might cause her. No, she wasn't a virgin, but by the looks of those scars it was entirely possible there was further damage where he was to tread. He felt the tremors course her body. "I— I am just as frightened as you."

She saw the moisture at the crease of his eye, realized the truth of what she had asked of him, then nodded. He advanced slowly, achingly slow. Imploring her to hold his gaze. Her eyes flared as he entered. There were long scars even here against his smooth skin and he cringed, sinking as far as her body would allow. He rested, unmoving as he searched her eyes. She lifted her hips slightly and he groaned at the feel of her warmth surrounding him, urging him on.

His hips pulsed once, and he reached between them and slowly, methodically began a cadence that would march them both to the same finale. The hot buttered cinnamon of her irises lightened, becoming more melted butterscotch, her pupils dilating as he watched her and she him. Her breath quickened and he put his mouth against her neck, feeling her heartbeat racing beneath the skin he kissed.


She pulled his head up, tangling her fingers in his hair as she searched the green glowing depths of his eyes, growing deeper, more hypnotic, more demanding, more desperate. She started to panic as she felt her heart increase its rhythm and his movement mirrored it. Threads of electricity coursed along her skin, rushing to her center, carrying with them all of her hopes, her fears, her dreams, her nightmares. She felt her body react to his, the increasing power like riding a horse at full speed; the pulse increasing, the muscles stretching and tightening. Her hands fisted in his hair.

She was a flower blooming at sunrise and closing for the day as the sun set, but her sun kept rising and setting. Faster and faster her world spun, the flower opening and closing its petals until finally it was a blur and she screamed, pushing her hands, and him, away from her.

He rose above her, taut like a hunter's bow as he pressed into her hard, his seed captured by a lambskin cap before entering her womb. His body jerked and he lay over her, their limbs tangled together, sated passion thick between them.

He loosed her hands from his hair, then massaged the red marks on her palms that her tension had made with slow, careful circles. She moved her fingers, releasing the cramps as he worked them, and drifted off to sleep without a word.

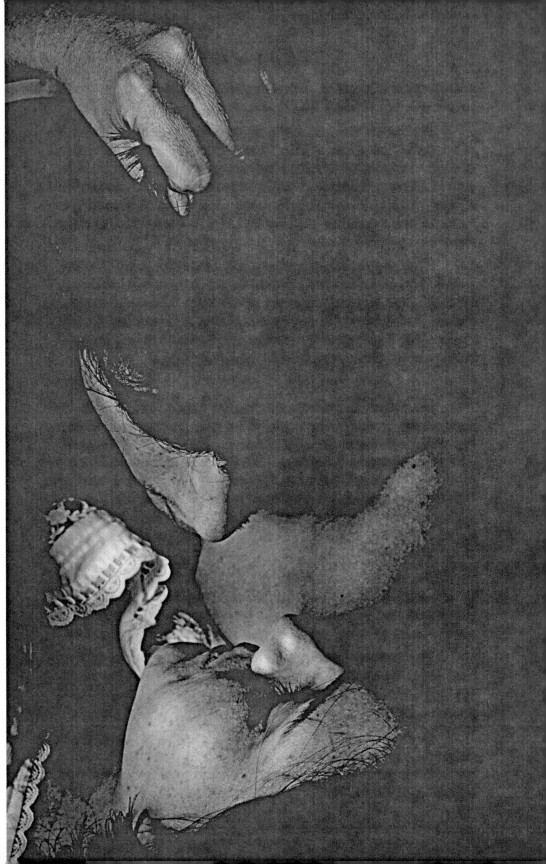

Perry awoke as the train slowed and took a bend, bringing the sun into full view from the window. The light invaded the train car and his dreams, preventing any further peace he hoped to claim. He unfolded his cramped muscles from the tangle of limbs around him. A delicate sigh broke the shuffle, and he stilled, realizing his current state of entanglement wasn't his usual sort.

Lilly slept peacefully. Her hair caught the sun, highlighting streaks of red and even deep brown. He had not noticed the strands before, as she kept them carefully tucked beneath a mobcap for working. He knew they'd had a great chore of getting the tangles out when her physical state was in such a desperate condition. But now her hair shone in an arresting shade of deepest auburn. She stirred as he stretched, arching her back like a cat beneath him, pressing her body into his ready form, then pausing as her very skin began to tremble.

Perry wasn't sure how to proceed. The last thing he wanted was to startle her. His hand covered her eyes to keep them closed, his mouth traveling softly from her shoulder to her neck. "You remember me, Lilly, you remember my gentle touch—I am so very gentle. Do not look, do not think. Just feel."

She breathed deeply, arching further, testing her surroundings while her eyelashes fluttered beneath his palm in acquiescence. He tilted her mouth toward his so he could capture her lips.

"Milord," she whispered against his mouth.

He stilled and lifted his heavy frame from her, the sudden rush of cool air between their bodies sending a shiver through her. Her hands clutched at his shoulders.

"No, milord, I—"

He cut her off with his thumb pressed across her mouth. "In this arena you really must use my name, or you may effect a change you are not entirely willing to succumb to, my sweet."

"I— I do not understand."

"Lilly, if I am your lord then I am also your master and will act as such. Is that what you wish?"

She breathed heavily, her breasts brushing against him in rhythm. She lifted her hands to his face. "Perry," she whispered, the sound no more than a breath. He smiled, then turned his head slightly and placed a kiss in her palm.

"Lilly, my sweet, the rules of our engagement have not changed a bit. You are in control, and at any moment you may bring this engagement to an end."

She smiled and drew his lips to hers, opening her mouth beneath his. He submitted to her, parting his lips and allowing her the innocent access she desired, letting her play, touch, feel, and taste of him. He allowed her to move as she would, to discover what she wanted. He was finding his submission rather the headiest brew of lust he'd ever managed to encounter.

She pushed against his chest until he was forced to roll to his back. She followed quickly, drawing herself along his side and propping her head on her hand. She moved her other hand to his eyes, gently pressing the lids closed, compelling him to keep them that way. He tensed, his flesh tingling with anticipation as the sheet drifted away.

She traced his jaw, the scruff of his beard scratching at her fingertips as her hand traveled. Her thumb drew along his mouth and it parted for her, allowing her access, willing her intrusion, begging to be satisfied, but the thumb disappeared along with her hand.

His eyelids fluttered with impatience, but he stayed them to her will. His jaw clenched against a hiss of a breath as her hand reappeared, this time gently tracing one of his wide nipples. His hands contracted like claws at his sides as she traced each ridge below his chest, counting his sturdy ribs, palming each band of hard muscle, stroking the soft valleys between the ridges before her eyes moved on.

He guessed where her gaze fell next, and he hardened impossibly as he groaned, a low guttural sound that resonated from deep within his cavernous chest, vibrating between their naked bodies and charging the nerves below her skin. His muscles tensed, and she felt the length of his body tighten against the softness of hers.

She drew in a deep breath to steady her rioting nerves and reached out. The first touch was a mere two fingers, sweeping down the upturned ridge of his manhood. The caress so delicate, so gentle, that it drew a deep but startled cry from him.

He lifted his head but clenched his eyes to remain in submission. She rested her palm across him fully, looking up to gauge his reaction. She moved slowly, watching the minute changes in his face, the sweeping and ebbing of tension across his visage. She increased the pressure, and the undulation of his muscles carried to his neck, then the rest of his body.

He was suddenly terrified of embarrassing himself, and he lifted one hand, wrapping it around her wrist and drawing her arm away. "If you continue on this tack, you will find little satisfaction for yourself, my sweet, and you may want to consider that," he said breathlessly, hoping she understood his meaning.

"Mil— Perry, I believe where I might find my satisfaction and where you believe I may find my satisfaction to be two entirely different things," she said brazenly.

He opened his eyes—the sparkle in them could not be captured, even by his thick lashes—and she grinned before chastening him. "Oh no, Perry, I'm quite far from finished," she said, holding his gaze.

He laid his head back and closed his eyes, releasing her wrist. He realized her speech and intonation mocked his status, and he marveled at her cunning. She didn't seem the same missish innocent he'd convinced to bed last night. Her hand returned to him, wrapping deftly around the silk-encased hardness. His body shifted under her ministrations, and he ground his teeth, pushing his head back into the pillow, his body drawn tight.

She lifted to her knees beside him and he tensed further. Stroking gently with one hand, the other slowly reached down, surrounding the rest of him in her hot grasp. His body bucked at the sudden sensation, and he wrapped his hands tightly in the sheets at his sides. Her rhythm steadied upon him, and he felt as if he would cease to exist.

His hips caught her rhythm and she glanced back to his face, seeing confusion and pain. She stopped instantly, shocked, and pulled her hands away as he opened his eyes to her.

He waited, his entire body thrumming with the built up passion she'd demanded from him. "Lilly, my God. What—"

She shook her head. "Did I… Did I hurt you?"

"No. God, no. Sweet Lilly, there is no pain here," he said, trying to calm his frustrated body. He took her hand and placed a kiss in her palm, then glanced around the berth and stood. He walked over to a cheval mirror that was attached to the wall with a silk cord and placed it at the end of the bed, turning it toward her. Then he returned. He moved her as she fought him instinctively, urging her on her knees to face the mirror. She grasped the sheets and pulled them around her.

"No, Lilly, you are going to look on yourself, and me. You are going to learn what passion looks like. You are going to recognize this in me, and in yourself." His voice was like the flames of a fire. The sound licked at her senses, heated her skin, forced the breath from her lungs.

"Yes, milord," she said quietly.

He growled at her and kneeled at the foot of the bed in front of her. His hands burned into the skin of her thighs, flaring her senses as he smoothed them up toward her hips, and she fought to keep still. He saw her closed eyes and tightened his grip tenderly. "Look," he breathed.

She opened her eyes. His large hands wrapped about her thighs, squeezing gently, moving softly on her. Her jaw dropped and her eyes fell shut again.

"Look," he said with greater intensity. He felt a shudder course her body then her lids flickered open. Her head fell back slightly and her gaze traveled to the thick dark hair reflected before her. He pulled her forward at the end of the bed and unfolded her legs, placing them over his broad shoulders as he bowed his head to her.

She cried out, her hands flying out to steady herself. He looked up at her again. "Watch," he commanded.

She did. She watched as he bowed his head and she felt his warm, wet tongue lick and explore. Her breath fled and her lungs heaved, trying to catch air. She saw her skin flush, her breasts lift, the nipples tightly ruching. Her face contorted, and she watched the fleeting expressions change; she saw what she had seen in him, And she realized these were all the faces of passion. His tongue dipped and she cried out again, gasping a breath as one of her hands flew to tangle in his hair.

Her body tensed, her legs fell open, her knees drew up, her toes curled against his shoulders, and her fingers bunched. She felt the tension grow then pulse, and she screamed. He stood before her swiftly and pushed into her, and in two thorough strokes she broke, writhing on the bed beneath him while he held her close.

Perry caressed her dewed skin, drawing a flush across her body, willing it to his command. He moved her back to the kneeling position and went to the basin, replacing the cap he'd used to prevent her becoming with child. He mounted the bed behind her on his knees. Sliding her onto his lap, he entered her once again—this time from behind—and she cried out.

"Watch," he reminded her, and her head fell back to his sturdy shoulder, her eyes open, staring into the mirror. His arms wrapped about her, one hand going to the soft mound at the crux of her hips, the other claiming one of her pale breasts, teasing it to fullness. He found in this position he was required to hold on tighter to her, against the sway and the speed of the train. He trailed kisses down the side of her neck, breathing heavily at her jaw.

She felt his pace, matched to the chug of the train on the track, and followed him fitfully toward the shining release she knew awaited her. He lifted his gaze as he slowed their pace, his eyes catching hers in the glass.

His hands caressed and held, and he bade her follow them, trailing down to her knees, then back to her thighs, to her hips, then to where he gently rubbed her soft, untouched, stomach. His hands sinking lower with each stroke.

"Watch," he said again. He spread her knees further apart so she could easily see his intimate stroke, the caress of his cadence.

She was mesmerized, overtaken by the sight of him entering and retreating, the sound of their heavy mingling breaths, the feel of his strength so close to her, surrounding her, penetrating her, carrying her, pushing her, pulling her, drawing her toward a second higher peak. Her lids fell again.

"Watch!" he commanded. His jaw clenched, and she saw the fear and the pain flash across his face and it drove her to the edge, forced her over. She collapsed and he caught her, their eyes holding as her pulsing sheath drew him along.

The second his release came she saw his face change; his jaw released and his eyes drifted closed, his hands clenched and lifted from the bed, taking her with him, pulling her onto him and fusing them together, the sway of the train lulling their passion.

# THIRTY-NINE

A loud knock sounded at the door, and Perry swept the blankets over Lilly as he sat up in the bed. "Come."

"Milord, the tray you requested," the porter said as he entered. Perry waved him toward the table and he moved quickly, bowing before he left. Perry pulled his drawers on, then walked over to fill a plate with fruits, cheeses, and crusty breads. He brought it back to the bed, pulling the blankets down to find Lilly wide-eyed but still in her little cocoon. He smiled.

"Lilly, my sweet, you should eat. We will be reaching Manchester soon, where we will be allowed a short foray into town." She shifted, wiggling her way up to sit. She rested against the pillows and looked at him patiently. "How are you?"

She smiled serenely, and he noted it wasn't quite the smile he was familiar with seeing on a partner after a full day of such passion. She still appeared wary and overwrought, not quite as sated as he was known to leave women. It brought him a sense of incompletion, almost incompetence, which unseated the masculine feeling of victory that traditionally elated his mood after a tryst.

He lifted a strawberry to her mouth and watched as her lips parted. When she took it in, his stomach tensed. In the entirety of his life he'd never felt so affected by a woman. He now realized the piece that had always been missing from his liaisons was the need to protect. Never had he wanted to protect a woman, to safeguard not only her body, but her mind.

He followed the strawberry with a scone and some clotted cream. She followed that with moans and sighs.

An hour later they were dressed and descending to the platform, Lilly clutching his greatcoat as she had when they'd first arrived at that inn. He decided what she really needed was a good dose of confidence, though retaining a healthy bit of that wariness would go far for her self-preservation. Somewhere between caution and self-assurance was the precarious position that would keep her from again being targeted as someone's victim.

He unlatched her from the folds of his greatcoat and pulled her to his side, placing her hand on his arm and drawing her spine straight and tall next to him. She tensed, and he moved his other hand to cover hers, willing the security he provided to pacify her nerves. He saw her features relax incrementally, and as they walked through the station, she glanced around with a quick grin.

"What do you intend to do in London?" he asked as their next train lurched forward.

"Whatever you wish, milord," she replied quietly from the seat across from him.

"I realize that you feel you have no choice but to do as I wish, but I would hope you understand that our relationship has much changed since I informed you of your status in my household as a servant."

"Yes, milord, but there's no chance of anythin' between us, even were I to wish it. I would never find comfort in your world. 'Tis not possible."

"I'm well aware of our current dilemma and the need for privacy. What I want to know is what need you have of me at this point. I don't want to make it seem as though I have ulterior motives in this, and I believe the best way to go about our relationship is to be perfectly honest with one another. As I've said, and will remind you again, you are charged with our present, and our future. I will do nothing you are not comfortable with, I will do nothing you do not want. For however long you wish to be obliged."

She blushed at his speech and attempted to dodge his gaze, but he wouldn't allow her to look away. "Milord, I— I'd appreciate a position within your household. So that I may, uh—" She closed her eyes, then looked into his directly. "So that we may continue. I believe I've much to learn, and I believe, if you're willing, you've much to teach me." She took a deep breath. "I know at some point we must part, and keeping that in mind, being truly careful, you can still help me. I understand your life, and I won't keep you from it. You are a rake. It is your nature, as I understand it, to not settle."

He watched as her hands trembled, twisting in her skirts. "Lilly, for as long as we are together, there will be none other. I would not

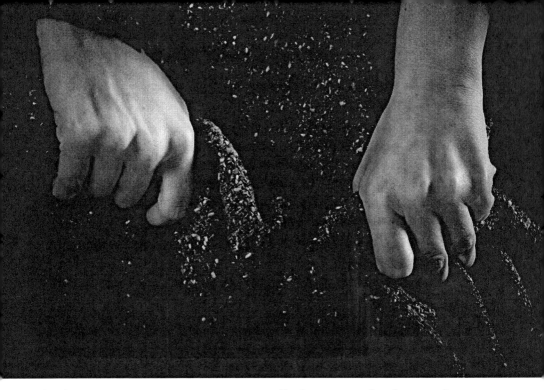

do that to anyone, not even to you. I will of course make the rounds, present myself to the *ton* as is expected of me, but I will not extend any private invitations for as long as you have need of me."

Her eyes grew wide and her mouth dropped into an *O*. Then she looked away, flustered. "I would not ask that of you. I don't want for you to change. There is no need," she whispered.

He reached across to her and stroked her hand, then lifted it and placed a kiss in her palm. She watched his movements carefully as her skin prickled with the awareness of his proximity. She hoped she would be able to remain in his household without the entire staff being made aware of her position. *Positions*, she thought, and pressed a fist to her forehead.

She stood and leaned toward the window, letting the chill of the night sink into her hands through her gloves. She heard him rise, felt him move to her, then closed her eyes on the anticipation of what he intended. His hands came to the window just outside of her own. She felt his tongue rise from the edge of her blouse to the nape of her neck, and she shivered at the long stroke.

His hands left the window and went to her gloves, slowly pulling them off. Tendrils of excitement spread through her fingers as they were swept away. She shook her head and felt him step back, then lost the warmth of her cape when he took it from her shoulders. She was not long bereft, for his warm hands sank through the fabric covering her shoulders, then lower, unbuttoning her blouse and loosening the simple corset.

He pushed her forward, her breasts meeting the glass of the window. She gasped from the chill as he raised her skirts.

"You want the rake?"

"I do not know what I want."

"Tell me what you want."

"I do not know what I want. How can I know what I want?"

"Perhaps some variety will narrow down the choices."

He pulled her back against him. She realized he had released his manhood and now pressed it against her backside.

"Milord."

"I warned you not to call me that."

"Don't stop."

He didn't.

She hadn't exactly planned for this. She thought she would be sad, letting him touch her, letting him *teach* her, and then walking away. But she'd measured the options. It had all happened so fast the night before that there was no real consideration. They drove each other easily to the act, pushing one another as the other pulled back, until ultimately there was no room for retreat.

This morning, as the sun broke and she watched his face come back to a wakeful state, she became aware of her peril. He was devastatingly handsome. She knew she'd thought so before, but the realization hit her like waves upon the beach. It would drift away, then come crashing down on her suddenly, without warning, stealing her very breath.

Even if she were to fall in love with this man, even if she were to lose herself in those eyes, she knew beyond doubt that being *with* him was impossible. She promised herself she would be happy to learn from him. To let him teach her what she wanted to know; to help her overcome the fears that plagued her, to feel anything again without pain, to not be afraid. She promised this, but feared that it was merely a delay of the inevitable.

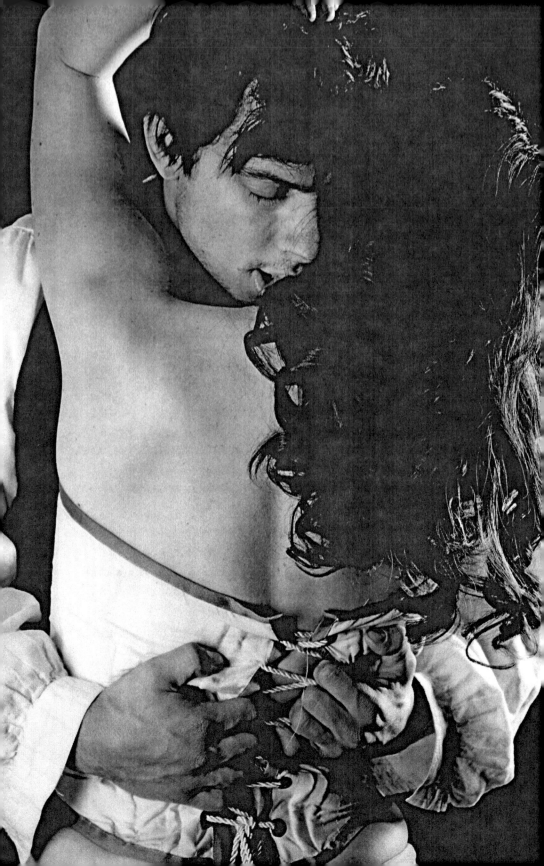

# FORTY

erry breezed into his town house on Grosvenor that afternoon, throwing his hat and gloves to Harper who held the door wide for his arrival.

"I've added to the staff," Perry said as he glanced around. "Uh, I thought she would have been behind me, but—" He walked back toward the door and looked out, then up and down the street. "Kerrigan," he called back to his man, who was halfway upstairs with a trunk.

"Yes, milord?"

"Where's Miss Lilly?"

"Not sure I know, milord. I thought as she was behind us."

Perry ran down the front steps, looking for the small figure he had become so well accustomed to having around. He stuck his head inside the landau and found her, still quietly sitting in the corner. "Lilly! You had me worried. What are you still doing here?" He reached across the carriage for her hand.

"Not sure as I know, milord, I was just waiting. I— I do not know how to do this. I simply do not." She shook her head.

"Sweet Lilly, I would like for you to be a guest for a few days, until you get your bearings. If this is difficult or too awkward after that, I will escort you to His Grace's town house to join his staff."

She took his hand and allowed him to lower her to the ground, placing her hand on his sleeve.

The look he received from Harper was enough to shake his composure. "Harper, a change of plans. This is Miss Lilly. She will be a guest here for a few days. After that we will determine where she belongs, be that here or at His Grace's."

Harper sized up the girl, and Perry.

"A guest, Harper," Perry said sardonically.

"Pardon, milord," he said with a lift of his brow. "Miss Lilly," he said, bowing before her. He looked back to Perry. "The blue room, milord?"

Perry cleared his throat. He knew he wasn't to be held accountable by his servants, but he felt guilty nonetheless. Everything about this girl had him off-kilter. "Yes, Harper the blue room, thank you. I will…see her up. Perhaps you could have Cook prepare a tray?"

Harper nodded and turned for the kitchens.

"Lilly," Perry said as he opened the receiving door at her suite, "you are welcome to stay here for as long as necessary." He stepped through the small entry and opened the second door. "There are a few things you should be aware of. First, you may have use of a maid if you would like, or not. Either way, if you have need of anything here you are to use the pull. Please do not try to accomplish everything on your own, as much as you would like to. Second," he said as he strode past the large four poster bed toward the far wall, motioning for her to follow him, "the bathing room is just here, behind this door." He waited until she reached the door, then continued. "The door at the other end of the bathroom reaches my bedchamber—directly."

Her jaw fell open. Deafening silence ensued.

"Sweet, if you would prefer—" She shook her head, cutting him off. He cleared his throat. "Is there—is there something else?"

"No, milord, just, I…well. This room you've seen to give me, 'tis for your wife," she whispered reverently.

"Yes, sweet, but as I have no wife, currently the room is for whomever I choose. As well, if you were to be in a guest chamber, I would not hear should you have any night terrors."

"Your household?"

"My household is quite familiar with my odd choices in manner. My household will think and do as I ask of them."

She felt a shiver traverse her shoulders as he approached her slowly.

"Have no fear, my sweet. Whatever happens here remains between us. Even as it pertains to my staff." He reached out and held her elbow, gently stroking her arm with his thumb.

Her breath caught and she looked up at him. He felt her muscles tense. This was different, though. This wasn't her usual reaction to being touched. This was not a knee-jerk reaction, but something else. She blinked, then returned to her steady regard of his face.

He saw the astonishment cross her features, then realized where it came from. He had touched her, and she hadn't jumped away, pulled back, flinched, or injured him. Not even a little, not in the least.

A bright smile broke her expression and she threw her arms around his neck, pulling his mouth to hers.

His eyes flew wide but he acquiesced quickly, drawing her up to him, lifting her feet from the floor as he straightened.

Lips locked in shared smiles, her hands tangled in his hair while his fingers spread at her back, holding her close. Their kiss broke, and he leaned his forehead against hers. "I would venture to say that was a step in the right direction."

She nodded against his forehead, her eyes sparkling. Then she looked down at her feet, suspended above the ground. He laughed and lowered her slowly, then released her completely when they heard the knock at her door. He followed her back into the bedchamber and motioned Harper toward the table before the fire. She removed her cape, carrying it to the wardrobe.

"Milord, will there be anything else this evening?" Harper asked.

"Has Louisa seen to the bath?" he asked.

"Yes my lord."

"Then nothing further, Harper. The household is free to retire."

Harper bowed and closed the door behind him as he backed out.

Perry took her hand and pulled her over to the dinner tray. "Sit, eat, please. I need to go blow the dust off from the journey." He turned back when he heard water rushing to the tub in the bathing room. "I will take my bath while you have your fill, then you can do the same."

She smiled up at him and he placed a kiss in her palm, then left her to her supper.

Perry sank into the water, allowing the heat to soothe his muscles and his will. He leaned his head back and let it seep slowly to his bones. "Lilly," he whispered as he closed his eyes. He breathed slowly, the scent

of the herbs in the water pacifying him. Louisa always prepared the most comforting and soothing of baths. He drifted off for a while, only awakening when his senses picked up a sweeter note in the air. His lids lifted and he found Lilly crouching next to the tub, her gaze moving across his form appreciatively. His heartbeat picked up and he shifted, causing a ripple to collide with the side of the tub.

She wasn't sure exactly when he awakened, but she was sure when he became aware of her presence. That particular part of him that announced his masculinity pulsed, straightened, shifted, and grew before her eyes.

His hand grasped her wrist and pulled her across him, obliging her to lift from the floor and lean far over the maw of the heavy clawfoot tub.

Her eyes widened with the force of his intent as his other hand wrapped around her hip, pressing her until she slipped into the water.

Her arms landed on his shoulders as she held her face out of the splashing water. It launched over the rim, flooding the room.

His hands searched through her sodden clothes, finding the roundness of her buttocks then kneading through the layers of fabric.

She looked down upon his face as his eyes lifted to hers. She watched, mesmerized, as his tongue swept his lower lip, then the upper. Her skin tingled as his gaze roved across her, her nipples tightening. She felt a shiver grow from her belly and spread in a circular pattern, her breath increasing exponentially. She was lightheaded, dizzy.

His smile became territorial in nature and he lifted up, capturing her mouth in a possessive kiss. Her hands slipped across his chest, sinking into the water around him, their bodies compressed. Her legs straddled his flanks and she held fast to his shoulders. With his hands on the sides of the tub, he pushed up with her wrapped tightly around his torso. Then his hands grasped her buttocks, shifting her weight on his frame as he bruised her mouth with his heavy kisses. She held tighter. Water poured from their joined figures, refilling the tub and spilling over to the floor.

He swept his hands down her thighs, urging her to stand before him. Without breaking their kiss, he worked his fingers on her ties, ribbons, buttons, and sashes until her saturated clothing fell away with a heavy slap on the side of the tub. His hands moved back to her hips, pulling her body tight against his.

She cried out and her hands fisted in his hair, pulling and holding him to her.

They shared breath, they shared cries, and they shared words within their joined lips.

Once again he lifted her to him, wrapping her legs around his long thighs as he stepped carefully from the tub, checking his footing on the tile to keep from slipping. He moved to her door then across the rug, finally laying her on the velvet and satin counterpane beneath him. He slid her body across the slick and soft fabric, pulling sighs from deep within.

He smiled against her, the sounds sinking to his very soul. He reached for pillows, stacking them and rolling her over them onto her stomach, then set to worshiping her. He ran his hands up her body, soothing and holding. He shifted his hands around her torso, finding her succulent breasts and teasing them to fullness. His arousal rode against her thigh, against the scars left behind. She tensed, and he paused, breathing heavily by her ear.

"Sweet Lilly," he panted, his breath coursing over her cheek. He moved back slowly, pulling the length of his body alongside her, watching her face.

Her eyes were wide in the dim light, her mouth open to him, taking in as much air as possible. His hand rested gently on her back, smoothing circles into her flesh.

"Sweet Lilly, tell me."

She moved before he could catch her, pushing him flat on his back and straddling him, high on her knees. She clenched her eyes, impaling herself on him as he writhed, slow to comprehend her movements, shocked to catch up to her will. She sank, her head falling back as she cried out.

He grasped her hips, pushing her down and back, burying himself to the hilt in her sweetness. She moved her hands to his chest and, leaning heavily, she raised up, then pushed down again, picking up the rhythm he set. She looked into his face. The shock, the worry, and the unmistakable rise of passion fought to overtake him.

Her nails dug in as her body started to tremble. Her response forced away his shock, and he took control of her movements until he drove her straight to the finale she yearned for. She screamed and tightened around him, drawing him deeper. He thrust and joined her pleasure with his as she collapsed on his chest.

Perry had no idea how long they lay joined, his mind turning and twisting violently. He drifted in and out of sleep, always aware of her relaxed breathing. Her hands, her arms, all the way down to her toes, she relaxed. Slumbered.

He allowed himself to drift, cradling her body against his.

When he felt her shift, he moved with her, helping her unfold and stretch out next to him. He smoothed her hair back from her face, then slid from the bed and lifted her. He pulled the counterpane down and snuggled her beneath it before easing in to warm her.

"How are you?" he asked quietly.

"I am, I…am," she repeated after a thought.

"I won't be here when you wake."

She frowned. "You'll stay here, for now?"

"Rest. Tomorrow— Well, later today there is more to learn."

She giggled, and he could see a blush color her cheeks. "You think I've more to learn?"

"Oh yes, my sweet, much more."

She sighed and wiggled into his strong frame, pulling a deep growl from his chest. "Lay still, or there will be no rest for us anytime soon."

She did and he wrapped her up in his arms, holding her close.


As expected, she woke the next day alone. Even knowing she would be, she was still disappointed. She prepared for the day slowly, enjoying her solitude. She dressed in her best dress, still heavy and drab, and went below stairs to find the household's dining room. She assumed it would be off the kitchen, so she followed her nose. As she rounded a corner she bumped into a footman carrying a tray of eggs.

"Miss, what are ye about?" he asked brusquely.

"I was only looking for the dining hall to break my fast. Is it near the kitchens?"

"You may follow me to the breakfast room. 'Tis on the ground floor, at the back of the town house, not below stairs."

"No, I beg pardon, I'm looking for the household's dining room, not the formal dining room," she said as she followed.

He stopped halfway up the stairs and turned back on her, stopping her suddenly. "You are a guest, miss, therefore you'll dine in the formal room above stairs, not below stairs with the likes of us."

She frowned. "I don't want to, I wish to be a member of the household."

"Apparently, miss, what you want and what milord wants are two separate facts. Unfortunate as 'tis for you, in this house Lord Trumbull has his say." He turned and proceeded to the breakfast room.

She sighed and followed. Being set apart from the household wasn't going to garner her any consideration from his staff. It was going to set her away from them, and she would never belong then. She shook her head and followed him in.

Perry stood when he realized the small figure behind the footman wasn't yet another of his staff, but Lilly. "What, pray tell, are you doing entering from the servants' passage?"

She shook her head and he saw the sadness in her eyes, then motioned her to a chair next to him.

"They'll never accept me here. As well they shouldn't, if I'm to be set apart. They'll never see me as one of them."

Perry studied her severe expression. There was no way around that fact. "Sweet Lilly, you will take a position in another household when you are no longer my guest. Until then, please act as my guest. You must have attended enough to know what their place is. There's no need to make my household more uncomfortable with your position here in my town house, but I will speak with them. There's no fighting me on this. You're my guest for now, and you're to behave as my guest. I thought that understood."

She looked as if she was about to cry, and his heart wrenched in his chest. He took a deep breath. "To that end, and no doubt to your own mortification, I have requested a seamstress to come today to aid with your wardrobe."

Her eyes went wide and her spine straightened. She shook her head again. He patently ignored her reaction, though taking note of it. "I understand, Lilly, but as you have so clearly pointed out already, you are no longer one of the underservants. You are my guest, you do not fit in, there's no reason for you to dress as a servant. You will accept a wardrobe from me, as well as some tutoring. Perhaps you would make a lady's maid someday."

"I did not expect this of you and I cannot accept it, milord. There's no need to dress me. My wardrobe is perfectly acceptable for who I am. I do not want to change. I asked for your help in one area, nothing more."

Perry glanced at the footmen, who were obviously faking their unaware countenances, something they often did in his house. "Lilly, you asked for my help, which I have given and will continue to give," he said under his breath. "But where my help ends isn't up to you, but me, and to be seen with me anywhere in London, you cannot be attired in such a fashion. I have a reputation, and I would prefer it remain intact. Everyone is buzzing of my charges, so they will merely assume you are one of them. Which is perfectly acceptable as far as I am concerned. When my charges are finally presented to the ton, none will be the wiser."

Lilly glanced around the room at the faces she was familiar

with for their station, if not their family. She'd put herself on this path and would not be able to return to the quiet life she'd become so well accustomed to. She lifted her hand to her face, tracing the faint scars on one cheek. She felt as though she didn't belong anywhere anymore. Her hand shook, and a single tear escaped her, running to the tip of her finger.

She looked up to Perry's concerned face, then stood, forcing him by courtesy to stand next to her. "I do not like what has been done to me." Her jaw dropped, shocked at her own admission. It seemed obvious, but she had never voiced it before; she had always been accepting of her status and position in the world. Her injuries. She was one to be used.

She stared at Perry. "This is not my position, this is not my choice. Simply because I was born to serve does not mean that anyone can choose to use me, to push me 'round. I'm angry!" she yelled.

"I understand," he whispered. "I don't wish to force you into anything, and yet—"

"And yet you have!"

His head dropped penitently.

"The hand of God points to this one and that one, touches them, blesses them with status and money. Then shuns the others, those not worthy. How is the man who did this to me worthy of the hand of God? How is he to be held in a position of authority, one to be cowered from, respected? How does God choose one and not the other?

"I do not wish to punish you for something that was not your doing, milord. But I do ask you to be more aware of my wishes. If I am truly a guest, you will make requests of me, not demands. I do have something to say, but nobody seems to listen." She paused, and was immediately contrite. "If it pleases you." She looked to the footmen, who had not moved the least, not even flinched. She knew what was to happen next, and knew that rumors of this scene would spread like wildfire through the town house, then beyond. She glanced at Perry, expecting to see the anger she so richly deserved. She sank to the chair and steeled herself for what would come.

He watched when she looked at the footmen as if they were suddenly the enemy. "As it happens, it does please me, Lilly, and I must beg your forgiveness, for we all know I am accustomed to women who are readily accepting of my charms and my sponsorship. You are welcome to refuse me and I suppose I haven't behaved in a manner that would presuppose that. No doubt I've crossed a line, and no doubt I will do so again. I will endeavor, however, to ask your opinion and permission in the future."

She nodded nervously. He followed his apology with a wave to the footmen, who finally moved forward to bring the trays of food to them. "Lilly, my household is very well compensated, so you never need fear rumors. Gossipmongers are not welcome here, and the pay is outrageous enough to keep every one of my men quiet." He observed her from the corner of his eye, wondering at her disposition as he thought back to his brother's betrothed, Francine.

"I had a notion," he said carefully, "that you might be in need of a few dresses suitable for London." Her eyes narrowed on him. "Might I send for a dressmaker to accommodate you?" He took a bite and suppressed a grin.

"Well, milord, when you put it that way, I simply cannot refuse. I would be happy to be…accommodated," she said in her best haughty accent.

He could see she was biting back a smile and his broadened in response. *I could get used to this.* He finished breakfast and stood, motioning to her to stay. "I have to be on with my work. Please take your time. I believe the seamstress will be here within the hour, and Harper will set you up in the parlor. If you have need of anything, do not hesitate to ask me." He smiled down at her until she met his eye. "Do not hesitate," he repeated.

She watched him move to the door. It was the first time she had been able to inspect his stride. He moved swiftly with economy of motion, no doubts in his movement, in his carriage or his direction. He was powerfully compelling, and she could easily see what made him so successful. Well, this and a few other things.

# FORTY-ONE

Hepplewort trudged across the entry of his manor.

"Fergus!" rang the shrill voice from the front parlor. It rankled his hide like nails on a blackboard. His head sank between his shoulders and he turned away, skittering in the opposite direction, but the sharp pain in his ear stopped him in his tracks. He emitted a girlish squeal.

"Fergus!" his mother shouted again, this time at his shoulder, "what is the meaning of this? I know you heard my summons."

He felt the spittle hit the back of his neck as she pinched harder. "Mother..." he whined.

"Oh, do shut up, Fergus. You are such a ninny. It gets my hackles up. Come to the parlor, we must discuss your issue."

"I've no issue to discuss, Mother."

"Precisely what we are to discuss," she said as she turned and walked toward the front parlor without releasing his ear.

He followed, tripping on the hem of his robe as he tried to keep up with her whilst being dragged sideways across the foyer. She was surprisingly strong for a wrinkly sack of bones. She crossed the threshold and released him to the satin chaise, confident he was too lazy to run once seated.

"If you bear no issue, the earldom will secede from the Hepplewort lineage. Unacceptable. Absolutely. I will not see our wayward cousins take what is rightfully mine," she said bitingly.

Hepplewort grunted. His last foray into marriage wasn't much to convince him, as he was still recovering from his run in with the Viscount and Duke of Roxleigh. He tested his broken nose as he thought of them, wincing.

"Fergus! Your thoughts betray you, you slovenly coward! I've no understanding how I bore such a beast as you."

"Mother, I will find a bride, I will bear issue." He said it quietly, unconvincingly.

"Who, Fergus? Who will bear your children? You must find an acceptable bride worthy of carrying my grandchild!"

"Yes, Mother." He quieted, allowing her rant. He knew argument was of no use, so he would sit and take her tirade, then return to his ways. He no longer cared to continue his line. Truth be told, he'd never cared in the first place. His only interest was the fresh chits he met on the journey. A string of drool escaped his liver-spotted maw, landing on his collar.

"Fergus!" she yelled.

"Yes, Mother," he replied, smiling to himself as he thought of his next conquest.

"You depart for London this day. Those horrible men are away to Roxleighshire. This could be your only chance to find a bride."

He looked at her. "Yes, Mother."

Hepplewort dressed and departed with minimal arrangements. His mother was correct. Attending a few balls and taking a wife would be simple. His carriage was loaded, his men waited, and as soon as he mounted the brougham the party was underway.


Lilly returned to her room, determined to enjoy the viscount's attentions. Why shouldn't she? She'd never had a thought beyond serving, beyond rising above her station. There were those in her village who aspired to greater things, but she'd been happy to merely exist, and was doing just that until she met the beast who had derailed her future. She'd wanted no more from life than to find a position, marry a good man, bear him children, and raise them to be as happy as she had been. Kelso was a small town, but it was her life and she'd expected to be there forever.

She certainly wasn't there now. Far from it. London wasn't merely a physical distance from Kelso, but as far removed from her country life as one could be. Her track had changed, but she was determined to follow wherever it would lead.

She walked to the bathing room to prepare for her visit from the modiste. She'd always made her own clothing, or remade it from clothes given her. She'd never been fitted, though she had once attended a fitting. She didn't look forward to the experience, but her nightly endeavors with Perry were proving to make her more tolerant of attention.

She prepared her bath, adding a sprinkling of the herbs and oils sitting on the shelf near the tub. She smiled as the hearty, spicy scents wafted up, remembering whose figure this bath generally cleansed and soothed. Then she blushed, remembering their attempt at bathing the night before.

She stomped her foot to cease her mind's wanderings. She wasn't allowed to dwell on him, she couldn't permit herself to consider him the way her body wanted her to. She'd asked him to tutor her, and that was all she could take from him. There was nothing more he would be allowed to give. She smiled; as long as he would allow, she would accept everything he gave. Then she would move on, return home, or find a new village where nobody knew of her and she could begin her prescribed life.

She sank into the heated water, breathing the scent of him, but something was most definitely missing. She realized the body that absorbed these herbs must change them subtly. His scent—he—was more…something. She breathed deeply and tried to place the missing hue. She caught it on a soft breeze: salt, exertion, strength—that's what was missing. She opened her eyes and bolted upright as she glanced at the door to her room. It was closed. A shiver chased her spine, and she turned slowly.

"Hello," he said quietly from the opposite door.

She gasped and closed her eyes, willing the shudder to ease.

He shook his head. "We've still a ways to go, I suppose. I beg your pardon, I did not mean to startle you."

She shook her head. "No, I— I believe any woman intimate with the knowledge of you would have suffered that shiver," she said, looking up to his smoldering green eyes.

A smile grazed his features with understanding as he removed his jacket, rolled his sleeves, and sank to his knees next to the bath. He picked up a cloth and soaked it, then smoothed it with soap. "I apologize for not having a more feminine banquet of scents for you. I shall make an effort to change that for you today." He gave her a sultry smile as he smoothed the cloth over her back.

"Please, milord, I beg you not to make a fuss." She sighed, realizing she was already countering her previous vow to allow him whatever he wished of her.

He smiled. "Allow me. You will, won't you?"

She drew her legs up and rested her cheek, nodding against her knee as she watched his understanding dawn.

"If I must endeavor to ask your permissions, you must endeavor to accept my attentions, is that the tacit agreement?"

She nodded again as he gently pushed her backward and smoothed the cloth over each breast, then across her belly. She watched his hand move across her, and knew he watched her as well, waiting for the panic to set in. She tensed slightly as he reached the vee of her thighs, but arched into him as he trespassed there, dropping the cloth. Her eyes widened and caught his, then looked back to his roving hand.

He heard the door to his bedchamber open and pulled back, walking to the entry of the bathing room that he'd left open.

"Harper."

"My lord, the modiste has arrived for Miss Lilly."

"Of course. I will see that she makes her way to the parlor momentarily," he said rather off-handedly. Lilly exhaled. Without effort or realization, he was a constant reminder of the great divide between them.

Perry heard a soft click as her door closed behind him, and he was left alone. He exhaled and kicked his boot against the doorframe.


Lilly decided that acquiescing to the viscount would be more difficult than she had imagined. The modiste and her assistant had their hands all over her, and though she remained fully clothed, it made her wary and uncomfortable. She supposed this was her lesson for the day. Allowing others to handle her. It was an admirable trait for anyone of notable birth, but for her it was unnecessary and merely served to bother her already quite overwrought nerves. In future she need only ever be handled by one man: whoever deigned to take her to wife.

She closed her eyes and thought of Perry's hands…on her. Caressing, smoothing, softening, quieting the very nerves that exasperated her. She eased under the modiste's ministrations, then smiled. Lesson learned.

Perry glanced at the ledgers open on his desk, then stared hard at them. He picked up his pen and tracked his last entry, then stopped. It wasn't a number. It wasn't even recognizable. *Perhaps a ride in the curricle,* he thought. He couldn't take her to the park because it wasn't exactly a statement he wished to make to the grand dames of the *ton.* His forehead hit the desk. He now understood why his brother was often mounted and screeching hell-bent for nowhere.

A knock sounded at the door. "Enter," he said as he lifted his head, not realizing at first that the page he'd fallen to was now stuck to his forehead. He pulled it off quickly as Lilly swept into the room. He tensed and rose. She was a vision in pale yellow muslin, a simple dress, high-waisted and draped easily about her frame. It shifted as she walked, and the color brightened her person, lightening her smile.

"Oh."

She looked at him quizzically. "My lord, I wanted to thank ye, eh-hem, you. Again."

He shifted his stance as she approached and shook his head, his mouth suddenly dry. Quite, quite dry. He tried to clear his throat, but words weren't finding their way out.

She rounded his desk and reached up to his face. Her fragrance assailed him, mixing with his, a feminine twist to his own familiar scent.

He cleared his throat again. "What are you—"

She touched his forehead with her gloved hand and pulled back, showing him her blue thumb. "Milord...my lord...you seem to have some ink," she said with a hint of concentration to the set of her jaw.

He gazed at her thumb, taking her hand in his and stroking her fingers. He then realized what she was saying and turned, wiping his forehead with his handkerchief.

"I beg your pardon, my lord." Her speech was slow as she enunciated each word. "I did not mean to offend."

He shook his head. "And none is taken, sweet. Your speech is lovely," he added, trying to change the subject.

"The clothes, they seem to require it of me." She gave him another smile.

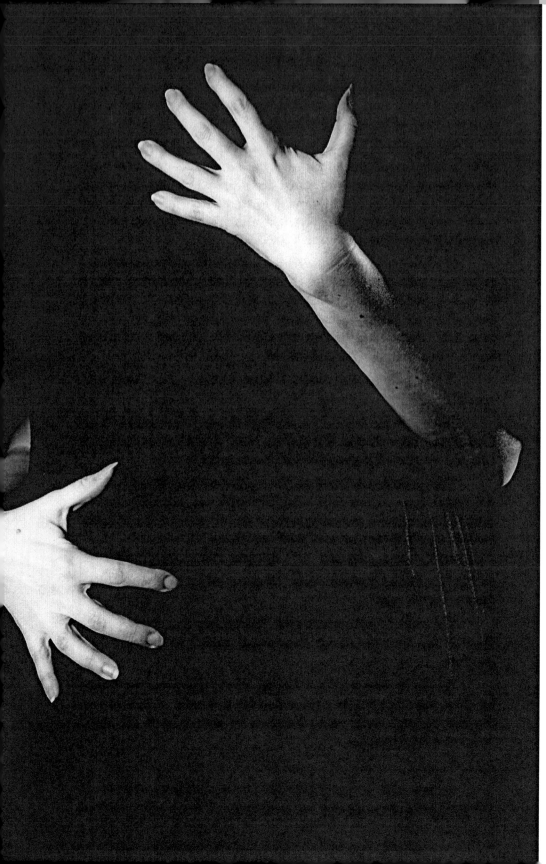

He watched her intently, saw how her face grew more serious with every word, then broke with a flashing smile at the end of the sentence. He couldn't help but to laugh and take her in his arms.

She seemed to melt against him, and he soaked in her warmth as her hands slipped around his waist to find the muscles of his back. His abdomen tightened as he stared down upon her. "You are simply amazing," he said, his hands moving to frame her face. He took her mouth then, capturing her sweet lips with his, driving yet holding, forcing while yielding, controlled yet wild.

Her hands smoothed across his muscles as they rolled and tensed under her touch. He slid his hands into her hair and held her, pulling her away from him slowly. He needed to harness his demons. His hands dropped to her shoulders and he set her back from him, though her arms still stretched toward him. He closed his eyes and took a deep breath. Then looked on her and smiled.

"I beg your pardon, sweet, I seem to have gotten away with myself."

She shook her head. "No, my lord, do not." She smiled. "I am fond of your, uh, well, this, as it is all we have." A blush raced across her face, and she turned, putting the desk between them.

Her words struck him then. The realization that all they had was this electric fire between them—this inimitable and intangible force of attraction that seemed to belong to them and no one else. It couldn't be the end, the all, the total sum of their experience.

"Sweet, if you will allow me a bit of time to finish here," he said quietly, "I would greatly appreciate it if you would accompany me on a drive in my curricle."

She nodded with a bright grin. "Oh yes, my lord, I'd very much like tha." She curtseyed deeply then turned and left him there, staring after her.

He finally took a decent lungful of air, filling and expanding his chest, then deflating in a great shudder of breath. He leaned over the desk, resting heavily on his hands as his body calmed. His smile, however, refused to fade.


Once outside the study, Lilly didn't know what to do with herself. What did ladies do when they had naught to do? She felt like polishing something. She stood in the entryway, looking around to the multitude of closed doors, and wondered where they all went. She knew there was a parlor, a study, and a dining room, and she imagined there was a library. There must also be a ballroom somewhere.

"Miss Lilly," Harper said from the back of the entry, making her jump.

"Oh, Mr. Harper, I didn't see you there."

"Perhaps you would like to wait in the library?"

"Would I?"

Harper gave her an easy smile.

"Well then, yes, sir, I believe I would."

Harper showed her to a door across the hall and handed her into the library.

"I shall inform Lord Trumbull of your whereabouts." He shut the door.

Lilly stared at the back of that solid door, the echo of that click resonating in her mind. She was completely alone in this room. She turned to see the shelves full of beautifully bound volumes. She had never actually appreciated a library, as she'd never been taught to read or write. She had only ever dusted and cleaned the most beautiful of libraries. Every one of them impressed her. Books drew her, their mysteries locked away from her so easily.

Not for the first time, she wished she knew how to read, if only to pass the time. She pulled down a large leather volume in deepest green with gilt edges. Her fingers played over the supple cover, then leafed through the pages. It was naught but a series of jumbled strokes of ink.

Her skin prickled, and she steeled herself. His deep voice came from just over her shoulder.

"The happiness of a man in this life does not consist in the absence, but in the mastery, of his passions."

She shivered.

"And have you mastered your passions, Lord Trumbull?"

"With every breath I take, I make an effort to master passion."

There it was again, that fine shiver that coursed her spine. He was very close behind her, the warmth of his body bringing her blood to the surface.

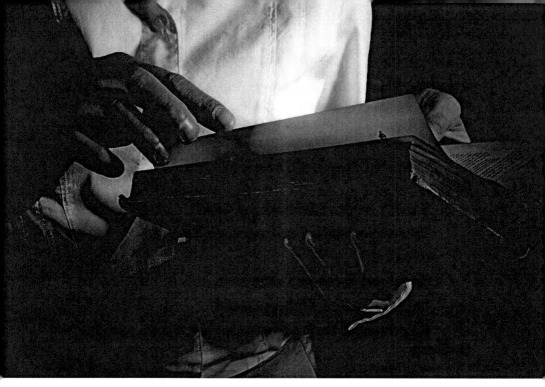

"That would be a first edition of Alfred Tennyson's *Poems*." His arm came around her and moved the pages, the fabric of his sleeve caressing her bare arm. She could feel the fine hairs stand on end as though they too wanted to be much closer to him.

"You can see here, on the flyleaf where it was inscribed to my mother, Melisande, the duchess." He said that almost as an afterthought, almost as a reminder that he was the son of a duke. A duke. But who was he trying to remind, himself? She was all too aware of his status, not to mention her own—which, previously, had never mattered in the least.

"They met at Buckingham, when Her Royal Highness was attempting to convince Tennyson to accept a baronetcy. He never has, of course." His laughter settled into her, and she shifted away from him suddenly.

"It is a beautiful book." She held it out, but he raised his hand.

"Please, if you would like to read it, you may keep it with you."

She shook her head, a certain sadness sinking in. "It must mean a great deal to you, if only for the remembrance of your mother."

"Yes, it does in fact have a distinct sentimental value for me, but idle pages are a devastating transgression, according to her, and as such she would have been overjoyed to have this book well read."

"I simply canna, I—" She turned away from him, holding the book reverently, trying to discern a solution. Her fingers played over the ridges and valleys of the intricate cover.

He took advantage of her distraction and wrapped his arms around her from behind, enclosing her in a solid embrace. "Merely one more lesson," he said against her ear.

She sighed then shuddered, a small tear escaping.

He kissed it away before it fell.

She leaned into his strong, secure form. "You—" She stopped herself. "My lord, you make me—"

"What is it, sweet?"

"I feel safe, I— I simply feel so very safe. It should not be like this between us. You, a chosen son, and I…"

His arms steeled around her, enveloping her. "You will always be safe with me." He allowed the words to lie between them, felt her realization settle in, felt a peace come over her. He began in that moment to figure out how he could ensure his words to be true.

They stood together until the long case clock in the entry rang, and he turned her toward him. He took her hands, kissed the tip of every finger, then the backs of her hands. Turning them over, he kissed her palms, shifting the book from one hand to the other before kissing the insides of her wrists.

"What is it?" she asked when she felt a smile against her wrist.

"You have it wrong. My brother is the chosen son, I'm merely the spare."

"You are also a rake, not nearly as safe as you profess to be."

His smile faded.

"I— Would you do me the honor of accompanying me on a ride through London?"

"I would very much appreciate a tour." Her smile broke the distinct concentration in her features as she endeavored to enunciate every word properly.

"Bring the book, perhaps we can stop at a park to read." He turned and pulled her hand to the crook of his elbow, holding it in place. His curricle was ready at the base of the town house stairs, behind a pair of matched greys. While his brother was enamored with his Friesians, Perry favored the large hunters he stabled.

He handed her up to the sporting carriage, then climbed to the seat next to her.

"Would you like to see the Palace and the Tower?"

She turned to him with wide eyes and a vibrant smile. "Oh yes, please."

He laughed and tickled his leader's ears, and they went bowling through the streets of London.

"My lord," she said slowly, turning the book in her hands.

"Yes, my sweet."

"I can never repay your favor. Though 'tis my greatest wish to do so," she rushed, slipping the moors from her newfound accent.

"Lilly, you have no need to repay anything. I do nothing I do not wish to do." He gave her a sideways glance, his primary attention still on the greys. "You should know this as well as you know my reputation."

Perry smiled and concentrated on steering his leader through a busy section toward the Thames. He enjoyed this. He had become so engrossed in his brother's new life and recent disregard for propriety, coupled with his own newfound responsibilities to his charges, that he had lost sight of what he always considered to be the crux of happiness.

Love—albeit a temporary and easily swayed feeling, in his experience. He believed the pursuit of love, the toe-tripping, mouth-watering, stomach-clenching wonderment of passion, was the noblest pursuit of all.

Love meant pure enjoyment, pure happiness; a feeling of freedom and possibility. He endeavored to find it with as many women as he could muster to his cause. Newfound love, precious and unknown, begging to be discovered and investigated, was a heady mix he found himself addicted to. And this with Lilly was no different, except that he was only feeling more and more passionate.

His smile faded as he considered this. In general his love waned with first completion. He frowned and snuck another sidelong glance at her. This was different. He could feel it burgeoning, increasing exponentially inside him. Begging to be released and set free.

He couldn't breathe. He pulled the carriage aside and jumped free, tying the ribbons and handing a coin to a boy who ran up to hold the harness. He turned back to Lilly, palm out, eyes pleading with her to wait. She nodded and he walked toward the bridge over the Thames, knowing her gaze was on him.

*What is this?* He looked back at her again, then stared into the depths of the ruddy watercourse. He turned, leaning his hips on the short balustrade bordering the bridge, and tried to catch his breath. Did he love her? He rubbed his thumb the length of his chin.

The need to protect Lilly had far outweighed any other thought he had concerning her. Perhaps that was all it was, this need. It was reasonable to believe that was the extent of it, but the fact was that he was drawn to more than just her vulnerable nature. Buying her dresses and doing his best to hear her laugh and see her smile had nothing to do with her safety.

The more he considered it, the more he realized he had been drawn to her from the beginning, but her injuries had hindered his progress. Any other woman would have been between his sheets that first night, particularly after she had begged him to have her. But he had refused, and that was difficult.

"My Lord Trumbull, have I somehow offended you?"

His stomach curled. He'd known she wasn't going to stay in the carriage, but her patience had been commendable. He didn't look at her, but all the same he could feel her reaching out to touch him. His muscles tightened across his back in preparation. She was gentle, timid, cautious. He straightened suddenly, coming to his full commanding height.

Lilly startled and attempted to back away but he caught up her shoulders, pulling her against him—neck to knee—his eyes searching. She felt him looking beyond her surface, sharing her breath, taking it and giving it back. Then he stole it, his lips sealing over hers. His hands moved; one at her nape—holding—the other at her waist—trapping.

Her arms, anchored by his at her sides, wiggled, attempting freedom. He shifted slightly and they wrapped about him beneath his coat, clutching at his back, her fingers stroking his spine. He shuddered and released her on a gasp, brought to reality in the space of a heartbeat.

"Peregrine."

His eyes widened. "Lilly, I—"

A shocked mother steered her children back from whence they came, and a group of gentlemen scowled, staring from the base of the bridge. He released her reluctantly, smoothing her dress and straightening her short mantelet.

"I beg your pardon," he said breathlessly, "I don't know what has come over me. I— there is no recompense for my untoward behavior."

"My lord, I must beg pardon of you, for I see no issue with your passion, though I know for you there is. I understand the restrictions of propriety, but have never had need to hold to them in the same manner as you. Perhaps it's a freedom of my class you cannot enjoy."

Perry glanced around again, for the first time seeing the people his vision was more accustomed to glazing over: the other couples on a lovers' walk along the Thames. The lower class didn't have as much use for the strictures of the peerage. He looked back to Lilly, then took her arm and placed it on his sleeve, guiding her back to his carriage.

"Say it again," he said quietly.

"Pardon."

"Say my name, Lilly."

She stopped and looked up at him as they stood beside his curricle. "Peregrine," she whispered, turning toward him.

His hand rose to her cheek and he framed her jaw, running his thumb from her ear to her chin. Without looking to see who watched, he lowered his mouth again, closing his eyes and absorbing all the sensation his mind could accept.

She acceded to his touch, her lips parting, allowing his tongue entrance. He smiled against her and she giggled. Then he heard a clicking behind him.

He turned to see the boy who held his harness kicking the cobbles at his feet, avoiding the ire of the well-born gentleman who had no idea how to behave. He handed Lilly up to the carriage then turned to the boy, giving him several coins from his purse. The boy smiled brightly, transgressions forgotten, then released the harness and ran off.

Perry laughed and vaulted to the box seat next to Lilly, grasping the ribbons. So this was what his brother had run into headlong. Funny, his own situation carried much the same impediments as they feared Gideon's had. At least he knew who his beloved was, and where she hailed from. The only difficulty now was in figuring out how to get past that within the constraints of his position.

He groaned, remembering his stiff admonishments to his brother. He supposed this was his reward. He turned the curricle back to the street, intending to show Lilly the Tower then Buckingham Palace on the way back to Grosvenor, just as he'd said he would.

They bowled on along the Thames as Lilly watched the buildings. They were beautiful and intricate, but every once in a while she would look down a long street and catch the sight of the destitute, wandering aimlessly, spilling into the road where they pandered for coin. It saddened her. She caught sight of one girl about her age who looked like she had a scar tracing her jaw, and it stilled her to think of where she could have ended up had it not been for her family. She was compelled to reach out to Perry, her hand lightly grazing his knee.

Hepplewort entered his town house on Talbot Square under the cover of darkness. No need to tempt fate and draw unnecessary attention to his arrival.

"My lord, there is a gentleman in the parlor," his butler said stiffly. "He refused to leave, and it has been most inconvenient."

"Who is it?"

"He refused me his name, my lord, as he refused to leave until you arrived, without explanation."

"I see, and you didn't feel the need to contact the constabulary?"

"He inferred that would be a misstep on your behalf, my lord, and with your previous admonishment to tell no one of your arrival, we had no choice but to acquiesce."

Hepplewort grunted and walked to the parlor door as his butler moved ahead of him. He waited for it to open, then stood outside, wary, the words of the Duke of Roxleigh booming in his head.

*I know you, I know the things you have done, and if you think for one minute that you can continue, you are sorely mistaken. Consider yourself a recluse, never to be heard from again, by anyone, anywhere. Is that perfectly clear?*

Hepplewort shivered, then shook it off; there was no way they could know he was here.

"Hepplewort!" It was a voice that shook him to his toes, but it wasn't the one that scared him to death. He moved into the room and looked around. The man who belonged to the voice stood and turned on him.

"You have me at a disadvantage, sir, for I know not who you are."

"Who I am is not as important as who I work for." The large man stretched to his full height and towered menacingly over Hepplewort.

"Well, then, pray tell whom that may be," he said nervously.

"I think you know. I also think you know you should not have returned." Hepplewort kept the large chaise between them as he moved. "The men who set me on you don't appreciate being ignored." The stranger was tracking him.

"I imagine, seeing as how they have employed the likes of you. However, that still leaves me at a loss as to who *they* may be."

"Quit playing games, you can't be in debt to that many books," the man growled.

Hepplewort stopped, his eyes wide. The respite from his panic was only momentary as understanding spread across his face, followed soon by terror. It wasn't Roxleigh, but it wasn't good.

"I— Yes, I dare say I've been forced to remain in the country. I was unable to return as I'd promised. My wedding, you see, it never did take place, which is why I didn't return. It's of no matter. I can make arrangements with Gunn himself while I'm here."

"Yes, you will make arrangements with Gunn. In fact, you will be arranging things with Gunn at first light—you know where. And just to be sure, don't forget that I'll be watching. I knew you were here, I'll know if you attempt to skip."

Hepplewort nodded slowly, considering the toothy grin breaking across his intruder's face. He was no gentleman. Regardless of his speech and carriage. The man moved toward the door, glancing over his shoulder with a gruff chuckle before he walked calmly through the entry and out into the night.

Hepplewort moved as quickly as he could to the front window, but the man was gone before he reached it. He let out a relieved sigh. He wasn't sure whether this was better or worse than being on the wrong side of the viscount and duke.

He would have to meet with Gunn, he would need to square things with him sufficiently so he could find a bride and get back to his estate before Roxleigh and Trumbull got wind of him here in London. He knew they had not filed their grievance with the House of Lords as yet, because he hadn't been formally summoned. He assumed they would deal with it after Gideon's wedding, when a scandal would be less threatening. He hoped so, anyway.

Hepplewort turned and left the parlor. He wanted nothing more than to sleep.

"Will there be anything else, my lord?" the butler asked.

"No— Wait, yes. Have Cook send up a tray of cuts. No fruit, just cuts and sauce. Wine, too. Red." A bit of drool collected on his lower lip.

The butler grimaced and nodded. "Yes, my lord."

# FORTY-TWO

"illy." Perry sing-songed her name through the open doors between their bedchambers. "Oh sweet, sweet Lilly, I have a present for you."

Lilly stood from her dressing table, laying the brush aside as the sound of his sultry voice drifted to her ears. She smiled and turned.

"Yes, my lord," she enunciated perfectly, singing sweetly as she glided through the bath chamber toward him.

She crossed the threshold alert and aware of her surroundings. She'd never set foot in here. He was accustomed to visiting her bed, or her bath, or her sitting room. She had not yet had occasion to enter his inner sanctum. The tall heavy drapes were open to the full moon, which glistened through the windows on a cloudless night. The sight took her breath away, as though the moon was drawn up just for their pleasure.

The draperies and thick rug on the floor were a blue so deep they absorbed the night, and the bed, which caught her eye easily as the centerpiece of his room, was draped in the same deep tones. The sheets were a softer, more subtle color, but also in blue, made from dreamy, wispy fabrics that rested carefully on the surface as though the slightest breeze would carry them away.

A heavy velvet counterpane anchored the sheets at the end of the massive structure, which appeared to be carved out of the deepest of burgundy-colored hardwood. There were no patterns in the tall, sturdy posts that reached close to the ceiling, but there were rings built into them, three to each post, one low, one high, and one midway. They accented the square design of the bedframe nicely. She moved closer and noted the enormous headboard, which also boasted several decorative rings.

A breeze drifted in from the open window and the sheets on the bed fluttered invitingly, begging for occupation, touch, enjoyment. She sighed, her eyes falling wide as she finally caught sight of his figure on the other side of the bed.

He felled the tent where he stood, becoming momentarily hidden from view.

She waited, her breath heavy, beads of perspiration running down her rigid spine.

He watched her from just out of sight.

She knew he was there in the shadows; she could feel his eyes grazing her, even though she couldn't see him.

She shuddered, and he felt his stomach tighten as he saw her nipples harden beneath the thin fabric of her chemise. He groaned and she turned toward the sound, waiting patiently.

He heard the change in her breathing and waited for her to bolt, but she did not. He moved one hand to the post at the end of the bed and tapped it, the sturdy jingle of the rings drawing her gaze.

"What?" she asked as she lifted a ring with her finger.

"That, my sweet, is not a lesson for tonight. Tonight we'll learn our letters."

She shook her head and looked on him for the first time as more than a shadow, his large frame dwarfing her easily, naked as the moon hung in the sky before her. She gasped and turned away.

He chuckled and reached for her. "My innocent Lilly, are you ashamed by my body?"

"No," she breathed.

He grasped her wrist gently in the circle of his fingers. "Well then, my dear, why won't you look at me?"

"Oh, I— Oh my!" She exclaimed when she turned back and saw him in his full glory, lit now by the moonlight and the single candle in his hand. He glowed warmly, reflecting the glittering light, his body covered in painted symbols.

She stared boldly, inspecting the marks. "Is this what you have been doing through supper?"

He chuckled lowly, the circle painted around his belly button dancing. "Yes, my sweet, I couldn't have help with this endeavor. I had to complete my work in solitude. I realize now my approach may have been off. Perhaps for our next lesson, you will do the honors?" He gave her a wry smile as he pulled her close.

She was mesmerized by the living, breathing words before her. She lightly traced the letters, sending a current through his already heated skin. She glanced up to see his smoldering eyes locked on her hand. His breath stilled, and his muscles tensed. She pulled her hand back, drawing a thick groan from him.

"I'll never learn a thing this way."

He grunted and pulled her to him, placing gentle kisses on the edges of her mouth until he felt her shift. He pulled her with him to the bed, crawling across toward the large headboard. He spread her out next to him and removed her chemise. Then he leaned over her, reaching for something on his side table.

"You should keep your eyes open for this," he said.

She opened them slowly, not sure what to expect, then her breath hissed as she felt a cool, wet touch on her shoulder. She looked up to find him hovering over her with a paintbrush, tracing blue lines across her heated skin.

"A," he said quietly.

"A," she repeated.

"Find the A, my sweet."

She glanced up into his face, confused, and shook her head quickly.

He retraced the letter on her shoulder.

She concentrated, then looking him over carefully with the candle, she found the A in much the same place where he had placed it on her. She smiled. "A," she said proudly.

"A is the first letter in the word arm," he said, then paused to trail kisses from her wrist to her elbow.

She gasped and pulled away, and he laughed, pushing her flat on her back beneath him. He swiped the brush through the cup of paint then reached for her again, straddling her thighs. Her face flushed and her nipples hardened as the brush lit on her smooth round breast, tracing one cool, wet loop above, then one around her budding nipple. The way she responded to him was simply magnificent.

Lilly wriggled, clutching his thighs. "Oh my, oh—oh my." She looked to where the brush swept across her flesh. "What—oh—what letter is this?"

"You tell me, my sweet. If the A is upon your arm, what letter would lie here?"

"Upon my, ah, upon my breast." Her voice wavered as she sounded out the letter B.

Perry smiled. "Yes, my sweet Lilly, B is the letter I have written upon your shapely breast."

She stared at the center of his chest. "What's this? 'Tis a full word."

"Yes, above my heart there lies a word, which we will return to in due time." He dipped the paintbrush, then shifted lower across her knees and left a mark on her thigh.

She traced the matching one on his. "Leg?" she asked tentatively.

He beamed. "Yes, leg, the first letter being L."

She glanced back to the word over his heart. "L," she said quietly. "L, leg, la la, Lilly," she breathed, tracing the letters across his heart. "It says Lilly."

Her breath hitched, and she placed her hand full over his heart, over her name.

He leaned down and kissed her. "Yes, sweet, that is your name, just where it should be."

"Put your name on me, show me your name."

He sat back slowly. "Where would you have it, sweet? Where would you have my name on you?"

"Just the same, Perry," she said, staring into his eyes.

His hand trembled as he painted his name across her breast.

She touched it, feeling the wetness, and pulled her hand back, looking at the letters transposed across her palm. She pressed it to his abdomen, below her name.

"Perry, Perry, forever on my heart. Forever." She studied the shapes. "What letter is this?" She traced the first.

"You have jumped ahead of your lesson. I had so much more planned to teach you. That, my sweet, would be the letter P. What else begins with the letter P?" he asked with a wicked grin.

She smoothed her hands over his muscles and down his figure, quietly naming his unnameables until she reached his thighs. Between

them she found her letter. Her perfectly formed mouth dropped into the most precious little O and he smiled. Placing the brush in the paint cup on the side table, he pulled her up to sit before him as he remained straddling her thighs. His lips burned into hers, searing her mouth with the heat of his passion.

Surprised by the heat, her mouth fell open and he took advantage, sweeping boldly through her as he held her tightly to his chest.

Her fingers searched, reaching for him bravely, and found.

He gasped and leaned back on his heels, shaking his head with a deep chuckle. "There is so much for you to learn," he said gruffly.

Her smile beamed and she reached for the candle, twisting her legs and unseating him. He landed on his back and she loomed over him with the light, looking for unknown letters. She rested just above him, holding the candle close to see the slightly smudged letter encircling his bellybutton.

"This isn't a B," she said. "This has just the one circle."

"Yes, and what sound does your mouth make when it makes that shape?"

"Oh," she said, tracing her lips. "Oh?"

He smiled and nodded, then his stomach shook softly with laughter, bouncing the candle in her hand and spilling hot wax across his abdomen and into his belly button. He hissed at the shock, then glanced up as his jaw dropped. "Oh!"

"Oh!" she repeated, then leaned over to blow gently across his skin, hardening the wax before reaching out and peeling the trickle away from his stomach, lifting it from the indentation. She turned the long waxen thread over in her hand, examining the smooth side that had rested against his skin, the thick side where the wax had flowed, then the little cone of wax where it had filled him. She blew lightly across it, hardening it further as he watched, his eyes darkening in passion.

She placed the candle and the wax on the side table and reached for the paint cup and brush. She swept the paintbrush across his abdomen, cooling the thin red welt.

Perry groaned and shifted. She traced her name across his heart, saying it carefully, then painted it again with a shaky hand. "And this letter, what is this?" she asked, as her hand skimmed the letter around his nipple.

He choked out, "I've no breasts as you do, my sweet."

"Chest," she whispered.

"The letter you seek is C."

She smoothed over it again. "C," she whispered. "And this?" She followed a staggered letter. He swallowed beneath her brush. "Na, na, neck."

**He nodded and she laughed, the paintbrush streaking his chin.**

"Oh!"

"No," he said quietly. "N, for neck. Where was O?"

"O was here," she said, tracing it yet again. She shifted, looking at him with a twinkle in her eye. "And P—"

She cried out as he seized her wrists, the paint spilling over his abdomen, his muscles clenching.

He could no longer stand her attentions. "This was a mistake," he growled.

"Oh, no. No, please don't say that."

He smiled up at her, then pulled her across his paint-streaked

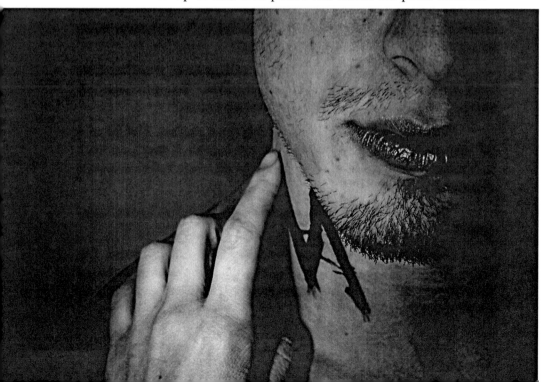

belly.

She slid up his torso, gliding on the wet splash of paint, laughing until he kissed her and captured the sweet sound between them.

He pushed his hands into her hair and held her right where he wanted her, just within reach. He spent the rest of the night teaching her letters, making it all the way to Q—for quiver.

Hepplewort left early, heading to Lower Queen Street on the Limehouse Reach, near the commercial docks. Mr. Gunn could be found every morning breaking his fast in an old pub house frequented by wharf-rats and sailors. The sign outside the pub dangled askew, the painted-on name long washed away with the weather. It was known as Queen's Pub and the owner never argued; as long as the patrons made their way in the door, he couldn't be bothered what his pub was called.

Hepplewort stumbled through the door, tripping on a loose piece of flashing meant to keep out the weather. Cursing, his gaze fell on Gunn, a lithe, dark man propped in the corner against a buxom woman. Hepplewort startled when he was prodded from behind, pushed farther into the pub. He turned to find the gentleman from the previous evening leaning jauntily on a cane.

"Humph," he said as he turned and walked toward Gunn. "Mr. Gunn," he said, grumpily sidling up to the table, "I am here to make arrangements for recompense as requested."

Gunn looked up, chewing a piece of ham as he considered the squat disrupter. "You disappeared," he grumbled. "You were to return straight from the wedding and make your reparations."

"I understand, Mr. Gunn. I do beg your pardon. Had bit of a tiff with an angry duke, you see. Lost my betrothed, but I am back in London to find another. Then I'm off to the estate before someone discovers."

"This someone you're hiding from, mightn't that be the angry duke?"

Hepplewort shifted uncomfortably. "One and the same, Mr. Gunn. Now, as you see, I have a schedule, and it is necessary that I get about my business and return to the country as soon as is possible. Let's get on about this, shall we?"

Gunn watched him.

"I have rooms on Talbot Square, off Oxford Street, as you apparently already know." Hepplewort glanced at the other gentleman. "I've no longer a need to be in the ton, and so would part with them. The rooms are easily worth more than your note on me. I will sign them to you the day I leave."

"You will sign them to me now, or not at all."

"Mr. Gunn, you do understand I have need for the rooms until I procure a bride and retire to the country? I also need to arrange to move the household items and—"

"You will sign the deed to me now. You may remain in the house until you remove to Shropshire. How long do you need?"

"I am unsure—merely as long as it takes to find a bride. If you are game to help, the sooner I'll quit London."

Mr. Gunn smiled wickedly. "I suppose you have requirements for this bride?"

Hepplewort nodded, wary of his new partner. "She must be chaste. And demure. I require a lady in bearing and upbringing. Nothing else will suit."

"*You* expect to fetch a highborn chit?" Gunn asked skeptically.

Hepplewort's eyes bulged. "I beg your pardon? I carry an earldom. Any well-bred lady would be honored to accept my suit and be my countess. The mother of the future Earl of Shropshire is a very tempting position, if I don't say so myself."

The other two men stared in shock and disgust. "You've quite the work cut out for you, Calder," Gunn said with a smile at the second gentleman.

Calder shifted his gaze from Hepplewort to Gunn and back again. His expression of shock deepened gradually until anger overtook him.

Gunn's shoulders shook with laughter. "You had better get yourself busy. You have balls to attend, invitations to accept."

Calder's eyes narrowed on Gunn, then he turned for the door, rapping his cane on the floor as he strode out. "Hepplewort!" he yelled from just outside the door.

Hepplewort jumped, then ran as fast as his pudgy little legs would carry him.

"There can be no doubt about who he is and what he is here for," the rumbling voice said.

Lilly stopped at the top of the stairs and went perfectly still.

"I can't believe he has the gall to show his face in London, after what we told him. After what happened." This came from Perry.

Lilly's heart stuttered and she sank to the top stair. "It's him," she whispered, her hand coming up to her mouth.

Perry felt her presence before he turned, hushing the gentleman with him. He saw her sitting at the top of the staircase, and his own heart skipped a pace at her pallor. "Lilly, sweet, are you ready to break your fast?" he asked casually, attempting a change of subject. It was obvious from her shocked expression that she'd heard at least some of their discussion.

"Don't." She pointed at him.

Perry glanced at the gentleman, then walked slowly toward the stairs. "Lilly, I—"

"It's him, isn't it? You are talking about him. The man who ruined me, who tried to kill me. The man who thought he had succeeded."

"Lilly—"

"Don't you dare, my lord Trumbull. Tell me the truth, or I will walk from this town house and never look back," she said severely.

Perry held out his hand. "You are safe here with me. My men are watching him. We will handle him, I promise you. You will not come to harm at his hands again. I promised to protect you, and. I. Will." The last came out so forcefully his jaw ached with it.

She stood and walked down the stairs toward him, her eyes narrowing as she descended. "It is not fear I feel," she said, taking his hand and a deep breath at the heavy, warm weight of him. "I feel perfectly safe here, with you."

"I am glad of it," Perry said. He turned her to the gentlemen. "May I present the most Honorable Thorne Magnus Calder, the Marquess of Canford, one of my cousins." He leaned toward her. "Future Duke of St.

Cyr."

Calder shook his head and bowed before Lilly, drawing a startled gasp from her throat.

"Oh, no, tell him," she said, hitting Perry's shoulder. "Tell him who I am, don't let him do that," she cried. "My lord, please!"

"Lilly." The voice rumbled forth from the future Duke of St. Cyr like a herd of beasts loosed on the meadow. "I know perfectly well who you are, and of whence you came. Trumbull here has no authority over me or my behavior, even with his advanced age." He grinned, slanting a devious look at his cousin. "I believe anyone with a heart as brave as yours deserves my unmitigated devotion, and so you have it."

Lilly shook her head, her hand tangled in the sleeve of Perry's coat. She but he caught her up, holding her against him.

Perry glanced at Calder, who turned and walked toward the breakfast room at the back of the town house.

"Lilly. Sweet, sweet Lilly, please do not distress yourself so."

"You canna understand, milord, what this means to me. I canna— Milord, he's a duke! I— even your brother I canna. Please," she cried.

"He isn't quite a duke yet. His sire would be most disappointed by your advancement of his son, as that would mean he missed his own funeral," Perry chided sweetly, trying to get her to laugh. "Calder is my cousin, one of the family. He will accept you as I have. He knows what an amazing woman you are."

She studied him, sinking into his eyes to harness the truth that swam just beyond her reach. She tried to smile. "Please, in the future, please at least give me some warning, so I don't make a complete fool of myself."

"He won't have noticed, I promise. Come, our guest is at breakfast, and we should join him."

"Our guest?" Lilly grasped his arm, allowing him to lead her to the breakfast room where Calder had gone before.

They entered and Perry placed his hand at the small of her back, urging her forward.

Lilly smiled, her spine straightening slightly, taking some of the confidence Perry sought to loan her. "My lord Canford, I beg your pardon—"

He cut her off with a wave as he stood to acknowledge her. "First off, you will address me as Calder, as all in the family have wont to do. Secondly, you will not apologize to me, as it is frightfully clear that my dear cousin quite rudely shocked you by having me here without so much as a warning. If anything, I should wish you would admonish him for his egregious error in judgment."

Lilly decided that Calder's demeanor quite undermined his rather large presence.

He leveled upon her a devastatingly charming smile.

Lilly took a sudden breath, then felt Perry edge her closer to a chair.

"Yes, I…yes," she said finally as she sat next to Perry, the marquess across from her.

Perry motioned to the footmen, who presented heaping trays of savory cuts of meat, thick heady sauces, and sweet jellies. Perry filled her plate.

She glanced up once, but he merely smiled. "You need your energy. This is no time to be dainty."

"So," she said, glancing at Calder, "tell me of him. Why is he here, and what have you to do with it?"

Calder grinned. "My, but she does recover well." He looked directly at her after receiving a nod from Perry. "I was charged with the duty of overseeing Hepplewort's town house on Talbot Square as Calder House, my own residence, is located on Sussex Square. It's a beautiful area, really, adjacent to Kensington Gardens. My rooms look out over the gardens at sunset, truly a marvelous sight—"

Perry cleared his throat, interrupting Calder's musings.

"Yes, well, the same rooms overlook the town houses across the Bathhurst Mews and Grand Junction Road. Hepplewort's being just across the road at Talbot's is easily visible from my highest floors. My majordomo was alerted to an arrival by the additional lights and bustle about the town house, and I went straightaway to handle him." He paused, looking to Perry to see if that was enough information.

He nodded again.

Calder cleared his throat. "Approaching Mr. Gunn wasn't at all a difficulty. Gunn is a well-known bookmaker, and as everyone is aware of Hepplewort's penchant for the cards, certain arrangements with the bookmaker were already in place should he turn up in town. Gunn, of course, could care less from whence his mark procured his tinker, so long as he procured it."

She stared at him for a moment, assessing, then glanced at Perry—something was being left out.

He watched her nervously for a moment. "It appears that Hepplewort has come to town to—uh, well, he is yet in need of a wife."

Her eyes fell and her breath stopped. Then she looked up for him to continue.

He took a deep breath. "Since Roxleigh divested him of Francine, he intends to find a different bride."

Lilly watched him carefully, then poked at the food piled on her plate before looking up to Calder, then Perry. "Well, he cannot be allowed to complete the task."

Perry and Calder shifted with discomfort, their need to control unsettling. They exchanged preemptive glances, and nodded. How and when Hepplewort was to be dealt with would be discussed soon, but it wasn't something Lilly would have any part of; she certainly had no need to be involved, as far as Perry was concerned.

Lilly pushed the cuts of meat and eggs around on her plate for a while as Perry and Calder attempted something resembling small talk.

"How is the duchess?"

"Mama is well—excited, of course, for Roxleigh to declare his troth. I suppose she is tired of fielding questions as he is so terribly unapproachable. It's a boon, really. No more trepidation in the ballrooms, all the mamas tossing their daughters in his path, and all of us waiting to see who he trips over in the end."

Perry smiled as he thought of Gideon and his Francine. He glanced up to see Lilly watching him from the safety of her eyelashes and his smile deepened to reassure her.

"I have to tell him," he said slowly.

Calder grunted. "You will do no such thing, Perry. Roxleigh is in the midst of his wedding celebration—which, by the way, you should be attending." He sent him a scornful glance. "As the head of the house of Trumbull is otherwise engaged, and you have quite enough to deal with at present, that puts me in line to take the reins. If Roxleigh has an issue with the decision, he can take it up with me after the wedding when we inform him of the outcome. As much as it was his decision to hold notification of the House of Lords until after their wedding, it has fallen to us to control the repercussions."

Perry groaned. "I believe I will take this young lady for a picnic, perhaps to Regent's Park, then a walk through the zoological gardens to see the royal collection."

"Capital idea. Perhaps you would stop by Calder House and take some other ladies with you? I've no doubt they would be enthralled with your miss, and they would also appreciate the respite from my attention."

"Oh? And who, pray tell me, does this party include?"

"Merely Izzy, Poppy, Saoirse, and Maebh," Calder said with a grin.

Perry shook his head. "They have terrible names."

"I beg your pardon?" Calder said, affronted.

"I only mean, I have been teaching our miss to read, and well, Isadore and Poppy are fine, but Saoirse and Maebh? I'll never be able to explain them."

"Try," Lilly said quietly.

"I will try." Perry gave her a smile.

Calder took the opportunity to stand. "I will leave you to your teaching," he said with a swift bow.

"Lessons," Perry said. "We call them lessons."

"Yes, well, a third hand in the pot certainly will be a distraction. I'll let the women know you will be around by noon."

Perry grimaced, then stood as his cousin left. He took his seat then turned her to face him.

"Seer-sha," he pronounced slowly, "is spelled S-A-O-I-R-S-E, and Maave is spelled M-A-E-B-H."

She stared at him, her eyes clouded.

He chuckled. "Their fiery mama, The Right Honorable Fallon Trumbull, Countess of Pemberley, is Gaelic. Now, remember the letter B?"

She blushed.

"In Gaelic, the B, coupled with the H…" He took her small hand in his and traced a H into her palm.

"H was for hand."

"Yes, the B and the H together make the sound of a V. Do you remember the V?" He wickedly held two fingers up in the shape of a V.

She nodded again, her breath catching as her mouth went dry.

Perry smiled and let go of her hand. "That wasn't very nice of me," he admitted with a slanted grin. "I very much enjoy the effect I have on you. You have much the same effect on me, in fact. *Indeed*, I'm not convinced this little garden party is all that good an idea."

"Oh, but it is. I would love to see Regent's and the Zoological Gardens. Once we leave here, I imagine I'll never return. Who, exactly, are Saoirse, Maebh, Poppy, and Isadore?"

"More cousins. There are eleven all told—the four ladies and seven gentlemen. They are all ladies of varying rank and of marriageable age. They came out together a year ago, to the disdain of the matchmaking mamas of the *ton*."

The truth was that every one of Perry's cousins was stunningly handsome. The male cousins were built like their common grandsire: tall, broad in the shoulder, and lean in the hip, while the ladies took on the figures of their respective mamas. But the wives and daughters of the Trumbull lineage were never hard to look at. As different as they all were, the common thread between them was a mesmerizing countenance. Beyond that distracting exterior they were willful and all-encompassing, a difficulty for any weak man—and their children followed suit.

Lilly stared at him in awe. She understood the sheer energy and power of Perry, and when his brother was involved it was multiplied, not merely doubled. She couldn't fathom what it would be like to be surrounded by seven men from the Trumbull lineage. She sighed. At least this would be the women. If they were anything like Francine she would certainly be terrified at first, but she hoped they would let her be.

Perry pushed back from the table. "Harper."

"Yes, my lord?"

"Have Gardner ready the landau, tell Kerrigan we are to be underway shortly, and have Cook prepare a basket for six, I believe."

"Yes, my lord."

Perry turned back to Lilly. "As for you, I will see you soon."

She smiled at him warily. "Just—" She looked up imploringly.

"Yes, my sweet?"

She reached up, her hands tracing the scars across her face as though they were Braille, then looked down. "What will they—"

"They won't. They know nothing of you, of your injuries, where you came from. They will accept you because you are with me. That is the only demonstration they will need to allow your presence." He paused, seeing the true question about her scars. He took her hand and pulled her up before him. "Wear the crimson—the reflection of the color on your skin is rather stunning," he said as he traced her chin. "It causes your cinnamon eyes to glow." He held her gaze. "And the sweet red of your mouth to deepen." He swept his thumb lightly across her lips. "No one will notice anything else. I certainly didn't when first I saw you in it."

She could scarcely breathe. "As you wish, my lord," she replied *sotto voce*.

His eyes narrowed upon her as he considered her words, then he released her quickly and turned and walked out. He had some plans to make for Lilly's next lesson, and not much time to complete them.

Perry stood at the base of the stairs in a dove grey suit with a violet waistcoat and grey neck cloth. Her heart seized. He held a matching grey top hat with a band in the same hue as his waistcoat. His trousers were pulled in a straight line to his shoes. He was pulling on his dark grey gloves as she started down the stairs, his thoughts traversing his face. Lilly was amazed at the way his expressions could both thrill and ease her.

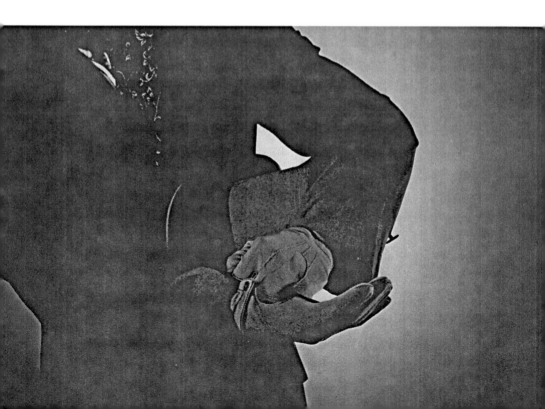

Perry looked up and graced her with a smile of pure excitement as he examined her crimson dress. It really did work to mask her scars in the most amazing way. The filtered light thorough her bonnet reflected off the bright colored dress and cast the same pale pink across her entire face, blending away the myriad of tiny scars until all one saw were her beautiful features. He would have to pay his respects to that seamstress. She was most certainly a master.

She returned the smile as he leaned toward her.

"The dress is beautiful, but the vision is quite breathtaking."

Lilly blushed violently. "Harper, we're off," Perry grunted.


The landau came to a halt in front of a lovely Georgian town house of five bays and three floors. The impressive columns stretched the full front of the façade and a large open porch which overlooked the central gardens on the square and Kensington Gardens just across the road. Several sets of French doors were set into it, and as Perry reached to pull Lilly from the carriage, the central door swept open and a bustle of silks and satins burst forth.

"Perry, don't you dare, we are so desperate for entertainment we've been watching the street for your arrival! Let's be off, not another moment to spare," said an excited woman with a riot of untamed curls flailing in all directions about her.

Perry chuckled and released Lilly, letting her slip back to the seat.

"Perry, top down! Top down! It's a beautiful day, what are you hiding in there? Goodness, if I didn't know better, I would guess—"

"Poppy dear, we were in such a rush to attend you we hadn't the time," Perry cut in.

"Oh, well, of course, I beg your pardon. However, now you're here, we can pause one moment to set the roof aside," Poppy said with a brilliant grin.

Perry looked to Gardner and Kerrigan, who jumped from the box to fold the enclosure and open the carriage.

"Much better—oh!" exclaimed a tiny, fairy-like girl with skin of porcelain and hair like the sun-kissed curling wisps of clouds.

The gaggle of cousins swarmed around Perry to get a look at the girl inside the coach, eyes wide and jaws dropped.

Perry cleared his throat. "Might I present Miss Lilly Steele, of Kelso," he said resolutely.

A collective gasp sounded from the group and Perry chuckled. "Ladies, please, if you might stop swarming about, I could introduce each of you."

"Oh my, of course," came the voice from the girl closest the door.

Perry bowed and handed her carefully into the landau. "Miss Lilly, I present you Lady Isadore Calder. You met her brother, the Marquess of Canford, earlier," he reminded her.

Lilly smiled as Isadore took the space nearest her.

"So very pleased to make your acquaintance, my dear," Isadore said as she patted her on the knee. "What a beautiful dress. You must tell me the name of your seamstress. Why, it's most beguiling!"

"Thank you, my lady," Lilly said, watching her speech carefully. "You would need to ask Perry about the maker, though. He would know better than I."

Isadore laughed and cast a sideways glance at Perry, who shifted uncomfortably. "You don't say. Well, I will do that, but I beg you, call me Izzy. We'll all get confused with all the *my lady's* floating around, and everyone in the family calls me Izzy, so you must as well." She gave Lilly a bright smile and patted her knee again.

Lilly looked up to see Perry quickly handing another girl in.

"Lilly, I would like to present Lady Saoirse." He pronounced the name carefully. "And Lady Maebh."

"Well, I must say you are a beautiful respite from the usual—"

"Maebh! Hush now, do not endeavor to embarrass our treasured cousin." Saoirse turned and sat directly across from Lilly, pulling Maebh with her.

Lilly looked into the vivid faces of the sisters. Saoirse was tiny, her skin smooth and creamy and glowing amidst the wild mane of ginger curls that seemed to move on the breeze with a life of their own. Maebh was similar—at least in spirit—to the curls that adorned her sister, but her form was tall and willowy, her long ginger locks twisted on her crown.

"So you hail from Kelso—does this mean you are familiar with Roxleigh? Have you seen his Friesians?" Saoirse asked excitedly.

Lilly smiled at the girls, but Perry interjected another cousin before she could reply.

"_Et en fin_, the Lady Poppy," he said, handing her into the landau and following her up. Poppy perched on the edge of the seat next to Lilly.

"Lilly, I'm so pleased to make your acquaintance, as we all are. I'm a bit surprised that Thorne managed to arrange this outing without a word as to the company."

Lilly smiled at Poppy, watching her bounce and sway on the seat as she talked, her dark curls arranged over a pair of the deepest green eyes, wide as saucers, bright and sparkling like Perry's.

"Calder did mention a surprise," sweet, blonde Isadore said.

"I had no idea it would be this type of surprise," Maebh said, inspecting Perry. It wasn't often he introduced a lady to his cousins. In general, they were noticed in passing at the balls or on the town.

Perry looked from one bench to the next, wondering where to part the sea of silks to have a seat. He felt like a giant towering over a conquest.

As if in answer, Saoirse pushed Maebh over and patted the seat between them with a grin.

Perry sat carefully between them, avoiding their finery. He leaned back into the seat and stretched his arms out along the back of the carriage to prevent crushing his cousins.

"We're off, Gardner." He then gave a nod to Kerrigan, who mounted the rear of the landau with wide eyes.

The girls' giggling sounded like a cacophony of sweet songbirds taking flight. Only Maebh didn't join in their mirth.

Perry saw her glare and knew instantly the reason for her ill temper. A family outing was never used for his kind of conquest; it was sacrosanct, something for the family and those who were to be family. He shifted under her unspoken scrutiny, then returned the glare.

Maebh looked away, concentrating on the girl Perry had brought into the fold. There was something about Lilly she couldn't quite grasp. She wished she could get a clear view of her face beneath that bonnet. She wanted to study her eyes and discover what it was that had Perry captured.

Perry grinned when she looked away, ever wary of the danger of his empathic cousin, then rested his gaze on Lilly, who was attempting to keep up with the countless questions volleyed her way. He prepared himself to intercede the moment she became unsure or uncomfortable.

"No—yes—yes—well, I don't—oh, you mean—no, no, I didn't— well, I never did becau—oh, all right." She fielded the questions admirably, much to his delight.

Perry had Gardner circle the park toward the outside lane, then pull up adjacent to the lake. His men jumped from the carriage and Kerrigan retrieved rugs from the boot and spread them near a giant oak, then ran back for several large baskets of provisions.

Perry stood at the landau, handing down the endless train of females to the emerald carpet of the sprawling lawns before them. They milled in a swish of skirts and parasols, awaiting the last of them to alight. Only after Lilly descended did they turn as one, heading jovially toward the repast. Perry did not lose her hand once she was afoot; he wrapped it around his arm, escorting her to the picnic.

"Well, sweet, how do you feel?" he murmured as he leaned into her.

Lilly smiled up at him from below the brim of her bonnet.

"You are the most surprising young lady I have ever met. You have my cousins enraptured," he said softly. "And you have me beguiled, captivated, enamored." He whispered the last words, his breath wafting gently over her ear.

She shuddered. "Maebh—"

"Don't be concerned with Maebh, she isn't like most. She feels deeply with her heart, yet as precious as she is to me, she has never approved of my, eh— Well. Let us just say she feels for the women who thought more of their position with me than I did." He frowned; it wasn't a very becoming statement, he supposed. "I only meant that—"

She waved him off. "Don't, I beg you. I understand what you're saying, as I also understand what she's feeling. I admire you for recognizing her concerns."

They reached the rugs under the watchful gaze of the four cousins who had preceded them. Perry handed Lilly down to sit first. His cousins followed in succession like a flower opening to the sun, each petal a different color. They laughed, enjoying the company.

Perry laid out the feast, passing loaded plates to each of the cousins and Lilly before filling his own plate and stretching out on the ground behind her to enjoy the peace.

Lilly turned to find him smiling up at the heavens, his eyes closed, absentmindedly munching an apple. She smiled in return, wondering what his daydreams contained.

"Saoirse, let's walk around the lake," Maebh said as she glanced at Lilly, then stood.

Saoirse also looked at Lilly and smiled, then grabbed Isadore, who grabbed Poppy, and they walked, arms linked, toward the peaceful water.

"It seems we have been left to our own devices," Perry said without opening his eyes.

"We— Oh." Lilly looked around, then her gaze landed on Perry's relaxed visage. She enjoyed the play of sun and shadow across his cheeks. "Will they be all right on their own?"

"Oh, quite. However, I've no doubt Kerrigan is following and Gardner is watching."

She glanced again to find Kerrigan following an easy distance behind the ladies, Gardner standing not far away from them while scanning the landscape. She smiled; he knew his men well.

"Sweet, how do you find my cousins?"

"Oh, they are wonderful—really, truly wonderful. I miss Meggie," she said suddenly. "I think I would like to go home." The realization struck her without warning.

Perry heard the note of sadness underlying her tone and opened his eyes to study her. "Only say the word and I will have you returned to my brother's household. In fact, my cousins will be quitting London soon to join Roxleigh for the wedding festivities." His voice carried a note of sadness. "I don't wish to keep you where you don't wish to be."

Lilly shook her head. "'Tisn't that," she said, slipping into her comfortable brogue. "'Tis jus' that I've never been without my family. Meggie and I were never apart till she joined the duke's household, and of course I never expected to be far from her."

Perry turned and moved in front of her, sitting up. "We have never discussed what is happening here, Lilly. That could be an egregious error on my part. It would damage me to know that I had hurt you in some way." He looked off into the distance, realizing at that moment that it wasn't she he was worried about as much as himself. His emotions had never traveled to the place they currently inhabited, not before her.

"No, *my lord*." She emphasized his title and picked up her proper speech patterns again. "I *know* my place in this world, just as well as I know yours. There is no doubt in me that this—" She gestured between them. "—goes no further than where we are now. I will always hold a place for you, if not in my heart then in my soul. For what you have done for me." She twisted her skirt between her fingers. "There is simply no way for me to repay so many kindnesses."

Perry scowled. "Don't think for one minute that I take nothing from this, my sweet," he said sardonically. "I am enjoying myself and our *activities* rather thoroughly. After all, that is who I am and what I do, is it not? That is recompense enough."

Lilly's jaw dropped, and he saw her eyes glaze over with tears.

Perry stood quickly and walked away from her to lean against the nearby tree. He should never have been so callous. His forehead hurt from the strain in his mind. Her words had done what he knew they would. She was correct, but he was broken. He would never be right, not without her by his side. Something had changed within him; the shift was complete. He could never return to his old ways, he could never look at another woman the way he had in the past.

He pounded a fist against the trunk of the tree, looking up into the leaves as he thought about her. The way she moved. The way she smiled. Yes, his cousins accepted her now, but they had no idea who she was. Would his family accept her when they did know? Calder hadn't had any difficulty acknowledging her, but he assumed Calder only thought her to be a temporary fixture in his life. But then if that were true, why would Calder recommend she meet the ladies of the family? He wouldn't have. If Calder could accept Lilly without qualm, then so would the rest of the family.

Perry shook his head and turned to apologize, to beg forgiveness, but she was gone.

R

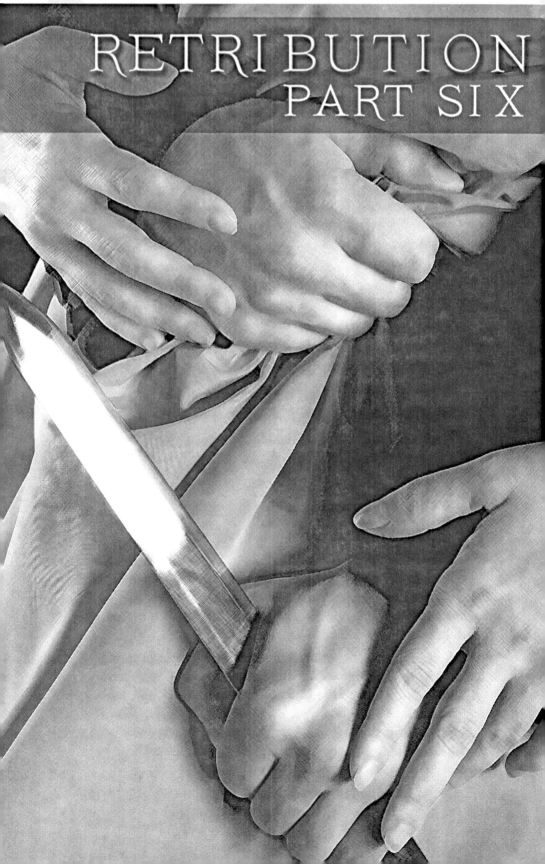

# RETRIBUTION
## PART SIX

# FORTY-THREE

Perry's entire body tensed as he scanned the park for Lilly's petite figure. His cousins and men were the only people in sight. *Oh God* he was an ass, if something happened to her now because of him—

"Lilly!" he bellowed, startling the four ladies. He paid them no heed. "Lilly!"

*Callous bastard.* He shook his head. He should have known better. Why was it that Lilly could unman him so easily, turn his mind to pudding? He truly needed to get his wits about him.

They rushed toward him, Gardner and Kerrigan in tow.

"What have you done, Perry?" Maebh asked.

"Maebh. What I have done I am all too eager to remedy. Do not cast aspersions on my soul just yet. Right now I simply need to find her."

"Perry—"

"No! I've no time for this! Gardner! Kerrigan!"

"But Perry—"

"Not. Now. Maebh!"

Shock in her eyes Maebh turned from him as he sent Gardner off with Isadore and Poppy and Kerrigan with Maebh and Saoirse in another direction. She threw one last glance at Perry then moved off, around the lake.

He stared across the park without seeing. His mind considered options, but he didn't pay much attention as he blindly strode away from the lake, deeper into the park. He had to find her, and soon. It wasn't just that he had to find a way to apologize, but if Hepplewort—he stopped the train of thought. There were stands of trees breaking up the vastness of the sweeping green lawns. He peered into each copse as he passed, his eyes searching for a slash of crimson.

Several times he ran for a tree, only to find the breeze playing tricks on him. He turned and walked toward a thicket bordering another copse and paused, pulling a flower from a bush and crushing it in his hand, letting the petals fall to the ground slowly as he moved deeper into the trees.

*How could I have been so cold as to speak to her that way? How am I going to repair this?* Regardless of station, regardless of possibility and future, he knew she deserved more from him, no matter how deeply that affected his way of life. He needed to stop thinking of her as the poor damaged servant girl from Kelso.

He groaned. He suddenly wanted the impossible from her, the responsibility of her. But she was a lowly scullery maid, possibly someday to rise as high as lady's maid, but no more—never to a rank suitable for his attention, never to a status at which he could offer. He really wasn't himself if he was considering marrying a scullery maid.

He shook his head, leaning back against a tree. She could be anywhere by now and she had every right to run, to leave. He had treated her as badly as Hepplewort—no, worse. Hepplewort had never made her promises, spoken or unspoken, so there was no basis for *his* destruction. Hepplewort was a stranger, but Perry had given Lilly kindness, sensitivity, and a certain regard—then he took it all back in one fell swoop.

His jaw clenched, and he closed his eyes tight against the sting behind them.

He felt irretrievably broken for his actions. He wouldn't find peace until he found Lilly and repaired this damage. Yet he didn't think it possible, and had no right to try. She certainly shouldn't accept it, she shouldn't accept him. In fact, she should stay away. It would be far better for her if he never saw her again—but he couldn't imagine never seeing her again. And then there was Hepplewort. Still…somewhere. He panicked at the thought, his chest seizing and his eyes flying wide as he tried to breathe.

He turned to head back toward the open lawns and—

She was there, too far to touch but close enough he caught the scent of his own bath oils on her skin. Her eyes were on fire, her spine rigid, her hands clasped in her skirts. She had never been so beautiful.

"Lilly!" He collapsed before her, his breath finally loosed. Sitting back on his knees, he tangled his hands in her skirts and pulled her to him as though he needed proof of her existence. He buried his face in the folds. She smelled of fresh cut lawn and warmed sugar and him. "I thought the worst possible, oh God I thought—"

Her hands opened in panic at her sides.

"I beg you, I never should have said what I said," he said. "I was— You should never forgive me. I beg you forgive me. You have me at such a disadvantage, I have never felt—" He shook his head. "I don't know what I feel." He couldn't bear to look at her, knowing how she must look upon him, knowing he would see her anger. He couldn't see her anger again. His shoulders shook.

"Perry," she breathed.

He moved his arms around her knees and pulled her closer still, turning his head to the side and holding her closely.

"I think it would be better if I left," she whispered, her hand coming down to stroke his hair.

"No, please—"

"I don't think this is a situation we can remedy. Your station will always get the better of you, as will mine. There can be no future for us. To continue now would be to demand failure, as well as more pain." She tugged gently at his hair, urging him to look up.

"Lilly." He released her, placing his hands on his knees as he tried to gather his composure. He stared at the ground between them. "I can't imagine— I can't even begin to fathom how it would be to never see you again. And I can't grasp how I would see you but be unable to have you."

Breathing slowly, he managed to rein the most powerful of his emotions that demanded he hold onto her and not release her until she acceded to his will. His fingers dug into the flesh of his thighs.

"I cannot imagine this either, at this point. You have brought me to life, given me time. I would never have lived had I not come with you, had you not agreed to—to what you agreed to." She shook the thoughts of his lessons away. She needed to see his eyes but he refused to look at her. Perhaps that was better; if she actually saw his pain, this might be impossible. It was difficult enough watching him in this defeated posture.

She didn't understand why she affected him so deeply. He could have any woman he wanted. She should have merely been a plaything, a temporary muse. "I had no idea," she whispered. "I never should have

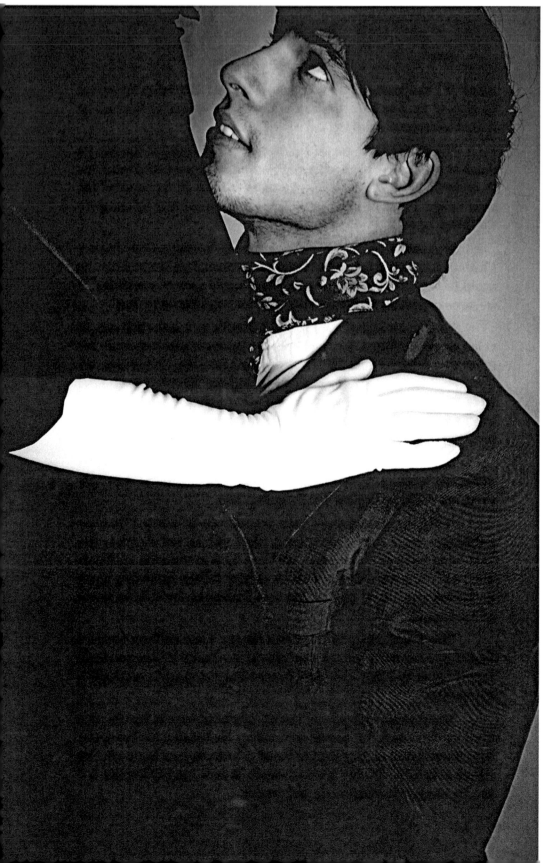

asked. If I had known what this would do, I—" Her voice broke and he glanced up. She lifted her hand to cover her quivering lips and he looked away again swiftly.

"Don't say that," he said fiercely. "You've changed me just as much as you say I've changed you. I was lost, and you found me. I ran from my brother's house, yet now I understand that all the reasons I left were wrong. I understand how he felt, I understand why he could do the things he did."

He stood, his voice rising with each word. "I relinquish my station. I'll disappear, with you, because I now understand. I understand how he could shun convention and propriety and nearly give up everything he is—no—everything he was meant to be. For her, Lilly, all for her."

Their gazes locked, he lowered his voice to a tenor that caught at her soul and refused to release, that low resonant tone that made her skin aware of his very breath. "He would do it for the joy in her eyes, the light in her smile, the sweet sound of her laughter." His eyes traveled her body. "The sway of her hips, the delight in her sighs as he fulfilled— her every wish." His eyes caught hers again, and he moved to stand a hair's breadth away.

Her breath hitched, and she raised her hands instinctively as protection between them, but his hands had already made their way about her waist, pulling her solidly against him.

"Lilly, my sweet Lilly, I have injured you in a way I have no justification for. I do not understand why I did so, and therefore can offer no excuse nor recompense. All I can do is promise on my honor that I will endeavor with every breath to keep it from happening again for the rest of my days." He held her close, leaning his head down to rest on her bonnet.

"You'll not relinquish your title for me. I should leave here— I should go, it would be better for you if I did. I— I cannot allow you to do something so foolish. I truly don't know what you mean to accomplish by doing so."

"Let me show you what it means." His hand went to her chin. He tilted her head back, his mouth descending. He brushed his lips across hers, warming them, begging her blood to rush, to heat her body. She sighed as he took, delving into her mouth to taste her, explore her, feel her. He was gentle, considerate and careful.

Drawing back slightly, he opened his eyes. And as her lips chased his, wanting to be kissed more thoroughly, he watched her and waited.

Frustrated at being so close but not being allowed her desire, Lilly opened her eyes and looked into his smoldering gaze. What she saw there, in their depths, shook her.

"I love you, Lilly, sweet Lilly. I love you, I love you, I love you." He pulled her ever tighter against him, caressing her lips with his words.

The reverberation of his voice against her mouth sent a shiver through her and she couldn't help but to sigh again. She melted into him, a single tear running down her cheek.

He kissed it away, then kissed her again, the salt of her tear flavoring their passion, fueling their connection.

"You cannot leave me," he said quietly, "for I am naught without you."

She shook her head, not wanting to break the cloud of emotion that enveloped them but knowing she must. "No, milord, it isn't right. It isn't."

"I see that I will need to convince you still."

He released her, and she nearly fell to the earth with the sudden loss of his powerful embrace.

He lifted her in his arms and marched for the carriage, her skirts trailing behind them like the abandoned ribbons of a maypole.

The rest of the luncheon party had gathered by the barouche, waiting.

Maebh caught sight of them first and strode forward.

Perry stopped just short of her and placed Lilly on her feet. She immediately ducked behind him as he caught Maebh's gaze. "Not one word Maebh, not one."

She glanced from Perry to Lilly, whose expression was overwhelmed and discontent, then back to Perry. Her eyes softened and Perry sighed. "I only— I didn't mean to say what I said. I just—"

"It matters not. You've found her." She dropped her voice until it was nearly inaudible over the gentle breeze. "She's not like us, Perry, and I believe you take that for granted."

"I'm attempting to show her, Maebh. I am attempting to do what's right."

"I understand that you are, but can you not realize that a week of explaining cannot possibly eradicate a lifetime of learning one's place?"

"What do you know of her place?"

"It's more than obvious: she dodges eye contact, flushes when any of us say her name, is terrified of using *our* names. Certainly you can see this as well?"

He nodded. "I can, and perhaps she needs more than a week, but—"

"Or perhaps she needs to return to what she is familiar with."

"No— I cannot, I couldn't bear to—"

"*You* cannot bear— Perry." Maebh carefully reached out and took his hand in hers. "What is best for her?"

He'd done his level best to convince himself that *he* was what was best for her. He moved uncomfortably, remembering his previous words to Lilly regarding his reputation as a rake: *that is who I am and what I do.* His gaze shifted penitently from Maebh.

Lilly shifted behind him, trying to hide her discomfiture. She latched onto him as she had their first night at the inn, and he softened instantly. He turned and wrapped her in the safety of his arms. Steadying her physically while also attempting to steady her nerves.

"Hush, sweet Lilly," he whispered into her hair.

Maebh shifted; this wasn't the Lilly they had met this morning. The girl was rather shy, of course, but all Maebh could see now was what appeared to be one of the most fragile beings she'd ever encountered.

None of her family was so fragile; they were all very strong and sure. In all her experience, she'd never met someone so timid and terrified. Her upbringing hadn't allowed for weakness of any kind, and Lilly's fear emanated from her so powerfully it was a tangible force. Lilly's raw need for protection and care called out to her soul, demanding shelter.

Maebh composed herself quickly and stepped forward, but was then struck by her cousin's strong, tall form wrapped cautiously, yet firmly, around the other woman. Perry's demonstration with Lilly—the way he shielded her from their environment, enveloping her so carefully as to cut off all outward effects on her senses—was mystifying. Maebh could feel the calm surrounding them. She turned then and walked back to the carriage.

"Kerrigan, fetch a hack," she said quickly.

"What are you about?" Saoirse asked.

"We are going home directly, as are they are as well. However, we are to part ways here." She glanced over her shoulder. The two figures hadn't moved. "Calder would never allow us to run through London without an escort. I know Kerrigan to be admirable and dedicated, so he will see us home in the barouche while Perry escorts Lilly in the hack."

"Shouldn't we say our goodbyes? We leave for Eildon Hill for Roxleigh's wedding on the morrow," said a concerned Isadore.

"There will be no interrupting them. What is happening there—" She nudged her head toward Perry. "—is beyond anything we are prepared for. I don't believe I ever understood the depth of his character until today. We are to leave them. He will understand, and she will be grateful. She doesn't need us…she has what she needs." Maebh looked away, then turned back when Kerrigan ran up.

"Hack is ready, milady. I'll load the barouche. Am I to see you ladies home?"

Maebh nodded. "Thank you, Kerrigan, we'll await you at the carriage." She took Saoirse by the arm and approached the barouche with Isadore and Poppy following. Saoirse never looked back; she understood and trusted her sister's words without a second thought, but that trust came from doubting her countless times in the past and being proven wrong.

Isadore and Poppy glanced behind them several times, concerned for their new friend. As Gardner handed the ladies into the carriage, Kerrigan booted the picnic, then gave instructions to the driver of the hack and handed over enough coin to keep him for any amount of time. He added a caution that if the driver were to leave as soon as the barouche was away, then he would be found post-haste and dealt with.

The driver nodded and looked at the figures in the distance. He tied off the reins and leaned back in the box, putting his feet up and his cap over his eyes. Then he crossed his arms across his chest and settled in for a nap. "Odd sort, the gentry," he mumbled to himself. "But his coin pays my rest, so I wait until he calls."

The sound of Perry's horses rumbling down the road was the only thing that could have broken his concentration. He focused his attention back on Lilly. She was no longer shaking and her breath had steadied, her tension drained. He loosened his hold slowly, waiting for her to look up from his chest. He ran his hand up and down her spine,

continuing to steady her.

Although her expression was still confused when she finally looked up, it was also more serene. Her eyes met his and held, the green of the grass around them reflecting and rioting within their depths. She took a deep breath, her chest filling and expanding, colliding with the wall of his.

He moved one hand to her jaw and she leaned into his palm, closing her eyes. "Will I ever find this with someone else?" she whispered.

"Why should you, when you have this with me?"

She started to shake her head but he held her still. She opened her eyes, but he was close, the sight of him stealing the breath she would have used to argue.

"I love you, Lilly." His lips moved against hers. This kiss was different from any kiss before. This kiss wasn't meant to rouse. This kiss was meant to prove, compel, and bind.

She grasped his coat in her hands and pulled him closer, ever closer. The embrace reached through to her soul and deepened, yet still did not push. She realized his intention, felt his testimony against her mouth, understood in that moment the truth of his words, his conviction. She should never have doubted him.

He moved to her side and swept her off her feet again, then carried her to the hack he assumed his man had arranged.

"Ho!"

The driver started, sitting up and pulling off his cap, then jumped down to wrench the door open.

Perry carefully placed Lilly inside the small carriage then followed her up. He gave instructions to the driver, who closed the door behind him and leapt up to the hack, sending the horse down the lane.

"From here on," Perry said, turning to her and taking her hand, "my intentions toward you are to be taken as honorable. You are to remove to Roxleigh House across the square and take residence there as a guest. I will arrange for one of my aunts to act as chaperone, and I will provide my own men for your safety."

"I do not understand," she whispered.

He took a deep breath. "I am to court you, Lilly, with the intention of taking you to wife."

# FORTY-FOUR

illy's eyes grew wide, sparkling in the dimness of the carriage. She started to shake her head but he caught her hand in his again.

"No, we'll have no more of this between us. No more confusion, no more questions. I have made my intentions clear. You will need to decide what path to choose." She opened her mouth to argue and he placed a thumb over it gently. "But not today. You will allow me to court you properly, you will allow yourself to be courted properly. You will decide your path when I ask you to be my wife. Make no mistake, I have not done so yet."

Lilly blinked. She nodded once, and he released her and withdrew to the opposite corner of the hack, which wasn't all that far as the combination of his size and the cramped interior of the carriage didn't allow for much space.

They soon arrived back at the town house and Perry handed her to the pavement. He heard his carriage and horses in the back mews and smiled, knowing his cousins were already safely at home.

He turned to the driver and handed him an extra coin.

The driver hesitated, then smiled. "Anytime yer in need, milord," he said with a stiff nod.

Perry escorted Lilly inside, then paused and turned to her. "As I imagine you are quite weary, I would think you'd enjoy a bath while I make out some instructions and send them off. We'll move you to Roxleigh House on the morrow, for my family is quitting London for the wedding and I need to make arrangements before everyone is away."

"A bath does sound quite nice, in fact," she said in her best speech. "Perhaps when you are finished you will join me upstairs? We missed the lesson you had planned for today, and I would hate to be a poor student."

Perry was momentarily taken aback by her change in demeanor, but then he kicked the corner of his mouth into a grin. "I would love to attend you, my dear, as we will have little opportunity after tomorrow. Though poor is far from the descriptions I would choose for you."

She turned and walked toward the stairs, allowing her hips to sway enticingly, her skirts swishing across the floor at her feet like a wide broom. She ascended the steps carefully, knowing he was watching her every move.

Perry's mouth went dry. He had the rather sudden thought that he wanted to see her in pearls. And not much else.

Harper cleared his throat politely, bringing Perry around.

"I'll be in my study, no visitors," he said.

Harper nodded and, taking Perry's gloves and hat, he retreated.

Perry went straight to his desk to write to one of his aunts and explain the circumstances...carefully. He considered his options. Lady Wyntor might not be in town as she'd never been fond of the Season, and as she had only the two sons, she wasn't particularly needed there, either. Lady Trumbull was too feisty for his purposes. He didn't need another willful and overbearing Irish woman in his nose; his experience with her daughter Maebh this morning was proof of that.

So it was left between the dowager Duchess of Warrick and the Duchess of St. Cyr. He would need to prepare Lilly to be in the company of either. Perry thought the latter duchess to be just the thing. Her son Calder was obviously of a mind to appreciate the difficult situation Perry found himself in, and since she'd raised Calder to be such a man, he knew she would be of a like mind. Not only that, but in the Trumbull hierarchy she was the reigning matron, one who ruled Society's opinions with an iron fist of butterflies. She should be the first to sing the praises of his precious lady.

He took his quill from the desk and dipped, then blotted it.

Madame,

It would be my honor if you would extend your time in London to be introduced to a recent acquaintance of mine. In truth, she is in need of a chaperone, such as we know you to be, for perhaps a fortnight until I return to Eildon. I would consider it the greatest honor if you were to act in her interest and stay with her, as she will be a guest of my brother at Roxleigh House as of the morrow.

If you would be so good as to attend a small dinner at my own town house this evening, you may be introduced and I will endeavor to explain everything then.

Shall we say nine o'clock?

Very respectfully, your devoted nephew,

Peregrine

The duchess studied the formal writing on the outside of the missive, then shrugged as she broke the seal. "Hmmm…" She looked at the faces of her sisters, sons, daughter, nieces, and nephews, who were all taking tea with her in the parlor.

*Her Grace, Auberry Leigh Calder,*
*The Duchess of St. Cyr*
*Sussex Square, Kensington Gardens*

"What is it, Mama?" asked Isadore.

"Well, it appears that all the excitement of your excursion has brought a difficulty with which my dear nephew needs my support."

Isadore watched her mother fold the missive and tuck it into the hidden pocket of her skirt. The duchess was petite, as she was, with rolling blonde curls the color of cornsilk. Her vivid eyes were either bright green or blue, depending on the environs, and Isadore always thought her gaze magical in that respect. Whenever she spoke, the color of her eyes shifted as she looked around a room, reflecting what her gaze was cast upon. She, intent on its occupants. Her mother carried the look of a wiser woman than she, but still the duchess was often mistaken for her sister instead of her parent.

Isadore, in fact, didn't realize that she was the mirror image of her mother in a younger day. "And are you willing to help?" Isadore asked.

The duchess glanced at her daughter. "I am of a mind, of course. As you are off to Eildon with family there is no need of me. You, and your cousins, shall be surrounded by willing chaperones. I see no harm in staying behind and helping Perry with this difficulty, whatever it may be. We will join the party in a fortnight—plenty of time to commune before the ceremonies begin."

Isadore looked to her cousins as the duchess called to their butler, Albert.

"Your Grace." He bowed reverently.

"I imagine Trumbull's man is awaiting my response?"

"He is, Your Grace."

"By all means, send him in."

Albert backed out of the room, allowing Kerrigan to enter.

Kerrigan bowed. "Your Grace," he said, then swept his eyes over the room. "—es," he added slowly, along with a precarious "My lords and ladies."

The duchess smiled and waved at him to stand. "I realize I must thank you for attending the ladies and returning them safely to Calder House. I am most appreciative of your service to my family."

"'Twas my honor, Your Grace, as ever."

"If you would be so kind, inform your household to expect fifteen for dinner, and notify Lord Trumbull that his family has accepted his invitation."

Kerrigan's eyes widened, for he knew Perry wasn't expecting the family to descend on his meager—by comparison—town house, as he also knew that there was no way for him to argue on his behalf. Unfortunately for his master, Kerrigan also realized that he wouldn't be prepared, as he'd given explicit orders to be left undisturbed until his guests arrived. However, for this bit of chaos, disturbing him may be the lesser of two evils.

The duchess' eyes twinkled up at him knowingly.

"As you wish, Your Grace," Kerrigan said with another bow.

The duchess nodded and he backed out of the room swiftly, a sweat breaking across his brow. Some simple dinner this was to be. "Fifteen?" he said under his breath as he walked from the house. "He'll have my arse for this!" he exclaimed as he mounted his horse and turned for Grosvenor.

The duchess giggled as the front door closed behind Perry's man. She looked around the room to find wide-eyed stares on all fronts. "What?"

"You could have sent that man straight to the gallows and he'd have gone more happily, Mama," Calder said.

The duchess laughed loudly, the sweet, hearty sound carrying throughout the room and relaxing the rest of her family. "Perry should have known better than to send an invitation to dinner, to me—at Calder House—at *tea*," she said with a grin. "I daresay there was hardly a way I could slight my dear family when an invitation was delivered with everyone in attendance."

"And I daresay it will never happen again," her younger son Jerrod injected.

Isadore looked up at her twin brother who stood at her shoulder. "Jerrod!" she whispered.

The duchess reached across the chaise and patted her daughter on the knee. "Oh, Isadore, my sweet, don't trouble yourself. Thorne?"

"Yes, Mama?" Calder responded.

"You will fetch your father and uncles from White's, won't you? They aren't aware we have a dinner to attend this evening." Though it was phrased as a request, everyone knew it was truly a command.

"Of course, Mama. Might I implore Jerrod, Quentin, Grayson, and Timothy to accompany me?" he said in the same tone.

"Don't dare manage me, sweet. You'll not emerge unscathed."

He bowed, hiding a sly grin.

She laughed and waved off all the men in the room. "Be gone with you. The parlor at tea is a lady's domain, and you, sweet gentlemen, are no ladies," she said with a bright smile.

Calder leaned down to kiss her on the cheek and whisper in her ear before he brushed a kiss across the hand of every woman in the room. His brothers and cousins followed suit, then they all gathered in the hall, laughing as the doors shut.

"Good God, man, how long were we to endure that?" Lord Timothy Wyntor, Earl of Vaughn, asked. "Your summons didn't refer to tea," he said grumpily.

"I was already to White's. You could have found me there," his brother Quentin added.

"I wasn't entirely confident in what form our cousin's need would surface. I merely assumed that Calder House would be the best place to find the result," Calder answered. "Along that line, I won't be quitting London with the family. I'll stay in residence to assist Perry as need arises, until we all return to Eildon," he said as he donned his top hat.

"Then I remain as well." This from Grayson, the Duke of Warrick.

Calder nodded and gestured to the door. "Shall we?"

# FORTY-FIVE

illy felt better after her bath. She started to dress for the evening, then realized it wasn't yet needed. She picked up the book Perry had given her of Tennyson's poems and sat in the chaise next to the fire. Some of the words popped off the page, while others sank into the delicate paper, hiding from her. She made some mental notes about which words she needed help with as she spent her time perusing the volume.

It was the most wonderful gift she had ever been given. It wasn't the exceptional first edition Perry kept in his library, but to her this one meant more. He had inscribed the flyleaf, most of which she was still unable to read, and what words she could understand seemed inconsequential, up unto the last of them.

My something Lilly,

I something tell you how something I am with you something day. How something I am of you, how much I hope you have a something something, with a something something who will give you all the something and something your something something.

At times I wish that something be me, but as you keep something it can something be; it can something be.

Something something that I something you, you have something me much joy, and opened my eyes to a new sort of something.

I love you for that,

Perry

She sighed. *He has hope, and he loves me for—something.* She sank back into the cushions to rest her eyes, clutching the book to her breast.

Perry heard the long case clock and stopped in the entry to his suite, the realization of his error slowly dawning on him. "No," he whispered. His arms fell limp at his sides and his jaw clenched in a violent frown. He turned to stop Kerrigan, but realized quickly there was no hope of catching him. Kerrigan was faster on his mount than any man in London, an asset that made him an invaluable man to keep.

He shook his head and shut the door behind him, then walked to his chest of drawers. He pulled the amethyst pin from his cravat and placed it in the tray as he unwound the long grey fabric.

He was shrugging out of his jacket when he heard a bloodcurdling scream. He bolted without thinking, tearing his jacket clean in two. He slid through the bathing room, the floor still wet from Lilly's bath, and landed with a loud thud in the doorway, looking around the room.

Lilly was stretched out on the long chaise by the fire, her hands held out in front of her, her face twisted in terror. He stood, daring to breathe again when he realized that Lilly's attacker was only in her dream. He strode swiftly to the chaise and rested on the edge next to her, taking her hands gently in his and pulling her forward.

She fought against him as he pulled her up. He wrapped her hands around him, holding her as close as he could.

"Wake up, I beg you. Shh, sweetheart. It's a dream, Lilly, naught but a dream." He felt her tension fade, then shift, and her hands clutched at the back of his shirt.

"My lord, I—" She sobbed. "'Twas him, I thought he were here, I thought as how he'd followed me. I—" She shook in his arms.

"Shh, sweet, shh. I'm here, he is not. And he never will be. I'll protect you," he said quietly, brushing her hair from her face.

"No, you can't. You can't possibly always be there. I don't want you to always be there. I don't want to feel trapped by your presence. I want to enjoy you, I want to be near you, I don't want to feel as though you *must* be there to protect me. You must understand the difference."

She twisted her fingers together.

He nodded. "I do understand the difference, which means we'll have to see to Hepplewort in a more permanent manner." His hands fisted. "And we will—we have plans for him. For now, however, I will protect you. If I am not close by, then my men will be there in my stead, as will Her Grace."

She looked up at him and nodded, then reached for her book, which had slipped to the floor while she slept. "Will you read to me?"

"Of course, what would you like to hear?"

"The inscription."

"No, sweet, I'll not read that for you. You have to learn those words for yourself. It is...important."

She frowned, then turned the pages to find a poem that had some of the words she needed to learn and handed it to him.

"Clever girl." He stretched out along the chaise and pulled her atop him. Her head and hands rested on his broad chest as he started to read, pointing to each word as he spoke. When he came to the word she wished to learn he slowed, teasing her.

"Beautiful," he said, stroking her jaw softly.

She smiled and reached for the book, turning to the inscription. "I hope you have a beautiful *something*." She sighed and looked up. "Just one?" she pleaded.

He laughed and it shook her head to toe. "All right, one. But remember, sweet, I wrote this inscription days ago. Things have changed."

She looked happily into his eyes and nodded.

"I hope you have a beautiful future." He set the book on the side table.

She stretched toward him, their lips meeting halfway. His hands wrapped around her, finding her soft round bottom. He lifted her, sliding her along his rigid form until her mouth melded solidly with his. Her legs fell to both sides of his thighs, drawing her body down. He groaned, pushing against her, and she felt the evident ridge of his arousal pressing between her legs.

She arched away from his chest, bringing herself down hard

upon his erection. She could feel it close to where she wanted it, and she shifted forward, crying out as his hands kneaded her backside and pulled her tightly to him.

"Ah, Perry!"

"Lilly, sweet, wait. I beg you."

"No, Perry, I need you, I need you now." And she did. Beyond anything else she could feel, beyond anything else she knew, she needed him inside her. Her body ached for the missing thread of him between her thighs. She reached down and pulled at the hem of her chemise, hitching it to her waist. "Now, Perry, now." She took his shirt and sent buttons flying, then helped to remove it.

"Lilly!"

"Shh." Her hands went between them, feeling along the front of his trousers, unbuttoning them.

"Lilly, I need to—"

"Please. Now."

Her frenzy startled him, and he moved his hands between them. "Lilly, just wait— just..." He slid his trousers down far enough and she grasped his shaft, guiding him to her entrance. She sank down, crying out, and he clutched her hips to slow her descent.

"Oh God, Lilly, you are so…perfect," he groaned as she rested fully on him.

Her legs straddled his and the chaise, stretched wide, and she bent her knees and hooked her feet on his legs behind her, then she shifted forward with a shriek.

"God, Lilly, please. You—" He grunted.

She shifted again, rounding her back and pressing her hands into his chest. As she moved forward she arched and felt his hands reach up to her breasts. She shifted and pushed down as hard as she could, taking all of him.

"Slow— Slow down."

"I can't," she cried. "I need, ah! I feel... No, I can't." She needed him, she needed to feel him, all of him in a physical, tangible way. She pulled at her gown. "Take this, get this off, I need to feel your skin against mine."

He grabbed the gown, tearing it asunder. Her rhythm increased, and he reached back up to grasp her breasts.

"Stay with me, Lilly."

"Perry, Perry, Perry!"

"Come off for me, Lilly, come off for me." He lifted and closed his mouth around one nipple, then the other. She arched away from him, her screams deepening as her body clenched tightly around his. "Oh God, yes, Lilly. There, sweet—there."

He leaned back on one elbow, his other hand holding her hip, his thumb resting by her belly button. He held her down and thrust up into her one last time before she collapsed on his chest and his release spilled, flooding her womb. He groaned and fell back, wrapping his arms around her sated body, his hands running up and down her back, his eyes wide. He was quite sure she wasn't aware of what she'd done, while he was all too aware of the cad he'd been for allowing it.

"Lilly, that wasn't exactly a good idea."

She lifted up suddenly, a blush painting her cheeks. "Why?"

"Well— Before, I took measures to help prevent you becoming with child." He moved slowly, still buried within her. "But you didn't give me a chance to do so here," he said quietly.

"Oh," she said, the realization sinking in. "Oh!" She pushed against his chest.

He groaned. "Oh, Lilly, you… You probably shouldn't move like that." He wrapped his arms tightly about her to hold her still.

Her eyes grew wide and her mouth opened in another O.

He cleared his throat and grasped her hips, lifting her up from him.

A small cry of disappointment escaped her as he turned to his side and set her on the chaise facing him, his erection cradled by her soft belly. He breathed slowly, willing his passion to subside until a more convenient moment.

"You would be disappointed if I were to become with child."

"Not for the reasons I assume you are thinking. And don't think for one moment that this is a disappointing turn for me."

"For what reason, then?" she implored, shifting her hips to

become more comfortable.

His hand grasped her hip again, this time more firmly. "You must stop wiggling, or we will not be leaving this chaise anytime soon." He grunted. "The reason being that I would prefer you were not with child until *after* I take you to wife. I would think that to be obvious. I

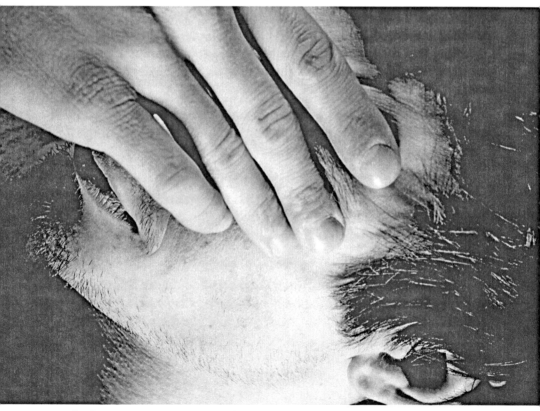

don't want Society to think for one moment that I wed you only because I bedded you." He pinched the bridge of his nose. "Is that understood?"

She nodded, trying to keep her body as still as possible, a hopeful smile on her face.

Perry laughed and rolled away from her, holding on to his trousers as he stood. "You, come with me, just as you are," he commanded.

She stood carefully, unfolding her legs and stretching her muscles.

As he watched her, his mouth went dry and his need pulsed heavily in his blood. He marched for his room, stripping off the rest of his clothes as he went.

He spent the remainder of the day making proper love to the woman he knew he would take to wife—if he had any say—very soon.

Perry bathed while Lilly slept. Telling her that his entire family was on the verge of descending on them wasn't something he looked forward to. She still seemed wary of her new position in his life, and becoming immersed in the entirety of the Trumbull clan would be a daunting task for any person, much less this precious soul. He was honestly worried for her and how she would react during the next few hours.

He heard a sweet sigh behind him and turned, leaning his arms on the side of the tub and resting his chin on them. Lilly stood in the doorway, wrapped in one of his bed linens. "Hello, my sweet."

"Hello, my love," she returned with a smile.

He smiled at the moniker, hiding his face momentarily behind his arm. The endearment touched him in a way he'd never expected. "I've just finished. I'll drain the tub and leave you to it."

She smiled again and nodded.

He turned and stood, the water coursing off his figure before her eager eyes. He stepped from the bath and wrapped himself in a fresh, warmed towel. "You might want to step back a touch," he said as he tucked the corner of the towel at his waist and grasped the tub, lifting it to let the water rush to the drain.

The water flooded to the floor as the drain backed up from the volume.

"Don't worry, sweet. The pipes simply aren't big enough to handle the rush of water, and I've not the patience to pour slowly."

She laughed and watched the muscles working in his arms and abdomen as he sat the tub back on its feet.

"Call your maid and have her fill it for you." He paused. "One more thing," he said, approaching her slowly. "The duchess has agreed to come to supper, and she is bringing the family with her."

"Family? You mean your cousins?"

"I imagine my cousins, both the gentlemen and the ladies, as well as my other aunts and my uncles. Everyone has gathered in London to travel to Eildon Hill together by train."

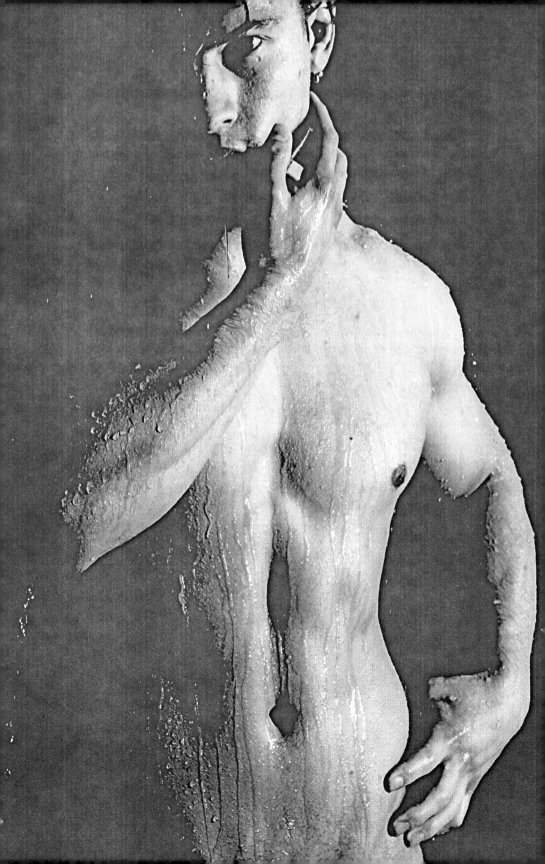

"That's a rather large number of people, then," she said with wide eyes.

"Yes, I must apologize. I hadn't thought before sending the request to Her Grace. I should have known better." He waited patiently, studying her face. "Are you well?" he finally asked.

She nodded, but she appeared concerned.

"I will endeavor to be at your side the entire evening."

She nodded again. He ran his thumb over her mouth, then entered his room, gently pulling his sheet and a squeal from her as he went.

Lilly obsessed about what to wear to meet the clan. She couldn't even keep track of the four—no, five—she had met, so she wasn't sure about all of them. Some seemed nice, some seemed not so sure of her. She shouldn't expect any less from them. She rubbed her forehead. If she were to take on this life with him, she would be forever wary, and what kind of life would that be?

She pulled out the nicest dress in her closet—a color similar to the bonnet that had garnered so many compliments earlier in the day.

She fastened the dress as much as she was able then laced up the

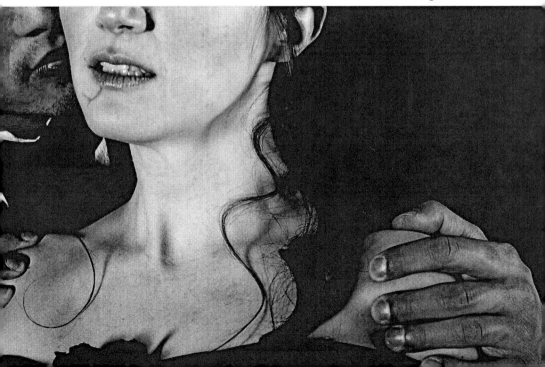

simple black ankle boots and wrapped a shawl around her shoulders. Her hair was drawn back in a chignon with a few loose curls framing her face, casting shadows over her scars. She sat at the small vanity and stared at her image, studying the way the light reflected off her skin. She practiced the perfect angles to hold her chin, to tilt her cheek. If she was very careful, she didn't think anyone would notice. Surely nobody in this company would deign to be so rude as to stare or examine her too closely.

"Nobody will be able to get past your beautiful eyes to see any of the little details you're obsessing over," Perry said from the adjoining doorway.

"You realize it's these little details that caused us to be together to begin with," she said quietly. "You always say such wonderful things."

"They are only wonderful because they are true. No lie would have that effect on a person because they would know the truth of the matter." He walked up behind her and rested his hands on her bare shoulders, lightly stroking.

She looked forward, catching his reflected gaze in the mirror. "My lord, you do have me at a disadvantage," she said breathlessly.

"And what disadvantage, pray tell, would that be?"

"You, my lord, hold every possible advantage there is," she said, enunciating carefully. "You are tall, strong, brave, titled, connected, well-spoken, feared, revered—" She ticked off each word with her fingers as she spoke.

His hand moved up her neck to her mouth, his thumb stopping the words that poured forth. "I wish you to see what I see," he murmured. "Watch your eyes." He held her face as he kissed his way down her ear, nibbling at her earlobe, then continued kissing a path down the side of her throat, suckling gently at the hollow of her shoulder where he could see her pulse. He glanced up and smiled; she followed directions well.

She swallowed and he moved to her shoulder, slipping her dress down her arm just a bit, his hand warming the skin at the edge of the dress. He stood and met her smoldering gaze. "What do you see?"

"You," she whispered.

He smiled and replaced the shoulder of her dress, smoothing his hands down her arms and gently gripping her. "I have something for you to wear."

She watched as he lowered a necklace over her head, letting a red stone dip below her neckline before pulling the chilly metal up to rest in the hollow at the base of her neck. She gasped as it dragged across her skin, then reached up to touch it. "I can't wear this, someone will say something. It belongs to your family."

"Actually, no, I had this piece made recently. The family jewels belong to my brother as the head of the family. This belongs to me."

She ran her hand down the necklace. The stone at the base of her throat filled the indent perfectly, just as he'd planned.

He lifted her up and turned her toward him, running his finger along the chain. "These are white sapphires, and this—" He outlined the stone. "—is a ruby."

She watched him examine the ruby against her skin, and a shiver ran the length of her spine. His gaze on her was so determined, intense, his eyes seeming to glow with an inner light. She took a deep breath, her chest filling, her breasts brushing against his arm, and his gaze jumped to hers.

"I knew this was your color when I saw the bonnet. I had no idea how truly perfect it would be." He leaned toward her as she lifted up, and he placed a single gentle kiss on the corner of her mouth. "Now, let us see to your dress. I'm sorry my household is lacking in the lady's maid department, though I have been told in the past that I'm rather adept at both the undressing and dressing of ladies."

He fastened the dress and straightened her shawl, then turned suddenly, walking to the entry of her room. "I will go greet the guests. Please join us when you are ready." He opened the door to the corridor. "And Lilly," he said, smiling at her over his shoulder, "everything will be just fine."

She wasn't sure if he was speaking to her or to himself.

"Trumbull, old man, I'd no idea you were keen on settling in," his Uncle Bridger Trumbull, Earl of Pemberley said, clapping him on the back.

Perry turned his gaze on the earl's daughters, Maebh and Saoirse, who were suddenly ensconced in conversation with their mama, Fallon, the countess. Perry smiled, suffering the earl's pontification.

Most of his guests had arrived, but a multitude of carriages were lined up out front, still waiting patiently for others to disembark. Perry greeted each branch of the family with as much enthusiasm as he could muster. His main concern, truly his only concern, was their reception of Lilly.

The next carriage bore Auberry and Vincent Calder, the Duke and Duchess of St. Cyr, and their three children, two of which Lilly had already met: Calder and Isadore. The third, Jerrod, she had not. Their carriage continued down the street and another took its place. Georgia Grace Danforth, Dowager Duchess of Warrick, had arrived on the arm of her son, Grayson Locke Danforth, Duke of Warrick, and with her daughter, Lady Poppy. As Warrick would be staying behind with Perry to watch over Lilly, it was important that she know him.

The final carriage held Helena Wyntor, Marchioness of Cheshire, and her two sons, Lord Vaughn and Lord Quintin.

Perry let out a breath, sweeping his gaze over the heads of his family with a smile. As terrified as he was of this moment, he was equally happy to have everyone together under one roof. The family migrated naturally, his uncles in one group, aunts in another, while his cousins drifted off in the entryway, lords and ladies slowly shifting away from one another, just like the elders.

He was roused from his inspection of his family by a nudge at his elbow. Surprised, he turned to find Harper pointing surreptitiously up the stairs.

"Lilly." It was more a breath of a vow than a word. He looked around the room. There was no way for him to move everyone into the parlor where they could receive Lilly quietly. He saw her begin to walk down the stairs. He pushed through the throng, vaulting up the steps and drawing every eye with him.

A collective hush fell over the entry as Perry stood one step below her, holding up his hand.

Lilly placed her hand in his, letting it disappear into his clasp as she looked up and saw nothing but his eyes on her.

Perry turned to descend the stairs, his gaze still holding hers, willing her strength, lending her his, and guiding her into the next chapter of her life.

A brilliant smile lit her face, and he knew she would win them, each and every one.

"I say, Trumbull," the Marquess of Cheshire said, "wasn't quite expecting this here." He looked at his wife, who took his arm and smiled at him.

"Dear man, let the boy be." She patted his arm.

The marquess grunted and turned back to the stairs.

Lady Fallon watched her daughters carefully, particularly Maebh, who stood arm-in-arm with Saoirse as the two descended the stairs.

Perry never took his eyes off of Lilly as he led her down the steps. When they reached the last step he stopped her. "Lilly, I would like to present you my family." He turned, slowly gazing at each of his family members with a silent caution. "I present you, Miss Lilly Steele of Kelso."

He guided Lilly around the entry, introducing and reintroducing her to each member of the family, purposely coming to Her Grace, the Duchess of St. Cyr, at the end. "Your Grace, Miss Lilly Steele. Miss Steele, Her Grace, the Duchess of St. Cyr." He noted the concern in his own voice.

Lilly curtseyed deeply, rising only when she felt a touch on her shoulder.

"Please, child, there is no need of such formalities here. This is family. As you have been invited among us, you will follow accordingly."

Lilly nodded. "Of course, Your Grace."

Auberry glanced at Perry, then back to Lilly. "Miss Steele, if you throw a *Your Grace* around here, you'll garner the attention of no less than three of us. That being said, *my ladiy* and *my lord* would serve a slightly more difficult proposition, and so *that* being said, with our host's permission, we will do away with all formalities for the night. You will address me as Auberry." She smiled warmly.

Lilly started to shake her head, and Perry saw the panic flash across her face. He took her hand and drew it through his arm as he captured her attention with a brilliant smile.

"As awkward as this may seem for my guest, I have no doubt she will endeavor to follow your wishes, though because she has such a great deal of respect for propriety, she may slip at times."

Auberry nodded with a smile, patting Lilly's hand.

# FORTY-SIX

"Dearest nephew," Auberry began, "do tell us of this woman Roxleigh is to wed. None of us have had the chance to see much of her, other than the ball where— Well." She cleared her throat. "When he proposed rather…unceremoniously."

"Ah, yes, her coming out sent her right back in, did it not? Amazing how that all went," he said with a grin. "In truth, she is a wonderful lady, and perfectly suited to him, as he is to her. A weaker woman would never suffice, of course, and she has enough will to keep him on his toes and enough brains to prevent him wandering."

"I see. So she truly is a Trumbull wife?"

"Oh yes, Your Grace, she is very much a Trumbull wife. Of the first order, I daresay."

"What of her family? I heard she was from France, but weren't there complications, or—"

Perry chuckled. "My dearest Aunt Auberry, you are so well practiced at beating the bush you never do have to chase your prey, do you?"

Auberry merely smiled.

"I now have responsibility for three young ladies. As my wards they will reside at Westcreek Park until they are presented to Society and married off in the proper fashion. Of course, Lady Francine is one of those wards, so I will have only two charges when I return for the wedding."

Auberry looked around the room curiously.

"They stayed behind at Eildon Hill Park to help with the wedding plans while I came to London to…complete some business since I had quit with such haste." It wasn't so much of a stretch—he had quit with haste, they were left behind, and the details were unnecessary. Or so he thought.

"I'm to assume we shall meet your charges when we arrive at

Eildon this week, then. That will be pleasant."

"I imagine." He pondered. "I haven't had much cause to spend time with them as of yet, but I'm beginning to look forward to getting to know them." He looked at Lilly.

"And you, Miss Lilly, you hail from Kelso. Have you met Trumbull's wards?"

"I have, but not formally. They were being well looked after by the governess. She was quite protective and strict," Lilly responded quietly.

"You will need to learn to speak up, especially at tables as large as this. You see, my sons at the other end looked quite interested in any word of Perry's charges, but were unable to hear your response," Auberry said with a smile. "Don't you worry, I've no doubt Perry would rather they were left without the information," she added with a quiet laugh.

"Thank you, Your Grace." She closed her eyes for a moment, hoping only to survive the rest of dinner.

"Auberry," the duchess replied.

"Beg pardon, Auberry, I might not remember all the names here tonight, but yours is quite beautiful." She tried to smile, but believed it looked a bit crooked.

"Why, thank you, that's very kind of you to say."

Lilly nodded, then looked down the table.

"Perry, you brought me here for a specific purpose. I imagine it's time for you to explain yourself," Auberry said.

Perry choked and covered his mouth politely with a linen, his eyes growing wide as he glanced down the table. She followed his glance to see fifteen pairs of eyes—and then hers—on him. "Hmm." He groaned, placing the linen back in his lap. "I, well, I was hoping for a more private audience with Your Grace," he said politely.

"Of course you were," she said, giving him a preemptive glare.

"Yes, well... Lilly will be my brother's guest at his town house across the Park. She will need a chaperone while there, until we return to Eildon for the wedding." Lilly turned abruptly toward him, and he smiled, continuing. "Naturally I thought of you, as you adore shaping the young ladies of the *ton*, bending them to your will and mastery."

"Naturally," she said with a grin. "Nonsense, however," she added. "Who is to remain with you in London? Calder, I assume, and who else,

Warrick?"

Perry nodded as Calder looked to Warrick with a shrug. He had long since ceased being surprised when his mother knew more than they believed she ought.

"Well, the answer is clear. No need to open Roxleigh House, as she will come to Calder House. You won't remove this poor old duchess to a new location against her will. Calder House may not be as impressive as Gideon's grand town house, but it is sufficient."

Perry laughed and shook his head. "Sufficient, is it, Your Grace? You are well aware that Calder House is more than adequate, and nearly on the same grand scale as Roxleigh House. Impressions are not what counts under these circumstances, merely Lilly's safety."

"I see. A bit more than a chaperone," she said *sotto voce*.

Auberry looked at Lilly, who shied under the sudden scrutiny. She knew she could see the network of scars covering her face. Auberry captured her attention and smiled warmly, setting her back at ease after her untoward scrutiny. Then one of Perry's hands went under the table and wrapped securely over her knee. She concentrated on the steady warmth and smiled back at the duchess.

Auberry looked to Perry and nodded as the final course of dinner was served.

Lilly looked down the table, watching the rest of the family interacting so easily and calmly together. She had always imagined that the people of this status acted in a proper manner at all times, even in their own company. Perhaps the majority of them did, perhaps it was merely this family that was different. Whatever the reason, she loved their jovial banter, the ease with which they conversed. It reminded her much of her own family.

As dinner finished and the women rose, drawing the men politely from their seats, Perry requested an audience with Auberry, who acquiesced. He made his apologies to the men, who awaited a round of port, and escorted the duchess and Lilly to his study.

He led them to the settee in front of the fireplace, then took a seat in a chair nearby.

"Well, I take this meeting to mean we have certain points that must be explained," Auberry said.

Perry nodded. "I would never, upon my honor, place you in a

position where you might find yourself in defense of your own propriety. For that reason, I wish for you to know everything there is to know, and I've no doubt you will know best how to proceed from there."

She looked to Lilly, who appeared a bit peaked. Auberry reached out and patted her hand, reassuring her, and Lilly smiled up at her, not quite lifting her head from where she gazed at the floor.

"Miss Steele came to be known to me when I returned to Eildon with my brother," Perry began quietly, then explained Lilly's upbringing, her injuries, and how they met.

Auberry listened intently, occasionally looking to see how Lilly was faring.

Perry paused after explaining how he found Lilly in his carriage.

"I assume that brings us to London and the need for a chaperone."

Perry smiled and inclined his head. "Not quite."

Lilly blushed and Auberry took her hand. Perry explained, in vague terms, Lilly's requet to him. It weighed the air upon them like a heavy blanket as the room sat in silence and she considered his words. Then she spoke.

"Believe me when I say that the fact you have the support of Calder and Maebh speaks volumes about what has happened between the two of you since you arrived here. I don't require you to give more details, but I imagine my nephew here has done creative and impressive things to fulfill your request for help. "

Lilly looked at the small hand resting on hers and smiled shakily up at her.

"You really have done very well with your speech practice, yes?" Auberry asked.

Lilly nodded.

"I imagine my nephew has been teaching you to read and write?"

Lilly nodded again, a heavy blush traveling her face.

"Well, we may not be able to have quite as much fun in our lessons, but we will continue nonetheless. And while you are under my protection, it will be my duty to protect you, even from my nephew, so I'm afraid those particular lessons will be suspended for now."

"As you wish, Your Grace—Auberry," Lilly said.

"You must be very well versed in proper behavior since you were being groomed to attend our Gideon's household, correct?"

"For a time."

"Perfect. That will come in handy when I take you out with me. We won't endeavor to attend any balls or great functions, but we shall attend tea with acquaintances should we be invited, and we shall take a few turns around the park. This will not be simple for you, my dear. A bit of a trial by fire, I'd say, but as you did exceptionally well being surrounded by my clan, I would guess you'll fare well regardless of the situation."

Perry smiled and stood. "Shall we return to the parlor to join the rest of the family?"

Auberry stood and pulled Lilly up from the settee. "We'll go find the ladies. Chances are the gents are still avoiding our company." Auberry then turned to Perry. "We'll also be able to talk more easily without you brooding over your charge."

Perry cleared his throat. "I would prefer she not be referred to in that manner as I do have three already, to whom I do not have the same intention."

Auberry smacked his arm. "You may be a rake of the first order, but we are ladies of the highest order and you will remember yourself in our presence," she said haughtily, her grin sparkling in the dim study.

Perry glanced at Lilly, whose spine straightened and chin rose perceptibly.

"As you wish, Your Grace. I will see you both soon."

Lilly curtseyed. "Until then, my lord."

Perry took her hand and placed a kiss across her knuckles, then turned it over, placing a kiss in her palm and a final kiss on the inside of her wrist.

Lilly's skin tingled and she smiled brilliantly.

"Peregrine Afton Trumbull, you will behave!" Auberry admonished.

He stood straight then nodded to his aunt. "Yes, Your Grace." Then he turned and walked out of his study to find the men and their spirits.

"Oh, you have done him well, my dear. He is quite thoroughly besotted."

Lilly smiled, uncertain.

"Make no mistake, hearts are breaking across London and well across England this very night. My nephew is no longer available to the matchmaking mamas."

They returned to the parlor, to the rest of the Trumbull women.

Lilly watched them carefully, noticing the small actions and demeanors that set them apart from her class, and indeed from their own and one another as well. Quite before she was ready, the door opened and the parlor was flooded with the men of the family, each one finding a place next to a wife or sister as Perry came to stand at her shoulder.

"Well," Auberry said, "it is late, and my family has an early train to catch. We should be off." She turned to Lilly. "Gather your things, dear, time to remove to Calder House."

Lilly's eyes grew wide, and Perry's hands clutched her shoulders rather suddenly. "Aunt, I had intended to bring Lilly to Calder House in the morning. I—"

Auberry waved him off. "Peregrine, you have charged me with a duty. It matters not what you intended or what you believed. She is now my responsibility and as such I cannot allow her to remain in your care."

Perry's jaw tensed and he walked around the chair Lilly rested in, drawing her to her feet and escorting her from the room silently.

A few moments later, as the family gathered in the entrance, sorting out their capes and mantles, Lilly and Perry descended the steps to the throng. He led her to Auberry.

"You'll not snub me, sweet boy. As aggravated as you might be with me, you still adore me unquestionably. Say goodbye to your aunt properly," she said, tilting her cheek to him.

Perry shook his head and fought a smile as he leaned down and placed a gentle kiss on her cheek. He squeezed her hand. "I'll be calling on you early."

"And you'll be turned away," she replied. "We have much to accomplish. You will continue to try, and will be consistently turned down. I'll allow it, eventually," she said with a grin.

Perry growled and the group silenced before hearty chuckles caught and rolled throughout the entry. He pulled his hand from her and pointed at each of his male cousins. "I look forward to the day you are to receive such treatment," he said with a glare, then pointed to the ladies. "And don't think for one moment you will escape this hawkery. I intend to watch over each one of you, terrifying every suitor who deigns to approach your person."

The group silenced sufficiently, Auberry patted Perry on the arm. "Well done, nephew, well done. Now, let's be off."

He grasped Lilly's arm as she turned to follow Auberry. He lifted her hand and placed a last kiss in her palm, then closed her fingers over it and released her. She stood mesmerized.

"Tut-tut, Miss Lilly, let's not have a scene," Auberry said over her shoulder.

Lilly turned slowly and followed her out.

The next morning the family quit London by rail, set to arrive in Carlisle late that evening, then to proceed to Roxleighshire by carriage the following day.

Perry grimaced at the morning. He readied then watched the maid gather the rest of Lilly's belongings—checking under the bed for a missing slipper, finding it under the chair. He was going to miss Lilly dreadfully.

Less than an hour after breakfast, the curricle was loaded and he was rumbling through the streets of London to deliver his beloved's accoutrements to his cousin's town house. He'd never realized just how far a drive it was to Calder House; he always thought it close, but it was nearly thirty minutes by carriage. That meant at least fifteen minutes by mount.

He jumped to the pavement in front of the beautiful home as footmen rushed about, pulling her trunks from the boot and the roof. He ran up the grand stairway to the portico.

The front door opened to him slowly and Perry nodded impatiently to Albert as he walked through the foyer and swept into the front parlor.

Albert took Perry's gloves and hat. "Her Grace is in the morning parlor, my lord. She is expecting you."

The morning parlor was opened up to let in the fresh summer sunshine. Lilly rested on a chaise by one of the French doors which overlooked the park, her smile brighter than the sun. Auberry was with her.

"Sweet Lilly," Perry said, almost like a benediction as his eyes found her.

"Come, Perry, off with you. I believe Calder and Warrick await you at White's."

Perry looked at Auberry and frowned. "I brought Lilly's things. I thought perhaps—"

"You thought, but no such thing will happen. Make your peace and be off with you now."

Perry shook his head. Perhaps he should have chosen Fallon for a guardian.

He laughed uncomfortably and kissed Lilly's hand. Auberry's polite clearing of her throat stopped him from turning it over. He walked from the room, bowing deeply from the entry before pulling the door closed behind him.

"I thought he would never leave," Auberry said. "Goodness, that boy dawdles."

Lilly smiled nervously as she stared at the door.

"What is it?"

"Only that I don't believe this entire thing is in his best interest," Lilly said quietly.

"You don't say?"

Lilly shook her head. "What I asked of him—" Her face warmed and she dropped her gaze to the floor. "Was patently improper. I understand that. I know that, I knew that at the time. But I was so afraid. I had carried this bit of terror with me everywhere I went."

The duchess took her hand and held it in both of hers.

"You do understand what I asked of him, don't you? You do understand what it was he agreed to?" Lilly asked without meeting her gaze.

"I understand you had been violently misused, and you requested my nephew to demonstrate the proper way a man should touch a woman."

Lilly blanched and looked up, surprised the duchess had responded so bluntly.

"Dear Lilly, you have survived a thing no one would ever expect to, and many would wish not to. I believe it admirable that you were brave enough to know that you needed help with the horrid memories in your mind. I understand completely why you would choose my nephew. It is no secret he is well versed in the area of expertise you sought, and considering your history I don't find it shocking, appalling, inappropriate, or improper. Though, of course, in polite company we should never speak on it."

"I found it so comforting to have someone to speak with about what happened, and now you. It was difficult with my family—though I know they would do anything for me, I think they felt guilty that they couldn't protect me, and therefore, I felt guilty about wanting to speak with them. I kept it all inside. The thing is, I know I am in love with him, but I don't think being with me is the best thing for him. I want him to be accepted, to be comfortable, to continue to do everything he has always done so readily, happily. I think it would be better for him were I to leave. I believe I could. I believe now I could find a nice man to marry me. I wouldn't scream at his touch, I wouldn't shy away at his glance, I wouldn't shudder at the thought of his intimacy."

Auberry studied her charge closely. "But what you haven't considered is that such a thing might not be possible. Have you considered that the reason my nephew is able to approach you—intimately—is simply because it is *him*? I don't believe you understand what has happened here." Auberry squeezed her hands, then straightened. "Once again you have impressed me, and should you choose to disappear I would be one who could help you with this. But only if you truly decide that's in his best interest—and at this point, I'm not convinced it is. Maebh told me of your outing to Regent's Park. I told you last night that it was due to Calder and Maebh's assurances that I believed you to be a worthy person for our family gathering. What I didn't tell you was what Maebh explained to me."

Lilly scarcely remembered the day in the park beyond what had happened between she and Perry; she wasn't entirely sure what Maebh would have to vouch for.

"My precious niece Maebh feels emotions on a much deeper level than most of us do. She knew you were sweet and innocent the moment she laid eyes on you, and for that she was upset with Perry, because she believed him to be taking advantage of you."

"I do remember her being quite short of temper with him."

Auberry nodded. "After they looked for you and he found you, she felt your pain. She felt how deeply you had been hurt and she believed it to have been at his hand." Auberry held up her hand to stave off an argument. "She realized, in watching him, that it was he who was helping you, with his very presence. She could see in the way he sheltered you, that in fact he was more honorable in his intentions toward you than she understood."

Lilly stood and walked to the French doors that opened out onto the large front porch of the town house. She breathed deeply of the floral scent carried to her on the breeze as it swept the loose curls back from her face. She turned.

"'Tis true," she said, "I have never felt such a peace as I feel with him. I have never felt so at ease as I do with him." She looked down at her hands as she considered. "But that is not to say that he should be required to spend the balance of his life taking care of my upended nerves. He deserves better. He should have a woman who can stand at his side and command his staff, run his household, oversee his family. Someone who will add good blood to his lineage."

Auberry stood in front of her, stopping the recitation. "For Perry, what he wants and what he needs may just be one and the same. He does not have the same responsibility to the family as his brother has. He does not hold the dukedom, but a mere viscountcy, and from what I've already seen here, your blood is rich with history, knowledge, compassion, thought, and so many traits our aristocracy needs infused in it—in abundance."

Auberry reached out and embraced Lilly. "Nobody is saying this will be an easy transition—" She stood back, holding her shoulders. "God only knows your family will probably disapprove as much as you seem to believe we should. But somehow we will figure this out. Because for my nephews, all of them, finding them love is of the utmost importance to me. I had neither hand nor choice in Gideon's wild romance, but if there is a way I can help Perry…believe that I will." The two women were the same height, and as different as they were in appearance and bearing, that small bit of common ground warmed Lilly.

"I hadn't even considered my family. I suppose I hadn't thought past the fact that he shouldn't look to me for his future. My family is devoted to the duke and his household. They have served at Eildon Hill for as long as a Trumbull has held the lands. My father looks to Roxleigh as the most important peer in the country, aside from Her Majesty. Along that vein, I'm not sure how His Grace will look on this. I understand him to be very protective of all those in his purview. Until recently, I was considered such."

"Don't think on it. I'll handle the duke if he needs handled, or I'll have his future wife do so as I understand her to be able. Regardless, we won't be arriving until the wedding, so he will have no time to complain before he is shackled and off to Italy or wherever they will be spending their first moon together."

Lilly nodded warily.

"Now, we should look at your things. I'm sure your trunks have been settled in your new room. Shall we?"

Lilly curtseyed, then followed.

Auberry looked through Lilly's wardrobe carefully, inspecting each of her dresses to determine what more she might need. "Perry did very well by you. I'll need to find out who he sent for—her choice of colors was absolute genius, and the designs prevent too much scrutiny, are unpretentious, and frankly quite perfect for your figure."

Lilly smiled. "I thought for sure I'd need no more garments for years. I still can't imagine I need more now."

Auberry returned the smile. "Well, dear, you will have to attend one or two higher functions, and if you attend the wedding, you will need a suitable ball gown, there is no way around that. We will procure you a few things, not much. Do you have a riding habit?"

Lilly shook her head. "I've never ridden sidesaddle. I wouldn't know what to do. We have but the one horse back home, and one saddle to fit him, so if I rode it was astride. My pa never thought anything of it, of course."

"Of course not, and why would he? There is no cause to, as the *ton* is much removed from the country. Truth be told, I much prefer to ride as the men do, though they would have conniptions if they were aware of it."

"Lady Francine wears riding trousers," Lilly said suddenly.

"Well, that is fabulous, I say. I am going to like that one. I look forward to meeting her. We, however, will have you fitted for a habit so as not to attract undue attention. There are ways of cutting them that will be comfortable for riding astride, perhaps a fuller skirt as was fashionable earlier in the century. People will hardly know you to be astride," she said with a smile. "I'll ask Perry about the seamstress. We'll need to find different ways to use this color, but it is most categorically *your* color."

Lilly smiled, but it fell far short of being genuine.

Auberry walked up to her and took her hand. "And how are you faring, my dear? It must be difficult to be away from him."

Lilly looked up and nodded. "More so than I would have thought." She shook her head. "When will he be allowed to visit?"

"When it is proper, he may call in the early afternoon, or with my permission, he may escort us to a ball. But as we discussed before, I'll be turning him away for a time. I do regret that on your behalf, but it is in your best interest. It pains you to be away from each other, but the lesson learned in the separation is insurmountable any other way. Consider it the truest test of my nephew. Though I've not a doubt he is smitten, his true nature will out or, more prudently, we hope it will."

"And what of his true nature? If he returns to his former life, then—"

"Oh, you misunderstand, my dear. That which he has done and lived and cultivated in the most recent past is not his true nature. It is his nature, as with all the Trumbull men, to find the one woman who will master him. The one woman to whom he will defer. I believe that woman to be you. Come to think on it, I am not surprised by you at all. Trumbull women tend to appear from the most unlikely of sources," she said with a grin. "It appears to be a necessity."

"And you, Your Grace? From where were you found?"

"I was born a Trumbull, though finding my own duke, well, that is a story we will dwell on at another time. We've much to accomplish. As for your lessons, you'll need to watch me, for you will have the management duties of your own household soon enough, and you need to learn everything that entails. I've no doubt you are well versed in the basics of household management, but there are things you may not be aware of from the top end."

Lilly nodded and felt instantly overwhelmed. Perhaps disappearing would be better for her as well as Perry. There was so much she didn't know about being a member of the peerage. A member of the peerage… She shook her head. Who would ever believe this? Meggie would never believe. How was she to explain this to her sister?

"Damn time you showed your face," Warrick grumbled. "You'd

not believe who is in the back room."

Perry raised a brow. He supposed he was delayed some, stopping by the shop to purchase a rather long strand of pearls. "Who might that be, and good day to you as well."

"Hepplewort," Calder said, folding the paper he'd been perusing and laying aside his cigar to stand and shake Perry's hand.

Perry scowled and Warrick moved to his other side. He placed a firm hand on Perry's shoulder. "We are not to have a scene at White's, Trumbull—much too great a disservice to the place."

"Also, should Hepplewort see you or me, or rather the two of us together, he'll know what we're about. Frankly, it came as a shock that he would show here," Calder added.

Just then Warrick grunted and moved forward, pushing his cousins toward the wall. "Your lackadaisical attitude toward this man is going to find you both swimming in the Thames," he growled. "Pay attention, at least."

Perry moved around a set of four chairs to sit. Calder followed suit, both men facing away from the room and the entry. Warrick slid past them to rest in the chair with the best view.

"We should discuss how we are to proceed," Perry said.

"How *are* we to proceed?" asked Calder.

"I'm not sure there *is* a way to proceed," Warrick replied. "The man has been warned, and until he does something he shouldn't, what are we to do? We cannot undercut Roxleigh's plea to the House. It wouldn't be the thing."

Perry shook his head. "And so we wait," he said angrily.

Warrick's gaze shifted to the main door, then he nodded at Perry. "He's leaving."

Perry jumped up and turned to the door before Warrick or Calder could think to stop him. He rushed across the room, following the pudgy man from the building.

Hepplewort held a slovenly countenance that sent Perry's hackles to standing. The earl's eyes were buried deep in his folded face and his corpulent jowls hung far past his chin. He *would* be dressed nice enough—if he were a rakish fop in Louis XIV's court. But since he wasn't, and it wasn't, his appearance merely served to turn Perry's stomach.

He stopped outside at the base of the stairs, a smile slowly breaking his stern features as he imagined Hepplewort's surprise upon seeing him. Calder and Warrick flanked Perry, not sure what else to do, and the three men waited patiently for the earl to turn and spy them.

"Get the damn carriage over here now. I asked to you hold it here. I wasn't expecting to be here overlong!" Hepplewort spat at the attendant.

"Of course, my lord, we had several arrivals. Your driver was merely asked to circle back to make room."

"Ridiculous what this place has come to. Back in my youth the thought of moving an earl's coach for the likes of some lower gentry was unheard of!" Hepplewort shouted.

"Pardon again, my lord, but truth be told, 'twas these gentlemen here what displaced your coach, not the lower gentry." The attendant motioned behind Hepplewort. He obviously hoped the sight of the Duke of Warrick, the Marquess of Canford, and Viscount Roxleigh would suffice to stop the man's ranting.

It did.

Hepplewort turned to find the three men occupying the lowest step of White's, every pair of eyes on him. He took a step back and nearly fell from the curb. "Why— Why, my lord, I—I—"

Perry cut him off. "I don't believe you're acquainted with my cousins as yet. Might I present His Grace, Grayson Danforth, Duke of Warrick, and the Most Honorable Thorne Calder, Marquess of Canford. Oh no, I beg your pardon. You have met Canford, have you not?"

"My lord, Your Grace, I—" He stopped himself, bowing deeply before the three gentlemen. When he stood he looked directly at Perry. "My lord, I understand you must be shocked to see me here in London. Might I explain? I was merely, uh—"

It was at that moment Hepplewort looked at Calder again, his eyes widening.

Calder smiled down on him. "Do tell, old man, what *are* you doing in London?"

Perry stepped down, drawing as close to Hepplewort as he dared come to his repugnant person. "It seems, my lord, that we have suffered a failure in communications. I was operating under the impression that you were not to return to London—ever. As you are here, I must have missed something. Perhaps you might be willing to clarify?"

"I, uh, well. Plainly, my lord, the duke has robbed me." He stopped when Perry's eyebrows rose. "I—no—the duke is to be happily married, and I am left to obtain a bride for the continuation of my titled lands as is required. I need to bear issue."

"Hmm. Again, as I remember it, your line was set to die with you. You were not to take a wife or bear any heirs, and the title was to fall where it may, without your help. Did I misunderstand His Grace's directive?"

"No, my lord, just that, well, you met my mother. She's quite insistent that I take a wife and continue—"

"*You* will take *nothing* but your leave of this place. Is that understood?"

Hepplewort looked from one face to the next as he stuttered incoherently, trying to find his verbal footing. "Yes, I— Yes, my lord," he said meekly as his carriage pulled up behind him.

Perry glanced up to find the same stout driver who had once been mastered at his hand staring down angrily. Perry walked to the box and yanked him down. The oversized man swung his arms, but Warrick pinned his hands behind his back, forcing him to his knees as Perry stepped back and straightened his jacket.

"You have been warned before as well. If you'll not adhere to the warnings, not even that man's title will be enough to save you from the gallows. Are you aware of that?" Perry ground out through clenched teeth.

"Yes, milord," the man grumbled.

The scuffle was attracting the attention of passersby. Calder nudged Perry's arm. "We should be moving on," he said quietly.

Perry nodded and caught Hepplewort's eye. "Leave London today and do not return. If I hear the slightest mention of you, anything Roxleigh had planned will be minor in comparison. I want you away from the people you have damaged."

Hepplewort nodded as he crawled up into his carriage.

Warrick released the driver, letting him stand before pushing him toward the box and forcing him up.

The White's attendant released the horses and the carriage rolled down the street. Calder nodded surreptitiously to a street urchin halfway down the block and the boy ran behind the carriage, grabbing the footman's hold at the back and pulling himself to the step. He nodded to Calder as the carriage disappeared around a corner.

Perry looked back at Calder, who shrugged.

"What? You did request I keep track of him while he was here in London. I'd say I've done so admirably, wouldn't you, Warrick?"

"Yes, quite," Warrick said, nodding at Perry. "You know him best. Is he leaving?"

"No, he'll be looking to complete his mother's orders in any fashion he can. He won't leave without a bride, which means we just moved up his deadline to tonight." Perry glanced at Calder. "We'll know where he'll be this evening?"

"Yes, we should know of his plans for the afternoon within the hour, as well as the ones for this evening. I assume he'll pick his attendance carefully, judging by where he believes we'll be."

"But we'll be wherever he will be, which means—" Warrick looked at Perry and held his gaze. "—this will end tonight."

Hepplewort stormed into his house, Morgan on his heels. "Damn him. Damn *them*."

"Perhaps, milord, we should leave. Find you a bride on the way out of town."

"I cannot. Mother would...I need an appropriate bride, a girl of the *ton*. I cannot just pick a girl from the road."

"Yes, milord. There is the Grenvilles' ball tonight. You did send word."

"Yes, yes. Nasty bit of business, this. Hopefully there will be someone there." He removed his hat and gloves and threw them at a chair, then shrugged out of his coat. When his arms were trapped, Morgan gave the capes a little tug to free him. He grunted his thanks.

"Fergus!"

Hepplewort froze.

"Mother." His eyes widened at Morgan, not knowing what to do. She saved him the trouble of thought, as she usually did, and walked out of the parlor. He bowed deferentially, pasting a warm smile on his face. "Dear Mother, I wasn't aware you intended to join me here. I—"

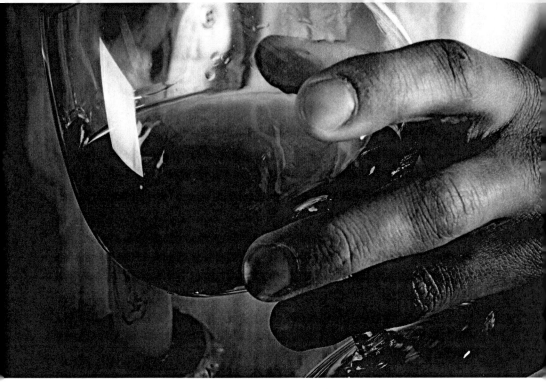

"Hush, Fergus. I considered how successful you were in bringing your bride home—twice—and determined I needed to be here to help."

"Mother, I had plans. I do not need you here."

"Don't speak to your mother in such a manner. Now, as I am here, I will help. You must have plans tonight. What are they?"

"The Grenvilles."

"Send a missive, let them know to expect me as well."


Calder and Warrick arrived at Trumbull House early that evening and waited in Perry's study for him to come down.

"You're sure he's attending the Grenvilles?" asked Warrick.

"Absolutely. His response was...intercepted."

Perry entered the study and poured himself a brandy. "Does this mean that if he doesn't attend he will be missed?"

"Not at all, merely that I've no doubt where he's expected to be," Calder replied.

Perry nodded, holding the balloon over the warming candle lit on the sideboard next to the tantalus. He swirled the fine liquor, watching it catch the light and bend it to its will. He turned toward the chairs where his cousins rested. "Do we have any sort of plan as to how we should proceed?"

Warrick looked up from beneath his eyelashes. It had been years since Perry had spent much time with him, as he'd recently returned from abroad, where he'd spent most of his adult life. The sudden death of his father had required a hasty return, and there were many unanswered questions as to where he'd been and what he'd been doing for all of a decade. "I've an inkling, though I don't imagine it's going to go well. The trouble, as I see it, is that for there to be cause, he must be caught in the act of doing something quite indefensible."

"We *know* his acts to be indefensible." Perry groaned.

"Don't be foolish, Perry," Calder said. "We all want to see him taken care of, but not at the expense of something as vital as your life."

"I want him dead," he replied easily.

"That can be arranged, of course." Perry and Calder turned at how easily Warrick had dispensed those words. He took no notice. "In which case you should be nowhere near this man."

Perry and Calder glanced at each other, eyes wide in consideration. "Warrick is right," Perry said after a pause. "Without cause, we should not proceed. Perhaps we merely wait. He cannot possibly stay true to his word for long, and *you* are no longer able to disappear into the night with that title hanging over your head."

Warrick scowled, seemingly angered by his bonds. "This was not my choice, merely an accident of birth. I didn't live by the rules of the peers while I was…" He shook his head. "And I do not wish to live by them now."

Calder exchanged a glance with Perry as he stood. "Let's be off, shall we?" he said jovially, trying to break the heavy mood.

Warrick nodded and followed. He was the tallest of the cousins by inches, and the most intense by demeanor.

"You make Roxleigh look like a puppy," Perry said with a wink to Calder.

Calder chuckled, clapping Perry on the back. "I do believe you are quite accurate in that assessment," he said, looking at Warrick. "And what will the *ton* think of you?"

Warrick grunted as Perry studied him.

"I've yet to be introduced to the *ton*, particularly as I've yet to be interested in the *ton*," Warrick said.

"You'll find they need you, more than you need them," Perry replied.

"Well, are we off to Lady Grenville's?" Calder asked impatiently.

"By all means," Warrick muttered.

Perry set his brandy on the sideboard and followed Calder through the hall. Harper was waiting with his cape, top hat, gloves, and cane.

"What the bloody hell is that?" Warrick asked, kicking at Perry's walking stick. "I'd no idea you were quite so fashionable," he said with a half grin.

Perry smiled. "Cunning, chap. In fact, this would be my only weapon when I travel the streets of London unescorted." He lifted the cane and pulled the end. The intricately carved handle clicked and slid from the base, revealing a narrow silver blade.

Warrick's face broke in a smile as he reached for it. The blade sang from its unconventional sheath and he smoothed his hands down the well-honed steel. "This is no toy." He tested the blade with his thumb. He flicked it, then measured the weight in his hand. "Well balanced, though the hilt is a bit awkward at first." Warrick thrust, then swept the blade in front of him, testing the feel as Calder and Perry backed away and Harper stepped behind them. "I want one."

Perry laughed. "Well, if you don't mind looking *fashionable* I'll have one made for you, only you'll need to choose the hilt and pommel. Consider it a welcome home gift."

Warrick smiled and nodded, holding the sword carefully at the hilt and gesturing for the scabbard. Perry handed it to him, and Warrick sheathed the delicately carved blade, listening to the solid click as it seated. "Impressive, very well crafted," he said approvingly.

Perry took the weapon when offered. "Should I be concerned that this is the most animated and interested I've seen you since we were both in short coats?"

Warrick's mouth curved in a genuine smile, and Perry realized just how much he had in common with Gideon. Perry could see the unadulterated appreciation in his expression. Much like Gideon and his horses, or his lands, or Francine. It was a striking exhibition on one who was generally so bereft of discernible happiness. While Perry ruminated, Warrick looked around for Harper, who seemed to have disappeared.

As it happened Harper was just outside the foyer, patiently waiting for the men to quit their perusal of the blade. He stepped into the foyer when Perry took the cane, moving to retrieve the duke's cape and hat.

"You know, if you like this blade you should see the weapon I carried in the navy. I didn't have much cause to test it, but know it to be a very well-honed rapier," Perry said.

"Yes," Warrick said, "I would like to, at some point. Perhaps we should spar," he offered as they walked out the door.

"By all means. I've no doubt that would be quite enjoyable. Let us meet over foils," Perry said with a twinkle in his eye.

"Should I feel left out for not having any weaponry training?" Calder asked jovially.

"Yes," Perry and Warrick replied in tandem.

They laughed as they mounted the carriage and were swept off in the night toward Stanhope Place off Hyde Park.


Morgan watched as the carriage pulled away from the Grosvenor Square town house, grumbling as he looked up to the dimmed windows. He snapped the rein, moving the carriage through the street around the park. Roxleigh House at the other end of the square was equally dark and hadn't been warmed since the duke quit London a month prior.

He didn't know of a residence for the Duke of Warrick, though he must be somewhere near the upper end. He groaned and snapped the rein again, bound for Calder House. If any of the Trumbull clan were left behind, Calder House was where they would be.

Hepplewort wanted some sport. His mother showing up had raised his dander. Morgan had been sent to find the girl who was fueling the rumors throughout the *ton*. A bride for a bride.


Lilly looked at her form in the mirror. She was amazed what a well-trained seamstress could accomplish in one afternoon. The dress was the same color everyone said belonged to her, a vibrant crimson in long flowing silks. She had also been fitted into a snug whalebone corset and multiple petticoats over a steel cage support that drew the majority of the fabric up in billowy gathers at the back. The dress was trimmed in a matching georgette, finishing the neckline to perfection.

The maid assigned to help her had drawn her hair up into a large, rolling pile of curls woven through with red satin ribbons. The curls spilled from the top of the pile to bounce cheerfully around her cheeks and over her forehead.

She caressed the necklace that Perry had given her. He had given it to his aunt for Lilly to wear, should they attend a suitable event. She pulled the long pale gloves up over her elbows, until they nearly touched the sleeves of her ball gown, and shook her head.

She heard a quiet knock at her door and turned. "Yes?"

The door swept open to reveal the duchess all done up in a lavender creation, her blonde locks tied up with ribbons of every color.

"Oh, Lilly, you're a vision!" she exclaimed, walking forward to take her hands.

"I'm quite uneasy, Your Grace. I'm not entirely sure of this."

"Don't trouble yourself. The lady is a dear friend of mine, and we shall sit and enjoy her company. Nothing more than companionship will be required of you tonight. I'll make your apologies for you so you won't be requested to dance."

Lilly shook her head. "It all seems so simple when you explain it."

"That's because it is simple. Let's be off." Auberry pulled Lilly down the stairs and to the entry, where Albert waited with their capes.


"Sarah Jane, how wonderful it is to see you," Auberry said, taking her friend's hand and sitting in the chaise next to her. She looked back to Lilly, then pulled her down to sit at her other side.

"Is this the bit of distraction that has kept your Trumbull from attending the Season?" Sarah Jane whispered behind her fan.

"Why, yes, in fact." Auberry pushed the fan aside with a wink. "Might I present you Miss Lilly Steele of Kelso. Lilly, this is the Lady Grenville. She—"

"What, pray tell, are you ladies doing here?"

Lilly jumped. She didn't need to look to know who was standing behind her. She turned to find Perry with his cousins flanking him and smiled nervously, deferring to the duchess.

"Why, Trumbull, what do you mean by asking what we're doing here? Whyever are *you* here? I thought for certain you would be at Lord

Tremayne's this evening."

"And with me safely at Tremayne's you ladies are able to gad about town attending unscheduled routs?" He had seen Lilly the second she entered the ballroom, as had every virile man within the walls. His eyes traveled the length of her, twice, from her broad sweeping crimson skirts to the tightly fitted bodice that held her posture perfectly, to the sheer sleeves that, along with the low neckline, framed the necklace he'd had made for her.

He couldn't help but to gaze at the heavy stone resting at the base of her throat. It moved with her pulse, ever so gently. The large gaslight chandeliers cast a glow about the room, making her hair shine. The loose curls which framed her face cast dancing shadows across her skin.

He was suddenly frustrated that everyone felt the need to hide her scars. He thought she was beautiful, regardless. Her face was perfect, her eyes glowing, her lips full and sweet, her nose pert and slightly turned up at the end. She was stunning, and he felt like nobody had ever noticed save him. Then he looked around the room to find that once again every gent in attendance *was* taking note. He was well and thoroughly distracted by her.

Perry heard the opening strains of a waltz and leaned over to whisper in Lilly's ear. "Do you waltz?"

"With my father and my brothers at the local fairs. I don't know that it would have been considered proper."

"I suppose we'll find out," he said as he turned to Warrick. "Mind my stick?"

"Not at all, Perry, but—"

Perry waved him off, never taking his eyes from Lilly. Warrick took the cane, twirling it in his hand as he balanced the weight.

"Give the man a weapon and he becomes all too genial." Calder chuckled as Warrick ran his hand over the concealed blade.

Perry turned to Lilly and, taking her hand, he led her to the edge of the dance floor. He stepped out and swept her in front of him, her skirts making a great arc, drawing the attention of the room. He pulled her around the room, her head falling back as she laughed. He saw the light glint off her hair, the sparkle in her eyes, the brightness in her smile, and he felt for all the world a success.

She was a treasure, and right now she was his. He had every

intention of making that permanent.

His hand tightened on hers and she looked up at him, amazed by the reflected joy in his eyes. She felt the movement of his muscles in his shoulder, the hand on her waist, the other holding hers warmly, leading her through turns, sweeping her in giddy circles.

The music faded and she frowned. He pulled her in two more sweeping turns as the floor cleared, then he bowed before her. Her fingertips brushed her mouth as she laughed. He took her hand, placing it on his arm to lead her to the terrace.

"My sweet Lilly, you are the most stunning woman I have ever laid eyes upon."

Once outside he leaned against the balustrade and took her hand, unbuttoning the row of tiny pearls at the inside of her wrist. He placed a gentle kiss inside the loosed fabric, then pinching the tips of her fingers to loosen her glove. He pulled it off slowly, sparking the nerves in her skin. Then he kissed the tips of each finger, stroking the inside of her wrist with his thumb.

"You have stolen my heart. I've no idea how you've done so. You must be a sprite, sent to bewitch me."

Lilly laughed. "I don't know anything of that."

Perry held her hand, slowly running his fingers up her arm and back again. "I was concerned about you holding your own in a venue of this sort. Clearly, there was no reason to be."

"I am still shaking. But now that you're here, I'm feeling much better."

"We must go back inside. The duchess will be wondering where I've taken you." He smoothed the glove back up her arm, straightening out the creases as he went.

"Must we?"

"I'm afraid we must." He straightened from the balustrade and tried to button the tiny pearls on her glove, but his fingers were too wide. He gave up and took her hand and placed it on his sleeve, leading her back through the French doors.

Perry was watching her face as they navigated the ballroom. As quickly as frost melts in sunlight, her features shifted to confusion and then to anger. He stopped and turned to face her, blocking the rest of the room. "Lilly," he said, taking her hands in his as he scanned the guests above her head.

"He's here." She paled.

"He." Perry shifted them, watching the room, scanning the faces. He caught the attention of his cousins, who weren't far away.

Perry surrounded her with his broad shoulders and strong arms, and walked toward the main entry. "I will get you out of here, I will keep you safe." What he should have done was insist she and his aunt leave the moment he saw them. But he'd been so taken with her, had wanted only one waltz. But at what price?

They left the ballroom without looking back. Once they crossed the threshold he swept Lilly from her feet, carrying her through the entry toward a parlor on the opposite side. They were followed closely by his cousins, his aunt, and the lady of the house.

Perry set Lilly on a long chaise and turned on Warrick. "He's here."

"I'm aware." Warrick held his hands up to stave off the rant. "We caught sight of him when you went out to the terrace."

"Where is he now?" Perry asked.

Warrick shook his head. "He was in the ballroom, but we lost him after he saw you and Lilly."

"Damn him. I should have removed them. This is my fault." Perry started to turn for the door, but Lilly held him.

"Let *them* call for the carriage, please. You can't walk away from me now." Her hands were shaking like autumn leaves from trees.

"As you wish." He turned to Calder. "We need to get them away from here."

"Mama, you are to stay with Warrick and Perry. Do not leave." Calder strode from the room.

"Someone needs to explain what's happening," Lady Grenville said.

"Oh, Sarah Jane, I do beg your pardon. It appears you have an unwelcome guest," Auberry said. "But not to worry—Calder and Warrick will handle it and none will be the wiser."

Calder came back into the room and spoke in Warrick's ear. Warrick went to Perry and Lilly. His large hand came down on Lilly's shoulder so very delicately, like an elephant on a spider's web. "He's out front, and demanding an audience."

She stood suddenly. "If you go, I go."

"Lilly, I—"

"If you go, I go."

Warrick led Perry while Lilly and Calder followed. They found Perry's men guarding the door, Hepplewort pacing at the base of the steps in front of his carriage, his horses shifting nervously.

"Hepplewort, you are supposed to have left London. Why are you here?" Warrick asked.

"I am here for reparations."

"You are due no further reparations from me, or anyone here," Perry said.

"He's well into his cups, that one is." Auberry looked down her nose at the earl. Perry scowled when he realized his aunt had followed them out as well.

"Perhaps I've had a drink or two, but that is irrelevant."

Perry shifted and Hepplewort caught a glimpse of Lilly. "What's this, then?" He stopped his pacing. "Here's a girl. Do you know we've made quite the rounds in an attempt to find one girl to return home with? And here's one right now, tucked safely behind the man who helped to steal my bride."

Calder and Warrick flanked Lilly, and she stepped forward, her other hand holding tightly to Perry's. "And why would you be looking for me? I thought I was just a passing fancy, a bit of fun you picked up."

Hepplewort sent her a confused glare. "What are you talking about? I only want to steal his bit of tail."

"You've no idea who I am, then?"

Perry squeezed her hand. "Lilly."

"Who you are? You're nobody, you're irrelevant, just a tool I wish to use."

Lilly stepped forward, her grip on Perry loosening while his grip on her tightened. "I see, but you don't. You've already used me, and quite thoroughly I might add, to sate your *need*." She took another step as he glared at her, allowing the light to strike her face.

"There is something about your— Oh." A devilish grin broke a crooked line across his pudgy face. "Why, I thought you were dead."

Lilly's jaw dropped and Perry stepped forward, taking him up by the collar and throwing him to the ground. "You son of a bitch! How dare you! You have no right to even address her! Much less to behave in such a callous manner."

Hepplewort scooted back, then sat up. "Well, she wasn't so brave and powerful when last we met, were you, chit?"

Perry lunged. Warrick reached out and caught him, pulling him back to the stairs.

"You have no right to even look on her, much less speak with her!" Perry roared.

"And what of you here, a viscount putting out for a ruined scullery maid? Ridiculous. At least I used her in her place and left her there. You—What? Look to pull her up to your station? You ignorant twap. I cannot even imagine what your family must think of that sort of thing."

Perry turned and glanced up at Lilly, who stood straight and tall on the top step.

She spoke so quietly that only Perry could hear. "This lesson, while the one I feared the most, has been quite possibly one of the most valuable. There is no cause to fear that man. He is not at all terrifying."

Perry forgot the man behind him, lost in Lilly's peaceful expression.

"Time for you to quit the ball, Hepplewort," Perry said without turning back.

Kerrigan and Gardner pulled Hepplewort up by the shoulders and shoved him at the carriage.

"You don't tell me when to leave!" he squawked.

Perry turned. "Don't I?" He walked toward the carriage, and with every step closer it seemed Hepplewort shrank further into his collar. "Get in your carriage and quit London tonight, or by God you will not live another day." He felt Warrick's hand on his shoulder, but shook him off. "You are not welcome here. You are not welcome anywhere. I believed you understood us when we told you this the first time, or even the second, but it is apparent you do not. I will not tell you again. Be gone."

Hepplewort fell backward into the carriage as Kerrigan swept the door open behind him, and Perry walked to the driver.

"Morgan, I believe you have been warned as well. I'll see you hanged before I see you near my family again. Don't think I won't." The man's eyes narrowed but Perry dismissed him, turning away and returning to Lilly.

He heard Kerrigan slam the carriage door, then Warrick crack the harness on the rear end of one of the horses "Ha!" The startled beasts took off down the street, and everyone walked back to the front of the house. Where he stood with Lilly. He still didn't take his eyes from her.

"Warrick. Inform Her Grace that Lilly will accompany me to my town house tonight. She may consider my offer official. Let her know that if she were to come and attempt to collect her, she'll be turned away, as we have much to accomplish. She may continue to try, but will be consistently turned down." He raised a brow. Lilly blanched when he used the very words his aunt had used against him.

"And Warrick—"

"Yes, Perry?"

"My stick?"

Warrick grumbled and handed it to him. Perry finally broke his hold on Lilly's gaze and turned down the steps, bringing Lilly with him when Gardner brought the carriage up to the curb. Perry handed Lilly in, then followed. He felt Kerrigan's weight on the back of the carriage and tapped the roof. "Home, Gardner, swiftly."

Perry turned to Lilly. "I told you my intentions were to court you, with the intention of taking you to wife."

Lilly looked at him in the dark, light from the gas lamps on the street crossing his features as the carriage rocked down the cobbled and dirt streets toward Grosvenor. "Yes, you informed me of such. You also informed me that you had not yet proposed, and that when you did, I would know."

"Lilly, that time is now. I cannot wait, I will not survive another day not knowing. I won't have you attending balls without me on your arm. I will not let you out of my sight without first putting my ring on your hand for everyone to see." He grasped that hand, pulling it up to his mouth. "Lilly, will you be my wife, in name and deed? Will you take up honorable residence in my house? Will you bear my children and raise them as you see fit? Will you spend the rest of my days making me the happiest man in all of Great Britain? In all of the United Kingdom? Even if it means we live a happily ostracized life in the country?"

"No, milord, I will not," she said quietly.

"Lilly, I—" His heart skipped. He gazed at her solemn expression as the lights flashed over her face.

"Milord, I cannot take this lightly. It is beyond me to be more than I am—"

"I'm not asking for—"

"Hush." She lifted her hand to his mouth to quiet him. "You have asked that I be your wife and said that if we are not accepted by the *ton*, that we will hide at your estate, live out our days happily never to be heard from again. I refuse to rob London of such a beautiful force. It would not be fair of me." She pressed harder on his lips when he tried to plead again. "What I mean to say is, I will never leave. I will never hide. I will be your wife in all things for as long as I shall live, be it with you or without you. You have stolen my heart, my very life, there is no living for me where you are not concerned. I will fight. I will stand tall and proud. I will endure whatever is sent my way. I will be strong. I will not hide. I will do as you wish. And I will spend the balance of *my* days doing so."

Perry held her, his thumbs tracing her lower lip. "You are the most beautiful woman I have ever met, Lilly Steele of Kelso. Beautiful within and without." He smoothed her hair back from her face. "Don't you ever hide your face from anyone. Not ever again, do you hear me? I am the only one ever allowed to see a bit of this hair long and flowing around you. Is that perfectly understood?"

She nodded and reached up to the ribbon that wove its way through her curls. Giving it a slight tug, she felt it untie, then unravel, her hair spilling around her shoulders as he watched.

He grabbed handfuls of her hair, smoothing it and pushing it away from her face. "I have waited all of my life to find you, sweet Lilly. If only I had known where you were, I could have saved you from all the pain."

She let her speech slip. "No, milord, 'twould have done not a bit of good. For were I not this person, with all my damage, and were you not this man, with all his experience, we, neither one of us, would have looked to the other for one moment, much less endeavored to do what we have done."

Perry considered what she said. He nodded as understanding set in. Were he not the rake, and she not broken, there would have been no need for them to meet. No need whatsoever. Under other circumstances he would never have noticed her.

Lilly smiled up at him, nestling into his side. "And how many children do you want?"

"As many as Westcreek Park will hold, I imagine, though perhaps we should get married and be done with my guardianship before we start on another brood."

"And when will we be married?"

He looked forward as he rubbed his chin. "We will be married within a sennight. We will quit London immediately and head to Gretna, where I will pledge my troth and you will be my wife. Then we will spend a few nights hidden away somewhere, returning to Eildon Hill in time to see my brother fall to his fate."

"I like it, I think it perfect, and I cannot wait to tell my family, to see my family, when we arrive for His Grace's wedding."

"They'll probably not recognize you. After all, they won't be looking for you in this dress."

"This dress? I have others I could wear."

Perry shook his head firmly. "Oh no, my sweet Lilly, this dress that my aunt had made will be the perfect dress to wear to my brother's wedding. I cannot wait to see you in it again. Tomorrow we should go by Calder House to explain what will happen next, or the duchess will have the entire country set out to find us, and that certainly will not do. But for tonight, tonight you are mine." His hands grasped her hips and drew her toward him. "You'll be in my bed, and we'll not be disturbed. Tonight, I make you my wife in deed," he said gruffly. The rocking of the carriage shifting them as one, as he let his pronouncement sink in, the only sounds the creak of the springs and the breath between them.

"Lilly?"

"Yes?"

"Would you like your family at our wedding? We could arrange for Kelso. It might require a favor or two, but I could make this happen."

"Perry," she said, with no more than a breath.

"Yes, my sweet?"

"I love you."

"And I love you, well beyond the boundaries of my heart."

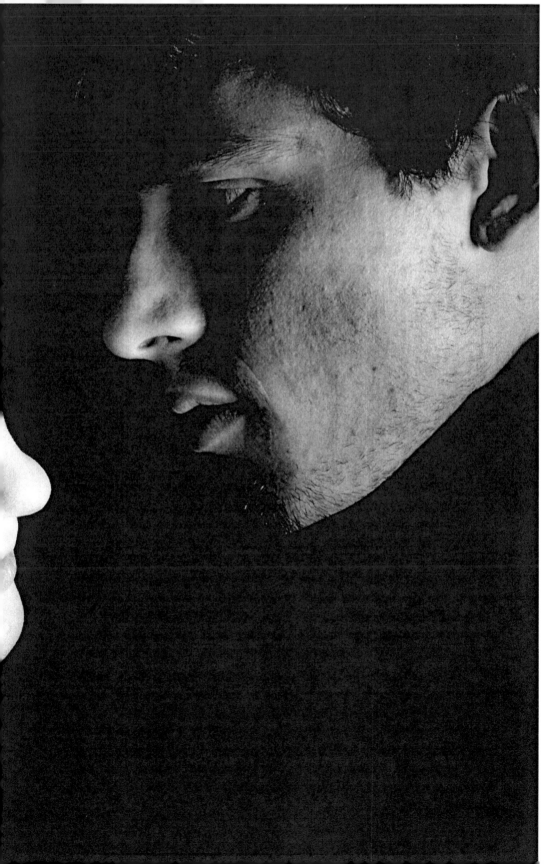

# FORTY-SEVEN

erry sat at the keys and considered the night before. He leaned across the board. Resting his elbow on the piano, he started a scale, his fingers gliding across the keys like the wings of a butterfly. The tones started rich and deep, then rose to fight his somber mood.

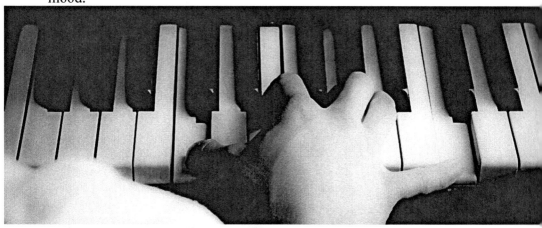

It was difficult to believe that Hepplewort was still causing problems. He had to protect Lilly, particularly since Hepplewort was now aware of her. The scale trilled up and back down and he shifted forward on the bench. Lilly, who he had left to sleep in after the trials he put her through once they'd made it back to the house. He had given her the pearls, and they had been truly beautiful. It had been the most passionate night of his life. His other hand met the first and he commanded the notes to come forth, fill the room, his senses, his need.

It must have been all the emotion roiling through them. In his life he'd never expected to be so close to another human. He'd never expected to share such a glorious connection. And they were to be married soon. He needed to send a message to Calder House, to let his aunt know they would be late. Lilly needed rest. He felt his cock stir at the very thought of their exertion. She had allowed so much, learned so much, given so much, and he was forever in her hold. Mastered. The crescendo grew.

He heard movement behind him and shifted, quickly closing the fall over the keys and rising from the bench.

"Lilly. I didn't know you were here. I—" He cleared his throat. She watched him closely as he stumbled out from behind the bench.

"You play." It was a quiet statement, not a question.

"Well. Yes, I do. I don't very well announce such, though. The image of tortured artist would do wonders for my rakehell reputation," he said sardonically.

She pursed her lips. "Your reputation. I see. Still quite concerned with that, are you, my lord?"

He stopped. "I—well. There, you have me."

Her smile broadened and she pulled a chair closer to the bench. "Well, then?" she said, sweeping her hand toward the instrument.

He turned, his knee brushing the corner of the bench and making him stumble again. He caught it before it toppled and cast her a nervous grin. He sat down, his wrists hovering above the keys, his fingers gently caressing the ivory just below. He cleared his throat, then clasped his hands, cracking his knuckles before repositioning his fingers.

Lilly waited serenely, her eyes trained on those long fingers she had come to know so well. They fluttered over the keys again and he heard her breath catch.

With that small sound the music flowed through him, to the strings of the piano, each note carried in precise tension throughout the room.

Her breathing caught the rhythm of the notes, her chest rising and falling in deep waves. He saw her knees tighten, her fingers curl into her skirts.

He built the crescendo, drawing the tension as far as he could before letting it drift softly back to earth. He closed his eyes and his body swayed. He felt the strain of the notes, pulled them into his gut then let them spiral through his veins, flowing back out to circle again toward him.

Lilly had never seen anyone play, much less been close enough to feel the tremor from the instrument below her feet as the chords left the strings and traveled to her. She watched closely as Perry's eyes fell closed and his brow stitched, the concentration in every line of his body. This wasn't something she had imagined when considering this man. The beauty and the passion. Her gaze fell once again to his fingers; watching them skim the ivory had her belly in knots, and she clenched her knees together to fight the sudden whirls of energy fluttering inside her.

She stood ever so slowly, not wanting to disturb his concentration but needing to feel. She slipped her shoes off and stepped quietly to the side of the grand piano to lean into it. She placed her hands on the giant lid that was closed over the strings to mute the sound. Spreading her fingers, she felt the reverberation of each note. She closed her eyes and her breath quickened.

Then the music fell away.

She turned to find him regarding her.

"That is the most beautiful thing I have ever heard in my life."

"Well, you have led a most sheltered life."

She noted there were no music sheets. "How..."

"It just comes to me, or I remember it. My mother was very talented. She used to play, and I was able to pick things up by ear. Later my father paid for a few lessons. Possibly to keep me from underfoot while he dealt with my brother."

"What of your mother then?"

"She was already gone."

Lilly turned away as he stood.

His hand reached up to her face, his thumb brushing the tear from her cheek. "There is no need to cry for the past."

She leaned into him. "It was not for the past, but for the music. I do not know how to describe how it felt. It filled me, it was..." She shook her head.

He turned her and lifted her, setting her upon the lid. "Let me tell you about my piano."

She protested and he moved closer, wrapping his arms around her waist and leaning toward her.

"This is an 1868 Streicher Concert Grand. Handmade of rosewood, for me, in Vienna." He ran his hand over the smooth surface. "The very same type of piano that Brahms uses for his compositions." He looked at her hopefully.

She shook her head.

He pulled her skirts up and wrapped her legs around his waist, then lifted her from the piano. She squealed and locked her arms around his neck.

"Perry!"

He rounded the piano, setting her petite frame on the lid at the front of the piano. His fingers traced down the backs of her thighs. His hands caught beneath her knees as he lifted her away from him, opened the fall, and placed her feet wide on the keyboard with a low and high complaint from the piano.

"Perry, not the keys, I—"

"Shhh. You are interrupting genius here," he said, then kissed her blunt on the lips and sat in front of her, looking at his hands on the keys. "Every genius needs a muse and I—" He glanced up and his breath caught as he took in the view he'd created. Lilly, wide on his piano. "I, my sweet, sweet Lilly, I'm no different." He shifted on the bench. "Perhaps this was a bad idea," he mumbled, moving his fingers, which seemed to tangle themselves before even attempting a chord.

He started in on a lilting melody; he thought a tribute to Brahms in order considering the lesson on his piano, but then when he glanced

up again he fumbled, losing the tune.

"I believe this calls for something a bit more, eh, up tempo?" He repositioned his hands. He started slow and lilting, then beat at the keys, the sound emanating loud and raucous. The entire piano shook beneath her, the vibrations coursing through her toes and resting in her hips. He smiled up at her. "Brahms would burn this piano for this one!" he yelled over the tune.

Lilly laughed and held on to the edge of the piano lid tightly, for fear of being bounced off. "What...whatever is this?" she asked through her giggles.

"This, my dear, is something my mother used to play for me. I haven't heard it anywhere else. I believe it to be American." He continued his harassment of the keys. Lilly was laughing so hard her foot slipped from the keyboard and she landed rather unceremoniously in Perry's lap.

"Well, my dear, you have but to ask me the one time." He gathered her to him, kissing and pulling and tearing at her clothes until they were joined beneath her ruined skirts, both screaming and grunting as they worked hard toward their end.

"Lilly...Lilly!" he yelled as he fell back and she followed, the two of them landing on the floor behind him, his breath knocked out.

She sat up quickly with a start, her hands touching either side of his jaw. "Perry? Are you all right?" She moved his head back and forth to rouse him.

His hands on her hips startled her. "Lilly, don't move, I— Lord, just...give me a moment, I beg you."

She leaned over him, kissing everywhere she could reach.

"Perry, I'm so sorry!"

He coughed, then breathed deeply and opened his eyes. Lifted his knees and kicked the piano bench away. He cleared his throat.

"It wasn't your fault. I should never have set you on my instrument," he said with a sly grin.

She wiggled her hips. "Your instrument seems to have survived." She leaned over his chest on her crossed hands.

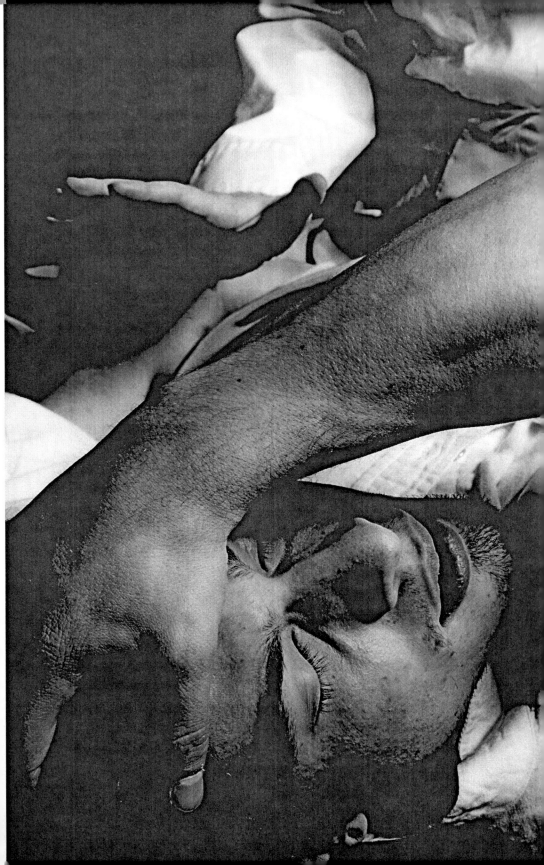

He pressed into her. "I leave you with no doubt as to the condition of said instrument."

Her eyes closed and her mouth parted as his rhythm gained. She pushed against his chest, rising to give him more depth, and cried out on his thrust.

"What...was...that...song?" she breathed.

"She called it the *Pineapple Rag.*"

"I don't know what that means, but I love it."

Lilly collapsed on a cry, melting into his tensed body.

Then, once he caught his breath: "Shall I play it again?"

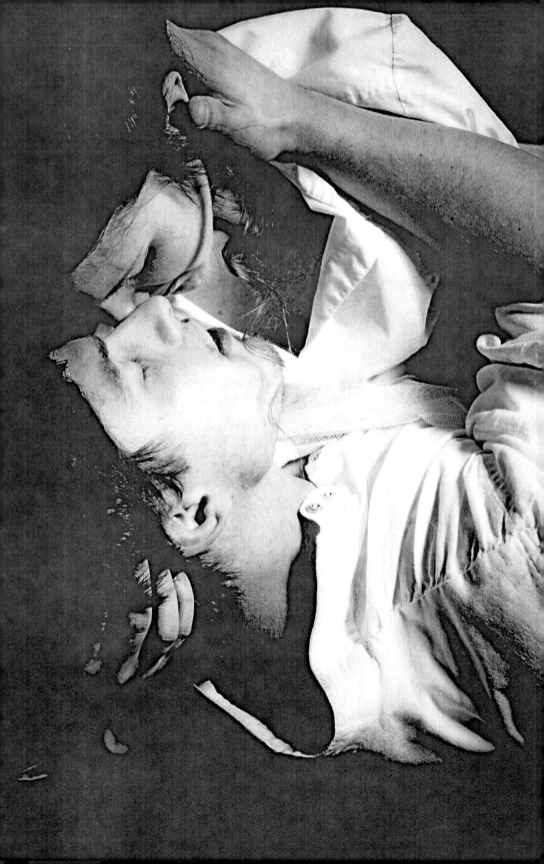

# FORTY-EIGHT

heir peaceful reverie was broken by a knock at the main door so powerful they heard it at the back of the house.

"Damn."

Lilly lifted her head from his chest and smiled, then began the slow process of extracting herself from his arms. "I'll leave you to it, I need to freshen up a bit. Again."

Perry grumbled as he heard the butler moving from his study to the parlor and knew the music room was about three doors farther on his hunt. He fastened his trousers and righted the piano bench—noting a pronounced wobble—then stood and attempted to reorder himself before the door swung wide.

"Milord, Warrick and Calder." Perry turned quickly at the tenor in his voice. "The entry, my lord, they say there's no time."

Perry glanced around the room to ensure Lilly was safely with him, then remembered she'd gone upstairs to change. He walked to the front of the house.

"Warrick, Calder."

"Perry, they've found a girl."

Perry stilled. "Where?"

"Hyde. At the Serpentine, near Rotten Row," Calder answered solemnly.

"It was him." His cousins nodded in agreement. "And where is he?" Perry looked to Calder.

"The man I had on him hasn't been heard from since Grenville's, which doesn't bode well for him."

Perry rubbed his temple. "That's still Westminster, but I'm assuming CID is involved. Who do we know?"

"Chief Inspector Cutbush," Warrick said quietly.

Perry and Calder turned to him. "Can he be trusted?"

Warrick shook his head stiffly.

Perry groaned. "Is anyone still at Hyde or have they taken her—Good lord. Do they know who she is?"

"No, according to Cutbush she wasn't readily recognizable. Her clothing might be working class or it could be that it was just severely damaged by whatever was done to her and she is lower gentry. They aren't yet sure," Calder said.

Perry's stomach twisted. He should never have let Hepplewort out of his sight. He looked to Warrick. "Find him. Now."

"I'm working on it. I believe he may have left London, but I wouldn't be too sure. Don't leave Lilly alone."

"Aunt—"

"My men are with her," Calder said quickly. Perry nodded, his head pounding with the movement. His only concern the night before had been Lilly, and now—*now*. He felt someone take his shoulder; he felt the squeeze and the brisk shake. He felt it all as though he were merely an observer.

"Perry—"

He wasn't sure who said it.

"Don't. I'll see to Lilly. We are to quit London. But Hepplewort—"

"I will see to Hepplewort." This was definitely from Warrick.

"I'll never forgive myself."

"For what?"

They all turned on Lilly in unison and she stepped back a pace, her smile falling. "For...what?" she asked again, warily. Perry looked back to his cousins, then took Lilly's hand and led her to his study.

For a time there was no sound. Then a deafening shriek carried from the study and Calder looked to Warrick. "He must be found." Warrick nodded once, then turned for the door.


Hepplewort paced in the inn as Morgan tracked him over the edge of his pint.

"Damn it, Morgan. Why did he have to make me angry? Why

did he do that? Shouldn't he understand by now that I am no one to be trifled with?"

Morgan continued to watch. He was growing weary of the man's constant gibbering. It had been worth it to stay with him since his propensities leaned close to his own, specifically where women were concerned. And he was easily led. But he was tired of the man's incessant maundering and questioned whether it was worth the effort. The duke and viscount were likely to end him soon anyway, so he would do well to be gone by then.

"Morgan! Aren't you listening?"

Morgan grunted.

"I want the girl. I want Lilly."

Morgan smiled.

# FORTY-NINE

Warrick's first stop was Alsatia, to meet with Gunn, Hepplewort's book maker. He had no luck, other than to learn Hepplewort had notified Gunn the day before that his rooms on Talbot Street were now his. It appeared likely that Hepplewort had taken their threats at face value and was determined to quit London. If he'd no place to stay, it meant he intended to leave.

Warrick went to the rooms next anyway and found them empty
. He wasn't sure about the mother, though she hadn't attended the ball, so perhaps he sent her off early yesterday. There were no servants left behind, no men to speak on what had happened. It seemed to be yet another dead end.

He made his way to Scotland Yard to speak with Cutbush. He might not trust him, but Cutbush knew better than to cross Warrick. He hoped he could glean some information. It turned out they already suspected Hepplewort, but Cutbush wouldn't say why. The information wasn't going to help him find the earl, but it would get him closer to his ultimate goal.

Chasing more tails, Warrick only managed to discover that accounts were closed, debts reconciled, and Hepplewort was merely a shadow.

He was gone.


Perry held Lilly. He'd never felt so hopeless in all his life. It felt as though his heart would stop, then only because he forced it to, would start again. There was no consoling her.

"I want to take you home."

"What?" She blinked tears from her lashes, her fingers stiff from holding onto him so tight.

"Let me take you home. I need to get you away from here. I need for you to be safe. Warrick will find Hepplewort, of this I've no doubt.

But I want for you to be safe. I think you need your family just now."

"And you?"

"It is time I spoke with your father."

"I'm not sure I'm prepared to face them," she said quietly. He considered this, and was suddenly wary. He was the one who wouldn't be accepted. He was a peer, he had no right. What if her father refused—could he? Could he refuse to allow Lilly to marry him? But Mr. Steele looked up to Roxleigh. Yes, Roxleigh. Not him, the irreverent rake brother, but Roxleigh. He was terribly unsure of his next move. He knew without a doubt he wasn't worthy of this woman. Perhaps to Gretna first to be married, then on to Kelso? He wasn't feeling so brave at the prospect of facing Lilly's father.

"We will face them together. What's the worst that could happen? I would have to steal you away to be married by the blacksmith?" Kelso was in Scotland, after all.

"He's my uncle," she said with a small grin. Perry paused.

"To...a blacksmith...in another town?" he choked out. Lilly laughed quietly, wiping the tears from her eyes.

"Perry, I— Oh, I don't know. You are quite wicked."

"So I've been told. I should make some arrangements. Since we are both residents of Scotland we shouldn't have a problem being married anywhere we choose within the borders. I can only hope your father will approve of me." His voice faded at the end. *Quite the turn. Funny, that.*

"You are truly worried, aren't you?"

He knew his eyes were wider than they ought to be; he was also aware that his palms were a bit clammy. He wiped them down his trousers and looked back to Lilly. "Of course I'm not worried. If we can't get married over the anvil as they do in Gretna, we'll find some other thing to get married over—a saddle, perhaps. Have you any relation to the saddler?"

Lilly laughed, and the sound made him grin so broadly he thought his face would crack. But it was then the thought of the poor Serpentine girl crept back in, and he set himself to action.

"Lilly, it's time we quit London. I shall have my men pack your things and send them on to Eildon. You'll stay with me."

"You'll do no such thing. I can pack my things. Have someone stand at my door if you must. *You* stand at my door. But I'll not have your men digging through my underthings."

"Quite right. Very well then, but we leave post haste. To Kelso."

Calder wandered Perry's house. He'd stayed behind because Warrick would fare better alone, and he knew Perry would have need of him—once Lilly calmed. He found the music room and approached the piano. He knew of Perry's talent, but like most of the family, had never heard him play. He touched the keys gently, then leaned on the bench as if to sit, but one of the legs gave way and he ended up on the floor.

"Good God, man, what are you doing? That is a one-of-a-kind instrument! Have you damaged the bench?"

Calder looked to Perry, only to catch the hint of a smile. "Funny. I suppose the bench was already damaged then?" He stood and straightened his pants, brushing at his knees.

"Yes, there was an...incident. Warrick?" he asked, changing tack abruptly.

"Doing what he does. Not a word."

"I'm to Kelso. I'm taking Lilly to her family. She needs them at the moment, after everything. I am leaving Hepplewort to you and Warrick, because my responsibility needs to be Lilly. Exclusively."

"I could never do that, leave the outcome to someone else. He knows who she is."

"I'm not leaving the outcome to just anyone, I'm leaving it to you and Warrick. And I refuse to leave her side. If Gideon were here, he would agree. I won't make the same mistake we made with Francine."

Lilly gathered enough clothing for a fortnight. The wedding was only a few more days out, and they would spend time with her family. Her family. Perry. Viscount Roxleigh, spending time with her family. Where would he sleep? Would her mother allow them in her old room? Should they stay at the inn? They should stay at the inn.

She pulled her brush off the vanity and put it on top of her dresses.

Warrick walked into the building where Hepplewort's mother maintained rooms apart from her son. It had taken him most of the day to track the information down, but he finally found something he could chase and he felt all the better for it.

"Your cousins have done their utmost to damage the Hepplewort line."

"My cousins? Are you possibly referring to His Grace, The Duke of Roxleigh, and The Right Honorable Viscount Roxleigh? I don't believe you should address them in so familiar a manner," Warrick said stiffly. This woman rankled beyond reason. Were he raised in her household, he quite believed he would be a different man. As it happened, he turned out to be as he was, for better or more possibly worse. Though he did, at the very least, respect women.

She wrinkled her nose at him, but seemed to take the warning. He knew his presence could be ominous, even beyond his rather large frame. He used that to his advantage quite often.

"I will not help you find my son."

"Would you like to visit Brixton? I can arrange for that. Your son, however, will be taken to Newgate after he stands trial for this latest murder." He saw her eyes widen, then her steel control snapped down and any emotion on her face was gone.

"Murder."

"You heard me."

"My son left after the ball, you told him to leave— He left." She waved a hand in the air.

"In which direction?"

"I believe he was going to the seat. Home." She didn't flinch. She was good. Even Warrick had to be slightly impressed by her control.

"Then we shall retrieve him there." Now it was a game. He wanted to see her flinch, he wanted to see how much it would take for her to break. He knew he could do it.

"You will do no such thing. There can be no evidence of any wrongdoing on his part."

"No? Then why am I here?"

Her nostrils flared, he nearly missed it.

"Because your family"—and this was said with such disdain he truly felt a triumph—"wishes to see the fall of mine."

"Pray tell, enlighten me to what end exactly. You have nothing any of us want."

"Save that woman."

"Yes, in fact, we did save that woman. From your son."

Her hands tightened one over the other.

"Madam, I expect you to aid the investigation, or I will see you hanged alongside your son, law or no."

She took one step backward into her room, then swung the door shut, narrowly missing his nose. He smiled. That was rather satisfying.

Kerrigan entered the study and bowed quickly. "Milord, His Grace's railcar is ready to depart at first light."

"Thank you. Make sure our cases are delivered and the car is guarded."

"Yes, milord."

Perry turned back to the paperwork on his desk that he'd been ignoring. He had to get a few missives off before they quit London because he'd promised Gideon he would handle these things, but he had been distracted.

He smiled at the thought; his recent bit of distraction was so much more than anything he had ever encountered before. He dropped his pen and stood, then scrubbed his hands though his hair, sat down again, and took the pen back up. He had to finish.

But then Lilly needed to know they wouldn't be leaving until dawn.

He stood.

Of course she would come find him when she was ready to depart, and he needed to finish the paperwork.

He sat. Then he growled, an actual feral moan.

The door swung open.

"They are leaving to return to Kelso. He has arranged to take

Roxleigh's private car."

Hepplewort watched Morgan's grin spread wide across his face.

"Well then, perhaps we can arrange to be aboard the same train? Kelso is so far from London, it would be much easier to corner my quarry there."

"I will arrange it, milord."

"Don't forget Mother."


"He's headed back to Shropshire, to his estate." Warrick entered without preamble.

Perry stood, again. "You're sure?" He waved his hand. "Of course you're sure." He watched as Warrick's brows rose nearly imperceptibly. "Then we are safe heading to Kelso. You and Calder will corner him in Shropshire."

"Perry, I—"

This time Perry's eyebrows rose. This was Warrick, usually so full of formality.

"Trumbull. I'm not entirely sure that would be the wisest move, either."

"You know you may address me as Perry." He still had no intention of calling him anything but Warrick, regardless that he'd never been invited to. His cousin didn't seem anything other than Warrick at this point, even though he'd only recently become such.

"If Hepplewort is to Shropshire—and where, pray tell, did you come by this information?"

"His mother." Warrick motioned at Perry's head, and Perry attempted to straighten his rather disheveled hair as he grumbled.

"Ah...the devil's mistress herself. If Hepplewort is to Shropshire, then we are safe heading to Kelso." Perry walked over to the sideboard, suddenly in need of a drink when he heard himself repeat those words. Who was he trying to convince? He tipped the whiskey decanter to Warrick, who raised his hand to stay him.

"But that man never stays where he's put."

"Unless his mother puts him there. So I am even more of a mind to go." He downed the whiskey and poured another finger. "What choice have I? Stay here in fear waiting for him to show his cards? I cannot leave her side so I am of no use to you. Hepplewort won't expect Kelso." He tried to shake the thought from his head. "Did you inform Cutbush of the mother's whereabouts?" Perry sat in a chair away from his desk and motioned Warrick to join him.

"I did, but he isn't interested in her."

"No, I don't suppose he would be. She's an old woman—harmless, really. Horrible and nagging, but rather harmless."

"Where's Calder?" Warrick asked.

"He's gone to check on Calder House. Did you notify Cutbush that Hepplewort is for Shropshire?"

"Not yet, I thought we should decide what happens next. If Cutbush goes off half-cocked, we may never find Hepplewort."

"He has no authority there, he would have to make arrangements with the local constabulary. Do we know anyone there?"

"I doubt that. As it would be under Hepplewort's purview. Chances are the local police would defer to him, regardless. You don't bite the hand that feeds, no matter how filthy."

Perry swirled the whiskey, watching it catch the light, then he cleared his throat. "We have a bit of time before Calder returns, and—"

Warrick's gaze sharpened on him and Perry felt suddenly flushed. He cleared his throat again. "I just thought we could catch up, eh?"

Warrick leaned back in the chair and watched him.

"Is this how you got information from Hepplewort's mother? Because I'm damned about to tell you everything since leaving my shortcoats."

A wicked grin crossed Warrick's face and Perry laughed. It was almost like the devious grin he remembered from their adolescence, the one he would see shortly before they all fell to a horrible fate of switches behind the barn, for one transgression or another.

Lilly finished packing the trunk and went to find Perry. It had been more than an hour, and she knew he had paperwork to catch up on. She headed straight for the study but stopped short of opening the door when she heard men's voices beyond. Not just men's voices, though—it was more of a happy banter. She didn't want to interrupt the bit of camaraderie, so she headed for the library to find a few books to take on the train.

She pulled a book from the shelf and backed herself to the chair to read. She heard the laughter across the foyer gain, then fade again, and she looked to the door to find Perry striding for the stairs. She stood quickly. She hadn't meant to worry him, but knew that's exactly what had happened. She caught him halfway to the first floor.

"I'm sorry, you were all having such a nice chat. I didn't want to interrupt." She blinked her lashes rapidly at him when he turned, and he laughed.

"Forgiven, but please, until this is settled—"

"I'll interrupt you, every chance I have. On my honor."

He took her hand and kissed her palm, then turned to head back down the stairs.

"Are we leaving soon or…?"

"At dawn. We are taking Roxleigh's private car—did I already tell you this?" He waved his hand as if to dismiss it. "They are preparing it now so they can hook it to the line, and we'll depart on the first train in the morning. It was to be delivered before the wedding, so we merely pushed that up a few days."

"Perry."

He turned on the bottom stair to look up at her. "Yes?"

"The girl."

"We will be notified as soon as her identity is discovered. If it isn't, we will handle all the arrangements, however you would feel comfortable."

"Are they aware? I don't want her in a pauper's grave or—"

"Yes. We will take care of her."

Kerrigan knocked and entered his chamber. "Milord, the railcar is prepared. It has been guarded through the night. Your cases have been transported, and we are ready to depart."

"Thank you, Kerrigan. We'll be out in a moment." Perry turned back into his chamber and moved through the bathing room toward Lilly's room, where she'd gone to prepare for the trip. She turned when he entered.

"I'm nervous."

"About?" he asked as he took her hands in his.

"My family."

Perry shook his head, hoping that the smile on his face appeared more confident than it felt. "It will be fine."

"I sent word to Meggie that I was returning to Kelso. I sent word to Mrs. Weston that I wasn't returning to the duke's household."

"Good. Then hopefully Meggie will be there when we arrive."

Perry had also made some arrangements. He'd arranged with the vicar in Kelso for a wedding ceremony to be held two days before Gideon's. A Thursday. He wanted to be sure they could be married before he returned to Eildon, partly so his brother could not do anything to attempt to influence his decision, and partly so he would be better able to protect Lilly.

Perry turned for the door and pulled Lilly along with him. "Let's get out of London."

Calder and Warrick arrived at the earl's Shropshire estate in the afternoon, prepared to haul Hepplewort back to face his charges. "There doesn't seem to be anyone here," Calder said.

"Would you work for these people?" Warrick replied.

"No, but it seems quite abandoned altogether."

Warrick reached up and let the heavy brass knocker fall to the door three times, then they waited. He was about to reach for it again when he heard shuffling from the other side of the door. He stood back, preparing for the worst. Calder eyed him nervously, then followed suit.

The door swung inward, the hinges groaning beneath the weight and lack of care. The man on the other side was haggard, old, and didn't seem to be happy to have been disturbed. He didn't make a sound, so Calder stepped forward.

"We are here for Hepplewort."

"You and everyone else, but he is not here."

"What do you mean 'everyone else?'"

"Debtors, primarily. I'm merely here for the dispensation of this property. Hepplewort and Madame quit the estate nearly a fortnight ago, with no intention of returning. They are ruined. He needed a wife to save the land. He never found one."

Calder closed his eyes and felt Warrick tense beside him.

"We are a full day behind them."


Perry was sold on the private car the minute they laid eyes on it. Fitted with brass fixtures and polished copper rails and piping, the car gleamed like nothing he'd ever seen. The interior was plush and comfortable, the heavy furniture meant to keep its place regardless of the sway and speed of the train. But what he appreciated the most was the enormous four poster bed set at the center, near the back. Just how he had envisioned it. It was rather unsettling at first.

If one lay in this bed, one could watch the countryside disappear from view out the back of the train. The windows were a masterful work of heavy curved glass, wrapping around the rear end of the car and providing breathtaking views. If he had Lilly in this bed, the view would be good no matter where he looked. It was the most beautiful room he'd ever seen, save the duchess' suite at Eildon. His brother truly had a romantic streak to him. Perry made a mental note to outdo him—in the very near future.

"This is...I've never seen anything quite like this." Lilly's voice was a breath on her lips as she watched the sun begin to climb its way from the edge of the world outside the car.

They had been so taken with the railcar itself, they'd missed the signals and were only aware they were set to depart by the first lurch of the train. Then the muffled scream of the steam whistle—so many cars ahead of them—blew and Perry set his arm around Lilly and walked her to the seating area near the center of the car. They sat on a great plush settee, immense in size and weight, each of them feeling the fabrics and wondering at the expense.

"I suppose the estate is finally prospering well under Gideon's hand for him to have enough blunt for this." He looked to the side to see Lilly leaning forward, inspecting the pockets in the dust ruffles with a curious gaze.

"Books!" he said suddenly. Lilly startled, looking up to him. "Gideon told me of these pockets he'd come up with because Francine leaves books lying all over the place. He had them sewn into the dust ruffles to save her books from the floor." Perry bent forward and stuck his hand in one of the pockets. "I had no idea what he was getting on about."

Lilly giggled. "Well, that is a good idea. So Francine loves to read, does she?"

"Yes. She loves to read, and she has a heart big enough to hold all of England."

"I remember. When they first returned to Eildon after— Well, after. She came straight up to me, she knew who I was. Meggie said she was very comforting when she received the missive about my injuries as well. She seems a good sort."

"A good sort. Yes, she is a good sort. What does that make me?" he asked suddenly.

"You! Oh, my lord, you are the worst sort of good."

"Am I now?"

"Yes. You are rather a sight better than you believe you are." He lifted his brows. "Well, you profess to be such a bad man, but I have seen neither hide nor hair of this bad man since we've met. Have I?"

Perry was struck then by the reality of his reputation, the one he had worked so meticulously to craft. He stood and took her hand to pull her up to him Then untied his cravat and unbuttoned his waistcoat.

"Come." Lilly stumbled, tripping over her skirts as he pulled her toward the giant mass of a bed. He handed her the cravat. "I seem to remember you mentioning that you don't know what you want, because you haven't much experience yet. Is this still true?"

Lilly shook her head as she watched him undress. Then, naked as the day, he ran the length of the car to the door and locked it, pulling the shades.

*Oh! He did that without a stitch on. Anyone could have seen—* Her hand lifted to cover her mouth as he ran back to her across the car.

"Now, where were we?" he asked as he grabbed her hips through all her layers. "What will you have me do...to you?"

She watched over his broad shoulder as the sun made its final push from behind the horizon, coming into full view and lighting up his naked skin with the warmest glow of sunrise. It chased away the chill of the early morning and rather quickly she was overly warm in her traveling dress and cloak. She felt wicked, standing here in this borrowed car, fully dressed. With him, fully bare, embracing her.

"Perry, this is your brother's car," she tried feebly.

"Mmm...hmmm..." He nibbled on her ear and she shuddered.

"But won't he mind?"

"How will he know?"

She pushed at his shoulders and gave him a scathingly shocked look.

"You are quite beautiful when you scowl at me that way. And it gives me various ideas...things to do with you," he said quietly, his gaze moving across her, willing her body to submit.

"Oh, Perry, you have me, whatever you wish."

"And I find myself blessed. Now, tell me: What will you have me do? To you. Or would you prefer to do to me?" He took the cravat she still held and grasped both ends, turning his hands, one over the other until it wrapped round his wrists and locked them together. He raised his hands before her eyes and over her head, trapping her against his body as he breathed heavily against her neck, and she attempted to gather her scattered thoughts.

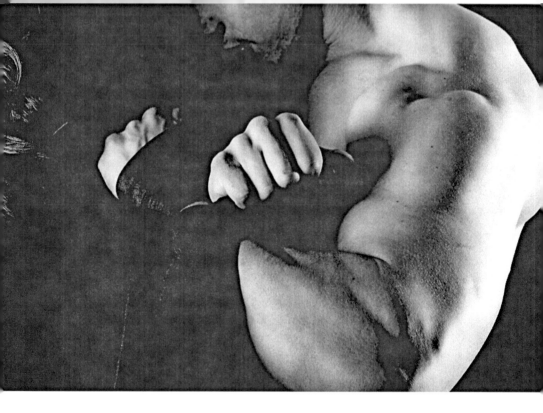

When someone knocked at the door, Hepplewort stood and ducked into the dressing room, leaving Morgan to deal with it.

"Are there two on this ticket, sir?"

Morgan nodded to the door Hepplewort cowered behind. "He is indisposed." He patted his stomach. "Trains." he said quietly.

The porter nodded and ripped the ticket, then moved on. Morgan shut the door, returning to his seat. He waited for Hepplewort to open the door, but it didn't move so he got up and knocked on it.

"Are we clear?"

Morgan groaned. "Yes, milord, just checking tickets." He returned to his seat again.


When Lilly woke, her sight was filled with Perry's perfectly round rear end leaning over the rail at the back of the car.

Outside. Naked. Still in broad daylight. She laughed and shook her head, then looked around as though there would be someone else around to see, besides herself and the red deer in the forest.

She pulled the blanket around her and moved toward him,

catching herself on one of the bed posts when the train suddenly rocked to the left. She stood behind him, appreciating his structure, the shift of his muscles beneath his skin as he corrected for the jerk and sway on the tracks. She then leaned forward and licked his spine from one end to the other. Bottom to top, as it were.

"Dear God, woman!" He straightened as she moved up, then turned, allowing her to wrap him inside the heavy counterpane.

She beamed up at him.

"What, exactly, made you do that?" he groaned as he sent his arms around her waist and pulled her tight.

"You. You just looked so—mmm. It seemed like a good idea at the time. I remember you doing that to me, so...I suppose I learned my lesson."

"Oh, did you now?"

"I did." She nodded.

"Well, let's have a few more lessons then. I quite like what you've been learning." He lifted her and carried her back through the door, kicking at the heavy fabric around his feet to keep from tripping. "To begin with, allow me to show you a few more uses for that cravat."


"They're in the last car, milord, and his men have the private berths at the end of the car before it. There's no way to get to them."

"Goddamnit, Morgan! I want that girl. I want her!" Hepplewort screeched. The door opened without a preemptive knock and his mother swept through.

"Keep your voice down, Fergus. You'll draw attention to yourself. I heard you all the way down the hall."

"Mother."

Morgan stood and cast his eyes down.

"Sit. I don't need you looming over me."

He did.


Perry and Lilly watched from the platform as they uncoupled the car in Carlisle for the train to continue on the main line to Edinburgh.

Eventually the branch line to Roxleighshire would make its way to Kelso, but they intended to reach the end of the line there, leave Gideon's car for him, and continue on by carriage.

The mainline train whistled and moved on, and they waited for the track to clear so the branch line could couple with Gideon's car.

"It really is a beautiful railcar," Perry said. "Ours will require a few more features, however."

Lilly turned to him. "Ours?"

"Oh yes, I'm not one to be outdone by my brother. I will need to make arrangements as soon as we return to London. Just think, by the time our car is finished, the line should move straight through to Kelso and on to Berwick-upon-Tweed. We'll take your family to the sea."

She stared at him. A private railcar. Their private railcar. "I'm not sure my family can change as much as you hope they can."

"I'll not ask them to. I will do as much for them as they will allow, as much as a son would be allowed to do for his parents. I will endeavor to not step on any toes." Her eyes grew wide and he took her hand. "What is it?"

"Daniel." She had completely forgotten him, but returning home, he was rather like one of the family. At least he had been. Well, he still was, he just— She sighed.

"Who... is Daniel?"

"A suitor."

"A—what?" Perry felt his chest tighten. He had never considered that she would have had a suitor, another man, at home.

"We were to be married." Her voice wavered, and he pulled her to a bench on the platform as a whistle blew and the other cars from the branch line started backing up toward their car.

"Tell me." He sounded nervous. He didn't like it.

"He is a simple man, sweet. His farm abuts my father's. He works with him, takes care of the animals. He's good with animals." She smiled warmly, and his gut twisted.

"But not with you?"

"No, not after Hepplewort."

"I don't understand. You were to be married? Or are to be—"

"No! No, I would never have— I...no. He... Well, after—after, I suppose all he saw was what was done." She fisted her hands in her skirts, and he put his over them, to steady her.

"I'm sorry." He would kill him. Or thank him. He was rather torn at the moment, considering that she had been brutalized and the one person meant to take care of her beyond her family had effectively abandoned her because of it. Horrible.

"Please, don't be. I know now that I could never have been happy with such a small life. You have shown me so much more...just more. I cannot imagine having less."

"But Daniel...he lives close by?"

"Yes, and he is over for dinner often. He has always been simply part of the family."

He didn't understand why they still allowed for him. "Is he handsome?" Perry cringed, the shallow words out before he realized. Her face turned to his suddenly.

"Is he— Are you jealous?"

"Me? No. Not at all. He works the land, so he must be strapping, well built?"

"Perry, I—"

"And clever, I imagine, if your family loves him."

"Perry, no, I— Actually, I don't know how close they are at this point. He just stopped coming over after I was hurt, that's why I left for Eildon."

"Well, we will have to see about this chap."

"What does that mean, we'll see about him?"

Perry shook his head as a giant clash of metal on metal made her jump from her seat. He stood next to her and squeezed her hand. "It's the train coupling," he whispered. She leaned into him.

"You must understand. His issue with me after... It was the best possible thing to happen. Please don't be angry with him, for if he hadn't, there wouldn't be you."

"I understand. Actually I don't, but I will endeavor to try. And I will be on my best behavior."

Hepplewort watched from inside the station as they spoke on the platform, acting so familiar, inappropriately close. Too intimate. *These damn Trumbull brothers have no idea how to handle a woman, how to behave like a gentleman, a peer of the realm.* He grunted.

"Fergus, come away from there."

"What exactly is your purpose in coming with me, Mother? You could have stayed in London."

"You are my son. Where else should I be?"

"Not here, not now."

"What is it you are planning?"

"None of your concern. Simply stay out of my way."

"Where are we headed? Are we taking the next train?"

"No, Mother, Morgan is hiring a carriage."

They arrived and settled relatively well with Lilly's family. Her mother, ever the hard working respectful woman insisted they stay with them, and not at the inn. She even tried to insist Perry take the master bedroom, but he refused. So he was placed in Lilly's old room, while she slept with Meggie.

He quite liked her family. They were real, honest, true. Every one of them worked hard, her father, her brothers, her mother and sister. It was a large, very close family and he certainly felt like an interloper.

Then there was Daniel.

Perry cut the bale of hay, then looked over his shoulder to see where he was. They'd worked their way down opposite sides of the stable row, mucking stalls, and now they were laying the bedding. He was currently one stall ahead because Daniel had stopped to remove his shirt. Perry turned back toward the entry to the stables and saw why; Lilly and Meggie were walking toward them with glasses of lemonade. It was then he wasn't sure if he'd won the battle or lost the war. He grumbled.

Daniel was actually a decent man. He had been confused by Lilly's injuries and her family had requested he stay away, to protect her. They had sheltered her so much that it eventually drove her from them. It wasn't his fault at all, and it turned out that he didn't blame them for it. Daniel said he held no grudge, he still felt part of the family, even if he and Lilly weren't to be wed. Perry admired his strength of character, though he wondered if Lilly had returned with another working man, whether the situation would be the same.

The gauntlet thrown with a simple piece of linen tossed casually over a stall gate, Perry decided he needed to remove his shirt as well, perhaps with a bit more gusto.

"I canna believe you and Lord Trumbull. I'm just— I'm shocked. Poor Mama, I thought she would faint! And when you came and he just requested to speak with Papa? Oh dear, Lilly. Lilly! You have to tell me what happened!"

"I cannot, I mean— I can tell you that he helped me to heal. Meggie, I owe him my life. I was nothing when I left Eildon. I wanted to fade away and he brought me back. I am so terribly taken with him."

"Do you pinch yourself to check if you're dreaming?" Meggie reached out and pinched her sister.

"Meggie!" She pinched her back.

"Ow! Sorry, I just, I feel like this is a dream; and Daniel, what is with him and Daniel?"

"I believe he might be a bit jealous."

Meggie stopped in her tracks. "Of...Daniel? But he is Daniel."

Lilly laughed at the absurdity of it. They were nowhere near the same man, and it had little to do with the title. "Yes. Daniel."

Meggie shook her head, then moved forward again. "And he keeps telling me to call him...*by his name.* Doesn't he understand?"

Lilly laughed. "No, Megs, he does not. Believe me, I have tried to explain it, but he does not. He simply doesn't see himself that way at all. It's quite the same in his world. He simply believes I should be accepted without qualm. And here, at my family's home, he wants to be seen as just a man. Nothing more."

"But he isn't."

"I understand that, Meggie, but please just try."

Meggie gave her a skeptical glance. "I don't know if Mama and Papa will survive this. Or Daniel."

"Daniel made his choice."

"More like it was made for him."

"We are all better for it, though," Lilly said quietly. "He will find someone more suited to him."

Meggie smiled.

"Has he already?" Lilly asked. Meggie shrugged.

"Is it wrong? When you left he needed a friend, he came to me. I was the closest to you. I do not know if we will...we are yet mere friends."

"He has always been part of the family Meggie."

Meggie shrugged and looked to the barn. "I'm surprised Lord Trumbull allows Daniel to stay here."

"He hasn't a choice, it is not his home."

"Well, no, but he is who he is and he could just ask Papa to send him away."

"He wouldn't! It's not like that, it's only that I was to marry someone else."

"He really loves you, doesn't he?"

"Yes, he does, Megs."

"But he was a rake, Lilly! Don't you worry?" They approached the paddock and Lilly stopped.

"He *was* a rake. Which is one of the reasons we ended up...where we are. But Meggie, he is so very different from what everyone thinks."

"Truly? I don't need to worry?"

"No. You really don't need to worry. You really don't. I love him."

"Do you now?" The rumble of his baritone caught them off guard as he marched across the paddock toward them, sweeping his shirt off over his head as he came.

Meggie blushed and started to curtsey, but Lilly grabbed her arm. She whispered, "Don't, Megs, he's your brother—or will be, hopefully, and he doesn't want that here."

"I don't know how you can deal with this. He is *still* who he is," she whispered back, casting her eyes down.

Perry flung his shirt—he'd decided with a great deal of gusto was

appropriate—across the paddock rail, then jumped on the lower rung and leaned toward them, taking a glass of the cool lemonade. He stood tall, holding the rail with one hand as he downed the glass. It was quite a show, and it caused Lilly's mouth to go dry. She looked at her sister, whose wide eyes were on his boots.

Lilly shook her head, then saw Daniel walk out from the stable behind him. She waved then nudged her sister. Meggie took the tray and walked over to Daniel to offer him a glass.

Perry's throat stopped moving. He lowered the glass and swiped his bare forearm across his mouth as he looked at Lilly. She lifted the hem of her skirts and grabbed the rail, lifting herself to meet his eyes. He took her about the waist and drew her toward him. Their precarious balance forced him to chase her mouth a bit before he caught her and kissed her within an inch of salvation.

She grabbed him hard about the waist to steady herself and he threw a leg over the top rail, pulling her to sit across his lap.

"This is beautiful country."

"Is it?" she asked quietly as she looked up at him.

"Yes, I begin to understand what Gideon loves about this land. I always found something to do, but I was much too restless to simply enjoy it all."

She settled her cheek against his chest, tucking a hand into his waistband to hold onto him.

"I could stay here forever."

"If you like."

She looked up as he looked down to her, then shook her head. "No, my mother needs a respite. She would never survive were we to live nearby."

He grinned. "No, I don't think she would. I feel terrible about that, by the way. I wish there was something I could do."

"Just continue to be your wonderful charming self. I have no doubt you'll win her over eventually." He laughed, and her whole body shook against him, causing a delightful friction.

"There's something I would like to show you. I'm going to saddle a horse—does it matter which?"

"The grey is ours, the rest are boarded. Will you be gone long?"

"As long as you wish it, as you are coming with me."

Hepplewort followed Morgan and his mother into the inn at Kelso. He ordered three rooms and asked that his borrowed team be seen to. The innkeeper gave him a wary glance, then handed off three keys and turned the register for him to sign.

"Supper is served at seven."

Hepplewort grunted and turned for the stairs.

Perry turned their mount into the wooded area. He loved turning the horse because it gave him the opportunity to graze her breasts with his forearms. He had started a slow burn way back at the edge of her father's property and he just knew Lilly was going to bubble over if they didn't get to their destination soon.

She kept shifting in the saddle as though to rub against the pommel in front of her, the side effect of which was the cockstand now resting at her backside.

"Perry, please."

He pushed the horse a little faster, smoothing out his gait as he leaned into her, pushing her gently into the pommel on each landing.

"Oh, God, Perry."

He pulled her skirt up and inched his hand between her and the pommel, sliding his fingers through her slick folds as his other arm held tight to her waist and the rein.

"God, you're wet, Lilly," he breathed against her ear.

Her hands clasped his forearms, her fingers digging into his flesh as the horse jumped some branches. She broke around him, coming apart as they flew into the clearing, and she screamed. The sound was like a hawk taking flight in search of something and he stopped the horse, holding her tightly against him as she came down, collapsing into him.

He turned the horse, spinning him as she relaxed further against him. The horse's hooves crushed the blooming heather in the clearing and created a cloud of musky scent around them sending his senses soaring, his memories reeling.

"Oh, Perry, that was...that was amazing,"

"I'm not quite done." He lifted one leg over the horse's neck, pulling her along, and jumped to the ground. She watched as he undressed her; she was a flag caught in the breeze of him, her trappings falling away as he worked efficiently, then turned those hands on himself.

"No, let me." She paused at his waistband and looked up with a smile. "You see, the tables have quite turned, for it is I that stands naked in the outdoors and you with all your clothes on."

He shook his head and smiled. "Be done with this or I will." Her eyes widened at his tone and her fingers moved swiftly, divesting him of his clothing as easily as he had hers.

He took her wrist and pulled her to the crystal clear pond. "Can you swim?"

"Yes, I—"

He lifted her as he walked across the big flat rock then tossed her in, diving in next to her. He grabbed her underwater and kissed her, hard, the bubbles of their breath mingling as they surfaced together.

"You horrible, evil, awful—"

He kissed her again to quiet her rant and pulled her toward the center of the pond.

"Have you been here before?" he asked.

"No. We used to go to a pond on my father's land. I really never came this direction—toward Eildon, I mean. We knew it was the duke's land, so we steered clear."

"Well, this is one of the places where he and I spent a great deal of time as children. Mostly naked, swimming all summer. I only asked because perhaps you spied on us, here in our private swimming hole."

Her jaw dropped and she smacked his shoulder when they stopped. "That's horrible! I would never!"

"No, I don't think you would have. Then."

"I do remember you younger. I have ridden with you before, you know, not quite like this, but..."

She blushed and it was beautiful. He took her in his arms, amazed he had been so lucky to meet her.

"I came to visit my father when he was in charge of the stable, and you—"

"I remember you— You were naught but a little thing. That was you?" He smiled against her mouth. "Oh dear, I thought you were the prettiest girl."

"You did not."

"I did! All that hair. It was past your waist! The sun made it glow, and when we cantered through the meadow it soared around my face like the waves in the ocean. It was incredible."

"Stop."

"I won't. I've thought of that girl since then, but the minute I met you she was no longer in my thoughts. I suppose I've been looking for you all along. I didn't even remember your name. But I remembered your hair, and that the heather was in bloom then as well. I have always loved the smell of crushed heather."

"It is a rather heady fragrance. And why wouldn't you remember my name?" She pulled back and looked at him, wrapping her legs around his waist under the water.

He shook his head. "I didn't need you back then."

She gasped and he delved into her mouth, deeper than she thought possible, shifting her hips against him, and though the pond was fairly cold, and he thought it not possible, his cock twitched and rose to meet her.

Meggie opened the door expecting to see Perry and Lilly, but instead was met with a carriage and four pulling through the far gate.

"Papa, there's someone here." She turned to find him coming from the kitchen, where he'd been trying to convince her mother that everything would work itself out. He stood at the front door and watched the team approach, then turned to Meggie. "Get Daniel, go to town, tell the men to come, and if you see Lord Trumbull and Lilly tell them to stay away."

Meggie panicked and looked back at the carriage.

"Go now! Take your mother, go out the back, Meggie. Go! *Now!*" He turned her and pushed her toward the kitchens and she ran.

He strode swiftly to the closet and pulled out his shotgun, then walked out to his front stoop and looked up at the giant on the box seat. "If that's who I think it is in that carriage, you should turn and leave this land now."

Morgan pulled the brake on the carriage and stopped the horses just shy of the house.

Hepplewort kicked the stairs down and descended.

"I told your man, and now I'm telling you, get off of my land."

"You've no right to talk to me that way! I am Hepplewort."

"I know who you are. You attacked my girl Lilly. You left her for dead. You've murdered others. You are not welcome here and if you wish to live, you will leave—for make no mistake, I will end you."

He heard the pounding of hoofbeats and turned again toward the far gate to see two men on horseback coming up his drive. Hepplewort turned to look as well, and Mr. Steele cocked his weapon, firing at the ground in front of the earl and startling the horses. Hepplewort shrieked and stepped back.

"I told you to get off my property and I expect you to do so. Immediately." Mr. Steele cocked the second barrel on his pinfire shotgun and pointed it at him.

"Stop! Papa, no!" Lilly and Perry came running around the house.

"I told Meggie to send you away."

"Papa don't, please, they'll take you from us."

"Sir, please give me the weapon," Perry said quietly as they walked toward him. Mr. Steele sighted the weapon at Hepplewort's head, his hands shaking violently. Long moments passed, then he relaxed, handing the gun to Perry.

Calder and Warrick jumped from their mounts, letting them continue their run toward the stable and paddock as Morgan fought with the team. The two cousins flanked Perry as Hepplewort looked on in astonishment.

"You, sir, are not welcome here," Calder said. "That has been made quite clear. We do, however, happen to know a place where you are welcome. Newgate." .

"You are much too cordial," Warrick grumbled.

"No need to be rude. Hepplewort is going to cooperate…aren't you?" Calder said as he held his gaze.

Perry looked to Morgan, who was still wrestling with the startled team, then back to Hepplewort. His eyes narrowed and Lilly turned. She could tell from Perry's reaction that this wasn't good. He reached for her, tucking her safely behind him on the front steps. "Why are you here?" he asked.

"You've ruined me."

"You've ruined yourself. Everything you've done, the women you have abused and murdered, that was all your doing. No one else helped with that."

Hepplewort looked to Morgan, drawing everyone's gaze, and Morgan ducked his head, avoiding Perry's glance as he held the reins and pressed harder on the carriage brake.

"Hepplewort, we are taking you back to London to face the charges brought against you concerning the murder of a Miss Anna Cole. If you do not cooperate with us, we will take you however we can get you, breathing or not," Warrick said.

*Anna Cole.* Lilly squeezed Perry's hand, and he returned the pressure.

Hepplewort's eyes looked as though they would pop right form his head. "You can't be serious. I'm an earl, she was nothing."

"You are mistaken, actually, she wasn't nothing. She was the daughter of Sir Davis Cole, and you, sir, left enough proof behind that they are merely waiting for your return."

"Why was she alone? Why would a lady be—"

"It. Matters. *Not!*" Calder railed, and everyone turned to look at him. He straightened his waistcoat, then his hat, and tightened his gloves as his composure returned. "It matters not what she was doing. In fact, it matters not who she was. You are a murdering bastard and we are here to see that you face the charges brought against you."

They watched as Hepplewort panicked, his feet shuffling, his brain obviously working out what he should do next. Perry's grip tightened on the barrel of the shotgun, and he glanced down to see that the second barrel was, in fact, loaded, the striker cocked.

Calder nodded to Warrick, and they stepped forward, blocking Perry's view as they approached Hepplewort. Perry pulled Lilly to his side, his arm around her shoulders, and kissed her temple. He closed his eyes and she felt his mouth move against her, maybe a silent prayer offered for the girl, for Anna Cole. She leaned into him.

Hepplewort had his hands up and was backing away from the men. Lilly watched him carefully, couldn't take her eyes from him, this man who had dragged her through the forest near her home, raped her, then raped her with a bottle and God knows what else. Left her for dead, didn't even give her a second thought, all because she wasn't touched by the hand of God, all because she hadn't been chosen to be born into the peerage. Her eyes narrowed on his face, and then time seemed to stand still.

His arm jerked forward, and he had a gun pointed at Warrick, then Calder, because he was that sort of vacillating weakling. Perry was still holding her, his eyes closed, and she pulled her father's shotgun up in his hand and positioned it against her hip as Perry's arm tightened on her shoulder and he started to shift.

Hepplewort finally took aim, at her, and pulled the trigger. Warrick lunged to block her, and as he fell, Lilly pulled, the shotgun knocking her off her feet as it bucked into her hip.

Lilly opened her eyes to see Perry's terrified face hovering over her. She let go of the shotgun and pulled herself up to sit with his help. Morgan was fighting the horses and losing, and Hepplewort was on the ground. Calder tossed aside the gun he took from Hepplewort, then bent over Warrick, rolling him. Morgan stood in the box, attempting to control his team, his full weight on the brake, his arms straining his jacket.

Calder yelled at Perry, motioning to the startled team on Hepplewort's carriage. Perry let go of Lilly and he and her father ran to Warrick, helping Calder pull him up the steps to where Lilly sat. Hepplewort's mother descended the carriage then, her eyes falling to Hepplewort as he writhed on the ground.

"My *son!*" she screamed, and the startled horses reared. She paid no heed as she threw herself upon Hepplewort. The violent movement of the horses broke the shaft and the front of the carriage lurched, throwing Morgan to the ground between the team, releasing the brake and the only thing holding them back. They jumped against their harnesses, coming down on Hepplewort and his mother before they careened toward the meadow, leaving death in their path.

Perry pulled Lilly into his embrace, blocking the gruesome view.

"Oh, God. Perry, did they— Was that? Oh, God help them!"

Perry glanced over his shoulder. "God is truly the only one who can help them now. Warrick?"

"Fine, I'm— I seem to be fine." Warrick shook off his coat and inspected the growing red stain on his shoulder. Calder descended the steps and walked to the mother, turning away suddenly when he got close. Then he glanced at Morgan, apparently determining he didn't even need to approach to find out whether he had survived.

Lilly watched the red stain as it saturated Warrick's sleeve, then pushed Perry away, lifting her skirt and tearing her petticoat. She folded a thick pad, then pressed it to the wound and tied another piece of her petticoat around it, apologizing when he winced.

When she was finished he put one hand on her shoulder, waiting until she looked him in the eye. "This outcome, while disagreeable, could not have been easily avoided. I would much prefer that my cousin be standing beside you, rather than that man. Remember that, above all else," he said gruffly.

Lilly nodded. Perry's arms came around her as he checked the pressure on Warrick's wound.

Warrick pushed him off then stood, as did Perry, the two of them pulling Lilly up with them. Perry saw the trembling in her arms subsiding. He smoothed the long curls back from her face and turned her to look at him.

"Believe Warrick, if no other, for he will tell you true like no other. There is nothing more you could have done here."

"I killed him."

"No, he was still alive—" He stopped and considered what he'd nearly said. "No, Lilly, *you* did not kill him."

She turned back to Warrick. "Why did you—" He shrugged, then winced, and she reached for him, but he raised his hand to stay her.

Perry crushed her to him. "God, Lilly, I love you."

"And I love you, milord," she replied on a breath.

"Must I warn you again?" he asked with a smile, trying to break the mood.

"No, milord, not at all. I know exactly what it is I'm asking for."

Lilly's father placed his hand on Perry's shoulder. "Son, I have to thank you for protecting my daughter. About that question you had for me. Ask me again. This time the answer will be yes."

Lilly's jaw dropped. "You said no?"

"As is his right," Perry said quietly, "though I had planned to convince him soon enough."

Lilly's father laughed. "You've succeeded." He pushed Perry away and took Lilly in his arms. "I am so proud of you. My Lilly."

"Oh, Papa." She looked up into his teary eyes and smiled. "Don't you know I didn't have a choice? I'm brave because I'm your daughter." He hugged her again, and Lilly thought he might break her, his embrace was so tight. When he finally released her, she glanced around to find that someone had covered the dead with blankets and Perry was at the base of the steps, speaking with Calder and Warrick.

She could tell he was having a difficult time suppressing a smile, his face taking on an awkward grimace as they discussed what should happen next. She found it rather difficult herself, so she turned to go into the house, away from all the death.

# FIFTY

My precious Lilly,

  I cannot tell you how amazed I am with you every day. How proud I am of you, how much I hope you have a beautiful future, with a wonderful husband, who will give you all the children and happiness your heart desires.

  At times I wish that would be me, but as you keep saying it can never be; it can never be.

  Simply know that I treasure you. You have brought me much joy, and opened my eyes to a new sort of happiness.

  I love you for that,

  Perry

Lilly read the inscription in the book again then looked up to the church, her hand resting on her father's arm. This was it. Had it only been a fortnight since she'd crawled into Perry's carriage and hid under the bench? So much had happened.

"It's time." Her father's voice cracked on the words, and she turned to him.

"I love you, Papa."

"I love you, Lillybug."

"He is a good man, Papa."

"He is that. Are you ready?"

She nodded and turned to the doors of the church. They were swept open before her and it took Lilly's breath away. The floor was littered with crushed purple heather, the earthy scent released into the air with every step she took down the aisle. Her gaze followed the heather to the steps, then up to the man at the altar. He was dressed in a kilt, with a crisp white shirt, black wool coat, and tartan sash displaying several bejeweled emblems pinned across his chest. The sun through the stained glass struck his chest as she moved toward him, and the walls of the church reflected the light from the sparkling jewels like dancing fire.

Her eyes drifted to the vicar, then down, and she realized he was standing in front of a beautifully tooled, deep-brown saddle. The heather was woven through the legs of the stand it rested on, and a long strand of pearls wrapped around one of the stirrups. She looked back to Perry, whose smile was so broad she couldn't see anything else. Except his eyes. Which twinkled devilishly.

She held tight to her father as he led her toward her future. It was a heady mix: the heather, her family, and the man. It was all she could do to keep her heart in her chest and make it the last few feet down the aisle to pledge her troth. Over a saddle. Woven with heather and pearls.

# FIFTY-ONE

Perry felt the tremble course Lilly's spine as the carriage ground to a halt in front of Eildon Manor.

"The last time I arrived here it was as a servant."

He almost didn't hear the words, as softly as they were spoken. He pulled her closer and kissed her temple, nudging the curls aside with the tip of his nose. "You will never arrive as a servant anywhere again."

She pressed her cheek into his, then trapped his face to hers with her palm against the other. He felt her breath in the rise and fall of her chest and moved both arms around her, pulling her into his strength, willing it to infuse her.

"I love you so, Perry, and I've survived much. But I'm not sure how I shall survive this."

He laughed then was immediately repentant, knowing she spoke the truth. Gideon wasn't merely possessive of his lands but of all those under his purview. He held each life as sacred, and when Lilly had been found injured he saw to it she had been cared for, then brought to his home for protection.

"We shall survive this together. Believe me, I know my brother. I'll speak with him, and you will be family. You *are* family."

"Name does not denote family," she whispered, a chill coursed his spine as her lips moved against his jaw.

"Lilly. Sweet, precious, Lilly," he groaned. "I know what you're about, but we cannot return to the inn. We've a wedding to attend."

She pushed him away and pouted. Her hands clasped in her lap. Perry returned her to his embrace and teased her mouth, willing her to submit—and she did, soon melting into his sturdy form.

The door opened and he turned to the footman as she straightened her skirts. He jumped down then lifted her from the carriage. As he placed her hand on his arm he guided her to the entry, searching for familiar faces among the workers who milled about.

"Miss Faversham!" he called as he crossed the threshold and spied the governess leading his charges toward the great staircase. "Miss Faversham, you are looking well. Ladies, it's good to see you." They curtseyed, and he nodded. "Miss Faversham, would you do me a great honor and allow my beautiful bride to accompany the three of you while I find my brother?"

Her eyes grew impossibly wide, and he watched warily as she glanced at Lilly. It wasn't until Miss Faversham cleared her throat that he realized he was quite remiss. "I beg your pardon. Miss Faversham, might I present my wife, the Viscountess of Roxleigh, Lady Trumbull."

Miss Faversham smiled and curtseyed. "So very lovely to meet you, my lady, and these are Lord Trumbull's charges, Amelié and Maryse." The girls curtseyed again and Miss Faversham lifted a hand. "Please do join us. We're about to have a warm cup of chocolate in the family parlor while we wait for the ceremony to begin."

Perry reluctantly relinquished Lilly's hand to Miss Faversham, who squeezed it before smiling at him. "We'll be fine, my lord. You know where to find us, and if you get caught up before the celebration, I'll ensure she's by my side until you're available. Go on now. His Grace is in his suite getting ready."

Perry nodded, placed a quick kiss on Lilly's cheek, and vaulted up the stairs, heading straight for Gideon's chambers. He stood outside the door and straightened his cravat. Smoothed his lapels. Checked his seams. His breath didn't seem to want to calm, and his heartbeat increased to an inconsolable cadence. Apparently he didn't believe his own words to Lilly. In fact, he was amazed he'd managed to keep her calm.

Placing his hand on the door latch, Perry was shocked to notice a slight tremor as he took a deep breath and pushed.

Ferry poked and prodded the cravat which was the brightest white Gideon had ever seen. He was quite worried the level of brightness below his chin might blind his guests. Or that Francine wouldn't be able to see him at all above the glow. Ferry made one final adjustment then nearly smiled, and Gideon knew it was his best knot to date. He watched his valet turn to the rack behind him for his jacket and garter sash, something Gideon was looking forward to wearing, though he wasn't quite sure why.

"Pulling out the crown jewels, are we, brother? Afraid Francine will turn you down if you don't impress?"

Gideon turned and in two great strides met Perry at the center of the room. He paused, attempting to read his brother's disposition, then took Perry's face between his hands and kissed him on the cheek before pulling him into a fierce embrace.

Perry laughed, then smacked his back when he wouldn't let go. "Good lord, Gideon, it has been naught but a fortnight."

"Yet if feels much longer. I've missed you."

"Well, I didn't miss your unsightly face one bit. I imagined Francine was keeping you entirely too busy to wonder about me, regardless. Now unhand me." He laughed.

Gideon took his brother by the shoulders, still reluctant to release him. He heard a grunt from across the room and turned to find Ferry scowling. Gideon's hand went straight to the neck cloth. "Ferry, a moment."

Ferry bowed stiffly and disappeared behind the fireplace.

"Come." Gideon motioned to the chairs at the fireplace as he unraveled the rumpled cravat. "I cannot tell you what it means to me that you've returned. I haven't heard from you in days, and there was no message with the railcar. They told me you had brought it up yourself. What did you think?"

"I...quite enjoyed the railcar, in fact. The accommodations were luxurious, appointments beautiful, and the ride was quite— Well." Perry rubbed his thumb down his jaw and Gideon knew there was more. He sat back in the chair and crossed his ankles in front of him, waiting.

Perry appeared hale and whole, his hair a bit long, but there wasn't much to be surprised about. His clothes were well suited to the occasion, he was not injured, his hand glinted in the sun— He was...he was married? Gideon caught the shine of the band on Perry's finger and watched as the hand it belonged to slid next to Perry's jaw. Back and forth.

"Married?" Gideon caught his brother's eye. He thought back to the night in London when he'd told Perry about Francine. "Is that a marriage band?"

Perry froze then moved his hand, twisting the ring on his finger. "Gideon. Let me—"

Gideon raised his hands, spread them wide in invitation, and set about waiting...once again.

Perry smiled, and it was the most overwhelming smile Gideon had ever witnessed on his brother's face. He knew. Gideon brought his hands together in his lap and fought to suppress his answering grin. And continued waiting.

"I understand. I understand completely why you did everything you did. I was wrong to speak in such a manner. I was wrong to accuse you, to berate you, to—"

Gideon waved his hand as if to wipe the slate clean. "Perry. Nobody in my life has been more supportive of me, or more correct in their assessment of my behavior. You were in the right to call me out. It was beneath me to act in such a way and it was demeaning to my Francine. I will not hear another word on it. We have already discussed this." He leaned forward. "Who is she? Is she here? Do I know her?"

"You already know her, and yes, she's here." Perry stared at the ring on his finger.

"Out with it. Your nerves are unsettling."

Perry looked up at him, clenching his fists on his knees.

"Her name is Lilly. Lilly Steele. Well, it was Lilly Steele."

Perry was watching him closely, and for some reason the name resonated with Gideon. *Lilly Steele. Lilly. Lady Steele? Miss Steele? Lilly. Oh, dear God—Lilly Steele of Kelso.*

Gideon stood. "Lilly? Meggie's Lilly? They told me she returned to her family. Why was she with you? She is one of my people, Peregrine." He took a step forward. "What have you done? That girl…what was done to her… What have you done?" Gideon heard the echo of his words resound through the room and hoped his walls were sturdy enough to contain it.

Perry stood and reached out to his brother—whether to console him or stay his advance, he wasn't sure. But he was quite sure he'd better start talking, and quickly. He put the chair between them. "Please listen to me, Gideon. I need you… I need you to hear me."

Perry felt as though he were being weighed and measured, a prized animal being prepared for sale and slaughter: the benefit of every inch of him accounted for, the leftovers considered, the comparison between the good and the bad closely examined. He felt any sudden movement could be disastrous.

Perry paced before the fireplace, angling to keep Gideon in his perifery. A safe distance from his brother, with two chairs and a chaise now between them. "She was in my carriage when I quit Eildon that night. She heard us argue, and she stowed away. It wasn't long before I found her. Once I saw her face, once I knew... There was nothing I could do. I couldn't leave her stranded, and she refused to return to Eildon..."

Perry wove his tale and did his utmost to stay true to the story while protecting Lilly as best he could. He knew full well how intimate was her struggle to be free of her demons. Relating their history to Gideon was perhaps the most difficult thing he'd ever done. He knew there was no way around it. His brother was the head of the family and could demand the marriage be annulled. He had the power to leave Lilly destitute, though Perry believed in his bones Gideon would never do such a thing. He might skin *him* to the core, but he knew Lilly would forever be protected.

"Perry." His brother was turning him; he hadn't realized he'd stopped talking. He hadn't heard Gideon approach. Hadn't felt his hands on his shoulders. Perry didn't move. He felt his arm twitch, perhaps wanting to rub his jaw, but he didn't. Gideon's eyes narrowed on him and he tensed.

"I should have been there." The words came through a clenched jaw, tight lips, closed teeth. "I should have stood by you when you pledged your troth. It's my place, I should have been allowed to stand by your side. This is unforgivable."

"Gideon, I'm sorry. I was concerned—"

"That I would stop you? Well, that would have been entirely up to her, of course." Perry wasn't prepared for his smile, and it overtook him. "Perry, I've always known you to be honorable. Trustworthy. Steadfast and true. I believe every word you've spoken. Did you really insult her the night you met?"

Perry shook his head in disbelief then nodded. "I did, quite egregiously. It was atrocious the way I spoke to her. She should never have let me apologize. But she simply unmans me, and I don't know how to react. I feel so out of control when she's in danger. I know, Gideon, I truly *know*." His brother moved across the room toward the tantalus. "Gideon, I honestly don't understand... It was naught but a fortnight!"

"I knew the moment I met Francine. No, not then. I knew the moment she railed at me across my guest room. The first time she prodded my waistcoat with that dainty finger, I knew." Gideon poured two glasses of rich brown whiskey and turned to Perry.

"You were in a right state when you arrived in London."

Gideon laughed. "I was. Then I spoke with you and understood. Perry, I'm terribly impressed with you. I don't know that I could have done what you did for Lilly." Gideon handed him one of the glasses, then they clinked the rims and he downed the contents.

"Well, I am a rake, after all." Perry raised the glass and inhaled, the heady smell of Gideon's prized whiskey burning its way through his senses and relaxing his mind. He downed it then turned back to his brother. "I only wish you'd been there—at the wedding, I mean."

Gideon smiled. "As do I. I do, however, have another question for you."

"Anything."

"The railcar."

The grin slid across Perry's face before he could stop it, and his hand went to his chin.

Gideon's eye narrowed on him again. "I see. Well, I believe I'll commission a new one. You may consider that one your wedding gift." Gideon raised a brow. "What exactly will I tell my wife when we have to wait for another car to be finished for our honeymoon?"

"I am terribly sorry." Perry couldn't stop grinning.

"Are you?"

"Not at all." He shook his head and chuckled. "Not a bit."

"I thought not."

"There's one other thing."

"Yes?"

"Hepplewort is dead. As is his mother."

"Truly?" Gideon asked.

Perry saw a certain stress leave his brother then. It was nearly imperceptible. If he hadn't been watching for it, he never would have seen the slight lift of his shoulders, the tension in his forehead drift.

"Yes, there's no doubt. But you are to be married, and we haven't much time for these stories now. I just thought you should know this one last thing before..."

"Before I'm to be married." Gideon beamed. "I am so glad you made it home for this." Gideon put his glass down with a thump. "She must be a terrible mess, waiting." He headed for the door. "Where is she?" Gideon left his chambers.

"Gideon." Perry panicked and ran to catch up.

"Family parlor? Must be. I can't imagine where else she would be."

"Gideon." Perry grabbed his shoulder as his brother reached for the door.

"Not to worry, Perry. But I can't wait another moment to greet my sister." He stopped. "A sister! Who would have thought? I certainly never did. Not with you for a brother, at any rate." As Perry started to smile, Gideon turned the latch on the parlor door and stepped in.

Lilly was sitting with the girls by the French doors. The doors stood open to a slight breeze, and the three of them looked so young and happy. Gideon looked back and when he laughed, Perry knew he was gazing at her with one of those ridiculous besotted faces he usually attempted to hide.

"Oh yes, brother, you're in this one for good, I see."

Perry may have actually blushed then, and Gideon marched for Lilly.

"I'm told I have a sister." Gideon said it quietly so as not to startle her or the girls. She stood instantly, and cowered. Exactly what Perry had been hoping to avoid. He tried to go to her, to move around Gideon, but Gideon threw his hand out to stay him. "Lady Trumbull, it is my greatest honor to meet the woman who has captured my brother's heart." He took another step toward her, and she straightened as he approached, like a flower warming to the sun. Perry's heart picked up a beat, and his shoulders started to relax.

The duke moved toward Lilly like a tangible force. She felt as though she'd been laid bare before him, unable to hide her face, unable to bow her head as was comfortable for her in her former station. She'd forgotten how easily one could hide in plain sight with a simple submissive bow of the head. "Your Grace."

"Gideon, please."

"Gideon." Perry said it over his shoulder but the duke brushed him off.

"Please, my lady, address me as Gideon while in our home."

She felt as though her eyes might roll down her cheeks and plop to the floor, they were so wide. She attempted to rein her shock as he reached for her hands, and she watched, telling her hands to still. Willing them to calm. Hoping he couldn't see her terror. Then he took her in an embrace, and kissed her cheek, and Perry was the one who stood by in shock.

"Gideon," she whispered. "Lilly." That was all she could manage after.

"Lilly." She felt it rumble through him, loosing her nerves and melting her tension. Why had she always been afraid of this man? "I cannot wait for you to meet Francine properly. She will be so thrilled for you, and for Perry. I hope you have a wonderful time today. If you need anything, please come to me directly and I will see to it. Perry is useless when it comes to getting anything done, as you are probably already aware."

Gideon placed her hand in Perry's. "I wasn't at your wedding, though I should have been." he glanced at Perry, then held their hands bound together. "Know now, that you have my blessing, whether you wish it or not. And we are family." He released their hands and stepped back. "We have much to discuss, but for now I must see to my cravat. I'm afraid Ferry will be in a right state. He simply won't allow me to be married in a rumpled neck cloth."

He beamed at Lilly, and she was caught. This was why her mother told her to never meet a man's eyes. She felt perfectly snared. Perry took her hand and squeezed it, and she nodded then moved toward him. Gideon turned to leave, then stopped at the entry. "Perry, please be sure to tell your lovely bride of your wedding gift from Francine and I." He smiled.

Perry laughed, then nodded. "On that note, Gideon, as I am quite unprepared for today's event, might I extend the same to you? Please, let me commission yours. It would be my honor."

She turned to look up at him. The hand not holding hers was placed over his heart in a pledge, and he winked at her. When she glanced back at the door the duke was gone, his laughter echoing back from the grand entry.

"Perry?"

"Yes, my lovely, sweet, wonderful woman?"

Lilly looked up at him again. "What exactly is this gift?"

He bowed swiftly to the girls, who had watched the entire scene unfold quietly, and pulled Lilly out the French doors to the balcony. "A new railcar." She felt the words as a whisper across her ear and knew she blushed from the heat in her cheeks.

"You didn't tell him."

"I didn't have to. He knows me too well."

"So I *am* to be laid bare before him because he knows you so well?"

"An unfortunate side effect, I have to say, but this works both ways. You'll come to know Gideon better than all of England. Save, of course, for myself and Francine."

She smiled and smoothed his jacket over his sturdy shoulders, then turned her face to the sun.

"What is it?" he asked quietly.

"He said 'our home', Perry."

"Of course he did. As it is. Would you like to see our suite?" he asked casually.

She thought she'd swoon. "I need a moment. Perhaps after the ceremony? Give me at least a moment for all of this"—she waved her hand above her head—"to settle in. It's a bit much for a girl, don't you know? Three days ago I was naught but Lilly Steele."

"And now?"

"And now, this!" She waved her hands about again. She saw Miss Faversham herding the girls from the parlor and shied away from the doors, realizing she was being a bit loud. Perhaps she needed more than a moment, she thought absently. She turned for the staircase at the end of the balcony.

"Lilly?"

She turned back to him, took his face between her hands, and kissed him until their souls met between their lips in a soaring shout the angels would certainly hear. "Perry, I love you. I truly do. I'm not going anywhere. I won't disappear, I won't wander off. I'm here, wherever here may be with you. I simply need a moment. Never fear."

He smiled and wrapped his arms around her waist, lifting and swinging her in a grand circle. Her skirts flew out behind her, carrying her laughter along to the breeze as his face nestled comfortably in her bosom.

"Lilly, my lady?" he said as he slowed and gazed up at her.

"Yes, my dear?"

"I love you."

"Yes, my lord, my Perry, I believe you do."

*The End*

# EPILOGUE

he alarm went off on bed 23a and Dr. Roman Wyntor glanced toward it. "Is that the first time that alarm has gone off?" he asked the nurse at the station.

"No, it's been going off all night, but I keep checking on her. Her stats are steady."

He considered the woman in the bed. She should be awake by now. The nurse moved toward her.

"No, I'll go," he said quietly. He took the chart and read over it again. He hadn't been there for a couple of days, but he'd been in the trauma center when the woman was brought in. He remembered her eyes above all else, like the ocean at high tide on Garrapata Beach in California, close to where he was born.

Roman pushed the alarm button to silence it, then reached out to her wrist, checking her pulse. It fluttered steadily beneath his fingertips, and he squeezed her hand reassuringly, then released her. He sat in the chair next to the bed and watched. The accident she'd been in had caused a severe concussion, and she had multiple abrasions but nothing she shouldn't recover from eventually.

He wasn't sure why he was drawn to this patient above the others. Something in her eyes that day had caught him and pulled him in. She had looked so terrified, and it grasped at something deep inside him. He knew she would recover. He knew this. He merely had to wait for the trauma to fade.

He went over the notes in her chart from the past few days, checking and double checking her care and the procedures. He considered ordering another MRI to be sure they hadn't missed anything, perhaps calling in Dr. Bohden to consult on the case. While reading over the previous night's notes, he saw a movement over the top edge of the chart and looked up.

Concentrated.

Nothing.

His eyes traveled her form beneath the blanket, head to toe. Not a single sign of activity. He looked back down to the chart only to see something again, and this time, he was sure of it. He watched as she tensed and released her muscles as though taking stock of every one, top to bottom. Her fingers moved, then her thighs shifted and her knees bent slightly, then her feet twirled under the blanket and her toes curled.

He stood and moved to her, speaking quietly. "My name is Dr. Wyntor. You are in Denver General. Take it slow and easy, you've been through quite an ordeal."

He waited.

Her eyelids shifted and she clenched her eyes tightly, then relaxed ever so slowly. Her eyes opened on him, and his breath pulled in suddenly, stolen from him with the remembrance of that gaze.

"My name is Dr. Wyntor—" he started again, then shook his head, realizing he'd already said that. "What's your name?" He took her wrist under the pretense of checking her pulse. Something in him needed to hold her, comfort her.

Her eyes narrowed on him, then relaxed.

"Take it easy, let everything come slowly. Do you remember what happened?"

The woman shook her head but didn't move her eyes from him.

"Where are you from?" Still no response. He released her wrist, knowing he'd been holding on for entirely too long, but she reached out and took his hand.

Her mouth parted on a breath and his gaze was drawn to her lips. He shook his head again. He tried to pull from her hold and bring down the shield of professionalism, but he just couldn't force himself away.

"I am here to help you." It was a quiet admission, and meant as a promise. He set aside her chart and swept a tendril of hair from her forehead. "If you need anything at all, you can ask for me." He reached for the button at her side, to show her how to call for help, and she took his hand again.

"Madeleine."

It was so quiet he thought he'd imagined it. His gaze went back to her mouth to see if there was any sign of movement.

"Pardon?"

"Madeleine," she repeated, and this time he saw it more than heard it. The movement of her mouth had him spellbound, and he repeated the name.

"Madeleine."

She smiled.

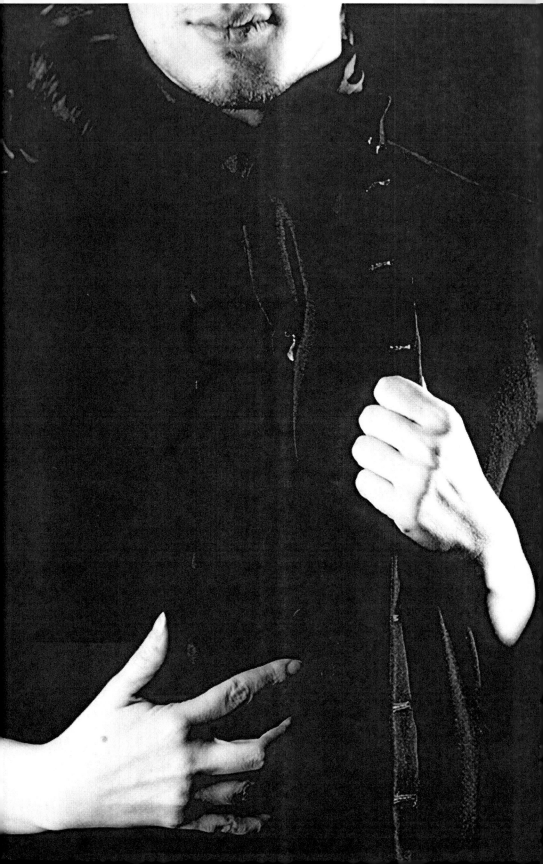

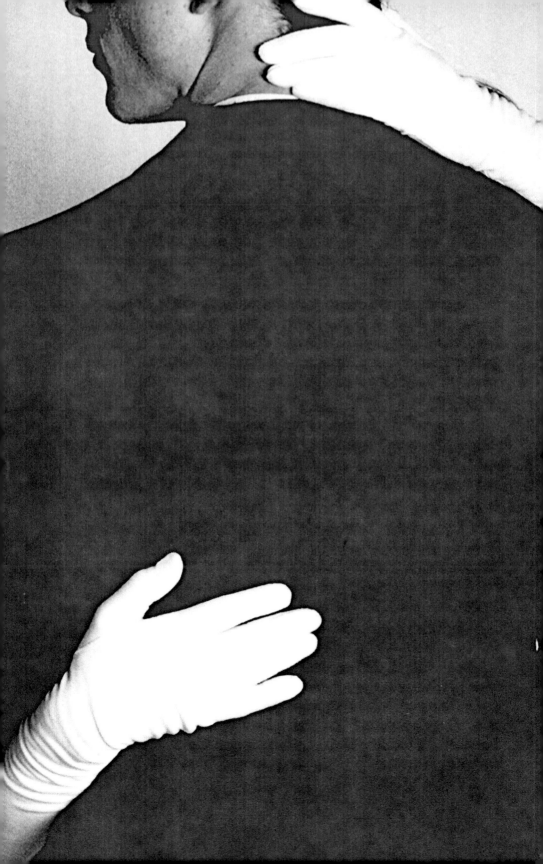

*Dearest reader,*

My deepest, most heartfelt thank you, for reading my novel.

It has been a long road from the dream to this reality and the fact that you're here reading it still astounds me. I certainly hope you enjoyed reading it as much as I've enjoyed writing, photographing, designing and bringing it to you.

A note about a couple things in the book. While, in general, there aren't duplicate location titles in the peerage, there are a few that I found in my research. In fact the first pair of titles sharing location I found was in my own family history wherein there was a Baron and Earl of the same title. *(Name withheld to protect me from being made fun of)*

From what I gathered it happened primarily in borderlands where there was a dispute. A new title of a higher rank was bestowed when a lesser title was already held. In general a second son wouldn't have a title at all unless it was bestowed upon him by the Queen (or King) for duties performed in his own right.

I placed the Roxleigh seat near the border of England and Scotland, on the Scotland side, because at one time the book dealt with the border disputes and all the intricacies of how the United Kingdom came to be, through all the wars and complaints. However, most of that information was removed from the final manuscript.

Roxleigh was meant to be a powerful Duke, to illustrate this he was placed at the border, which would have been one of the foothold seats that held the Scots from the Sassenachs. At any rate, the backstory cometh and the editor taketh away and I was left with no explanation as to why there were both Duke and Viscount Roxleigh. Also, the reason he is referred to as Lord Trumbull is because Roxleigh is Roxleigh. And as in *Highlander* - There can be only one. The Duke being the highest rank recieves the right to be referred to as *THE* Roxleigh.

I thought about changing Trumbull's title to make it easier but decided, since it was already out there, that I didn't want to create a new level of confusion for my first readers.

Perry has become a beloved character in his own right that changing his name was unteneble to me.

There was also, at one point, a great deal of information about mental illness and the handling of mentally ill people in the Victorian era *(it was not very well done)*. Bethlem Royal Hospital was the main dumping ground for the mentally deficient, and it's nickname, Bedlam, has become synonymous with chaos.

Mental illness touches my family closely, and it's a theme that I dealt with carefully. One of the biggest problems that I see, personally, with mentally ill people is misunderstanding. That is something I hope I brought across in this book.

I love to chat so feel free to come find me on Facebook, Twitter or my blog. If you would like to use TRATR for a book club, online or in person, I would love to be included and I am more than happy to chat with your group!

Again, Thank you, thank you, without you, my guys would be nowhere. With you they have a new life in every word you read.

*Thank you,*

*Jenn*

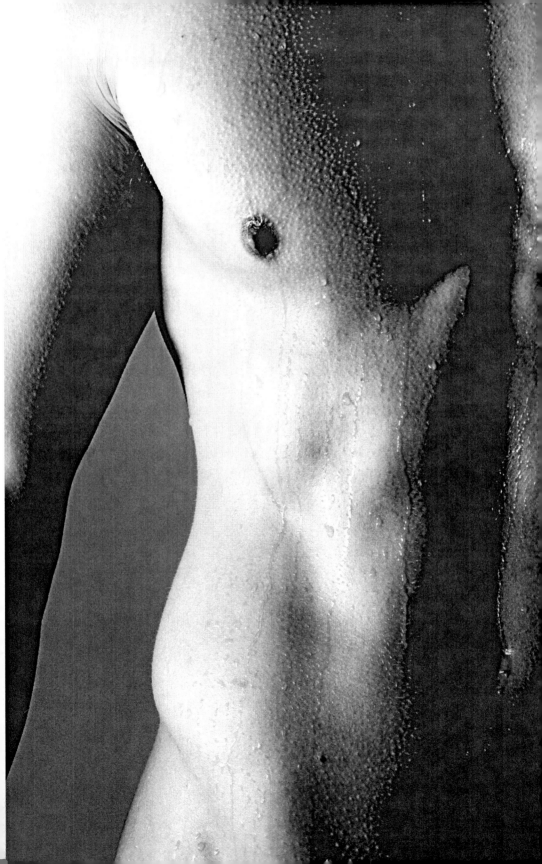

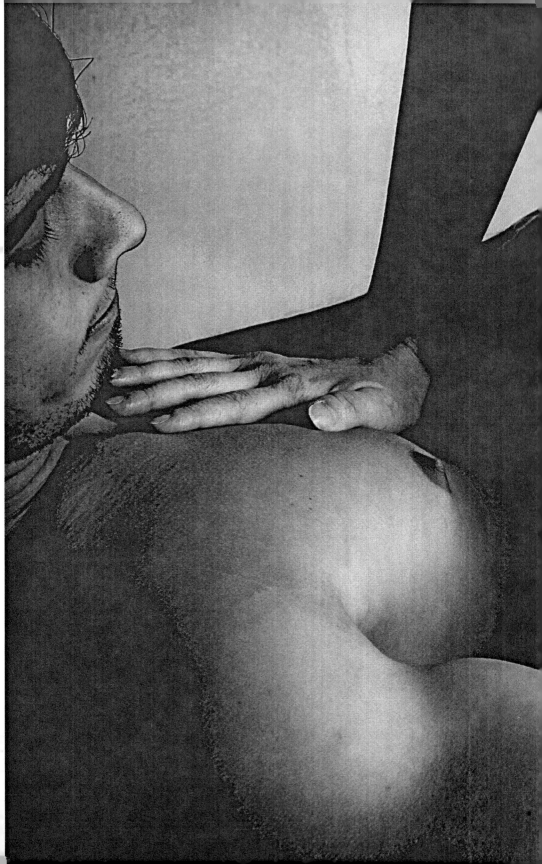

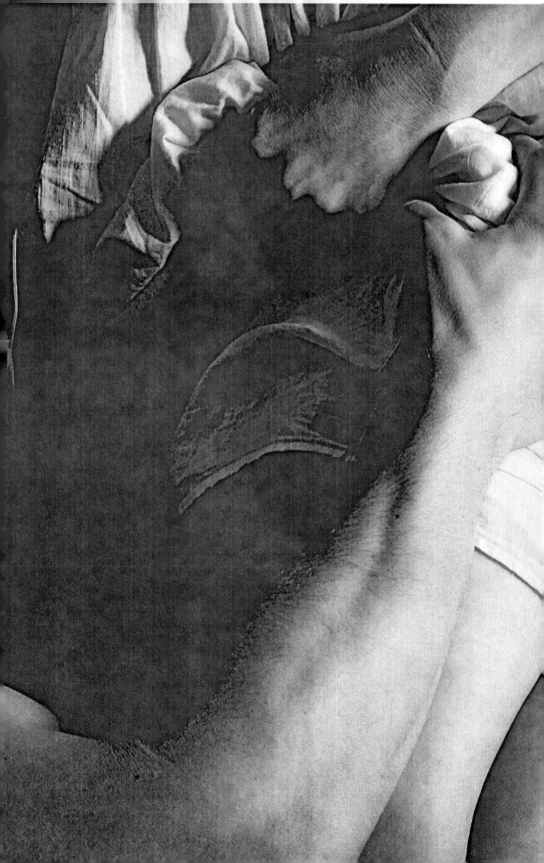

"And what is the use of a book,"
thought Alice,
"without pictures or conversations?"

Alice's Adventures in Wonderland
Lewis Carroll

JennLeBlanc.com

@JennLeBlanc

IllustratedRomance.com

Facebook.com/IllustratedRomance